THE EDINBURGH EDITION OF
THE WAVERLEY NOVELS

EDITOR-IN-CHIEF
Professor David Hewitt

VOLUME TWENTY-ONE

THE FAIR MAID OF PERTH

EDINBURGH EDITION OF THE
WAVERLEY NOVELS

to be complete in thirty volumes

Each volume will be published separately but original conjoint publication of certain works is indicated in the EEWN volume numbering [4a, b; 7a, b, etc.]. Where EEWN editors have been appointed, their names are listed

1	Waverley [1814] P. D. Garside
2	Guy Mannering [1815] P. D. Garside
3	The Antiquary [1816] David Hewitt
4a	The Black Dwarf [1816] P. D. Garside
4b	The Tale of Old Mortality [1816] Douglas Mack
5	Rob Roy [1818] David Hewitt
6	The Heart of Mid-Lothian [1818] David Hewitt & Alison Lumsden
7a	The Bride of Lammermoor [1819] J. H. Alexander
7b	A Legend of the Wars of Montrose [1819] J. H. Alexander
8	Ivanhoe [1820] Graham Tulloch
9	The Monastery [1820] Penny Fielding
10	The Abbot [1820] Christopher Johnson
11	Kenilworth [1821] J. H. Alexander
12	The Pirate [1822] Mark Weinstein with Alison Lumsden
13	The Fortunes of Nigel [1822] Frank Jordan
14	Peveril of the Peak [1822] Alison Lumsden
15	Quentin Durward [1823] G. A. M. Wood and J. H. Alexander
16	Saint Ronan's Well [1824] Mark Weinstein
17	Redgauntlet [1824] G. A. M. Wood with David Hewitt
18a	The Betrothed [1825] J. B. Ellis
18b	The Talisman [1825] J. B. Ellis
19	Woodstock [1826] Tony Inglis
20	Chronicles of the Canongate [1827] Claire Lamont
21	The Fair Maid of Perth [1828] A. Hook and D. Mackenzie
22	Anne of Geierstein [1829] J. H. Alexander
23a	Count Robert of Paris [1831] J. H. Alexander
23b	Castle Dangerous [1831] J. H. Alexander
24	*Stories from* The Keepsake [1828] Graham Tulloch
25a	Introductions and Notes from the *Magnum Opus* edition of 1829–33
25b	Introductions and Notes from the *Magnum Opus* edition of 1829–33

WALTER SCOTT

THE FAIR MAID OF PERTH

Edited by
A. D. Hook
and
Donald Mackenzie

EDINBURGH
University
Press

© The University Court of the University of Edinburgh 1999
Edinburgh University Press
22 George Square, Edinburgh

Typeset in Linotronic Ehrhardt
by Speedspools, Edinburgh
and printed and bound in Great Britain
on acid-free paper at the University Press, Cambridge

ISBN 0 7486 0585 1

A CIP record for this book is available from the British Library

FOREWORD

THE PUBLICATION of *Waverley* in 1814 marked the emergence of the modern novel in the western world. It is difficult now to recapture the impact of this and the following novels of Scott on a readership accustomed to prose fiction either as picturesque romance, 'Gothic' quaintness, or presentation of contemporary manners. For Scott not only invented the historical novel, but gave it a dimension and a relevance that made it available for a great variety of new kinds of writing. Balzac in France, Manzoni in Italy, Gogol and Tolstoy in Russia, were among the many writers of fiction influenced by the man Stendhal called 'notre père, Walter Scott'.

What Scott did was to show history and society in motion: old ways of life being challenged by new; traditions being assailed by counter-statements; loyalties, habits, prejudices clashing with the needs of new social and economic developments. The attraction of tradition and its ability to arouse passionate defence, and simultaneously the challenge of progress and 'improvement', produce a pattern that Scott saw as the living fabric of history. And this history was rooted in *place*; events happened in localities still recognisable after the disappearance of the original actors and the establishment of new patterns of belief and behaviour.

Scott explored and presented all this by means of stories, entertainments, which were read and enjoyed as such. At the same time his passionate interest in history led him increasingly to see these stories as illustrations of historical truths, so that when he produced his final *Magnum Opus* edition of the novels he surrounded them with historical notes and illustrations, and in this almost suffocating guise they have been reprinted in edition after edition ever since. The time has now come to restore these novels to the form in which they were presented to their first readers, so that today's readers can once again capture their original power and freshness. At the same time, serious errors of transcription, omission, and interpretation, resulting from the haste of their transmission from manuscript to print can now be corrected.

DAVID DAICHES

EDINBURGH
University
Press

CONTENTS

Acknowledgements viii

General Introduction xi

THE FAIR MAID OF PERTH

Volume I 1

Volume II 129

Volume III 257

Essay on the Text 389

genesis 389

composition 393

later editions 402

the present text 410

Emendation List 421

End-of-line Hyphens 462

Historical Note 464

Explanatory Notes 469

Glossary 520

ACKNOWLEDGEMENTS

The Scott Advisory Board and the editors of the Edinburgh Edition of the Waverley Novels wish to express their gratitude to The University Court of the University of Edinburgh *for its vision in initiating and supporting the preparation of the first critical edition of Walter Scott's fiction. Those Universities which employ the editors have also contributed greatly in paying the editors' salaries, and awarding research leave and grants for travel and materials. Particular thanks are due to the* University of Glasgow *and the* University of Aberdeen.

Although the edition is the work of scholars employed by universities, the project could not have prospered without the help of the sponsors cited below. Their generosity has met the direct costs of the initial research and of the preparation of the text of the first ten novels to appear in this edition.

BANK OF SCOTLAND

The collapse of the great Edinburgh publisher Archibald Constable in January 1826 entailed the ruin of Sir Walter Scott who found himself responsible for his own private debts, for the debts of the printing business of James Ballantyne and Co. in which he was co-partner, and for the bank advances to Archibald Constable which had been guaranteed by the printing business. Scott's largest creditors were Sir William Forbes and Co., bankers, and the Bank of Scotland. On the advice of Sir William Forbes himself, the creditors did not sequester his property, but agreed to the creation of a trust to which he committed his future literary earnings, and which ultimately repaid the debts of over £120,000 for which he was legally liable.

In the same year the Government proposed to curtail the rights of the Scottish banks to issue their own notes; Scott wrote the 'Letters of Malachi Malagrowther' in their defence, arguing that the measure was neither in the interests of the banks nor of Scotland. The 'Letters' were so successful that the Government was forced to withdraw its proposal and to this day the Scottish Banks issue their own notes.

A portrait of Sir Walter appears on all current bank notes of the Bank of Scotland because Scott was a champion of Scottish banking, and because he was an illustrious and honourable customer not just of the Bank of Scotland itself, but also of three other banks now incorporated within it—the British Linen Bank which continues today as the merchant banking arm of the Bank of Scotland, Sir William Forbes and Co., and Ramsays, Bonars and Company.

Bank of Scotland's *support of the EEWN continues its long and fruitful involvement with the affairs of Walter Scott.*

THE BRITISH ACADEMY

The assistance of the British Academy and the Humanities Research Board in awarding a series of Major Research Grants in support of the Edition's Research Fellows has been of the greatest consequence, has been much appreciated, and has been received with gratitude.

OTHER BENEFACTORS

The Advisory Board and editors also wish to acknowledge with gratitude the generous grants, gifts and assistance to the EEWN from the P. F. Charitable Trust, the main charitable trust of the Fleming family which founded and still has a controlling interest in the City firm of Robert Fleming Holdings Limited; *the Edinburgh University General Council Trust, now incorporated within the* Edinburgh University Development Trust, *and the alumni who contributed to the Trust;* Sir Gerald Elliott; *the* Carnegie Trust for the Universities of Scotland; *and particularly the* Robertson Trust *whose help has been especially important in the production of this volume.*

LIBRARIES

Without the generous assistance of the two great repositories of Scott manuscripts, the National Library of Scotland *and the* Pierpont Morgan Library, New York, *it would not have been possible to have undertaken the editing of Scott's novels, and the Board and editors cannot overstate the extent to which they are indebted to their Trustees and staffs.*

THE FAIR MAID OF PERTH

The incomplete manuscript of The Fair Maid of Perth *is owned by the National Library of Scotland. The editors wish to thank the Library for its generous agreement to transfer the manuscript to the University of Glasgow Library for an extended period. Thanks are also due to Hugh Stevenson, Curator at the Kelvingrove Art Gallery in Glasgow, for allowing access to the half-folio of the manuscript owned by the Gallery, and to Jane Millgate for alerting the editors to the existence of the other half of the same folio in the Houghton Library of Harvard University. For a description of the manuscript, Claire Lamont's account in her EEWN edition of* Chronicles of the Canongate First Series *was an indispensable resource. Other manuscripts consulted in preparing this edition – such as Cadell's Diary and Letterbooks – are held by the National Library, and without access to these materials (made possible by the University of Edinburgh Library when the National Library was closed for over a year) it would have been impossible to produce a properly scholarly edition. For helpful access to early editions of* The Fair Maid, *and other materials, special thanks are due to the staff of the Special Collections sections of both Glasgow and Strathclyde University Libraries.*

Editing Scott requires knowledge, expertise and resources of time beyond the capacity of individuals, and many people have helped the present editors. The

EEWN Research Fellow, Alison Lumsden, has been an invaluable assistant in a variety of ways, including the examination of variant textual readings, and the checking of information and quotations; Gerard Carruthers made an important contribution to the early collation procedure. John Cairns proved a mine of information on matters relating to Scots law; Thomas Craik offered specialist advice on Shakespearean references, Roy Pinkerton on classical ones, and Caroline Jackson-Houlston on popular song, while Donald Meek translated the Gaelic in the text of the novel. Ted Cowan, and in particular Stephen Boardman, provided guidance on Scottish history. Thanks are also due to the following for specific information, assistance or guidance: J. H. Alexander, Richard Cronin, Robert Cummings, Angus Kennedy, Bernard Lloyd, Bob Maslen, David Newell and Des O'Brien. The proof-readers were Ian Clark, Gillian Hughes and Sheena Sutherland and the editors are indebted to them not just for spotting typographical errors but for pointing out many issues which might otherwise have been overlooked. Finally the editors wish to record their profound gratitude to the Editor-in-Chief, David Hewitt: his dedicated industry, and widely-ranging knowledge of Scott, have contributed immensely to the production of this volume.

The General Editor for this volume was David Hewitt.

GENERAL INTRODUCTION

What has the Edinburgh Edition of the Waverley Novels achieved? The original version of this General Introduction said that many hundreds of readings were being recovered from the manuscripts, and commented that although the individual differences were often minor, they were 'cumulatively telling'. Such an assessment now looks tentative and tepid, for the textual strategy pursued by the editors has been justified by spectacular results.

In each novel up to 2000 readings never before printed are being recovered from the manuscripts. Some of these are major changes although they are not always verbally extensive. The restoration of the pen-portraits of the Edinburgh literati in *Guy Mannering*, the reconstruction of the way in which Amy Robsart was murdered in *Kenilworth*, the recovery of the description of Clara Mowbray's previous relationship with Tyrrel in *Saint Ronan's Well*—each of these fills out what was incomplete, or corrects what was obscure. A surprising amount of what was once thought loose or unidiomatic has turned out to be textual corruption. Many words which were changed as the holograph texts were converted into print have been recognised as dialectal, period or technical terms wholly appropriate to their literary context. The mistakes in foreign languages, in Latin, and in Gaelic found in the early printed texts are usually not in the manuscripts, and so clear is this manuscript evidence that one may safely conclude that Friar Tuck's Latin in *Ivanhoe* is deliberately full of errors. The restoration of Scott's own shaping and punctuating of speech has often enhanced the rhetorical effectiveness of dialogue. Furthermore, the detailed examination of the text and supporting documents such as notes and letters has revealed that however quickly his novels were penned they mostly evolved over long periods; that although he claimed not to plan his work yet the shape of his narratives seems to have been established before he committed his ideas to paper; and that each of the novels edited to date has a precise time-scheme which implies formidable control of his stories. The Historical and Explanatory Notes reveal an intellectual command of enormously diverse materials, and an equal imaginative capacity to synthesise them. Editing the texts has revolutionised the editors' understanding and appreciation of Scott, and will ultimately generate a much wider recognition of his quite extraordinary achievement.

The text of the novels in the Edinburgh Edition is normally based on the first editions, but incorporates all those manuscript readings which were lost through accident, error, or misunderstanding in the process of converting holograph manuscripts into printed books. The Edition is the first to investigate all Scott's manuscripts and proofs, and all the printed editions to have appeared in his lifetime, and it has adopted the textual strategy which best makes sense of the textual problems.

It is clear from the systematic investigation of all the different states of Scott's texts that the author was fully engaged only in the early stages (manuscripts and proofs, culminating in the first edition), and when preparing the last edition to be published in his lifetime, familiarly known as the Magnum Opus (1829–33). There may be authorial readings in some of the many intermediate editions, and there certainly are in the third edition of *Waverley*, but not a single intermediate edition of any of the nineteen novels so far investigated shows evidence of sustained authorial involvement. There are thus only two stages in the textual development of the Waverley Novels which might provide a sound basis for a critical edition.

Scott's holograph manuscripts constitute the only purely authorial state of the texts of his novels, for they alone proceed wholly from the author. They are for the most part remarkably coherent, although a close examination shows countless minor revisions made in the process of writing, and usually at least one layer of later revising. But the heaviest revising was usually done by Scott when correcting his proofs, and thus the manuscripts could not constitute the textual basis of a new edition; despite their coherence they are drafts. Furthermore, the holograph does not constitute a public form of the text: Scott's manuscript punctuation is light (in later novels there are only dashes, full-stops, and speech marks), and his spelling system though generally consistent is personal and idiosyncratic.

Scott's novels were, in theory, anonymous publications—no title page ever carried his name. To maintain the pretence of secrecy, the original manuscripts were copied so that his handwriting should not be seen in the printing house, a practice which prevailed until 1827, when Scott acknowledged his authorship. Until 1827 it was these copies, not Scott's original manuscripts, which were used by the printers. Not a single leaf of these copies is known to survive but the copyists probably began the tidying and regularising. As with Dickens and Thackeray in a later era, copy was sent to the printers in batches, as Scott wrote and as it was transcribed; the batches were set in type, proof-read, and ultimately printed, while later parts of the novel were still being written. When typesetting, the compositors did not just follow what was before them, but supplied punctuation, normalised spelling, and corrected minor errors. Proofs were first read in-house against the transcripts, and, in addition to the normal checking for mistakes, these proofs were used to improve the punctuation and the spelling.

When the initial corrections had been made, a new set of proofs went to James Ballantyne, Scott's friend and partner in the printing firm which bore his name. He acted as editor, not just as proof-reader. He drew Scott's attention to gaps in the text and pointed out inconsistencies in detail; he asked Scott to standardise names; he substituted nouns for pronouns when they occurred in the first sentence of a paragraph, and inserted the names of speakers in dialogue; he changed incorrect punctuation, and added punctuation he thought desirable; he corrected grammatical errors; he removed close verbal repetitions; and in a cryptic correspondence in the margins of the proofs he told Scott when he could not follow what was happening, or when he particularly enjoyed something.

These annotated proofs were sent to the author. Scott usually accepted Ballantyne's suggestions, but sometimes rejected them. He made many more changes; he cut out redundant words, and substituted the vivid for the pedestrian; he refined the punctuation; he sometimes reworked and revised passages extensively, and in so doing made the proofs a stage in the creative composition of the novels.

When Ballantyne received Scott's corrections and revisions, he transcribed all the changes on to a clean set of proofs so that the author's hand would not be seen by the compositors. Further revises were prepared. Some of these were seen and read by Scott, but he usually seems to have trusted Ballantyne to make sure that the earlier corrections and revisions had been executed. When doing this Ballantyne did not just read for typesetting errors, but continued the process of punctuating and tidying the text. A final proof allowed the corrections to be inspected and the imposition of the type to be checked prior to printing.

Scott expected his novels to be printed; he expected that the printers would correct minor errors, would remove words repeated in close proximity to each other, would normalise spelling, and would insert a printed-book style of punctuation, amplifying or replacing the marks he had provided in manuscript. There are no written instructions to the printers to this effect, but in the proofs he was sent he saw what Ballantyne and his staff had done and were doing, and by and large he accepted it. This assumption of authorial approval is better founded for Scott than for any other writer, for Scott was the dominant partner in the business which printed his work, and no doubt could have changed the practices of his printers had he so desired.

It is this history of the initial creation of Scott's novels that led the editors of the Edinburgh Edition to propose the first editions as base texts. That such a textual policy has been persuasively theorised by Jerome J. McGann in his *A Critique of Modern Textual Criticism* (1983) is a bonus: he argues that an authoritative work is usually found not in the artist's manuscript, but in the printed book, and that there is a collective responsibility in converting an author's manuscript into print, exercised by author, printer and publisher, and governed by the nature of the understanding between the author and the other parties. In Scott's case the exercise of such a collective responsibility produced the first editions of the Waverley Novels. On the whole Scott's printers fulfilled his expectations. There are normally in excess of 50,000 variants in the first edition of a three-volume novel when compared with the manuscript, and the great majority are in accordance with Scott's general wishes as described above.

But the intermediaries, as the copyist, compositors, proof-readers, and James Ballantyne are collectively described, made mistakes; from time to time they misread the manuscripts, and they did not always understand what Scott had written. This would not have mattered had there not also been procedural failures: the transcripts were not thoroughly checked against the original manuscripts; Scott himself does not seem to have read the proofs against the manuscripts and thus did not notice transcription errors which made sense in their context; Ballantyne continued his editing in post-authorial proofs. Furthermore, it has become increasingly evident that, although in theory Scott as partner in the printing firm could get what he wanted, he also succumbed to the pressure of printer and publisher. He often had to accept mistakes both in names and the spelling of names because they were enshrined in print before he realised what had happened. He was obliged to accept the movement of chapters between volumes, or the deletion or addition of material, in the interests of equalising the size of volumes. His work was subject to bowdlerisation, and to a persistent attempt to have him show a 'high example' even in the words put in the mouths of his characters; he regularly objected, but conformed nonetheless. From time to time he inserted, under protest, explanations of what was happening in the narrative because the literal-minded Ballantyne required them.

The editors of modern texts have a basic working assumption that what is written by the author is more valuable than what is generated by compositors and proof-readers. Even McGann accepts such a position, and argues that while the changes made in the course of translating the manuscript text into print are a feature of the acceptable 'socialisation' of the authorial text, they have authority only to the extent that they fulfil the author's expectations about the public form of the text. The editors of the Edinburgh Edition normally choose the first edition of a novel as base-text, for the first edition usually represents the culmination of the initial creative process, and usually seems closest to the form of his work Scott wished his public to have. But they also recognise the failings of the first editions, and thus after the careful collation of all pre-publication materials, and in the light of their investigation into the factors governing the writing and printing of the Waverley Novels, they incorporate into the base-text those manuscript readings which were lost in the production process through accident, error, misunderstanding, or a misguided attempt to 'improve'. In certain cases they also introduce into the base-texts revisions found in editions published almost immediately after the first, which they believe to be Scott's, or which complete the intermediaries' preparation of the text. In addition, the editors correct various kinds of error, such as typographical and copy-editing mistakes including the misnumbering of chapters, inconsistencies in the naming of characters, egregious errors of fact that are not part of the fiction, and failures of sense which a simple emendation can restore. In doing all this the editors follow the model for editing the Waverley Novels which was provided by Claire Lamont in her edition of *Waverley* (Oxford, 1981): her base-text is the first edition emended in the light of the manuscript. But they have also developed that model because working on the Waverley Novels as a whole has greatly increased knowledge of the practices and procedures followed by Scott, his printers and his publishers in translating holograph manuscripts into printed books. The result is an 'ideal' text, such as his first readers might have read had the production process been less pressurised and more considered.

The Magnum Opus could have provided an alternative basis for a new edition. In the Advertisement to the Magnum Scott wrote that his insolvency in 1826 and the public admission of authorship in 1827 restored to him 'a sort of parental control', which enabled him to re-issue his novels 'in a corrected and . . . an improved form'. His assertion of authority in word and deed gives the Magnum a status which no editor can ignore. His introductions are fascinating autobiographical essays which write the life of the Author of Waverley. In addition, the Magnum has a considerable significance in the history of culture. This was the first time all Scott's works of fiction had been gathered together, published in a single uniform edition, and given an official general title, in the process converting diverse narratives into a literary monument, the Waverley Novels.

There were, however, two objections to the use of the Magnum as the base-text for the new edition. Firstly, this has been the form of Scott's work which has been generally available for most of the nineteenth and twentieth centuries; a Magnum-based text is readily accessible to any-one who wishes to read it. Secondly, a proper recognition of the Magnum does not extend to approving its text. When Scott corrected his novels for the Magnum, he marked up printed books (specially pre-pared by the binder with interleaves, hence the title the 'Interleaved Set'), but did not perceive the extent to which these had slipped from the text of the first editions. He had no means of recognising that, for example, over 2000 differences had accumulated between the first edi-tion of *Guy Mannering* and the text which he corrected, in the 1822 octavo edition of the *Novels and Tales of the Author of Waverley*. The printed text of *Redgauntlet* which he corrected, in the octavo *Tales and Romances of the Author of Waverley* (1827), has about 900 divergences from the first edition, none of which was authorially sanctioned. He himself made about 750 corrections to the text of *Guy Mannering* and

200 to *Redgauntlet* in the Interleaved Set, but those who assisted in the production of the Magnum were probably responsible for a further 1600 changes to *Guy Mannering*, and 1200 to *Redgauntlet*. Scott marked up a corrupt text, and his assistants generated a systematically cleaned-up version of the Waverley Novels.

The Magnum constitutes the author's final version of his novels and thus has its own value, and as the version read by the great Victorians has its own significance and influence. To produce a new edition based on the Magnum would be an entirely legitimate project, but for the reasons given above the Edinburgh editors have chosen the other valid option. What is certain, however, is that any compromise edition, that drew upon both the first and the last editions published in Scott's lifetime, would be a mistake. In the past editors, following the example of W. W. Greg and Fredson Bowers, would have incorporated into the first-edition text the introductions, notes, revisions and corrections Scott wrote for the Magnum Opus. This would no longer be considered acceptable editorial practice, as it would confound versions of the text produced at different stages of the author's career. To fuse the two would be to confuse them. Instead, Scott's own material in the Inter-leaved Set is so interesting and important that it will be published separately, and in full, in the two parts of Volume 25 of the Edinburgh Edition. For the first time in print the new matter written by Scott for the Magnum Opus will be wholly visible.

The Edinburgh Edition of the Waverley Novels aims to provide the first reliable text of Scott's fiction. It aims to recover the lost Scott, the Scott which was misunderstood as the printers struggled to set and print novels at high speed in often difficult circumstances. It aims in the Historical and Explanatory Notes and in the Glossaries to illuminate the extraordinary range of materials that Scott weaves together in creating his stories. All engaged in fulfilling these aims have found their en-quiries fundamentally changing their appreciation of Scott. They hope that readers will continue to be equally excited and astonished, and to have their understanding of these remarkable novels transformed by reading them in their new guise.

DAVID HEWITT
January 1999

ST VALENTINE'S DAY;

OR,

THE FAIR MAID OF PERTH.

BY

THE AUTHOR OF "WAVERLEY," &c.

FORMING THE

Second Series

OF CHRONICLES OF THE CANONGATE.

SIC ITUR AD ASTRA.

Motto of the Canongate Arms.

SECOND EDITION.

IN THREE VOLUMES.

VOL. I.

EDINBURGH:

PRINTED FOR CADELL AND CO., EDINBURGH;
AND SIMPKIN AND MARSHALL, LONDON.

1828.

CHRONICLES
OF
THE CANONGATE

Second Series

VOLUME I

━━━━━━━

Chrystal Croftangry's Narrative

The ashes here of murder'd Kings
Beneath my footsteps sleep;
And yonder lies the scene of death,
Where Mary learn'd to weep.
CAPTAIN MARJORIBANKS

EVERY QUARTER of Edinburgh has its own peculiar boast, so that the city together combines within its precincts, (if you take the word of the inhabitants on the subject,) as much variety as beauty, as much of historical interest as of natural sublimity. Our claims in behalf of the Canongate are not the slightest or least interesting. The Castle may excel us in extent of prospect and natural sublimity of site; the Calton had always the superiority of its unrivalled panorama, and has of late added to them that of its towers, bridges, and triumphal arches. The High Street, we acknowledge, had the distinguished honour of being defended by fortifications, of which we can show no vestiges. We will not descend to notice the claims of mere upstart districts, called Old New Town and New New Town, not to mention the favourite Moray Place, which is the newest New Town of all. We will not match ourselves except with our equals, and with our equals in age only, for in dignity we admit of none. We boast being the Court end of the town, possessing the Palace and the sepulchral remains of ancient Monarchs, and that we have the power to excite, in a degree unknown

3

to the less honoured quarters of the city, the dark and solemn recollections of the ancient grandeur, which occupied the precincts of our venerable Abbey from the time of St David, till her deserted halls were once more made glad, and her long silent echoes awakened, by the visit of our present gracious Sovereign.

My long habitation in the neighbourhood, and the quiet respectability of my habits, have given me a sort of intimacy with good Mrs ——, the housekeeper in that most interesting part of the old building, called Queen Mary's Apartments. But a circumstance which lately happened has conferred upon me greater privileges; so that, indeed, I might, I believe, venture on the exploit of Chatelet, who was executed for being found secreted at midnight in the very bedchamber of Scotland's Mistress.

It chanced that the good lady I have mentioned, was, in the discharge of her function, showing the apartments to a cockney from London;—not one of your quiet, dull, common-place visitors, who gape, yawn, and listen with an acquiescent *umph* to the information doled out by the provincial cicerone. No such thing—this was the brisk, alert agent of a great house in the city, who missed no opportunity of doing business, as he termed it, that is, of putting off the goods of his employers, and improving his own account of commission. He had fidgeted through the suite of apartments, without finding the least opportunity to touch upon that which he considered as the principal end of his existence. Even the story of Rizzio's assassination presented no ideas to this emissary of commerce, until the housekeeper appealed, in support of her narrative, to the dusky stains of blood upon the floor.

"These are the stains," she said; "nothing will remove them from the place—there they have been for two hundred and fifty years—and there they will remain while the floor is left standing—neither water nor anything else will ever remove them from that spot."

Now, our cockney, amongst other articles, sold Scouring Drops, as they are called, and a stain of two hundred and fifty years standing was interesting to him, not because it had been caused by the blood of a Queen's favourite, slain in her apartment, but because it offered so admirable an opportunity to prove the efficacy of his unequalled Detergent Elixir. Down on his knees went our friend, but neither in horror nor devotion.

"Two hundred and fifty years, ma'am, and nothing take it away? Why, if it had been five hundred, I have something in my pocket will fetch it out in five minutes. D'ye see this elixir, ma'am? I will show you the stain vanish in a moment."

Accordingly, wetting one end of his handkerchief with the all-deterging specific, he began to rub away on the planks, without heeding the remonstrances of Mrs ———. She, good soul, stood at first in astonishment, like the Abbess of St Bridget's, when a profane visitant drank up the vial of brandy which had long passed muster among the relics of the cloister for the tears of the blessed saint. The venerable guardian of St Bridget probably expected the interference of her patroness—She of Holy Rood might, perhaps, hope that David Rizzio's spectre would arise to prevent the profanation. But Mrs ——— stood not long in the silence of horror. She uplifted her voice, and screamed as loudly as Queen Mary herself, when the dreadful deed was in the act of perpetration—

"Harrow now out! and walawa!" she cried.

I happened to be taking my morning walk in the adjoining gallery, pondering in my mind why the Kings of Scotland, who hung around me, should be each and every one painted with a nose like the knocker of a door, when lo! the walls once more re-echoed with such shrieks, as formerly were as often heard in the Scottish palaces as were sounds of revelry and music. Somewhat surprised at such an alarm in a place so solitary, I hastened to the spot, and found the well-meaning traveller scrubbing the floor like a housemaid, while Mrs ———, dragging him by the skirts of the coat, in vain endeavoured to divert him from his sacrilegious purpose. It cost me some trouble to explain to the zealous purifier of silk-stockings, embroidered waistcoats, broadcloth, and deal planks, that there were such things in the world as stains which ought to remain indelible, on account of the associations with which they are connected. Our good friend viewed everything of the kind only as the means of displaying the virtue of his vaunted commodity. He comprehended, however, that he would not be permitted to proceed to exemplify its powers on the present occasion, so took his leave, muttering that he had always heard the Scots were a nasty people, but had no idea they carried it so far as to choose to have the floors of their palaces blood-boltered, like Banquo's ghost, when to remove them would have cost but a hundred drops of the Infallible Detergent Elixir, prepared and sold by Messrs Scrub and Rub, in five shilling and ten shilling bottles, each bottle being marked with the initials of the inventor, to counterfeit which would be to incur the pains of forgery.

Freed from the odious presence of this lover of cleanliness, my good friend Mrs ——— was profuse in her expressions of thanks; and yet her gratitude, instead of exhausting itself in these declarations, according to the way of the world, continues as lively at this moment as if she had never thanked me at all. It is owing to her recollection of this piece of good service, that I have the permission of wandering, like the ghost of some departed gentleman-usher, through these deserted halls, sometimes, as the old Irish ditty expresses it,

Thinking on things that are long enough ago;

and sometimes wishing I could, with the good luck of most editors of romantic narrative, light upon some hidden crypt or massive antique cabinet, which should yield to my researches an almost illegible manuscript, containing the authentic particulars of some of the strange deeds of those wild days of the unhappy Mary.

My dear Mrs Baliol used to sympathize with me when I regretted that all the Godsends of this nature had ceased to occur, and that an author might chatter his teeth to pieces by the seaside, without a wave ever wafting to him a casket containing such a history as that of Automathes; that he might break his shins in stumbling through a hundred vaults, without finding anything but rats and mice, and become the tenant of a dozen sets of shabby tenements, without seeing any manuscript but the weekly bill for board and lodging. A dairy-maid of these degenerate days might as well wash and deck her dairy in hopes of finding the fairy tester in her shoe.

"It is a sad, and too true a tale, cousin," said Mrs Baliol. "I am sure we all have occasion to regret the want of these ready supplements to a failing invention. But you, most of all, have right to complain that the fairies have not favoured your researches—you who have shown the world that the Age of Chivalry still exists—you, the Knight of Croftangry, who braved the fury of the 'London 'prentice bold,' in behalf of the fair Dame ——, and the memorial of Rizzio's slaughter. Is it not a pity, cousin, considering the feat of chivalry was otherwise so much according to rule—is it not, I say, a great pity that the lady had not been a little younger, and the legend a little older?"

"Why, as to the age at which a fair dame loses the benefits of chivalry, and is no longer entitled to crave boon of brave knight, that I leave to the statutes of the Order of Errantry; but for the blood of Rizzio, I take up the gauntlet, and maintain against all and sundry, that I hold the stains to be of no modern date, but to have been actually the consequence and the record of that terrible assassination."

"As I cannot accept the challenge to the field, fair cousin, I am contented to require proof."

"The unaltered tradition of the Palace, and the correspondence of the existing state of things with that tradition."

"Explain, if you please."

"I will.—The universal tradition bears, that when Rizzio was dragged out of the chamber of the Queen, the heat and fury of the assassins, who struggled which should deal him most wounds, dispatched him at the door of the ante-room. There, therefore, the greater quantity of the blood was spilled, and there the marks of it are still shown. It is reported further by historians, that Mary continued her entreaties for his life, mingling her prayers with screams and exclamations, until she knew that he was assuredly slain; on which she wiped her eyes and said, 'I will now study revenge.'"

"All this is granted.—But the blood? would it not wash out, or waste out, think you, in so many years?"

"I am coming to that presently. The constant tradition of the Palace says that Mary discharged any measures to be taken to remove the marks of slaughter, which she had resolved should remain as a memorial to quicken and confirm her purposed vengeance. But it is added, that, satisfied with the knowledge that it existed, and not desirous to have the ghastly evidence always under her eye, she caused a traverse, as it is called, (that is, a temporary screen of boards,) to be drawn along the under part of the anteroom, a few feet from the door, so as to separate the place stained with the blood from the rest of the apartment, and involve it in considerable obscurity. Now this temporary partition still exists, and by running across and interrupting the plan of the roof and cornices, plainly intimates that it has been intended to serve some temporary purpose, since it disfigures the proportions of the room, interferes with the ornaments of the ceiling, and could only have been put there for some such purpose as hiding an object too disagreeable to be looked upon. As to the objection that the blood-stains would have disappeared in course of time, I apprehend that if measures to efface them were not taken immediately after the affair happened—if the blood, in other words, were allowed to sink into the wood, the stain would become almost indelible. Now, not to mention that our Scottish palaces were not particularly well washed in those days, and that there were no Patent Drops to assist the labours of the mop, I think it very probable that these dark relics might subsist for a long course of time, even if Mary had not desired or directed that they should be preserved, but screened by the traverse from public sight. I know several instances of similar blood-stains remaining for a great many years, and I doubt whether, after a certain time, anything can remove them, save the carpenter's plane. If any Seneschal, by way of increasing the interest of the apartments, had, by means of paint, or any other mode of imitation, endeavoured to palm upon posterity supposititious stigmata, I conceive that the impostor would have chosen the Queen's cabinet and the bedroom for the scene of his trick, placing his bloody tracery where it could be distinctly seen by visitors, instead of hiding it behind the traverse in this manner. The existence of the said traverse, or temporary partition, is also extremely difficult to be accounted for, if the common and ordinary tradition be rejected. In short, all the rest of this striking locality is so true to the historical fact, that I think it may well bear out the additional circumstance of the blood on the floor."

"I profess to you," answered Mrs Baliol, "that I am very willing to be converted to your faith. We talk of a credulous vulgar, without always recollecting that there is a vulgar incredulity, which, in historical matters, as well as in those of religion, finds it easier to doubt than to examine, and endeavours to assume the credit of an *esprit fort*, by denying whatever happens to be a little beyond the very limited comprehension of the sceptic.—And so, that point being settled, and you possessing, as we understand, the Open Sesamum into these secret apartments, how, if we may ask, do you intend to avail yourself of your privilege?—Do you propose to pass the night in the royal bedchamber?"

"For what purpose, my dear lady?—if to improve the rheumatism, this east wind may serve the purpose."

"Improve the rheumatism—Heaven forbid! that would be worse than adding colours to the violet. No, I mean to recommend a night on the couch of the Rose of Scotland, merely to improve the imagination. Who knows what dreams might be produced by a night spent in a mansion of so many memories! For aught I know, the iron door of the postern stair might open at the dead hour of midnight, and, as at the time of the conspiracy, forth might sally the phantom assassins, with stealthy step and ghastly look, to renew the semblance of the deed. There comes the fierce fanatic Ruthven—party hatred enabling him to bear the armour which would otherwise weigh down a form extenuated by wasting disease. See how his writhen features show under the hollow helmet, like those of a corpse tenanted by a demon, whose vindictive purpose looks out at the flashing eyes, while the visage has the stillness of death.—Yonder appears the tall form of the boy Darnley, as goodly in person as vacillating in resolution; yonder he advances with hesitating step, and yet more hesitating purpose, his childish fear having already overcome his childish passion. He is in the plight of a mischievous boy who has fired a mine, and who now, expecting the explosion in remorse and terror, would give his life to quench the train which his own hand lighted.—Yonder—yonder—But I forget the rest of the worthy cut-throats. Help me, if you can."

"Summon up," said I, "the Postulate, George Douglas, the most active of the gang. Let him arise at your call—the claimant of wealth which he does not possess—the partaker of the illustrious blood of Douglas, but which in his veins is sullied with illegitimacy. Paint him the ruthless, the daring, the ambitious—so nigh greatness, yet debarred from it—so near to wealth, yet excluded from possessing it —a political Tantalus, ready to do or dare anything to terminate his necessities and assert his imperfect claims."

"Admirable, my dear Croftangry! But what is a Postulate?"

"Pooh, my dear madam, you disturb the current of my ideas—The Postulate was, in Scottish phrase, the candidate for some benefice which he had not yet attained—George Douglas, who stabbed Rizzio, was the Postulate for the temporal possessions of the rich Abbey of Arbroath."

"I stand informed—Come, proceed; who comes next?"

"Who comes next? Yon tall, thin-made, savage-looking man, with the petronel in his hand, must be Andrew Ker of Faldonside, a brother's son, I believe, of the celebrated Sir David Ker of Cessford; his look and bearing those of a Border freebooter; his disposition so savage, that, during the fray in the cabinet, he presented his loaded piece at the bosom of the young and beautiful Queen, that Queen also being within a few weeks of becoming a mother."

"Bravo, *beau cousin!*—Well, having raised your bevy of phantoms, I hope you do not intend to send them back to their cold beds to warm them? You will put them to some action, and since you do threaten the Canongate with your desperate quill, you surely mean to novelize, or to dramatize if you will, this most singular of all tragedies?"

"Worse—that is less interesting periods of history have been, indeed, shown up, for furnishing amusement to the peaceable ages which have succeeded; but, dear lady, the events are too well known in Mary's days, to be used as vehicles of romantic fiction. What can a better writer than myself add to the elegant and forcible narrative of Robertson? So adieu to my vision—I awake, like John Bunyan, and behold it is a dream.—Well, enough that I awake without a sciatica, which would have probably rewarded my slumbers had I profaned Queen Mary's bed, by using it as a mechanical resource to awaken a torpid imagination."

"This will never do, cousin," answered Mrs Baliol; "you must get over all these scruples, if you would thrive in the character of a romantic historian, which you have determined to embrace. What is the classic Robertson to you? The light which he carried was that of a lamp to illuminate the dark events of antiquity; yours is a magic lantern to raise up wonders which never existed. No reader of sense wonders at your historical inaccuracies, any more than he does to see Punch in the show-box seated on the same throne with King Solomon in his glory, or to hear him hallowing out to the patriarch, amid the deluge, 'Mighty hazy weather, Master Noah.'"

"Do not mistake me, my dear madam," said I; "I am quite conscious of my own immunities as a tale-teller. But even the mendacious Mr Fagg assures us, that though he never scruples to tell a lie at his master's command, yet it hurts his conscience to be found out. Now, this is the reason why I avoid in prudence all well-known paths of history, where every one can read the finger-posts carefully set up to advise them of the right turning; and the very boys and girls, who learn the history of Britain by way of question and answer, hoot at a poor author if he abandons the highway."

"Do not be discouraged, however, Cousin Chrystal. There are plenty of wildernesses in Scottish history, through which, unless I am greatly misinformed, no certain paths have been laid down from actual survey, but which are only described by imperfect tradition, which fills up with wonders and with legends the periods in which no real events are recognized to have taken place. Even thus, as Mat Prior says—

Geographers on pathless downs,
Place elephants for want of towns."

"If such be your advice, my dear lady," said I, "the course of my story shall take its rise upon this occasion at a remote period of history, and in a province removed from my natural sphere of the Canongate."

It was under the influence of those feelings that I undertook the following Historical Romance, which, often suspended and flung aside, is now arrived at a size too important to be altogether thrown away, although there may be little prudence in sending it to the press.

I have not placed in the mouth of the characters the Lowland Scotch dialect now spoken, because unquestionably the Scottish of that day resembled very closely the Anglo-Saxon, with a sprinkling of French or Norman to enrich it. Those who wish to investigate the subject, may consult the Chronicles of Winton, and the History of Bruce, by Archdeacon Barbour. But supposing my own skill in the ancient Scottish were sufficient to invest the dialogue with its peculiarities, a translation must have been necessary for the benefit of the general reader. The Scottish dialect may be therefore considered as laid aside, unless where the use of peculiar words may add emphasis or vivacity to the composition.

Saint Valentine's Day;

OR,

THE FAIR MAID OF PERTH

Chapter One

"Behold the Tiber," the vain Roman cried,
Viewing the ample Tay from Beglie's side;
But where's the Scot that would the vaunt repay,
And hail the puny Tiber for the Tay?

AMONG all the provinces in Scotland, if an intelligent stranger were asked to describe the most varied and the most beautiful, it is probable he would name the county of Perth. A native also of any other district, though his partialities might lead him to prefer his native county in the first instance, would certainly class that of Perth in the second, and thus give its inhabitants a fair right to plead that—prejudice apart—Perthshire forms the fairest portion of Caledonia. It is long since Lady Mary Wortley Montague, with that excellent taste which characterises her writings, expressed her opinion that the most interesting portion of every country, and that which exhibits the varied beauties of natural scenery in greatest perfection, is that where the mountains sink down upon the champaign, or more level land. The most picturesque, if not the highest hills, are to be found there. The rivers find their way out of the mountainous region by the wildest leaps, and through the most romantic passes. Above, the vegetation of a happier climate and soil is mingled with the magnificent characteristics of mountain-scenery, and woods, groves, and thickets in profusion clothe the base of the hills, ascend up the ravines, and mingle with the precipices. It is in such favoured regions that the traveller finds what the poet Gray, or some one else, has termed, Beauty lying in the lap of Terror.

From the same advantage of situation, this favoured province presents a variety of the most pleasing character. Its lakes, woods, and mountains, may vie in beauty with any that the Highland tour exhibits; while Perthshire contains, amidst this romantic scenery, and in some places in connexion with it, many fertile and habitable tracts, which may vie with the richness of merry England herself. The country has also been the scene of many remarkable exploits and events, some of historical importance, others interesting to the poet and romancer, though recorded in popular tradition alone. It was in these vales that the Saxons of the plain, and the Gael of the mountains, had many a desperate and bloody encounter, in which it was frequently impossible to decide the palm of victory between the mailed chivalry of the Low Country, and the plaided clans whom they opposed.

Perth, so eminent for the beauty of its situation, is a place of great antiquity; and old tradition assigns to the town the importance of a Roman foundation. That victorious nation, it is said, pretended to recognize the Tiber in the much more magnificent and navigable Tay, and to acknowledge the large level space, well known by the name of the North Inch, as having a near resemblance to their Campus Martius. The city was often the residence of our monarchs, who, although they had no palace at Perth, found the Cistercian Convent amply sufficient for the reception of their court. It was here that James the First, one of the wisest and best of the Scottish kings, fell a victim to the jealousy of the vengeful aristocracy. Here also occurred the mysterious conspiracy of Gowrie, the scene of which has only of late been effaced, by the destruction of the ancient palace in which the tragedy was acted. The Antiquarian Society of Perth, with just zeal for the objects of their pursuit, have published an accurate plan of this memorable mansion, with some remarks upon its connexion with the narrative of the plot, which display equal acuteness and candour.

One of the most beautiful points of view which Britain, or perhaps the world, can afford, is, or rather we may say was, the prospect from a spot called the Wicks of Beglie, being a species of niche at which the traveller arrived, after a long stage from Kinross, through a waste and uninteresting country, and from which, as forming a pass over the summit of a ridgy eminence which he had gradually surmounted, he beheld, stretching beneath him, the valley of the Tay, traversed by its ample and lordly stream; the town of Perth, with its two large meadows, or Inches, its steeples, and its towers; the hills of Moncrieff and Kinnoul faintly rising into picturesque rocks, partly clothed with woods; the rich margin of the river, studded with elegant mansions; and the distant view of the huge Grampian mountains, the northern screen of this exquisite landscape. The alteration of the road, greatly, it must be owned, to the improvement of general intercourse, avoids this magnificent point of view, and the landscape is introduced more gradually and partially to the eye, though the approach must be still considered as extremely beautiful. There is still, we believe, a footpath left open, by which the station at the Wicks of Beglie may be approached; and the traveller, by quitting his horse or equipage, and walking a few hundred yards, may still compare the real landscape with the sketch which we have attempted to give. But it is not in our power to communicate, or in his to receive, the exquisite charm which

surprise gives to pleasure, when so splendid a view arises when least
expected or hoped for, and which Chrystal Croftangry experienced
when he beheld, for the first time, the matchless scene.

Childish wonder, indeed, was an ingredient in my delight, for I was
not above fifteen years old; and as this had been the first excursion
which I was permitted to make on a pony of my own, I also experienced the glow of independence, mingled with that degree of anxiety
which the most conceited boy feels when he is first abandoned to his
own undirected counsels. I recollect pulling up the reins without
meaning to do so, and gazing on the scene before me as if I had been
afraid it would shift like those in a theatre before I could distinctly
observe its different parts, or convince myself that what I saw was real.
Since that hour, and the period is now more than fifty years past, the
recollection of that inimitable landscape has possessed the strongest
influence over my mind, and retained its place as a memorable thing,
when much that was influential on my own fortunes has fled from my
recollection. It is therefore natural, that, whilst deliberating on what
might be brought forward for the amusement of the public, I should
pitch upon some narrative connected with the splendid scenery which
made so much impression on my youthful imagination, and which
may perhaps have that effect in setting off the imperfections of the
composition, which ladies suppose a fine set of china to possess in
heightening the flavour of indifferent tea.

The period at which I propose to commence, is, however, considerably earlier than either of the remarkable historical transactions to
which I have already alluded, as the events which I am about to
recount occurred during the last years of the fourteenth century, when
the Scottish sceptre was swayed by the gentle, but feeble hand of John,
who reigned under the title of Robert the Third.

Chapter Two

PERTH, boasting, as we have already mentioned, so large a portion of
the beauties of inanimate nature, has at no time been without its own
share of those charms which are at once more interesting and more
transient. To be called the Fair Maid of Perth, would at any period
have been a high distinction, and have inferred no mean superiority in
beauty, where there were many to claim that much-envied attribute.
But, in the feudal times, to which we now call the reader's attention,
female beauty was a quality of much higher importance than it has
been since the ideas of chivalry have been in a great measure extinguished. The love of the ancient cavaliers was a licensed species of

idolatry, which the love of Heaven alone was theoretically supposed to approach in intensity, and which in practice it seldom equalled. God and the Ladies were familiarly appealed to in the same breath; and devotion to the fair sex was as peremptorily enjoined upon the aspirant to the honour of chivalry, as that which was due to Heaven. At such a period in society, the power of beauty was almost unlimited. It could level the highest rank with that which was immeasurably inferior.

It was but in the reign preceding that of Robert III., that beauty alone had elevated a person of inferior rank and indifferent morals to share the Scottish throne; and many women, less artful or less fortunate, had risen to greatness from a state of concubinage, for which the manners of the times made allowance and apology. Such views might have dazzled a girl of higher birth than Catherine, or Katie Glover, who was universally acknowledged to be the most beautiful young woman of the city or its vicinity, and whose renown, as the Fair Maid of Perth, had drawn on her much notice from the young gallants of the Royal Court, when it chanced to be residing in or near Perth; insomuch, that more than one nobleman of the highest rank, and most distinguished for deeds of chivalry, were more attentive to exhibit feats of horsemanship as they passed the door of old Simon Glover, in what was called Couvrefew, or Curfew Street, than to distinguish themselves in the tournaments, where the noblest dames of Scotland were spectators of their address.

But the Glover's daughter—for, as was common with citizens and artizans of that early period, her father, Simon, derived his sirname from the trade which he practised,—showed no inclination to listen to any gallantry which came from those of a station highly exalted above that which she herself occupied; and though probably in no degree insensible to her personal charms, seemed desirous to confine her conquests to those who were within her own sphere of life. Indeed, her beauty being of that kind which we connect more with the mind than with the person, was, notwithstanding her natural kindness and gentleness of disposition, rather allied to reserve than to gaiety, even when in company with her equals; and the earnestness with which she attended upon the exercises of devotion, induced many to think that Catherine Glover nourished the private wish to retire from the world, and bury herself in the recesses of the cloister. But to such a sacrifice, should it be meditated, it was not to be expected her father, reputed a wealthy man, and having this only child, would yield a willing consent.

In her resolution of avoiding the addresses of the gallant courtiers, the reigning Beauty of Perth was confirmed by the sentiments of her parent. "Let them go," he said; "let them go, Catherine, those gallants, with their capering horses, their jingling spurs, their plumed bonnets, and their trim moustaches; they are not of our class, nor will we aim at pairing with them. To-morrow is Saint Valentine's Day, when every bird chooses her mate; but you will not see the linnet pair with the sparrow-hawk, nor the robin red-breast with the kite. My father was an honest burgher of Perth, and could use his needle as well as I can. Did there come war to the gates of our fair burgh, down went needles, thread, and shamoy leather, and out came the good head-piece and target from the dark nook, and the long lance from above the chimney. Show me a day that either he or I were absent when the Provost made his musters? Thus we have led our lives, my girl, working to win our bread, and fighting to defend it. I will have no son-in-law that thinks himself better than me; and for these lords and knights, I trust thou wilt always remember thou art too low to be their lawful love, and too high to be their unlawful loon. And now lay by thy work, lass, for it is holytide eve, and it becomes us to go to the evening service, and pray that Heaven may send thee a good Valentine to-morrow."

So the Fair Maid of Perth laid aside the splendid hawking glove which she was embroidering for the Lady Drummond, and putting on her holiday kirtle, prepared to attend her father to the Blackfriars Monastery, which was adjacent to Couvrefew Street in which they lived. On their passage, Simon Glover, an ancient and esteemed burgess of Perth, somewhat stricken in years and increased in substance, received from young and old the homage due to his velvet jerkin and his gold chain, while the beauty of Catherine, though concealed beneath her screen—which resembled the mantilla still worn in Flanders—called both obeisances and doffings of the bonnet from young and old.

As the pair moved on arm in arm, they were followed by a tall handsome young man, dressed in a yeoman's habit of the plainest kind, but which showed to advantage his fine limbs, as the handsome countenance that looked out from a quantity of curled tresses, surmounted by a small scarlet bonnet, became that species of head-dress. He had no other weapon than a staff in his hand, it not being thought fit that persons of his degree, (for he was an apprentice to the old Glover,) should appear on the street armed with sword or dagger, a privilege which the jack-men, or military retainers of the nobility, esteemed exclusively their own. He attended his master at holytide, partly in the character of a domestic, or protector, should there be cause for his interference; but it was not difficult to discern, by the earnest attention which he paid to Catherine Glover, that it was to her, rather than to her father, that he desired to dedicate his good offices. Generally speaking, there was no opportunity for his zeal displaying itself; for a common feeling of respect induced passengers to give way to the father and daughter.

But when the steel caps, barrets, and plumes, of squires, archers, and men-at-arms, began to be seen among the throng, the wearers of these warlike distinctions were more rude in their demeanour than the quiet citizens. More than once, when from chance, or perhaps from an assumption of superior importance, such an individual took the wall of Simon in passing, the Glover's youthful attendant bristled up with a look of defiance, and the air of one who sought to distinguish his zeal in his mistress's service by its ardour. As frequently did Conachar, for such was the lad's name, receive a check from his master, who gave him to understand that he did not wish his interference before he required it. "Foolish boy," he said, "hast thou not lived long enough in my shop to know that a blow will breed a brawl—that a dirk will cut the skin as fast as a needle pierces leather—that I love peace, though I never feared war, and care not which side of the causeway my daughter and I walk upon, so we may keep our road in peace and quietness?"—Conachar excused himself as zealous for his master's honour, yet was scarce able to pacify the old citizen.—"What have we to do with honour?" said Simon Glover. "If thou wouldst remain in my service, thou must think of honesty, and leave honour to the swaggering fools who wear spurs at their heels and iron on their shoulders. If you wish to wear and use such garniture, you are welcome, but it shall not be in my house or in my company."

Conachar seemed rather to kindle at this rebuke than to submit to it. But a sign from Catherine, if that slight raising of her little finger was indeed a sign, had more effect than the angry reproof of his master; and the youth laid aside the military air which seemed natural to him, and relapsed into the humble follower of a quiet burgher.

Meantime the little party were overtaken by a tall young man wrapped in a cloak, which obscured or muffled a part of his face, a practice often used by the gallants of the time, when they did not wish to be known, or were abroad in quest of adventures. He seemed, in short, one who might say to the world around him, "I desire, for the present, not to be known, or addressed in my own character; but, as I am answerable to myself alone for my actions, I wear my incognito but for form's sake, and care little whether you see through it or not." He came on the right side of Catherine, who had hold of her father's arm, and slackened his pace as if joining their party.

"Good even to you, goodman."

"The same to your worship, and thanks.—May I pray you to pass on?—our pace is too slow for that of your lordship—our company too mean for that of your father's son."

"My father's son can best judge of that, old man. I have business to talk of with you and with my fair St Catherine here, the loveliest and most obdurate saint in the calendar."

"With deep reverence, my lord," said the old man, "I would remind you that this is good St Valentine's Eve, which is no time for business, and that I can have your worshipful commands by your serving man as early as it pleases you to send them."

"There is no time like the present," said the persevering youth, whose rank seemed to be of a kind which set him above ceremony. "I wish to know whether the buff doublet be finished which I commissioned some time since;—and from you, pretty Catherine, (here he sank his voice to a whisper,) I desire to be informed whether your fair fingers have been employed upon it, agreeably to your promise? But I need not ask you, for my poor heart has felt the pang of each puncture that pierced the garment which was to cover it. Traitress, how wilt thou answer for thus tormenting the heart that loves thee so dearly!"

"Let me entreat you, my lord, to forego this wild talk—it becomes not you to speak thus, or me to listen. We are of poor rank, but honest manners; and the presence of the father ought to protect the child from such expressions, even from your lordship."

This she spoke so low that neither her father nor Conachar could understand what she said.

"Well, tyrant," answered the persevering gallant, "I will plague you no longer now, providing you will let me see you from your window to-morrow, when the sun first peeps over the eastern hill, and give me right to be your Valentine for the year."

"Not so, my lord; my father has but now told me that hawks, far less eagles, pair not with the humble linnet. Seek some court lady, to whom your favours will be honour; to me—your Highness must permit me to speak the plain truth—they can be nothing but disgrace."

As they spoke thus, the party arrived at the gate of the church. "Your lordship will, I trust, permit us here to take leave of you," said her father. "I am well aware how little you will alter your pleasure for the pain and uneasiness you may give to such as us; but from the throng of attendants at the gate, your lordship may see that there are others in the church, to whom even your gracious lordship must pay respect."

"Yes—respect; and who pays any respect to me?" said the haughty young lord. "A miserable artizan and his daughter, too much honoured by my slightest notice, have the insolence to tell me that my notice dishonours them. Well, my princess of doe-skin and blue silk, I will teach you to rue this."

As he murmured thus, the Glover and his daughter entered the

Dominican Church, and their attendant, Conachar, in attempting to follow them closely, jostled, perhaps not unwillingly, the young nobleman. The gallant, starting from his unpleasing reverie, and perhaps considering this as an intentional insult, seized on the young man by the breast, struck him, and threw him from him. His irritated opponent recovered himself with difficulty, and grasped towards his own side, as if seeking a sword or dagger in the place where it was usually worn; but finding none, he made a gesture of disappointed rage, and entered the church. During the few seconds he remained, the young nobleman stood with his arms folded on his breast, with a haughty smile, as if defying him to do his worst. When Conachar had entered the church, his opponent, adjusting his cloak yet closer about his face, made a private signal by holding up one of his gloves. He was instantly joined by two men, who, disguised like himself, had waited his motions at a little distance. They spoke together earnestly, after which the young nobleman retired in one direction, his friends or followers going off in another.

Simon Glover, before he entered the church, cast a look towards the group, but had taken his place among the congregation before they separated themselves. He knelt down with the air of a man who has something burthensome on his mind; but when the service was ended, he seemed free from anxiety, as one who had referred himself and his troubles to the disposal of Heaven. The ceremony of High Mass was performed with considerable solemnity, a number of noblemen and ladies of rank being present. Preparations had indeed been made for the reception of the good old King himself, but some of those infirmities to which he was subject had prevented Robert III. from attending the service, as was his wont. When the congregation were dismissed, the Glover and his beautiful daughter lingered for some time, for the purpose of making their several shrifts in the confessionals, where the priests had taken their places for discharging that part of their duty. Thus it happened that the night had fallen dark, and the way was solitary, when they returned along the now deserted streets to their own dwelling. Most persons had betaken themselves to home and to bed. They who still lingered in the street were nightwalkers or revellers, the idle and swaggering retainers of the haughty nobles, who were much wont to insult the peaceful passengers, relying on the impunity which their masters' court favour was too apt to secure them.

It was, perhaps, in apprehension of mischief from some character of this kind, that Conachar, stepping up to the Glover, said, "Master, walk faster—we are dogg'd."

"Dogg'd, sayest thou? By whom and by how many?"

"By one man muffled in his cloak, who follows us like our shadow."

"Then will I never mend my pace along the Couvrefew Street, for the best one man that ever trode it."

"But he has arms," said Conachar.

"And so have we, and hands and legs and feet. Why sure, Conachar, you are not afraid of one man?"

"Afraid!" answered Conachar, indignant at the insinuation; "you shall soon know if I am afraid."

"Now you are as far on the other side of the mark, thou foolish boy —thy temper has no middle course; there is no occasion to make a brawl, though we do not run. Walk thou before with Catherine, and I will take thy place. We cannot be exposed to danger so near home as we are."

The Glover fell behind accordingly, and certainly observed a person keep so close to them, as, the time and place considered, justified some suspicion. When they crossed the street, he also crossed it, and when they advanced or slackened their pace, the stranger's was in proportion accelerated or diminished. The matter would have been of very little consequence had Simon Glover been alone; but the beauty of his daughter might render her the object of some profligate scheme, in a country where the laws afforded such slight protection to those who had not the means to defend themselves. Conachar and his fair charge having arrived on the threshold of their own apartment, which was opened to them by an old female servant, the burgher's uneasiness was ended. Determined, however, to ascertain, if possible, whether there had been any cause for it, he called out to the man whose motions had occasioned the alarm, and who stood still, though he seemed to keep out of reach of the light. "Come, step forward, my friend, and do not play at bo-peep; knowest thou not, that they who walk like phantoms in the dark, are apt to encounter the conjuration of a quarter-staff? Step forward, I say, and show us thy shapes, man."

"Why, so I can, Master Glover," said one of the deepest voices that ever answered question. "I can show my shapes well enough, only I wish they could bear the light something better."

"Body of me," exclaimed Simon, "I should know that voice!—And is it thou, in thy bodily person, Harry Gow?—nay, beshrew me if thou passest this door with dry lips. What, man, curfew has not rung yet, and if it had, it were no reason why it should part father and son. Come in, man; Dorothy shall get us something to eat, and we will jingle a can ere thou leave us. Come in, I say; my daughter Kate will be right glad to see thee."

By this time he had pulled the person, whom he welcomed so cordially, into a sort of kitchen, which served also upon ordinary occasions the office of parlour. Its ornaments were trenchers of pewter, mixed with a silver cup or two, which, in the highest degree of cleanliness, ornamented a range of shelves like those of a beauffet, popularly called the Bink. A good fire, with the assistance of a blazing lamp, spread light and cheerfulness through the apartment, and a savoury smell of some victuals which Dorothy was preparing, did not at all offend the unrefined noses of those whose appetite they were destined to satisfy.

Their unknown attendant now stood in full light among them, and though his appearance was neither dignified nor handsome, his face and figure were not only deserving of attention, but seemed in some manner to command it. He was rather below the middle stature, but the breadth of his shoulders, length and brawniness of his arms, and the muscular appearance of the whole man, argued a most unusual share of strength, and a frame kept in vigour by constant exercise. His legs were somewhat bent, but not in a manner which could be said to approach to deformity; on the contrary, which seemed to correspond to the strength of his frame, though it injured in some degree its symmetry. His dress was of buff-hide; and he wore in a belt around his waist a heavy broad-sword, and a dirk or poniard, as if to defend his purse, which (burgher-fashion) was attached to the same cincture. The head was well proportioned, round, close cropped, and curled thickly with black hair. There was daring and resolution in the dark eye, but the other features seemed to express a bashful timidity, mingled with good humour, and obvious satisfaction at meeting with his old friends. Abstracted from the bashful expression, which was that of the moment, the forehead of Henry Gow, or Smith, (for he was indifferently so called, as both words equally indicated his profession,) was high and noble, but the lower part of the face was less happily formed. The mouth was large, and well-furnished with a set of firm and beautiful teeth, the appearance of which corresponded with the air of personal health and muscular strength, which the whole frame indicated. A short thick beard, and moustaches which had lately been arranged with some care, completed the picture. His age could not exceed eight-and-twenty.

The family appeared all well pleased with the unexpected appearance of an old friend. Simon Glover shook his hand again and again, Dorothy made her compliments, and Catherine herself offered freely her hand, which Henry held in his massive grasp as if he designed to carry it to his lips, but, after a moment's hesitation, desisted, from fear lest the freedom might be ill taken. Not that there was any resistance on the part of the little hand which lay passive in his grasp; but there was a smile mingled with the blush on her cheek, which seemed to increase the confusion of the gallant.

Her father, on his part, called out frankly, as he saw his friend's hesitation, "Her lips, man, her lips! and that's a proffer I would not make to every one who crosses my threshold. But, by good St Valentine, (whose holiday will dawn to-morrow,) I am so glad to see thee in the bonny city of Perth again, that it would be hard to tell the thing I could refuse thee."

The Smith,—for, as has been said, such was the craft of this sturdy artizan,—was encouraged modestly to salute the Fair Maid, who yielded the courtesy with a smile of affection that might have become a sister, saying, at the same time, "Let me hope that I welcome back to Perth a repentant and amended man."

He held her hand as if about to answer, then suddenly, as one who lost courage at the moment, relinquished his grasp; and drawing back as if afraid of what he had done, his dark countenance glowing with bashfulness, mixed with delight, he sate down by the fire on the opposite side from that which Catherine occupied.

"Come, Dorothy, speed thee with the food, old woman;—and Conachar—where is Conachar?"

"He is gone to bed, sir, with a head-ache," said Catherine, in a hesitating voice.

"Go, call him, Dorothy," said the old Glover; "I will not be used thus by him; his Highland blood, forsooth, is too gentle to lay a trencher or spread a napkin, and he expects to enter our ancient and honourable craft without duly waiting and tending upon his master and teacher in all matters of lawful obedience. Go, call him, I say; I will not be thus neglected."

Dorothy was presently heard screaming up stairs, or more probably up a ladder, to the cock-loft, to which the recusant apprentice had made an untimely retreat; a muttered answer was returned, and soon after Conachar appeared in the eating apartment. There was a gloom of deep sullenness on his haughty, though handsome features, and as he proceeded to spread the board, and arrange the trenchers, with salt, spices, and other condiments—to discharge, in short, the duties of a modern domestic, which the custom of the time imposed upon all apprentices—he was obviously disgusted and indignant with the mean office imposed upon him. The Fair Maid of Perth looked with some anxiety at him, as if apprehensive that his evident sullenness might increase her father's displeasure; but it was not till her eyes had sought out his for a second time, that Conachar condescended to veil his dissatisfaction, and throw a greater appearance of willingness and submission into the services which he was performing.

And here we must acquaint our reader, that though the private

interchange of looks betwixt Catherine Glover and the young mountaineer indicated some interest on the part of the former in the conduct of the latter, it would have puzzled the strictest observer to
discover whether that feeling exceeded in degree what might have
been felt by a young person towards a friend and inmate of the same
age, with whom she had lived on habits of intimacy.

"Thou hast had a long journey, son Henry," said Glover, who had
always used that affectionate style of speech, though noways akin to
the young artizan; "ay, and hast seen many a river besides Tay, and
many a fair bigging besides St Johnstoun."

"But none that I like half so well, and none that are half so much
worth my liking," answered the Smith; "I promise you, father,
that when I crossed the Wicks of Beglie, and saw the bonny city lie
stretched fairly before me like a Fairy Queen in romance, whom the
Knight finds asleep among a wilderness of flowers, I felt even as a
bird, when it folds its wearied wings to stoop down on its own nest."

"Aha! so thou canst play the Makar* yet?" said the Glover. "What,
shall we have our ballets, and our roundels again? our lusty carols for
Christmas, and our mirthful springs to trip it round the May-pole?"

"Such toys there may be forthcoming, father," said Henry Smith,
"though the blast of the bellows and the clatter of the anvil make but
coarse company to lays of minstrelsy; but I can afford them no better,
since I must mend my fortune, though I mar my verses."

"Right again—my own son just," answered the Glover; "and I trust
thou has made a saving voyage of it?"

"Nay, I made a thriving one, father—I sold the steel habergeon that
you wot of for four hundred marks, to the English Warden of the East
Marches, Sir Magnus Redman. He scarce scrupled a penny after I
gave him leave to try a sword-dint upon it. The beggarly Highland
thief who bespoke it boggled at half the sum, though it had cost me a
year's labour."

"What dost thou start at, Conachar?" said Simon, addressing himself, by way of parenthesis, to the mountain disciple; "wilt thou never
learn to mind thy own business, without listening to what is passing
round thee? What is it to thee that an Englishman thinks that cheap
which a Scottishman may hold dear?"

Conachar turned round to speak, but, after a moment's consideration, looked down, and endeavoured to recover his composure, which
had been deranged by the contemptuous manner in which the Smith
had spoken of his Highland customers. Henry went on without paying
any attention to him.

"I sold at high prices some swords and whingers when I was at

*Old Scottish for *Poet*.

Edinburgh. They expect war there; and if it please God to send it, my merchandize will be worth its price. St Dunstan make us thankful, for he was of our craft. In short, this fellow (laying his hand on his purse) who, thou knowest, father, was somewhat lank and low in condition when I set out four months since, is now as round and full as a six-weeks' porker."

"And that other leathern-sheathed iron-hilted fellow who hangs beside him," said the Glover, "has he been idle all this while?—Come, jolly Smith, confess the truth—how many brawls hast thou had since crossing the Tay?"

"Nay, now you do me wrong, father, to ask me such a question, (glancing a look at Catherine,) in such a presence," answered the armourer; "I make swords, indeed, but I leave it to other people to use them. No, no—seldom have I a naked sword in my fist, save when I am turning them on the anvil or grindstone; and they slandered me to your daughter Catherine, that led her to suspect the quietest burgess in Perth of being a brawler. I wish the best of them would dare say such a word at the Hill of Kinnoul, and never a man on the green but he and I."

"Ay, ay," said the Glover, laughing, "we should then have a fine sample of your patient sufferance—Out upon you, Henry, that you will speak so like a knave to one who knows thee so well! You look at Kate, too, as if she did not know that a man in this country must make his hand keep his head, unless he will sleep in slender security. Come, come; beshrew me if thou hast not spoiled as many suits of armour as thou hast made."

"Why, he would be a bad armourer, father Simon, that could not with his own blow make proof of his own workmanship. If I did not sometimes cleave a helmet, or strike a sword's point through a harness, I should not know what strength of fabric to give them; and might jingle together such pasteboard work as yonder Edinburgh smiths think not shame to put out of their hands."

"Aha—now would I lay a gold crown thou hast had a quarrel with some Edinburgh Burn-the-wind upon that very ground?"

"A quarrel!—no, father," replied the Perth armourer, "but a measuring of swords with such a one upon St Leonard's Crags, for the honour of my bonny city, I confess. Surely you do not think I would quarrel with a brother craftsman?"

"Ah, to a surety, no. But how did your brother craftsman come off?"

"Why, as one with a sheet of paper on his bosom might come off from the stroke of a lance—or rather, indeed, he came not off at all; for, when I left him, he was lying in the Hermit's Lodge daily expecting death, for which Father Gervis said he was in heavenly preparation."

"Well—any more measuring of weapons?" said the Glover.

"Why, truly, I fought an Englishman at Berwick besides, on the old question of the Supremacy, as they call it—I am sure you would not have me slack at that debate?—and I had the luck to hurt him on the left knee."

"Well done for St Andrew!—to it again.—Whom next had you to deal with?" said Simon, laughing at the exploits of his pacific friend.

"I fought a Scotsman in the Torwood," answered Henry Smith, "upon a doubt which was the better swordsman, which, you are aware, could not be known or decided without a trial. The poor fellow lost two fingers."

"Pretty well for the most peaceful lad in Perth, who never touches a sword but in the way of his profession.—Well, anything more to tell us?"

"Little—for the drubbing of a Highlandman is a thing not worth mentioning."

"For what didst thou drub him, O man of peace?" inquired the Glover.

"For nothing that I can remember," replied the Smith, "except his presenting himself on the south side of Stirling Bridge."

"Well, here is to thee, and thou art welcome to me after all these exploits.—Conachar, bestir thee. Let the cans clink, lad, and thou shalt have a cup of the nut-brown for thyself, my boy."

Conachar poured out the good liquor for his master and for Catherine, with due observance. But that done, he set the flagon on the table, and sate down.

"How now, sirrah!—be these your manners? Fill to my guest, the worshipful Master Henry Smith."

"Master Smith may fill for himself, if he wishes for liquor," answered the youthful Celt. "The son of my father has demeaned himself enough already for one evening."

"That's well crowed for a cockeril," said Henry; "but thou art so far right, my lad, that the man deserves to die of thirst who will not drink without a cup-bearer."

But his entertainer took not the contumacy of the young apprentice with so much patience.—"Now, by my honest word, and by the best glove I ever made," said Simon, "thou shalt help him with liquor from that cup and flagon, if thee and I are to abide under one roof."

Conachar arose sullenly upon hearing this threat, and, approaching the Smith, who had just taken the tankard in his hand, and was raising it to his head, he contrived to stumble against him and jostle him so awkwardly, that the foaming ale gushed over his face, person, and dress. Good-natured as the Smith, in spite of his warlike propensities, really was in the utmost degree, his patience failed under such a provocation. He seized the young man's throat, being the part which came readiest to his grasp, as Conachar arose from the pretended stumble, and pressing it severely as he cast the lad from him, exclaimed, "Had this been in another place, young gallows-bird, I had stowed the lugs out of thy head, as I have done to some of thy clan before thee."

Conachar recovered his feet with the activity of a tiger, and exclaiming, "Never shall you live to make that boast again!" drew a short sharp knife from his bosom, and springing on Henry Smith, attempted to plunge it into his body over the collar-bone, which must have been a mortal wound. But the object of this violence was so ready to defend himself by striking up the assailant's hand, that the blow only glanced on the bone, and scarce drew blood. To wrench the dagger from the boy's hand, and to secure him with a grasp like that of his own iron vice, was, for the powerful Smith, the work of a single moment. Conachar felt himself at once in the absolute power of the formidable antagonist whom he had provoked; he became deadly pale, as he had been the moment before glowing red, and stood mute with shame and fear, until, relieving him from his powerful hold, the Smith quietly said, "It is well for thee that thou canst not make me angry—thou art but a boy, and I, a grown man, ought not to have provoked thee. But let this be a warning."

Conachar stood an instant as if about to reply, and then left the room, ere Simon had collected himself enough to speak. Dorothy was running hither and thither for salves and healing herbs. Catherine had swooned at the sight of the trickling blood.

"Let me depart, father Simon," said Henry Smith, mournfully; "I might have guessed I should have my old luck, and spread strife and bloodshed where I would wish most to bring peace and happiness. Care not for me—look to poor Catherine; the fright of such an affray hath killed her, and all through my fault."

"Thy fault, my son!—It was the fault of yon Highland cateran, whom it is my curse to be cumbered with; but he shall go back to his glens to-morrow, or taste the tolbooth of the burgh. An assault upon the life of his master's guest in his master's house!—It breaks all bonds between us. But let me see to thy wound."

"Catherine!" repeated the armourer, "look to Catherine."

"Dorothy will see to her," said Simon; "surprise and fear kill not—skenes and dirks do. And she is not more the daughter of my blood than thou, my dear Henry, art the son of my affections. Let me see the wound. The skene-occle is an ugly weapon in a Highland hand."

"I mind it no more than the scratch of a wild-cat," said the armourer; "and now that the colour is coming to Catherine's cheek again, you shall see me a sound man in a moment." He turned to a corner in which hung a small mirror, and hastily took from his purse some dry lint to apply to the slight wound he had received. As he unloosed the leathern jacket from his neck and shoulders, the manly and muscular form which they displayed, was not more remarkable than the fairness of his skin, where it had not, as in hands and face, been exposed to the effects of rough weather, and of his laborious trade. He hastily applied some lint to stop the bleeding, and a little water having removed all other marks of the fray, he buttoned his doublet anew, and turned again to the table where Catherine, still pale and trembling, was, however, recovered from her fainting fit.

"Would you but grant me your forgiveness for having offended you in the very first hour of my return? The lad was foolish to provoke me, and yet I was more foolish to be provoked by such as he. Your father blames me not, Catherine, and cannot you forgive me?"

"I have no power to forgive," answered Catherine, "where I have no title to resent. If my father chooses to have his house made the scene of night brawls, I must witness them—I cannot help myself. Perhaps it was wrong in me to faint and interrupt, it may be, the farther progress of a fair fray. My apology is that I cannot bear the sight of blood."

"And is this the manner," said her father, "in which you receive my friend after his long absence?—my friend, did I say?—nay, my son. He escapes being murdered by a fellow whom I will to-morrow clear this house of, and you treat him as if he had done wrong in dashing from him the snake which was about to sting him!"

"It is not my part, father," returned the Maid of Perth, "to decide who had the right or wrong in the present brawl; nor did I see what happened distinctly enough to say which was assailant or which defender. But sure our friend, Master Henry, will not deny that he lives in a perfect atmosphere of strife, blood, and quarrels. He hears of no swordsman but he envies his reputation, and must needs put his valour to the proof. He sees no brawl but he must strike into the midst of it. Has he friends, he fights with them for love and honour—has he enemies, he fights with them for hatred and revenge. And those men who are neither his friends nor foes, he fights with them because they are on this or that side of a river. His days are days of battle, and doubtless he acts them over again in his dreams."

"Daughter," said Simon, "your tongue wags too freely. Quarrels and fights are men's business, not women's, and it is not maidenly to think or speak of them."

"But if they are so rudely enacted in our presence," said Catherine, "it is a little hard to expect us to think or speak of anything else. I will grant you, my father, that this valiant burgess of Perth is one of the best-hearted men that draws breath within its walls—that he would walk a hundred yards out of the way rather than step upon a worm—that he would be as loath, in wantonness, to kill a spider, as if he was a kinsman to King Robert of happy memory—that in the last quarrel before his departure he fought with four butchers to prevent their killing a poor mastiff that had misbehaved in the bull-ring, and narrowly escaped the fate of the cur that he was protecting. I will grant you also, that the poor never pass the house of the wealthy armourer but they are relieved with food and alms. But what avails all this, when his sword makes as many starving orphans and mourning widows as his purse relieves?"

"Nay, but Catherine, hear me but a word before going on with a string of reproaches against my friend, that sound something like sense, while they are, in truth, inconsistent with all we hear and see around us. What," continued the Glover, "do our King and our court, our knights and ladies, our abbots, monks, and priests themselves, so earnestly crowd to see? Is it not to behold the display of chivalry, to witness the gallant actions of brave knights in the tilt and tourney-ground, to look upon deeds of honour and glory achieved by arms and bloodshed? What is it these proud knights do, that differs from what our good Henry Gow works out in his sphere? Who ever heard of his abusing his skill and strength to do evil or forward oppression, and who knows not how often it has been employed in the good cause of the burgh? And shouldst not thou? of all women, deem thyself honoured and glorious that so true a heart and so strong an arm has termed himself thy bachelor? In what do the proudest dames take their loftiest pride, save in the chivalry of their knight; and has the boldest in Scotland done more gallant deeds than my brave son Henry, though but of low degree? Is he not known to Highland and Lowland as the best armourer that ever made sword, and the truest soldier that ever drew one?"

"My dearest father," answered Catherine, "your words contradict themselves, if you will permit your child to say so. Let us thank God and the good saints, that we are in a peaceful rank of life, below the notice of those whose high birth, and yet higher pride, lead them to glory in their bloody works of cruelty, which the proud and lordly term deeds of chivalry. Your wisdom will allow that it would be absurd in us to prank ourselves in their dainty plumes and splendid garments—why, then, should we imitate their full-blown vices? Why should we assume their hard-hearted pride and relentless cruelty, to which murder is not only a sport, but a subject of vainglorious triumph? Let those whose rank claims as its right such bloody homage, take pride and pleasure in it;—we, who have no share in the sacrifice, may the better pity the sufferings of the victim. Let us thank our lowliness, since it secures us from temptation.—But forgive me, father, if I have stepped over the limits of my duty in contradicting the views which you entertain, with so many others, on these subjects."

"Nay, thou hast ever too much talk for me, girl," said her father, somewhat angrily. "I am but a poor workman, whose best knowledge is to distinguish the left-hand glove from the right. But if thou wouldst have my forgiveness, say something of comfort to my poor Henry. There he sits, confounded and dismayed with all the preachment thou hast heaped together; and he, to whom a trumpet sound was like the invitation to a feast, is struck down at the sound of a child's whistle."

The armourer, indeed, while he heard the lips that were dearest to him paint his character in such unfavourable colours, had laid his head down on the table, upon his folded arms, in an attitude of the deepest dejection, or almost despair. "I would to Heaven, my dearest father," answered Catherine, "that it were in my power to speak comfort to Henry, without betraying the sacred cause of the truths I have just told you. And I may,—nay, I must have such a commission," she continued, with something that the earnestness with which she spoke, and the extreme beauty of her features, caused for the moment to resemble inspiration. "The truth of Heaven," she said, in a solemn tone, "was never committed to a tongue, however feeble, but it gave a right to that tongue to announce mercy, while it declared judgment.—Arise, Henry—rise up, noble-minded, good, and generous, though widely mistaken man—thy faults are those of this cruel and remorseless age—thy virtues all thine own."

While she thus spoke, she laid her hand upon the Smith's arm, and extricating it from under his head by a force which, however gentle, he could not resist, she compelled him to raise towards her his manly face, and the eyes into which her expostulations, mingled with other feelings, had summoned tears. "Weep not," she said, "or rather weep on—but weep as those who have hope. Abjure the sins of pride and anger which most easily beset thee—Fling from thee the cursed weapons, to the fatal and murderous use of which thou art so easily tempted."

"You speak to me in vain, Catherine," returned the armourer; "I may, indeed, turn monk and retire from the world, but while I live in it I must practise my trade; and while I form armour and weapons for others, I cannot myself withstand the temptation of using them. You would not reproach me as you do, if you knew how inseparably the means by which I gain my bread are connected with that warlike spirit which you impute to me as a fault, though it is the consequence of inevitable necessity. While I strengthen the shield or corslet to withstand wounds, must I not have constantly in remembrance the manner and strength with which they may be dealt; and when I forge the sword and temper it for war, is it practicable for me to avoid the recollection of its use?"

"Then throw from you, my dear Henry," said the enthusiastic girl, clasping with both her slender hands the nervous strength and weight of one of the muscular armourer's, which they raised with difficulty, permitted by its owner, yet without receiving assistance from his volition—"cast from you, I say, the art which is a snare to you. Abjure the fabrication of weapons which can only be useful to abridge human life, already too short for repentance, or to encourage with a feeling of safety those whom fear might otherwise prevent from risking themselves in peril. The art of forming arms, whether offensive or defensive, is alike sinful in one to whose violent and ever vehement disposition the very working upon them proves a sin and a snare. Resign utterly the manufacture of weapons of every description, and deserve the forgiveness of Heaven, by renouncing all that can lead to the sin which most easily besets you."

"And what," murmured the armourer, "am I to do for my livelihood, when I have given over the art of forging arms, for which Henry of Perth is known from the Tay to the Thames?"

"Your art itself," said Catherine, "has innocent and laudable resources. If you renounce the forging of swords and bucklers, there remains to you the task of forming the harmless spade, and the honourable as well as useful ploughshare,—of those implements which contribute to the support of life, or to its comforts. Thou canst frame locks and bars to defend the property of the weak against the stouthrief and oppression of the strong. Men will still resort to thee, and repay thy honest industry"——

But here Catherine was interrupted. Her father had heard her declaim against war and tournaments with a feeling, that though her doctrines were new to him, they might not, nevertheless, be entirely erroneous. He felt, indeed, a wish that his proposed son-in-law should not commit himself voluntarily to the hazards which the daring character and great personal strength of Henry the Smith had hitherto led him to incur too readily; and so far he would rather have desired that Catherine's arguments should have produced some effect upon the mind of her lover, whom he knew to be as ductile, when influenced by his affections, as he was fierce and intractable when assailed by hostile remonstrances or threats. But it entered into none of his views, when he heard her enlarge upon the necessity of his designed son-in-law resigning a trade which brought in more ready income than any at that time practised in Scotland, and more profit to Henry of Perth in particular, than to any armourer in the nation. He had some indistinct idea, that it would not be amiss to convert, if possible, Henry Smith from his too frequent use of arms, even though he felt some pride in being connected with one who wielded with such superior excellence those weapons, which in that warlike age it was the boast of all men to manage with spirit. But when he heard his daughter recommend, as the readiest road to this pacific state of mind, that her lover should renounce the gainful trade in which he was held unrivalled, and which, from the constant private differences and public wars of the time, was sure to afford him a large income, he could withhold his wrath no longer. The daughter had scarce recommended to her lover the fabrication of the implements of husbandry, than, feeling that certainty of being right, of which in the earlier part of their debate he had been somewhat doubtful, the father broke in with—

"Locks and bars, plough-graith and harrow-teeth!—and why not grates and fire-prongs, and Culross girdles, and an ass to carry the merchandize through the country—and thou for another ass to lead it by the halter? Why, Catherine, girl, has sense altogether forsaken thee, or dost thou think that in these hard and iron days men will give ready silver for anything save that which can defend their own life, or enable them to take that of their enemy? We play for our lives now, thou silly wench, and not for the bread supports them—for that part those who are strong take, those who are weak yield, and happy is the man who, like my worthy son, has means of obtaining his living otherwise than by the point of the sword which he makes. Preach peace to him as much as thou wilt—I will never be he will say thee nay; but as for bidding the first armourer in Scotland forego the forging of swords, curtal-axes, and harness, it is enough to drive patience itself mad—Out from my sight!—and next morning I prithee remember, that shouldst thou have the luck to see Henry Smith, which is more than thy usage of him has deserved, you see a man who has not his match in Scotland at the use of broadsword and battle-axe, and who can work for five hundred merks a year without breaking a holiday."

The daughter, on hearing her father speak thus peremptorily, made a low obeisance, and without further good-night, withdrew to the chamber which was her usual sleeping apartment.

Chapter Three

THE ARMOURER'S HEART swelled big with various and contending sensations, so that it seemed it would burst the leathern doublet under which it was shrouded. He arose—turned away his head, and extended his hand towards the Glover, while he averted his face, as if desirous that his emotion should not be read upon his countenance.

"Nay, hang me if I bid you farewell, man," said Simon, striking the flat of his hand against that which the armourer expanded towards him. "I will shake no hands with you for an hour to come at least. Tarry but a moment, man, and I will explain all this; and surely a few drops of blood from a scratch, and a few silly words from a foolish wench's lips, are not to part father and son, when they have been so long without meeting? Stay then, man, if ever you would wish for a father's blessing and St Valentine's, whose blessed eve this chances to be."

The Glover was soon heard loudly summoning Dorothy, and, after some clanking of keys and trampling up and down stairs, Dorothy appeared bearing three large rummer cups of green glass, which were then esteemed a great and precious curiosity, and the Glover followed with a huge bottle, equal at least to three quarts of these degenerate days.—"Here is a cup of wine, Henry, older by half than I am myself; my father had it in a gift from stout old Crabbe the Flemish engineer, who defended Perth so stoutly in the minority of David the Second. We Glovers could always do something in war, though our connexion with it was less than yours who work in steel and iron. And my father had pleased old Crabbe—some other day I will tell you how, and also how long these bottles were concealed under ground to save them from the reiving Southron. So I will empty a cup to the health of my honoured father—May his sins be forgiven him! Dorothy, thou shalt drink this pledge, and then be gone to thy cock-loft. I know thine ears are itching, girl, but I have that to say which no one must hear save Henry Smith, the son of mine adoption."

Dorothy did not venture to remonstrate, but taking off her glass, or rather her goblet, with good courage, retired to her sleeping apartment according to her master's commands. The two friends were left alone.

"It grieves me, friend Henry," said Simon, filling at the same time his own glass and his guest's, "it grieves me from my soul that my daughter retains this idle humour; but also, methinks, thou mightst mend it. Why wouldst thou come hither clattering with thy sword and dagger, when the girl is so silly that she cannot bear the sight of them? Dost thou not remember that thou hadst a sort of quarrel with her even thou hast left Perth, because thou wouldst not go like other honest quiet burgesses, but must be ever armed, like one of the rascally jackmen that wait on the nobility? Sure it is time enough for decent burgesses to arm at the tolling of the common bell, which calls us out bodin in effeir of war."*

"Why, my good father, that was not my fault; but I had no sooner quitted my nag than I run hither to tell you of my return, thinking, if it were your will to permit me, that I would get your advice about being Mistress Catherine's Valentine for the year; and then I heard from Mrs Dorothy that you were gone to hear mass at the Black Friars. So I thought I would follow thither, partly to hear the same mass with you, and partly—Our Lady and St Valentine forgive me—to look upon one who thinks little enough of me—And, as you entered the church, methought I saw two or three dangerous-looking men holding counsel together, and gazing at you and at her, and in especial Sir John Ramorny, whom I knew well enough, for all his disguise, and the velvet patch over his eye, and his cloak so like a serving man's. So methought, father Simon, that as you were old, and yonder slip of a Highlander something too young to do battle, I would, even walk quietly after you, not doubting, with the tools I had about me, to bring any one to reason that might disturb you on your way home. You know that yourself discovered me, and drew me into the house, whether I would or no. Otherwise, I promise you, I would not have seen your daughter till I had donn'd the new jerkin which was made at Berwick after the latest cut; nor would I have appeared before her with these weapons, which she mislikes so much—although, to say truth, so many are at deadly feud with me for one unhappy chance or another, that it is as needful for me as for any man in Scotland to go by night with weapons about me."

"The silly wench never thinks of that," said Simon Glover; "she never has sense to consider, that in our dear native land of Scotland every man deems it his privilege and duty to avenge his own wrong. But, Harry, my boy, thou art to blame for taking her talk so much to heart. I have seen thee bold enough with other wenches—wherefore so still and tongue-tied with her?"

"Because she is something different from other maidens, father Glover—because she is not only more beautiful, but wiser, higher, holier, and seems to me as if she were made of better clay than we that

* That is, not in dread of war, but in the guise which *effeirs*, or belongs, to war; in arms, namely, offensive and defensive. "Bodin in feir of war," a frequent term in old Scottish history and muniments, means arrayed in warlike guise.

approach her. I can hold my head high enough with the rest of the lasses round the Maypole; but somehow, when I approach Catherine, I feel myself an earthly, coarse, ferocious creature, scarce worthy to look on her, much less to contradict the precepts which she expounds to me."

"You are an imprudent merchant, Henry Smith," replied Simon; "and rate too high the goods you wish to purchase. Catherine is a good girl, and my daughter; but if you make her a conceited ape by your bashfulness and your flattery, neither you nor I will see our wishes accomplished."

"I often fear it, my good father," said the Smith; "for I feel how little I am worthy of Catherine."

"Feel a thread's end!" said the Glover; "feel for me, friend Smith, for Catherine and me. Think how the poor thing is beset from morning to night, and by what sort of persons. We were accosted to-day by one too powerful to be named, though windows be down and doors shut—Ay, and he showed his displeasure openly, because I would not permit him to gallant my daughter in the church itself, when the priest was saying mass. There are others scarce less reasonable. I sometimes wish that Catherine were some degrees less fair, that she might not catch that dangerous sort of admiration, or somewhat less holy; that she might sit down like an honest woman, contented with stout Henry Smith, who could protect his wife against every sprig of chivalry in the Court of Scotland."

"And if I did not," said Henry, thrusting out a hand and arm which might have belonged to a giant for bone and muscle, "I would I may never bring hammer upon anvil again. Ay, an it were come but that length, my fair Catherine should see that there is no harm in a man having the trick of defence. But I believe she thinks the whole world is one great Minster-church, and that all who live in it should behave as if they were at an eternal mass."

"Nay, in truth," said the father, "she has strange influence over those who approach her—the Highland lad, Conachar, with whom I have been cumbered for these two or three years, although you may see he has the natural spirit of his people, obeys the least sign which Catherine makes him, and, indeed, will hardly be ruled by any one else in the house. She takes much pains with him to bring him from his rude Highland habits."

Here Harry Smith became uneasy in his chair, lifted the flaggon, set it down, and at length exclaimed, "The devil take the young Highland whelp and his whole kindred!—what has Catherine to do to instruct such a fellow as him? He will be just like the wolf-cub that I was fool enough to train to the offices of a dog, and every one thought him reclaimed, till, in an ill hour, I went to walk on the hill of Moncrieff, when he broke loose on the Laird's flock, and made a havock that I might well have rued, had the Laird not wanted harness at the time. And I marvel that you, being a sensible man, father Glover, will keep this Highland young fellow—a likely one, I promise you—so nigh to Catherine, as if there were no other than your daughter to serve him for schoolmistress."

"Fie, my son, fie,—now you are jealous," said Simon, "of a poor young fellow, who, to tell you the truth, resides here because he may not so well live on the other side of the hill."

"Ay, ay, father Simon," retorted the Smith, who had all the narrow-minded feelings of the burghers of his time, "an it were not for fear of offence, I would say that you have even too much packing and peeling with yonder loons out of burgh."

"I must get my deer-hides, kid-skins, and so forth, somewhere, my good Harry,—and Highlandmen give good bargains."

"They can afford them," replied Henry, drily; "for they sell nothing but stolen gear."

"Well, well,—be that as it may, it is not my business where they get the bestial, so I get the skins. But as I was saying, there are certain considerations why I am willing to oblige the father of this young man by keeping him here. And he is but half a Highlander neither, and wants a thought of the dour spirit of a Glune-amie;—after all, I have seldom seen him so fierce as he showed himself but now."

"You could not, unless he had killed his man," replied the Smith, in the same dry tone.

"Nevertheless, if you wish it, Harry, I'll set all other respects aside, and send the landlouper to seek other quarters to-morrow morning."

"Nay, father," said the Smith, "you cannot suppose that Harry Burn-the-wind cares the value of a smithy-dander* for such a cub as yonder cat-a-mountain? I care little, I promise you, though all his clan were coming down the Shoe-gate with slogan crying, and pipes playing; I would find fifty blades and bucklers would send them back faster than they came. But, to speak truth, though it is a fool's speech too—I care not to see the fellow so much with Catherine. Remember, father Glover, your trade keeps your eyes and hands close employed, and must have your heedful care, even if this lazy lurdane wrought at it, which you know yourself he seldom does."

"And that is true," said Simon; "he cuts all his gloves out for the right hand, and never could finish a pair in his life."

"No doubt his notions of skin-cutting are rather different," said Henry. "But with your leave, father, I would only say, that work he, or

*Cinder.

be he idle, he has no bleared eyes,—no hands seared with the hot iron, and welked by the use of the fore-hammer,—no hair rusted in the smoke, and singed in the furnace like the hide of a badger, rather than what is fit to be covered with a Christian bonnet. Now, let Catherine be as good a wench as ever lived, and I will uphold her to be the best in Perth, yet she must see and know that these things make a difference betwixt man and man, and that the difference is not in my favour."

"Here is to thee with all my heart, son Harry," said the old man, filling a brimmer to his companion, and another to himself; "I see, that good smith as thou art, thou ken'st not the mettle that women are made of. Thou must be bold, Henry; and bear thyself not as if thou wert a witch going to the gallow-lee, but a gay young fellow who knows his own worth, and will not be slighted by the best grandchild Eve ever had. Catherine is a woman like her mother, and thou thinkest foolishly to suppose they are all set on what pleases the eye. Their ear must be pleased too, man; they must know that he whom they favour is bold and buxom, and might have the love of twenty, though he is sueing for theirs. Believe an old man, women walk more by what others think than by what they think themselves; and when she asks for the boldest man in Perth, whom shall she hear named but Harry Burn-the-wind? —The best armourer that ever fashioned weapon on anvil?—why Harry Smith again—The tightest dancer at the May-pole?—why, the lusty smith—The gayest troller of ballads?—why, who but Harry Gow?—The best wrestler, sword-and-buckler player—the king of the weapon-shawing—the breaker of mad horses—the tamer of wild Highlandmen?—Ever more it is thee—thee—no one but thee. —And shall Catherine prefer yonder slip of a Highland boy to thee? —pshaw! she might as well make a steel gauntlet out of kid's leather. I tell thee, Conachar is nothing to her, but so far as she would fain prevent the devil having his due of him, as of other Highlandmen— God bless her, poor thing, she would bring all mankind to better thoughts if she could."

"In which she will fail to a certainty," said the Smith, who, as the reader may have noticed, had no good will to the Highland race. "I will wager on Old Nick, of whom I should know something, he being indeed a worker in the same element with myself, against Catherine on that debate—the devil will have the tartan; that is sure enough."

"Ay, but she hath a second thou knowest little of—Father Clement has taken the young catheran in hand, and he fears a hundred devils as little as I do a flock of geese."

"Father Clement?" said the Smith; "you are always making some new saint in this godly city of Saint Johnstoun. Pray who, for a devil's drubber, may he be?—one of your hermits that trains for the work like a wrestler for the ring, and brings himself to trim by fasting and penance—is he not?"

"No, that is the marvel of it," said Simon; "Father Clement eats, drinks, and lives much like other folks—all the rules of the Church, nevertheless, strictly observed."

"Oh, I comprehend!—a buxom priest that thinks more of good living than of good life—tipples a can on Fastern's Eve to enable him to face Lent—has a pleasant *in principio*—and confesses all the prettiest women about town?"

"You are on the bow-hand still, Smith. I tell you, my daughter and I could nose out either a fasting hypocrite or a full one. But Father Clement is neither one nor the other."

"But what is he then, in Heaven's name?"

"One who is either greatly better than half his brethren of Saint Johnstoun put together, or so much worse than the worst of them, that it is sin and shame that he is suffered to cumber the country."

"Methinks it were easy to tell whether he be the one or the other," said the Smith.

"Content you, my friend," said Simon, "with knowing, that if you judge Father Clement by what you see him do and hear him say, you will think of him as the best and kindest man in the world, with a comfort for every man's grief, a counsel for every man's cumber, the rich man's surest guide, and the poor man's best friend. But if you listen to what the Dominicans say of him, he is—Benedicite! (here the Glover crossed himself on brow and bosom)—a foul heretic, who ought by means of earthly flames to be sent to those which burn eternally."

The Smith also crossed himself, and exclaimed—"Saint Mary! father Simon, and do you, who are so good and prudent that you have been called the Wise Glover of Perth, let your daughter attend the ministry of one who—the Saints preserve us!—may be in league with the foul fiend himself? Why, was it not a priest who raised the devil in the Meal Vennel when Hodge Jackson's house was blown down in the great wind?—did not the devil appear in the midst of the Tay, dressed in a priest's scapular, gambolling like a pellach amongst the waves, the morning when our stately bridge was swept away?"

"I cannot tell whether he did or no," said the Glover; "I only know I saw him not. As to Catherine, she cannot be said to use Father Clement's ministry, seeing her confessor is old Father Francis the Dominican, from whom she had her shrift to-day. But women will sometimes be wilful, and sure enough she consults with Father Clement more than I could wish; and yet when I have spoken with him myself, I have thought him so good and holy a man, that I could have trusted my own salvation with him. There are bad reports of him among the Dominicans, that is certain. But what have we laymen to do with such things, my son? Let us pay Mother Church her dues, give our alms, confess and do our penances duly, and the saints will bear us out."

"Ay, truly; and they will have consideration," said the Smith, "for any rash and unhappy blow that a man may deal in a fight, when his party was on defence, and standing up to him. And that's the only creed a man can live upon in Scotland, let your daughter think what she pleases; marry, a man must know his fence, or have a short lease of his life, in any place where blows are going so rife. Five nobles to our altar have cleared me for the best man I ever had misfortune with."

"Let us finish our flask, then," said the old Glover; "for I reckon the Dominican tower is tolling midnight. And hark thee, son Henry. Be at the lattice window on our east gable by the very peep of dawn, and make me aware thou art come by whistling the Smith's call gently. I will contrive that Catherine shall look out at window, and thus thou wilt have all the privileges of being a gallant Valentine through the rest of the year; which if thou canst not use to thine own advantage, I shall be led to think, that for all thou be'st covered with the lion's hide, Nature has left thee the long ears of the ass."

"Amen, father," said the armourer; "a hearty good night to you; and God's blessing on your roof-tree, and those whom it covers. You shall hear the Smith's call sound by cock-crowing; I warrant I put Sir Chanticleer to shame."

So saying, he took his leave; and moved through the deserted streets like one upon his guard though completely undaunted, to his own dwelling, which was situated in the Mill Wynd, at the western end of Perth.

Chapter Four

THE STURDY ARMOURER was not, it may be well believed, slack in keeping the appointment assigned by his intended father-in-law. He went through the process of his toilette with more than ordinary care, throwing, as far as he could, those points which had a military air into the shade. He was far too noted a person to venture to go entirely unarmed in a town where he had indeed many friends, but also, from the character of some of his former exploits, several deadly enemies, at whose hands, should they take him at advantage, he knew he had little mercy to expect. He, therefore, wore under his jerkin a *secret*, or coat of chain-mail, so light and flexible that it interfered as little with his movements as a modern under-waistcoat, yet of such proof as he might safely depend upon, every ring of it having been wrought and joined by his own hands. Above this he wore, like others of his age and degree, the Flemish hose and doublet, which, in honour of the holy tide, were of the best superfine English broad cloth, light blue in colour, slashed out with black satin, and passamented (laced, that is) with embroidery of black silk. His walking boots were of Cordovan leather; his cloak of good Scottish grey, which served to conceal a whinger, or *couteau de chasse*, that hung at his belt, and was his only offensive weapon, for he carried in his hand but a rod of holly. His black velvet bonnet was lined with steel, quilted between the metal and his head, and thus constituted a means of defence which might safely be trusted to.

Upon the whole, Henry had the appearance, to which he was well entitled, of a burgher of wealth and consideration, assuming in his dress as much consequence as he could display, without stepping beyond his own rank, and encroaching that of the gentry. Neither did his frank and manly deportment, though indicating a total indifference to danger, bear the least resemblance to that of the bravoes or swash-bucklers of the day, amongst whom Henry was sometimes unjustly ranked by those who imputed the frays, in which he was so often engaged, to a quarrelsome and violent temper, resting upon consciousness of his personal strength and knowledge of his weapon. On the contrary, every feature bore the easy and good-humoured expression of one who neither thought of inflicting mischief, nor dreaded it from others.

Having attired himself in his best, the honest armourer next placed nearest to his heart (which throbbed at its touch,) a little gift which he had long provided for Catherine Glover, and which his quality of Valentine would now give him the title to present, and her to receive, without regard to maidenly scruples. It was a small ruby cut into the form of a heart, transfixed with a golden arrow, and was inclosed in a small purse made of links of the finest work in steel, as if it had been designed for a hauberk to King Oberon. Round the verge of the purse were these words—

> Love's darts
> Cleave hearts
> Through mail-shirts.

This device had cost the armourer some thought, and he was much satisfied with his composition, because it seemed to imply that his skill could defend all hearts saving his own. He wrapped himself in his cloak, and hastened through the still silent streets, determined to appear at the window appointed a little before dawn.

With this purpose he passed up the High Street, and turned down the opening where Saint John's Church now stands, in order to proceed to Couvrefew Street; when it occurred to him, from the appearance of the sky, that he was at least an hour too early for his purpose, and that it would be better not to appear at the place of rendezvous till nearer the time assigned. Other gallants were not unlikely to be on the watch as well as himself about the house of the Fair Maid of Perth; and he knew his own foible so well as to be sensible of the great chance of a scuffle arising betwixt them. "I have the advantage," he thought, "by my father Simon's friendship; and why should I bloody my fingers with the poor creatures that are not worth my notice? No—no—I will be wise for once, and keep at a distance from all temptation to a broil. They shall have no more time to quarrel with me than just what it may require for me to give the signal, and for my father Simon to answer it. I wonder how the old man will contrive to bring her to the window? I fear, if she knew his purpose, he would find it difficult to carry it into execution."

While these lover-like thoughts were passing through his brain, the armourer loitered in his pace, often turning his eyes eastward, and eying the firmament, on which slight shades of grey were beginning to flicker, but too faintly and indistinctly to announce the certain approach of dawn which, to the impatience of the stout armourer, seemed on that morning to abstain longer than usual from occupying her eastern barbican. He was now passing slowly under the wall of Saint Anne's Chapel, (not failing to cross himself and say an *ave*, as he trode the consecrated ground,) when a voice, which seemed to come from behind one of the flying buttresses of the chapel, said, "He lingers that has need to run."

"Who speaks?" said the armourer, standing and looking around him, somewhat startled at an address so unexpected, both in its tone and tenor.

"No matter who speaks," answered the same voice. "Do thou make great speed, or thou wilt scarce make good speed. Bandy not words, but begone."

"Saint or sinner, angel or devil," said Henry, crossing himself, "your advice touches me but too dearly to be neglected—Saint Valentine be my speed!"

So saying, he instantly changed his loitering pace to one with which few people could have kept up, and in an instant was in Couvrefew Street. He had not made three steps towards Simon Glover's, which stood in the midst of the narrow street, when two men started from under the houses on different sides, and advanced, as it were by concert, to intercept his passage. The imperfect light only permitted him to discern that they wore the Highland mantle.

"Clear the way, catheran," said the armourer, in the deep stern voice which corresponded with the breadth of his chest.

They did not answer, at least intelligibly; but he could see that they drew their swords, with the purpose of withstanding him by violence. Conjecturing some evil, but of what kind he could not anticipate, Henry instantly determined to make his way through whatever odds, and defend his mistress, or at least die at her feet. He cast his cloak over his left arm as a buckler, and advanced rapidly and steadily to the two men. The first of them thrust at him, but Henry Smith, parrying the blow with his cloak, dashed his arm in the man's face, and tripping him at the same time gave him a severe fall on the causeway; while almost in the same instant he struck a blow with his whinger at the fellow who was upon his right hand, so severely applied that he also lay prostrate by his associate. Meanwhile, the armourer pushed forwards in alarm, for which the circumstances of the street being guarded or defended by strangers who conducted themselves with such violence, afforded sufficient reason. He heard a suppressed whisper and a bustle under the Glover's windows—those very windows from which he had expected to be hailed by Catherine as her Valentine. He held to the opposite side of the street, that he might reconnoitre their number and purpose. But one of the party, who were beneath the windows, observing or hearing him, crossed the street also, and taking him doubtless for one of the sentinels, asked, in a whisper, "What noise was yonder, Kenneth? Why gave you not the signal?"

"Villain!" said Henry, "you are discovered, and you shall die the death!"

As he spoke thus, he dealt the stranger a blow with his weapon, which would probably have made his words good, had not the man, raising his arm, received on his hand the blow meant for his head. The wound must have been a severe one, for he staggered and fell with a deep groan. Without noticing him further, Henry Smith sprung forwards upon a party of men who seemed engaged in placing a ladder against the latticed window in the gable. Henry did not stop either to count their numbers or to ascertain their purpose. But crying the alarm-word of the town, and giving the signal at which the burghers were wont to collect, he rushed on the nightwalkers, one of whom was in the act of ascending the ladder. The Smith seized it by the rounds, threw it down on the pavement, and placing his foot on the body of the man who had been mounting, prevented him from regaining his feet. His accomplices struck fiercely at Henry to extricate their companion. But his mail-coat stood him in good stead, and he repaid their blows with interest, shouting aloud, "Help, help, for bonnie St Johnstoun!

—Bows and blades, brave citizens! bows and blades!—they break into our houses under cloud of night."

These words, which resounded far through the streets, were accompanied by as many fierce blows, dealt with good effect among those whom the armourer assailed. In the meantime, the inhabitants of the street began to awaken and appear on the street in their shirts, with swords and targets, and some of them with torches. The assailants now endeavoured to make their escape, which all of them effected excepting the man who had been thrown down along with the ladder. Him the intrepid armourer had caught by the throat in the scuffle, and held as fast as the greyhound holds the hare. The other wounded men were borne off by their comrades.

"Here are a sort of knaves breaking peace within burgh," said Henry to the neighbours who began to assemble; "make after the rogues. They cannot all get off, for I have maimed some of them; the blood will guide you to them."

"Some Highland catherans—" said the citizens,—"up and chase, neighbours!"

"Ay, chase—chase,—leave me to manage this fellow," continued the armourer.

The assistants dispersed in different directions, their lights flashing, and their cries resounding through the whole adjacent district.

In the meantime the armourer's captive entreated for freedom, using both bribes and threats to obtain it. "As thou art a gentleman," he said, "let me go, and what is past shall be forgiven."

"I am no gentleman," said Henry—"I am Hal of the Wynd, a burgess of Perth; and I have done nothing to need forgiveness."

"Villain, thou hast done thou knowest not what! But let me go, and I will fill thy bonnet with gold pieces."

"I shall fill thy bonnet with a cloven head presently," said the armourer, "unless thou stand still as a true prisoner."

"What is the matter, my son Harry?" said Simon, who now appeared at the window.—"I hear thy voice in another tone than I expected.—What is all this noise and why are the neighbours gathering to the affray?"

"There have been a proper set of limmers about to scale your windows, father Simon; but I am like to prove godfather to one of them, whom I hold here as fast as ever vice held iron."

"Hear me, Simon Glover," said the prisoner; "let me but speak one word with you in private and rescue me from the gripe of this iron-fisted and leaden-pated clown, and I will show thee that no harm was designed to thee or thine; and, moreover, tell thee what shall much advantage thee."

"I should know that voice," said Simon Glover, who now came to the door with a dark-lantern in his hand. "Son Smith, let this young man speak with me—there is no danger in him, I promise you. Stay but an instant where you are, and let no one enter the house, either to attack or defend. I will be answerable that this galliard meant but some Saint Valentine's jest."

So saying, the old man pulled in the prisoner and shut the door, leaving Henry a little surprised at the unexpected light in which his father-in-law had viewed the affray. "A jest!" he said; "it might have been a strange jest, if they had got into the maiden's sleeping room!—And they would have done so, had it not been for the honest friendly voice from behind the buttress, which, if it were not that of the blessed Saint, (though what am I that the holy person should speak to me?) could not sound in that place without her permission and assent, and for which I will promise her a wax candle at her shrine, as long as my whinger,—and I would I had had my two-handed broadsword in stead, both for the sake of St Johnstoun and of the rogues—for of a certain, those whingers are pretty toys, but more fit for a boy's hand than a man's. Oh, my old two-handed Trojan, hadst thou been in my hands, as thou hang'st presently at the tester of my bed, the legs of those rogues had not carried their bodies so clean off the field.—But there come lighted torches and drawn swords.—So ho—stand!—Are you for St Johnstoun?—If friends to the bonnie burgh, you are well come."

"We have been but bootless hunters," said the townsmen. "We followed by the tracks of the blood into the Dominican burial-ground, and we started two fellows from amongst the tombs, supporting betwixt them a third, who had probably got some of your marks about him, Harry. They got to the postern gate before we could overtake them, and rang the sanctuary bell,—the gate opened, and in went they. So they are safe in girth and sanctuary, and we may go to our cold beds and warm us."

"Ay," said one of the party, "the good Dominicans have always some devout brother of their convent sitting up to open the gate to any poor soul that is in trouble, and desires shelter in the church."

"Ay, if the poor soul can pay for it," said another; "but, truly, if he be poor in purse as well as in spirit, he may stand on the outside till the hounds come up with him."

A third, who had been poring for a few minutes upon the ground by advantage of his torch, now looked upwards and spoke. He was a brisk, forward, rather corpulent little man, called Oliver Proudfute, reasonably wealthy, and a leading man in his craft, which was that of bonnet-makers; he, therefore, spoke as one in authority.—"Canst tell us, jolly Smith,"—for they recognised each other by the lights which were brought into the streets,—"what manner of fellows they were who raised up this fray within burgh?"

"The two that I first saw," answered the armourer, "seemed to me, as well as I could observe them, to have Highland plaids about them."

"Like enough—like enough," answered the citizens, shaking their heads. "It's a shame the breaches in our walls are not repaired, and that these land-louping Highland scoundrels are left at liberty to take honest men and women out of their beds any night that is dark enough."

"But look here, neighbours," said Oliver Proudfute, showing a bloody hand which he had picked up from the ground; "when did such a hand as this tie a Highlandman's brogues? It is large indeed, and bony, but as fine as a lady's, with a ring that sparkles like a gleaming candle. Simon Glover has made gloves for this hand before now, if I am not much mistaken, for he works for all the courtiers." The spectators here began to gaze on the bloody token with various comments.

"If that is the case," said one, "Harry Smith had best show a clean pair of heels for it, since the Justiciar will scarce think the protecting a burgess's house an excuse for cutting off a gentleman's hand. There be hard laws against mutilation."

"Fie upon you, that you will say so, Michael Wabster," answered the bonnet-maker; "are we not representatives and successors of the stout old Romans, who built Perth as like to their own city as they could? And have we not charters from all our noble kings and progenitors, as being their loving liegemen? And would you have us now yield up our rights, privileges, and immunities, our outfang and infang, our hand-habend and back-bearand, and our blood-suits and amerciaments, escheats and commodities, and suffer an honest burgess's house to be assaulted without seeking for redress? No—brave citizens, craftsmen, and burgesses, the Tay shall flow back to Dunkeld before we submit to such an injustice!"

"And how can we help it?" said a grave old man, who stood leaning on a two-handed sword—"What would you have us do?"

"Marry, Bailie Craigdallie, I wonder that you of all men ask the question. I would have you pass like true men from this very place to the King's Grace's presence, raise him from his royal rest, and presenting to him the piteous case of our being called forth from our beds at this season, with little better covering than these shirts, I would show him this bloody token, and know from his Grace's own royal lips, whether it is just and honest that his loving lieges should be thus treated by the knights and nobles of his deboshed court. And this I call pushing our cause warmly."

"Warmly, sayst thou?" replied the old burgher; "why, so warmly that we shall all die of cold, man, before the porter turn a key to let us into the royal presence.—Come, friends—the night is bitter—we have kept our watch and ward like men, and our jolly Smith hath given a warning to those that would wrong us, which shall be worth twenty proclamations of the King. To-morrow is a new day; we will consult on this matter on this self-same spot, and consider what measures should be taken for discovery and pursuit of the villains. And therefore let us dismiss before the heart's-blood freeze in our veins."

"Bravo, bravo, neighbour Craigdallie—St Johnstoun for ever!"

Oliver Proudfute would still have spoken; for he was one of those pitiless orators who think that their eloquence can overcome all inconveniences in time, place, and circumstances. But no one would listen; and the citizens dispersed to their own houses by the light of the dawn, which began now to streak the horizon.

They were scarce gone ere the door of Glover's house opened, and seizing the Smith by the hand, the old man pulled him in.

"Where is the prisoner?" demanded the armourer.

"He is gone—escaped—fled—what do I know of him?" said the Glover. "He got out at the back door, and so through the little garden. —Think not of him, but come and see the Valentine, whose honour and life you have saved this morning."

"Let me but sheathe my weapon," said the Smith—"let me but wash my hands."

"There is not an instant to lose, she is up and almost dressed— Come on, man—She shall see thee with thy good weapon in thy hand, and with villain's blood on thy fingers, that she may know what is the value of a true man's service. She has stopped my mouth over long with her pruderies and her scruples. I will have her know what a brave man's love is worth, and a bold burgess's to boot."

Chapter Five

STARTLED from her repose by the noise of the affray, the Fair Maid of Perth had listened in breathless terror to the sounds of violence and outcry which arose from the street. She had sunk on her knees to pray for assistance, and as she distinguished the voices of neighbours and friends collected for her protection, she remained in the same posture to return thanks. She was still kneeling when her father almost thrust her champion, Henry Smith, into her apartment; the bashful lover hanging back at first, as if afraid to give offence, and, on observing her posture, from respect to her devotion.

"Father," said the armourer, "she prays—I dare no more speak to her than to a bishop when he says mass."

"Now go thy ways for a right valiant and courageous blockhead," said her father; and then speaking to his daughter, he added,—"Heaven is best thanked, my daughter, by gratitude shown to our fellow-creatures. Here comes the instrument by whom God has rescued thee from death, or perhaps from dishonour worse than death. Receive him, Catherine, as thy true Valentine, and him whom I desire to see my affectionate son."

"Not thus—father," replied Catherine. "I can see—can speak to no one now. I am not ungrateful—perhaps I am too thankful to the instrument of our safety—but let me thank the guardian Saint who sent me this timely relief—and give me but a moment to don my kirtle."

"Nay, God-a-mercy, wench, it were hard to deny thee time to busk thy body-clothes, since the request is the only words like a woman that thou hast uttered for these ten days.—Truly, son Harry, I would my daughter would put off being entirely a saint till the time comes for her being canonized for St Catherine the Second."

"Nay, jest not, father; for I will swear she has at least one sincere adorer already, who hath devoted himself to her pleasure, so far as sinful man may.—Fare-thee-well then, for the moment, fair maiden," he concluded, raising his voice, "and Heaven send thee dreams as peaceful as thy waking thoughts. I go to watch thy slumbers, and woe with him that shall again intrude on them!"

"Nay, good and brave Henry, whose warm heart is at such variance with thy reckless hand, thrust thyself into no further quarrels to-night—but take the kindest thanks, and with these, try to assume the peaceful thoughts which you assign to me. To-morrow we will meet that I may assure you of my gratitude—Farewell."

"And farewell, lady and light of my heart!" said the armourer, and, descending the stair which led to Catherine's apartment, was about to sally forth into the street, when the Glover caught him by the arm.

"I shall love the ruffle of to-night," said he, "better than I ever thought to do the clashing of steel, if it brings my daughter to her senses, Harry, and teaches her what thou art worth. By St Macgrider! I even love these roysterers, and am sorry for that poor lover who will never wear left-handed chevron again. Ay! He has lost that which he will miss all the days of his life, especially when he goes to pull on his gloves,—Ay, he will pay but half a fee to my craft in future.—Nay, not a step from this house to-night," he continued. "Thou dost not leave us, I promise thee, my son."

"I do not mean it. But I will, with your permission, watch in the street. The attack may be renewed."

"And if it is," said Simon, "thou wilt have better access to drive them back, having the vantage of the house. It is the way of fighting which suits us burghers best—that of resisting from behind stone walls. Our duty of watch and ward teaches us that trick; besides, enough are awake and astir to ensure us peace and quiet till morning. So come in this way."

So saying, he drew Henry, nothing loath, into the same apartment where they had supped, and where the old woman, who was still on foot, disturbed as others had been by the nocturnal affray, soon roused up the fire.

"And now, my doughty son," said the Glover, "what liquor wilt thou pledge thy father in?"

Henry Smith had suffered himself to sink mechanically upon a seat of old black oak, and now gazed on the fire, that flashed back a ruddy light over his manly features. He muttered to himself half audibly—"*Good* Henry—*brave* Henry—Ah! had she but said, *dear* Henry!"

"What liquors be these?" said the old Glover, laughing. "My cellar holds none such; but if sack, or rhenish, or wine of Gascony can serve, why, say the word and the flagon foams—that is all."

"The *kindest* thanks," said the armourer, still musing; "that's more than she ever said to me before—the *kindest* thanks—what may not that stretch to?"

"It shall stretch like kid's leather, man," said the Glover, "if thou wilt but be ruled, and say what thou wilt take for thy morning's draught."

"Whatever thou wilt, father," answered the armourer carelessly, and relapsed into the analysis of Catherine's speech to him. "She spoke of my warm heart; but she also spoke of my reckless hand. What earthly can I do to get rid of that fighting fancy? Certainly I were best strike my right hand off, and nail it to the door of a church, that it may never do me discredit more."

"You have chopped off hands enough for one night," said his friend, setting a flagon of wine on the table. "Why dost thou vex thyself, man? She would love thee twice as well did she not see how thou doatest upon her. But it becomes serious now. I am not to have the risk of my booth being broken, and my house plundered, by the hell-raking followers of the nobles, because she is called the Fair Maid of Perth, and please ye. No, she shall know I am her father, and will have that obedience to which law and gospel give me right. I will have her thy wife, Henry, my heart of gold—thy wife, my man of metal, and that before many weeks are over. Come, come, here is to thy merry bridal, jolly Smith."

The father quaffed a large cup, and filled it to his adopted son, who raised it slowly to his head; then, ere it had reached his lips, replaced it suddenly on the table and shook his head.

"Nay, if thou wilt not pledge me to such a health, I know no one who will," said Simon. "What canst thou mean, thou foolish lad? Here is a chance happened, which in a manner places her in thy power, since from one end of the city to the other all would cry fie on her if she should say thee nay. Here am I her father, not only consenting to the cutting out of the match, but willing to see you two as closely united together, as ever needle stitched buckskin. And with all this on thy side, fortune, father, and all, thou lookest like a distracted lover in a ballad, more like to pitch thyself into the Tay than to woo a lass that may be had for the asking, if you choose the lucky minute."

"Ay, but that lucky minute, father! I question much if Catherine ever has such a moment to glance on earth and its inhabitants, as might lead her to listen to a coarse ignorant borrel man like me. I cannot tell how it is, father; elsewhere I can hold up my head like another man, but with your saintly daughter I lose heart and courage, and I cannot help thinking that it would be well nigh robbing a holy shrine if I could succeed in surprising her affections. Her thoughts are too much fitted for heaven to be wasted on such a man as I am."

"E'en as you like, Henry," answered the Glover. "My daughter is not courting you any more than I am—a fair offer is no cause of feud; —Only if you think that I will give into her foolish notions of a convent, take it with you that I will never listen to them. I love and honour the Church," he said, crossing himself. "I pay her rights duly and cheerfully; tithes and alms, wine and wax, I pay them as duly as any man in Perth of my means; but I cannot afford the Church my only and single ewe-lamb that I have in the world. Her mother was dear to me on earth, and is now an angel in heaven. Catherine is all I have to remind me of her I have lost; and if she goes to the cloister, it shall be when these old eyes are closed for ever, and not sooner.—But as for you, Master Gow, I pray you will act according to your own best liking. I want to force no wife on you, I promise you."

"Nay, now, you beat the iron twice over," said Henry. "It is thus we always end, father, by your being testy with me for not doing that thing in the world which would make me happiest, were I to have it in my power. Why, father, I would the keenest dirk I ever forged were sticking in my heart at this moment, if there is one single particle in it that is not more your daughter's property than my own. But what can I do? I cannot think less of her, and more of myself, than we both deserve; and what seems to you so easy and certain, is to me as difficult as it would be to work a steel hauberk out of hards of flax.—

But here is to you, father," he added, in a more cheerful tone; "and here is to my fair Saint and Valentine, as I hope your Catherine will be mine for the season. And let me not keep your old head longer from the pillow, but make interest with your feather-bed till day-break; and then you must be my guide to your daughter's chamber-door, and my apology for entering it, to bid her good morrow, for the brightest that the sun will awaken in the city or for miles round it!"

"No bad advice, my son," said the honest Glover. "But you, what will you do? Will you lie down beside me, or take a part of Conachar's bed?"

"Neither," answered Harry Gow; "I should but prevent your rest; and for me this easy-chair is worth a down bed, and I will sleep like a sentinel, with my graith about me."

As he spoke, he laid his hand on his sword.

"Nay, Heaven send us no more need of weapons.—Good night, or rather, good morrow, till day-peep—and the first who wakes calls up the other."

Thus parted the two burghers. The Glover retired to his bed, and, it is to be supposed, to rest. The lover was not so fortunate. His burly frame easily bore the fatigue which he had encountered in the course of the night, but his mind was of a different and more delicate mould. In one point of view, he was but the stout burgher of his period, proud alike of his art in making weapons, and wielding them when made; his professional jealousy, personal strength, and skill in the use of arms, brought him into many quarrels, which had made him generally feared, and in some instances disliked. But with these qualities were united the simple good-nature of a child, and at the same time an imaginative and enthusiastic temper, which seemed little to correspond with his labours at the forge, or his combats in the field. Perhaps a little of the hair-brained and ardent feeling which he had picked out of old ballads, or from the metrical romances which were his sole source of information or knowledge, may have been the means of pricking him on to some of his achievements, which had often a rude strain of chivalry in them. At least, it was certain that his love to the fair Catherine had in it a delicacy such as might have become the Squire of low degree, who was honoured, if song speaks truth, with the smiles of the King of Hungary's daughter. His sentiments towards her were certainly as exalted as if they had been fixed upon an actual angel, which made old Simon, and others who watched his conduct, think that his passion was too high and devotional to be successful with maiden of mortal mould. They were mistaken, however. Catherine, coy and reserved as she was, had a heart which could feel and understand the nature and depth of the armourer's passion; and whether she was able to repay it or not, she had as much secret pride in the attachment of the redoubted Henry Gow, as a lady of romance may be supposed to have in the company of a tame lion, who follows to provide for her and defend her. It was with sentiments of the most sincere gratitude that she recollected, as she awoke at dawn, the services of Henry during the course of the eventful night, and the first thought which she dwelt upon was the means of making him understand her feelings.

Arising hastily from bed, and half blushing at her own purpose—"I have been cold to him, and perhaps unjust; I will not be ungrateful," she said to herself, "though I cannot yield to his suit. I will not wait till my father compels me to receive him as my Valentine for the year; I will seek him out, and choose him myself—I have thought other girls bold when they did something like this; but I shall thus best please my father, and but discharge the rites due to good Saint Valentine by showing my gratitude to this brave man."

Hastily slipping on her dress, which, nevertheless, was left a good deal more disordered than usual, she tripped down stairs and opened the door of the chamber in which, as she had guessed, her lover had passed the hours after the fray. Catherine paused at the door, and became half afraid of executing her own purpose, which not only permitted but enjoined the Valentines of the year to begin their connexion with a kiss of affection. It was looked upon as a peculiarly propitious omen if the one party could find the other asleep, and awaken him or her by performance of this interesting ceremony.

Never was a fairer opportunity offered for commencing this mystic tie than that which now presented itself to Catherine. After many and various thoughts, sleep had at length overcome the stout armourer in the chair in which he had deposited himself. His features, in repose, had a more firm and manly cast than Catherine, who saw them generally fluctuating between shamefacedness and apprehension of her displeasure, had been used to connect with them.

"He looks very stern," she said; "if he should be angry—and then when he awakes we are alone—if I should call Dorothy—if I should wake my father—But no!—it is a thing of custom, and done in all maidenly and sisterly love and honour—I will not suppose that Henry can misconstrue it, and I will not let a childish fear put my gratitude to sleep."

So saying, she tripped along the floor of the apartment with a light, though hesitating step, and a cheek crimsoned at her own purpose; and gliding to the chair of the sleeper, dropped a kiss upon his lips as light as if a rose-leaf had fallen on them. The slumbers must have been slight which such a touch could dispel, and the dreams of the sleeper must needs have been connected with the cause of the interruption, since Henry, instantly starting up, caught the maiden in his arms, and attempted to return in ecstasy the salute which had broken his repose. But Catherine struggled in his embrace; and as her efforts implied alarmed modesty, rather than maidenly coyness, her bashful lover suffered her to escape a grasp, from which twenty times her strength could not have extricated her.

"Nay, be not angry, good Henry," said Catherine, in the kindest tone, to her surprised lover. "I have paid my vows to Saint Valentine to show how I value the mate which he has sent me for the year. Let but my father be present, and I will not dare to refuse thee the revenge you may claim for a broken sleep."

"Let not that be a hinderance," said the old Glover, rushing in ecstasy into the room—"to her, Smith—to her—strike while the iron is hot, and teach her what it is not to let sleeping dogs lie still."

Thus encouraged, Henry, though perhaps with less alarming vivacity, again seized the blushing maiden in his arms, who submitted with a tolerable grace to receive repayment of her salute, a dozen times repeated, and with an energy very different from that which had provoked such severe retaliation. At length, she again extricated herself from her lover's arms, and, as if frightened and repenting what she had done, threw herself into a seat, and covered her face with her hands.

"Cheer up, thou silly girl," said her father, "and be not ashamed thou hast made the two happiest men in Perth, since thy old father is one of them. Never was kiss so well bestowed, and meet it is that it should be suitably returned. Look up, my darling, look up and let me see thee but give one smile. By my honest word, the sun that now rises over our fair city shows no sight that can give me greater pleasure.— What," he continued, in a jocose tone, "thou thoughtst thou hadst Jamie Keddie's ring, and couldst walk invisible? but not so, my fairy of the dawning. Just as I was about to rise, I heard thy chamber door open, and watched thee down stairs—not to protect thee against this sleepy-headed Henry, but to see with my own delighted eyes my beloved girl do that which her father most wished.—Come, put down these foolish hands, and though thou blushest a little it will only the better grace St Valentine's morn, when blushes best become a maiden's cheek."

As Simon Glover spoke, he pulled away, with gentle violence, the hands which hid his daughter's face. She blushed deeply, indeed, but there was more than maiden's shame in her face, and her eyes were fast filling with tears.

"What! weeping, love?" continued her father,—"nay, nay, this is more than need—Henry, help me to comfort this little fool."

Catherine made an effort to collect herself and to smile, but the smile was of a melancholy and serious cast.

"I only meant to say, father," said the Fair Maid of Perth with continued exertion, "that in choosing Henry Gow for my Valentine, and rendering to him the rights and greeting of the morning, according to wonted custom, I meant but to show my gratitude to him for his manly and faithful service, and my obedience to you.—But do not lead him to think—and, oh, dearest father, do not yourself entertain an idea, that I meant more than what the promise to be his faithful and affectionate Valentine through the year requires of me."

"Ay—ay—ay—ay—we understand it all," said Simon, in the soothing tone which nurses apply to children—"We understand what the meaning is; enough for once—enough for once. Thou shalt not be frightened or hurried.—Loving, true, and faithful Valentines are ye, and the rest as Heaven and opportunity shall permit. Come, prithee, have done—wring not thy tiny hands, nor fear further persecution now. Thou hast done bravely—excellently—and now, away to Dorothy, and call up the old sluggard. We must have a substantial breakfast, after a night of confusion and a morning of joy; and thy hand will be needed to prepare for us some of these delicate cakes which no one can make but thyself; and well hast thou a right to the secret, seeing who taught it thee.—Ah! health to the soul of thy dearest mother," he added, with a sigh; "how blithe would she have been to see this happy St Valentine's morning!"

Catherine took the opportunity of escape which was thus given her, and glided from the room. To Henry it seemed as if the sun had disappeared from the heaven at mid-day, and left the world in sudden obscurity. Even the high-swelled hopes with which the late incident had filled him began to quail, as he reflected upon her altered demeanour; the tears in her eyes; the obvious fear which occupied her features; and the pains she had taken to show, as plainly as delicacy would permit, that the advances which she had made to him were limited to the character with which the rites of the day had invested him. Her father looked on his fallen countenance with something like surprise and displeasure.

"In the name of good St John, what has befallen you that makes you look as grave as an owl, when a lad of your spirit, having really such a fancy for this poor girl as you pretend, ought to be as blithe as a lark?"

"Alas, father!" replied the crest-fallen lover, "there is that written on her brow which says she loves me well enough to be my Valentine, especially since you wish it—but not well enough to be my wife."

"Now, a plague on thee for a cold, down-hearted goose-cap," answered the father. "I can read a woman's brow as well, and better than thou; and I can see no such matter on hers. What the foul fiend, man! there thou wast lying like a lord in thy elbow-chair, as sound asleep as a judge, when, hadst thou been a lover of any spirit, thou wouldst have been watching the east for the first ray of the sun. But there thou layest, snoring, I warrant, thinking nought about her, or anything else; and the poor girl rises at peep of day, lest any one else should pick up her most precious and vigilant Valentine, and wakes thee with a grace, which—so help me St Macgrider!—would have put life in an anvil; and thou awakest to hone, and pine, and moan, as if she had drawn a hot iron across thy lips! Now I would to St John she had sent old Dorothy on the errand, and bound thee for thy Valentine service to that bundle of dry bones, with never a tooth in her head. She were fittest Valentine in Perth for so craven a wooer."

"As to craven, father," answered the Smith, "there are twenty good cocks, whose combs I have plucked, can tell thee if I am craven or no. And Heaven knows, that I would give my good land, held by burgess' tenure, with smithy, bellows, tongs, anvil, and all, providing it would make your view of this matter the true one. But it is not of her coyness, or her blushes, that I speak; it is of the paleness which so soon followed the red, and chased it from her cheeks; and it is of the tears which succeeded. It was like the April shower stealing up on and obscuring the fairest dawning that ever beamed over the Tay."

"Tutti taitti," replied the Glover; "neither Rome nor Perth were built in a day. Thou hast fished salmon a thousand times, and mightst have taken a lesson. When the fish has taken the fly, to pull a hard strain on the line would snap the tackle to pieces, were it made of wire. Ease your hand, man, and let him rise; take leisure, and in half-an-hour thou layest him on the bank.—There is a beginning, as fair as you could wish, unless you expect the poor wench to come to thy bed-side, as she did to thy chair; and that is not the fashion of modest maidens. But mind me; after we have had our breakfast, I will take care thou hast an opportunity to speak thy mind; only beware thou be neither too backward, nor press her too hard. Give her line enough; but do not slack too fast, and my life for yours upon the issue."

"Do what I can, father," answered Henry, "you will always lay the blame on me; either that I give too much head, or that I strain the tackle. I would give the best habergeon I ever wrought, that the difficulty in truth rested with me; for there were then the better chance of its being removed. I own, however, I am but an ass in bringing such discourse as is to the purpose."

"Come into the booth with me, my son, and I will furnish thee with a fitting theme. Thou knowest the maiden who ventures to kiss a sleeping man wins of him a pair of gloves. Come to my booth—thou shalt have a pair of delicate kid, that will exactly suit her hand and arm.—I was thinking of her poor mother when I shaped them," added honest Simon, with a sigh; "and except Catherine, I know not the woman in Scotland whom they would fit, though I have measured most of the high beauties in the court. Come with me, I say, and thou art provided with a theme to wag thy tongue, providing thou have courage and caution to stand by thee in thy wooing."

Chapter Six

Never to man shall Catherine give her hand.
Taming of a Shrew

THE BREAKFAST was served, and the thin soft cakes, made of flour and honey according to the family receipt, were not only commended with all the partiality of a father and a lover, but done liberal justice to in the mode which is best proof of cake as well as pudding. They talked, jested, and laughed. Catherine, too, had recovered her equanimity where the dames and damsels of the period were apt to lose theirs—in the kitchen, namely, and in the superintendence of household affairs, in which she was an adept. I question much if the perusal of Seneca for as long a period would have had equal effect in composing her mind.

Old Dorothy sate down at the board-end, as was the homespun fashion of the period; and so much were the two men amused with their own conversation, and Catherine occupied either in attending to them, or with her own reflections, that the old woman was the first who observed the absence of the boy Conachar.

"It is true," said the Master Glover; "go call him, the idle Highland loon. He was not seen last night during the fray neither, at least I saw him not. Did any of you observe him?"

The reply was negative; and Henry's observation followed—"There are times when Highlanders can couch like their own deer,—ay, and run from danger too as fast—I have seen them myself for that matter of it."

"And there are times," replied Simon, "when King Arthur and his Round Table could not make stand against them. I wish, Henry, you would speak more reverently of the Highlanders. They are often in Perth, both alone and in numbers; and you ought to keep peace with them, so long as they will keep peace with you."

An answer of defiance rose to Henry's lips, but he prudently suppressed it.

"Why, thou knowest, father," he said, smiling, "that we handicrafts best love the folks we live by; now, my craft provides for valiant and noble knights, gentle squires and pages, stout men-at-arms, and others that wear the arms which we make. It is natural I should like the Ruthvens, the Lindsays, the Ogilvys, the Oliphants, and so many others of our brave and noble neighbours, who are sheathed in steel of my making like so many Paladins, better than those naked, snatching mountaineers, who are ever doing us wrong, especially since no five of each clan have a rusty shirt of mail—and that as old as their *brattach** and but the work of the clan-smith after all, who is no member of our honourable mystery, but simply works at the anvil, where his father wrought before him. I say, such people can have no favour in the eyes of an honest craftsman."

"Well, well," answered Simon; "I prithee let the matter rest even now, for here comes the loitering boy; and though it is a holiday morn, I want no more bloody puddings."

The youth entered accordingly. His face was pale, his eyes red; and there was an air of discomposure about his whole person. He sate down at the lower end of the table, opposite to Dorothy, and crossed himself, as if preparing for his morning's meal. As he did not help himself to any food, Catherine handed to him a platter containing some of the cakes which had met with such general approbation. At first he rejected her offered kindness rather sullenly; but on her repeating the offer with a smile of good-will, he took a cake in his hand, broke it, and was about to eat a morsel, when the effort to swallow seemed almost too much for him; and though he succeeded, he did not repeat it.

"You have a bad appetite for Saint Valentine's morning, Conachar," said his good-humoured master; "and yet I think you must have slept soundly the night before, since I conclude you were not disturbed by the noise of the scuffle. Why, I thought a lively Glunami would have been at his master's side, dirk in hand, at the first sound of danger which arose within a mile of us."

"I heard but an indistinct noise," said the youth, his face glowing suddenly like a heated coal, "which I took for the shout of some merry reveller; and you are wont to bid me never open door or window, or alarm the house, on the score of such folly."

"Well, well," said Simon; "I thought a Highlander would have known better the difference betwixt the clash of swords and the twanging on harps, the wild war-cry and the merry hunts up. But let it pass, boy; I am glad thou art losing thy quarrelsome fashions. Eat thy breakfast, any way, as I have that to employ thee which requires haste."

* Standard.

"I have breakfasted already, and am in haste myself. I am for the hills.—Have you any message to my father?"

"None," replied the Glover, in some surprise; "but art thou beside thyself, boy? or what a vengeance takes thee from the city, like the wing of the whirlwind?"

"My warning has been sudden," said Conachar, speaking with difficulty; but whether arising from the hesitation incidental to the use of a foreign language, or whether from some other cause, could not easily be distinguished. "There is to be a meeting—a great hunting——" Here he stopped.

"And when are you to return from this blessed hunting?" said his master; "that is, if I may make so bold as to ask."

"I cannot justly answer," replied the apprentice. "Perhaps never—if such be my father's pleasure," continued Conachar, with assumed indifference.

"I thought," said Simon Glover, rather seriously, "that all this was to be laid aside, when at earnest intercession I took you under my roof. I thought that when I undertook, being very loath to do so, to teach you an honest trade, we were to hear no more of hunting, or hosting, or clan-gatherings, or any matters of the kind?"

"I was not consulted when I was sent hither," said the lad, haughtily. "I cannot tell what the terms were."

"But I can tell you, Sir Conachar," said the Glover, angrily, "that there is no fashion of honesty in binding yourself to an honest craftsman, and spoiling more hides than your own is worth; and now, when you are of age to be of some service, you take up the disposal of the time as if it were your own property, not your master's."

"Reckon with my father about that," answered Conachar; "he will pay you gallantly—a French mutton* for every hide I have spoiled, and a fat cow or bullock for each day I have been absent."

"Close with him, friend Glover—close with him," said the armourer, drily. "Thou wilt be paid gallantly at least, if not honestly. Methinks I would like to know how many purses have been emptied to fill the goatskin sporran† that is to be so free of its gold, and whose pastures the bullocks have been calved in that are to come down from the Grampian passes."

"You remind me, friend," said the Highland youth, turning haughtily towards the Smith, "that I have also a reckoning to hold with you."

---

*Mouton, a French gold coin, so called from its being impressed with the image of a lamb.

†The Highland pouch, generally formed of goatskin, and worn in front of the garb, is called in Gaelic a *Sporran*. A *sporran-moullach* is a shaggy pouch, formed, as they usually are, of goatskin, or some such material, with the rough side outermost.

"Keep at arm's-length, then," said Henry, extending his brawny arm,—"I will have no more close hugs—no more bodkin work, like last night. I care little for a wasp's sting, yet I will not allow the insect to come near me if I have warning."

Conachar smiled contemptuously. "I meant thee no harm," he said. "My father's son did thee but too much honour to spill such churlblood. I will pay you for it by the drop, that it may be dried up, and no longer soil my fingers."

"Peace, thou bragging ape!" said the Smith; "the blood of a true man cannot be valued in gold. The only expiation would be to come a mile into the Low Country with two of the strongest gallo-glasses of thy clan; and while I dealt with them, I would leave thee to the correction of my apprentice, little Jankin."

Here Catherine interposed. "Peace," she said, "my trusty Valentine, whom I have a right to command; and peace you, Conachar, who ought to obey me as your master's daughter. It is ill done to awaken again on the morrow the evil which has been laid to sleep at night."

"Farewell, then, master," said Conachar, after another look of scorn at the Smith, which he only answered with a laugh, "Farewell! and I thank you for your kindness, which has been more than I deserved. If I have at times seemed less than thankful, it was the fault of circumstances, and not of my will. Catherine——" He cast upon the maiden a look of strong emotion, in which various feelings were blended, hesitated, as if to say something, and at length turned away with the single word *farewell*. Five minutes afterwards, with Highland buskins on his feet, and a small bundle in his hand, he passed through the north gate of Perth, and directed his course to the Highlands.

"There goes enough of beggary and of pride for a whole Highland clan," said Henry. "He talks as familiarly of gold pieces as I would of silver pennies; and yet I will be sworn that the thumb of his mother's worsted glove might hold the treasure of the whole clan."

"Like enough," said the Glover, laughing at the idea; "his mother was a large-boned woman, especially in the hand and wrist."

"And as for cattle," continued Henry, "I reckon his father and brothers steal sheep by one at a time."

"The less we say of them the better," said the Glover, becoming again grave. "Brothers he hath none; his father is a powerful man— hath long hands—reaches as far as he can, and hears farther than it is necessary to talk of him."

"And yet bound his only son apprentice to a glover in Perth?" said Henry. "Why, I would have thought the Gentle Craft, as it is called, of

St Crispin, would have suited him best; and that if the son of some great Mac or O was to become an artizan, it could only be in the craft where princes set him the example."

This remark, though ironical, seemed to awaken our friend Simon's sense of professional dignity, which was a prevailing feeling that marked the manners of the artizans of the time.

"You err, son Henry," he replied, with much gravity; "the glovers are the more honourable craft, in regard they provide for the accommodation of the hands, whereas the shoemakers and cordwainers do but work for the feet."

"Both equally necessary members of the body corporate," said Henry, whose father had been a cordwainer.

"It may be so, my son," said the Glover; "but not both alike honourable. Bethink you, that we employ the hands as pledges of friendship and good faith, and the feet have no such privilege. Brave men fight with their hands—cowards employ their feet in flight. A glove is borne aloft, a shoe is trampled in the mire;—a man greets a friend with his open hand; he spurns a dog, or one whom he holds as mean as a dog, with his advanced foot. A glove on the point of a spear is a sign and pledge of faith all the wide world through, as a gauntlet flung down is a gage of knightly battle; while I know no other emblem belonging to an old shoe, except that some crones will fling them after a man by way of good luck, in which practice I for one entertain no confidence."

"Nay," said the Smith, amused with his friend's eloquent pleading for the dignity of the art he practised, "I am not the man, I promise you, to disparage the glover's mystery. Bethink you, I am myself a maker of gauntlets. But the dignity of your ancient craft removes not my wonder, that the father of this Conachar suffered his son to learn a trade of any kind from a Lowland craftsman, holding us, as they do, altogether beneath their magnificent degree, and a race of contemptible drudges, unworthy of any other fate than to be ill used and plundered, as often as these bare-breeched Dunniewassals see safety and convenience for doing so."

"Ay," answered the Glover, "but there were powerful reasons for— for——" He withheld something which seemed upon his lips, and went on, "for Conachar's father acting as he did.—Well, I have played fair with him, and I do not doubt but he will act honourably by me.—But Conachar's sudden leave-taking has put me to some inconvenience. He had things under his charge. I must look through the booth."

"Can I help you, father?" said Henry Gow, deceived by the earnestness of his manner.

"You?—no,"—said Simon, with a dryness which made Henry so sensible of the simplicity of his proposal that he blushed to the eyes at his own dulness of comprehension, in a matter where love ought to have induced him to take his cue easily up. "You, Catherine," said the Glover as he left the room, "entertain your Valentine for five minutes, and see he departs not till my return.—Come hither with me, old Dorothy, and bestir thy limbs in my behalf."

He left the room, followed by the old woman; and Henry Smith remained with Catherine, almost for the first time in his life, entirely alone. There was embarrassment on the maiden's part, and awkwardness upon that of the lover, for about a minute; when Henry, calling up his courage, pulled the gloves out of his pocket with which Simon had supplied him, and asked her to permit one who had been so highly graced that morning, to pay the usual penalty for being asleep at the moment when he would have given the slumbers of a whole twelvemonth to be awake for a single minute.

"Nay, but," said Catherine, "the fulfilment of my homage to St Valentine infers no such penalty as you desire to pay, and I cannot therefore think of accepting them."

"These gloves," said Henry, advancing his seat insidiously towards Catherine as he spoke, "were wrought by the hands that are dearest to you; and see—they are shaped for your own." He extended them as he spoke, and taking her arm in his robust hand, spread the gloves beside to show how well they fitted. "Look at that taper arm," he said, "look at these small fingers; think who sewed these seams of silk and gold, and think whether the glove, and the arm that alone the glove can fit, ought to remain separate, because the poor glove has had the misfortune to be for a passing minute in the grasp of a hand so swart and rough as mine."

"They are welcome as coming from my father," said Catherine; "surely not less so as coming from my *friend*, (there was an emphasis on the word,) and my preserver."

"Let me aid to do them on," said the Smith, bringing himself yet closer to her side; "they may seem a little over tight at first, and you may require some assistance."

"You are skilful in such service, good Henry Gow," said the maiden, smiling, but at the same time drawing farther from her lover.

"In good faith no," said Henry, shaking his head; "my experience has been in donning steel gauntlets on mailed knights, more than in fitting embroidered gloves upon maidens."

"I will trouble you then no further, and Dorothy shall aid me— though there needs no assistance—my father's eye and fingers are faithful to his craft; what work he puts through his hands is always true to the measure."

"Let me be convinced of it," said the Smith; "let me see that these slender gloves actually match the hands they were made for."

"Some other time, good Henry," answered the maiden; "I will wear the gloves in honour of St Valentine, and the mate he has sent me for the season. I would to heaven I could pleasure my father as well in weightier matters—at present the perfume of the leather harms the head-ache I have had since morning."

"Head-ache! fair Catherine?" echoed her lover.

"If you call it heart-ache, you shall not mis-name it," said Catherine with a sigh, and proceeded to speak in a very serious tone. "Henry," she said, "I am going perhaps to be as bold as I gave you reason to think me this morning; for I am about to speak the first upon a subject, on which, it may well be, I ought to wait till I had to answer you. But I cannot, after what has happened this morning, suffer my feelings towards you to remain unexplained, without the possibility of my being greatly misconceived.—Nay, do not answer till you have heard me out.—You are brave, Henry, beyond most men, honest and true as the steel you work upon"——

"Stop—stop, Catherine, for mercy's sake! You never said so much that was good concerning me, save to introduce some bitter censure, of which your praises were the harbingers. I am honest, and so forth, you would say, but a hot-brained brawler, and common sworder or stabber."

"I should injure both myself and you in calling you such. No, Henry, to no common stabber, had he worn a plume in his bonnet, and gold spurs on his heels, would Catherine Glover have offered the little grace she has this day voluntarily done to you. If I have at times dwelt severely upon the proneness of thy spirit to anger and of thy hand to strife, it is because I would have thee, if I could so persuade thee, hate in thyself the sins of vanity and wrath, by which thou are most easily beset. I have spoken on the topic more to alarm your own conscience than to express my opinion. I know as well as my father, that in these forlorn and desperate days the whole customs of our nation, nay, of every Christian nation, may be quoted in favour of bloody quarrels for trifling causes; the taking of deadly and deep revenge for slight offences; and the slaughter of each other for emulation of honour, or often in mere sport. But I know that for all these things we shall one day be called into judgment; and fain would I convince thee, my brave and generous friend, to listen oftener to the dictates of thy good heart, and take less pride in the strength and dexterity of thy unsparing arm."

"I am—I am convinced, Catherine," exclaimed Henry; "thy words shall henceforwards be a law to me. I have done enough, far too much indeed, for proof of my bodily strength and courage; but it is only from you, Catherine, that I can learn a better way of thinking. Remember, my fair Valentine, that my ambition of distinction in arms, and my love of strife, if it can be called such, do not fight even-handed with my reason and my milder dispositions, but have their patrons and sticklers to egg them on. Is there a quarrel,—I, thinking on your counsels, am something loth to engage in it,—believe you I am left to decide between peace or war at my own choosing? Not so, by St Mary! there are a hundred round me to stir me on. 'Why, how now, Smith, is thy mainspring rusted,' says one. 'Jolly Henry is deaf on the quarrelling ear this morning,' says another. 'Stand to it, for the honour of Perth,' says my Lord the Provost. 'Harry against them for a gold noble,' cries your father, perhaps. Now, what can a poor fellow do, Catherine, when all are hollowing him on in the devil's name, and not a soul putting in a word on the other side?"

"Nay, I know the devil has factors enough to utter his wares," said Catherine; "but it is our duty to fling aside such idle arguments, though they be pleaded even by those to whom we owe much love and honour."

"Then there are the minstrels, with their romaunts and ballads, which place all a man's praise in receiving and repaying hard blows. It is sad to tell, Catherine, how many of my sins that Blind Harry the Minstrel hath to answer for. When I hit a downright blow, it is not, (so save me, St John!) to do any man injury, but only to strike as William Wallace struck."

The Minstrel's namesake spoke this in such a tone of rueful seriousness that Catherine could scarce forbear smiling; but nevertheless she assured him that the danger of his own and other men's lives ought not for a moment to be weighed against such simple toys.

"Ay, but," replied Henry, emboldened by her smiles, "methinks now the good cause of peace would thrive all the better for an advocate. Suppose, for example, that when I am pressed and urged to lay hand on my weapon, I could recollect that there was a gentle and guardian angel at home, whose image would seem to whisper— 'Henry, do no violence; it is my hand which you crimson with blood— Henry, rush upon no idle danger; it is my breast which you expose to injury;' such thoughts would do more to restrain my mood than if every monk in Perth should call 'Hold thy hand, on pain of bell, book, and candle.'"

"If such a warning as could be given by the voice of sisterly affection can have weight in the debate," said Catherine, "think that in striking you empurple this hand, in receiving wounds you harm this heart."

The Smith took courage at the sincerely affectionate tone in which these words were delivered.

"And wherefore not stretch your regard a degree beyond these cold

limits? Why, since you're so kind and generous as to own some interest in the poor ignorant sinner before you, should you not at once
adopt him as your scholar and your husband? Your father desires it;
the town expects it; glovers and smiths are preparing their rejoicings;
and you, only you, whose words are so fair and so kind, you will not
give your consent!"

"Henry," said Catherine, in a low and tremulous voice, "believe me
I should hold it my duty to comply with my father's commands were
there not obstacles invincible to the match which he proposes."

"Yet think—think but a moment. I have little to say for myself in
comparison of you, who can both read and write. But then I love to
hear reading, and could listen to your sweet voice for ever. You love
music, and I have been taught to play and sing as well as some minstrels. You love to be charitable, I have enough to give and enough to
keep; as large a daily alms as a deacon gives would never be missed by
me. Your father gets old for work; he would live with us, as I should
truly hold him for my father also. I would be as chary of mixing in
causeless strife as of thrusting my hand into my own furnace; and if
there came on us unlawful violence, its wares would be brought to an
ill-chosen market."

"May you experience all the domestic happiness which you can
conceive, Henry,—but with some one more happy than me."

So spoke, or rather so sobbed, the Fair Maiden of Perth, who
seemed choking in the attempt to restrain her tears.

"You hate me, then?" said the lover, after a pause.

"Heaven is my witness, No."

"Or you love some other better?"

"It is cruel to ask what it cannot avail you to know. But you are
entirely mistaken."

"Yon cat-a-mountain Conachar, perhaps?" said Henry. "I have
marked his looks"——

"You avail yourself of this painful situation to insult me, Henry,
though I have little deserved it. Conachar is nothing to me, more than
the trying to tame his wild spirit by instruction might lead me to take
some interest in a mind abandoned to prejudices and passions—and
therein, Henry, not unlike your own."

"It must then be some of these flaunting silk-worm Sirs about
the court," said the armourer, his natural heat of temper kindling
from disappointment and vexation; "some of those who think they
carry it off through the height of their plumed bonnets and the
jingle of their spurs. I would I knew who it was, that, leaving his
natural mates, the painted, perfumed dames of the court, comes to
take his prey among the simple maidens of the burgher crafts. I

would I knew but his name and surname!"

"Henry Smith," said Catherine, shaking off the weakness which seemed to threaten to overpower her a moment before, "this is the language of an ungrateful fool, or rather of a frantic madman. I have told you already, there was no one who stood, at the beginning of this conference, more high in my opinion than he who is now losing ground with every word he utters in the tone of unjust suspicion and senseless anger. You had no title to know even what I have told you; which, I pray you to observe, implies no preference to you over others, though it disowns any preference of another to you. It is enough you should know that there is as insuperable an objection to what you desire as if an enchanter had a spell over my destiny."

"Spells may be broken by true men," said the Smith. "I would it were come to that. Thorbiorn, the Danish armourer, spoke of a spell he had for making breastplates, by singing a certain song while the iron was heating. I told him that his runic rhymes were no proof against the weapons which fought at Loncarty—what farther came of it it is needless to tell—but the corslet and the wearer, and the leech who salved his wound, know if Henry Gow can break a spell or no."

Catherine looked at him as if about to return some answer little approving of the exploit he had vaunted, which the downright Smith had not recollected was of a kind that exposed him to her frequent censure. But ere she had given words to her thoughts, her father thrust his head in at the door.

"Henry," he said, "I must interrupt your more pleasing affairs, and request you to come into my working room in all speed, to consult about certain matters deeply affecting the weal of the burgh."

Henry, making his obeisance to Catherine, left the apartment upon her father's summons. Indeed it was probably in favour of their future friendly intercourse that they were parted on this occasion, at the turn which the conversation seemed likely to take. For as the wooer had begun to hold the refusal of the damsel as somewhat capricious and inexplicable after the degree of encouragement, which, in his opinion, she had afforded; Catherine, on the other hand, considered him rather as an encroacher upon the grace which she had shown him, than one whose delicacy rendered him deserving of such favour.

But there was living in their bosoms towards each other a reciprocal kindness, which on the termination of the dispute was sure to revive, inducing the maiden to forget her offended delicacy, and the lover his slighted warmth of passion.

Chapter Seven

This quarrel may draw blood another day.
Henry VI. Part I

THE CONCLAVE of citizens appointed to meet for investigating the affray of the preceding evening, had now assembled. The work-room of Simon Glover was filled to crowding by personages of no little consequence, some of whom wore black velvet cloaks, and gold chains around their necks. They were, indeed, the fathers of the city; and there were bailies and deacons in the honoured number. There was an ireful and offended air of importance upon every brow, as they conversed together, rather in whisper than aloud or in detail. Busiest among the busy, the little important assistant of the previous night, Oliver Proudfute by name, and bonnet-maker by profession, was bustling among the crowd; much after the manner of the sea-gull, which flutters, screams, and sputters most at the commencement of a gale of wind, though one can hardly conceive what the bird has better to do than to fly to its nest, and remain quiet till the gale is over.

Be that as it may, Master Proudfute was in the midst of the crowd, his fingers upon every one's button, and his mouth in every man's ear, embracing such as were near to his own stature, that he might more closely and mysteriously utter his sentiments; and standing on tip-toe, and supporting himself by the cloak-collars of tall men, that he might dole out to them also the same share of information. He felt himself one of the heroes of the affair, being conscious of the dignity of superior information on the subject as an eye-witness, and much disposed to push his connexion with the affray a few points beyond the modesty of truth. It cannot be said his communications were in especial curious and important, consisting chiefly of such assertions as these:—

"It is all true, by St John. I was there and saw it myself—was the first to run to the fray; and if it had not been for me and another stout fellow, who came in about the same time, they had broken into Simon Glover's house, cut his throat, and carried his daughter off to the mountains. It is too bad—not to be suffered, neighbour Crookshank, —not to be endured, neighbour Glass—not to be borne, neighbours Balneaves, Rollock, and Chrysteson. It is a mercy that I and that stout fellow came in—Is it not, neighbour and worthy Bailie Craigdallie?"

These speeches were dispersed by the busy bonnet-maker into sundry ears. Bailie Craigdallie, a portly guild-brother, the same who had advised the prorogation of their civic council to the present place and hour, a big, burly, good-looking man, shook him from his cloak with pretty much the grace with which a large horse shrugs off the importunate fly that has beset him for ten minutes, and exclaimed, "Silence, good citizens; here comes Simon Glover, in whom no man ever saw falsehood. We will hear the outrage from his own mouth."

Simon being called upon to tell his tale, did so with obvious embarrassment, which he imputed to a reluctance that the burgh should be put in deadly feud with any one upon his account. It was, he dared to say, a masquing or revel on the part of the young gallants about court; and the worst that might come of it would be that he would put iron stancheons on his daughter's window, in case of such another frolic.

"Why, then, if this was a mere masquing or mummery," said Craigdallie, "our townsman, Harry of the Wynd, did far wrong to cut off a gentleman's hand for such a harmless pleasantry, and the town may be brought to a heavy fine for it, unless we secure the person of the mutilator."

"Our Lady forbid," said the Glover. "Did you know what I do, you would be as much afraid of handling this matter as if it were glowing iron. But, since you will needs put your fingers in the fire, truth must be spoken. And come what will, I must say that the matter might have ended ill for me and mine, but for the opportune assistance of Henry Gow, the armourer, well known to you all."

"And mine also was not awanting," said Oliver Proudfute, "though I do not profess to be utterly so good a swordsman as our neighbour, Henry Gow.—You saw me, neighbour Glover, at the beginning of the fray?"

"I saw you after the end of it, neighbour," answered the Glover, drily.

"True, true; I had forgot you were in your house while the blows were going, and could not survey who were dealing them."

"Peace, neighbour Proudfute; I prithee, peace," said Craigdallie, who was obviously tired of the tuneless screeching of the worthy Oliver. "There is something mysterious here; but I think I spy the secret. Our friend Simon is, as you all know, a peaceful man, and one that will rather sit down with wrong than put a friend, or say a neighbourhood, in danger, to seek his redress. Thou, Henry, who art never wanting where the burgh needs a defender, tell us what *thou* knowest of this matter."

Our Smith told his story to the same purpose which we have already related; and the meddling maker of bonnets added as before, "And thou sawest me there, honest Smith, didst thou not?"

"Not I, in good faith, neighbour," answered Henry; "but you are a little man, you know, and I might overlook you."

This reply produced a laugh at Oliver's expense, who laughed for company, but added, "I was one of the foremost to the rescue for all that."

"Why, where wert thou then, neighbour?" said the Smith; "for I saw you not, and I would have given the worth of the best suit of armour I ever wrought to have seen as stout a fellow as thou at my elbow."

"I was no farther off, however, honest Smith; and whilst thou wert laying on blows as if on an anvil, I was parrying those that the rest of the villains aimed at thee behind thy back; and that is the cause thou sawest me not."

"I have heard of Smiths of old time who had but one eye," said Henry. "I have two, but they are both set in my forehead, and so I could not see behind my back, neighbour."

"The truth is, however," persevered Master Oliver, "there I was, and I will give Master Bailie my account of the matter; for the Smith and I were first up to the fray."

"Enough at present," said the Bailie, waving to Master Proudfute an injunction of silence. "The precognition of Simon Glover and Henry Gow would bear out a matter less worthy of belief.—And now, my masters, your opinion what should be done. Here are all our burgher rights broken through and insulted, and you may well fancy that it is by some man of main, since no less dared have attempted such an outrage. My masters, it is hard on flesh and blood to submit to this. The laws have framed us of lower rank than the princes and nobles, yet it's against reason to suppose that we'll suffer our houses to be broken into, and the honour of our women insulted, without some redress."

"It is not to be endured," answered the citizens unanimously.

Here Simon Glover interfered with a very anxious and ominous countenance. "I hope still that all was not meant so ill as it seemed to us, my worthy neighbours; and I for one would cheerfully forgive the alarm and disturbance to my poor house, providing the Fair City were not brought into jeopardy for me. I beseech you to consider who are to be our judges that are to hear the case, and give or refuse redress. I speak among neighbours and friends, and therefore I speak openly. The King, God bless him! is so broke in mind and body that he will but turn us over to some great man amongst his councillors, who shall be in favour for the time—Perchance he will refer us to his brother the Duke of Albany, who will make our petition for righting of our wrongs the pretence for squeezing money out of us."

"We will none of Albany for our judge," answered the meeting with the same unanimity as before.

"Or perhaps," added Simon, "he will bid the Duke of Rothsay take charge of it; and the wild young prince will regard the outrage as something for his gay companions to scoff at, and his minstrels to turn into a song."

"Away with Rothsay! he is too gay to be our judge," again exclaimed the citizens.

Simon, emboldened by seeing he was reaching the point he aimed at, yet pronouncing the dreaded name with a half whisper, next added, "Would you like the Black Douglas better?"

There was no answer. They looked on each other with fallen countenances and blanched lips. But Henry Smith spoke out boldly, and in a decided voice, the sentiments which all felt, but none else dared give words to—"The Black Douglas to judge betwixt a burgher and a gentleman, nay, a nobleman for all I know or care?—The black devil of hell sooner! You are mad, father Simon, so much as to name so wild a proposal."

There was again a silence of fear and uncertainty, which was at length broken by Craigdallie, who, looking significantly to the speaker, replied, "You are confident in a stout doublet, neighbour Smith, or you would not speak so boldly."

"I am confident of a good heart under my doublet, such as it is, Bailie," answered the undaunted Henry; "and though I speak but little, my mouth shall never be padlocked by any noble of them all."

"Wear a thick doublet, good Henry, or do not speak so loud," reiterated the Bailie, in the same significant tone. "There are Border men in the town who wear the Bloody Heart on their shoulder.—But all this is no rede. What shall we do?"

"Short rede, good rede," said the Smith. "Let us to our Provost, and demand his countenance and assistance."

A murmur of applause went through the party, and Oliver Proudfute exclaimed, "That is what I have been saying for this half hour, and not one of ye would listen to me. Let us go to our Provost, said I. He is a gentleman himself, and ought to come between the burgh and the nobles in all matters."

"Hush, neighbours, hush; be wary what you say or do," said a thin meagre figure of a man, whose diminutive person seemed still more reduced in size, and more assimilated to a shadow, by his efforts to assume an extreme degree of humility, and make himself, to suit his argument, look meaner yet, and yet more insignificant than nature had made him.

"Pardon me," said he; "I am but a poor Pottingar. Nevertheless, I have been bred in Paris, and learned my humanities and my *cursus medendi* as well as some that call themselves learned leeches.

Methinks I can tent this wound, and treat it with emollients. Here is our friend Simon Glover, who is, as you all know, a man of worship. Think you he would not be the most willing of us all to pursue harsh courses here, since his family honour is so nearly concerned? And since he blenches away from the charge against these same revellers, consider if he may not have some good reason more than he cares to utter for letting the matter sleep. It is not for me to put my finger on the sore; but, alack! we all know that young maidens are what I call fugitive essences. Suppose now, an honest maiden—I mean in all innocence—leaves her window unlatched on St Valentine's morn that some gallant cavalier may (in all honesty, I mean) become her Valentine for the season; and suppose the gallant be discovered, may she not scream out as if the visit were unexpected, and—and—bray all this in a mortar, and then consider, will it be a matter to place the town in feud for?"

The Pottingar delivered his opinion in a most insinuating manner; but he seemed to shrink into something less than his natural tenuity when he saw the blood rise in the old cheeks of Simon Glover, and inflame to the temples the complexion of the redoubted Smith. The last, stepping forward and turning a stern look on the alarmed Pottingar, broke out as follows:—"Thou walking skeleton! thou asthmatic gallipot! thou poisoner by profession! if I thought that the puff of vile breath thou hast left could blight for the tenth part of a minute the fair fame of Catherine Glover, I would pound thee, quacksalver! in thine own mortar, and beat up thy wretched carrion with flower of brimeston, the only real medicine in thy booth, to make a salve to rub mangy hounds with!"

"Hold, son Henry, hold!" cried the Glover in a tone of authority,—"no man has title to speak of this matter but me.—Worshipful Bailie Craigdallie, since such is the construction that is put upon my patience, I am willing to pursue this riot to the uttermost; and though the issue may prove we had better have been patient, you will all see that my Catherine hath not by lightness or folly of hers afforded grounds for this great scandal."

The Bailie also interposed. "Neighbour Henry," said he, "we came here to consult and not to quarrel. As one of the fathers of the Fair City, I command thee to forego all evil will and maltalent you may have against Master Pottingar Dwining."

"He is too poor a creature, Bailie," said Henry Gow, "for me to harbour feud with—me that could destroy him and his booth with one blow of my fore-hammer."

"Peace, then, and hear me," said the official. "We all are as much believers in the honour of the Fair Maiden of Perth, as in that of our

Blessed Lady." Here he crossed himself devoutly. "But touching our appeal to our Provost—Are you agreed, neighbours, to put matter like this into our Provost's hand, being against a powerful noble, as is to be feared?"

"The Provost being himself a nobleman—" squeaked the Pottingar, in some measure released from his terror by the intervention of the Bailie—"and God knows, I speak not to the disparagement of an honourable gentleman, whose forebears have held the office he now holds for many years"——

"By free choice of the citizens of Perth," said the Smith, interrupting the speaker with the tones of his deep and decisive voice.

"Ay, surely," said the disconcerted orator, "by the voice of the citizens. How else?—I pray you, friend Smith, interrupt me not. I speak to our worthy and eldest Bailie, Craigdallie, according to my poor mind. I say that, come amongst us how he will, still this Sir Patrick Charteris is a nobleman, and hawks will not pick hawks' eyes out. He may well bear us out in a feud with the Highlandmen, and do the part of our Provost and leader; but whether he that himself wears silk will take our part against broidered cloak and cloth of gold, though he may do so against tartan and Irish frieze, is something to be questioned. Take a fool's advice. We have saved our Maiden, of whom I never meant to speak harm, as truly I knew none. They have lost one man's hand at least, and with thanks to Harry Smith."

"And to me," added the little important bonnet-maker.

"And to Oliver Proudfute, as he tells us," continued the Pottingar, who contested no man's claim to glory, provided he was not himself compelled to tread the perilous paths which lead to it. "I say, neighbours, since they have left a hand as a pledge they will never come in Couvrefew street again, why, in my simple mind, we were best to thank our stout townsman, and the town having the honour and these rakehells the loss, that we should hush the matter up and say no more about it."

These pacific counsels had their effect with some of the citizens, who began to nod and look exceedingly wise upon the advocate of acquiescence, with whom, notwithstanding the offence so lately given, Simon Glover seemed also to agree in opinion. But not so Henry Smith, who, seeing the consultation at a stand, took up the speech in his downright way.

"I am neither the oldest nor the richest among you, neighbours, and I am not sorry for it. Years will come, if one lives to see them; and I can win and spend my penny like another, by the blaze of the furnace and the wind of the bellows. But no man ever saw me sit down with wrong done in word or deed to our fair town, if man's tongue and hands could right it. Neither will I sit down with this outrage, if I can help it. I will go to the Provost myself if no one will go with me. He is a knight, it is true, and a gentleman of free and true-born blood, as we all know, since Wallace's time, who settled his great-grandsire amongst us. But if he were the proudest nobleman in the land, he is Provost of Perth, and for his own honour must see the freedoms and immunities of the burgh preserved—ay, and I know he will—I have made a steel doublet for him, and have a good guess at the kind of heart that it was meant to cover."

"Surely," said Bailie Craigdallie, "it would be to no purpose to stir at court without Sir Patrick Charteris's countenance; the ready answer would be, Go to your Provost, you borrel loons. So, neighbours and townsmen, if you will stand by my side, I and our Pottingar Dwining will repair presently to Kinfauns, with Sim Glover, the jolly Smith, and gallant Oliver Proudfute, for witnesses to the onslaught, and speak with Sir Patrick Charteris in name of the Fair Town."

"Nay," said the peaceful man of medicine, "leave me behind, I pray you; I lack audacity to speak before a belted knight."

"Never regard that, neighbour, you must go," said Bailie Craigdallie. "The town hold me a hot-headed carle for a man of threescore—Sim Glover is the offended party—we all know that Harry Gow spoils more harnesses with his sword than he makes with his hammer—and our neighbour Proudfute,—who, take his own word, is at the beginning and end of every fray in Perth,—is of course a man of action. We must have at least one advocate amongst us for peace and quietness; and thou, Pottingar, must be the man. Away with you, sirs, get your boots and your beasts—horse and hattock, I say—and let us meet at the East Port—that is, if it is your pleasure, neighbours, to trust us with the matter."

"There can be no better rede, and we will all avouch it," said the citizens. "If the Provost take our part, as the Fair Town hath a right to expect, we may bell-the-cat with the best of them."

"It is well, then, neighbours," answered the Bailie; "so said, so shall be done. Meanwhile, I have called the whole town-council together about this hour, and I have little doubt," looking around the company, "that as so many of them who are in this place have resolved to consult with our Provost, the rest will be compliant to the same resolution. And therefore, neighbours, and good burghers of the Fair City of Perth—horse and hattock, as I said before, and meet me at the East Port."

A general acclamation concluded the sitting of this species of Privy Council, or Lords of the Articles; and they dispersed, the deputation to prepare for the journey, and the rest to tell their impatient wives and daughters of the measures they had taken to render their chambers safe in future against the intrusion of gallants at unseasonable hours.

While nags are saddling, and the town-council debating, or rather putting in form what the leading members of their body had already adopted, it may be necessary for some readers to learn in distinct terms what is more circuitously intimated in the course of the former discussion.

It was the custom at this period, when the strength of the feudal aristocracy controlled the rights, and frequently insulted the privileges, of the Royal Burghs of Scotland, that the latter, where it was practicable, often chose their Provost, or Chief Magistrate, not out of the order of the merchants, shopkeepers, and artizans, who inhabited the town itself, and filled up the roll of the ordinary magistracy, but elected to that pre-eminent state some powerful nobleman, or baron, in the neighbourhood, who was expected to stand their friend at court in such matters as concerned their common weal, and to lead their civic militia to fight, whether in general battle or in private feud, reinforcing them with his own feudal retainers. This protection was not always gratuitous. The Provosts sometimes availed themselves of their situation to an unjustifiable degree, and obtained grants of lands and tenements belonging to the common good, or public property of the burgh, and thus made the citizens pay dear for the countenance which they afforded. Others were satisfied to receive the powerful aid of the townsmen in their own feudal quarrels, with such other marks of respect and benevolence as the burgh over which they presided were willing to gratify them with, in order to secure their active services in case of necessity. The Baron, who was the regular protector of a Royal Burgh, accepted such free-will offerings without scruple, and repaid them by defending the rights of the town, by arguments in the Council, and by bold deeds in the field.

The citizens of the town, or, as they loved better to call it, the Fair City of Perth, had for several generations found a protector of this kind in the family of Charteris, Lords of Kinfauns, in the neighbourhood of the burgh. It was scarce a century (in the time of Robert III.) since the first of this distinguished family had settled in the strong castle which now belonged to them, with the picturesque and fertile scenes adjoining to it. But the history of the first settler, chivalrous and romantic in itself, was calculated to facilitate the settlement of an alien in the land in which his lot was cast. We relate it as it is given by an ancient and uniform tradition, which carries in it great indications of truth, and is warrant enough, perhaps, for its insertion in graver histories than the present.

During the brief career of the celebrated patriot Sir William Wallace, and when his arms had for a time expelled the English invaders from his native country, he is said to have undertaken a voyage to France, with a small band of trusty friends, to try what his presence (for he was respected through all countries for his prowess) might do to induce the French monarch to send to Scotland a body of auxiliary forces, or other assistance, to aid the Scots in regaining their independence.

The Scottish Champion was on board a small vessel, and steering for the port of Dieppe, when a sail appeared in the distance, which the mariners regarded with doubt and apprehension, and at last with confusion and dismay. Wallace demanded to know what was the cause of their alarm. The captain of the ship informed him that the tall vessel which was bearing down, with the purpose of boarding that which he commanded, was the ship of a celebrated rover, equally famed for his courage, strength of body, and successful piracies. It was commanded by a gentleman named Thomas de Longueville, a Frenchman by birth, but by practice one of those pirates who called themselves friends to the sea, and enemies to all who sailed upon it. He attacked and plundered vessels of all nations, like one of the ancient Norse Sea-kings, as they were termed, whose dominion was upon the mountain waves. The master added that no vessel could escape the rover by flight, so speedy was the bark he commanded; and that no crew, however hardy, could hope to resist him, when, as was his usual mode of combat, he threw himself on board at the head of his followers.

Wallace smiled sternly, while the master of the ship, with alarm in his countenance, and tears in his eyes, described to him the certainty of their being captured by the Red Rover, a name given to De Longueville, because he usually displayed the blood-red flag, which he had now hoisted.

"I will clear the narrow seas of this rover," said Wallace.

Then calling together some ten or twelve of his own followers, Boyd, Kerlie, Seton, and others, to whom the dust of the most desperate battle was like the breath of life, he commanded them to arm themselves, and lie flat upon the deck, so as to be out of sight. He ordered the mariners below, excepting such as were absolutely necessary to manage the vessel; and he gave the master orders, upon pain of death, so to steer as, while the vessel had an appearance of attempting to fly, he should in fact permit the Red Rover to come up with them and do his worst. Wallace himself then lay down on the deck that nothing might be seen which could intimate any purpose of resistance. In a quarter of an hour De Longueville's vessel ran on board that of Wallace, and the pirate captain casting out grappling irons to make sure of his prize, jumped on the deck in complete armour, followed by his men, who gave a terrible shout as if victory had been already secured. But the armed Scots started up at once, and the rover found himself unexpectedly engaged with men accustomed to consider victory as secure, when they were only opposed as one to two or three. Wallace himself rushed on the pirate captain, and a dreadful strife began with such fury that the others suspended their own battle to look on, and seemed by common consent to refer the issue of the strife to the fate of the combat between the two chiefs. The pirate fought as well as man could do; but Wallace's strength was beyond that of ordinary mortals. He dashed the sword from the rover's hand, and placed him in such peril, that, to avoid being cut down, he was fain to close with the Champion of Scotland, in hopes of overpowering him in the grapple. In this also he was foiled. They fell on the deck, locked in each other's arms, but the Frenchman fell undermost; and Wallace, fixing his grasp upon his gorget, compressed it so closely, notwithstanding it was made of the finest steel, that the blood gushed from his eyes, nose, and mouth, and he was only able to ask for quarter by signs. His men threw down their weapons and begged for mercy, when they saw their leader thus severely handled. Wallace granted them all their lives, but took possession of their vessel, and detained them prisoners.

When he came in sight of the French harbour, Wallace alarmed the place by displaying the rover's colours, as if De Longueville was coming to pillage the town. The bells were rung backward; horns were blown, and the citizens were hurrying to arms, when the scene changed. The Scottish Lion in his shield of gold was raised above the piratical flag, and announced the Champion of Scotland was approaching, like a falcon with his prey in his clutch. He landed with his prisoner, and carried him to the court of France, where, at Wallace's request, the robberies which the pirate had committed were forgiven, and the King even conferred the honour of knighthood on Sir Thomas de Longueville, and offered to take him into his service. But the rover had contracted such a friendship for his generous victor that he insisted on uniting his fortunes with those of Wallace, with whom he returned to Scotland, and fought by his side in many a bloody battle, where the prowess of Sir Thomas de Longueville was remarked as inferior to that of none, save of his heroic conqueror. His fate also was more fortunate than that of his patron. Being distinguished by the beauty as well as strength of his person, he rendered himself so acceptable to a young lady, heiress of the ancient family of Charteris, that she chose him for her husband, bestowing on him with her hand the fair baronial Castle of Kinfauns, and the domains annexed to it. Their descendants took the name of Charteris, as connecting themselves with their maternal ancestors, the ancient proprietors of the property, though the name of Thomas de Longueville was equally honoured amongst them; and the large two-handed sword with which he mowed the ranks of war, was, and is still, preserved among the family muniments. Another account is, that the family name of De Longueville himself was Charteris. The estate afterwards passed to a family of Blairs, and is now the property of Lord Gray.

These barons of Kinfauns, from father to son, held, for several generations, the office of Provost of Perth; the vicinity of the castle and town rendering it a very convenient arrangement for mutual support. The Sir Patrick of this history had more than once led out the men of Perth to battles and skirmishes with the restless Highland depredators, and with other enemies, foreign and domestic. True it is, he used sometimes to be weary of the slight and frivolous complaints unnecessarily brought before him, and in which he was requested to interest himself. Hence he had sometimes incurred the charge of being too proud as a nobleman, or too indolent as a man of wealth, and one who was too much addicted to the pleasures of the field, and the exercise of feudal hospitality, to bestir himself upon all and every occasion when the Fair Town would have desired his active interference. But notwithstanding that this occasioned some slight murmuring, upon any serious cause of alarm the citizens were wont to rally around their Provost, and were warmly supported by him both in council and action.

Chapter Eight

THE CHARACTER and quality of Sir Patrick Charteris, the Provost of Perth, being such as we have sketched in the last chapter, let us now return to the deputation which was in the act of rendezvousing at the East Port, in order to wait upon that dignitary with their complaints at Kinfauns.

And first appeared Simon Glover, on a pacing palfrey, which had sometimes enjoyed the honour of bearing the fairer as well as the lighter weight of his beautiful daughter. His cloak was muffled round the lower part of his face, as a sign to his friends not to interrupt him by any questions while he passed through the streets, and partly, perhaps, on account of the coldness of the weather. The deepest anxiety was seated on his brow, as if the more he meditated on the matter he was engaged in, the more difficult and perilous it appeared. He only greeted by silent gestures his friends as they came to the rendezvous.

A strong black horse, of the old Galloway breed, of an under size, not exceeding fourteen hands, but high-shouldered, strong-limbed, well-coupled, and round-barrelled, bore to the East Port the gallant Smith. A judge of the animal might see in his eye a spark of that vicious temper which is frequently the accompaniment of the form that is most vigorous and enduring; but the weight, the hand, and the seat of the rider, added to the late regular exercise of a long journey, had subdued its stubbornness for the present. He was accompanied by the honest Bonnet-maker, who, being, as the reader is aware, a little round man, had planted himself like a red pin-cushion, (for he was wrapped in a scarlet cloak, over which he had slung a hawking pouch,) on the top of a great saddle, which he might be said rather to be perched upon than to bestride. The saddle and the man were girthed on the ridge-bone of a great trampling Flemish mare, with a nose turned up in the air like a camel, a huge fleece of hair at each foot, and each foot full as large in circumference as a frying-pan. The contrast between the beast and the rider was so extremely extraordinary that whilst chance passengers contented themselves with wondering how he got up, his friends were anticipating with sorrow the perils which must attend his coming down again; for the high-seated horseman's feet did not by any means come beneath the laps of the saddle. He had associated himself to the Smith, whose motions he had watched for the purpose of joining him; for it was Oliver Proudfute's opinion that men of action showed to most advantage when beside each other; and he was delighted when some wag of the lower class had gravity enough to cry out, without laughing outright, "There goes the pride of Perth —there go the slashing craftsmen, the jolly Smith of the Wynd, and the bold Bonnet-maker!"

It is true the fellow who gave this all-hail thrust his tongue in his cheek to some scapegraces like himself; but as the Bonnet-maker did not see this by-play, he generously threw him a silver penny to encourage his respect for martialists. This munificence occasioned their being followed by a crowd of boys, laughing and hallowing, until Henry Smith, turning back, threatened to switch the foremost of them; a resolution which they did not wait to see put in execution.

"Here are we the witnesses," said the little man on the large horse, as they joined Simon Glover at the East Port; "but where are they that should back us? Ah, brother Henry! authority is a load for an ass rather than a spirited horse; it would but clog the motions of such young fellows as you and me."

"I could well wish to see you bear ever so little of that same weight, worthy Master Proudfute," replied Henry Gow, "were it but to keep you firm in the saddle; for you bounce about as if you were dancing a jig on your seat without any help from your legs."

"Ay, ay! I raise myself in my stirrups to avoid the jolting. She is cruelly hard set this mare of mine—But she has carried me in field and forest, and through some passages that were something perilous—so Jezabel and I part not—I call her Jezabel, after the Princess of Castille."

"Isabel, I suppose you mean," answered the Smith.

"Ay—Isabel or Jezabel,—'tis the same, you know. But here comes Bailie Craigdallie at last, with that poor, creeping, cowardly creature the Pottingar. They have brought two town-officers with their partizans, to guard their fair persons, I suppose.—If there is one thing I hate more than another, it is such a sneaking varlet as that Dwining!"

"Have a care he does not hear you say so," said the Smith. "I tell thee, Bonnet-maker, that there is more danger in yonder slight wasted anatomy, than in twenty stout fellows like yourself."

"Pshaw! Bully Smith, you are but jesting with me," said Oliver,— softening his voice, however, and looking towards the Pottingar, as if to discover in what limb or lineament of his wasted face and form lay any appearance of the menaced danger; and his examination reassuring him, he answered boldly, "Blades and bucklers, man, I would stand the feud of a dozen such as Dwining. What could he do to any man with blood in his veins?"

"He could give him a dose of physic," answered the Smith, drily.

They had no time for further colloquy, for Bailie Craigdallie called to them to take the road to Kinfauns, and himself showed the example. As they advanced at a leisurely pace, the discourse turned on the reception which they were to expect from their Provost, and the interest which he was like to take in the aggression which they complained of. The Glover seemed particularly desponding, and spoke more than once in a manner which implied a wish that they would yet consent to let the matter rest. He did not speak out very plainly, however, fearful, perhaps, of the malignant interpretation which might be derived from any appearance of his flinching from the assertion of his daughter's reputation. Dwining seemed to agree with him in opinion, but spoke more cautiously than in the morning.

"After all," said the Bailie, "when I think of all the propines and good gifts which have passed from the good town to my Lord Provost's, I cannot think he will be backward to show himself. More than one lusty boat, laden with Bourdeaux wine, has left the South Shore to discharge its burden under the Castle of Kinfauns. I have some right to speak of that, who was the merchant importer."

"And," said Dwining, with his squeaking voice, "I could speak of delicate confections, curious comfits, loaves of wastel bread, and even cakes of that rare and delicious condiment which men call sugar, that have gone thither to help out a bridal banquet, or a kirstening feast, or such like. But alack, Bailie Craigdallie, wine is drunk, comfits are eaten, and the gift is forgotten when the flavour is past away. Alas, neighbour! the banquet of last Christmas is gone like the last year's snow."

"But there have been gloves filled full of gold pieces," said the Magistrate.

"I should know that who wrought them," said Simon, whose professional recollections still mingled with whatever else might occupy his mind. "One was a hawking glove for my lady. I made it something wide. Her ladyship found no fault, in consideration of the intended lining."

"Well, go to," said Bailie Craigdallie, "the less I lie; and if these are not to the fore, it is the Provost's fault, and not the town's; they could neither be eat nor drunk in the shape in which he got them."

"I could speak of a brave armour too," said the Smith; "but, *cogan na schie!* as John Highlandman says, I think the Knight of Kinfauns will do his devoir by the burgh in peace or war; and it is needless to be reckoning the town's good deeds till we see him thankless for them."

"So say I," cried our friend Proudfute, from the top of his mare. "We roystering blades never bear so base a mind as to reckon up for wine and walnuts with a friend like Sir Patrick Charteris. Nay, trust me, a good woodsman like Sir Patrick will prize the right of hunting and sporting over the lands of the burgh—an high privilege, and his Majesty the King's Grace excepted, neither granted to lord nor loon save to our Provost alone."

As the Bonnet-maker spoke, there was heard on the left hand the cry of, "*So so—waw waw—haw,*" being the shout of a falconer to his hawk.

"Methinks yonder is a fellow using the privilege you mention, who, from his appearance, is neither King nor Provost," said the Smith.

"Ay, marry, I see him," said the Bonnet-maker, who imagined the occasion presented a chief occasion to win honour. "Thou and I, jolly Smith, will prick towards him and put him to the question."

"Have with you, then," cried the Smith; and his companion spurred his mare and went off, never doubting that Gow was at his heels.

But Craigdallie caught Henry's horse by the reins. "Stand fast by the standard," he said; "let us see the luck of our light horseman—if he procures himself a broken pate, he will be quieter for the rest of the day."

"From what I already see," said the Smith, "he may easily come by such a boon. Yonder fellow who stops so impudently to look at us, as if he were engaged in the most lawful sport in the world—I guess him, by his trotting hobbiler, his rusty head-piece with the cock's feather, and long two-handed sword, to be the follower of some of the South-land lords—men who live so near the Southron that the black jack is never off their backs, and who are as free of their blows as they are light in their fingers."

Whilst they were thus speculating on the issue of the rencounter, the valiant Bonnet-maker began to pull up Jezabel, in order that the Smith, who he still concluded was close behind, might overtake him, and either advance first, or at least abreast of himself. But when he saw him at a hundred yards' distance, standing composedly with the rest of the group, the flesh of the champion, like that of the old Spanish general, began to tremble in anticipation of the dangers into which his own venturous spirit was about to involve it. Yet the consciousness of being countenanced by the neighbourhood of so many friends; the hopes that the appearance of such odds must intimidate the single intruder, and the shame of abandoning an enterprise in which he had volunteered, and when so many persons must witness his disgrace, surmounted the strong inclination which prompted him to wheel Jezabel to the right about, and return to the friends whose protection he had quitted, as fast as her legs could carry them. He accordingly continued his direction towards the stranger, who increased his alarm considerably by putting his little nag in motion, and riding to meet him at a brisk trot. On observing this apparently offensive movement, our hero looked over his left shoulder more than once, as if reconnoitring the ground for a retreat, and in the meanwhile came to a decided halt. But the Philistine was upon him ere the Bonnet-maker could decide whether to fight or fly, and a very ominous-looking Philistine he was. His figure was gaunt and lathy, his visage marked by two or three ill-favoured scars, and the whole man had much the air of one accustomed to say, "Stand and deliver," to a true man.

This individual began the discourse by exclaiming, in tones as sinister as his looks,—"The devil catch you for a cuckoo, why do you ride across the moor to spoil my sport?"

"Worthy stranger," said our friend, in the tone of pacific remonstrance, "I am Oliver Proudfute, a burgess of Perth, and a man of substance; and yonder is the worshipful Adam Craigdallie, the oldest Bailie of the burgh, with the fighting Smith of the Wynd, and three or four armed men more, who desire to know your name, and how you come to take your pleasure over these lands belonging to the burgh of Perth—although, natheless, I will answer for them, it is not their wish to quarrel with a gentleman, or stranger, for any accidental trespass;

only it is their use and wont not to grant such leave, unless it is duly asked; and—and—therefore I desire to know your name, worthy sir."

The grim and loathly aspect with which the falconer had regarded Oliver Proudfute during his harangue had greatly disconcerted him, and altogether altered the character of the inquiry which, with Henry Gow to back him, he would probably have thought fitting for the occasion.

The stranger replied to it, modified as it was, with a most inauspicious grin, which the scars of his visage made appear still more menacing. "You want to know my name?—My name is the Devil's Dick of Hellgarth-hill, well known in Annandale for a gentle Johnstone. I follow the stout Laird of Wamphray, who rides with his kinsman the redoubted Lord of Johnstone, who is banded with the doughty Earl of Douglas; and the Earl and the Lord, and the Laird and I the Esquire, fly our hawks where we find our game, and ask no man whose ground we ride over."

"I will do your message, sir," replied Oliver Proudfute, meekly enough; for he began to be very desirous to get free of the embassy which he had so rashly undertaken, and was in the act of turning his horse's head when the Annandale man added, "And take you this to boot, to keep you in mind that you met the Devil's Dick, and to teach you another time to beware how you spoil the sport of any who wears the flying spur on his shoulder."

With these words he applied two or three smart blows of his riding-rod upon the luckless Bonnet-maker's head and person. Some of them lighted upon Jezabel, who, turning sharply round, laid her rider upon the moor, and galloped back towards the party of citizens.

Proudfute, thus overthrown, began to cry for assistance in no very manly voice, and almost in the same breath to whisper for mercy; for his antagonist, dismounting almost as soon as he fell, offered a whinger, or large wood knife, to his throat, while he rifled the pockets of the unlucky citizen, and even examined his hawking bag, swearing two or three grisly oaths that he would have what it contained, since the wearer had interrupted his sport. He pulled the belt rudely off, terrifying the prostrate Bonnet-maker still more by the regardless violence which he used, as, instead of taking the pains to unbuckle the strap, he drew till the fastening gave way. But apparently it contained nothing to his mind. He threw it carelessly from him, and at the same time suffered the dismounted cavalier to rise, while he himself remounted his hobbiler, and looked towards the rest of Oliver's party, who were now advancing.

When they had seen their delegate over-thrown, there was some laughter; so much had the vaunting humour of the Bonnet-maker prepared his friends to rejoice, when, as Henry Smith termed it, they saw their Oliver meet with a Rowland. But when he saw his adversary bestride him, and handle him in the manner described, the armourer could hold out no longer. "Please you, good Master Bailie, I cannot endure to see our townsman beaten and rifled and like to be murdered before us all. It reflects upon the Fair Town; and if it is neighbour Proudfute's misfortune, it is our shame. I must to his rescue."

"We will all go to his rescue," answered Bailie Craigdallie: "but let no man strike without order from me. We have more feuds on our hands, it is to be feared, than we have strength to bring to good end. And therefore I charge you all, more especially you, Henry of the Wynd, in the name of the Fair City, that you make no stroke but in self-defence." They all advanced, therefore, in a body; and the appearance of such a number drove the plunderer from his booty. He stood at gaze, however, at some distance, like the wolf, which, though it retreats before the dogs, cannot be brought to absolute flight.

Henry, seeing this state of things, spurred his horse and advanced far before the rest of the party, up toward the scene of Oliver Proudfute's misfortune. His first task was to catch Jezabel by the flowing rein, and his next to lead her to meet her discomfited master, who was crippling toward him, his clothes much soiled with his fall, his eyes streaming with tears, from pain as well as mortification, and altogether so unlike the spruce and dapper importance of his ordinary appearance that the honest Smith felt compassion for the little man, and some remorse at having left him exposed to such disgrace. All men, I believe, enjoy an ill-natured joke. The difference is, that an ill-natured person can drink out to very dregs the amusement which it affords, while the better-moulded mind soon loses the sense of the ridiculous in sympathy for the pain of the sufferer.

"Let me pitch you up to your saddle again, neighbour," said the Smith, dismounting at the same time, and assisting Oliver to scramble into his war-saddle as a monkey might have done.

"May God forgive you, neighbour Smith, for not backing of me! I would not have believed in it, though fifty credible witnesses had sworn it of you."

Such were the first words, spoken in sorrow more than anger, by which the dismayed Oliver vented his feelings.

"The Bailie kept hold of my horse by the bridle; and besides," Henry continued, with a smile, which even his compassion could not suppress, "I thought you would have accused me of diminishing your honour if I brought you aid against a single man. But cheer up! the villain took foul odds of your horse not being well at command."

"That is true—that is true," said Oliver, eagerly catching at the apology.

"And yonder stands the faitour, rejoicing at the mischief he has done, and triumphing in your overthrow, like the King in the romance, who played upon the fiddle whilst a city was burning. Come thou with me, and thou shalt see how we will handle him—Nay, fear not that I will desert thee this time."

So saying, he caught Jezabel by the rein, and galloping alongside of her, without giving Oliver time to express a negative, he rushed toward the Devil's Dick, who had halted on the top of a rising ground at some distance. The gentle Johnstone, however, either that he thought the contest unequal, or that he had fought enough for the day, snapping his fingers, and throwing his hand out with an air of defiance, spurred his horse into a neighbouring bog, through which he seemed to flutter like a wild duck, swinging his lure round his head, and whistling to his hawk all the while, though any other horse and rider must have been instantly bogged up to the saddle-girths.

"There goes a thorough-bred moss-trooper," said the Smith. "That fellow will fight or flee as suits his humour, and there is no use to pursue him, any more than to hunt a wild goose. He has got your purse, I doubt me, for they seldom leave off till they are full-handed."

"Ye—ye—yes," said Proudfute, in a melancholy tone; "he has got my purse—but there is less matter since he hath left the hawking-bag."

"Nay, the hawking-bag had been an emblem of personal victory, to be sure—a trophy, as the minstrels call it."

"There is more in it than that, friend," said Oliver, significantly.

"Why, that is well, neighbour; I love to hear you speak in your own scholarly tone again. Cheer up, you have seen the villain's back, and regained the trophies you had lost when taken at advantage."

"Ah, Henry Gow—Henry Gow," said the Bonnet-maker, and stopped short with a deep sigh, nearly amounting to a groan.

"What is the matter?" asked his friend; "what is it you vex yourself about now?"

"I have some suspicion, my dearest friend, that the villain fled for fear of you, not of me!"

"Do not think so," replied the armourer; "he saw two men and fled, and who can tell whether he fled for one or the other? Besides, he knows by experience your strength and activity; we all saw how you kicked and struggled when you were on the ground."

"Did I?" said poor Proudfute; "I do not remember it—but I know it is my best point—I am a strong dog in the loins. But did they all see it?"

"All as much as I," said the Smith, smothering an inclination to laughter.

"But thou wilt remind them of it?"

"Be assured I will," answered Henry, "and of thy desperate rally even now. Mark what I say to Bailie Craigdallie, and make the best of it."

"It is not that I require any evidence in my favour, for I am as brave by nature as most men in Perth—but only——" Here the man of valour paused.

"But only what?" inquired the armourer.

"But only I am afraid of being killed. To leave my pretty wife and my young family, you know, would be a sad change, Smith. You will know this when it is your own case, and will feel abated in courage."

"It is like that I may," said the armourer, musing.

"Then I am so accustomed to the use of arms, and so well breathed, that few men can match me. It's all here," said the little man, expanding his breast like a trussed fowl, and patting himself with his hands; "here is room for all the wind machinery."

"I dare say you are long-breathed—long-winded,—at least your speech bewrays"——

"My speech?—You are a wag—but I have got the stern post of a dromond brought up the river from Dundee."

"The stern post of a Drummond!" exclaimed the armourer, "conscience, man, it will put you in feud with the whole clan—not the least wrathful in the country, as I take it."

"St Andrew, man, you put me out!—I mean a dromond, that is, a large ship. I have fixed this post in my yard. It is carved something like a Soldan or Saracen, and with him I breathe myself, and will wield my two-handed sword against him, thrust or point, for an hour together."

"That must make you familiar with the use of your weapon," said the Smith.

"Ay, marry does it—and sometimes I will place you a bonnet (an old one most likely) on my Soldan's head, and cleave it with such a downright blow that, in troth, the infidel has but little of his skull remaining to hit at."

"That is unlucky, for you will lose your practice," said Henry.—
"But how say you, Bonnet-maker? I will put on my head-piece and corslet one day, and you shall hew at me, allowing me my broadsword to parry and pay back? Eh, what say you?"

"By no manner of means, my dear friend. I should do you too much evil—Besides, to tell you the truth, I strike far more freely at a helmet or bonnet, when it is set on my wooden Soldan—then I am sure to fetch it down. But when there is a plume of feathers in it that nod, and two eyes gleaming fiercely from under the shadow of the visor, and when the whole is dancing about here and there, I acknowledge it puts out my hand of fence."

"So, if men would but stand stock still like your Soldan, you would play the tyrant with them, Master Proudfute?"

"In time, and with practice, I conclude I might," answered Oliver. —"But here we come up with the rest of them; Bailie Craigdallie looks angry—but it is not his kind of anger that frightens me."

You are to recollect, gentle reader, that as soon as the Bailie, and those who attended him, saw that the Smith had come up to the forlorn Bonnet-maker and that the stranger had retreated, they gave themselves no trouble about advancing further to his assistance, which they regarded as quite insured by the presence of the redoubted Henry Gow. They had resumed their straight road to Kinfauns, desirous that nothing should delay the execution of their mission. As some time had elapsed ere the Bonnet-maker and the Smith rejoined the party, Bailie Craigdallie asked them, and Henry Smith in particular, what they meant by dallying away precious time by riding up hill after the falconer.

"By the mass, it was not my fault, Master Bailie," replied the Smith. "If ye will couple up an ordinary low-country greyhound with a highland wolf-dog, you must not blame the first of them for taking the direction in which it pleases the last to drag him on. It was so, and not otherwise, with my neighbour Oliver Proudfute. He no sooner got up from the ground, but he mounted his mare like a flash of lightning, and enraged at the unknightly advantage which yonder rascal had taken of his stumbling horse, he flew after him like a dromedary. I could not but follow, both to prevent a second stumble, and secure our over bold friend and champion from the chance of some ambush at the top of the hill. But the villain, who is a follower of some Lord of the Marches, and wears a winged spur for his cognizance, fled from our neighbour like fire from flint."

The senior Bailie of Perth listened with surprise to the legend which it had pleased Gow to circulate; for, though not much caring for the matter, he had always doubted the Bonnet-maker's romancing account of his own exploits, which hereafter he must hold as in some degree orthodox. The shrewd old Glover looked closer into the matter.

"You will drive the poor Bonnet-maker mad," he whispered to Henry, "and set him a-ringing his clapper as if he were a town-bell on a rejoicing day, when for order and decency it were better he were silent."

"O, by Our Lady, father," replied the Smith, "I love the poor little

braggadocio, and could not think of him sitting rueful and silent in the
Provost's hall, while all the rest of them, and in especial that venomous
Pottingar, were telling their mind."

"Thou art even too good-natured a fellow, Henry," answered
Simon. "But mark the difference betwixt these two men. The harmless little Bonnet-maker assumes the airs of a dragon, to disguise his
natural cowardice; while the Pottingar wilfully desires to show himself
timid, poor-spirited, and humble, to conceal the danger of his temper.
The adder is not the less deadly that he creeps under a stone. I tell
thee, son Harry, that for all his sneaking looks and timorous talking,
this wretched anatomy loves mischief more than he fears danger.—
But here we stand in front of the Provost's castle; and a lordly place is
Kinfauns, and a credit to the city it is to have the owner of such a
gallant castle for their chief magistrate."

"A goodly fortalice, indeed," said the Smith, looking at the broad
winding Tay, as it swept under the bank on which the castle stood, like
its modern successor, and seemed the queen of the valley, although,
on the opposite side of the river, the strong walls of Elcho appeared to
dispute the pre-eminence. Elcho, however, was in that age a peaceful
nunnery, and the walls with which it was surrounded were the barriers
of secluded vestals, not the bulwarks of an armed garrison. "'Tis a
brave castle," said the armourer, again looking at the towers of Kinfauns, "and the breast-plate and target of the bonnie course of the
Tay. It were worth lipping* a good blade before wrong were offered to
it."

The porter of Kinfauns, who knew from a distance the persons and
characters of the party, had already undone the court-yard gate for
their entrance, and sent notice to Sir Patrick Charteris, that the eldest
Bailie of Perth, with some other good citizens, were approaching the
castle. The good knight, who was getting ready for a hawking party,
heard the intimation with pretty much the same feelings that the
modern representative of a burgh hears of the menaced visitation of a
party of his worthy electors, at a time rather unseasonable for their
reception. That is, he internally devoted the intruders to Mahound
and Termagant, and outwardly gave orders to receive them with all
decorum and civility; commanded the sewers to bring hot venison
steaks and cold baked meats into the knightly hall with all dispatch,
and the butler to broach his casks and do his duty; for if the Fair City
of Perth sometimes filled his cellar, her citizens were always equally
ready to assist at emptying his flagons.

The good burghers were reverendly marshalled into the hall, where
the knight, who was in a riding-habit, and booted up to the middle of

* *Lipping*, *i. e.* making notches in a sword or knife.

his thighs, received them with a mixture of courtesy and patronizing condescension; wishing them all the while at the bottom of the Tay, on account of the interruption their arrival gave to his proposed amusement of the morning. He met them in the midst of the hall, with bare head and bonnet in hand, and some such salutation as the following:—"Ha, my Master Eldest Bailie, and you, worthy Simon Glover, fathers of the Fair City;—and you, my learned Pottingar;—and you, stout Smith;—and my slashing Bonnet-maker too, who cracks more skulls than he covers, how come I to have the pleasure of seeing so many friends so early? I was thinking to see my hawks fly, and your company will make the sport more pleasant—(*Aside*, I trust in Our Lady they may break their necks!)—that is, always, unless the city have any commands to lay on me—Butler Gilbert, dispatch, thou knave—But I hope you have no more grave errand than to try if the malvoisie holds its flavour?"

The city delegates answered to their Provost's civilities by inclinations and congees, more or less characteristic, of which the Pottingar's bow was the lowest, and the Smith's the least ceremonious. Probably he knew his own value as a fighting man upon occasion. To the general compliment the elder Bailie replied.

"Sir Patrick Charteris, and our noble Lord Provost," said Craigdallie, gravely, "had our errand been to enjoy the hospitality with which we have been often regaled here, our manners would have taught us to tarry till your lordship had invited us, as on other occasions. And as to hawking, we have had enough on't for one morning; since a wild fellow, who was flying a falcon hard by on the moor, unhorsed and cudgelled our worthy friend Oliver Bonnet-maker, or Proudfute, as some men call him, merely because he questioned him, in your honour's name, and the town of Perth's, who or what he was that took so much upon him."

"And what account gave he of himself?" said the Provost. "By St John! I will teach him to forestall my sport!"

"So please your lordship," said the Bonnet-maker, "he did take me at disadvantage. But I got on horseback again afterwards, and pricked after him gallantly. He calls himself Richard the Devil."

"How, man? he that the rhymes and romances are made on?" said the Provost. "I thought that smaik's name had been Robert."

"I trow they be different, my lord; I only graced this fellow with the full title, for indeed he called himself the Devil's Dick, and said he was a Johnstone, and a follower of the lord of that name. But I put him back into the bog, and recovered my hawking bag, which he had taken when I was at disadvantage."

Sir Patrick paused for an instant. "We have heard," said he, "of the

Lord of Johnstone, and of his followers. Little is to be had by meddling with them.—Smith, tell me, did you endure this?"

"Ay, faith did I, Sir Patrick; having command from my betters not
to help."

"Well, if thou satst down with it," said the Provost, "I see not why
we should rise up; especially as Master Oliver Proudfute, though
taken at advantage at first, has, as he has told us, recovered his reputation and that of the burgh. But here comes the wine at length—fill
round to my good friends and guests till the wine leap over the cup—
Prosperity to St Johnstoun, and a merry welcome to you all, my honest
friends! And now sit you to eat a morsel, for the sun is high up and it
must be long since you thrifty men have broken your fast."

"Before we eat, my Lord Provost," said the Bailie, "let us tell you
the pressing cause of our coming, which as yet we have not touched
upon."

"Nay, prithee, Bailie," said the Provost, "put it off till thou hast
eaten. Some complaint against the rascally jackmen and retainers of
the nobles, for playing at foot-ball on the streets of the burgh, or some
such goodly matter."

"No, my lord," said Craigdallie, stoutly and firmly. "It is the jack-
mens' masters of whom we complain, for playing at foot-ball with the
honour of our families, and using as little ceremony with our daughters' sleeping chambers, as if they were in a bordel at Paris. A party of
riving night-walkers,—courtiers and men of rank, as there is but too
much reason to believe,—attempted to scale the windows of Simon
Glover's house last night, stood in their defence with drawn weapons
when they were interrupted by Henry Smith, and fought till they were
driven off by the rising of the citizens."

"How?" said Sir Patrick, setting down the cup which he was about
to raise to his head. "Cocksbody, make that manifest to me, and by the
soul of Thomas of Longueville I will see you righted with my best
power, were it to cost me life and land.—Who attests this?—Simon
Glover, you are held an honest and a cautious man—Do you take the
truth of this charge upon your conscience?"

"My lord," said Simon, "understand I am no willing complainer in
this weighty matter. No damage has arisen, save to the breakers of the
peace themselves. I fear only great power could have encouraged such
lawless audacity; and I were unwilling to put feud between my native
town and some powerful nobleman on my account. But it has been
said that if I hang back in prosecuting this complaint, it will be as much
as admitting that my daughter expected such a visit, which is a direct
falsehood. Therefore, my lord, I will tell your lordship what happened, so far as I know, and leave further proceeding to your

wisdom." He then told, from point to point, all that he had seen of the attack.

Sir Patrick Charteris, listening with much attention, seemed particularly struck with the escape of the man who had been made prisoner. "Strange," he said, "that you did not secure him when you had him. Did you not look at him so as to know him again?"

"I had but the light of a lantern, my Lord Provost; and as to suffering him to escape, I was alone," said the Glover, "and old. But yet I might have kept him, had I not heard my daughter shriek in the upper room; and ere I had returned from her chamber the man had escaped through the garden."

"Now, armourer, as a true man and a good soldier," said Sir Patrick, "tell me what you know of this matter."

Henry Gow, in his own decided style, gave a brief but clear narrative of the whole affair.

Honest Proudfute being next called upon, began his statement with an air of more importance. "Touching this awful and astounding tumult within the burgh, I cannot altogether, it is true, say with Henry Gow, that I saw the very beginning. But it will not be denied that I beheld a great part of the latter end, and especially that I procured the evidence most effectual to convict the knaves."

"And what is it, man?" said Sir Patrick Charteris. "Never lose time fumbling and prating about it. What is it?"

"I have brought your lordship, in this pouch, what one of the rogues left behind him," said the little man. "It is a trophy which, in good faith and honest truth, I do confess I won not by the blade, but I claim the credit of securing it with that presence of mind which few men possess amidst flaming torches and clashing weapons. I secured it, my lord, and here it is."

So saying, he produced, from the hawking pouch already mentioned, the stiffened hand which had been found on the scene of the skirmish.

"Nay, Bonnet-maker," said the Provost, "I'll warrant thee man enough to secure a rogue's hand after it is cut from the body.—What do you look so busily for in your bag?"

"There should have been—there was—a ring, my lord, which was on the knave's finger. I fear I have been forgetful, and left it at home, for I took it off to show to my wife, as she cared not to look upon the dead hand, as women love not such sights. But yet I thought I had put it on the finger again. Nevertheless, it must, I bethink me, be at home. I will ride back for it, and Henry Smith will trot along with me."

"We will all trot with thee," said Sir Patrick Charteris, "since I am for Perth myself. Look you, honest burghers and good neighbours of

Perth. You may have thought me unapt to be moved by light complaints and trivial breaches of your privileges, such as small trespasses on your game, the barons' followers playing foot-ball in the street, and such like. But, by the soul of Thomas of Longueville, you shall not find Patrick Charteris slothful in a matter of this importance.—This hand," he continued, holding up the severed joint, "belongs to one who hath worked no drudgery. We will put it in a way to be known and claimed if the owner or his comrades of the revel have but one spark of honour in them.—Here you, Gerard—get me some half-score of good men instantly to horse, and let them take jack and spear. Meanwhile, neighbours, if feud arise out of this, as is most likely, we are to come to each other's support. If my poor house be attacked, how many men will you bring to my support?"

The burghers looked at Henry Gow, to whom they instinctively turned when such matters were discussed. "I will answer," said he, "for fifty good fellows to be assembled ere the common bell has rung ten minutes; for a thousand, in the space of an hour."

"It is well," answered the gallant Provost; "and in the case of need, I will come to aid the Fair City with such men as I can make. And now, good friends, let us to horse."

Chapter Nine

IT WAS EARLY in the afternoon of St Valentine's Day that the Prior of the Dominicans was engaged in discharge of his duties as Confessor to a penitent of no small importance. This was an elderly man, of a goodly presence, a florid and healthful cheek, the under part of which was shaded by a venerable white beard, which descended over his bosom. The large and clear blue eyes, with the broad expanse of brow, expressed dignity; but it was of a character which seemed more accustomed to receive honours voluntarily paid than to enforce them when they were refused. The good-nature of the expression was so great as to approach to defenceless simplicity or weakness of character, unfit, it might be inferred, to repel intrusion or subdue resistance. Amongst the grey locks of this personage was placed a small circlet or coronet of gold, upon a blue fillet. His beads, which were large and conspicuous, were of native gold, rudely enough wrought, but ornamented with Scottish pearls of rare size and beauty. These were his only ornaments; and a long crimson robe of silk, tied by a sash of the same colour, formed his attire. His shrift being finished, he arose heavily from an embroidered cushion upon which he kneeled during his confession, and by the assistance of a crutch-headed staff of ebony, moved ungracefully, and with apparent pain, to a chair of state, which, surmounted by a canopy, was placed for his accommodation by the chimney of the lofty and large apartment.

This was Robert, third of the name, and second of the ill-fated family of Stewart, who filled the throne of Scotland. He had many virtues, and was not without talent; but it was his great misfortune, that, like others of his devoted line, his merits were not of a kind suited to the part which he was called upon to perform in life. The King of so fierce a people as the Scots then were ought to have been warlike, prompt, and active, liberal in rewarding services, strict in punishing crimes; one whose conduct should make him feared as well as beloved. Robert the Third was the reverse of this. In youth he had indeed seen battles; but, without incurring disgrace, he had never manifested the chivalrous love of war and peril, or the eager desire to distinguish himself by dangerous achievement, which in that age was expected from all who were of noble birth, and had claims to authority.

Besides, his military career was very short. Amidst the tumult of a tournament, the young Earl of Carrick, such was then his title, received a kick from the horse of Sir James Douglas of Dalkeith; in consequence of which he was lame for the rest of his life, and absolutely disabled from taking share either in warfare, or in the military sports and tournaments which were its image. As Robert had never testified much predilection for violent exertion, he did not probably much regret the incapacities which exempted him from these active scenes. But his misfortune, or rather its consequences, lowered him in the eyes of a fierce nobility and warlike people. He was obliged to repose the principal charge of his affairs now in one member, now in another, of his family; sometimes with the actual rank, and always with the power of Lieutenant-general of the kingdom. His paternal affection would have induced him to use the assistance of his eldest son, a young man of spirit and talent, whom his fond father had created Duke of Rothsay, in order to give him the present possession of a dignity next to that of the throne. But the young Prince's head was too giddy, and his hand too feeble, to wield with dignity the delegated sceptre. However fond of power, pleasure was the Prince's favourite pursuit; and the court was disturbed, and the country scandalized, by the number of fugitive amours and extravagant revels practised by him who should have set an example of order and regularity to the youth of the kingdom.

The license and impropriety of the Duke of Rothsay's conduct was the more reprehensible in the public view, that he was a married person; although some, over whom his youth, gaiety, grace, and good temper had obtained influence, were of opinion, that an excuse for his libertinism might be found in the circumstances of the marriage itself. They reminded each other that his nuptials were entirely conducted by his uncle, the Duke of Albany, by whose counsels the infirm and timid King was much governed at the time, and who had the character of managing the temper of his brother and sovereign so as might be most injurious to the interests and prospects of the young heir. By Albany's machinations the hand of the heir apparent was in a manner put up to sale, as it was understood publicly that the nobleman in Scotland who would give the largest dower to his daughter might aspire to raise her to the bed of the Duke of Rothsay.

In the competition which ensued, George, Earl of Dunbar and March, who possessed, by himself or his vassals, a great part of the eastern frontier, was preferred to other competitors; and his daughter was, with the mutual good will of the young couple, actually contracted to the Duke of Rothsay.

But there remained a third party to be consulted, and that was no other than the tremendous Archibald, Earl of Douglas, terrible alike from the extent of his lands, from the offices and jurisdictions with which he was invested, and from his personal qualities of wisdom and valour, mingled with indomitable pride, and more than the feudal love of vengeance. The Earl was also nearly related to the throne, having married the eldest daughter of the reigning Monarch.

After the espousals of the Duke of Rothsay with the Earl of March's daughter, Douglas, as if he had postponed his share in the negotiation to show that it could not be concluded with any one but himself, entered the lists to break off the contract. He made a larger offer with his daughter Marjory than the Earl of March had proffered; and secured by his own cupidity and fear of the Douglas, Albany exerted his influence with the timid monarch till he was prevailed upon to break the contract with the Earl of March, and wed his son to a woman whom he could not love. No apology was offered to the Earl of March, excepting that the espousals betwixt the Prince and Elizabeth of Dunbar had not been approved by the States of Parliament, and that till such ratification the contract was liable to be broken off. The Earl deeply resented the wrong done to himself and his daughter, and was generally understood to study revenge, which his great influence on the English frontier was like to place within his power.

In the meantime, the Duke of Rothsay, incensed at the sacrifice of his hand and his inclinations to this state-intrigue, took his own mode of venting his displeasure, by neglecting his wife, contemning his formidable and dangerous father-in-law, and showing little respect to the authority of the King himself, and none whatever to the remonstrances of Albany his uncle, whom he looked upon as his confirmed enemy.

Amid these internal dissensions of his family, which extended themselves through his councils and administration, introducing everywhere the baneful effects of uncertainty and disunion, the feeble Monarch had for some time been supported by the counsels of his Queen Annabella, a daughter of the noble House of Drummond, and gifted with a depth of sagacity and firmness of mind, which exercised some restraint over the levities of a son who respected her, and sustained on many occasions the wavering resolution of her royal husband. But after her death the imbecile Sovereign resembled nothing so much as a vessel drifted from her anchors, and tossed about amidst contending currents. Abstractedly considered, Robert might be said to doat upon his son,—to entertain respect and awe for the character of his brother Albany, so much more decisive than his own,—to fear the Douglas with a terror which was almost instinctive, and to suspect the constancy of the bold but fickle Earl of March. But his feelings towards these various characters were so mixed and complicated that from time to time they showed entirely different from what they really were; and according to the interest which had been last exerted over his flexible mind, the King would change from an indulgent, to a strict and even cruel father—from a confiding, to a jealous brother—or from a benignant and bountiful, to a grasping and encroaching Sovereign. Like the chameleon, his feeble mind reflected the colour of that firmer character upon which at the time he reposed for counsel and assistance. And when he disused the advice of one of his family, and employed the counsel of another, it was no unwonted thing to see a total change of measures, equally disrespectable to the character of the King, and dangerous to the safety of the state.

It followed as a matter of course that the clergy of the Catholic Church acquired influence over a man whose intentions were so excellent, and his resolutions so infirm. Robert was haunted, not only with a due sense of the errors he had really committed, but with the tormenting apprehensions of those peccadilloes which beset a superstitious and timid mind. It is scarce necessary, therefore, to add that the churchmen of various descriptions had no small influence over this facile prince, though indeed theirs was, at that period, an influence from which few or none escaped, however resolute and firm of purpose in affairs of a temporal character.—We now return from this long digression, without which what we have to relate could not perhaps have been well understood.

The King had moved with ungraceful difficulty to the cushioned chair, which, under a state or canopy, stood prepared for his accommodation, and upon which he sank down with enjoyment, like an indolent man, who had been for some time confined to a constrained position. When seated, the gentle and venerable looks of the good old man showed benevolence. The Prior, who now remained standing opposite to the royal seat, with an air of deep deference which cloaked the natural haughtiness of his carriage, was a man betwixt forty and fifty years of age, but every one of whose hairs still retained their natural dark colour. Acute features, and a penetrating look, attested the talents by which the venerable father had acquired his high station in the community over which he presided; and, we may add, in the councils of the kingdom in whose service they were often exercised. The chief objects which his education and habits taught him to keep in view were the extension of the dominion and the wealth of the Church, and the suppression of heresy, both of which he endeavoured to accomplish by all the means which his situation afforded him. But he honoured his religion by the sincerity of his own belief and the morality which guided his conduct in all ordinary situations. The faults of the Prior Anselm, though they led him into grievous error, and even cruelty, were perhaps rather those of his age and profession —his virtues were his own.

"These things done," said the King, "and the lands I have mentioned secured by my gift to this monastery, you are of opinion, father, that I stand as much in the good graces of our Holy Mother Church as to term myself her dutiful son?"

"Surely, my liege," said the Prior; "would to God that all her children brought to the efficacious sacrament of confession as deep a sense of their errors, and as much will to make amends for them. But I speak these comforting words, my liege, not to Robert King of Scotland, but only to my humble and devout penitent, Robert Stewart of Carrick."

"You surprise me, Father," answered the King; "I have little check on my conscience for aught that I have done in my kingly office, seeing that I use therein less mine own opinion than the advice of the most wise counsellors."

"Even therein lieth the danger, my liege," replied the Prior. "The Holy Father recognises in your Grace, in every thought, word, and action, an obedient vassal of the Holy Church. But there are perverse counsellors, who obey the instinct of their wicked hearts, while they abuse the good-nature and ductility of their monarch, and, under colour of serving his temporal interests, take steps which are prejudicial to those that last to eternity."

King Robert raised himself upright in his chair, and assumed an air of authority, which, though it well became him, he did not usually display.

"Prior Anselm," he said, "if you have discovered anything in my conduct, whether as a king or a private individual, which may call down such censures as your words intimate, it is your duty to speak plainly, and I command you to do so."

"My liege, you shall be obeyed," answered the Prior, with an inclination of the body. Then raising himself up, and assuming the dignity of his rank in the Church, he said, "Hear from me the words of our Holy Father the Pope, the successor of St Peter, to whom have descended the Keys both to bind and to unloose. 'Wherefore, O Robert of Scotland, hast thou not received into the See of St Andrews, Henry of Wardlaw, whom the Pontiff hath nominated to fill that See? Why dost thou make profession with thy lips of dutiful service to the Church, when thy actions proclaim the pravity and disobedience of thy inward soul? Obedience is better than sacrifice.'"

"Sir Prior," said the Monarch, bearing himself in a manner not unbecoming his lofty rank, "we may well dispense with answering you upon this subject, being a matter which concerns us and the Estates of our kingdom, but does not affect our private conscience."

"Alas," said the Prior, "and whose conscience will it concern at the last day? Which of your belted lords or wealthy burgesses will then step between their King and the penalty which he has incurred, by following of their secular policy in matters ecclesiastical? Know, mighty King, that, were all the chivalry of thy realm drawn up to shield thee from the red levin-bolt, they would be consumed like scorched parchment before the blaze of a furnace."

"Good Father Prior," said the King, on whose timorous conscience this kind of language seldom failed to make an impression, "you surely argue over rigidly in this matter. It was during my last indisposition, while the Earl of Douglas held, as Lieutenant-general, the regal authority in Scotland, that the obstruction to the reception of the Primate unhappily arose. Do not, therefore, tax me with what happened when I was unable to conduct the affairs of the kingdom, and compelled to delegate my power to another."

"To your subject, Sire, you have said enough," replied the Prior. "But, if the impediment arose during the lieutenancy of the Earl of Douglas, the Legate of his Holiness will demand wherefore it has not been instantly removed, when the King resumed in his royal hands the rein of authority? The Black Douglas can do much—more perhaps than a subject should have power to do in the kingdom of his sovereign—but he cannot stand betwixt your Grace and your own conscience, or release you from the duties to the Holy Church, which your situation as a king imposes upon you."

"Father," said Robert, somewhat impatiently, "you are over per-
emptory in this matter, and ought at least to wait a reasonable season,
until we have time to consider of some remedy. Such disputes have
happened repeatedly in the reigns of our predecessors; and our royal
and blessed ancestor, Saint David, did not resign his privileges as a
monarch without making a stand in their defence, even though he was
involved in arguments with the Holy Father himself."

"And therein was that great and good king neither good nor
saintly," said the Prior; "and therefore was he given to be a rout and a
spoil to his enemies, when he raised his sword against the banners of
St Peter, and St Paul, and St John of Beverley, in the war, as it is still
called, of the Standard. Well was it for him, that, like his namesake,
the son of Jesse, his sin was punished upon earth, and not entered
against him at the long and dire day of accounting."

"Well, good Prior—well—enough of this for the present. The Holy
See shall, God willing, have no title to complain of me. I take Our
Lady to witness, I would not for the crown I wear take the burden of
wronging our Mother Church. We have ever feared that the Earl of
Douglas kept his eyes too much fixed on the fame and the temporalities of this frail and passing life, to feel altogether as he ought to the
claims that refer to a future world."

"It is but lately," said the Prior, "that he hath taken up forcible
quarters in the Monastery of Aberbrothock, with his retinue of a
thousand followers; and the abbot is compelled to furnish him with all
he needs for horse and man, which the Earl calls exercising the hospitality which he hath a right to expect from the foundation to which
his ancestors were contributors. Certain, it were better to return
to the Douglas his lands than to submit to such exaction, which more
resembles the masterful license of Highland thiggers and sorners than
the demeanour of a Christian baron."

"The Black Douglasses," said the King, with a sigh, "are a race
which will not be said nay. But, Father Prior, I am myself, it may be, an
intruder in this kind; for my sojourning hath been long among you,
and my retinue, though far fewer than the Douglas's, are nevertheless
enough to cumber you for their daily maintenance; and though our
order is to send out purveyors to lessen your charge as much as may
be, yet if there be inconvenience, it were fitting we should remove in
time."

"Now, Our Lady forbid," said the Prior, who, if desirous of power,
had nothing meanly covetous in his temper, but was even magnificent
in his hospitality; "certainly the Dominican Convent can afford to her
Sovereign the hospitality which the House offers to every wanderer of

whatever condition, who will receive it at the hands of the poor ser-vants of our patron. No, my royal liege; come with ten times your present train, they shall neither want a grain of oats, a pile of straw, a morsel of bread, nor an ounce of food, which our convent will not supply them. It is one thing to employ the revenues of the Church, which are so much larger than monks ought to need or wish for, in the suitable and dutiful reception of your royal Majesty, and another to have it wrenched from us by the hands of rude and violent men, whose love of rapine is only limited by the extent of their power."

"It is well, good Prior," said the King; "and now to turn our thoughts for an instant from state affairs, can thy reverence inform us how the good citizens of Perth have begun their Valentine's Day?—Gallantly and merrily, and peacefully, I hope."

"For gallantly, my liege, I know little of such qualities. For peace-fully, there were three or four men, two cruelly wounded, came this morning before day-light to seek the privilege of girth and sanctuary, pursued by a hue and cry of citizens in their shirts, with clubs, bills, Lochaber axes, and two-handed swords, crying kill and slay, each louder than another. Nay, they were not satisfied when our porter and watch told them that those they pursued had taken refuge in the Galilee of the Church; but continued for some minutes clamouring and striking upon the postern door, demanding that the men who had offended should be delivered up to them.—I was afraid their rude noise might have broken your Majesty's rest, and raised some sur-prise."

"My rest might have been broken," said the Monarch. "But that sounds of violence should have occasioned surprise—alas, reverend Father, there is in Scotland only one place where the shriek of the victim, and threats of the oppressor are not heard—and that, Father, is—the grave."

The Prior stood in respectful silence, sympathizing with the feel-ings of a monarch, whose tenderness of heart suited so ill with the condition and manners of his people.

"And what became of the fugitives?" asked Robert, after a minute's pause.

"Surely, Sire," said the Prior, "they were dismissed, as they desired to be, before day-light; and after we had sent out to be assured that no ambush of their enemies watched them in the vicinity, they went their way in peace."

"You know nothing," inquired the King, "who the men were, or the cause of their taking refuge with you?"

"The cause," said the Prior, "was the riot with the townsmen; but how arising is not known. The custom of our house is to afford twenty-four hours of uninterrupted refuge in the sanctuary of St Dominic, without asking any question at the poor unfortunates who have sought relief there. If they desire to remain for a longer space, the cause of their resorting to sanctuary must be put upon the register of the convent; and, praised be our holy Saint, many persons escape the weight of the law by his protection, whom, did we know the character of their crimes, we might have found ourselves obliged to render up to their pursuers and persecutors."

As the Prior spoke, a dim idea occurred to the Monarch, that the privilege of sanctuary thus peremptorily executed must prove a severe interruption to the course of justice through his realm. But he repelled the feeling, as if it had been a suggestion of Satan, and took care that not a single word should escape to betray to the churchman that such a profane thought had ever occupied his bosom; on the contrary, he hasted to change the subject.

"The sun," he said, "moves slowly on the index. After the painful information you have given me, I expected the Lords of my Council ere now to take order with the ravelled affairs of this unhappy riot. Evil was the fortune which gave me rule over a people, among whom it seems to me I am in my own person the only man who desires rest and tranquillity."

"The Church always desires peace and tranquillity," added the Prior, not suffering even so general a proposition to escape the poor King's oppressed mind, without insisting on a saving clause for the Church's honour.

"We meant nothing else," said Robert. "But, Father Prior, you will allow that the Church, in quelling strife, as is doubtless her purpose, resembles the busy housewife who puts in motion the dust which she means to sweep away."

To this remark the Prior would have made some reply, but the door of the apartment was opened, and a gentleman usher announced the Duke of Albany.

Chapter Ten

If I know how to manage these affairs,
Thus thrust disorderly upon my hands,
Never believe me——
Richard II

THE DUKE OF ALBANY was, like his royal brother, named Robert. The Christian name of the latter had been John until he was called to the throne; when the superstition of the times observed that the name had been connected with misfortune in the lives and reigns of John of

England, John of France, and John Baliol of Scotland. It was therefore agreed that, to elude the bad omen, the new King should assume the name of Robert, rendered dear to Scotland by the recollections of Robert Bruce. We mention this to account for the existence of two brothers of the same Christian name in one family, which was not certainly an usual occurrence, more than at the present day.

Albany, also an aged man, was not supposed to be much more disposed for warlike enterprise than the King himself. But if he had not courage, he had wisdom to conceal and cloak over his want of that quality, which, once suspected, would have ruined all the plans which his ambition had formed. He had also pride enough to supply, in extremity, the want of real valour, and command enough over his nerves to conceal their agitation. In other respects, he was experienced in the ways of courts, calm, cool, and crafty, fixing upon the points which he desired to attain while they were yet far removed, and never losing sight of them, though the winding paths in which he trode might occasionally seem to point to a very different direction. In his person he resembled the King, for he was noble and majestic both in stature and countenance. But he had the advantage of his elder brother in being unencumbered with any infirmity, and in every respect lighter and more active. His dress was rich and grave, as became his age and rank, and, like his royal brother, he wore no arms of any kind, a case of small knives supplying at his girdle the place usually occupied by a dagger, whether sword were worn or no.

At the Duke's entrance the Prior, after making an obeisance, respectfully withdrew to a recess in the apartment, at some distance from the royal seat, in order to leave the conversation of the brothers uncontrolled by the presence of a third person. It is necessary to mention that the recess was formed by a window, placed in the inner front of the monastic buildings called the Palace, from its being the frequent residence of the Kings of Scotland, but which was, in fact, the residence of the Prior or Abbot. The window was placed over the principal entrance to the royal apartments, and commanded a view of the internal quadrangle of the convent, formed on the right hand by the length of the magnificent church, on the left by a building containing the range of cellars, with the refectory, chapter-house, and other conventual apartments rising above them, for such existed altogether independent of the space occupied by King Robert and his attendants; while a fourth row of buildings, showing a noble outward front to the rising sun, consisted of a large *hospitium* for the reception of strangers and pilgrims, and many subordinate offices, warehouses, and places of accommodation for the ample stores which supplied the magnificent hospitality of the Dominican fathers. A lofty vaulted entrance led through this eastern front into the quadrangle, and was precisely opposite to the window at which Prior Anselm stood, so that he could see underneath the dark arch, and observe the light which gleamed beneath it from the eastern and open portal; but, owing to the height to which he was raised, and the depth of the vaulted archway, his eye could but indistinctly reach the opposite and external portal. It is necessary to notice these localities. We return to the conversation between the princely brothers.

"My dear brother," said the King, raising the Duke of Albany as he stooped to kiss his hand; "my dear, dear brother, wherefore this ceremonial? Are we not both sons of the same Steward of Scotland, and of the same Elizabeth Muir?"

"I have not forgot that it is so," said Albany, arising; "but I must not forget, in the familiarity of the brother, the respect that is due to the King."

"Oh, true, most true, Robin," answered the King. "The throne is like a lofty and barren rock, upon which flower or shrub can never take root. All kindly feelings, all tender affections, are denied to a monarch. A king must not fold a brother to his heart—he dare not give way to fondness for a son!"

"Such, in some respects, is the doom of greatness, Sire," answered Albany; "but Heaven, who removed to some distance from your Majesty's sphere the members of your own family, has given you a whole people to be your children."

"Alas! Robert," answered the Monarch, "your heart is better framed for the duties of a sovereign than mine. I see from the height at which fate has placed me, that multitude whom you call my children— I love them, I wish them well—but they are many, and they are distant from me. Alas! even the meanest of them has some beloved being whom he can clasp to his heart, and upon whom he can lavish the fondness of a father! But all that a king can give to a people is a smile, such as the sun bestows on the snowy peaks of the Grampian mountains, as distant and as ineffectual. Alas, Robin! our father used to caress us, and if he chid us it was with a tone of kindness; yet he was a monarch as well as I, and wherefore should not I be permitted, like him, to reclaim my poor prodigal by affection as well as severity?"

"Had affection never been tried, my liege," replied Albany, in the tone of one who delivers sentiments which he grieves to utter, "means of gentleness ought assuredly to be first made use of. Your Grace is best judge whether they have been long enough persevered in, and whether those of discouragement and restraint may not prove a more effectual corrective. It is exclusively in your royal power to take what measures with the Duke of Rothsay as you think will be most available to his ultimate benefit, and that of the kingdom."

"This is unkind, brother," said the King; "you indicate the painful path which you would have me pursue, yet you offer me not your support in treading it."

"My support your Grace may ever command," replied Albany; "but would it become me, of all men on earth, to prompt to your Grace severe measures against your son and heir? Me—on whom, in case of failure—which Heaven forefend—of your Grace's family, this fatal crown might descend? Would it not be thought and said by the fiery March and the haughty Douglas, that Albany had sown dissension between his royal brother and the heir to the Scottish throne, perhaps to clear the way for the succession of his own family?—No, my liege— I can sacrifice my life to your service, but I must not place my honour in danger."

"You say true, Robin—you say very true," replied the King, hastening to put his own interpretation upon his brother's words. "We must not suffer these powerful and dangerous lords to perceive that there is aught like discord in the royal family. That must be avoided of all things; and therefore we will still try indulgent measures, in hopes of correcting the follies of Rothsay. I behold sparks of hope in him, Robin, from time to time, that are well worth cherishing. He is young —very young—a prince, and in the hey-day of his blood. We will have patience with him, like a good rider with a hot-tempered horse. Let him exhaust this idle humour, and no one will be better pleased with him than yourself. You have censured me in your kindness for being too gentle, too retired—Rothsay has no such defects."

"I will pawn my life he has not," replied Albany, drily.

"And he wants not reflection as well as spirit," continued the poor King, pleading the cause of his son to his brother. "I have sent for him to attend council to-day, and we shall see how he acquits himself of his devoir. You yourself allow, Robin, that the Prince wants neither shrewdness nor capacity for affairs, when he is in the humour to consider them."

"Doubtless, he wants neither, my liege," replied Albany, "when he *is* in the humour to consider them."

"I say so," answered the King; "and am heartily glad that you agree with me, Robin, in giving this poor hapless young man another trial. He has no mother now to plead his cause with an incensed father. That must be remembered, Albany."

"I trust," said Albany, "the course which is most agreeable to your Grace's feelings will also prove the wisest and the best."

The Duke well saw the simple stratagem by which the King was endeavouring to escape from the conclusions of his reasoning, and to adopt, under pretence of his sanction, a course of proceeding the reverse of what it best suited him to recommend. But though he saw he could not guide his brother to the line of conduct he desired, he would not abandon the reins, but resolved to watch for a fitter opportunity of obtaining the sinister advantages to which new quarrels betwixt the King and Prince were soon, he thought, likely to give rise.

In the meantime, King Robert, afraid lest his brother should resume the painful subject from which he had just escaped, called aloud to the Prior of the Dominicans, "I hear the trampling of horse. Your station commands the court-yard, reverend Father. Look from the window, and tell us who alights—Rothsay, is it not?"

"The noble Earl of March with his followers," said the Prior.

"Is he strongly accompanied?" said the King. "Do his people enter the inner-gate?"

At the same moment, Albany whispered the King, "Fear nothing—the Brandanes* of your household are under arms."

The King nodded thanks, while the Prior from the window answered the question he had put. "The Earl is attended by two pages, two gentlemen, and four grooms. One page follows him up the main stair-case, bearing his lordship's sword. The others halt in the court, and—Benedicite, how is this?—Here is a strolling glee-woman with her viol, preparing to sing beneath the royal windows, and in the cloister of the Dominicans, as she might in the yard of an hostelrie! I will have her presently thrust forth."

"Not so, Father," said the King. "Let me implore grace for the poor wanderer. The joyous science, as they call it, which they profess, mingles sadly with the distresses to which want and calamity condemn a strolling race; and in that they resemble a King, to whom all men cry, 'All hail!' while he lacks the homage and obedient affection which the poorest yeoman receives from his family. Let the wanderer remain undisturbed, Father; and let her sing if she will to the yeomen and troopers in the court—it will keep them from quarrelling with each other, belonging, as they do, to such unruly and hostile masters."

So spoke the well-meaning and feeble-minded Prince, and the Prior bowed in acquiescence. As he spoke, the Earl of March entered the hall of audience, dressed in the ordinary riding garb of the time, and wearing his poniard: he had left in the anteroom the page of honour who carried his sword. The Earl was a well-built, handsome man, fair-complexioned, with a considerable profusion of light-coloured hair, and bright blue eyes, which gleamed like those of a falcon. He exhibited in his countenance, otherwise pleasing, the marks of a

---

*The men of the Isle of Bute were called Brandanes; from what derivation is uncertain. The island was the King's own patrimony, and its natives his personal followers.

hasty and irritable temper, which his situation as a high and powerful feudal lord had given him but too many opportunities of indulging.

"I am glad to see you, my Lord of March," said the King, with a gracious inclination of his person. "You have been long absent from our councils."

"My liege," answered March, with a deep reverence to the King, and a haughty and formal inclination to the Duke of Albany, "if I have been absent from your Grace's councils, it is because my place has been supplied by more acceptable, and, I doubt not, abler counsellors. And now I come but to say to your Highness, that the news from the English frontier make it necessary that I should return without delay to my own estates. Your Grace has your wise and politic brother, my Lord of Albany, with whom to consult, and the mighty and warlike Earl of Douglas to carry your councils into effect. I am of no use save in my own country; and thither, with your Highness's permission, I am purposed instantly to return, to attend my charge as Warden of the Eastern Marches."

"You will not deal so unkindly with us, cousin," replied the gentle Monarch. "Here are evil tidings on the wind. These unhappy Highland clans are again breaking into general commotion, and the tranquillity even of our own court requires the best of our council to advise, and the bravest of our barons to execute what may be resolved upon. The descendant of Thomas Randolph will not surely abandon the grandson of Robert Bruce at such a period as this?"

"I leave with him the descendant of the far-famed James of Douglas," answered March. "It is his lordship's boast, that he never puts foot in stirrup but a thousand horse mount with him as his daily lifeguard, and I believe the monks of Aberbrothock will swear to the fact. Surely, with all the Douglas's chivalry, they are fitter to restrain a disorderly swarm of Highland kerne than I can be to withstand the archery of England, and power of Henry Hotspur? And then, here is his Grace of Albany, so jealous in his care of your Highness's person, that he calls your Brandanes to take arms when a dutiful subject like myself approaches the court with a poor half-score of horse, the retinue of the meanest of the petty barons who own a tower and a thousand acres of barren heath. When such precautions are taken where there is not the slightest chance of peril—since I trust none was to be apprehended from me—your royal person will surely be suitably guarded in real danger."

"My Lord of March," said the Duke of Albany, "the meanest of the barons of whom you speak put their followers in arms, even when they receive their dearest and nearest friends within the iron gate of their castle; and, if it please Our Lady, I will not care less for the King's person than they do for their own. The Brandanes are the King's immediate retainers and household servants, and an hundred of them is but a small guard round his Grace, when yourself, my lord, as well as the Earl of Douglas, often ride with ten times the number."

"My lord duke," replied March, "when the service of the King requires it, I can ride with ten times as many horse as your grace has named; but I have never done so either traitorously to entrap the King, nor boastfully to overawe other nobles."

"Brother Robert," said the King, ever anxious to be a peace-maker, "you do wrong even to intimate a suspicion of my Lord of March. And you, cousin of March, misconstrue my brother's caution.—But hark —to divert this angry parley—I hear no unpleasing touch of minstrelsy. You know the gay science, my Lord of March, and love it well —Step to yonder window, by the holy Prior, at whom we make no question touching secular pleasures, and you will tell us if the music and lay be worth listening to. The notes are of France, I think—My brother of Albany's judgment is not worth a cockle-shell in such matters—'tis you, cousin, must report your opinion whether the poor glee-woman deserves recompense. Our son and the Douglas will presently be here, and then, when our council is assembled, we will treat of graver matters."

With something like a smile on his proud brow, March withdrew into the recess of the window, and stood there in silence beside the Prior like one who, while he obeyed the King's command, saw through and despised the timid precaution which it implied. The tune, which was played upon a viol, was gay and sprightly in the commencement, with a touch of the wildness of the Troubadour music. But as it proceeded, the faltering tones of the instrument, and of the female voice which accompanied it, became plaintive and interrupted, as if choked by the painful feelings of the minstrel.

The offended Earl, whatever might be his judgment in such matters on which the King had complimented him, paid, it may be supposed, little attention to the music of the female minstrel. His proud heart was struggling between the allegiance he owed his Sovereign, as well as the love he still found lurking in his bosom for the person of his well-natured King, and a desire of vengeance arising out of his disappointed ambition, and the disgrace done to him by the substitution of Marjory Douglas to be bride of the heir-apparent, instead of his betrothed daughter. March had the vices and virtues of a hasty and uncertain character, and even now, when he came to bid the King adieu, with the purpose of renouncing his allegiance as soon as he reached his own feudal territories, he felt unwilling, and almost unable, to resolve upon a step so criminal and so full of peril. It was with such dangerous cogitations that he was occupied during the beginning of the glee-maiden's lay; but objects which called his attention powerfully, as the songstress proceeded, affected the current of his thoughts, and riveted them on what was passing in the court-yard of the monastery. The song was in the Provençal dialect, well understood as the language of poetry in all the courts of Europe, and particularly in Scotland. It was more simply turned, however, than was the general caste of the Sirventes, and rather resembled the *lai* of a Norman Minstrel. It may be translated thus:

The Lay of poor Louise.

Ah, poor Louise! The live-long day
She roams from cot to castle gay;
And still her voice and viol say,
Ah, maids, beware the woodland way,
  Think on Louise!

Ah, poor Louise! The sun was high,
It smirch'd her cheek, it dimm'd her eye,
The woodland walk was cool and nigh,
Where birds with chiming streamlets vie
  To cheer Louise.

Ah, poor Louise! The savage bear
Made ne'er that lovely grove his lair;
The wolves molest not paths so fair—
But better far had such been there
  For poor Louise.

Ah, poor Louise! In woody wold
She met a huntsman fair and bold;
His baldrick was of silk and gold,
And many a witching tale he told
  To poor Louise.

Ah, poor Louise! Small cause to pine
Hadst thou for treasures of the mine;
For peace of mind, that gift divine,
And spotless innocence, were thine,
  Ah, poor Louise!

Ah, poor Louise! Thy treasure's reft!
I know not if by force or theft,
Or part by violence, part by gift;
But misery is all that's left
  To poor Louise.

Let poor Louise some succour have!
She will not long your bounty crave,
Or tire the gay with warning stave—
For Heaven has grace, and earth a grave
  For poor Louise.

The song was no sooner finished than, anxious lest the dispute should be revived betwixt his brother and the Earl of March, King Robert called to the latter, "What think you of the minstrelsy, my lord? —Methinks, as I heard it even at this distance, it was a wild and pleasing lay."

"My judgment is not deep, my lord; but the singer may dispense with my approbation, since she seems to have received that of his Grace of Rothsay—the first judge in Scotland."

"How!" said the King in alarm; "is my son below?"

"He is sitting on horseback by the glee-maiden," said March, with a malicious smile on his cheek, "apparently as much interested by her conversation as by her music."

"How is this, Father Prior?" said the King. But the Prior drew back from the lattice.

"I have no will to see, my lord, things which it would pain me to repeat."

"How is all this?" said the King, who coloured deeply, and seemed about to rise from his chair; but changed his mind, as if unwilling, perhaps, to look upon some unbecoming prank of the wild young Prince, which he might not have had heart to punish with necessary severity. The Earl of March seemed to have a pleasure in informing him of that of which doubtless he desired to remain ignorant.

"My liege," he cried, "this is better and better. The glee-maiden has not only engaged the ear of the Prince of Scotland, as well as every groom and trooper in the court-yard, but she has riveted the attention of the Black Douglas, whom we have not known as a passionate admirer of the gay science. But truly, I do not wonder at his astonishment, for the Prince has honoured the fair professor of song and viol with a kiss of approbation."

"How?" cried the King, "is Rothsay trifling with a glee-maiden, and his wife's father in presence?—Go, my good Father Abbot, call the Prince here instantly—Go, my dearest brother—Go, good cousin of March—there will be mischief, I am assured of it—I pray you go, cousin, and second my Lord Prior's prayers with my commands."

"You forget, my liege," said March, with the voice of a deeply offended person; "the father of Elizabeth of Dunbar were but an unfit intercessor between the Douglas and his royal son-in-law."

"I crave your pardon, cousin," said the gentle old man. "I own you have had some wrong—but my Rothsay will be murdered—I must go myself."

But as he arose precipitately from his chair, the poor King missed a footstep, stumbled, and fell heavily to the ground in such a manner that his head striking the corner of the seat from which he had risen, he became for a minute insensible. The sight of the accident at once overcame March's resentment, and melted his heart. He ran to the fallen monarch, and replaced him in his seat, using, in the tenderest and most respectful manner, such means as seemed most fit to recall animation. Robert opened his eyes, and gazed around with uncertainty.

"What has happened?—are we alone?—who is with us?"

"Your dutiful subject, March," replied the Earl.

"Alone with the Earl of March!" repeated the King, his still disturbed intellects receiving some alarm from the name of a powerful chief, whom he had reason to believe he had mortally offended.

"Yes, my gracious liege, with poor George of Dunbar; of whom many have wished your Majesty to think ill, though he will be found truer to your Majesty at the last than they will."

"Indeed, cousin, you have had too much wrong; and believe me, we shall strive to redress"——

"If your Grace thinks so, it may yet be righted," interrupted the Earl; "the Prince and Marjory Douglas are nearly related—the dispensation from Rome was informally granted—their marriage cannot be lawful—the Pope, who will do much for so godly a Prince, can set aside this unchristian union, in respect of the pre-contract. Bethink you well, my liege," continued the Earl, kindling with a new train of ambitious thoughts, to which the unexpected opportunity of pleading his cause personally had given rise,—"bethink you how you choose betwixt the Douglas and me. He is powerful and mighty, I grant. But George of Dunbar wears the keys of Scotland at his belt, and could bring an English army to the gates of Edinburgh ere Douglas could leave the skirts of Cairntable to oppose them. Your royal son loves my poor deserted girl, and hates the haughty Marjory of Douglas. Your Grace may judge the small account in which he holds her, by his toying with a common glee-maiden even in the presence of her father."

The King had hitherto listened to the Earl's argument with the bewildered feelings of a timid horseman, borne away by an impetuous steed, whose course he can neither arrest nor direct. But the last words awakened in his recollection the sense of his son's immediate danger.

"Oh, ay, most true—my son—the Douglas—Oh my dear cousin, prevent blood, and all shall be as you will.—Hark, there is a tumult—that was the clash of arms!"

"By my coronet—by my knightly faith, it is true!" said the Earl, looking from the window upon the inner square of the convent, now filled with armed men and brandished weapons, and resounding with the clash of armour. Even the deep-vaulted entrance was crowded with warriors at its farthest extremity, and blows seemed to be in the act of being exchanged betwixt some who were endeavouring to shut the gate, and others who contended to press in.

"I will go instantly," said the Earl of March, "and soon quell this sudden broil. Humbly, I pray your Majesty to think on what I have had the boldness to propose."

"I will—I will, fair cousin," said the King, scarce knowing to what he pledged himself—"Do but prevent tumult and bloodshed!"

Chapter Eleven

WE MUST here trace, a little more distinctly, the events which had been indistinctly seen from the window of the royal apartments, and yet more indistinctly reported by those who witnessed them. The glee-maiden, already mentioned, had planted herself, where a rise of two large broad steps, giving access to the main gateway of the royal apartments, gained her an advantage of a foot and a half in height over those in the court, amongst whom she hoped to form an audience. She wore the dress of her calling, which was more gaudy than rich, and showed the person more than did the garb of other females. She had laid aside an upper mantle, and a small basket which contained her slender stock of necessaries, and a little French spaniel dog lay beside them as their protector. An azure-blue jacket, embroidered with silver, and sitting close to the person, was open in front, and showed several waistcoats of different-coloured silks, calculated to set off the symmetry of the shoulders and bosom, and remaining open at the throat. A small silver chain round her neck involved itself amongst these brilliant-coloured waistcoats, and was again produced from them to display a medal of the same metal, which intimated, in the name of some court or guild of minstrels, the degree she had taken in the gay or joyous science. A small scrip, suspended over her shoulders by a blue silk ribband, hung on her left side.

Her sunny complexion, snow-white teeth, brilliant black eyes, and raven locks, marked her country which lay far in the south of France, and the arch smile and dimpled chin bore the same character. Her luxuriant locks, twisted around a small gold bodkin, were kept in their position by a net of silk and gold. Short petticoats, deep-laced with silver, to correspond with the jacket, red stockings which were visible to near the calf of the leg, and buskins of Spanish leather, completed her adjustment, which, though far from new, had been saved as an untarnished holiday suit which much care had kept in good order. She seemed at least twenty-five years old; but perhaps fatigue and wandering had, anticipating the touch of time, obliterated the freshness of early youth.

We have said the glee-maiden's manner was lively, and we may add, that her smile and repartee were ready. But her gaiety was assumed as a quality essentially necessary to her trade, of which it was one of the miseries that the professors were obliged frequently to cover an aching heart with a compelled smile. This seemed to be the case with Louise, who, whether she was actually the heroine of her own song, or whatever other cause she might have for sadness, showed at times a strain of deep melancholy thought, which interfered with and controlled the natural flow of lively spirits, which the practice of the joyous science especially required. She lacked also, even in her gayest sallies, the decided boldness and effrontery of her sisterhood, who were seldom at a loss to retort a saucy jest or turn the laugh against any who interrupted or interfered with them.

It was impossible that this class of women could bear a character generally respectable. They were, however, protected by the manners of the age; and such were the immunities they possessed by the rights of chivalry, that nothing was more rare than to hear of these errant damsels sustaining injury or wrong, and they passed and repassed safely where armed travellers would probably have encountered a bloody opposition. But though licensed and protected in honour of their tuneful art, the wandering minstrels, male or female, like other ministers to the public pleasure, itinerant musicians and strolling comedians of our day, led a life too irregular and precarious to be accounted a creditable part of society. Indeed among the stricter Catholics the profession was considered as unlawful.

Such was the damsel, who, with viol in hand, and stationed on the slight elevation we have mentioned, stepped forward and announced herself as a mistress of the gay science, duly qualified by a brief from a Court of Love and Music held at Aix, in Provence, under the countenance of the flower of chivalry, the gallant Count Aymer; and now she prayed that the cavaliers of merry Scotland, who were known over the wide world for bravery and courtesy, would permit a poor stranger to try whether she could afford them any amusement by her art. The love of song was like the love of fight, a common passion of the age, which all at least affected whether they actually possessed it or no; therefore the acquiescence in Louise's proposal was universal. At the same time, an aged, dark-browed monk who was among the bystanders thought it necessary to remind the glee-maiden, that, since she was tolerated within these precincts, which was an unusual grace, he trusted nothing would be sung or said inconsistent with the holy character of the place.

The glee-maiden bent her head low, shook her sable locks, and crossed herself reverentially, as if she disclaimed the possibility of such a transgression, and then began the song of Poor Louise, which we gave at length in the last chapter.

Just as she commenced, she was stopped by a cry for "Room—room —place for the Duke of Rothsay!"

"Nay, hurry no man on my score," said a gallant young cavalier, who entered on a noble Arabian horse, which he managed with exquisite grace, though by such slight handling of the reins, such imperceptible pressure of the limbs and sway of the body, that to any eye save that of an experienced horseman the animal seemed to be putting forth his paces for his own amusement, and bearing forwards thus gracefully a rider who was too indolent to give himself any trouble about the matter.

The Prince's apparel, which was very rich, was put on with slovenly carelessness. His form, though his stature was low and his limbs extremely slight, was elegant in the extreme; and his features no less handsome. But there was on his brow a haggard paleness, which seemed the effect of care or of dissipation, or of both these wasting causes combined. His eyes were sunk and dim, as from late indulgence in revelry on the preceding evening, while his cheek was inflamed with unnatural red, as if either the effect of the Bacchanalian orgies had not passed away from the constitution, or a morning draught had been resorted to in order to remove the effects of the night's debauchery.

Such was the Duke of Rothsay, and heir of the Scottish crown, a sight at once of interest and compassion. All unbonneted and made way for him, while he kept repeating carelessly, "No haste—no haste —I shall arrive soon enough at the place I am bound for.—How's this —a damsel of the joyous science? Ay, by St Giles! and a comely wench to boot. Stand still, my merry men; never was minstrelsy marred for me.—A good voice, by the mass! Begin me that lay again, sweetheart."

Louise did not know the person who addressed her; but the general respect paid on all hands, and the easy and indifferent manner in which it was received, showed her she was addressed by a man of the highest quality. She sung her best accordingly and the young Duke seemed thoughtful and rather affected towards the close of the ditty. But it was not his habit to cherish such melancholy affections. "This is a melancholy song, my nut-brown maid," said he, chucking the retreating glee-maiden under the chin, and detaining her by the collar of her dress, which was not difficult, as he sat on horseback so close to the steps on which she stood. "But I warrant me you have livelier notes at will, *ma bella tenebrosa;* ay, and canst sing in bower as well as wold, and by night as well as day."

"I am no nightingale, my lord," said Louise, endeavouring to escape a species of gallantry which ill-suited the place and presence, circumstances of which he who addressed it to her seemed contemptuously indifferent.

"What hast thou there, darling?" he added, removing his hold from her collar, to the scrip which she carried.

Glad was Louise to escape his grasp, by slipping the knot of the ribband, and leaving the little bag in the Prince's hand, as, retiring back beyond his reach, she answered, "Nuts, my lord, of the last season."

The Prince pulled out a handful of nuts accordingly. "Nuts, child! —they will break thine ivory teeth—hurt thy pretty voice," said Rothsay, cracking one with his teeth, like a village schoolboy.

"They are not the walnuts of my own sunny clime, my lord," said Louise; "but they hang low, and are within the reach of the poor."

"You shall have something to give you better fare, poor wandering ape," said the Duke, in a tone in which feeling predominated more than in the affected and contemptuous gallantry of his first address to the glee-maiden.

At this moment, as he turned to ask an attendant for his purse, the Prince encountered the stern and piercing look of a tall black man, seated on a powerful iron-grey horse, who had entered with attendants while he was engaged with Louise, and had remained stupified and almost turned to stone by his surprise and anger. Even one who had never seen Archibald Earl of Douglas, called THE GRIM, must have known him by his swart complexion, his gigantic frame, his buffcoat of bull's-hide, and his air of courage, firmness, and sagacity, mixed with the most indomitable pride. The loss of an eye in battle, though not perceptible at first sight, as the ball of the injured organ remained similar to the other, gave yet a stern immovable glare to the whole aspect.

The meeting of the royal son-in-law with his terrible step-father was in circumstances which arrested the attention of all present; and the by-standers waited the issue with silence and suppressed breath, lest they should lose any part of what was to ensue.

When the Duke of Rothsay saw the expression which occupied the stern features of Douglas, and remarked that the Earl did not make the least motion towards respectful or even civil salutation, he seemed determined to show him how little respect he was disposed to pay to his displeased looks. He took his purse from his chamberlain.

"Here, pretty one," he said. "I put one gold piece in thy little purse for the song thou hast sung me, and another for the nuts I have stolen from thee, and a third for the kiss thou art about to give me. For know, my pretty one, that when fair lips make music for my pleasure, I am sworn to St Valentine to press them to mine."

"My song is recompensed nobly—" said Louise, shrinking back; "my nuts are sold to a good market—farther traffic, my lord, were neither befitting you nor beseeming me."

"What! you coy it, my nymph of the highway?" said the Prince, contemptuously. "Know, damsel, that one asks you a grace who is unused to denial."

"It is the Prince of Scotland"—"the Duke of Rothsay,"—said the courtiers around, to the terrified Louise, pressing forward the trembling young woman; "you must not thwart his humour."

"But I cannot reach your lordship," she said, "you sit so high on horseback."

"If I must alight," said Rothsay, "there shall be the heavier penalty —What does the wench tremble for? Place thy foot on the toe of my boot, give me hold of thy hand—Gallantly done!" He kissed her as she stood thus suspended in the air, perched upon his foot, and supported by his hand; saying, "There is thy kiss, and there is my purse to pay it; and to grace thee farther, Rothsay will wear thy scrip for the day." He suffered the frightened girl to spring to the ground, and turned his looks from her to bend them contemptuously on the Earl of Douglas, as if he had said, "All this I do in despite of you and of your daughter's claims."

"By St Bride of Douglas!" said the Earl, pressing towards the Prince, "this is too much, unmannered boy, as void of sense as honour! You know what considerations restrain the hand of Douglas, else had you never dared"——

"Can you play at spang-cockle, my lord?" said the Prince, placing a nut on the second joint of his forefinger, and spinning it off by a smart application of the thumb. The nut struck on Douglas's broad breast, who burst out into a dreadful exclamation of wrath, inarticulate, but resembling the growl of a lion in depth and sternness of expression. "I cry your pardon, most mighty lord," said the Duke of Rothsay, scornfully, while all around trembled; "I did not conceive my pellet could have wounded you, seeing you wear a buff-coat. Surely, I trust, it did not hit your eye?"

The Prior had by this time made way through the crowd, and laying hold on Douglas's rein, in a manner that made it impossible for him to advance, reminded him that the Prince was the son of his

Sovereign, and the husband of his daughter.

"Fear not, Sir Prior," said Douglas. "I despise the beardless boy too much to raise a finger against him. But I will return insult for insult.— Here, any of you who love the Douglas—spurn me this quean from the Monastery gates; and let her be so scourged that she may bitterly remember to the last day of her life, how she gave means to an unrespective boy to affront the Douglas!"

Four or five retainers instantly stepped forth to execute commands which were seldom uttered in vain, and heavily would Louise have atoned for an offence of which she was alike the innocent, unconscious, and unwilling instrument, had not the Duke of Rothsay interfered.

"Spurn the poor glee-woman?" he said, in high indignation; "scourge her for obeying my commands?—Spurn thine own oppressed vassals, rude Earl—scourge thine own faulty hounds—but beware how you touch so much as a dog that Rothsay hath patted on the head, far less a female whose lips he hath kissed!"

Before Douglas could give an answer, which would certainly have been in defiance, there arose that great tumult at the outward gate of the Monastery, already noticed, and men both on horseback and on foot began to thrust headlong in, not actually fighting, but certainly in no peaceable manner.

The contending parties, seemingly, were partizans of Douglas, known by the cognizance of the Bloody Heart, and citizens of the town of Perth. It appeared they had been skirmishing in earnest when without the gates, but, out of respect to the sanctified ground, they lowered their weapons when they entered, and confined their strife to a war of words and mutual abuse.

The tumult had this good effect, that it forced asunder, by the weight and press of numbers, the Prince and Douglas, at a moment when the levity of the former, and the pride of the latter, were urging them to the utmost extremity. But now peace-makers interfered on all sides. The Prior and the monks threw themselves among the multitude, and commanded peace in the name of Heaven, and reverence to their sacred walls, under penalty of excommunication; and their expostulations began to be listened to. Albany, who was dispatched by his royal brother at the beginning of the fray, had not arrived till now on the scene of action. He instantly applied himself to Douglas, and in his ear conjured him to temper his passion.

"By St Bride of Douglas, I will be avenged!" said the Earl. "No man shall brook life after he has passed an affront on Douglas."

"Why so you may be avenged in fitting time," said Albany; "but let it not be said, that, like a peevish woman, the Great Douglas could choose neither time nor place for his vengeance. Bethink you, all that we have laboured at is like to be overset by an accident. George of Dunbar hath had the advantage of an audience with the old man; and though it lasted but five minutes, I fear it may endanger your family match, which we brought about with so much difficulty. The authority from Rome has not yet been obtained."

"A toy!" answered Douglas, haughtily,—"they dare not dissolve it."

"Not while Douglas is at large, and in possession of his power," answered Albany. "But, noble Earl, come with me, and I will show you at what disadvantage you stand."

Douglas dismounted and followed his wily accomplice in silence. In a lower hall they saw the ranks of the Brandanes drawn up, well-armed in caps of steel and shirts of mail. Their captain, making an obeisance to Albany, seemed to desire to address him.

"What now, MacLouis?" said the Duke.

"We are informed the Duke of Rothsay has been insulted, and I can scarce keep the Brandanes within door."

"Gallant MacLouis," said Albany, "and you, my trusty Brandanes, the Duke of Rothsay, my princely nephew, is as well as a hopeful gentleman can be. Some scuffle there has been, but all is appeased." He continued to draw the Earl of Douglas forward. "You see, my lord," he said in his ear, "that if the word *arrest* was to be once spoken, it would be soon obeyed, and you are aware your attendants are few."

Douglas seemed to acquiesce in the necessity of patience for the time. "If my teeth," he said, "should bite through my lips, I will be silent till it is the hour to speak out."

George of March, in the meanwhile, had a more easy task of pacifying the Prince. "My Lord of Rothsay," he said, approaching him with grave ceremony, "I need not tell you that you owe me something for reparation of honour, though I blame not you personally for the breach of contract which has destroyed the peace of my family. Let me conjure you by what observance your Highness may owe an injured man, to forego for the present this scandalous dispute."

"My lord, I owe you much," replied Rothsay; "but this haughty and all-controlling lord has wounded mine honour."

"My lord, I can but add, your royal father is ill—hath swooned with terror for your Highness's safety."

"Ill!—the kind, good old man—swooned, said you, my Lord of March?—I am with him in an instant."

The Duke of Rothsay sprung from his saddle to the ground, and was dashing into the palace like a greyhound, when a feeble grasp was laid on his cloak, and the faint voice of a kneeling female exclaimed,

"Protection, my noble Prince!—Protection for a helpless stranger!"

"Hands off, stroller!" said the Earl of March, thrusting the suppliant glee-maiden aside.

But the gentler Prince paused. "It is true," he said, "I have brought the vengeance of an unforgiving devil upon this helpless creature. O heaven! what a life is mine, so fatal to all who approach me!—What to do in the hurry?—She must not go to my apartments—And all my men are such born reprobates.—Ha! thou at mine elbow, honest Harry Smith? What dost thou here?"

"There has been something of a fight, my lord, between the townsmen and the Southland loons who ride with the Douglas; and we have swinged them as far as the Abbey-Gate."

"I am glad of it—I am glad of it. And you beat the knaves fairly?"

"Fairly, does your Highness ask?" said Henry. "Why, ay! We were stronger in numbers, to be sure; but no men ride better armed than those who follow the Bloody Heart. And so in a sense we beat them fairly; for as your Highness knows, it is the smith who makes the men-at-arms, and men with good weapons are a match for great odds."

While they thus talked, the Earl of March, who had spoke with some one near the palace gate, returned in anxious haste. "My Lord Duke, my Lord Duke!—Your father is recovered, and if you haste not speedily, my Lord of Albany and the Douglas will have possession of his ear."

"And if my royal father is recovered," said the thoughtless Prince, "and is holding, or about to hold, council with my gracious uncle and the Earl of Douglas, it befits neither your lordship nor me to intrude till we are summoned. So there is time for me to speak of my little business with mine honest armourer here."

"Does your Highness take it so?" said the Earl, whose sanguine hopes of a change of favour at court had been too hastily excited, and were as speedily checked,—"Then so let it be for George of Dunbar."

He glided away with a gloomy and displeased aspect; and thus out of the two most powerful noblemen in Scotland, at a time when the aristocracy so closely controlled the throne, the reckless heir-apparent had made two enemies; the one by scornful defiance, and the other by careless neglect. He heeded not the Earl of March's departure, however, or rather he felt relieved from his importunity.

The Prince went on in indolent conversation with our armourer, whose skill in his art had made him known to many of the great lords about the court.

"I had something to say to thee, Smith—canst thou take up a fallen link in my Milan hauberk?"

"As well, please your Highness, as my mother could take up a stitch in the nets she wove—The Milaner shall not know my work from his own."

"Well, but that was not what I wished of thee just now," said the Prince, recollecting himself; "this poor glee-woman, good Smith, must be placed in safety. Thou art man enough to be any woman's champion, and thou must conduct her to some place of safety."

Henry Smith was, as we have seen, sufficiently rash and daring when weapons were in question. But he had also the pride of a decent burgher, and was unwilling to place himself in what might be thought equivocal circumstances by the sober part of his fellow-citizens.

"May it please your Highness," he said, "I am but a poor craftsman. But though my arm and sword are at the King's service and your Highness's, I am, with reverence, no squire of dames. Your Highness will find among your own retinue knights and lords willing enough to play Sir Pandarus of Troy—it is too knightly a part for poor Hal of the Wynd."

"Umph—hah!"—said the Prince. "My purse, Edgar—(his attendant whispered him)—True, true—I gave it to the poor wench.—I know enough of your craft and of craftsmen in general to be aware that men lure not hawks with empty hands; but I suppose my word may pass for the price of a good armour, and I will pay it thee with thanks to boot, for this slight service."

"Your Highness may know other craftsmen," said the Smith; "but, with reverence, you know not Henry Gow. He will serve you in making a weapon or in wielding one, but he knows nothing of this petticoat service."

"Hark thee, thou Perthshire mule," said the Prince, yet smiling, while he spoke, at the sturdy punctilio of the honest burgher,—"the wench is as little to me as she is to thee. But in an idle moment, as you may learn from those about thee if thou sawest it not thyself, I did her a passing grace, which is likely to cost the poor wretch her life. There is no one here whom I can trust to protect her against the discipline of belt and bowstring with which the Border brutes who follow Douglas will beat her to death, since such is his pleasure."

"If such be the case, my liege, she has a right to every honest man's protection; and since she wears a petticoat,—though I would it were longer, and of a less fanciful fashion,—I will answer for her protection as well as a single man may. But where am I to bestow her?"

"Good faith, I cannot tell," said the Prince. "Take her to Sir John Ramorny's lodging—But, no—no—he is ill at ease, and besides, there are reasons—take her to the devil if thou wilt, but take her safe, and oblige David of Rothsay."

"My noble Prince," said the Smith, "I think—always with reverence—that I would rather take a defenceless woman to the care of the devil than of Sir John Ramorny. But though the devil be a worker in fire like myself, yet I know not his haunts, and with aid of Holy Church hope to keep him on terms of defiance. And, moreover, how I am to convey her out of this crowd, or through the streets, in such a mumming habit, may be well made a question."

"For the leaving the convent," said the Prince, "this good monk (seizing upon the nearest by his cowl,) Father Nicholas or Boniface"——

"Poor brother Cyprian, at your Highness's command," said the father.

"Ay, ay, brother Cyprian," continued the Prince, "yes. Brother Cyprian shall let you out at some secret passage which he knows of, and I will see him again to pay a Prince's thanks for it."

The churchman bowed in acquiescence, and poor Louise, who, during this debate, had looked from the one speaker to the other, hastily said, "I will not scandalize this good man with my foolish garb —I have a mantle for ordinary wear."

"Why, there, Smith, thou hast a friar's hood and a woman's mantle to shroud thee under. I would all my frailties were as well shrouded! Farewell, honest fellow; I will thank thee hereafter."

Then, as if afraid of farther objection on the Smith's part, he hurried into the palace.

Henry Gow remained stupified at what had passed, and at finding himself involved in a charge at once inferring much danger, and an equal risk of scandal, both which, joined to a principal share which he had taken, with his usual forwardness, in the fray, might, he saw, do him no small injury in the suit he pursued most anxiously. At the same time, to leave a defenceless creature to the ill usage of the barbarous Galwegians and licentious followers of the Douglas, was a thought which his manly heart could not brook for an instant.

He was roused from his reverie by the voice of the Monk, who, sliding out his words with the indifference which the holy fathers entertained, or affected, towards all temporal matters, desired them to follow him. The Smith put himself in motion, with a sigh much resembling a groan, and, without appearing exactly connected with the Monk's motions, he followed him into a cloister, and through a postern door, which, after looking once behind him, the priest had left ajar. Behind them both followed Louise, who had hastily assumed her small bundle, and, calling her little four-legged companion, had eagerly followed in the path which opened an escape from what had shortly before seemed a great and inevitable danger.

Chapter Twelve

THE PARTY were now, by a secret passage, admitted within the church, the outward doors of which, usually left open, had been closed against every one in consequence of the recent tumult, when the rioters of both parties had endeavoured to rush into it for other purposes than those of devotion. They traversed the gloomy aisles, whose arched roof resounded to the heavy tread of the armourer, but was silent under the sandal'd foot of the Monk and the light step of poor Louise, who trembled excessively, as much from fear as cold. She saw that neither her spiritual nor temporal conductor looked kindly upon her. The former was an austere man, whose looks seemed to hold the luckless wanderer in some degree of horror, as well as contempt; while the latter, though, as we have seen, one of the best natured men living, was at present grave to the pitch of sternness, and not a little displeased with having the part he was playing forced upon him, without, as he was constrained to feel, a possibility of his declining it.

His dislike at his task extended itself to the innocent object of his protection, and he internally said to himself, as he surveyed her scornfully,—"A proper queen of beggars to walk the streets of Perth with, and I a decent burgher! This tawdry minion must have as ragged a reputation as the rest of her sisterhood, and I am finely sped if my chivalry in her behalf comes to Catherine's ears. I had better have slain a man, were he the best in Perth; and, by hammer and nails! I would have done it on provocation, rather than convoy this baggage through the city."

Perhaps Louise suspected the cause of her conductor's anxiety, for she said, timidly and with hesitation, "Worthy sir, were it not better I should stop one instant in that chapel and don my mantle?"

"Umph, sweetheart, well proposed," said the armourer; but the Monk interfered, raising at the same time the finger of interdiction.

"The Chapel of Holy St Madox is no tyring room for vile jugglers and strollers to shift their trappings in. I will presently show thee a vestiary more suited to thy condition."

The poor young woman hung down her humbled head, and turned from the chapel door which she had approached, with the deep sense of self-abasement. Her little spaniel seemed to gather from his mistress's looks and manner, that they were unauthorized intruders on the holy ground which they trode, and hung his ears, and swept the pavement with his tail, as he trotted slowly and close to Louise's heels.

The Monk moved on without a pause. They descended a broad flight of steps, and proceeded through a labyrinth of subterranean passages, dimly lighted. As they passed a low-arched door, the Monk turned, and said to Louise, with the same stern voice as before,—"There, daughter of folly, there is a robing-room, where many before you have deposited their vestments!"

Obeying the least signal with ready and timorous acquiescence, she pushed the door open, but instantly recoiled with terror. It was a charnel-house, half filled with dry skulls and bones.

"I fear to change my dress there, and alone—But if you, father, command it, be it as you will."

"Why, thou child of vanity, the remains on which thou lookest are but the earthly attire of those who, in their day, led or followed in the pursuit of worldly pleasure. And such shalt thou be, for all thy mincing and ambling, thy piping and thy harping; thou, and all such ministers of frivolous and worldly pleasure, must become like these poor bones, whom thy idle nicety fears and loaths to look upon."

"Say not with idle nicety, reverend father," answered the glee-maiden, "for Heaven knows, I covet the repose of these poor bleached bones; and if by stretching my body upon them, I could, without sin, bring my state to theirs, I would choose that charnel heap for my place of rest, beyond the fairest and softest couch in Scotland."

"Be patient, and come on," said the Monk, in a milder tone. "The reaper must not leave the harvest-work till the sunset gives the signal."

They walked forward. Brother Cyprian, at the end of a long gallery, opened the door of a small apartment, or perhaps a chapel, for it was decorated with a crucifix, before which burned four lamps. All bent and crossed themselves; and the priest said to the minstrel maiden, pointing to the crucifix, "What says that emblem?"

"That HE invites the sinner as well as the righteous to approach."

"Ay, if the sinner put from him his sin," said the Monk, whose tone of voice was evidently milder. "Prepare thyself here for thy journey."

Louise remained an instant or two in the chapel, and presently reappeared in a mantle of coarse grey cloth, in which she had closely muffled herself, having put such of her more gawdy habiliments as she had time to take off, in the little basket which held her ordinary clothes.

The Monk presently afterwards unlocked a door which led to the open air. They found themselves in the garden which surrounded the monastery of the Dominicans. "The southern gate is on the latch, and through it you can pass unnoticed," said the Monk. "Bless thee, my son; and bless thee too, unhappy child. Remembering where you put off your idle trinkets, may you take care how you again resume them!"

"Alas, father!" said Louise, "if the poor foreigner could supply the mere wants of life by any more creditable occupation, she has small wish to profess her idle art. But"——

But the Monk had vanished, nay, the very door through which she had just passed appeared to have vanished also, so curiously was it concealed beneath a flying buttress, and among the profuse ornaments of Gothic architecture. "Here is a woman let out by this private postern, sure enough," was Henry's reflection. "Pray Heaven the good fathers never let any in! The place seems convenient for such games at bo-peep.—But, benedicite, what is to be done next? I must get rid of this quean as fast as I can—And I must see her safe. For let her be at heart what she may, she looks too modest, now she is in decent dress, to deserve the usage which the wild Scot of Galloway, or the Devil's legion from the Liddell, are like to afford her."

Louise stood as if she waited his pleasure which way to go. Her little dog, relieved by the exchange of the dark subterranean vault for the open air, sprung in wild gambols through the walks, and jumped upon his mistress; and even, though more timidly, circled close round the Smith's feet to express its satisfaction to him also, and conciliate his favour.

"Down, Charlot, down!" said the glee-maiden. "You are glad to get into the blessed sunshine; but where shall we rest at night, my poor Charlot?"

"And now, mistress," said the Smith,—not churlishly, for it was not in his nature, but bluntly, as one who is desirous to finish a disagreeable employment,—"which way lies your road?"

Louise looked on the ground, and was silent. On being again urged to say which way she desired to be conducted, she again looked down, and said, she could not tell.

"Come, come," said Henry, "I understand all that—I have been a goliard—a reveller in my day—but it's best to be plain. As matters are with me now, I am an altered man for these many, many months; and so, my quean, you and I must part sooner than perhaps a light o' love such as you expected to part with—a likely young fellow."

Louise wept silently, with her eyes still cast on the ground, as one who felt an insult which she had not a right to complain of. At length, perceiving that her conductor was grown impatient, she faltered out, "Noble sir—"

"*Sir* is for a knight," said the impatient burgher, "and *noble* is for a baron. I am Harry of the Wynd, an honest mechanic, and free of my guild."

"Good craftsman, then," said the minstrel woman, "you judge me harshly, but not without seeming cause. I would relieve you immediately of my company, which, it may be, brings little credit to good men, did I but know which way to go."

"To the next wake or fair, to be sure," said Henry roughly, having no doubt that this distress was affected for the purpose of pinning herself upon him, and perhaps dreading to throw himself into the way of temptation; "and that is the feast of St Madox, at Auchterarder. I warrant thou wilt find the way thither well enough."

"Aftr—Achter—" repeated the glee-maiden, her southern tongue in vain attempting the Celtic accentuation. "I am told my poor lays will not be understood if I go nearer to yon dreadful range of mountains."

"Will you abide, then, in Perth?"

"But where to lodge?" said the wanderer.

"Why, where lodged you last night?" replied the Smith. "You know where you came from surely, though you seem doubtful where you are going?"

"I slept in the hospital of the Convent. But I was only admitted upon great importunity, and I was commanded not to return."

"Nay, they will never take you in with the brand of the Douglas upon you, that is even too true. But the Prince mentioned Sir John Ramorny's—I can take you to his lodgings through by-streets—though it is short of an honest burgher's office, and my time presses."

"I will go anywhere—I know I am a scandal and incumbrance—there was a time when it was otherwise—But this Ramorny, who is he?"

"A courtly knight, who lives a jolly bachelor's life, and is Master of the Horse, and privado, as they say, to the young Prince."

"What! to the wild, scornful young man who gave occasion to yonder scandal?—Oh, take me not thither; good friend, is there no Christian woman, who would give a poor creature rest in her cow-house, or barn, for one night? I will be gone with early daybreak. I will repay her richly. I have gold—and I will repay you too, if you will take me where I may be safe from that wild reveller, and from the followers of that dark Baron, in whose eye was death."

"Keep your gold for those who like it, mistress," said Henry, "and do not offer to honest hands the money that is won by violing, and tabouring, and toe-tripping, and perhaps worse pastimes. I tell you plainly, mistress, I am not to be fooled. I am ready to take you to any place of safety you can name, for my promise is as strong as an iron shackle. But you cannot persuade me that you do not know what earth to make for. You are not so young in your trade as not to know there are hostelries in every town, much more in a city like Perth, where such as you may be harboured for your money, if you cannot find some gulls, more or fewer, to pay your lawing. If you have money, mistress, my care about you need be the less; and truly I see little but pretence in all that excessive grief and fear of being left alone, in one of your occupation."

Having thus, as he conceived, signified that he was not to be deceived by the ordinary arts of a glee-maiden, Henry walked a few paces sturdily, endeavouring to think he was doing the wisest and most prudent thing in the world. Yet he could not help looking back to see how Louise bore his departure, and was shocked to see that she had sunk upon a bank, with her arms resting on her knees, and her head on her arms, in a situation expressive of the utmost desolation.

The Smith tried to harden his heart. "It is all a sham," he said; "the gouge* knows her trade, I'll be sworn by Saint Ringan."

At the instant, something pulled the skirts of his cloak; and, looking round, he saw the little spaniel, who immediately, as if to plead his mistress's cause, got on his hind legs and began to dance, whimpering at the same time, and looking back to Louise, as if to solicit compassion for his forsaken owner.

"Poor thing," said the Smith, "there may be a trick in this too, for thou dost but as thou art taught.—Yet, as I promised to protect this poor creature, I must not leave her in a swoon, if it be one, were it but for manhood's sake."

Returning and approaching his troublesome charge, he was at once assured, from the change of her complexion, either that she was actually in the deepest distress, or had a power of dissimulation beyond the comprehension of man—or woman either.

"Young woman," he said, with more of kindness than he had hitherto been able even to assume, "I will tell you frankly how I am placed. This is St Valentine's Day, and by custom I was to spend it with my fair Valentine. But blows and quarrels have occupied all the morning, save one poor half hour. Now, you may well understand where my heart and my thoughts are, and where, were it only in mere courtesy, my body ought to be."

The glee-maiden listened, and appeared to comprehend him.

"If you are a true lover, and have to wait upon a chaste Valentine, God forbid that one like me should make disturbance between you! Think about me no more. I will ask of that great river to be my guide to where it meets the ocean, where I think they said there was a seaport; I will sail from thence to La Belle France, and find myself once more in a country in which the roughest peasant would not wrong the poorest female."

"You cannot go to Dundee to-day," said the Smith. "The Douglas's people are in motion on both sides of the river, for the alarm of

* Gouge, in old French, is almost equivalent to wench.

the morning has reached them ere now; and all this day, and the next, and the whole night which is between, they will gather to their leader's standard like Highlandmen at the fiery cross. Do you see yonder five or six men, who are riding so wildly on the other side of the river? These are Annandale men; I know them by the length of their lances, and by the way they hold them. An Annandale man never slopes his spear backwards, but always keeps the point upright, or pointed forward."

"And what of them?" said the glee-maiden. "They are men-at-arms and soldiers—They would respect me for my viol and my helplessness."

"I will say them no scandal," answered the Smith. "If you were in their own glens, they would use you hospitably, and you would have nothing to fear; but they are now on an expedition. All is fish that comes to their net. There are amongst them who would take your life for the value of your gold ear-rings. Their whole soul is settled in their eyes to see prey, and in their hands to grasp it. They have no ears either to hear lays of music, or listen to prayers for mercy. Besides, their leader's order is gone forth concerning you, and it is of a kind sure to be obeyed. Ay, great lords are sooner listened to if they say, 'Burn a church,' than if they say, 'Build one.'"

"Then," said the glee-woman, "I were best sit down and die."

"Do not say so," replied the Smith. "If I could but get you a lodging for the night, I would carry you the next morning to Our Lady's Stairs, from whence the vessels go down the river for Dundee, and put you on board with some one bound that way, who should see you safely lodged where you would have fair entertainment and kind usage."

"Good—excellent—generous man!" said the glee-maiden, "do this, and if the prayers and blessings of a poor unfortunate should ever reach Heaven, they will rise thither in thy behalf. We will meet at yonder postern door, at whatever time the boats take their departure."

"That is at seven in the morning when the day is but young."

"Away with you, then, to your Valentine;—and if she loves you, oh, deceive her not!"

"Alas, poor damsel! I fear it is deceit hath brought thee to this pass. But I must not leave you thus unprovided. I must know where you are to pass the night."

"Care not for that," replied Louise—"the heavens are clear—there are bushes and boskets enough by the river side; Charlot and I can well make a sleeping room of a green arbour for one night; and tomorrow will, with your promised aid, see me out of reach of injury and wrong. Oh, the night soon passes away when there is hope for tomorrow!—Do you still linger, with your Valentine waiting for you?

Nay, I shall hold you but a loitering lover, and you know what belongs
to a minstrel's reproaches."

"I cannot leave you, damsel," answered the armourer, now completely melted. "It were mere murder to suffer you to pass the night
exposed to the keenness of a Scottish night in February. No, no—my
word would be ill kept in this manner; and if I should incur some risk
of blame, it is but just penance for thinking of thee, and using thee,
more according to my own prejudices, as I now well believe, than thy
merits. Come with me, damsel—thou shalt have a sure and honest
lodging for the night, whatsoever may be the consequence. It would be
an evil compliment to my Catherine were I to leave a poor creature to
be starved to death, that I might enjoy her company an hour sooner."

So saying, and hardening himself against all anticipations of the ill
consequences or scandal which might arise from such a measure, the
manly-hearted Smith resolved to set evil report at defiance, and give
the wanderer a night's refuge in his own house. It must be added that
he did this with extreme reluctance, and in a sort of enthusiasm of
benevolence.

Ere our stout son of Vulcan had fixed his worship on the Fair Maid
of Perth, a certain wildness of disposition had placed him under the
influence of Venus, as well as that of Mars; and it was only the effect of
a sincere attachment which had withdrawn him entirely from such
licentious pleasures. He was therefore justly jealous of his newly-
acquired reputation for constancy, which his conduct to this poor
wanderer must expose to suspicion—a little doubtful, perhaps, of
exposing himself too venturously to temptation—and in despair to
lose so much of St Valentine's Day, which custom not only permitted,
but enjoined him to pass beside his mate for the season. The journey
to Kinfauns, and the various transactions which followed, had consumed the day, and it was now nearly even-song time.

As if to make up by a speedy pace for the time he was compelled to
waste upon a subject so foreign to that which he had most at heart, he
strode on through the Dominicans' gardens, entered the town, and
casting his cloak around the lower part of his face, and pulling down
his bonnet to conceal the upper, he continued the same pace through
by-streets and lanes, hoping to reach his own house in the Wynd
without being observed. But when he had continued his rate of hard
walking for ten minutes, he began to be sensible it might be too rapid
for the young woman to keep up with him. He accordingly looked
behind him with a degree of angry impatience, which soon turned into
compunction, when he saw that she was almost utterly exhausted by
the speed which she had exerted.

"Now, marry, hang me up for a brute," said Henry to himself. "Was my own haste ever so great, could it give that poor creature wings? And she loaded with baggage too! I am an ill-nurtured beast, that is certain, wherever women are in question; and always sure to do wrong when I have the best will to act right.—Hark thee, damsel; let me carry these things for thee. We shall make better speed that I do so."

Poor Louise would have objected, but her breath was too much exhausted to express herself; and she permitted her good-natured guardian to take her little basket, which when the dog beheld he came straight before Henry, stood up, and shook his fore-paws, whining gently as if he too wanted to be carried.

"Nay, then, I must needs lend thee a lift too," said the Smith, who saw the creature was tired.

"Fie, Charlot!" said Louise; "thou knowest I will carry thee myself."

She endeavoured to take up the little spaniel, but it escaped from her; and going to the other side of the Smith, renewed its supplications that he would carry it.

"Charlot's right," said the Smith; "he knows best who is ablest to bear him. This lets me know, my pretty one, that you have not been always the bearer of your own mail—Charlot can tell tales."

So deadly a hue came across the poor glee-maiden's countenance as Henry spoke, that he was obliged to support her, lest she should have dropped to the ground. She recovered again, however, in an instant or two, and with a feeble voice requested her guide would go on.

"Nay, nay," said Henry, as they began to move, "keep hold of my cloak, or my arm, if it helps you forward better. A fair sight we are; and had I but a rebeck or guitar at my back, and a jackanapes on my shoulder, we should seem as joyous a brace of strollers as ever struck string at a castle gate.—S'nails!" he ejaculated internally, "were any neighbour to meet me with this little harlotry's basket at my back, her dog under my arm, and herself hanging on my cloak, what could they think but that I had turned mumper in good earnest? I would not for the best harness I ever laid hammer on, that any of our long-tongued neighbours met me in this guise; it were a jest would last from St Valentine's Day to next Candlemas."

Stirred by these thoughts, the Smith, although at the risk of making much longer a route which he wished to traverse as swiftly as possible, took the most indirect and private course which he could find in order to avoid the main streets, still crowded with people, owing to the late scene of tumult and agitation. But unhappily his policy availed him nothing; for in turning into an alley, he met a man with his cloak muffled around his face, from a desire like his own to pass unobserved, though the slight insignificant figure, the spindle-shanks, which showed themselves beneath the mantle, and the small dull eye that blinked over its upper folds, announced the Pottingar as distinctly as if he had carried his sign in front of his bonnet. His unexpected and most unwelcome presence overwhelmed the Smith with confusion. Ready evasion was not the property of his bold, blunt temper; and knowing this man to be a curious observer, a malignant tale-bearer, and by no means well disposed to himself in particular, no better hope occurred to him than that the worshipful apothecary would give him some pretext to silence his testimony, and secure his discretion, by twisting his neck round.

But far from doing or saying anything which could warrant such extremities, the Pottingar, seeing himself so close upon his stalwart townsman that recognition was inevitable, seemed determined it should be as slight as possible; and without appearing to notice any-thing peculiar in the company or circumstances in which they met, he barely slid out these words as he passed him, without even a glance towards his companion after the first instant of their meeting,—"A merry holiday to you once more, stout Smith. What! thou art bringing thy cousin, pretty Mistress Joan Letham, with her mail, from the water-side—fresh from Dundee, I warrant? I heard she was expected at the old cordwainer's."

As he spoke thus, he looked neither right nor left, and exchanging a "Save you!" with a salute of the same kind which the Smith rather muttered than uttered distinctly, he glided forward on his way like a shadow.

"The foul fiend catch me if I can swallow that pill," said Henry Smith, "how well soever it may be gilded. The knave has a shrewd eye for a kirtle, and knows a wild-duck from a tame, as well as e'er a man in Perth—He were the last in the Fair City to take sour plums for pears, or my round-about cousin Joan for this piece of fantasy work. I fancy his bearing was as much as to say, I will not see what you might wish me blind to—and he is right to do so, as he might easily purchase himself a broken pate by meddling with my matters—and so he will be silent for his own sake. But whom have we next—By St Dunstan! the chattering, bragging, cowardly knave, Oliver Proudfute!"

It was, indeed, the bold Bonnet-maker whom they next encoun-tered, who, with his cap on one side, and trolling the ditty of

> Thou art over long at the pot, Tom, Tom,

gave plain intimation that he had made no dry meal.

"Ha! my jolly Smith," he said, "have I caught thee in the manner? —What, can the true steel bend?—Can Vulcan, as the minstrel says, pay Venus back in her own coin?—Faith, thou wilt be a gay Valentine before the year's out, that begin the very holiday so jollily."

"Hark ye, Oliver," said the displeased Smith, "shut your eyes and pass on, crony. And hark ye again, stir not your tongue about what concerns you not, as you value having an entire one in your head."

"I betray counsel?—I bear tales, and that against my brother mar-tialist?—I scorn it—I would not tell it even to my timber Soldan!—Why, I can be a wild galliard in a corner as well as thou, man—And now I think on't, I will go with thee somewhere, and we will have a rouse together, and thy Dalilah shall give us a song. Ha! said I not well?"

"Excellently," said Henry, longing the whole time to knock his brother martialist down, but wisely taking a more peaceful way to rid himself of the incumbrance of his presence—"Excellently well!—I may want thy help too—for here be five or six of the Douglasses before us—they will not fail to try to take the wench from a poor burgher like myself, so I will be glad of the assistance of a tearer such as thou art."

"I thank ye—I thank ye," answered the Bonnet-maker—"but were I not better run, and cause ring the common bell, and get my great sword?"

"Ay, ay—run home as fast as you can, and say nothing of what you have seen."

"Who, I?—Nay, fear me not. Pah! I scorn a tale-bearer with my heels."

"Away with you, then;—I hear the clash of armour."

This put life and mettle into the heels of the Bonnet-maker, who, turning his back on the supposed danger, set off at a pace which the Smith never doubted would speedily bring him to his own house.

"Here is another chattering jay to deal with," thought the Smith; "but I have a hank over him too. The minstrels have a fabliau of a daw with borrowed feathers,—why, this Oliver is the very bird, and, by St Dunstan, if he lets his chattering tongue run on at my expense, I will so pluck him as never hawk plumed a partridge. And this he knows."

As these reflections thronged upon his mind, he had nearly reached the end of his journey; and, with the glee-maiden still hanging on his cloak, exhausted, partly with fear, partly with fatigue, he at length arrived at the middle of the Wynd, which was honoured with his own habitation, and from which, in the uncertainty that then attended the application of surnames, he derived one of his own appellatives. Here, on ordinary days, his furnace was seen to blaze, and four half-stripped knaves stunned the neighbourhood with the clang of hammer and stithy. But St Valentine's holiday was an excuse for these men of steel having shut the shop, and for the present being absent on their own errands of devotion or pleasure. The house which adjoined to the smithy called Henry its owner; and though it was small, and situated in a narrow street, yct, as there was a considerable garden with fruit trees behind, it constituted upon the whole a pleasant dwelling. The Smith, instead of knocking or calling, which would have drawn neighbours to doors and windows, drew out a pass-key of his own fabrication, then a great and envied curiosity, and opening the door of his house introduced his companion into his habitation.

The apartment which received Henry and the glee-maiden was the kitchen, which served amongst those of the Smith's station for the family sitting-room, although one or two individuals, like Simon Glover, had an eating-room apart from that in which their victuals were prepared. In the corner of this apartment, which was arranged with an unusual attention to cleanliness, sat an old woman, whose neatness of attire, and the precision with which her scarlet plaid was drawn over her head, so as to descend to her shoulders on each side, might have indicated a higher rank than that of Luckie Shoolbred, the Smith's housekeeper. Yet such and no other was her designation; and not having attended mass in the morning, she was quietly reposing herself by the side of the fire, her beads, half told, hanging over her left arm; her prayers, half said, loitering upon her tongue; her eyes, half closed, resigning themselves to slumber, while she expected the return of her foster-son, without being able to guess at what hour it was likely to happen. She started up at the sound of his entrance, and bent her eye upon his companion, at first with a look of the utmost surprise, which gradually was exchanged for one expressive of great displeasure.

"Now the Saints bless mine eye-sight, Henry Smith!—" she exclaimed, very devoutly.

"Amen, with all my heart. Get some food ready presently, good nurse, for I fear me this traveller hath dined but lightly."

"And again I pray that Our Lady would preserve my eyesight from the delusions of Satan!"

"So be it, I tell you, good woman. But what is the use of all this pattering and prayering? Do you not hear me? or will you not do as I bid you?"

"It must be himself, then, whatever is of it—but oh! it is more like the foul fiend in his likeness, to have such a baggage hanging upon his cloak.—O Harry Smith, men called you a wild lad for less things! But who would ever have thought that Harry would have brought a light leman under the roof that sheltered his worthy mother, and where his own nurse has dwelt for forty years!"

"Hold your peace, old woman, and be reasonable," said the Smith.

"This glee-woman is no leman of mine, nor of any other person that I know of; but she is going off for Dundee to-morrow by the boats, and we must give her quarters till then."

"Quarters!" said the old woman. "You may give quarters to such cattle if you like it yourself, Harry Wynd; but the same house shall not quarter that trumpery quean and me, and of that you may assure yourself."

"Your mother is angry with me," said Louise, misconstruing the connexion of the parties. "I will not remain to give her any offence. If there is a stable or a cowhouse, an empty stall will be bed enough for Charlot and me."

"Ay, ay; I am thinking it is the quarters you are best used to," said Dame Shoolbred.

"Hark ye, Nurse Shoolbred," said the Smith. "You know I love you for your own sake, and for my mother's; but by St Dunstan, who was a saint of my own craft, I will have the command of my own house; and if you leave me without any better reason but your own nonsensical suspicions, you must think how you will have the door open to you when you return; for you shall have no help of mine, I promise you."

"Aweel, my bairn, and that will never make me risk the honest name I have kept for sixty years. It was never your mother's custom, and it shall never be mine, to take up with ranters, and jugglers, and singing women; and I am not sae far to seek for a dwelling, that the same roof should cover me and a tramping princess like that."

With this the refractory gouvernante began in great hurry to adjust her tartan mantle for going abroad, by pulling it so far forward as to conceal the white linen cap, the edges of which bordered her shrivelled but still fresh and healthful countenance. This done, she seized upon a staff, the trusty companion of her journeys, and was fairly trudging towards the door, when the Smith stepped between her and the passage.

"Wait at least, old woman, till we have cleared scores. I owe you for fee and bountith."

"An' that's e'en a dream of your own fool's head. What fee or bountith am I to take from the son of your mother, that fed, clad, and bielded me as if I had been a sister?"

"And well you repay it, nurse, leaving her only child at his utmost need."

This seemed to strike the obstinate old woman with compunction. She stopped and looked at her master and the minstrel alternately; then shook her head, and seemed about to resume her motion towards the door.

"I only receive this poor wanderer under my roof," urged the

Smith, "to save her from the prison and the scourge."

"And why should you save her?" said the inexorable Dame Shool-bred. "I dare say she has deserved them both as well as ever thief deserved a hempen collar."

"For aught I know she may, or she may not. But she cannot deserve to be scourged to death, or imprisoned till she is starved to death; and that is the lot of them that the Black Douglas bears maltalent against."

"And you are ganging to thraw the Black Douglas for the sake of a glee-woman? This will be the worst of your feuds yet.—Oh, Henry, Henry, there is as much iron in your head as in your anvil!"

"I have sometimes thought this myself, Mistress Shoolbred; but if I do get a cut or two on this new argument, I wonder who's to cure them, if you run away from me like a scared wild-goose? Ay, and moreover, who is to receive my bonny bride that I hope to bring up the Wynd one of these days?"

"Ah, Harry, Harry," said the old woman, shaking her head, "this is not the way to prepare an honest man's house for a young bride—you should be guided by modesty and discretion, and not by chambering and wantonness."

"I tell you again, this poor creature is nothing to me. I want her only to be safely cared for. I think the boldest Borderman in Perth will respect the bar of my door as much as the gate of Carlisle Castle.—I am going down to Sim Glover's—I may stay there all night, for the Highland cub is run back to the hills, like a wolf-whelp as he is, and so there is a bed to spare, and father Simon will make me welcome to the use of it. You will remain with this poor creature, feed her, and protect her, and I will call her before day; and thou mayst go with her to the boat thyself an thou wilt, and so thou wilt set the last eyes on her at the same time I shall."

"There is some reason in that," said Dame Shoolbred; "though why you should put your reputation in risk for a creature that would find a lodging for a silver twopence and less matter is a mystery to me."

"Trust me with that, old woman, and be kind to the girl."

"Kinder than she deserves, I warrant you; and truly, though I little like the company of such cattle, yet I think I am less like to take harm from her than you—unless she be a witch, indeed, which may well come to be the case, as the devil is very powerful with all this wayfaring clanjamfray."

"No more a witch than I am a warlock," said the honest Smith; "a poor broken-hearted thing, that, if she hath done evil, has dreed a sore weird for it. Be kind to her—And you, my musical damsel—I will call on you to-morrow morning and carry you to the water-side. This old woman will treat you kindly if you say nothing to her but what becomes honest ears."

The poor minstrel had listened to this dialogue, without understanding more than its general tendency; for, though she spoke English well, she had acquired the language in England itself, and the northern dialect was then, as now, of a broader and harsher character. She saw, however, that she was to remain with the old lady, and meekly folding her arms on her bosom, bent her head with humility. She next looked towards the Smith with a strong expression of thankfulness, then raising her eyes to heaven, took his passive hand, and seemed about to kiss the hard and sinewy fingers in token of deep and affectionate gratitude. But Dame Shoolbred did not give license to the stranger's mode of expressing her feelings. She thrust in between them, and pushing poor Louise aside, said, "No, no, I'll have none of that work. Go into the chimney nook, mistress, and when Harry Smith's gone, if you must have hands to kiss, you shall kiss mine as long as you like.—And you, Harry, away down to Sim Glover's, for if pretty Mistress Catherine hears of the company you have brought home she may chance to like them as little as I do.—What's the matter now?—is the man demented?—are you going out without your buckler, and the hail town in misrule?"

"You are right, dame," said the armourer; and throwing the buckler over his broad shoulders, he departed from his house without abiding farther question.

END OF VOLUME FIRST

SAINT VALENTINE'S DAY;
OR,
THE FAIR MAID OF PERTH
VOLUME II

Chapter One

WE MUST NOW leave the lower parties in our historical drama to
attend to the incidents which took place among those of a higher rank
and greater importance.

We pass from the hut of an armourer to the council-room of a
monarch; and resume our story just when, the tumult beneath being
settled, the angry chieftains were summoned to the royal presence.
They entered, displeased with and lowering upon each other, each so
exclusively filled with his own fancied injuries, as to be equally unwilling and unable to attend to reason or argument. Albany alone, calm
and crafty, seemed prepared to use their dissatisfaction for his own
purposes, and turn each incident as it should occur to the furtherance
of his own indirect ends.

The King's irresolution, although it amounted even to timidity, did
not prevent his assuming the exterior dignity of his situation. It was
only when hard pressed, as in the preceding scene, that he lost his
external composure. In general, he might be driven from his purpose,
but seldom from his dignity of manner. He received Albany, Douglas, March, and the Prior, (those ill-assorted members of his motley
council,) with a mixture of courtesy and dignity, which reminded each
haughty peer that he stood in the presence of his Sovereign, and
compelled him to do the beseeming reverence.

Having received their salutations, the King motioned them to be
seated; and they were obeying his command when Rothsay entered.
He walked gracefully up to his father, and, kneeling at his footstool,

requested his blessing. Robert, with a look in which fondness and sorrow were ill disguised, making an attempt to assume a look of reproof, laid his hand on the youth's head, as he said, with a sigh, "God bless thee, my thoughtless boy, and make thee a wiser man in thy future years!"

"Amen, my dearest father!" said Rothsay, in a tone of feeling such as his happier moments often evinced. He then kissed the royal hand, with the reverence of a son and a subject; and instead of taking a place at the council board, remained standing behind the King's chair, in such a position that he might, when he chose, whisper into his father's ear.

The King then made a sign to the Prior of St Dominic's to take his place at the table, on which there were writing materials, which, of all the company, Albany excepted, the churchman was alone able to use. The King then opened the purpose of their meeting by saying, with much dignity,

"Our business, my lords, respected these unhappy dissensions in the Highlands, which, we learn by our latest messengers, are about to occasion the waste and destruction of the country, even within a few miles of this our own court. But near as this trouble is, our ill fate, and the instigations of wicked men, have raised up one yet more near, by throwing strife and contention among the citizens of Perth and those attendants who follow your lordships, and others our knights and nobles. I must first, therefore, apply to yourselves, my lords, to know why our court is disturbed by such unseemly contendings, and by what means they ought to be repressed?—Brother of Albany, do you tell us first your sentiments on this matter."

"Sir, our royal Sovereign and brother," said the Duke, "being in attendance on your person when the fray began, I am not acquainted with its origin."

"And for me," said the Prince, "I heard no worse war-cry than a minstrel wench's ballad, and saw no more dangerous bolts flying than hazel nuts."

"And I," said the Earl of March, "could only perceive that the stout citizens of Perth had in chase some knaves who had assumed the Bloody Heart on their shoulders. They ran too fast to be actually the men of the Earl of Douglas."

Douglas understood the sneer, but only replied to it by one of those withering looks with which he was accustomed to intimate his mortal resentment. He spoke, however, with haughty composure.

"My liege," he said, "must see it is Douglas who must answer to this heavy charge; for when was there strife or bloodshed in Scotland, but there were foul tongues to asperse a Douglas or a Douglas's man, as having given cause to them? We have here a goodly train of witnesses. I speak not of my Lord of Albany, who has only said that he was, as well becomes him, by your Grace's side. And I say nothing of my Lord of Rothsay, who, as befits his rank, years, and understanding, was cracking nuts with a strolling musician.—He smiles—Here he may say his pleasure—I shall not forget a tie which he seems to have forgotten. But here is my Lord of March, who saw my followers flying before the clowns of Perth! I can tell that Earl, that the followers of the Bloody Heart advance or retreat when their chieftain commands, and the good of Scotland requires."

"And I can answer—" exclaimed the equally proud Earl of March, his blood rushing into his face, when the King interrupted him.

"Peace! angry lords, and remember in whose presence you stand! —And you, my Lord of Douglas, tell us, if you can, the cause of this mutiny, and why your followers, whose general good services we are most willing to acknowledge, were thus active in private brawl?"

"I obey, my lord," said Douglas, slightly stooping a head that seldom bent. "I was passing from my lodgings in the Carthusian Convent, through the High Street of Perth, with a few of my ordinary retinue, when I beheld some of the baser sort crowding around the Cross, against which there were nailed this placard, and that which accompanies it."

He took from a pocket in the bosom of his buff-coat a human hand and a piece of parchment. The King was shocked and agitated.

"Read," he said, "good Father Prior, and let that ghastly spectacle be removed."

The Prior read a placard to the following purpose:—

"Inasmuch as the house of a citizen of Perth was assaulted last night, being St Valentine's Eve, by a sort of disorderly night-walkers, belonging to some company of the strangers now resident in the Fair City: And whereas, this hand was struck from one of the lawless limmers in the fray that ensued, the Provost and Magistrates have directed that it should be nailed to the Cross, in scorn and contempt of those by whom such brawl was occasioned. And if any one of knightly degree shall say that this our act is wrongfully done, I, Patrick Charteris of Kinfauns, Knight, will justify this cartel in knightly weapons, within the barrace. Or, if any one of meaner birth shall deny what is here said, he shall be met with by a citizen of the Fair City of Perth, according to his degree. And so God and St John protect the Fair City!"

"You will not wonder, my lord," resumed Douglas, "that when my almoner had read to me the contents of so insolent a scroll, I caused one of my squires to pluck down a trophy so disgraceful to the chivalry and nobility of Scotland. Whereupon, it seems some of these saucy burghers took license to hoot at and insult the hindmost of my train, who wheeled their horses on them, and would soon have settled the feud, but for my positive command that they should follow me in as much peace as the rascaille vulgar would permit. And thus they arrived here in the guise of flying men, when, with my command to repel force by force, they might have set fire to the four corners of this wretched borough, and stifled the insolent churls like fox-cubs in a burning brake of furze."

There was a silence when Douglas had done speaking, until the Duke of Rothsay answered, addressing his father—"Since the Earl of Douglas possesses the power of burning the town where your Grace holds your court, so soon as the Provost and he differ about a night riot, or the terms of a cartel, I am sure we ought all to be thankful that he has not the will to do so."

"The Duke of Rothsay," said Douglas, who seemed resolved to maintain command of his temper, "may have reason to thank Heaven in a more serious tone than he now uses, that the Douglas is as true as he is powerful. This is a time when the subjects in all countries rise against the Law; we have heard of the insurgents of the Jacquerie in France; and of Jack Straw, and Hob Miller, and Parson Ball, among the Southron, and we may be sure there is fuel enough to catch such a flame, were it spreading to our frontiers. When I see peasants challenging noblemen, and nailing the hands of the gentry to their city Cross, I will not say I *fear* mutiny—for that would be false—but I foresee, and will stand prepared for it."

"And why does my Lord Douglas say," answered the Earl of March, "that this cartel has been done by churls? I see Sir Patrick Charteris's name there, and he, I ween, is of no churl's blood. The Douglas himself, since he takes the matter so warmly, might lift Sir Patrick's gauntlet without soiling of his honour."

"My Lord of March," replied Douglas, "should speak but of what he understands. I do no injustice to the descendant of the Red Rover when I say he is too slight to be weighed with the Douglas. The heir of Thomas Randolph might have a better claim to be answered."

"And, by my honour, it shall not miss for want of my asking the grace," said the Earl of March, pulling his glove off.

"Stay, my lord," said the King. "Do us not so gross an injury as to bring your feud to mortal defiance here; but rather offer your ungloved hand in kindness to the noble Earl, and embrace, in token of your mutual fealty to the Crown of Scotland."

"Not so, my liege," answered March; "your Majesty may command me to return my gauntlet, for that and all the armour it belongs to are at your command while I continue to hold my earldom of the Crown of Scotland—but when I clasp Douglas it must be with a mailed hand. Farewell, my liege. My counsels here avail not, and those of others are so favourably received, that perhaps farther stay were unwholesome for my safety. May God keep your Highness from open enemies and treacherous friends!—I am for my Castle of Dunbar, from whence I think you will soon hear news. Farewell to you, my Lords of Albany and Douglas; you are playing a high game, look you play it fairly— Farewell, poor thoughtless Prince, who art sporting like a fawn within spring of a tiger. Farewell all—George of Dunbar sees the evil he cannot remedy.—Adieu, all."

The King would have spoken, but the accents died on his tongue, as he received from Albany a look cautioning him to forbear. The Earl of March left the apartment, receiving the mute salutations of the members of the council whom he had severally addressed, excepting from Douglas alone, who returned to his farewell speech a glance of contemptuous defiance.

"The recreant goes to betray us to the Southron," he said; "his pride rests on his possessing that sea-worn Hold which can admit the English into Lothian.—Nay, look not alarmed, my liege, I will hold good what I say—Nevertheless, it is yet time. Speak but the word, my liege—say but 'Arrest him,' and March shall not yet cross the Earn on his traitorous journey."

"Nay, gallant Earl," said Albany, who wished rather that the two powerful lords should counterbalance each other than that one should obtain a decisive superiority, "that were too hasty counsel. The Earl of March came hither on the King's warrant of safe-conduct, and it may not consist with my royal brother's honour to break it. Yet, if your lordship can bring any detailed proof——"

Here they were interrupted by a flourish of trumpets.

"His Grace of Albany is unwontedly scrupulous to-day," said Douglas; "but it skills not wasting words—the time is past—these are March's trumpets, and I warrant me he rides at flight-speed so soon as he passes the South Port. We shall hear of him in time; and if it be as I have conjectured, he shall be met with though all England backed his treachery."

"Nay, let us hope better of the noble Earl of March," said the King, no way displeased that the quarrel betwixt March and Douglas had seemed to obliterate the traces of the disagreement betwixt Rothsay and his father-in-law; "he hath a fiery, but not a sullen temper—In some things he has been—I will not say wronged—but disappointed —and something is to be allowed to the resentment of high blood armed with great power. But thank Heaven, all of us who remain are of one sentiment and of one house; so that, at least, our councils cannot now be thwarted with disunion.—Father Prior, I pray you take your writing materials, for you must as usual be our clerk of council.— And now to business, my lords—and our first object of consideration must be this Highland cumber."

"Between the Clan Chattan and the Clan Quhele," said the Prior; "which, as our last advices from our brethren at Dunkeld inform us, is ready to break out into a more formidable warfare than has yet taken place between these sons of Belial, who speak of nothing else than of utterly destroying one another. Their forces are assembling on each side, and not a man claiming in the tenth degree of kindred but must repair to the Brattach* of his tribe, or stand to the punishment of fire and sword. The fiery cross hath fled like a meteor in every direction, and awakened strange and unknown tribes beyond the distant Murray Firth. May Heaven and St Dominic be our protection! But if your lordships cannot find remedy for evil, it will spread broad and wide and the patrimony of the Church in every direction be exposed to the fury of these Amalekites, with whom there is as little devotion to Heaven as there is pity or love to their neighbours—may Our Lady be our guard!—We hear some of them are yet utter heathens, and worship Mahound and Termagaunt."

"My lords and kinsmen," said Robert, "ye have heard the urgency of this case, and may desire to know my sentiments before you deliver what your own wisdom shall suggest. And, in sooth, no better remedy occurs to me than to send two commissioners, with full power from us to settle such debates as be among them; and at the same time to charge them, as they will be answerable to the law, to lay down their arms, and forbear all practices of violence against each other."

"I approve of your Grace's proposal," said Rothsay; "and I trust the good Prior will not refuse the honourable station of envoy upon this peace-making errand. And his reverend brother, the Abbot of the Carthusian convent, will contend for an honour which will certainly add two most eminent recruits to the large army of martyrs, since the Highlanders little regard the distinction betwixt clerk and layman in the ambassadors whom you send to them."

"My royal Lord of Rothsay," said the Prior, "if I am destined to the blessed crown of martyrdom, I shall be doubtless directed to the path by which I am to attain it. Meantime, if you speak in jest, may Heaven pardon you, and give you light to perceive it were better buckle on your arms to guard the possessions of the Church, so

---

* Standard—literally, cloth. The Lowland language still retains the word *brat*, which, however, is only applicable to a child's pinafore or a coarse towel. To such mean offices may words descend.

perilously endangered, than to employ your wit in taunting her ministers and servants."

"I taunt no one, Father Prior," said the youth, yawning; "nor have I
much objection to taking arms, excepting that they are a somewhat
cumbrous garb, and in February a furred mantle is more suiting the
weather than a steel corslet. And it irks me the more to put on cold
harness in this nipping weather that, would but the Church send a
detachment of their saints, (and they have some Highland ones well
known in this district, and doubtless used to the climate,) they might
fight their own battles like merry St George of England. But I know
not how it is, we hear of their miracles when they are propitiated, and
of their vengeance if any one trespasses on their patrimonies, and
these are urged as reasons for extending their lands by large grants;
and yet if there come down but a band of twenty Catherans, bell, book,
and candle make no speed, and the belted baron must be fain to
defend the lands which he has given to the Church, as much as if he
still enjoyed the fruits of them."

"Son David," said his father, "you give an undue license to your
tongue."

"Nay, sir, I am mute," replied the Prince. "I had no purpose to
disturb your Highness, or displease the Father Prior, who, with so
many miracles at his disposal, will not face, as it seems, a handful of
Highland catherans."

"We know," said the Prior, with suppressed indignation, "from
what source these vile doctrines are derived, which we hear with
horror from the tongue of your Highness. When princes converse
with heretics, their minds and manners are alike corrupted. They
show themselves in the streets as the companions of masquers and
harlots, and in the council as the scorners of the Church and of holy
things."

"Peace, good Father!" said the King. "Rothsay shall make amends
for what he has idly spoken. Alas! let us take counsel in friendly
fashion, rather than resemble a mutinous crew of mariners in a sinking vessel, when each is more intent on quarrelling with his neighbours than in assisting the exertions of the forlorn master for the safety
of the ship.—My Lord of Douglas, your house has been seldom to
lack, when the crown of Scotland desired either wise counsel or manly
achievement; I trust you will help us in this strait?"

"I can only wonder that the strait should exist, my lord," answered
the haughty Douglas. "When I was intrusted with the lieutenancy
of the kingdom, there were some of these wild clans came down
from the Grampians. I troubled not the council about the matter,
but made the Sheriff, Lord Ruthven, get to horse with the forces of

the Carse—the Hays, the Lindsays, the Ogilvies, and other gentle-men. By St Bride! when it was steel coat to frieze mantle, the thieves knew what lances were good for, and whether swords had edges or no. There were some three hundred of their best bonnets, besides that of their chief, Donald Cormac,* left on the moor of Thorn, and in Rochinroy Wood; and as many were gibbeted at Houghman Stairs, which has still the name from the hangman work that was done there. This is the way men deal with thieves in my country; and if gentler methods will succeed better with these Irish knaves, do not blame Douglas for speaking his mind.—You smile, my Lord of Rothsay. May I ask how I have a second time become your jest, before I have replied to the first which you passed on me?"

"Nay, be not wrathful, my good Lord of Douglas," answered the Prince; "I did but smile to think how your princely retinue would dwindle, if every thief were dealt with as the poor Highlanders at Houghman Stairs."

The King again interfered to prevent the Earl giving an angry reply. "Your lordship," said he to Douglas, "advises wisely that we should trust to arms when these men come out against our subjects on the fair and level plain; but the difficulty is to put a stop to their disorders while they continue to lurk within their mountains. I need not tell you that the Clan Chattan and the Clan Quhele are great confederacies, consisting each of various tribes who are banded together, each to support their own separate league, and who of late have had dissen-sions which have drawn blood wherever they have met, whether indi-vidually or in bands. The whole country is torn to pieces by their restless feuds."

"I cannot see the evil of this," said the Douglas; "the ruffians will destroy each other, and the deer of the Highlands will increase as the men diminish. We will gain as hunters the exercise we lose as war-riors."

"Rather say that the wolves will increase as the men diminish," replied the King.

"I am content," said Douglas; "better wild wolves than wild High-landers. Let there be strong forces maintained along the Highland frontier to separate the quiet from the disturbed country. Confine the fire of civil war within the Highlands; let it spend its uncontrolled ferocity, and it will be soon burnt out for want of fuel. The survivors will be humbled, and will be more obedient to a whisper of your Grace's pleasure than their fathers, or the knaves that now exist, have been to your strictest commands."

* Some authorities place this skirmish so late as 1443.

"This is wise but ungodly counsel," said the Prior, shaking his head; "I cannot take it upon my conscience to recommend it. It is wisdom, but it is the wisdom of Achitophel, crafty at once and cruel."

"My heart tells me so—" said Robert, laying his hand on his breast; "my heart tells me that it will be asked of me at the awful day, 'Robert Stewart, where are the subjects I have given thee?'—it tells me that I must account for them all, Saxon and Gael, Lowland, Highland, and Border man; that I will not be required to answer for those alone who have wealth and knowledge, but for those also who were robbers because they were poor, and rebels because they were ignorant."

"Your Highness speaks like a Christian King," said the Prior; "but you bear the sword as well as the sceptre, and this present evil is of a kind which the sword must cure."

"Hark ye, my lords," said the Prince, looking up as if a gay thought had suddenly struck him,—"Suppose we teach these savage mountaineers a strain of chivalry? It were no hard matter to bring their two great commanders, the captain of the Clan Chattan, and the chief of the no less doughty race of the Clan Quhele, to defy each other to mortal combat. They might fight here in Perth—we would lend them horse and armour: thus their feud would be stanched by the death of one, or probably both, of the villains, (for I think they would break their necks in the first charge,) my father's godly desire of saving blood would be attained—and we would have the pleasure of seeing such a combat between two salvage knights, for the first time in their lives wearing breeches, and mounted on horses, as has not been heard of since the days of King Arthur."

"Shame upon you, David!" said the King. "Do you make the distress of your native country, and the perplexity of our councils, a subject for buffoonery?"

"If you will pardon me, royal brother," said Albany, "I think that though my princely nephew hath started this thought in a jocular manner, there may be something wrought out of it, which might greatly remedy this pressing evil."

"Good brother," replied the King, "it is unkind to expose Rothsay's folly by pressing further his ill-timed jest. We know the Highland clans have not our customs of chivalry, nor the habit or mode of doing battle which it requires."

"True, royal brother," answered Albany; "yet I speak not in scorn, but in serious earnest. True, the mountaineers have not our forms and mode of doing battle in the lists, but they have those which are as effectual to the dispatch of human life; and so that the mortal game is played, and the stake won and lost, what signifies it whether they fight with sword and lance, as becomes belted knights, or with sand-bags like the crestless churls of England, or butcher each other with knives and skeans in their own barbarous fashion? Their habits, like our own, refer all disputed rights and claims to the decision of battle. They are as vain, too, as they are fierce; and the idea that these two clans would be admitted to combat in presence of your Grace and of your court will readily induce them to refer their difference to the fate of battle, even were such rough arbitrement less familiar to their customs, and that in any such numbers as shall be thought most convenient. We must take care that they approach not the court, save in such a fashion and number that they shall not be able to surprise us; and that point being provided against, the more that shall be admitted to combat upon either side, the greater will be the slaughter among their bravest and most stirring men, and the more the chance of the Highlands being quiet for some time to come."

"This were a bloody policy, brother," said the King; "and again I say that I cannot bring my conscience to countenance the slaughter of these rude men, that are so little better than so many benighted heathens."

"And are their lives more precious," asked Albany, "than those of nobles and gentlemen who by your Grace's license are so frequently admitted to fight in barrace, either for the satisfying of disputes at law, or simply to acquire honour?"

The King, thus hard pressed, had little to say against a custom so engrafted upon the laws of the realm and the usages of chivalry as the trial by combat; and he only replied, "God knows, I have never granted such license as you urge me with, unless with the greatest repugnance; and that I never saw men have strife together to the effusion of blood but what I could have wished to appease it with the shedding of my own."

"But, my gracious lord," said the Prior, "it seems that if we follow not some such policy as this of my Lord of Albany, we must have recourse to that of the Douglas; and, at the risk of the dubious event of battle, and with the certainty of losing many excellent subjects, do, by means of the Lowland swords, that which these wild mountaineers will otherwise perform with their own hand.—What says my Lord of Douglas to the policy of his Grace of Albany?"

"Douglas," said the haughty lord, "never counselled that to be done by policy which might be attained by open force. He remains by his opinion, and is willing to march at the head of his own followers, with those of the Barons of Perthshire and the Carse; and either bring these Highlanders to reason and subjection, or leave the body of a Douglas among their savage wildernesses."

"It is nobly said, my Lord of Douglas," said Albany; "and well might the King rely upon thy undaunted heart, and the courage of thy resolute followers. But see you not how soon you may be called elsewhere, where your presence and services are altogether indispensable to Scotland and her Monarch? Marked you not the gloomy tone in which the fiery Earl of March limited his allegiance and faith to our Sovereign here present, to that space for which he was to remain King Robert's vassal? And did not you yourself suspect that he was plotting a transference of his allegiance to England?—Other chiefs, of subordinate power and inferior fame, may do battle with the Highlanders; but if March admit the Percies and their Englishmen into our frontiers, who will drive them back if the Douglas be elsewhere?"

"My sword," answered Douglas, "is equally at the service of his Majesty, on the frontier, or in the deepest recesses of the Highlands. I have seen the backs of the proud Percy and George Dunbar ere now, and I may see them again. And, if it is the King's pleasure I should take measures against this probable conjunction of stranger and traitor, I admit that, rather than trust to an inferior or feebler hand the important task of settling the Highlands, I would be disposed to give my opinion in favour of the policy of my Lord of Albany, and suffer those savages to carve each other's limbs without giving barons and knights the trouble of hunting them down."

"My Lord of Douglas," said the Prince, who seemed determined to omit no opportunity to gall his haughty father-in-law, "does not choose to leave to us Lowlanders even the poor crumbs of honour which might be gathered at the expense of the Highland kerne, while he, with his Border chivalry, reaps the full harvest of victory over the English. But Percy hath seen men's backs as well as Douglas; and I have known as great wonders as that he who goes forth to seek wool should come back shorn."

"A phrase," said Douglas, "well becoming a prince who speaks of honour with a wandering harlot's scrip in his bonnet by way of favour."

"Excuse it, my lord," said Rothsay; "they who have matched unfittingly become careless in the choice of those whom they love *par amours*. The chained dog must snatch at the nearest bone."

"Rothsay, my unhappy son!" exclaimed the King, "art thou mad? or wouldst thou draw down on thee the full storm of a king and father's displeasure?"

"I am mute," returned the Prince, "at your Grace's command."

"Well then, my lord of Albany," said the King, "since such is your advice, and since Scottish blood must flow, how, I pray you, are we to prevail on these fierce men to refer their quarrel to such a combat as you propose?"

"That, my liege," said Albany, "must be the result of more mature deliberation. But the task will not be difficult. Gold will be needful to bribe some of the bards, and principal counsellors and spokesmen. The chiefs, moreover, of both these leagues must be made to understand that, unless they agree to this amicable settlement"——

"*Amicable*, Robert?" said the King, with emphasis.

"Ay, amicable, my liege," replied his brother, "since it is better the country were placed in peace, at the expense of losing a score or two of Highland kernes, than remain at war till as many thousands are destroyed by sword, fire, famine, and all the extremities of mountain warfare. To return to the purpose; I think that the first party to whom the accommodation is proposed will snatch at it eagerly; that the other will be ashamed to reject an offer to rest the cause on the swords of their bravest men; that the national vanity, and factious hate to each other, will prevent them from seeing our purpose in adopting such a rule of decision; and that they will be more eager to cut each other to pieces than we can be to halloo them on.—And now, as our councils are finished so far as I can aid, I will withdraw."

"Stay yet a moment," said the Prior, "for I also have a grief to disclose, of a nature so black and horrible, that your Grace's pious heart will hardly credit its existence; and I state it mournfully because, as certain as that I am an unworthy servant of St Dominick, it is the cause of the displeasure of Heaven against this poor country; by which our victories are turned into defeat, our gladness into mourning, our councils distracted with disunion, and our country devoured by civil war."

"Speak, reverend Prior," said the King; "assuredly, if the cause of such evils be in me, or in my house, I will take instant care to their removal."

He uttered these words with a faltering voice, and eagerly waited for the Prior's reply, in the dread, no doubt, that it might implicate Rothsay in some new charge of folly or vice. His apprehensions perhaps deceived him when he thought he saw the churchman's eye rest for a moment on the Prince, before he said, in a solemn tone, —"Heresy, my noble and gracious liege, heresy is among us. She snatches soul after soul from the congregation as wolves steal lambs from the sheepfold."

"There are enough of shepherds to watch the fold," answered the Duke of Rothsay. "Here are four convents of regular monks alone, around this poor hamlet of Perth, and all the secular clergy besides. Methinks a town so well garrisoned should be fit to keep out an enemy."

"One traitor in a garrison, my lord," answered the Prior, "can do much to destroy the security of a city which is guarded by legions; and if that one traitor is, either from levity, or love of novelty, or whatever other motive, protected and fostered by those who should be most eager to expel him from the fortress, his opportunities of working mischief will be incalculably increased."

"Your words seem to aim at some one in this presence, Father Prior," said the Douglas; "if at me, they do me foul wrong. I am well aware that the Abbot of Aberbrothick hath made some ill-advised complaints, that I suffered not his beeves to become too many for his pastures, or his stock of grain to burst the girnels of the monastery, while my followers lacked beef, and their horses corn. But bethink you, the pastures and cornfields which produced that plenty were bestowed by my ancestors on the house of Aberbrothick, surely not with the purpose that their descendant should starve in the midst of it; and neither will he, by St Bride! But for heresy and false doctrine," he added, striking his large hand heavily on the council-table, "who is it that dare tax the Douglas? I would not have poor men burned for silly thoughts; but my hand and sword are ever ready to maintain the Christian faith."

"My lord, I doubt it not," said the Prior; "so hath it ever been with your most noble house. For the Abbot's complaints, they may pass to a second day. But what we now desire is a commission to some noble lord of state, joined to others of Holy Church, to support by strength of hand, if necessary, the inquiries which the reverend official of the bounds, and other grave prelates, my unworthy self being one, are about to make into the cause of the new doctrines, which are now deluding the simple, and depraving the pure and precious faith, approved by the Holy Father and his reverend predecessors."

"Let the Earl of Douglas have a royal commission to this effect," said Albany; "and let there be no exception whatever from his jurisdiction, saving the royal person. For my own part, although conscious that I have neither in act nor thought received or encouraged a doctrine which Holy Church hath not sanctioned, yet I should blush to claim an immunity under the blood royal of Scotland, lest I should seem to be seeking refuge against a crime so horrible."

"I will have nought to do with it—" said Douglas; "to march against the English, and the Southron traitor March, is task enough for me. Moreover, I am a true Scotsman, and will not give way to aught that may put the Church of Scotland's head farther into the Roman yoke, or make the baron's coronet stoop to the mitre and cowl. Do thou, therefore, most noble Duke of Albany, place your own name in the commission; and I pray your grace so to mitigate the zeal of the men of Holy Church, who may be associated with you, that there be no over zealous dealings; for the smell of a faggot on the Tay would bring back the Douglas from the walls of York."

The Duke hastened to give the Earl assurance that the commission should be exercised with lenity and moderation.

"Without a question," said King Robert, "the commission must be ample; and did it consist with the dignity of our crown we would not ourselves decline its jurisdiction. But we trust, that while the thunders of the Church are directed against the vile authors of these detestable heresies, there shall be measures of mildness and compassion taken with the unfortunate victims of their delusions."

"Such is ever the course of Holy Church, my lord," said the Prior of St Dominic's.

"Why, then, let the commission be expedited with due care, in name of our brother Albany, and such others as shall be deemed convenient," said the King.—"And now once again let us break up our council; and, Rothsay, come thou with me, and lend me thine arm,—I have matter for thy private ear."

"Ho, la!"—exclaimed the Prince, in the tone in which he would have addressed a managed horse.

"What means this rudeness, boy?" said the King; "wilt thou never learn reason and courtesy?"

"Let me not be thought to offend, my liege," said the Prince; "but we are parting without learning what is to be done in the passing strange adventure of the dead hand, which the Douglas hath so gallantly taken up. We sit but uncomfortably here at Perth, if we are at variance with the citizens."

"Leave that to me," quoth Albany. "With some little grant of lands and money, and plenty of fair words, the burghers may be satisfied for this time; but it were well that the barons and their followers, who are in attendance on the court, were warned to respect the peace within burgh."

"Surely, we would have it so," said the King; "let strict orders be given accordingly."

"It is doing the churls but too much grace," said the Douglas; "but be it at your Highness's pleasure. I take leave to retire."

"Not before you taste a flagon of Gascon wine, my lord," said the King.

"Pardon," replied the Earl, "I am not athirst, and I drink not for fashion, but either for need or for friendship." So saying he departed.

The King, as if relieved by his absence, turned to Albany, and said, "And now, my lord, we should chide this truant Rothsay of ours. Yet he hath served us so well at council too, that we must receive his merits as some atonement for his follies."

"I am happy to hear it," answered Albany, with a countenance of pity and incredulity, as if he knew nothing of the supposed services.

"Nay, brother, you are dull," said the King, "for I will not think you envious. Did you not note that Rothsay was the first to suggest the mode of settling the Highlands, which your experience brought indeed into better shape, and which was generally approved of—and even now we had broken up, leaving a main matter unconsidered, but that he put us in mind of the affray with the citizens?"

"I nothing doubt, my liege," said the Duke of Albany, with the acquiescence which he saw was expected, "that my royal nephew will soon emulate his father's wisdom."

"Or," said the Duke of Rothsay, "I may find it easier to borrow from another member of my family, that happy and comfortable cloak of hypocrisy which covers all vices, and then it signifies little whether they exist or not."

"My Lord Prior," said the Duke, addressing the Dominican, "we will for a moment pray your reverence's absence. The King and I have that to say to the Prince which must have no further audience, not even yours."

The Dominican bowed and withdrew.

When the two royal brothers and the Prince were left together, the King seemed in the highest degree embarrassed and distressed; Albany sullen and thoughtful; while Rothsay himself endeavoured to cover some anxiety under his usual appearance of levity. There was a silence of a minute. At length Albany spoke.

"Royal brother," he said, "my princely nephew entertains with so much suspicion any admonition coming from my mouth, that I must pray your Grace yourself to take the trouble of telling him what it is most fitting he should know."

"It must be some unpleasing communication indeed, which my Lord of Albany cannot wrap up in honied words," said the Prince.

"Peace with thine effrontery, boy," answered the King, passionately. "You asked but now of the quarrel with the citizens— Who caused that quarrel, David?—what men were those who scaled the window of a peaceful citizen and liegeman, alarmed the night with torch and outcry, and subjected our subjects to danger and affright?"

"More fear than danger, I fancy," answered the Prince; "but how can I tell the men who made this nocturnal disturbance?"

"There was a follower of thine own there," continued the King; "a man of Belial, whom I will have brought to condign punishment."

"I have no follower, to my knowledge, capable of deserving your Highness's displeasure," answered the Prince.

"I will have no evasions, boy—Where wert thou on St Valentine's Eve?"

"It is to be hoped that I was serving the good Saint, as a man of mould might," answered the young man carelessly.

"Will my royal nephew tell us how his Master of the Horse was employed upon that holy Eve?" said the Duke of Albany.

"Speak, David—I command thee to speak," said the King.

"Ramorny was employed in my service—I think that answer may satisfy my uncle."

"But it will not satisfy *me*," said the angry father. "God knows, I never coveted man's blood, but that Ramorny's head I will have, if law can give it. He has been the encourager and partaker of all thy numerous vices and follies. I will take care he shall be so no more.—Call MacLouis, with a guard!"

"Do not injure an innocent man," interposed the Prince, desirous at every sacrifice to preserve his favourite from the menaced danger, —"I pledge my word that Ramorny was employed in business of mine, therefore could not be engaged in this brawl."

"False equivocator that thou art!" said the King, presenting to the Prince a ring, "behold the signet of Ramorny, lost in the infamous affray! It fell into the hands of a follower of the Douglas, and was given by the Earl to my brother. Speak not for Ramorny, for he dies; and go thou from my presence, and repent the flagitious councils which could make thee stand before me with a falsehood in thy mouth.—Oh, shame, David, shame! as a son, thou hast lied to thy father; as a knight, to the head of thy order."

The Prince stood before his father mute, conscience-struck, and self-convicted. He then gave way to the honourable feelings which at bottom he really possessed, and threw himself at his father's feet.

"The false knight," he said, "deserves degradation, the disloyal subject death; but, oh! let the son crave from the father pardon for the servant who did not lead him into guilt, but who reluctantly plunged himself into it at his command! Let me bear the weight of my own folly, but spare those who have been my tools rather than my accomplices. Remember, Ramorny was preferred to my service by my sainted mother."

"Name her not, David, I charge thee!" said the King; "she is happy that she never saw the child of her love stand before her doubly dishonoured, by guilt and by falsehood."

"I am indeed unworthy to name her," said the Prince; "and yet, my dear father, in her name I must petition for Ramorny's life."

"If I might offer my counsel," said the Duke of Albany, who saw that a reconciliation would soon take place betwixt the father and son,

"I would advise that Ramorny be dismissed from the Prince's household and society, with such further penalty as his imprudence may seem to merit. The public will be contented with his disgrace, and the matter will be easily accommodated or stifled, so that his Highness do not attempt to screen his servant."

"Wilt thou, for my sake, David," said the King, with a faltering voice, and the tear in his eye, "dismiss this dangerous man? for my sake, who could not refuse thee the heart out of my bosom?"

"It shall be done, my father—done instantly," the Prince replied; and seizing the pen, he wrote a hasty dismissal of Ramorny from his service, and put it into Albany's hands. "I would I could fulfil all your wishes as easily, my royal father," he added, throwing himself at the King's feet, who raised him up, and fondly folded him in his arms.

Albany scowled, but was silent; and it was not till after the space of a minute or two that he said, "This matter being so happily accommodated, let me ask if your Majesty is pleased to attend the Even-song service in the chapel?"

"Surely," said the King. "Have I not thanks to pay to God, who has restored union to my family? You will go with us, brother?"

"So please your Grace to give me leave of absence—No," said the Duke. "I must concert with the Douglas, and others, the manner in which we may bring these Highland vultures to our lure."

Albany retired to think over his ambitious projects, while the father and son attended divine service to thank God for their happy reconciliation.

Chapter Two

A FORMER CHAPTER opened in the royal confessional; we are now to introduce our readers to a situation somewhat similar, though the scene and persons were very different. Instead of a Gothic and darkened apartment in a monastery, one of the most beautiful prospects in Scotland lay extended beneath the hill of Kinnoul, and at the foot of a rock which commanded the view in every direction sat the Fair Maid of Perth, listening in an attitude of devout attention to the instructions of a Carthusian monk, in his white gown and scapular, who concluded his discourse with prayer, in which his proselyte devoutly joined.

When they had finished their devotions, the priest sat for some time with his eyes fixed on the glorious prospect, of which even the early and chilly season could not conceal the beauties, and it was some time ere he addressed his attentive companion.

"When I behold," he said at length, "this rich and varied land, with its castles, churches, convents, stately palaces, and fertile fields, these extensive woods, and that noble river, I know not, my dearest daughter, whether most to admire the bounty of God or the ingratitude of man. He hath given us the beauty and fertility of the earth, and we have made the scene of his bounty a charnel-house and a battle-field. He hath given us power over the elements, and skill to erect houses for comfort and defence, and we have converted them into dens for robbers and ruffians."

"Yet surely, my Father, there is room for comfort," replied Catherine, "even in the very prospect we look upon. Yonder four goodly convents, with their churches, and their towers, which tell the citizens with brazen voice, that they should think on their religious duties—their inhabitants, who have separated themselves from the world, its pursuits and its pleasures, to dedicate themselves to the service of Heaven—all bear witness, that if Scotland be a bloody and a sinful land, she is yet alive and sensible to the duties which religion demands of the human race."

"Surely, daughter, what you say seems truth; and yet, nearly viewed, too much of the comfort you describe will be found delusive. It is true, there was a period in the Christian world when good men, maintaining themselves by the work of their hands, assembled together, not that they might live easily or sleep softly, but that they might strengthen each other in the Christian faith, and qualify themselves to be teachers of the word to the people. Doubtless there are still such to be found in the holy edifices on which we now look. But it is to be feared that the love of many has waxed cold. Our churchmen have become wealthy, as well by the gifts of pious persons as by the bribes which wicked men have given in their ignorance, imagining that they can purchase that pardon for endowments to the Church which Heaven has only offered to sincere penitents. And thus, as the Church waxeth rich, her doctrines have unhappily become dim and obscure, as a light is less seen if placed in a lamp of chased gold, than beheld through a screen of glass. God knows, if I see these things and mark them, it is from no wish of singularity, or desire to make myself a teacher in Israel; but because the fire burns in my bosom, and will not permit me to be silent. I obey the rules of my order, and withdraw not myself from its austerities. Be they essential to our salvation, or be they mere formalities, adopted to supply the want of real penitence and sincere devotion, I have promised, nay vowed, to observe them; and they shall be respected by me the more, that otherwise I might be charged with regarding my bodily ease, when Heaven is my witness how light I value what I may be called on to act or suffer, if the purity of the Church could be restored, or the discipline of the priesthood replaced in its primitive simplicity."

"But, my Father," said Catherine, "even for these opinions men term you a Lollard and a Wickliffite, and say it is your desire to destroy churches and cloisters, and restore the religion of heathenesse."

"Even so, my daughter, am I driven to seek refuge in hills and rocks, and must be presently contented to take my flight amongst the rude Highlanders, who are thus far in a more gracious state than those I leave behind me, since theirs are crimes of ignorance, not of presumption. I will not omit to take such means of safety and escape from their cruelty as Heaven may open to me; for, while such appear, I shall account it a sign that I have still a service to accomplish. But when it is my Master's pleasure, He knows how willingly Clement Blair will lay down a vilified life upon earth, in humble hope of a blessed exchange hereafter.—But wherefore dost thou look northward so anxiously, my child?—thy young eyes are quicker than mine—dost thou see any one coming?"

"I look, Father, for the Highland youth, Conachar, who will be thy guide to the hills, where his father can afford thee a safe, if a rude retreat. This he has often promised, when we spoke of you and of your lessons—I fear he is now in company where he will soon forget them."

"The youth hath sparkles of grace in him," said Father Clement; "although those of his race are usually too much devoted to their own fierce and savage customs to endure with patience either the restraints of religion or those of the social law.—Thou hast never told me, daughter, how, contrary to all the usages either of the burgh or of the mountains, this youth came to reside in thy father's house?"

"All I know touching that matter," said Catherine, "is that his father is a man of consequence among those hill men, and that he desired as a favour of my father, who hath had dealings with them in the way of his merchandize, to keep this youth for a certain time; and that two days since they parted, as he was to return home to his own mountains."

"And why has my daughter," demanded the priest, "maintained such a correspondence with this Highland youth, that she should know how to send for him when she desired to use his services in my behalf? Surely, this is much influence for a maiden to possess over such a wild colt as this youthful mountaineer."

Catherine blushed, and answered with hesitation, "If I have had any influence with Conachar, Heaven be my witness I have only exerted it to enforce upon his fiery temper compliance with the rules of civil life. It is true, I have long expected that you, my Father, would be obliged to take to flight, and I therefore had agreed with him that he should meet me at this place, as soon as he should receive a message from me with a token, which I yesterday dispatched. The messenger was a light-footed boy of his own clan, whom he used sometimes to send on errands into the Highlands."

"And am I then to understand, daughter, that this youth, so fair to the eye, was nothing more dear to you than as you desired to enlighten his mind and inform his manners?"

"It is so, my Father, and no otherwise," answered Catherine; "and perhaps I did not do well to hold intimacy with him, even for his instruction and improvement. But my discourse never led farther."

"Then have I been mistaken, my daughter; for I thought I had seen in thee of late some change of purpose, and a looking back to this world, of which you were at one time resolved to take leave."

Catherine hung down her head, and blushed more deeply than ever, as she said, "Yourself, Father, were used to remonstrate against my taking the veil."

"Nor do I now approve of it, my child," said the priest. "Marriage is an honourable state, appointed by Heaven as the regular means of continuing the race of man; and I read not in the Scriptures, what human inventions have since affirmed concerning the superior excel-lence of a state of celibacy. But I am jealous of thee, my child, as a father is of his only daughter, lest thou shouldst throw thyself away upon some one unworthy of thee. Thy parent, I know, less nice in thy behalf than I am, countenances the addresses of that fierce and riot-ous reveller, whom they call Henry of the Wynd. He is rich, it may be; but a haunter of idle and debauched company—a common prize-fighter, who has shed human blood like water. Can such a one be a fit mate for Catherine Glover?—And yet report says they are soon to be united."

The Fair Maid of Perth's complexion changed hastily from red to pale, and from pale to red, as she replied, "I think not of him; though it is true some courtesies have passed betwixt us of late, both as he is my father's friend, and as being, according to the custom of the time, my Valentine."

"*Your* Valentine, my child?" said Father Clement. "And can your modesty and prudence have trifled so much with the delicacy of your sex, as to place yourself in such a relation to such a man as this artificer?—Think you that this Valentine, a godly saint and Christian bishop as he is said to have been, ever countenanced a silly and unseemly custom, more likely to have originated in the heathen wor-ship of Flora or Venus, when mortals gave the names of deities to their passions, and studied to excite instead of restraining them?"

"Father," said Catherine, in a tone of more displeasure than she had ever before assumed to the Carthusian, "I know not upon what ground you tax me thus severely for complying with a general practice, authorized by universal custom, and sanctioned by my father's authority. I cannot feel it kind that you put such misconstructions upon me."

"Forgive me, daughter," answered the priest, mildly, "if I have given you offence. But this Henry Smith is a forward, licentious man, to whom you cannot allow any uncommon degree of intimacy and encouragement, without exposing yourself to misconstruction,— unless, indeed, it be your purpose to wed him, and that very shortly."

"Say no more of it, my Father," said Catherine. "You give me more pain than you would desire to do—and I may be provoked to answer otherwise than as becomes me. Perhaps I have already had cause enough to make me repent my compliance with an idle custom. At any rate, believe that Henry Smith is nothing to me; and that even the idle intercourse arising from St Valentine's Day is utterly broken off."

"I am rejoiced to hear it, my daughter," replied the Carthusian; "and must now sound you on another subject, which renders me most anxious on your behalf. You cannot yourself be ignorant of it, although I could wish it were not necessary to speak of a thing so dangerous, even before these surrounding rocks, cliffs, and stones. But it must be said.—Catherine, you have a lover in the highest rank of Scotland's sons of honour?"

"I know it, Father," answered Catherine, composedly. "I would it were not so."

"So would I also," said the priest, "did I see in my daughter only the child of folly, which most young women are at her age, especially if possessed of the fatal gift of beauty. But as thy charms, to speak the language of an idle world, have attached to thee a wooer of such high rank, so I know that thy virtue and wisdom will maintain the influence over the Prince's mind which thy beauty hath acquired."

"Father," replied Catherine, "the Prince is a licentious gallant, whose notice of me tends only to my disgrace and ruin. Can you, who seemed but now afraid that I acted imprudently in entering into an ordinary exchange of courtesies with one of my own rank, speak with patience of the sort of correspondence which the heir of Scotland dares to fix upon me? Know that it is but two nights since he, with a party of his debauched followers, would have carried me by force from my father's house, had I not been rescued by that same rash-spirited Henry Smith,—who, if he be too hasty in venturing on danger on slight occasion, is always ready to venture his life in behalf of innocence, or in resistance of oppression. It is well my part to do him that justice."

"I should know something of that matter," said the monk, "since it was my voice that sent him to your assistance. I had seen the party by your door, and was hastening to Bailie Craigdallie's in order to raise assistance, when I perceived a man's figure coming slowly towards me. Apprehensive it might be one of the ambuscade, I stepped behind the buttresses of the chapel of St John, and seeing from a nearer view that it was Henry Smith, I guessed which way he was bound, and raised my voice in an exhortation, which made him double his speed."

"I am beholden to you, Father," said Catherine; "but all this, and the Duke of Rothsay's own language to me, only show that the Prince is a profligate young man, who will scruple no extremities which may gratify an idle passion, at whatever expense to its object. His emissary, Ramorny, has even had the insolence to tell me, that my father shall suffer for it, if I dare to prefer being the wife of an honest man to becoming the loose paramour of a married prince. So I see no other remedy than to take the veil, or run the risk of my own ruin and my poor father's. Were there no other reason, the terror of these threats from a man so notoriously capable of keeping his word, ought to prevent my becoming the bride of any worthy man, as it would prevent me from unlatching his door to admit murderers.—Oh, good Father! what a lot is mine! and how fatal am I likely to prove to my affectionate parent, and to any one with whom I might ally my unhappy fortunes!"

"Be yet of good cheer, my daughter," said the monk; "there is comfort for thee even in this extremity of apparent distress. Ramorny is a villain, and abuses the ear of his patron. The Prince is unhappily a dissipated and idle youth; but, unless my grey hairs have been strangely imposed on, his character is beginning to alter. He hath been awakened to Ramorny's baseness, and deeply regrets having followed his evil advice. I believe, nay I am well convinced, his passion for you has assumed a nobler and purer character, and that the lessons he has heard from me on the corruptions of the Church and of the times, will, if enforced from your lips, sink more deeply into his heart, and perhaps produce fruits for the world to wonder as well as rejoice at. Old prophecies have said that Rome shall fall by the speech of a woman."

"These are dreams, Father," said Catherine; "the visions of one whose thoughts are too much on better things to admit his thinking justly upon the ordinary affairs of earth. When we have looked long on the sun, everything else can only be seen indistinctly."

"Thou art over hasty, my daughter," said Clement, "and thou shalt be convinced of it. The prospect which I am to open to thee were unfit to be exposed to one of a less firm sense of virtue, or a more ambitious temper. Perhaps it is not fit that, even to you, I should display it. But my confidence is strong in thy wisdom and thy principles. Know, then, that there is much chance that the Church of Rome will dissolve the union which she has herself formed, and release the Duke of Rothsay from his marriage with Marjory Douglas."

Here he paused.

"And if the Church hath power and will to do this," replied the maiden, "what influence can the divorce of the Duke from his wife produce on the fortunes of Catherine Glover?"

She looked at the priest anxiously as she spoke, and he had some apparent difficulty in framing his reply, for he looked on the ground while he answered her.

"What did beauty do for Margaret Logie? Unless our fathers told us falsely, it raised her to share the throne of David Bruce."

"Did she live happy, or die regretted, good Father?" asked Catherine, in the same calm and steady tone.

"She formed her alliance from temporal and perhaps criminal ambition," replied Father Clement; "and she found her reward in vanity and vexation of spirit. But had she wedded with the purpose that the believing wife should convert the unbelieving, or confirm the doubting, husband, what then had been her reward? Love and honour upon earth, and an inheritance in Heaven with Queen Margaret, among those sovereigns who have been the nursing mothers of the Church."

Hitherto Catherine had sat upon a stone beside the priest's feet, and looked up to him as she spoke or listened; but now, as if animated by calm yet settled feelings of disapprobation, she rose up, and extending her hand towards the monk as she spoke, addressed him with a countenance and voice which might have become a cherub, pitying, and even as much as possible sparing, the feelings of the mortal whose errors he is commissioned to rebuke.

"And is it even so?" she said, "and can so much of the wishes, hopes, and prejudices of this vile world affect him who may be called to-morrow to lay down his life for opposing the corruptions of a wicked age and backsliding priesthood? Can it be the severely virtuous Father Clement who advises his child to aim at, or even to think of, the possession of a throne and a bed, which cannot become vacant but by an act of crying injustice to the present possessor? Can it be the wise reformer of the Church who wishes to rest a scheme, in itself so unjust, upon a foundation so precarious? Since when is it, good Father, that the principal libertine has altered his morals so much to be likely to court in honourable fashion the daughter of a Perth artizan? Two days must have wrought this change; for only that space has passed since he was breaking into her father's house at midnight, with worse mischief in his mind than that of a common robber. And think you that if Rothsay's heart could dictate so mean a match, he could achieve such a purpose without endangering both his succession and his life, assailed by the Douglas and March at the same time, for what they must receive as an act of injury and insult to both their houses? Oh! Father Clement, where was your principle, where your prudence, when they suffered you to be bewildered by so strange a dream, and placed the meanest of your disciples in the right thus to reproach you?"

The old man's eyes filled with tears, as Catherine, visibly and painfully affected by what she had said, was at length silent.

"By the mouths of babes and sucklings," he said, "hath He rebuked those who would seem wise in their generation. I thank Heaven that hath taught me better thoughts than my own vanity suggested, through the medium of so kind a monitress.—Yes! Catherine, I must not hereafter wonder or exclaim when I see those whom I have hitherto judged too harshly struggling for temporal power, and holding all the while the language of religious zeal. I thank thee, daughter, for thy salutary admonition, and I thank Heaven that sent it by thy lips rather than those of a sterner reprover."

Catherine had raised her head to reply, and bid the old man, whose humiliation gave her pain, be comforted, when her eyes were arrested by an object close at hand. Among the crags and cliffs which surrounded their place of seclusion, there were two which stood in such close contiguity that they seemed to have been portions of the same rock, which, rended by lightning or by an earthquake, now exhibited a chasm of about four feet in breadth betwixt the masses of stone. Into this chasm an oak tree had thrust itself, in one of the fantastic frolics which vegetation often exhibits in such situations. The tree, stunted and ill-fed, had sent its roots along the face of the rock in all directions to seek for supplies, and they lay like military lines of communication, contorted, twisted, and knotted like the immense snakes of the Indian archipelago. As Catherine's look fell upon the curious complication of knotty branches and twisted roots, she was suddenly sensible that two large eyes were fixed and glaring at her, like those of a wild animal in ambush. She started, and without speaking pointed out the object to her companion, and looking herself with more strict attention could at length trace out the bushy red hair and shaggy beard, which had hitherto been concealed by the drooping branches and contorted roots of the tree.

When he saw himself discovered, the Highlander, for such he proved, stepped forth from his lurking-place, and stalking forward, displayed a colossal person, clothed in a purple, red, and green-checked plaid, under which he wore a jacket of bull's hide. His bow and arrows were at his back, his head was bare, and a large quantity of tangled locks, like the glibbs of the Irish, served to cover the head and supplied all the purposes of a bonnet. His belt bore a sword and dagger, and he had in his hand a Danish pole-axe, more recently called a Lochaber axe. Through the same rude portal advanced, one by one, four men more, of similar size, and dressed and armed in the same manner.

Catherine was too much accustomed to the appearance of the inhabitants of the mountains so near to Perth to permit herself to be alarmed, as another Lowland maiden might have been on the same occasion. She saw with tolerable composure these gigantic forms arrange themselves in a semicircle around and in front of the monk and herself, all bending upon them in silence their large fixed eyes, expressing, as far as she could judge, a wild admiration of her beauty. She inclined her head to them, and uttered imperfectly the usual words of a Highland salutation. The elder and leader of the party returned the greeting, and then again remained silent and motionless. The monk told his beads; and even Catherine began to have strange fears for her personal safety, and anxiety to know whether they were to consider themselves at personal freedom. She resolved to make the experiment, and moved forward as if to descend the hill; but when she attempted to pass the line of Highlanders, they extended their pole-axes betwixt each other, so as effectually to occupy each opening through which she could have passed.

Somewhat disconcerted, yet not dismayed, for she could not conceive that any evil was intended, she sat down upon one of the scattered fragments of rock, and bade the monk, standing by her side, be of good courage.

"If I fear," said Father Clement, "it is not for myself; for whether I be brained with the axes of these wild men, like an ox when, worn out by labour, he is condemned to the slaughter, or whether I am bound with their bow-strings, and delivered over to those who will take my life with more cruel ceremony, it can but little concern me, if they suffer thee, dearest daughter, to escape uninjured."

"We have neither of us," replied the Maiden of Perth, "any cause for apprehending evil; and here comes Conachar to assure us of it."

Yet as she spoke, she almost doubted her own eyes; so altered were the manner and attire of the handsome, stately, and almost splendidly dressed youth, who, springing like a roebuck from a cliff of considerable height, lighted just in front of her. His dress was of the same tartan worn by those who had first made their appearance, but closed at the throat and elbows with a necklace and armlets of gold. The hauberk which he wore over his person was of steel, but so clearly

burnished that it shone like silver. His arms were profusely ornamented, and his bonnet, besides the eagle's feather, marking the
quality of chief, was ornamented with a chain of gold, wrapt several
times around it, and secured by a large clasp adorned with pearls. His
brooch, by which the tartan mantle, or plaid, as it is now called, was
secured on the shoulder, was also of gold, large and curiously carved.
He bore no weapon in his hand, excepting a small sapling stick with a
hooked head. His whole appearance and gait, which used formerly to
denote a sullen feeling of conscious degradation, was now bold, forward, and haughty; and he stood before Catherine with smiling confidence, as if fully conscious of his improved appearance, and waiting
till she should recognise him.

"Conachar," said Catherine, desirous to break this state of sus-
pense, "are these your father's men?"

"No, fair Catherine," answered the young man. "Conachar is no
more, unless in regard to the wrongs he has sustained, and the
vengeance which they demand. I am Ian Eachin MacIan, son to the
Chief of the Clan Quhele. I have moulted my feathers, as you see,
when I changed my name. And for these men, they are not my
father's followers, but mine. You see only one half of them collected;
they form a band consisting of my foster father and eight sons, who
are my body-guard, and the children of my belt, who breathe but to
do my will. But Conachar," he added, in a softer tone of voice,
"lives again so soon as Catherine desires to see him; and while he
is the young Chief of the Clan Quhele to all others, he is to her as
humble and obedient as when he was Simon Glover's apprentice.
See, here is the stick I had from you when we nutted together in
the sunny braes of Lednoch, when autumn was young in the year
that is gone. I would not part with it, Catherine, for the truncheon
of my tribe."

While Eachin thus spoke, Catherine began to doubt in her own
mind whether she had acted prudently in requesting the assistance of
a bold young man, elated, doubtless, by his sudden elevation from a
state of servitude to one which she was aware gave him extensive
authority over a very lawless body of adherents.

"You do not fear me, fair Catherine?" said the young Chief, taking
her hand. "I suffered my people to appear before me for a few minutes, that I might see how you could endure their presence; and
methinks you regarded them as if you were born to be a chieftain's
wife."

"I have no reason to fear wrong from Highlanders," said Catherine,
firmly; "especially as I thought Conachar was with them. Conachar
has drunk of our cup, and eaten of our bread; and my father has often

had traffic with Highlanders, and never was there wrong or quarrel betwixt him and them."

"No?" replied Hector, for such is the Saxon equivalent for Eachin, "what! never when he took the part of the Gow Chrom, (the bandy-legged Smith,) against Eachin MacIan?—Say nothing to excuse it, and believe it will be your own fault if I ever again allude to it. But you had some command to lay upon me—speak, and you shall be obeyed."

Catherine hastened to reply; for there was something in the young Chief's manner and language, which made her desire to shorten the interview.

"Eachin," she said, "since Conachar is no longer your name, you ought to be sensible that in claiming, as I honestly might, a service from my equal, I little thought that I was addressing a person of such superior power and consequence. You, as well as I, have been obliged to the religious instruction of this good man. He is now in great danger; wicked men have accused him with false charges, and he is desirous to remain in safety and concealment till the storm shall pass away."

"Ha! the good Clerk Clement? Ay, the worthy clerk did much for me, and more than my rugged temper was capable to profit by. I will be glad to see any one in the town of Perth persecute one who hath taken hold of MacIan's mantle!"

"It may not be safe to trust too much to that," said Catherine. "I nothing doubt the power of your tribe, but when the Black Douglas takes up a feud, he is not to be scared by the shaking of a Highland mantle."

The Highlander disguised his displeasure at this speech with a forced laugh.

"The sparrow," he said, "that is next the eye seems larger than the eagle that is perched on Bengoile. You fear the Douglasses most, because they sit next to you. But be it as you will—You will not believe how wide our hills, and vales, and forests extend beyond the dusky barrier of yonder mountains, and you think all the world lies on the banks of the Tay. But this good Clerk shall see hills that could hide him were all the Douglasses on his quest—ay, and he shall see men enough also to make them right glad to get once more southward of the Grampians.—And wherefore should you not go with the good man? I will send a party to bring him in safety from Perth, and we will set up the old trade beyond Loch Tay—only no more cutting out of gloves for me. I will find your father in hides, but I will not cut them, save when they are on the creatures' backs."

"My father will come one day and see your housekeeping, Conachar—I mean Hector.—But times must be quieter, for there is feud between the town's-people and the followers of the noblemen, and there is speech of war about to break out in the Highlands."

"Yes, by Our Lady, Catherine! and were it not for that same Highland war, you should not thus put off your Highland visit, my pretty mistress. But the race of the hills are no longer to be divided into two nations. They will fight like men for the supremacy, and he who gets it will deal with the King of Scotland as an equal, not as a superior. Pray that the victory may fall to MacIan, my pious St Catherine, for thou prayest for one who loves thee dearly."

"I will pray for the right," said Catherine; "or rather, I will pray that there be peace on all sides.—Farewell, kind and excellent Father Clement; believe I shall never forget thy lessons—remember me in thy prayers.—But how wilt thou be able to sustain a journey so toilsome?"

"They shall carry him if need be," said Hector, "if we go far without finding a horse for him. But you, Catherine—it is far from hence to Perth. Let me attend you thither as I was wont."

"If you were as you were wont, I would not refuse your escort. But gold brooches and bracelets are perilous company, where the Liddesdale and Annandale lancers are riding as throng upon the highway as the leaves at Hallowmass; and there is no safe meeting betwixt Highland tartans and steel jackets."

She hazarded this remark, as she somewhat suspected that, in casting his slough, young Eachin had not entirely surmounted the habits which he had acquired in his humbler state, and that, though he might use bold words, he would not be rash enough to brave the odds of numbers, to which a descent into the vicinity of the city would be likely to expose him. It appeared that she judged correctly; for, after a farewell, in which she compounded for the immunity of her lips by permitting him to kiss her hand, she returned towards Perth, and could obtain at times, when she looked back, an occasional glance of the Highlanders, as, winding through the most concealed and impracticable paths, they bent their way towards the North.

She felt in part relieved from her immediate anxiety as the distance increased betwixt her and these men, whose actions were only directed by the will of their chief, and whose chief was a giddy and impetuous boy. She apprehended no insult on her return to Perth from the soldiery of any party whom she might meet; for the rules of chivalry were in those days a surer protection to a maiden of decent appearance than an escort of armed men, whose cognizance might not be acknowledged as friendly by any other party whom they might chance to encounter. But more remote dangers pressed on her apprehension. The pursuit of the licentious Prince was rendered formidable by threats which his unprincipled counsellor, Ramorny, had not shunned to utter against her father, if she persevered in her coyness. These menaces, in such an age, and from such a character, were deep grounds for alarm; nor could she consider the pretensions to her favour which Conachar had scarce repressed during his state of servitude, and now avowed boldly, as less fraught with evil, since there had been repeated incursions of the Highlanders into the very town of Perth, and citizens had, on more occasions than one, been made prisoners, and carried off from their own houses, or died by the claymore in the very streets of their city. She feared, too, her father's importunity in behalf of the Smith, of whose conduct on St Valentine's day unworthy reports had reached her; and whose suit, had he stood clear in her good opinion, she dared not listen to while Ramorny's threats of revenge upon her father rung on her ear. She thought on these various dangers with the deepest apprehension, and an earnest desire to escape from them and herself, by taking refuge in the cloister; but saw no possibility of obtaining her father's consent to the only course from which she expected peace and protection.

In the course of these reflections, we cannot discover that she very distinctly regretted that her perils attended her because she was the *Fair Maid of Perth;* this was one point which marked that she was not yet altogether an angel; and perhaps it was another, that, in despite of Henry Smith's real or supposed delinquencies, a sigh escaped from her bosom when she thought upon St Valentine's dawn.

Chapter Three

WE HAVE SHOWN the secrets of the confessional; those of the sick chamber are not hidden from us. In a darkened apartment, where salves and medicines showed that the leech had been busy in his craft, a tall thin form lay on a bed, arrayed in a night-gown belted around him, with pain on his brow, and a thousand stormy passions agitating his bosom. Everything in the apartment indicated a man of opulence and of expense. Henbane Dwining, the apothecary, who seemed to have the care of the patient, stole with a crafty and cat-like step from one corner of the room to another, busying himself with mixing medicines and preparing dressings. The sick man groaned once or twice, on which the leech, advancing to his bed-side, asked whether these sounds were a token of the pain of his body, or of the distress of his mind.

"Of both, thou poisoning varlet," said Sir John Ramorny; "and of being encumbered with thy accursed company."

"If that is all, I can relieve your knighthood of one of these ills by presently removing myself elsewhere. Thanks to the feuds of this boisterous time, had I twenty hands, instead of these two poor servants of my art, (displaying his skinny palms,) there is enough of employment for them—well requited employment, too, where thanks and crowns contend which shall best pay my services; while you, Sir John, wreak upon your chirurgeon the anger you ought only to bear against the author of your wound."

"Villain, it is beneath me to reply to thee," said the patient; "but every word of thy malignant tongue is a dirk, inflicting wounds which set all the medicines of Arabia at defiance."

"Sir John, I understand you not; but if you give way to these tempestuous fits of rage, it is impossible but fever and inflammation must be the result."

"Why then dost thou speak in a sense to chafe my blood? Why dost thou name the supposition of thy worthless self having more hands than nature gave thee, while I, a knight and gentleman, am mutilated like a cripple?"

"Sir John," replied the chirurgeon, "I am no divine, nor a mainly obstinate believer in things which divines tell us. Yet I may remind you that you have been kindly dealt with; for if the blow which has done you this injury had lighted on your neck, as it was aimed, it would have swept your head from your shoulders instead of amputating a less considerable member."

"I wish it had, Dwining—I wish it had lighted as it was addressed. I should not then have seen a policy, which had spun a web so fine as mine, burst through by the brute force of a drunken churl. I should not have been reserved to see horses which I must not mount—lists which I must no longer enter—splendours which I cannot hope to share—or battles which I must not take part in. I should not, with a man's passions for power and for strife, be set to keep place among the women, despised by them too, as a miserable impotent cripple, unable to aim at obtaining the favour of the sex."

"Supposing all this to be so, I will yet pray of your knighthood to remark," replied Dwining, still busying himself with arranging the dresses of the wounds, "that your eyes, which you must have lost with your head, may, being spared to you, present as rich a prospect of pleasure as either ambition, or victory in the lists or in the field, or the love of woman itself, could have proposed to you."

"My sense is too dull to catch thy meaning, leech," replied Ramorny. "What is this precious spectacle reserved to me in such a shipwreck?"

"The dearest that mankind knows," replied Dwining; and then, in the accent of a lover who utters the name of his beloved mistress, and expresses his passion for her in the very tone of his voice, he added the word "REVENGE!"

The patient had raised himself on his couch to listen with some anxiety for the solution of the physician's enigma. He laid himself down again as he heard it explained, and after a short pause, asked, "In what Christian college learned you this morality, good Master Dwining?"

"In no Christian college," answered his physician; "for though it is privately received in most, it is openly and manfully adopted in none. But I have studied among the sages of Granada, where the fiery-souled Moor lifts high his deadly dagger as it drips with his enemy's blood, and avows the doctrine which the pallid Christian practises though coward-like he dare not name it."

"Thou art then a more high-souled villain than I deemed thee," said Ramorny.

"Let that pass," answered Dwining. "The waters that are the stillest are also the deepest; and the foe is most to be dreaded who never threatens till he strikes. You knights and men-at-arms go straight to your purpose with sword in hand. We who are clerks win our access with a noiseless step and an indirect approach, but attain our object not less surely."

"And I," said the knight, "who have trod to my revenge with a mailed foot, which made all echo around it, must now use such a slipper as thine? Ha!"

"He who lacks strength," said the wily mediciner, "must attain his purpose by skill."

"And tell me sincerely, mediciner, wherefore thou wouldst read me these devil's lessons—why wouldst thou thrust me further on to my vengeance than I may seem to thee ready to go of my own accord? I am old in the ways of the world, man; and I know that such as thou do not drop words in vain, or thrust themselves upon the dangerous confidence of such as I am, save with the prospect of advancing some purpose of their own. What interest hast thou in the road, whether peaceful or bloody, which I may pursue on these occurrents?"

"In plain dealing, Sir Knight, though it is what I seldom use," answered the leech, "my road to revenge is the same with yours."

"With mine, man?" said Ramorny, with a tone of scornful surprise. "I thought it had been high beyond thy reach. Thou aim at the same revenge with Ramorny!"

"Ay, truly," replied Dwining; "for the smithy churl under whose blow you have suffered has often done me despite and injury. He has thwarted me in council, and despised me in action. His brutal and unhesitating bluntness is a living reproach to the subtlety of my natural disposition. I fear him, and I hate him."

"And you hope to find an active coadjutor in me?" said Ramorny, in the same supercilious tone as before. "But know, the artizan fellow is too much below me in degree to be either the object of hatred or of fear to me. Yet he shall not escape. We hate not the reptile that has stung us, though we might shake it off the wound and tread upon it. I know the ruffian of old as a stout man-at-arms, and a pretender, as I have heard, to the favour of the scornful puppet, whose beauties, forsooth, spurred us to our wise and hopeful attempt.—Fiends, that direct this nether world! by what malice have you decided that the hand which has couched a lance against the bosom of a prince should be struck off like a sapling by the blow of a churl, and during the turmoil of a midnight riot!—Well, mediciner, thus far our courses hold together, and I bid thee well believe that I will crush for thee this reptile mechanic. But do not thou think to escape me, when that part of my revenge is done, which will be most easily and speedily accomplished."

"Not, it may be, altogether so easily accomplished," said the apothecary; "for if your knighthood will credit me, there will be found small ease or security in dealing with him. He is the strongest, boldest, and most skilful swordsman in Perth, and all the country around it."

"Fear nothing; he shall be met with had he the strength of Sampson. But then, mark me! Hope not thou to escape my vengeance, unless thou become my passive agent in the scene which is to follow. Mark me, I say once more. I have studied at no Moorish college, and lack some of thy unbounded appetite for revenge, but yet I will have my share of vengeance.—Listen to me, mediciner, while I shall thus far unfold myself; but beware of treachery, for powerful as thy fiend is, thou hast taken lessons from a meaner devil than mine. Hearken—the master whom I have served through vice and virtue, with too much zeal for my own character perhaps, but with unshaken fidelity to him —the very man, to soothe whose frantic folly I have incurred this irreparable loss, is, at the prayer of his doating father, about to sacrifice me, by turning me out of his favour, and leaving me at the mercy of the hypocritical relative, with whom he seeks a precarious reconciliation at my expense. If he perseveres in this most ungrateful purpose, thy fiercest Moors, were their complexion swarthy as the smoke of hell, shall blush to see their revenge outdone! But I will give him one chance more for honour and safety, before my wrath shall descend on him in unrelenting and unmitigated fury.—There then, thus far thou hast my confidence—Close hands on our bargain—close hands, did I say?—where is the hand that should be the pledge and representative

of Ramorny's plighted word?—is it nailed on the public pillory, or
flung as offal to the houseless dogs, who are even now snarling over it?
Lay thy finger on the mutilated stump then, and swear to be a faithful
actor in my revenge, as I shall be in yours.—How now, Sir Leech, look
you pale—you, who say to Death, Stand back or advance, can you
tremble to think of him or to hear him named? I have not mentioned
your fee, for one who loves revenge for itself requires no deeper bribe
—yet, if broad lands and large sums of gold can increase thy zeal in a
brave cause, believe me, these shall not be lacking."

"They tell for something in my humble wishes," said Dwining; "the
poor man in this bustling world is thrust down like a dwarf in a crowd,
and so trodden under foot—the rich and powerful rise like giants
above the press, and are at ease while all is turmoil around them."

"Then shalt thou arise above the press, mediciner, as high as gold
can raise thee. This purse is weighty, yet it is but an earnest of thy
guerdon."

"And this Smith? my noble benefactor—" said the leech, as he
pouched the gratuity—"This Henry of the Wynd or whatever is his
name—would not the news that he hath paid the penalty of his action
assuage the pain of thy knighthood's wound better than the balm of
Mecca with which I have salved it?"

"He is beneath the thoughts of Ramorny; and I have no more
resentment against him than I have ill-will at the senseless weapon
which he swayed. But it is just thy hate should be vented upon him.
Where is he chiefly to be met with?"

"That also I have considered," said Dwining. "To make the
attempt by day in his own house were too open and dangerous, for he
hath five servants who work with him at the stithy, four of them strong
knaves, and all loving to their master. By night were scarce less desperate, for he hath his doors strongly fastened with bolt of oak and bar
of iron, and ere the fastenings of his house could be forced the neighbourhood would rise to his rescue, especially as they are still alarmed
by the practice on St Valentine's Even."

"O ay, true, mediciner," said Ramorny, "for deceit is thy nature,
even with me—thou knewest my hand and signet, as thou said'st,
when my hand was found cast out on the street like the disgusting
refuse of a shambles,—why, having such knowledge, went'st thou
with these jolter-headed citizens to consult that Patrick Charteris,
whose spurs should be hacked off from his heels for the communion
which he holds with paltry burghers, and whom thou brought'st here
with the fools to do dishonour to the lifeless hand, which, had it held
its wonted place, he was not worthy to have touched in peace or faced
in war!"

"My noble patron, as soon as I had reason to know you had been the sufferer, I urged them with all my powers of persuasion to desist from prosecuting the feud, but the swaggering Smith, and one or two other hot heads, cried out for vengeance. Your knighthood must know this fellow calls himself bachelor to the Fair Maiden of Perth, and stands upon his honour to follow up her father's quarrel; but I have forestalled his market in that quarter, and that is something in earnest of revenge."

"How mean you by that, Sir Pottercarrier?" said the patient.

"Your knighthood shall conceive," said the mediciner, "that this Smith doth not live within compass, but is an outlier and a galliard. I met him myself on St Valentine's day, shortly after the affray between the townsfolks and the followers of Douglas. Yes, I met him sneaking through the lanes and by-passages with a common minstrel wench, with her messan and her viol on his one arm, and her buxom self hanging upon the other. What thinks your honour? Is not this a trim squire, to cross a prince's love with the fairest girl in Perth, strike off the hand of a knight and baron, and become gentleman-usher to a strolling glee-woman, all in the course of the same four-and-twenty hours?"

"Marry, I think the better of him that he is so much of a gentleman's humour, clown though he be," said Ramorny. "I would he had been a precisian instead of a galliard, and I would have had better heart to aid thy revenge;—and such revenge! revenge on a smith in the quarrel of a pitiful manufacturer of rotten cheverons!—And yet it shall be taken in full. Thou hast commenced it, I warrant me, by thine own manœuvres."

"In a small degree only," said the apothecary. "I took care that two or three of the most notorious gossips in Curfew Street, who liked not to hear Catherine called the Fair Maid of Perth, should be possessed of this story of her faithful Valentine. They opened on the scent so keenly that, rather than doubt had fallen on the tale, they would have vouched for it as if their own eyes had seen it. The lover came to her father's within an hour after, and your worship may think what a reception he had from the angry Glover, for the damsel herself would not be looked upon. And thus your honour sees I had a foretaste of revenge. But I trust to receive the full draught from the hands of your lordship, with whom I am in a brotherly"——

"Brotherly!" said the Knight, contemptuously. "But be it so, the priests say we are all of one common earth. I cannot tell—there seems to me some difference; but the better mould shall keep faith with the baser, and thou shalt have thy revenge. Call thou my page hither."

A young man made his appearance from the anteroom upon the physician's summons.

"Eviot," said the knight, "does Bonthron wait? and is he sober?"

"He is as sober as sleep can make him after a deep drink," answered the page.

"Then fetch him hither, and do thou shut the door."

A heavy step presently approached the apartment, and a man entered whose deficiency of height seemed made up in breadth of shoulders and strength of arm.

"There is a man thou must deal upon, Bonthron," said the knight.

The man smoothed his rugged features, and grinned a smile of satisfaction.

"That mediciner will show thee the party. Take such advantage of time, place, and circumstance as will ensure the result; and mind you come not by the worst, for the man is the fighting Smith of the Wynd."

"It will be a tough job," growled the assassin; "for if I miss my blow, I may esteem myself but a dead man. All Perth rings with the Smith's skill and strength."

"Take two assistants with thee," said the knight.

"Not I," said Bonthron. "If you double anything, let it be the reward."

"Account it doubled," said his master; "but see thy work be thoroughly executed."

"Trust me for that, Sir Knight—seldom have I failed."

"Use this sage man's directions," said the wounded man, pointing to the physician. "And hark thee—await his coming forth—and drink not till the business be done."

"I will not," answered the dark satellite; "my own life depends on my blow being steady and sure—I know whom I have to deal with."

"Vanish, then, till he summons you—and have axe and dagger in readiness."

Bonthron nodded and withdrew.

"Will your knighthood venture to intrust such an act to a single hand?" said the mediciner, when the assassin had left the room. "May I pray you to remember that yonder man did, two nights since, baffle six armed men?"

"Question me not, Sir Mediciner; a man like Bonthron, who knows time and place, is worth a score of confused revellers.—Call Eviot—thou shalt first exert thy powers of healing, and do not doubt that thou shalt, in the farther work, be aided by one who will match thee in the art of sudden and unexpected destruction."

The page Eviot again appeared at the mediciner's summons, and at his master's sign assisted the chirurgeon in removing the dressings from Sir John Ramorny's wounded arm. Dwining viewed the naked stump with a species of professional satisfaction, enhanced, no doubt, by the malignant pleasure which his evil disposition took in the pain and distress of his fellow-creatures. The knight just turned his eye on the ghastly spectacle, and uttered, under the pressure of bodily pain or mental agony, a groan which he would fain have repressed.

"You groan, sir," said the leech, in his soft insinuated tone of voice, but with a sneer of enjoyment, mixed with scorn, curling upon his lip, which his habitual dissimulation could not altogether disguise—"You groan—but be comforted. This Henry Smith knows his business— his sword is as true to its aim as his hammer to the anvil. Had a common swordman struck this fatal blow, he had harmed the bone and damaged the muscles, so that even my art might not have been able to repair them. But Henry Smith's cut is clean, and as sure as that with which my own scalpel could have made the amputation. In a few days you will be able, with care and attention to the ordinance of medicine, to stir abroad."

"But my hand—the loss of my hand—"

"It may be kept secret for a time," said the mediciner; "I have possessed two or three tattling fools, in deep confidence, that the hand which was found was that of your knighthood's groom, Black Quentin, and your knighthood knows that he is parted for Fife, in such sort as to make it generally believed."

"I know well enough," said Ramorny, "that the rumour may stifle the truth for a short time. But what avails this brief delay?"

"It may be concealed till your knighthood retires for a time from the court, and then, when new accidents have darkened the recollection of the present stir, it may be imputed to a wound received from the shivering of a spear, or from a cross-bow bolt. Your slave will find a suitable device, and stand for the truth of it."

"The thought maddens me," said Ramorny, with another groan of mental and bodily agony. "Yet I see no better remedy."

"There is none other," said the leech, to whose evil nature his patron's distress was delicious nourishment. "In the meanwhile it is believed you are confined by the consequences of some bruises, aiding the sense of displeasure at the Prince's having consented to dismiss you from his household, at the remonstrance of Albany; which is publicly known."

"Villain, thou rackest me," said the patient.

"Upon the whole, therefore," said Dwining, "your knighthood has escaped well, and saving the lack of your hand, a mischance beyond remedy, you ought rather to rejoice than to complain; for no barber-chirurgeon in France or England could have more ably performed the operation than this churl with one downright blow."

"I understand my obligation fully," said Ramorny, struggling with his anger, and affecting composure; "and if Bonthron pays him not with a blow equally downright, and rendering the aid of the leech unnecessary, say that John of Ramorny cannot requite an obligation."

"That is said like yourself, noble knight," answered the mediciner. "And let me further say that the operator's skill must have been vain, and the hæmorrhage must have drained your life-veins, but for the bandages, the cautery, and the styptics, applied by the good monks, and the poor services of your humble vassal, Henbane Dwining."

"Peace," exclaimed the patient, "with thy ill-omened voice, and worse-omened name!—Methinks, as thou mentionest the tortures I have undergone, my tingling nerves stretch and contract themselves as if they still actuated the fingers that could clutch a dagger."

"That," explained the leech, "may it please your knighthood, is a phenomenon well known to our profession. There have been those among the ancient sages who have thought that there still remained a sympathy between the severed nerves, and those belonging to the amputated limb; and that the severed fingers are seen to quiver and strain, as corresponding with the impulse which proceeds from their sympathy with the energies of the living system. Could we recover the hand from the Cross, or from the custody of the Black Douglas, I would be pleased to observe this wonderful operation of occult sympathies. But I fear me, one might as safely go to wrest the joint from the talons of an hungry eagle."

"And thou may'st as safely break thy malignant jests on a wounded lion as on John of Ramorny!" said the knight, raising himself in uncontrollable indignation. "Caitiff, proceed to thy duty; and remember that if my hand can no longer clasp a dagger, I can command an hundred."

"The sight of one drawn and brandished in anger were sufficient," said Dwining, "to consume the vital powers of your chirurgeon. But who then," he added, in a tone partly insinuating, partly jeering, "who then would relieve the fiery and scorching pain which my patron now suffers, and which renders him exasperated even with his poor servant for quoting the rules of healing, so contemptible, doubtless, compared with the power of inflicting wounds?"

Then, as daring no longer to trifle with the mood of his dangerous patient, the leech addressed himself seriously to salving the wound, and applied a fragrant balm, the odour of which was diffused through the apartment, while it communicated a refreshing coolness instead of the burning heat; a change so gratifying to the fevered patient that, as he had before groaned with agony, he could not now help sighing for pleasure, as he sunk back on his couch to enjoy the ease which the dressing bestowed.

"Your knightly lordship now knows who is your friend," said Dwining; "had you yielded to a rash impulse, and said, 'Slay me this worthless quack salver,' where, within the four seas of Britain, would you have found the man to have ministered to you as much comfort?"

"Forget my threats, good leech," said Ramorny, "and beware how you tempt me. Such as I brook not jests upon our agony. See thou keep thy scoffs to pass upon misers* in the hospital."

Dwining ventured to say no more, but poured some drops from a phial which he took from his pocket, into a small cup of wine allayed with water.

"This draught," said the man of art, "is medicated to produce a sleep which must not be interrupted."

"For how long will it last?" asked the knight.

"The period of its operation is uncertain—perhaps till morning."

"Perhaps for ever," said the patient. "Sir Mediciner, taste me that liquor presently, else it passes not my lips."

The leech obeyed him with a scornful smile. "I will drink the whole with readiness; but the juice of this Indian gum will bring sleep in the healthy man as well as upon the patient, and the business of the leech requires me to be a watcher."

"I crave your pardon, Sir Leech," said Ramorny, looking downwards, as if ashamed to have manifested suspicion.

"There is no room for pardon where offence must not be taken," answered the mediciner. "An insect must thank a giant that he does not tread on him—yet, noble knight, insects have their power of harming as well as physicians. What would it have cost me, save a moment's trouble, so to have drugged that balm as should have made your arm rot to the shoulder-joint, and your life-blood curdle in your veins to a corrupted jelly? What is there that prevented me to use means yet more subtle, and to taint your room with essences before which the light of life twinkles more and more dimly till it expires, like a torch amidst the foul vapours of some subterranean dungeon? You little estimate my power if you know not that these, and yet deeper modes of destruction, stand at command of my art. But a physician slays not the patient by whose generosity he lives, and far less will he, the breath of whose nostrils is the hope of revenge, destroy the vowed ally who is to favour his pursuit of it.—Yet one word;—should a necessity occur for rousing yourself,—for who in Scotland can promise himself eight hours uninterrupted repose?—then smell at the

---

*That is, miserable persons, as used in Spenser, and other writers of his time; though the sense is now restricted to those who are covetous.

strong essence contained in this pouncet-box.—And now, farewell, Sir Knight; and if you cannot think of me as a man of nice conscience acknowledge me at least as one of reason and of judgment."

So saying the mediciner left the room, his usual mean and shuffling gait elevating itself into something more noble, as conscious of a victory over his imperious patient.

Sir John Ramorny remained sunk in unpleasing reflections, until he began to experience the incipient effects of the soporific draught. He then roused himself for an instant, and summoned his page.

"Eviot! what ho! Eviot!—I have done ill to unbosom myself so far to this poisonous quack salver—Eviot!"

The page entered.

"Is the mediciner gone forth?"

"Yes, so please your knighthood."

"Alone, or accompanied?"

"Bonthron spoke apart with him, and followed him almost immediately—by your lordship's commands, as I understood him."

"Lack-a-day, yes!—he goes to seek some medicaments—he will return anon. If he be intoxicated see he come not near my chamber, and permit him not to enter into converse with any one. He raves when drink has touched his brain. He was a rare fellow before a Southron bill laid his brain-pan bare; but since that time he talks gibberish whenever the cup crosses his lips.—Said the leech aught to you, Eviot?"

"Nothing, save to reiterate his commands that your honour be not disturbed."

"Which thou must surely obey," said the knight. "I feel the summons to rest, of which I have been deprived since this unhappy wound —At least, if I have slept it has been but for a snatch. Aid me to take off my gown, Eviot."

"May God and the saints send you good rest, my lord," said the page, retiring after he had rendered his wounded master the assistance required.

As Eviot left the room, the knight, whose brain was becoming more and more confused, muttered over the page's departing salutation.

"God—saints—I *have* slept sound under such a benison. But now —methinks if I awake not to the accomplishment of my proud hopes of power and revenge, the best wish for me is that the slumbers which now fall around my head were the forerunners of that sleep which shall return my borrowed powers—to their original non-existence—I can argue it no farther."

Thus speaking, he fell into a profound sleep.

Chapter Four

THE NIGHT which sunk down on the sick-bed of Ramorny was not doomed to be a quiet one. Two hours had passed since curfew-bell, then rung at seven o'clock at night, and in those primitive times all were retired to rest, excepting such whom devotion, or duty, or debauchery made watchers; and the evening being that of Shrovetide, or, as it was called in Scotland, Fastern's E'en, the vigils of gaiety were by far the most frequented of the three.

The common people had, throughout the day, toiled and struggled at foot-ball; the nobles and gentry had fought cocks, and hearkened to the wanton music of the minstrel; the citizens had gorged themselves upon pancakes fried in lard, and brose, or brewis, that is the fat broth, in which salted beef had been boiled, poured upon highly-toasted oatmeal, a dish which even now is not ungrateful to simple old-fashioned Scottish palates. These were all exercises and festive dishes proper to the holiday. It was no less a solemnity of the evening that the devout Catholic should drink as much good ale and wine as he had means to procure; and, if young and able, that he should dance at the ring, or figure among the morrice-dancers, who, in the city of Perth as elsewhere, wore a peculiarly fantastic garb, and distinguished themselves by their address and activity. All this gaiety took place under the prudential consideration, that the long term of Lent, now approaching, with its fasts and deprivations, rendered it wise for mortals to cram as much idle and sensual indulgence as they could into the brief space which intervened before its commencement.

The usual revels had taken place, and in most parts of the city were succeeded by the usual pause. A particular degree of care had been taken by the nobility to prevent any renewal of discord betwixt their followers and the citizens of the town; so that the revels had proceeded with fewer casualties than usual, embracing only three deaths and certain fractured limbs, which, occurring to individuals of little note, were not accounted worth inquiring into. The Carnival was closing quietly in general, but in some places the sport was still kept up.

One company of revellers, who had been particularly noticed and applauded, seemed unwilling to conclude their frolic. The Entry, as it was called, consisted of thirteen persons habited in the same manner, having doublets of chamois leather sitting close to their bodies, curiously slashed and laced. They wore green caps with silver tassels, red ribbands, and white shoes, had bells hung at their knees and around their ankles, and naked swords in their hands. This gallant party, having exhibited a sword-dance before the King, with much clashing of weapons and fantastic interchange of postures, went on gallantly to repeat their exhibition before the door of Simon Glover, where, having made a fresh exhibition of their agility, they caused wine to be served round to their own company and the by-standers, and with a loud shout drank to the health of the Fair Maid of Perth. This summoned old Simon to the door of his habitation to acknowledge the courtesy of his countrymen, and in his turn to send the wine around in honour of the Merry Morrice Dancers of Perth.

"We thank thee, father Simon," said a voice, which strove to drown in an artificial squeak the pert conceited tone of Oliver Proudfute. "But a sight of thy lovely daughter had been more sweet to us young bloods than a whole vintage of Malvoisie."

"I thank you, neighbours, for your good-will," replied the Glover. "My daughter is ill at ease, and may not come forth into the cold night air—but if this gay gallant, whose voice methinks I should know, will go into my poor house, she will charge him with thanks for the rest of you."

"Bring them to us at the hostelrie of the Griffin," cried the rest of the ballet to their favoured companion; "for there will we ring in Lent, and have another rouse to the health of the lovely Catherine."

"Have with you in half an hour," said Oliver, "and see who will quaff the largest flagon or sing the loudest glee. Nay, I will be merry in what remains of Fastern's Even, should Lent find me with my mouth closed for ever."

"Farewell, then," cried his mates in the morrice; "farewell, slashing Bonnet-maker, till we meet again."

The morrice-dancers accordingly set out upon their further cruize, dancing and carolling as they went along to the sound of four musicians, who led the joyous band, while Simon Glover drew their Coryphæus into his house, and placed him in a chair by his parlour fire.

"But where is your daughter?" said Oliver. "She is the bait for us brave blades."

"Why, truly, she keeps her apartment, neighbour Oliver; and, to speak plainly, she keeps her bed."

"Why, then will I up stairs to see her in her sorrow—you have marred my ramble, Gaffer Glover, and owe me amends—a roving blade like me—I will not lose both the lass and the glass.—Keeps her bed, does she?

"My dog and I we have a trick
To visit maids when they are sick;
When they are sick and like to die,
O thither do come my dog and I.

"And when I die, as needs must hap,
Then bury me under the good ale-tap;
With folded arms there let me lie,
Cheek for jowl, my dog and I."

"Canst thou not be serious for a moment, neighbour Proudfute?"
said the Glover; "I want a word of conversation with you."

"Serious?" answered his visitor; "why, I have been serious all this
day—I can hardly open my mouth, but something comes out about
death, a burial, or such-like—the most serious subjects that I wot of."

"St John, man," said the Glover, "art thou fey?"

"No, not a whit—it is not of my own death which these gloomy
fancies foretell—I have a strong horoscope, and shall live for fifty
years to come. But it is the case of the poor fellow—the Douglas-man
whom I struck down at the fray of St Valentine's—he died last night—
it is that which weighs on my conscience and awakens sad fancies. Ah,
father Simon, we martialists that have spilt blood in our choler have
dark thoughts at times—I sometimes wish that my knife had cut
nothing but worsted thrums."

"And I wish," said Simon, "that mine had cut nothing but buck's
leather, for it has sometimes cut my own fingers. But thou mayst spare
thy remorse for this bout; there was but one man dangerously hurt at
the affray, and it was he from whom Henry Smith hewed the hand,
and he is well recovered. His name is Black Quentin, one of Sir John
Ramorny's followers. He has been sent privately back to his own
country of Fife."

"What, Black Quentin?—why, that is the very man. Henry and I, as
we ever keep close together, struck him at the same moment, only my
blow fell somewhat earlier. I fear further feud will come of it, and so
does the Provost.—And is he recovered? Why, then, I will be jovial,
and since thou wilt not let me see how Kate becomes her night-gear, I
will back to the Griffin to my morrice-dancers."

"Nay, stay but one instant. Thou art a comrade of Henry Wynd, and
hast done him the service to own one or two deeds, and this last among
others. I would thou couldst clear him of other charges with which
fame hath loaded him."

"Nay, I will swear by the hilt of my sword they are as false as hell,
father Simon. What!—blades and targets! shall not men of the sword
stick together?"

"Nay, neighbour Bonnet-maker, be patient: thou mayst do the

Smith a kind turn an thou takest this matter the right way. I have chosen thee to consult with anent this matter—not that I hold thee the wisest head in Perth, for should I say so I should lie."

"Ay, ay," answered the self-satisfied Bonnet-maker; "I know where you think my fault lies—you cool heads think we hot heads are fools—I have heard men call Henry Wynd such a score of times."

"Fool enough and cool enough may rhyme together passing well," said the Glover; "but thou art good-natured, and I think lovest this crony of thine. It stands awkwardly with us and him just now," continued Simon. "Thou knowest there hath been some talk of marriage between my daughter Catherine and Henry Gow?"

"I have heard some such song since St Valentine's Morn—Ah! he that hath the Fair Maid of Perth must be a happy man—and yet marriage spoils many a pretty fellow. I myself somewhat regret"——

"Prithee, truce with thy regrets for the present, man," interrupted the Glover, somewhat peevishly. "You must know, Oliver, that some of these talking women, who I think make all the business of the world their own, have accused Henry of keeping light company with glee-women and such-like. Catherine took it to heart; and I hold my child insulted, that he had not waited upon her like a Valentine, but had thrown himself into unseemly society on the very day when, by ancient custom, he might have had an opportunity to press his interest with my daughter.—Therefore when he came hither late on the evening of St Valentine's, I, like a hasty old fool, bid him go home to the company he had left, and denied him admittance. I have not seen him since, and I begin to think that I may have been too hasty in the matter. She is my only child, and the grave should have her sooner than a debauchee. But I have hitherto thought I knew Henry Gow as if he were my son. I cannot think he would use us thus, and it may be there are means of explaining what is laid to his charge. I was led to ask Dwining, who is said to have saluted the Smith while he was walking with this choice mate—If I am to believe his words, this wench was the Smith's cousin, Joan Letham. But thou knowest that the pottercarrier ever speaks one language with his visage, and another with his tongue—Now, thou, Oliver, hast too little wit—I mean, too much honesty—to belie the truth, and as Dwining hinted that thou also hadst seen her"——

"I see her, Simon Glover! Will Dwining say that I saw her?"

"No, not precisely that—but he says you *told* him you had met the Smith thus accompanied."

"He lies, and I will pound him into a gallipot!" said Oliver Proudfute.

"How? Did you never tell him then of such a meeting?"

"What an if I did?" said the Bonnet-maker. "Did not he swear he would never repeat again to living mortal what I communicated to him? and therefore in telling the occurrent to you he hath made himself a liar."

"Thou didst not meet the Smith, then," said Simon, "with such a loose baggage as fame reports?"

"Lack-a-day, not I—perhaps I did, perhaps I did not. Think, father Simon—I have been a three-year married man, and can you expect me to remember the turn of a glee-woman's ankle, the trip of her toe, the lace upon her petticoat and such toys? No, I leave that to unmarried wags like my gossip Henry."

"The upshot is, then," said the Glover, much vexed, "you *did* meet him on St Valentine's day walking the public streets"——

"Not so, neighbour; I met him in the most distant and dark lane in Perth, steering full for his own house with bag and baggage, which, as a gallant fellow, he carried in his arms, the puppy dog on one, and the jilt herself (and to my thought she was a pretty one) hanging upon the other."

"Now, by good St John," said the Glover, "this infamy would make a Christian man renounce his faith, and worship Mahound in very anger! But he has seen the last of my daughter. I would rather she went to the wild Highlands with a bare-legged catheran than wed with one who could, at such a season, so broadly forget honour and decency—Out upon him!"

"Tush! tush! father Simon," said the liberal-minded Bonnet-maker; "you consider not the nature of young blood. Their company was not long, for—to speak truth, I did keep a little watch on him—I met him before sunrise, conducting his errant damsel to the Lady's Stairs, that the wench might embark on the Tay from Perth; and I know for certainty, (for I made inquiry,) that she sailed in a gabbart for Dundee. So you see it was but a slight escape of youth."

"And he came here," said Simon, bitterly, "beseeching for admittance to my daughter, while he had his harlot awaiting him at home! I had rather he had slain a score of men.—It skills not talking, least of all to thee, Oliver Proudfute, who, if thou art not such a one as himself would fain be thought so. But"——

"Nay, think not of it so seriously," said Oliver, who began to reflect on the mischief his tattling was like to occasion to his friend, and on the consequences of Henry Gow's displeasure, when he should learn the disclosure which he had made, rather in vanity of heart than in evil intention. "Consider," he continued, "that there are follies belonging to youth. Occasion provokes men to such frolics, and Confession wipes them off. I care not if I tell thee that though my wife be as goodly a woman as the city has, yet I myself"——

"Peace, silly braggart," said the Glover, in high wrath; "thy loves
and thy battles are alike apocryphal. If thou must needs lie, which I
think is thy nature, canst thou invent no falsehood that may at least do
thee some credit? Do I not see through thee—as I could see the light
through the horn of a base lantern? Do I not know, thou filthy weaver
of rotten worsted, that thou dared no more cross the threshold of thy
own door if thy wife heard of thy making such a boast, than thou darest
cross naked weapons with a boy of twelve years old who has drawn a
sword for the first time in his life? By St John, it were paying you for
your tale-bearing trouble to send thy Maudie word of thy gay brags."

The Bonnet-maker, at this threat, started as if a cross-bow bolt had
whizzed past his head when least expected. And it was with a trembling voice that he replied, "Nay, good father Glover, thou takest too
much credit for thy grey hairs. Consider, good neighbour, thou art too
old for a young martialist to wrangle with. And in the matter of my
Maudie, I can trust thee, for I know no one who would be less willing
than thou to break the peace of families."

"Trust thy coxcomb no longer with me," said the incensed Glover;
"but take thyself, and the thing thou call'st a head, out of my reach, lest
I borrow back five minutes of my youth and break thy pate."

"You have had a merry Fastern's Even, neighbour," said the Bonnet-maker, "and I wish you a quiet sleep; we shall meet better friends
to-morrow."

"Out of my doors to-night!" said the Glover. "I am ashamed so idle
a tongue as thine can have power to move me thus."

"Idiot—beast—loose-tongued coxcomb!" he exclaimed, throwing
himself into a chair, as the Bonnet-maker disappeared; "that a fellow
made up of lies should not have had the grace to frame one when it
might have covered the shame of a friend! And I—what am I that I
should, in my secret mind, wish that such a gross insult to me and my
child had been glossed over? Yet such was my opinion of Henry, that I
should have willingly believed the grossest figment the swaggering ass
could have invented. Well!—it skills not thinking of it. Our honest
name must be maintained though everything else should go to ruin."

While the Glover thus moralized on the unwelcome confirmation
of the tale he wished to think untrue, the expelled morrice-dancer had
leisure, in the composing air of a cool and dark February night, to
meditate on the consequences of the Glover's wrath.

"But it is nothing," he bethought himself, "to the wrath of Henry
Wynd, who hath killed a man for much less than placing displeasure
betwixt him and Catherine, as well as her fiery old father. Certainly I
were better have denied everything. But the humour of seeming a

knowing gallant (as in truth I am) fairly overcame me. Were I best go to finish the revel at the Griffin?—But then Maudie will rampage on my return—But this being holiday even, I may claim a privilege.—I have it—I will not to the Griffin—I will to the Smith's, who must be at home, since no one hath seen him this day amid the revel. I will endeavour to make peace with him, and offer my intercession with the Glover. Harry is a simple downright fellow, and though I think he is my better in a broil, yet in discourse I can turn him my own way. The streets are now quiet—the night, too, is dark, and I may slip aside if I meet any rioters. I will to the Smith's, and, securing him for my friend, I care little for old Simon. Saint Ringan bear me well through this night, and I will clip my tongue out ere it shall run my head into such peril again! Yonder old fellow, when his blood was up, looked more like a carver of buff-jerkins than a clipper of kid-gloves."

With these reflections, the puissant Oliver walked swiftly, yet with as little noise as possible, towards the wynd in which the Smith, as our readers are aware, had his habitation. But his evil fortune had not ceased to pursue him. As he turned into the high, or principal street, he heard a burst of music very near him, followed by a loud shout.

"My merry mates, the morrice-dancers," thought he; "I would know old Jeremy's rebeck among an hundred. I will venture across the street ere they pass on—if I am espied, I shall have the renown of some private quest, which may do me honour as a roving blade."

With these longings for distinction among the gay and gallant, combated, however, internally, by more prudential considerations, the Bonnet-maker made an attempt to cross the street. But the revellers, whoever they might be, were accompanied by torches, the flash of which fell upon Oliver, whose light-coloured habit made him the more distinctly visible. The general shout of "A prize, a prize," overcame the noise of the minstrel, and before the Bonnet-maker could determine whether it were better to stand or fly, two active young men, clad in fantastic masking habits, resembling wild men, and holding great clubs, seized upon him, saying, in a tragical tone, "Yield thee, man of bells and bombast; yield thee, rescue or no rescue, or truly thou art but a dead morrice-dancer."

"To whom shall I yield me?" said the Bonnet-maker, with a faltering voice; for though he saw he had to do with a party of mummers who were a-foot for pleasure, yet he observed, at the same time, that they were far above his class, and he lost the audacity necessary to support his part in a game where the inferior was likely to come by the worst.

"Dost thou parley, slave?" answered one of the masquers; "and must I show thee that thou art a captive, by giving thee incontinently the bastinado?"

"By no means, puissant man of Ind," said the Bonnet-maker; "lo, I am conformable to your pleasure."

"Come, then," said those who had arrested him, "come and do homage to the Emperor of Mimes, King of Caperers, and Grand Duke of the Dark Hours, and explain by what right thou art so presumptuous as to prance and jingle, and wear out shoe-leather within his dominions without paying him tribute. Know'st thou not thou hast incurred the pains of high-treason?"

"That were hard, methinks," said poor Oliver, "since I knew not that his Grace exercised the government this evening. But I am willing to redeem the forfeit, if the purse of a poor Bonnet-maker may, by the mulct of a gallon of wine, or some such matter."

"Bring him before the Emperor," was the universal cry; and the morrice-dancer was placed before a slight, but easy and handsome figure of a young man, splendidly attired, having a cincture and tiara of peacock's feathers, then brought from the East as a marvellous rarity; a short jacket and under-dress of leopard's skin fitted closely the rest of his person, which was attired in flesh-coloured silk so as to resemble the ordinary idea of an Indian prince. He wore sandals, fastened on with ribbands of scarlet silk, and held in his hand a sort of fan, such as ladies then used, composed of the same feathers assembled into a plume or tuft.

"What mister wight have we here," said the Indian chief, "who dares to tie the bells of a morrice on the ankles of a dull ass?—Hark ye, friend, your dress should make you a subject of ours, since our empire extends over all Merryland, including mimes and minstrels of every description.—What, tongue-tied? He lacks wine—minister to him our nut-shell full of sack."

A huge calabash full of sack was offered to the lips of the supplicant, while this prince of revellers exhorted him, "Crack me this nut, and do it handsomely, and without wry faces."

But, however Oliver might have relished a moderate sip of the same good wine, he was terrified at the quantity he was required to deal with. He drank a draught, and then entreated for mercy.

"So please your princedom, I have yet far to go, and if I were to swallow your grace's bounty, for which accept my dutiful thanks, I should not be able to stride over the next kennel."

"Art thou in case to bear thyself like a galliard? Now, cut me a caper —ha! one—two—three—admirable!—again—give him the spur— (here a satellite of the Indian gave Oliver a slight twinge with his sword)—Nay, that is best of all—he sprang like a cat in a gutter!

Tender him the nut once more—nay, no compulsion, he has paid forfeit, and deserves not only free dismissal but reward. Kneel down, kneel, and arise Sir Knight of the Calabash! What is thy name? And one of you lend me a rapier."

"Oliver, may it please your honour—I mean your principality."

"Oliver, man? nay, then thou art one of the Douze peers already, and fate has forestalled our intended promotion. Yet rise up, sweet Sir Oliver Thatchpate, Knight of the honourable order of the Pumpkin— Rise up, in the name of Nonsense, and begone about thine own concerns, in the devil's name."

So saying, the prince of the revels bestowed a smart blow with the flat of the weapon across the Bonnet-maker's shoulders, who sprung to his feet with more alacrity of motion than he had hitherto displayed, and, accelerated by the laugh and halloo which arose behind him, arrived at the Smith's door before he stopped, with the same speed with which a hunted fox makes for his den.

It was not till the affrighted Bonnet-maker had struck a blow on the door, that he recollected he ought to have bethought himself before-hand in what manner he was to present himself before Henry, and obtain his forgiveness for his rash communications to Simon Glover. No one answered to his first knock, and, perhaps, as these reflections arose, in the momentary pause of recollection which circumstances permitted, the perplexed Bonnet-maker might have flinched from his purpose, and made his retreat to his own premises, without venturing upon the interview which he had purposed. But a distant strain of minstrelsy revived his apprehensions of falling once more into the hands of the gay masquers from whom he had escaped, and he renewed his summons on the door of the Smith's dwelling, with a hurried though faltering hand. He was then appalled by the deep, yet not unmusical voice of Henry Gow, who answered from within,— "Who calls at this hour?—and what is it that you want?"

"It is I—Oliver Proudfute," replied the Bonnet-maker; "I have a merry jest to tell you, gossip Henry."

"Carry thy foolery to some other market. I am in no jesting humour," said Henry. "Go hence—I see no one to-night."

"But, gossip—good gossip," answered the martialist without, "I am beset with villains, and beg the shelter of your roof!"

"Fool that thou art!" replied Henry; "no dunghill cock, the most recreant that has fought this Fastern's Even, would ruffle his feathers at such a craven as thee!"

At this moment another strain of minstrelsy, and, as the Bonnet-maker conceited, one which approached much nearer, goaded his apprehensions to the uttermost; and in a voice the tones of which expressed the undisguised extremity of instant fear, he exclaimed, "For the sake of our old gossipred, and for the love of Our blessed Lady, admit me, Henry, if you would not have me found a bloody corpse at thy door, slain by the bloody-minded Douglasses!"

"That would be shame to me," thought the good-natured Smith; "and sooth to say, his peril may be real. There are roving hawks that will strike at a sparrow as soon as a heron."

With these reflections, half-muttered, half-spoken, Henry undid his well-fastened door, proposing to reconnoitre the reality of the danger before he permitted his unwelcome guest to enter the house. But as he looked abroad to ascertain how matters stood, Oliver bolted in like a scared deer into a thicket, and harboured himself by the Smith's kitchen-fire, before Henry could look up and down the lane and satisfy himself there were no enemies in pursuit of the apprehensive fugitive. He secured his door, therefore, and returned into the kitchen, displeased that he had suffered his gloomy solitude to be intruded upon by sympathizing with apprehensions which he thought he might have known were so easily excited as those of his timid townsman.

"How now?" he said, coldly enough, when he saw the Bonnet-maker calmly seated by his hearth. "What foolish revel is this, Master Oliver?—I see no one near to harm you."

"Give me a drink, kind gossip," said Oliver; "I am choked with the haste I have made to come hither."

"I have sworn," said Henry, "that this shall be no revel night in this house. I am in my work-day clothes, as you see, and keep fast, as I have reason, instead of holiday. You have had wassail enough for the holiday evening for you speak thick already—If you wish more ale or wine you must go elsewhere."

"I have had over much wassail already," said poor Oliver, "and have been wellnigh drowned in it.—That accursed calabash!—A cup of water, kind gossip—you will not surely let me ask for that in vain? or, if it is your will, a cup of cold small ale."

"Nay, if that be all," said Henry, "it shall not be lacking. But it must have been much which brought thee to the pass of asking for either."

So saying, he filled a quart flagon from a barrel that stood nigh, and presented it to his guest. Oliver eagerly accepted it, raised it to his head with a trembling hand, imbibed the contents with lips which quivered with emotion, and, though the potation was as thin as he had requested, so much was he exhausted with the combined fears of alarm and of former revelry, that when he placed the flagon on the oak table he uttered a deep sigh of satisfaction, and remained silent.

"Well, now you have had your draught, gossip," said the Smith, "what is it you want? Where are those that threatened you? I could see no one."

"No—but there were twenty chased me into the wynd," said Oliver. "But when they saw us together, you know they lost the courage that brought all of them upon one of us."

"Nay, do not trifle, friend Oliver," replied his host; "my mood lies not that way."

"I jest not, by St John of Perth. I have been stayed and foully outraged (gliding his hand sensitively over the place afflicted) by mad David of Rothsay, roaring Ramorny, and the rest of them. They made me drink a firkin of Malvoisie."

"Thou speakest folly, man—Ramorny is sick nigh to death, as the pottercarrier everywhere reports; they and he cannot surely rise at midnight to do such frolics."

"I cannot tell," replied Oliver; "but I saw the party by torch-light, and I can make bodily oath to the bonnets I made for them since last Innocent's. They are of a quaint device, and I should know my own stitch."

"Well, thou mayst have had wrong," answered Henry. "If thou art in real danger, I will cause them get a bed for thee here. But you must fill it presently, for I am not in the humour of talking."

"Nay, I would thank thee for my quarters for a night, only my Maudie will be angry—that is, not angry, for that I care not for—but the truth is she is over anxious on a revel night like this, knowing my humour is like thine, for a word and a blow."

"Why, then, go home," said the Smith, "and show her that her treasure is in safety, Master Oliver—the streets are quiet—and, to speak a blunt word, I would be alone."

"Nay, but I have things to speak with thee of moment," replied Oliver, who, afraid to stay, seemed yet unwilling to go. "There has been a stir in our city council about the affair of St Valentine's Even. The Provost told me not four hours since, that the Douglas and he had agreed that the feud should be decided by a yeoman on either part, and that our acquaintance, the Devil's Dick, was to waive his gentry, and take up the cause for Douglas and the nobles, and that you or I should fight for the Fair City. Now, though I am the elder burgess, yet I am willing, for the love and kindness we have always borne to each other, to give thee the precedence, and content myself with the humbler office of stickler."*

Henry Smith, though angry, could scarce forbear a smile.

"If it is that which breaks thy quiet, and keeps thee out of thy bed at

---

*The seconds in ancient single combats were so called from the white sticks which they carried in emblem of their duty to see fair play between the combatants.

midnight, I will make the matter easy. Thou shalt not lose the advantage offered thee. I have fought a score of duels—far, far too many.
Thou hast, I think, only encountered with thy wooden Soldan—it
were unjust—unfair—unkind—in me to abuse thy friendly offer. So
go home, good fellow, and let not the fear of losing honour disturb thy
slumbers. Rest assured that thou shalt answer the challenge, as good
right thou hast, having had injury from this rough-rider."

"Gramercy, and thank thee kindly," said Oliver, much embarrassed
by his friend's unexpected deference; "thou art the good friend I have
always thought thee. But I have as much friendship for Henry Smith,
as he for Oliver Proudfute. I swear by St John, I will not fight in this
quarrel to thy prejudice. So, having said so, I am beyond the reach of
temptation, since thou wouldst not have me mansworn, though it were
to fight twenty duels."

"Hark thee," said the Smith, "acknowledge thou art afraid, Oliver;
tell the honest truth at once, otherwise I leave thee to make the best of
the quarrel."

"Nay, good gossip," replied the Bonnet-maker, "thou knowest I am
never afraid—But, in sooth, this is a desperate ruffian—and as I have
a wife—poor Maudie, thou knowest—and a small family—And
thou"——

"And I," interrupted Henry hastily, "have none, and never will
have."

"Why, truly—such being the case—I would rather thou fought'st
this combat than I."

"Now, by our holidame, gossip," answered the Smith, "thou art
easily gulled. Know, thou silly fellow, that Sir Patrick Charteris, who
is ever a merry man, hath but jested with thee. Dost thou think he
would venture the honour of the city on thy head? or that I would yield
thee the precedence in which such a matter was to be disputed? Lack-
a-day, go home, let Maudie tie a warm nightcap on thy head; get thee
a warm breakfast and a cup of distilled waters, and thou wilt be in case
to-morrow to fight thy wooden dromond, or Soldan as thou call'st
him, the only thing thou wilt ever lay downright blow upon."

"Ay, say'st thou so, comrade?" answered Oliver, much relieved, yet
deeming it necessary to seem in part offended. "I care not for thy
dogged humour; it is well for thee thou canst not wake my patience to
the point of falling foul. Enough—we are gossips, and this house is
thine. Why should the two best blades in Perth clash with each other?
What! I know thy rugged humour and can forgive it.—But is the feud
really soldered up?"

"As completely as ever hammer fixed rivet," said the Smith. "The
town hath given the Johnston a purse of gold for not ridding them of a

troublesome fellow called Oliver Proudfute, when he had him at his mercy; and this purse of gold buys for the Provost the Sleepless Isle, which the King grants him, for the King pays all in the long run. And thus Sir Patrick gets the comely Inch, which is opposite to his dwelling, and all honour is saved on both sides, for what is given to the Provost is given, you understand, to the town. Besides all this, the Douglas has left Perth to march against the Southron, whom men say are called into the Marches by the false Earl of March. So the Fair City is quit of him and his cumber."

"But, in St John's name, how came all that about?" said Oliver; "and no one spoken to about it?"

"Why, look thee, friend Oliver, this I take to have been the case. The fellow whom I cropped of a hand, is now said to have been a servant of Sir John Ramorny's, who hath fled to his motherland of Fife, to which Sir John himself is also to be banished, with full consent of every honest man. Now, anything which brings in Sir John Ramorny, touches a much greater man—I think Simon Glover told as much to Sir Patrick Charteris. If it be as I guess, I have reason to thank Heaven, and all the saints, I stabbed not him upon the ladder when I made him prisoner."

"And I too thank Heaven, and all saints, most devoutly," said Oliver. "I was behind thee, thou knowest, and"——

"No more of that, if thou be'st wise—There are laws against striking princes," said the Smith; "best not handle the horse-shoe till it cools. All is hushed up now."

"If this be so," said Oliver, partly disconcerted, but still more relieved, by the intelligence he received from his better informed friend, "I have reason to complain of Sir Patrick Charteris for jesting with the honour of an honest burgess, being as he is, Provost of our town."

"Do, Oliver; challenge him to the field, and he will bid his yeoman loose his dogs on thee.—But come, night wears apace, will you be shogging?"

"Nay, I had one word more to say to thee, good gossip. But first, another cup of your cold ale."

"Pest on thee, for a fool! Thou makest me wish thee where cold liquors are a scarce commodity.—There, swill the barrelful an thou wilt."

Oliver took the second flagon, but drank, or rather seemed to drink, very slowly, in order to gain time for considering how he should introduce his second subject of conversation, which seemed rather delicate for the Smith's present state of irritability. At length, nothing better occurred to him than to plunge into the subject at once, with, "I have seen Simon Glover to-day, gossip."

"Well," said the Smith, in a low, deep, and stern tone of voice—
"And what is that to me?"

"Nothing—nothing," answered the appalled Bonnet-maker. "Only
I thought you might like to know that he questioned me close if I had
seen thee on St Valentine's day, after the uproar at the Dominicans',
and in what company thou wert."

"And I warrant thou told'st him thou met'st me with a glee-woman
in the mirk loaning yonder?"

"Thou know'st, Henry, I have no gift at lying; but I made it all up
with him."

"As how, I pray you?" said the Smith.

"Marry, thus—father Simon, said I, you are an old man, and know
not the quality of us in whose veins youth is like quicksilver. You think
now he cares about this girl, said I, and, perhaps, that he has her
somewhere here in Perth in a corner? No such matter; I know, said I,
and I will make oath to it, that she left his house early next morning for
Dundee. Ha! have I helped thee at need?"

"Truly, I think thou hast, and if anything could add to my grief and
vexation at this moment, it is, that when I am so deep in the mire an ass
like thee should place his clumsy hoof on my head to sink me entirely.
Come, away with thee, and mayst thou have such luck as thy meddling
humour deserves, and then, I think, thou wilt be found with a broken
neck in the next gutter—Come you—out, or I will put you to the door
with head and shoulders forward."

"Ha, ha!" exclaimed Oliver, laughing with some constraint; "thou
art such a groom! But in sadness, gossip Henry, wilt thou not take a
turn with me as far as my own house in the Meal Vennal?"

"Curse thee, no," answered the Smith.

"I will bestow the wine on thee, if thou wilt go," said Oliver.

"I will bestow the cudgel on thee, if thou stay'st," said Henry.

"Nay, then, I will don thy buff-coat and cap of steel, and walk with
thy swashing step, and whistling thy pibroch of 'Broken Bones at
Loncarty;' and if they take me for thee, there dare not four of them
come near me."

"Take all, or anything thou wilt, in the fiend's name! only be gone."

"Well, well, Hal, we shall meet when thou art in better humour,"
said Oliver, who had put on the dress.

"Go—and may I never see thy coxcombly face again."

Oliver at last relieved his host by swaggering off, imitating, as well
as he could, the sturdy step and outward gesture of his redoubted
companion, and whistling a pibroch, composed on the rout of the
Danes at Loncarty, which he had picked up from its being a favourite

of the Smith's, whom he made a point of imitating as far as he could. But as the innocent though conceited fellow stepped out from the entrance of the wynd, where it communicated with the High Street, he received a blow from behind against which his head-piece was no defence, and he fell dead upon the spot; an attempt to mutter the name of Henry, to whom he always looked for protection, quivering upon his dying tongue.

Chapter Five

Nay, I will fit you for a young Prince.
FALSTAFF

WE RETURN to the revellers, who had, half an hour before, witnessed, with such boisterous applause, Oliver's feat of agility, being the last which the poor Bonnet-maker was ever to exhibit, and at the hasty retreat which had followed it, animated by their wild shout. After they had laughed their fill, they passed on their mirthful path in frolic and jubilee, stopping and frightening some of the people whom they met; but, it must be owned, without doing them any serious injury either in their person or feelings. At length, tired with his rambles, their chief gave a signal to his merrymen to close around him.

"We, my brave hearts and wise councillors, are," he said, "the real King over all in Scotland that is worth commanding. We command the hours when the wine-cup circulates and beauty becomes kind, when Frolic is awake and Gravity snoring upon his pallet. We leave to our vicegerent, King Robert, the weary task of controlling ambitious nobles, gratifying greedy clergymen, subduing wild Highlanders, and composing deadly feuds. And since our empire is one of joy and pleasure, meet it is that we should haste with all our forces to the rescue of such as own our sway, when they chance, by evil fortune, to become the prisoners of care and hypochondriac malady. I speak in relation chiefly to Sir John, whom the vulgar call Ramorny. We have not seen him since the onslaught of Curfew Street, and though we know he was somedeal hurt in that matter, we cannot see why he should not do homage in leal and duteous sort.—Here, you, our Calabash King-at-arms, did you legally summon Sir John to his part of this evening's revels?"

"I did, my lord."

"And did you acquaint him that we have for this night suspended his sentence of banishment, that since higher powers have settled that part, we must at least take a mirthful leave of an old friend."

"I so delivered it, my lord," answered the mimic herald.

"And sent he not a word in writing, he that piques himself upon being so great a clerk?"

"He was in bed, my lord, and I might not see him. So far as I hear, he hath lived very retired, harmed with some bodily bruises, malcontent with your Highness's displeasure, and doubting insult in the streets, since he had a narrow escape from the burghers, when the churls pursued him and his two servants into the Dominican Convent. The servants, too, have been removed to Fife, lest they should tell tales."

"Why, it was wisely done," said the Prince,—who, we need not inform the intelligent reader, had a better title to be so called than arose from the humours of the evening,—"it was prudently done to keep light-tongued companions out of the way. But Sir John's absenting himself from our solemn revels, so long before decreed, is flat mutiny and disclamation of allegiance. Or, if the knight be really the prisoner of illness and melancholy, we must ourself grace him with a visit, seeing there can be no better cure for those maladies than our own presence, and a gentle kiss of the calabash.—Forward, ushers, minstrels, guard, and attendants! Bear on high the great emblem of our dignity—Up with the calabash, I say! and let the merrymen who bear these firkins which are to supply the wine-cup with their life-blood, be chosen with regard to their state of steadiness. Their burden is weighty and precious, and if the fault is not in our eyes, they seem to us to reel and stagger more than were desirable. Now, move on, sirs, and let our minstrels blow their blithest and boldest."

On they went with tipsy mirth and jollity, the numerous torches flashing their red light against the small windows of the narrow streets, from whence night-capped householders, and sometimes their wives to boot, peeped out by stealth to see what wild wassail disturbed the peaceful streets at that unwonted hour. At length the jolly train halted before the door of Sir John Ramorny's house, which a small court divided from the street.

Here they knocked, thundered, and hollowed, with many denunciations of vengeance against the recusants who refused to open the gates. The least punishment threatened was imprisonment in an empty hogshead, within the Massamore of the Prince of Pastimes' feudal palace, videlicet, the ale-cellar. But Eviot, Ramorny's page, heard and knew well the character of the intruders who knocked so boldly, and thought it best, considering his master's condition, to make no answer at all in hopes that the revel would pass on, than to attempt to deprecate their proceedings, which he knew would be to no purpose. His master's bed-room looking into a little garden, his page hoped he might not be disturbed by the noise; and he was confident in the strength of the outward gate, upon which he resolved they should beat till they tired themselves, or till the tone of their drunken humour should change. The revellers accordingly seemed likely to exhaust themselves in the noise they made by shouting and beating the door, when their mock Prince (alas! too really such) upbraided them as lazy and dull followers of the god of wine and of mirth.

"Bring forward," he said, "our key—yonder it lies, and apply it to this rebellious gate."

The key he pointed at was a large beam of wood, left on one side of the street, with the usual neglect of order proper to a Scottish borough of the period.

The shouting men of Ind instantly raised it in their arms, and supporting it by their united strength, ran against the door with such force that hasp, hinge, and staple jingled, and gave fair promise of yielding. Eviot did not choose to wait the extremity of this battery; he came forth into the court, and after some momentary questions for form's sake, caused the porter to undo the gate, as if he had for the first time recognised the midnight visitors.

"False slave of an unfaithful master," said the Prince, "where is our disloyal subject, Sir John Ramorny, who has proved recreant to our summons?"

"My lord," said Eviot, bowing at once to the real and the assumed dignity of the leader; "my master is just now very much indisposed— he has taken an opiate—and—your Highness must excuse me if I do my duty to him in saying he cannot be spoke with without danger of his life."

"Tush! tell me not of danger, Master Teviot—Cheviot—Eviot— what is it they call thee?—But show me thy master's chamber, or rather undo me the door of his lodging, and I will make a good guess at it myself.—Bear high the calabash, my brave followers, and see that you spill not a drop of the liquor, which Dan Bacchus has sent for the cure of all diseases of the body and cares of the mind. Advance it, I say, and let us see the holy rind which encloses such precious liquor."

The Prince made his way into the house accordingly, and, acquainted with its interior, ran up stairs, followed by Eviot, in vain imploring silence, and, with the rest of the rabble rout, burst into the room of the wounded master of the lodging.

He who has experienced the sensation of being compelled to sleep in spite of racking bodily pains, by the administration of a strong opiate, and of having been again startled by noise and violence, out of the unnatural state of insensibility in which he had been plunged by the potency of the medicine, may be able to imagine the confused and alarmed state of Sir John Ramorny's mind, and the agony of his body, which acted and re-acted upon each other. If we add to these feelings the consciousness of a criminal command, sent forth and in the act of being executed, it may give us some idea of an awakening, to which, in the mind of the party, eternal sleep would be a far preferable doom. The groan which he uttered as the first symptom of returning sensation, had something in it so terrific that even the revellers were awed into momentary silence; and as, from the half recumbent posture in which he had gone to sleep, he looked around the room, filled with fantastic shapes, rendered still more so by his disturbed intellects, he muttered to himself, "It is thus then, after all, and the legend is true! These are fiends, and I am condemned for ever! The fire is not external but I feel it—I feel it at—my heart—burning as if the seven times heated furnace were doing its work within."

While he cast ghastly looks around him, and struggled to recover some share of recollection, Eviot approached the Prince, and falling on his knees implored him to allow the apartment to be cleared.

"It may," he said, "cost my master his life."

"Never fear, Cheviot," replied the Duke of Rothsay; "were he at the gates of death, here is what should make the fiends relinquish their prey.—Advance the calabash, my masters."

"It is death for him to taste it in his present state," said Eviot; "if he drinks wine he dies."

"Some one must drink it for him—he shall be cured vicariously—and may our great Dan Bacchus deign to Sir John Ramorny the comfort, the elevation of heart, the lubrication of lungs, and lightness of fancy, which are his choicest gifts, while the faithful follower, who quaffs in his stead, shall have the qualms, the sickness, the racking of the nerves, the dimness of the eyes, and the throbbing of the brain, with which our great master qualifies gifts which would else make us too like the gods.—What say you, Eviot? will you be the faithful follower that will quaff in your lord's behalf, and as his representative? Do this, and we will hold ourselves contented to depart, for, methinks, our subject doth look something ghastly."

"I would do anything in my slight power," said Eviot, "to save my master from a draught which may be his death, and your Grace from the sense that you had occasioned it. But here is one who will perform the feat of good-will, and thank your Highness to boot."

"Whom have we here?" said the Prince, "a butcher?—and I think fresh from his office. Do butchers ply their craft on Fastern's E'en? Foh, how he smells of blood!"

This was spoken of Bonthron, who, partly surprised at the tumult in the house where he had expected to find all dark and silent, and partly stupid through the wine which the wretch had drunk in great quantities, stood in the threshold of the door, staring at the scene before him, with his buff-coat splashed with blood, and a bloody axe in his hand, exhibiting a ghastly and disgusting spectacle to the revellers, who felt, though they could not tell why, fear as well as dislike at his presence.

As they approached the calabash to this ungainly and truculent-looking savage, and as he extended a hand soiled, as it seemed, with blood, to grasp it, the Prince called out, "Down stairs with him! let not the wretch drink in our presence; find him some other vessel than our holy calabash, the emblem of our revels—a swine's trough were best if it could be come by. Away with him! let him be drenched to purpose, in atonement for his master's sobriety.—Leave me alone with Sir John Ramorny and his page; by my honour, I like not his looks."

The attendants of the Prince left the apartment, and Eviot alone remained.

"I fear," said the Prince, approaching the bed in different form from that which he had hitherto used—"I fear, my dear Sir John, that this visit has been unwelcome; but it is your own fault. Although you know our old wont, and were yourself participant of our schemes for the evening, you have not come near us since St Valentine's—it is now Fastern's Even, and the desertion is flat disobedience and treason to our kingdom of mirth, and the statutes of the calabash."

Ramorny raised his head, and fixed a wavering eye upon the Prince; then signed to Eviot to give him something to drink. A large cup of ptisan was presented by the page, which the sick man swallowed with eager and trembling haste. He then repeatedly used the stimulating essence left for the purpose by the leech, and seemed to collect his scattered senses.

"Let me feel your pulse, dear Ramorny," said the Prince; "I know something of that craft.—How? Do you offer me the left hand, Sir John?—that is neither according to the rules of medicine nor of courtesy."

"The right has already done its last act in your Highness's service," muttered the patient, in a low and broken tone.

"How mean you by that?" said the Prince. "I am aware thy follower, Black Quentin, lost a hand; but he can steal with the other as much as will bring him to the gallows, so his fate cannot be much altered."

"It is not that fellow who has had the loss in your Grace's service—it is I—John of Ramorny."

"You!" said the Prince; "you jest with me, or the opiate still masters your reason."

"If the juice of all the poppies in Egypt were blended in one draught," said Ramorny, "it would lose influence over me when I look

upon this." He drew his right arm from beneath the cover of the bed-
clothes, and extending it towards the Prince, wrapped as it was in
dressings, "Were these undone and removed," he said, "your Highness would see that a bloody stump is all that remains of a hand ever
ready to unsheath the sword at your Grace's slightest bidding."

Rothsay started back in horror. "This," he said, "must be avenged."

"It is avenged in small part," said Ramorny; "that is, I thought I saw
Bonthron but now—or was it that the dream of hell that first arose in
my mind when I awakened summoned up an image so congenial?
Eviot, call the miscreant,—that is, if he is fit to appear."

Eviot retired, and presently returned with Bonthron, whom he had
rescued from the penance, to him no unpleasing infliction, of a second
calabash of wine, the brute having gorged the first without much
apparent alteration in his demeanour.

"Eviot," said the Prince, "let not that beast come nigh me. My soul
recoils from him in fear and disgust; there is something in his looks
alien from my nature, and which I shudder at as at a loathsome snake
from which my instinct revolts."

"First hear him speak, my lord," answered Ramorny; "unless a
wineskin were to talk, nothing could use fewer words.—Hast thou
dealt with him, Bonthron?"

The savage raised the axe which he still held in his hand, and
brought it down again edge-ways.

"Good. How knew you your man?—the night, I am told, is dark."

"By sight and sound, garb, gait, and whistle."

"Enough, vanish!—and, Eviot, let him have gold and wine to his
brutish contentment.—Vanish!—and go thou with him."

"And whose death is achieved?" said the Prince, released from the
feelings of disgust and horror under which he suffered while the
assassin was in presence. "I trust this is but a jest? Else must I call it a
rash and savage deed. Who has had the hard lot to be butchered by
this bloody and brutal slave?"

"One little better than himself," said the patient; "a wretched artizan, to whom, however, fate gave the power of reducing Ramorny to a
mutilated cripple—a curse go with his base spirit!—his miserable life
is but to my revenge what a drop of water would be to a furnace.—I
must speak briefly, for my ideas again wander; it is only the necessity
of the moment which keeps them together, as a thong combines a
handful of arrows. You are in danger, my lord—I speak it with certainty—you have braved Douglas, and offended your uncle—displeased your father—though that were a trifle were it not for the rest."

"I am sorry I have displeased my father," said the Prince, (entirely
diverted from so insignificant a thing as the slaughter of an artizan by

the more important subject touched upon,) "if indeed it be so. But if I live, the strength of the Douglas shall be broken, and the craft of Albany shall little avail him!"

"Ay—*if—if.* My lord," said Ramorny, "with such opposites, you must not rest upon *if* or *but*—You must resolve at once to slay or be slain."

"How mean you, Ramorny? your fever makes you rave," answered the Duke of Rothsay.

"No, my lord," said Ramorny, "were my frenzy at the highest, the thoughts that pass through my mind at this moment would qualify it. It may be that regret for my own loss has made me desperate; that anxious thoughts for your Highness's safety have made me nourish bold designs; but I have all the judgment with which Heaven has gifted me, when I tell you, that if ever you would brook the Scottish crown, nay more, if ever you would see another Saint Valentine's Day, you must"——

"What is it that I must do, Ramorny?" said the Prince, with an air of dignity; "nothing unworthy of myself, I hope?"

"Nothing, certainly, unworthy or misbecoming a Prince of Scotland, if the blood-stained annals of our country tell the tale truly—but that which might well shock the nerves of a prince of mimes and merry-makers."

"Thou art severe, Sir John Ramorny," said the Duke of Rothsay, with an air of displeasure; "but thou hast dearly bought a right to censure us by what thou hast lost in our cause."

"My Lord of Rothsay," said the knight, "the chirurgeon who dressed this mutilated stump told me that the more I felt the pain his knife and brand inflicted, the better was my chance of recovery. I shall not, therefore, hesitate to hurt your feelings, while by doing so I am able to bring you to a sense of what is necessary for your safety. Your Grace has been the pupil of mirthful folly too long; you must now assume manly policy, or be crushed like a butterfly on the bosom of the flower you are sporting on."

"I think I know your cast of morals, Sir John; you are weary of merry folly,—the churchmen call it vice,—and long for a little serious crime. A murder, now, or a massacre, would enhance the flavour of debauch, as the taste of the olive gives zest to wine. But my worst acts are but merry malice; I have no relish for the bloody trade, and abhor to see or hear of its being acted even on the meanest caitiff. Should I ever fill the throne, every Scots lad shall have his flagon in the one hand and the other around his lass's neck, and manhood shall be tried by kisses and bumpers, not by dirks and dourlachs; and they shall write on my grave, 'Here lies David, third of his name. He won not

battles like Robert the First. He rose not from a count to a king
like Robert the Second. He founded not churches like Robert the
Third, but was contented to live and die King of good fellows!'
Of all my two centuries of ancestors, I would only emulate the
fame of

> Old King Coul,
> Who had a brown bowl."

"My gracious lord," said Ramorny, "let me remind you that your
joyous revels involve serious evils. If I had lost this hand in fighting to
attain for your Grace some important advantage over your two powerful enemies, the loss would never have grieved me. But to be reduced
from helmet and steel-coat to biggen and night-gown, in a night-
brawl"——

"Why, there again, now, Sir John—" interrupted the reckless
Prince—"how canst thou be so unworthy as to be for ever flinging thy
bloody hand in my face, as the ghost of Gaskhall threw his head at Sir
William Wallace? Bethink thee, thou art more unreasonable than
Fawdyon himself; for Wallace had swept his head off in somewhat a
hasty humour, whereas I would gladly stitch thy hand on again, were
that possible. And, hark thee, since that cannot be, I will get thee such
a substitute as the steel hand of the old Knight of Carselogie, with
which he greeted his friends, caressed his wife, braved his antagonists,
and did all that a hand of flesh and blood might be do in offence or
defence. Depend on it, John Ramorny, we have much that is superflu-
ous about us. Man can see with one eye, hear with one ear, touch with
one hand, smell with one nostril; and why we should have two of
each, (unless to supply an accidental loss or injury,) I for one am at a
loss to conceive."

Sir John Ramorny turned from the Prince with a low groan.

"Nay, Sir John," said the Duke, "I am quite serious. You know the
truth of Steelhand better than I, since he was your own neighbour. In
his time that curious engine could only be made in Rome; but I will
wager an hundred merks with you, that, let the Perth armourer have
the use of it for a pattern, Henry of the Wynd will execute as complete
an imitation as all the smiths in Rome could accomplish, with all the
cardinals to bid a blessing on the work."

"I could venture to accept your wager, my lord," answered Ramorny, bitterly, "but there is no time for foolery. You have dismissed me
from your service, at command of your uncle?"

"At command of my father," answered the Prince.

"Upon whom your uncle's commands are imperative," replied
Ramorny. "I am a disgraced man, thrown aside, as I may now fling

away my right hand glove as a thing useless. Yet my head might help you though my hand be gone. Is your Grace disposed to listen to me for one word of serious import?—for I am much exhausted, and feel my force sinking under me."

"Speak your pleasure," said the Prince; "thy loss binds me to hear thee; thy bloody stump is a sceptre to control me. Speak, then, but be merciful in thy strength of privilege."

"I will be brief, for mine own sake as well as thine; indeed I have but little to say. Douglas places himself presently at the head of his vassals. He will assemble, in the name of King Robert, thirty thousand Borderers, whom he will shortly after lead into the interior to demand that the Duke of Rothsay receive, or rather restore, his daughter to the rank and privilege of his Duchess. King Robert will yield to any conditions which may secure peace—What will the Duke do?"

"The Duke of Rothsay loves peace," said the Prince, haughtily; "but he never feared war. Ere he take yonder proud peat to his table and his bed at the command of her father, Douglas must be King of Scotland."

"Be it so—but even this is the less pressing peril, especially as it threatens open violence, for the Douglas works not in secret."

"What is there which presses and keeps us awake at this late hour? I am a weary man, thou a wounded one, and the very tapers are blinking, as if tired of our conference."

"Tell me, then, who is it that rules this kingdom of Scotland?" said Ramorny.

"Robert, third of the name," said the Prince, raising his bonnet as he spoke; "and long may he sway the sceptre!"

"True, and amen," answered Ramorny; "but who sways King Robert and dictates almost every measure the King pursues?"

"My Lord of Albany, you would say," replied the Prince. "Yes, it is true my father is guided almost entirely by the counsels of his brother; nor can we blame him in our consciences, Sir John Ramorny, for little help hath he had from his son."

"Let us help him now, my lord," said Ramorny. "I am possessor of a dreadful secret—Albany hath been trafficking with me to join him in taking your Grace's life! He offers full pardon for the past—high favour for the future."

"How, man—my life?—I trust, though, thou dost only mean my kingdom?—it were impious!—he is my father's brother—they sat on the knees of the same father—lay in the bosom of the same mother— Out on thee, man! what follies they make thy sick-bed believe!"

"Believe, indeed?" said Ramorny. "It is new to me to be termed credulous. But the man through whom Albany communicated his

temptations is one whom all will believe so soon as he hints at mischief
—even the medicaments which are prepared by his hands have a
relish of poison."

"Tush! such a slave would slander a saint," replied the Prince.
"Thou art duped for once, Ramorny, shrewd as thou art. My uncle of
Albany is ambitious, and would secure for himself and for his house a
larger portion of power and wealth than he ought in reason to desire.
But to suppose he would dethrone or slay his brother's son—fie,
Ramorny! put me not to quote the old saw that evil doers are evil
dreaders—it is your suspicion, not your knowledge, which speaks."

"Your Grace is fatally deluded—I will put it to an issue. The Duke
of Albany is generally hated for his greed and covetousness—Your
Highness is, it may be, more beloved than—"

Ramorny stopped, the Prince calmly filled up the blank—"More
beloved than I am honoured. It is so I would have it, Ramorny."

"At least," said Ramorny, "you are more beloved than you are
feared, and that is no safe condition for a prince. But give me your
honour and knightly word that you will not resent what good service I
shall do in your behalf, and lend me your signet to engage friends in
your name, and the Duke of Albany shall not assume authority in this
court till the wasted hand which once terminated this stump shall be
again united to the body, and acting in obedience to the dictates of my
mind."

"You would not venture to dip your hands in royal blood!" said the
Prince, sternly.

"Fie, my lord—at no rate—blood need not be shed. Life may, nay,
will, be extinguished of itself—for want of trimming it with fresh oil,
or screening it from a breath of wind, the quivering light will die in the
socket—to suffer a man to die is not to kill him."

"True—I had forgot that policy. Well, then, suppose my uncle
Albany does not continue to live—I think that must be the phrase—
Who then rules the court of Scotland?"

"Robert the Third, with consent, advice, and authority of the most
mighty David, Duke of Rothsay, Lieutenant of the kingdom, and
ALTER EGO; in whose favour, indeed, the good King, wearied with
the fatigues and troubles of sovereignty, will, I guess, be well disposed
to abdicate. So long live our brave young monarch, King David the
Third!

> *Ille, manu fortis,*
> *Anglis ludebit in hortis.*"

"And our father and predecessor," said Rothsay, "will he continue
to live to pray for us, as our beadsman, by whose favour he holds the
privilege of laying his grey hairs in the grave as soon, and no earlier,

than the course of nature permits?—or must he also encounter some of those negligences, in consequence of which men cease to continue to live, and exchange the limits of a prison, or of a convent resembling one, for the dark and tranquil cell where the priests say that the wicked cease from troubling, and the weary are at rest?"

"You speak in jest, my lord," replied Ramorny; "to harm the good old King were equally unnatural and impolitic."

"Why shrink from that, man, when thy whole scheme," answered the Prince, in stern displeasure, "is one lesson of unnatural guilt mixed with short-sighted ambition?—If the King of Scotland can scarcely make head against his nobles, even now when he can hold up before them an unsullied and honourable banner, who will follow a prince that is blackened with the death of an uncle, and the imprisonment of a father? Why, man, thy policy were enough to revolt a heathen divan, to say nought of the council of a Christian nation.— Thou wert my tutor, Ramorny, and perhaps I might justly upbraid thy lessons and example for some of the follies which men chide in me. Perhaps, if it had not been for thee, I had not been standing at midnight in this fool's guise, (looking at his dress,) to hear an ambitious profligate propose to me the murder of an uncle, the dethroning of the best of fathers. Since it is my fault, as well as thine, that has sunk me so deep in the gulf of infamy, it were unjust that thou alone shouldst die for it. But dare not to renew this theme to me on peril of thy life! I will proclaim thee to my father—to Albany—to Scotland—throughout its length and breadth! As many market crosses as are in the land shall have morsels of the traitor's carcass, who dare counsel such horrors to the Heir of Scotland. Well hope I, indeed, the fever of thy wound, and the intoxicating influence of the cordials which act on thy infirm brain, have this night operated on thee, rather than any fixed purpose."

"In sooth, my lord," said Ramorny, "if I have said anything which could so greatly exasperate your Highness, it must have been by excess of zeal, mingled with imbecility of understanding. Surely I, of all men, am least likely to propose ambitious projects with a prospect of advantage to myself. Alas! my only future views must be to exchange lance and saddle for the breviary and the confessional. The convent of Lindores must receive the maimed and impoverished Knight of Ramorny, who will there have ample leisure to meditate upon the text, 'Put not thy faith in princes.'"

"It is a goodly purpose," said the Prince; "and we will not be lacking to promote it. Our separation, I thought, would have been but for a time—it must now be perpetual. Certainly, after such talk as we have held, it were meet that we should live asunder. But the convent of Lindores, or whatever other house receives thee, shall be richly endowed and highly favoured by us.—And now, Sir John of Ramorny, sleep—sleep—and forget this evil-omened conversation, in which the fever of disease and of wine has rather, I trust, held colloquy than your own proper thoughts.—Light to the door, Eviot."

A call from Eviot summoned the attendants of the Prince, who had been sleeping on the staircase and hall, exhausted by the revels of the evening.

"Is there none amongst you sober?" said the Duke of Rothsay, disgusted by the appearance of his attendance.

"Not a man—not a man," answered the followers, with a drunken shout; "we are none of us traitors to the Emperor of Merry-makers."

"And are all of you turned into brutes, then?" said the Prince.

"In obedience and imitation of your Grace," answered one fellow; "or, if we are a little behind you, one pull at the pitcher will"——

"Peace, brute!" said the Duke of Rothsay; "is there none of you sober, I say?"

"Yes, my noble liege," was the answer; "here is one false brother, Watkins the Englishman."

"Come hither then, Watkins, and aid me with a torch—give me a cloak, too, and another bonnet, and take away this trumpery," throwing down his coronet of feathers; "I would I could throw off all my follies as easily.—English Wat, attend me alone, and the rest of you end your revelry and doff your mumming habits. The holytide is expended and the Fast has begun."

"Our monarch has abdicated sooner than usual this night," said one of the revel rout; but as the Prince gave no encouragement, such as happened for the time to want the virtue of sobriety endeavoured to assume it as well as they could, and the whole of the late rioters began to adopt the appearance of a set of decent persons, who, having been surprised into intoxication, endeavour to disguise their condition by assuming a double portion of formality of behaviour. In the interim, the Prince, having made a hasty reform in his dress, was lighted to the door by the only sober man of the company, but, in his progress thither, wellnigh stumbled over the sleeping bulk of the brute Bonthron.

"How now—is that vile beast in our way once more?" said he, in anger and disgust. "Here, some of you, toss this caitiff into the horse-trough, that for once in his life he may be washed clean."

While the train executed his commands, availing themselves of a fountain which was in the outer court, and while Bonthron underwent a discipline which he was incapable of resisting, otherwise than by some inarticulate groans and snorts, like those of a dying boar, the Prince proceeded on his way to his apartments in a mansion called the

Constable's lodgings, from the house being the property of the Earls of Errol. On the way, to divert his thoughts from more unpleasing matters, the Prince asked his companion how he came to be sober, when the rest of the party had been so much overcome with liquor.

"So please your honour's Grace," replied English Wat, "I confess it was very familiar in me to be sober when it was your Grace's pleasure that your train should be mad drunk; but in respect they were all Scottishmen but myself, I thought it argued no policy in getting drunken in their company; seeing that they only endure me even when we are all sober, and if the wine were uppermost, I might tell them a piece of my mind and be paid with as many stabs as there are skenes in the good company."

"So it is your purpose never to join any of the revels of our household?"

"Under favour, yes; unless it be your Grace's pleasure that your train should remain one day sober to admit Will Watkins to get drunk without terror of his life."

"Such occasion may arrive.—Where dost thou serve, Watkins?"

"In the stable, so please you."

"Let our chamberlain bring thee into the household as a yeoman of the night-watch. I like thy favour, and it is something to have one sober fellow in the house, although he is only such through the fear of death. Attend, therefore, near our person, and thou shalt find sobriety a thriving virtue."

Meantime a load of care and fear added to the distress of Sir John Ramorny's sick-chamber. His reflections, disordered as they were by the opiate, fell into great confusion when the Prince, in whose presence he had suppressed its effect by strong resistance, had left the apartment. His consciousness, which he had possessed perfectly during the interview, began to be very much disturbed. He felt a general sense that he had incurred a great danger; that he had rendered the Prince his enemy, and that he had betrayed to him a secret which might affect his own life. In this state of mind and body, it was not strange that he should either dream, or else that his diseased organs should become subject to that species of phantasmagoria which is excited by the use of opium. He thought that the shade of Queen Annabella stood by his bedside, and demanded the youth whom she had placed under his charge, simple, virtuous, gay, and innocent.

"Thou hast rendered him reckless, dissolute, and vicious," said the shade of pallid majesty. "Yet I thank thee, John of Ramorny, ungrateful to me, false to thy word, and treacherous to my hopes. Thy hate shall counteract the evil which thy friendship has done to him. And well do I hope that, now thou art no longer his counsellor, a bitter

penance on earth may purchase my ill-fated child pardon and acceptance in a better world."

Ramorny stretched out his arms after his benefactress, and endeavoured to express contrition and excuse. But the countenance of the
apparition became darker and sterner, till it was no longer that of the
late Queen, but presented the gloomy and haughty countenance of
the Black Douglas—then the timid and sorrowful face of King Robert, who seemed to mourn over the approaching dissolution of his
royal house—and then a group of fantastic features, partly hideous,
partly ludicrous, which moped, and chattered, and twisted themselves
into unnatural and extravagant forms, as if ridiculing his endeavour
to obtain an exact idea of their lineaments.

Chapter Six

THE MORNING of Ash Wednesday arose pale and bleak, as usual at
this season in Scotland, where the worst and most inclement weather
often occurs in the early spring months. It was a severe day of fast, and
the citizens had to sleep away the consequences of the preceding
holiday's debauchery. The sun had therefore risen for an hour above
the horizon, before there was any general appearance of life among
the inhabitants of Perth. The rich or rather those who had spent
money on the preceding day slept off the remains of their unusual
revelry—the poor lay in bed to enjoy the unusual indulgences of the
morning. It therefore was some time after daybreak, when an early
citizen, going to mass, saw the body of the luckless Oliver Proudfute
lying on his face, across the kennel, in the manner in which he had
fallen under the blow, as our readers will easily imagine, of Antony
Bonthron, the "boy of the belt," that is, the executioner of the pleasure
of John of Ramorny.

This early citizen was Allan Griffin, so termed because he was
master of the Griffin inn; and the alarm which he raised soon brought
together, first straggling neighbours, and by and by a concourse of
citizens. At first, from the circumstance of the well-known buff-coat
and the crimson feather in the head-piece, the noise arose that it was
the stout Smith lay there slain. This false rumour continued for some
time; for the host of the Griffin, who himself had been a magistrate,
would not permit the body to be touched or stirred till Bailie Craigdallie arrived, so that the face was not seen.

"This concerns the Fair City, my friends," he said; "and if it is the
stout Smith of the Wynd who lies here, the man lives not in Perth who
will not risk land and life to avenge him. Look you, the villains have

struck him down behind his back, for there is not a man within ten Scottish miles of Perth, gentle or simple, Highland or Lowland, that would have met him face to face with such evil purpose. Oh, brave men of Perth! the flower of your manhood has been cut down, and that by a base and treacherous hand!"

A wild cry of fury arose from the people who were fast assembling.

"We will take him on our shoulders," said a strong butcher; "we will carry him to the King's presence at the Dominican convent."

"Ay, ay," answered a blacksmith, "neither bolt nor bar shall keep us from the King; neither monk nor mass shall break our purpose. A better armourer never laid hammer on anvil!"

"To the Dominicans! to the Dominicans!" shouted the assembled people.

"Bethink you, burghers," said another citizen, "our King is a good King, and loves us like his children. It is the Douglas and the Duke of Albany that will not let good King Robert hear the distresses of his people."

"Are we to be slain in our own streets for the King's softness of heart?" said the butcher. "The Bruce did otherwise. If the King will not keep us, we will keep ourselves. Ring the bells backward, every bell of them that is made of metal. Cry, and spare not, St Johnstoun's hunt is up!"

"Ay," cried another citizen, "and let us to the holds of Albany and the Douglas, and burn them to the ground. Let the fires tell far and near, that Perth knew how to avenge her stout Henry Gow! He has fought a score of times for the Fair City's right—let us show we can fight once to avenge his wrong. Hallo! ho! brave citizens, St Johnstoun's hunt is up!"

This cry, the well-known rallying word amongst the inhabitants of Perth, and seldom heard but on occasions of general uproar, was echoed from voice to voice; and one or two neighbouring steeples, of which the enraged citizens possessed themselves, either by consent of the priests or in spite of their opposition, began to ring out the ominous alarm notes, in which, as the ordinary succession of the chimes were reversed, the bells were said to be rung backward.

Still, as the crowd thickened, and the roar waxed more universal and louder, Allan Griffin, a burly man with a deep voice, and well respected among high and low, kept his station as he bestrode the corpse, and called loudly to the multitude to keep back and wait the arrival of the magistrates.

"We must proceed by order in this matter, my masters; we must have our magistrates at our head. They are duly chosen and elected in our town-hall, good men and true every one; we will not be called rioters or idle perturbators of the King's peace. Stand you still, and make room, for yonder comes Bailie Craigdallie, ay and honest Simon Glover, to whom the Fair City is so much bounden. Alas, alas, my kind townsmen! his beautiful daughter was a bride yesternight— this morning the Fair Maid of Perth is a widow before she has been a wife!"

This new theme of sympathy increased the rage and sorrow of the crowd the more, as many women now mingled with them, who echoed back the alarm cry to the men.

"Ay, ay, St Johnstoun's hunt is up. For the Fair Maid of Perth and the brave Henry Gow! Up, up, every man of you, spare not for your skin-cutting! To the stables! to the stables!—when the horse is gone the man-at-arms is useless. Cut off the grooms and yeomen—lame, maim, stab the horses—kill the base squires and pages. Let these proud knights meet us on their feet if they dare!"

"They dare not, they dare not," answered the men; "their strength is in their horses and armour; and yet the haughty and ungrateful villains have slain a man whose skill as an armourer was never matched in Milan or Venice. To arms! to arms, brave burghers! St Johnstoun's hunt is up!"

Amid this clamour, the magistrates and superior class of inhabitants with difficulty obtained room to examine the body, having with them the town-clerk to take an official protocol, or, as it is still called, a precognition, of the condition in which it was found. To these delays the multitude submitted, with a patience and order which strongly marked the national character of a people whose resentment has always been the more deeply dangerous, that they will, without relaxing their determination of vengeance, submit with patience to all delays which are necessary to ensure its attainment. The multitude, therefore, received their magistrates with a loud cry, in which the thirst of revenge was announced, together with the deferential welcome to the patrons by whose direction they expected to obtain it in right and legal fashion.

While these accents of welcome still rung above the crowd, who now filled the whole adjacent streets, receiving and circulating a thousand varying reports, the fathers of the city caused the body to be raised and more closely examined; when it was instantly perceived, and the truth publicly announced, that not the armourer of the Wynd, so highly, and according to the esteemed qualities of the time so justly popular among his fellow citizens, but a man of far less general estimation, though not without his own value in society, lay murdered before them—the brisk Bonnet-maker, Oliver Proudfute. The resentment of the people had so much turned upon the general opinion, that their frank and brave champion, Henry Gow, was the slaughtered person, that the contradiction of the report served to cool the general fury, although, if poor Oliver had been recognised at first, there is little doubt that the cry of vengeance would have been as unanimous as in the case of Henry Wynd. The first circulation of the unexpected intelligence even excited a smile among the crowd, so near are the confines of the ludicrous to those of the terrible.

"The murderers have without doubt taken him for Henry Smith," said Griffin, "which must have been a great comfort to him in the circumstances."

But the arrival of other persons on the scene soon restored its deeply tragic character.

Chapter Seven

Who's that that rings the bell, Diablo, ho!
The town will rise.——
Othello

THE WILD RUMOURS which flew through the town, speedily followed by the tolling of the alarm, spread general consternation. The nobles and knights, with their followers, gathered in different places of rendezvous where a defence could best be maintained; and the alarm reached the royal residence, where the young Prince was one of the first to appear to assist, if necessary, in the defence of the old King. The scene of the preceding night ran in his recollection; and, remembering the blood-stained figure of Bonthron, he conceived, though indistinctly, that his act had been connected with this uproar. The subsequent and more interesting discourse with Sir John Ramorny had, however, been of such an impressive nature as to obliterate all traces of what he had indistinctly heard of the bloody act of the assassin, excepting a confused recollection that some one or other had been slain. It was chiefly on his father's account that he had assumed arms with his household train, who, clad in bright armour and bearing lances in their hands, made now a figure very different from that of the preceding night, when they appeared as intoxicated Bacchanalians. The kind old monarch received this mark of filial attachment with tears of gratitude, and proudly presented his son to his brother Albany, who entered shortly afterwards. He took them each by the hand.

"Now are we three Stewarts," he said, "as inseparable as the holy Trefoil; and, as they say the wearer of that sacred herb mocks at magical delusion, so we, while we are true to each other, may set malice and enmity at defiance."

The brother and son kissed the kind hand which pressed theirs, while Robert III. expressed his confidence in their affection. The kiss of the youth was, for the time, sincere; that of the brother was the salute of the apostate Judas.

In the meantime the bells of Saint John's church alarmed, amongst others, the inhabitants of Curfew Street. In the house of Simon Glover, old Dorothy Glover, as she was called, (for she also took name from the trade she practised under her master's auspices,) was the first to catch the sound. Though somewhat deaf upon ordinary occasions, her ear for bad news was as sharp as a kite's scent for carrion; for Dorothy, otherwise an industrious, faithful, and even an affectionate creature, had that strong appetite for collecting and retailing bad news which is often to be marked in the lower classes. Little accustomed to be listened to, they love the attention which a tragic tale ensures to the bearer, and enjoy, perhaps, the temporary equality to which misfortune reduces those who are ordinarily accounted their superiors. Dorothy had no sooner possessed herself of a slight packet of the rumours which were flying abroad than she bounced into her master's bed-room, who had taken the privilege of age and the holytide to sleep longer than usual.

"There he lies, honest man!" said Dorothy, half in a screeching, and half in a wailing tone of sympathy,—"There he lies—his best friend slain, and he knowing as little about it as the babe new born that kens not life from death."

"How now!" said the Glover, starting up out of his bed,—"What is the matter, old woman? is my daughter well?"

"Old woman!" said Dorothy, who, having her fish hooked, chose to let him play a little. "I am not so old," said she, flouncing out of the room, "as to bide in the place till a man rises from his naked bed"—

And presently she was heard at a distance in the parlour beneath, melodiously singing to the scrubbing of her own broom.

"Dorothy—screech-owl—devil,—say but my daughter is well!"

"I am well, my father," answered the Fair Maid of Perth, speaking from her bed-room, "perfectly well; but what, for our Lady's sake, is the matter? The bells ring backward, and there is shrieking and crying in the streets."

"I will presently know the cause—Here, Conachar, come speedily and tie my points—I forgot—the Highland loon is far beyond Fortingall—Patience, daughter, I will presently bring you news."

"Ye need not hurry yourself for that, Simon Glover," quoth the obdurate old woman; "the best and the worst of it may be tauld before you could hobble over your door-stane. I ken the haill story abroad; for, thought I, our goodman is so wilful that he'll be for banging out to the tuilzie, be the cause what it like; and sae I maun e'en stir my shanks, and learn the cause of all this, or he will hae his auld nose in the midst of it, and maybe get it nipt off before he knows what for."

"And what *is* the news, then, old woman?" said the impatient Glover, still busying himself with the hundred points or latchets which were the means of attaching the doublet to the hose.

Dorothy suffered him to proceed in his task, till she conjectured it must be nearly accomplished; and foresaw that, if she told not the secret herself, her master would be abroad to seek in person for the cause of the disturbance. She therefore hollowed out—"Aweel, aweel, ye canna say it is my fault, if you hear ill news before you hear the morning mass. I would have kept it from ye till ye had heard the priest's word—But since you must hear it, you have e'en lost the truest friend that ever gave hand to another, and Perth maun mourn for the bravest burgher that ever took a blade in hand."

"Harry Smith! Harry Smith!" exclaimed the father and the daughter at once.

"Oh, ay, there ye hae it at last," said Dorothy; "and whase fault was it but your ain?—You made such a piece of work about his company-ing with a glee woman as if he had companied with a Jewess!"

Dorothy would have gone on long enough, but her master exclaimed to his daughter, who was still in her own apartment, "It is nonsense, Catherine—all the doting of an old fool—no such thing has happened. I will bring you the true tidings in a moment;" and catching up his staff, the old man hurried out past Dorothy, and into the street, where the throng of people were rushing towards the High Street. Dorothy, in the meantime, kept muttering to herself, "Thy father is a wise man, take his ain word for it. He will come next by some scathe in the hobbleshow, and then it will be, Dorothy, get the lint, and, Doro-thy, spread the plaster; but now it is nothing but nonsense, and a lie, and impossibility, that can come out of Dorothy's mouth—Imposs-ible!—Does auld Simon think that Harry Smith's head was as hard as his stithy, and a haill clan of Highlandmen dinging at him?"

Here she was interrupted by a figure like an angel, who came wandering by her with wild eye, cheek deadly pale, hair dishevelled, and an apparent want of consciousness, which terrified the old woman out of her discontented humour.

"Our Lady bless my bairn," said she. "What look you sae wild for?"

"Did you not say some one was dead?" said Catherine, with a frightful uncertainty of utterance, as if her organs of speech and hearing served her but imperfectly.

"Dead, hinny! Ay, ay, dead eneugh; ye'll no hae him to gloom at ony mair."

"Dead!" repeated Catherine, still with the same uncertainty of voice and manner. "Dead—slain—and by Highlanders?"

"I'se warrant by Highlanders,—the lawless loons. Wha is it else that kills maist of the folks about, unless now and than when the burghers take a tirrivie and kill ane another, or whiles that the knights and nobles shed blood? But I'se uphauld it's been the Highlandmen this bout. The man was no in Perth, laird or loon, durst have faced Henry Smith man to man. There's been sair odds against him; ye'll see that when it's looked into."

"Highlandmen!" repeated Catherine, as if haunted by some idea which troubled her senses. "Highlanders!—Oh, Conachar! Conachar!"

"Indeed, and I daresay you have lighted on the very man, Catherine—they quarrelled, as you saw, on the St Valentine's Even, and had a warstle—a Highlandman has a long memory for the like of that—gie him a cuff at Martinmas, and his cheek will be tingling at Whitsunday. But wha could have brought down the lang-legged loons to do their bloody wark within burgh?"

"Woe's me, it was I," said Catherine; "it was I brought the Highlanders down to the—I that sent for Conachar—ay, they have lain in wait—but it was I that brought them within reach of their prey. But I will see with my own eyes—and then—something we will do. Say to my father I will be back anon."

"Are ye distraught, lassie?" shouted Dorothy, as Catherine made past her towards the street door. "You wad na gang into the street with the hair hanging down your haffets in that guise, and you kenn'd for the Fair Maid of Perth?—Mass, but she's out in the street, come o't what like, and the auld Glover will be as mad as if I could withhold her, will she nill she, flyte she fling she.—This is a brave morning for an Ash-Wednesday!—What's to be done? If I were to seek my master amang the multitude, I were like to be crushed beneath their feet, and little moan made for the old woman—And I were to run after Catherine, why she's out of sight, and far lighter of foot than I am—So I will just down the gate to Nicol Barber's, and tell him a' about it."

While the trusty Dorothy was putting her prudent resolve into execution, Catherine ran through the streets of Perth in a manner which at another moment would have brought on her the attention of every one who saw her hurrying on with a reckless impetuosity, wildly and widely different from the ordinary decency and composure of her pace and manner, and without the plaid, scarf, or mantle, which "women of good," of fair character and decent rank, normally carried around them when they went abroad. But distracted as the people were, every one inquiring or telling the cause of the tumult, and most recounting it different ways, the negligence of her dress, and discomposure of her manner, made no impression on any one; and she was suffered to press forward on the path she had chosen, without attracting any more notice than the other females, who, stirred by anxious curiosity or fear, had come out to inquire the cause of an alarm so general, or, it might be, to seek for friends for whose safety they were interested.

As Catherine passed along, she felt all the wild influence of the agitating scene, and it was with difficulty she forbore from repeating the cries of lamentation and alarm, which were echoed around her. In the meantime, she rushed rapidly on, embarrassed like one in a dream, with a strange sense of dreadful calamity, the precise nature of which she was unable to define, but which implied the terrible consciousness, that the man who loved her so fondly, whose good qualities she so highly esteemed, and whom she now felt to be dearer than perhaps she would before have acknowledged to her own bosom, was murdered, and most probably by her means. The connexion betwixt Henry's supposed death, and the descent of Conachar and his followers, though adopted by her in a moment of extreme and engrossing emotion, was sufficiently probable to have been received for truth, even if her understanding had been at leisure to examine its credibility. Without knowing what she sought, except the general desire to know the worst of the dreadful report, she hurried forward to the very spot which of all others her feelings of the preceding day would have induced her to avoid.

Who would, upon the evening of Shrove-tide, have persuaded the proud, the timid, the shy, the rigidly decorous Catherine Glover, that before mass on Ash Wednesday she should rush through the streets of Perth, making her way amidst tumult and confusion, with her hair unbound, and her dress disarranged, to seek the house of that same lover who, she had reason to believe, had so grossly and indelicately neglected and affronted her as to pursue a low and licentious amour! Yet so it was; and her eagerness taking, as if by instinct, the road which was most free, she avoided the High Street, where the pressure was greatest, and reached the wynd by the narrow lanes and vennels on the northern skirt of the town, through which Henry Smith had formerly escorted Louise. But even these comparatively lonely passages were now astir with passengers, so general was the alarm. Catherine Glover made her way through them, while such as observed her looked on each other, and shook their heads in sympathy with her distress. At length, without any distinct idea of her own purpose, she stood before her lover's door, and knocked for admittance.

The silence which succeeded the echoing of her hasty summons increased the alarm which had induced her to take this desperate measure.

"Open,—open, Henry!" she cried. "Open, if you yet live!— Open, if you would not find Catherine Glover dead upon your threshold!"

As she cried thus franticly, to ears which she was taught to believe were stopped by death, the lover she invoked opened the door in person, just in time to prevent her sinking on the ground. The extremity of his ecstatic joy upon an occasion so unexpected, was qualified only by the wonder which forbade him to believe it real, and by his alarm at the closed eyes, half-opened and blanched lips, total absence of complexion, and apparently total cessation of breathing.

Henry had remained at home, in spite of the general alarm, which had reached his ears for a considerable time, fully determined to put himself in the way of no brawls that he could avoid; and it was only in compliance with a summons from the Magistrates, which, as a burgher, he was bound to obey, that, taking his sword and a buckler from the wall, he was about to go forth, for the first time unwillingly, to pay his service as his tenure bound him.

"It is hard," he said, "to be put forward in all the town feuds, when the fighting work is so detestable to Catherine. I am sure there are enough of wenches in Perth that say to their gallants, 'Go out—do your devoir bravely, and win your lady's grace;' and yet they send not for their lovers, but for me, who cannot do the duties of a man to protect a minstrel woman, or of a burgess who fights for the honour of his town, but this peevish peat Catherine uses me as if I were a brawler and bordeller!"

Such were the thoughts which occupied his mind, when, as he opened his door to issue forth, the person dearest to his thoughts, but whom he certainly least expected to see, was present to his eyes, and dropped into his arms.

His mixture of surprise, joy, and anxiety did not deprive him of the presence of mind which the occasion demanded. To place Catherine Glover in safety, and recall her to herself, was to be thought of before rendering obedience to the summons of the Magistrates, however pressingly that had been delivered. He carried his lovely burden, as light as a feather, yet more precious than the same quantity of purest gold, into a small bedchamber which had been his mother's. It was the most fit for an invalid, as it looked into the garden, and was separated from the noise of the tumult.

"Here, Nurse—Nurse Shoolbred—come quick—come for death and life—here is someone wants thy help!"

Up trotted the old dame. "If it should but prove any one that will keep thee out of the scuffle—" for she also had been aroused by the noise,—but what was her astonishment, when, placed in love and reverence upon the bed of her late mistress, and supported by the athletic arms of her foster son, she saw the apparently lifeless form of the Fair Maid of Perth. "Catherine Glover!" she said; "and, Holy Mother—a dying woman, as it would seem!"

"Not so, old woman," said her foster son; "the dear heart throbs— the sweet breath comes and returns! Come thou that mayst aid her more meetly than I—bring water—essences—whatever thy old skill can devise. Heaven did not place her in my arms to die, but to live for herself and me."

With an activity which her age little promised, Nurse Shoolbred collected the means of restoring animation; for, like many women of the period, she understood what was to be done in such cases, nay, possessed a knowledge of treating wounds of an ordinary description, which the warlike propensities of her foster son kept in pretty constant exercise.

"Come now," she said, "son Henry, unfold your arms from about my patient—though she is worth the pressing—and set thy arms at freedom to help me with what I want.—Nay, I will not insist on your quitting her hand, if you will beat the palm gently, as the fingers unclose their clenched grasp."

"Me beat her slight beautiful hand!" said Henry; "you were as well bid me beat a glass cup with a fore-hammer as tap her fair palm with my horn-hard fingers.—But the fingers do unfold, and we will find a better way than beating;" and he applied his lips to the pretty hand, whose motion indicated returning sensation. One or two deep sighs succeeded, and the Fair Maid of Perth opened her eyes, fixed them on her lover, as he kneeled by the bedside, and again sunk back on the pillow. As she withdrew not her hand from her lover's hold or from his grasp, we must in charity believe that the return to consciousness was not so complete as to make her aware that he abused the advantage by pressing it alternately to his lips and his bosom. At the same time we are compelled to own, that the blood was dawning in her cheek, and that her breathing was deep and regular for a minute or two during this relapse.

The noise at the door began now to grow much louder, and Henry was called for by all his various names, of Smith, Gow, and Hal of the Wynd, as heathens used to summon their deities by different epithets. At last, like Portuguese Catholics when exhausted with entreating their saints, the crowd without had recourse to vituperative exclamations.

"Out upon you, Henry! You are a disgraced man, mansworn to

your burgher-oath, and a traitor to the Fair City, unless you come instantly forth!"

It would seem that Nurse Shoolbred's applications were now so far successful, that Catherine's senses were in some measure restored; for, turning her face more towards that of her lover than her former posture permitted, she let her right hand fall on his shoulder, leaving her left still in his possession, and seeming slightly to detain him, while she whispered, "Do not go, Henry—stay with me—they will kill thee, these men of blood."

It is probable that this gentle invocation, the result of finding the lover alive whom she expected to have only recognised as a corpse, though it was spoken so low as scarce to be intelligible, had more effect to keep Henry Wynd in his present posture than the repeated summons of many voices from without had to bring him down stairs.

"Mass, townsmen," cried one hardy citizen to his companions, "the saucy Smith but jests with us! Let us into the house, and bring him out by the lug and the horn."

"Take care what you are doing," said a more cautious assailant. "The man that presses on Henry Gow's retirement may go into his house with sound bones, but will return with ready-made work for the surgeon.—But here comes one has good right to do our errand to him, and make the recreant hear reason on both sides of his head."

The person of whom this was spoken was no other than Simon Glover himself. He had arrived at the fatal spot where the unlucky Bonnet-maker's body was lying, just in time to discover, to his great relief, that when it was turned with the face upwards by Bailie Craigdallie's orders, the features of the poor braggart Proudfute were recognised, when the crowd expected to behold those of their favourite champion Henry Smith. A laugh, or something approaching to one, went amongst those who remembered how hard Oliver had struggled to obtain the character of a fighting man, however foreign to his nature and disposition, and remarked now, that he had met with a mode of death much better suited to his pretensions than to his temper. But this tendency to ill-timed mirth, which savoured of the rudeness of the times, was at once hushed by the voice, and cries, and exclamations of a woman who struggled through the crowd, screaming at the same time,—"Oh, my husband!—my husband!"

Room was made for the sorrower, who was followed by two or three female friends. Maudie Proudfute had been hitherto only noticed as a good-looking, black-haired woman, believed to be *dink** and disdainful to those whom she thought meaner or poorer than herself, and lady and empress over her late husband, whom she quickly caused to lower

* Contemptuous—scornful of others.

his crest when she chanced to hear him crowing out of season. But now, under the influence of powerful passion, she assumed a far more imposing character.

"Do you laugh," she said, "you unworthy burghers of Perth, because one of your own citizens has poured his blood into the kennel?—or do you laugh because the deadly lot has lighted on my husband? How has he deserved this?—Did he not maintain an honest house by his own industry, and keep a creditable board, where the sick had welcome, and the poor had relief?—Did he not lend to those who wanted,—stand by his neighbours as a friend, keep counsel and do justice like a magistrate?"

"It is true, it is true," answered the assembly; "his blood is our blood, as much as if it were Henry Gow's."

"You speak truth, neighbours," said Bailie Craigdallie; "and this feud cannot be patched up as the former was—citizens' blood must not flow unavenged down our kennels, as if it were ditch-water, or we shall soon see the broad Tay crimsoned with it. But this blow was never meant for the poor man on whom it has unhappily fallen. Every one knew what Oliver Proudfute was, how wide he would speak, and how little he would do. He has Henry Smith's buff-coat, target, and head-piece. All the town know them as well as I do; there is no doubt on't. He had the trick, as you know, of trying to imitate the Smith in most things. Some one, blind with rage, or perhaps through liquor, has stricken the innocent Bonnet-maker, whom no man either hated or feared, or indeed cared either much or little about, instead of the stout Smith, who has twenty feuds upon his hands."

"What then is to be done, Bailie?" cried the multitude.

"That, my friends, your magistrates will determine for you, as we shall instantly meet together when Sir Patrick Charteris cometh here, which must be anon. Meanwhile, let the chirurgeon Dwining examine that poor piece of clay, that he may tell us how he came by his fatal death; and then let the corpse be decently swathed in a clean shroud, as becomes an honest citizen, and placed before the high altar in the church of St John, the patron of the Fair City. Cease all clamour and noise, and every defensible man of you, as you would wish well to the Fair Town, keep his weapons in readiness, and be prepared to assemble on the High Street, at the tolling of the common bell from the Town-House, and we will either revenge the death of our fellow-citizen, or else we shall take such measure as Heaven will send us. Meanwhile avoid all quarrelling with the knights and their followers, till we know the innocent from the guilty.—But wherefore tarries this knave smith? He is ready enough in tumults when his presence is not wanted, and lags he now when his presence may serve the Fair City?

—What ails him, doth any one know? Hath he been upon the frolic last Fastern's Even?"

"Rather he is sick or sullen, Master Bailie," said one of the city's mairs, or sergeants; "for though he is within door, as his knaves report, yet he will neither answer to us nor admit us."

"So please your worship, Master Bailie," said Simon Glover, "I will go myself to fetch Henry Smith. I have some little difference to make up with him. And blessed be Our Lady, who hath so ordained it that I find him alive, as a quarter of an hour since I could never have expected!"

. "Bring the stout Smith to the Council-house," said the Bailie, as a mounted yeoman pressed through the crowd, and whispered in his ear,—"Here is a good fellow who says the knight of Kinfauns is entering the port."

Such was the occasion of Simon Glover presenting himself at the house of Henry Gow at the period already noticed.

Unrestrained by the considerations of doubt and hesitation which influenced others, he repaired to the parlour; and having overheard the bustling of Dame Shoolbred, he took the privilege of intimacy to ascend to the bed-room, and, with the slight apology of—"I crave your pardon, good neighbour," he opened the door, and entered the apartment, where a singular and unexpected sight awaited him. At the sound of his voice, May Catherine experienced a revival much speedier than Dame Shoolbred's restoratives had been able to produce; and the paleness of her complexion changed into a deep glow of the most lovely red. She pushed her lover from her with both hands, which, until that minute, her want of consciousness, or her affection, awakened by the events of the morning, had well nigh abandoned to his caresses. Henry Smith, bashful as we know him, stumbled as he rose up; and none of the party were without a share of confusion, excepting Dame Shoolbred, who was glad to make some pretext to turn her back to the others, in order that she might enjoy a laugh at their expense, which she felt herself utterly unable to restrain, and in which the Glover, whose surprise, though great, was of short duration, and of a joyful character, sincerely joined.

"Now, by good St John," he said, "I thought I had seen a sight this morning that would cure me of laughter, at least till Lent was over; but this would make me curl my cheek, if I were dying. Why, here stands honest Henry Smith, who was lamented as dead, and toll'd out for from every steeple in town, alive, merry, and, as it seems from his ruddy complexion, as like to live as any man in Perth. And here is my precious daughter, that yesterday would speak of nothing but the wickedness of the wights that haunt profane sports, and protect glee-maidens—Ay, she who set St Valentine and St Cupid both at defiance,—here she is, turned a glee-maiden herself, for what I can see! Truly, I am glad to see that you, my good Dame Shoolbred, who give way to no disorder, have been of this loving party."

"You do me wrong, my dearest father," said Catherine, as if about to weep. "I came here with far different expectations than you suppose. I only came because—because—"

"Because you expected to find a dead lover," said her father, "and you have found a living one, who can receive the tokens of your regard, and return them. Now, were it not a sin, I could find in my heart to thank Heaven, that thou hast been surprised at last into owning thyself a woman—Simon Glover is not worthy to have an absolute saint for his daughter.—Nay, look not so piteously, nor expect condolence from me! Only I will try not to look merry, if you will be pleased stop your tears, or confess them to be tears of joy."

"If I were to die for such a confession," said poor Catherine, "I could not tell what to call them. Only believe, dear father—and let Henry believe, that I would never have come hither, unless—unless"—

"Unless you had thought that Henry could not come to you," said her father. "And now, shake hands in peace and concord, and agree as Valentines should. Yesterday was Shrovetide, Henry—We will hold that thou hast confessed thy follies, hast obtained absolution, and art relieved of all the guilt thou stoodest charged with."

"Nay, touching that, father Simon," said the Smith, "now that you are cool enough to hear me, I can swear on the Gospels, and I can call my nurse, Dame Shoolbred, to witness"—

"Nay, nay," said the Glover, "wherefore rake up differences which should be forgotten?"

"Hark ye, Simon!—Simon Glover!" This was now echoed from beneath.

"True, son Smith," said the Glover seriously, "we have other work in hand. You and I must to the council instantly. Catherine shall remain here with Dame Shoolbred, who will take charge of her till we return; and then, as the town is in misrule, we two, Harry, will carry her home, and they will be bold men that cross us."

"Nay, my dear father," said Catherine, with a smile, "now you are taking Oliver Proudfute's office. That doughty burgher is Henry's brother-at-arms."

Her father's countenance grew dark.

"You have spoke a stinging word, daughter; but you know not what has happened. Kiss him, Catherine, in token of forgiveness."

"Not so," said Catherine; "I have done him too much grace already. When he has seen the errant damsel safe home, it will be time enough to claim his reward."

"Meantime," said Henry, "I will claim, as your host, what you will not allow me on other terms."

He folded the fair maiden in his arms, and was permitted to take the salute which she had refused to bestow.

As they descended the stair together, the old man laid his hand on the Smith's shoulder, and said, "Henry, my dearest wishes are fulfilled; but it is the pleasure of the saints that it should be in an hour of difficulty and terror."

"True," said the Smith; "but thou knowest, father, if our riots be frequent at Perth, at least they seldom last long."

Then, opening a door which led from the house into the smithy, "Here, comrades," he cried, "Anton, Cuthbert, Dingwell, and Ringan! None of you stir from the place till I return. Be as true as the weapons I have taught you to forge; a French crown and a Scottish merry-making for you, if you obey my command. I leave a mighty treasure in your charge. Watch the doors well—let little Jannekin scout up and down the wynd, and have your arms ready if any one approaches the house. Open the doors to no man, till father Glover or I return; it concerns my life and happiness."

The strong swarthy giants to whom he spoke, answered, "Death to him who attempts it!"

"My Catherine is now as safe," said he to her father, "as if twenty men garrisoned a royal castle in her cause. We shall pass most quietly to the Council-house by walking through the garden."

He led the way through a little orchard accordingly, where the birds, which had been sheltered and fed during the winter by the good-natured artizan, early in the season as it was, were saluting the precarious smiles of a February sun, with a few faint and interrupted attempts at melody.

"Hear these minstrels, father," said the Smith; "I laughed at them this morning in the bitterness of my heart, because the little wretches sung, with so much of winter before them. But now, methinks, I could bear a blithe chorus, for I have my Valentine as they have theirs; and whatever ill may lie before me for to-morrow, I am to-day the happiest man in Perth, city or county, burgh or landward."

"Yet I must allay your joy," said the old Glover, "though, Heaven knows, I share it.—Poor Oliver Proudfute, the inoffensive fool that you and I knew so well, has been found this morning dead in the streets."

"Only dead drunk, I trust?" said the Smith; "nay, a caudle and a dose of matrimonial advice will bring him to life again."

"No, Henry, no. He is slain—slain with a battle-axe, or some such weapon."

"Impossible!" replied the Smith; "he was light-footed enough, and would not for all Perth have trusted to his hands, when he could extricate himself by his heels."

"No choice was allowed him. The blow was dealt in the very back of his head; he who struck must have been a shorter man than himself, and used a horseman's battle-axe, or some such weapon, for a Lochaber-axe must have struck the upper part of his head—But there he lies dead, brained, I may say, by a most frightful wound."

"This is inconceivable," said Henry Wynd. "He was in my house at midnight, in a morricer's habit—seemed to have been drinking, though not to excess. He told me a tale of having been beset by revellers, and being in danger—but, alas! you know the man—I deemed it was a swaggering fit, as he sometimes took when he was in liquor—and, may the Merciful Virgin forgive me!—I let him go without company, in which I did him inhuman wrong—Holy St John be my witness! I would have gone with any helpless creature; and far more with him, with whom I have so often sat at the same board, and drunken of the same cup. Who, of the race of man, could have thought of harming a creature so simple, and so unoffending, excepting by his idle vaunts!"

"Henry, he wore thy headpiece, thy buff-coat, thy target—How came he by these?"

"Why, he demanded the use of them for the night, and I was ill at ease, and well pleased to be rid his company; having kept no holiday, and being determined to keep none, in respect of our misunderstanding."

"It is the opinion of Bailie Craigdallie, and all our sagest councillors, that the blow was intended for yourself, and that it becomes you to prosecute the due vengeance of our fellow-citizen, who received the death which was meant for you."

The Smith was for some time silent. They had now left the garden, and were walking in a lonely lane, by which they meant to approach the Council-house of the burgh, without being exposed to observation or idle inquiry.

"You are silent, my son, yet we two have much to speak of," said Simon Glover. "Bethink thee that this widowed woman Maudlin, if she should see cause to bring a charge against any one for the wrong done to her and her orphan children, must support it by a champion, according to law and custom; for be the murderer who he may, we know enough of these followers of the nobles to be assured, that the party suspected will appeal to the combat, in derision, perhaps, of those whom they will call the cowardly burghers. While we are men with blood in our veins, this must not be, Henry Wynd."

"I see where you would draw me, father," answered Henry, dejectedly; "and St John knows I have heard a summons to battle as willingly as war-horse ever heard the trumpet. But bethink you, father, how I have lost Catherine's favour repeatedly, and have been driven well nigh to despair of ever regaining it, for being, if I may say so, even too ready a man of my hands. And here are all our quarrels made up, and the hopes, that seemed this morning removed beyond earthly prospect, have become nearer and brighter than ever; and must I, with the dear one's kiss of forgiveness on my lips, engage in a new scene of violence, which you are well aware will give her the deepest offence?"

"It is hard for me to advise you, Henry," said Simon. "But this I must ask you—have you, or have you not, reason to think, that this poor unfortunate Oliver has been mistaken for you?"

"I fear it too much," said Henry. "He was thought something like me, and the poor fool had studied to ape my gestures and manner of walking, nay, the very airs which I have the trick of whistling, that he might increase a resemblance which has cost him dear. I have ill-willers enough, both in burgh and landward, to owe me a shrewd turn; and he, I think, could have none such."

"Well, Henry, I cannot say but my daughter will be offended. She has been much with Father Clement, and has received notions about peace and forgiveness, which methinks suit ill with a country where the laws cannot protect us, unless we have spirit to protect ourselves. If you determine for the combat, I will do my best to persuade her to look on the matter as the other good womanhood in the burgh will do; and if you resolve to let the matter rest—the man who has lost his life for yours remaining unavenged—the widow and the orphans without any reparation for the loss of a husband and father—I will then do you the justice to remember, that I, at least, ought not to think the worse of you for your patience, since it was adopted for love of my child. But, Henry, we must in that case remove ourselves from bonny St John-stoun, for here we will be but a disgraced family."

Henry groaned deeply, and was silent for an instant, then replied, "I would rather be dead than dishonoured, though I should never see her again. Had it been yester evening, I would have met the best blade among these men-at-arms as blithely as ever I danced at a May-pole. But to-day, when she had first as good as said, 'Henry Smith, I love thee!'—Father Glover, it is very hard. Yet it is all my own fault! I ought to have allowed him the shelter of my roof, when he prayed me in his agony of fear; or, had I gone with him, I should then have prevented or shared his fate. But I taunted him, ridiculed him, loaded him with maledictions, though the saints know they were uttered in idle peevishness of impatience. I drove him out from my doors, whom I knew so helpless, to take the fate which was perhaps intended for me. I must avenge him, or be dishonoured for ever. See, father—I have been called a man hard as the steel I work in—Does burnished steel ever drop tears like these?—Shame on me that I should shed them!"

"It is no shame, my dearest son," said Simon; "thou art as kind as brave, and I have always known it. There is yet a chance for us. No one may be discovered to whom suspicion attaches, and where none such is found, the combat cannot take place. It is a hard thing to wish that the innocent blood may not be avenged. But if the perpetrator of this foul murder be hidden for the present, thou wilt be saved from the task of seeking that vengeance which Heaven, doubtless, will take at its own proper time."

As they spoke thus, they arrived at the point of the High Street where the Council-house was situated. As they reached the door, and made their way through the multitude who still thronged the street, they found the avenues guarded by a select party of armed burghers, and about fifty spears belonging to the Knight of Kinfauns, who, with his allies the Grays, Blairs, Moncrieffs, and others, had brought to Perth a considerable body of horse, of which these were a part. So soon as the Glover and Smith presented themselves, they were admitted to the chamber in which the magistrates were assembled.

Chapter Eight

THE COUNCIL-ROOM of Perth presented a singular spectacle. In a gloomy apartment, ill and inconveniently lighted by two windows of different form and of unequal size, were assembled, around a large oaken table, a group of men, of whom those who occupied the higher seats were merchants, that is, guild brethren, or shopkeepers, arrayed in decent dresses becoming their station, but most of them bearing, like the Regent York, "signs of war around their aged necks;" gorgets, namely, and baldricks, which sustained their weapons. The lower places around the table were occupied by mechanics and artisans, the presidents, or deacons, as they were termed, of the working classes, in their ordinary clothes, somewhat better arranged than usual. These too wore pieces of armour of various description. Some had the black jack, or doublet, covered with small plates of iron of a lozenge shape, which, secured through the upper angle, hung in rows above each, and which, swaying with the motion of the wearer's person, formed a secure defence to the body. Others had buff-coats, which, as already mentioned, could resist the blow of a sword, and even a lance's point, unless propelled with great force. At the bottom of the table, surrounded as it was with this varied assembly, sat Sir Louis Lundin; no military man, but a priest and parson of St John's, arrayed in his canonical dress, and having his pen and ink before him. He was town-clerk of the burgh, and, like all the priests of the period, (who were called from that circumstance the Pope's knights,) received the honourable title of *Dominus*, contracted into Dom, or Dan, or translated into SIR, the title of reverence due to the secular chivalry.

On an elevated seat, at the head of the council board, was placed Sir Patrick Charteris, in complete armour, brightly burnished; a singular contrast to the motley mixture of warlike and peaceful attire exhibited by the burghers, who were only called to arms occasionally. The bearing of the Provost, while it completely admitted the intimate connexion which mutual interests had created betwixt himself, the burgh, and its magistracy, was at the same time calculated to assert the superiority, which, in virtue of gentle blood and chivalrous rank, the opinions of the age assigned to him over the members of the assembly in which he presided. Two squires stood behind him, one of them holding the knight's pennon, and another his shield, bearing his armorial distinctions, being a hand holding a dagger, or short sword, with the proud motto, *This is my charter*. A handsome page displayed the long sword of his master, and another bore his lance; all which chivalrous emblems and appurtenances were the more scrupulously exhibited, that the dignitary to whom they belonged was engaged in discharging the office of a burgh magistrate. In his own person the Knight of Kinfauns appeared to affect something of state and stiffness, which did not naturally pertain to his frank and jovial character.

"So, you are come at length, Henry Smith and Simon Glover," said the Provost. "Know that you have kept us waiting for your attendance. Should it so chance again while we occupy this place, we will lay such a fine on you as you will have small pleasure in paying. Enough—make no excuses. They are not asked now, and another time they will not be admitted. Know, sirs, that our reverend clerk hath taken down in writing, and at full length, what I will tell you in brief, that you may see what is to be required of you, Henry Smith, in particular. Our late fellow-citizen, Oliver Proudfute, hath been found dead in the High Street, close by the entrance into the wynd. It seemeth he was slain by a heavy blow with a short axe, dealt from behind and at unawares; and the act by which he fell can only be termed a deed of foul and fore-thought murder. So much for the crime. The criminal can only be indicated by circumstances. It is recorded in the protocol of the reverend Sir Louis Lundin, that divers well-reputed witnesses saw our deceased citizen, Oliver Proudfute, till a late period, accompanying the entry of the morrice-dancers, of whom he was one, as far as the house of Simon Glover, in Couvrefew Street, where they again played their pageant—That at this place he separated from the rest of the band, after some discourse with Simon Glover, and made an appointment to meet with the others of his company at the sign of the Griffin, there to conclude the holiday.— Now, Simon, I demand of you whether this be truly stated, so far as you know? and further, what was the purport of the defunct Oliver Proudfute's discourse with you?"

"My Lord Provost and very worshipful Sir Patrick," answered Simon Glover, "you and this honourable council shall know, that, touching certain reports which had been made of the conduct of Henry Smith, some quarrel had arisen between myself and another of my family, and the said Smith here present. Now, this our poor fellow-citizen, Oliver Proudfute, having been active in spreading these reports, as indeed his element lay in such gossipred, some words passed betwixt him and me on the subject; and, as I think, he left me with the purpose of visiting Henry Smith, for he broke off from the morrice-dancers, promising, as it seems, to meet them, as your honour has said, at the sign of the Griffin, in order to conclude the evening. But what he actually did, I know not, as I never again saw him in life."

"It is enough," said Sir Patrick, "and agrees with all that we have heard.—Now, worthy sirs, we next find our poor fellow-citizen environed by a set of revellers and maskers, who had assembled in the High Street; by whom he was shamefully ill intreated, being compelled to kneel down in the street, and there to quaff huge quantities of liquor against his inclination, until at length he escaped from them by flight. This violence was accomplished with drawn swords, loud shouts, and imprecations, so as to attract the attention of several persons, who, alarmed by the tumult, looked out from their windows, as well as of one or two passengers, who, keeping aloof from the light of the torches, lest they also had been maltreated, beheld the usage which our fellow-citizen received in the High Street of the burgh. And although these revellers were disguised, and used vizards, yet their disguises were well known, being a set of quaint masquing habits, prepared some weeks ago by command of Sir John Ramorny, Master of the Horse to his Royal Highness the Duke of Rothsay, Prince Royal of Scotland."

A low groan went through the assembly.

"Yes; so it is, brave burghers," continued Sir Patrick; "our inquiries have led us into conclusions both melancholy and terrible. But as no one can regret the point at which they seem likely to arrive more than I do, so no man living can dread its consequences less. It is even so—various artizans employed upon the articles have described the dresses prepared for Sir John Ramorny's masque as being exactly similar to those of the men by whom Oliver Proudfute was observed to be maltreated. And one mechanic, being Wingfield the feather-dresser, who saw the revellers when they had our fellow-citizen within their hands, remarked that they wore the cinctures and coronals of painted feathers, which he himself had made by the order of the Prince's Master of the Horse.

"After the moment of his escape from these revellers, we lose all trace of Oliver; but we can prove that the masquers went to Sir John Ramorny's, where they were admitted, after some show of delay.—It is rumoured, that thou, Henry Smith, sawest our unhappy fellow-citizen after he had been in the hands of these revellers—What is the truth of that matter?"

"He came to my house in the wynd," said Henry, "about half an hour before midnight; and I admitted him, something unwillingly, as he had been keeping carnival while I remained at home; and there is ill talk, says the proverb, betwixt a full man and a fasting."

"And in which plight seemed he when thou didst admit him?" said the Provost.

"He seemed," answered the Smith, "out of breath, and talked repeatedly of having been endangered by revellers. I paid but small regard, for he was ever a timorous, chicken-spirited, though well-meaning man, and I held that he was speaking more from fancy than reality. But I shall always account it for foul offence in myself, that I did not give him my company, which he requested; and if I live, I will found masses for his soul, in expiation of my guilt."

"Did he describe those from whom he received the injury?" said the Provost.

"Revellers in masquing habits," replied Henry.

"And did he intimate his fear of having to do with them on his return?" again demanded Sir Patrick.

"He alluded particularly to his being way-laid, which I treated as visionary, having been able to see no one in the lane."

"Had he then no help from thee, of any kind whatsoever?" said the Provost.

"Yes, worshipful," replied the Smith; "he exchanged his morrice dress for my head-piece, buff-coat, and target, which I hear were found upon his body; and I have at home his morrice-cap and bells, with the jerkin and other things pertaining. He was to return my garb of fence, and get back his own masquing suit this day, had the saints so permitted."

"You saw him not then afterwards?"

"Never, my lord."

"One word more," said the Provost. "Have you any reason to think that the blow which slew Oliver Proudfute was meant for another man?"

"I have," answered the Smith; "but it is doubtful, and may be dangerous to add such a conjecture, which is besides only a conjecture."

"Speak it out, on your burgher faith and oath—For whom think you the blow was meant?"

"If I must speak," replied Henry, "I believe Oliver Proudfute received the fate which was designed for myself; the rather that, in his folly, Oliver spoke of trying to assume my manner of walking, as well as my dress."

"Have you feud with any one, that you form such an idea?" said Sir Patrick Charteris.

"To my shame and sin be it spoken, I have feud with Highland and Lowland, English and Scot, Perth and Angus. I do not believe poor Oliver had feud with a new-hatched chicken.—Alas! he was the more fully prepared for a sudden call!"

"Hark ye, Smith," said the Provost,—"Answer me distinctly—Is there cause of feud between the household of Sir John Ramorny and yourself?"

"To a certainty, my lord, there is. It is now generally said, that Black Quentin, who went over Tay to Fife some days since, was the owner of the hand which was found in Couvrefew Street upon the eve of St Valentine. It was I who struck off that hand with a blow of my broadsword. As this Black Quentin was a chamberlain of Sir John, and much trusted, it is like there must be feud between me and his master's dependents."

"It bears a face, friend Smith," said Sir Patrick Charteris.—"And now, good brothers and wise magistrates, there lie two suppositions, each of which leads to the same conclusion. The masquers who seized our fellow-citizen, and misused him in a manner of which his body retains some slight marks, may have met with their former prisoner as he returned homewards, and finished their ill usage by taking his life. He himself expressed to Henry Gow fears that this would be the case. If this be really true, one or more of Sir John Ramorny's attendants must have been the assassins. But I think it more likely that one or two of the revellers may have remained on the field, or returned to it, having changed perhaps their disguise, and that to those men (for Oliver Proudfute, in his own personal appearance, would only have been a subject of sport) his apparition in the dress, and assuming, as he proposed to do, the manner, of Henry Smith, was matter of deep hatred; and that seeing him alone, they had taken, as they thought, a certain and safe mode to rid themselves of an enemy so dangerous as all men know Henry Wynd is accounted by those that are his unfriends. The same train of reasoning, again, rests the guilt with the household of Sir John Ramorny—How think you, sirs? Are we not free to charge the crime upon them?"

The Magistrates whispered together for several minutes, and then replied by the voice of Bailie Craigdallie. "Noble Knight, and our worthy Provost—We agree entirely in what your wisdom has spoken concerning this dark and bloody matter; nor do we doubt your sagacity in tracing to the fellowship and the company of John Ramorny of that Ilk, the villainy which hath been done to our deceased fellow-citizen, whether in his own character and capacity, or as mistaking him for our brave townsman, Henry of the Wynd. But Sir John, in his own behalf, and as the Prince's Master of the Horse, maintains an extensive household; and as of course the charge will be rebutted by a denial, we would ask, how we shall proceed in that case?—It is true, could we find law for firing the lodging, and putting all within it to the sword, the old proverb of 'short rede, good rede,' might here apply; for a fouler household of defiers of God, destroyers of men, and debauchers of women, are nowhere sheltered than are Ramorny's band. But I doubt that this summary mode of execution would scarce be borne out by the laws; and no tittle of evidence which I have heard will tend to fix the crime on any single individual or individuals."

Before the Provost could reply, the Town-Clerk arose, and stroking his venerable beard, craved permission to speak, which was instantly granted. "Brethren," he said, "as well in our fathers' time as ours, hath God, on being rightly appealed to, condescended to make manifest the crimes of the guilty, and the innocence of those who may have been rashly accused. Let us demand from our Sovereign Lord, King Robert, who, when the wicked do not interfere to pervert his good intentions, is as just and clement a Prince as our annals can show in their long line, in the name of the Fair City, and of all the commons in Scotland, that he give us, after the fashion of our ancestors, the means of appealing to Heaven for light upon this dark murder. We will demand the proof by *bier-right*, often granted in the days of our Sovereign's ancestors, approved of by bulls and decretals, and administered by the great Emperor Charlemagne in France, by King Arthur in

Britain, and by Gregory the Great, and the mighty Achaius, in this our land of Scotland."

"I have heard of the bier-right, Sir Louis," quoth the Provost, "and I know we have it in our charters of the Fair City; but I am something ill-learned in the ancient laws, and would pray you to inform me more distinctly of its nature."

"We will demand of the King," said Sir Louis Lundin, "my advice being taken, that the body of our murdered fellow-citizen be transported into the High Church of St John's, and suitable masses said for the benefit of his soul, and for the discovery of his foul murder. Meantime we will obtain an order that Sir John Ramorny give up a list of such of his household as were in Perth in the course of the night between Fastern's Even and this Ash-Wednesday, and become bound to present them on a certain day and hour, to be early named, in the High Church of St John's; there one by one to pass before the bier of our murdered fellow-citizen, and in the form prescribed to call upon God and his saints to bear witness that he is innocent of the acting, art or part, of the murder. And credit me, as has been indeed proved by numerous instances, that if the murderer shall endeavour to shroud himself by making such an appeal, the antipathy which subsists between the dead body, and the hand which dealt the fatal blow that divorced it from the soul, will awaken some imperfect life, under the influence of which the veins of the dead man will pour forth at the fatal wounds the blood which has been so long stagnant in the veins. Or, to speak more certainly, it is the pleasure of Heaven, by some hidden agency which we cannot comprehend, to leave open this mode of discovering the wickedness of him who has defaced the image of his Creator."

"I have heard this law talked of," said Sir Patrick, "and it was enforced in the Bruce's time. This surely is no unfit period to seek, by such a mystic mode of inquiry, the truth, to which no ordinary means can give us access, seeing that a general accusation of Sir John's household would full surely be met by a general denial. Yet, I must crave farther of Sir Louis, our reverend town-clerk, how we shall prevent the guilty person from escaping in the interim?"

"The burghers will maintain a strict watch upon wall and at gate, draw-bridges shall be raised, and portcullises lowered, from sunset to sunrise, and strong patrols maintained through the night. This guard the burghers will willingly maintain, to secure against the escape of the murderer of their townsman."

The rest of the councillors acquiesced, by word, sign, and look, in this proposal.

"Again," said their Provost, "what if any one of the suspected household refuse to submit to the ordeal of bier-right?"

"He may appeal to the ordeal of combat," said the reverend city scribe, "with an opponent of equal rank; because the accused person must have his choice, in the appeal to the judgment of God, by what ordeal he will be tried. But if he refuses both, he must be held as guilty, and so punished."

The sages of the council unanimously agreed with the opinion of their Provost and Town-Clerk, and resolved, in all formality, to petition the King, as a matter of right, that the murder of their fellow-citizen should be inquired into according to this ancient form, which was held to manifest the truth, and received as matter of evidence in case of murder, so late as towards the end of the seventeenth century. But before the meeting dissolved, Bailie Craigdallie thought it meet to inquire, who was to be the champion of Maudie, or Magdalen Proudfute, and her two children.

"There need but little inquiry about that," said Sir Patrick Charteris; "we are men, and wear swords, which should be broken over the head of any one amongst us, who will not draw it in behalf of the widow and orphans of our murdered fellow-citizen, and in brave revenge of his death. If Sir John Ramorny shall personally resent the inquiry, Patrick Charteris of Kinfauns will do battle with him to the outrance, whilst horse and man may stand, or spear and blade hold together. But in case the challenger be of yeomanly degree, well wot I that Magdalen Proudfute may choose her own champion among the bravest burghers of Perth, and shame and dishonour were it to the Fair City for ever, could she light upon one who was traitor and coward enough to say her nay! Bring her hither, that she may make her election."

Henry Smith heard this with a melancholy anticipation that the poor woman's choice would light upon him, and that his recent reconciliation with his mistress would be again dissolved, by his being engaged in a fresh quarrel, from which there lay no honourable means of escape, and which, in any other circumstances, he would have welcomed as a glorious opportunity of distinguishing himself, both in sight of the court and of the city. He was aware that under the tuition of Father Clement, Catherine viewed the ordeal of battle rather as an insult to religion, than an appeal to the Deity, and did not consider it as reasonable, that superior strength of arm, or skill of weapon, should be resorted to as the proof of moral guilt or innocence. He had, therefore, much to fear from her peculiar opinions in this particular, refined as they were beyond those of the age she lived in.

While he thus suffered under contending feelings, Magdalen, the widow of the slaughtered man, entered the court, wrapt in a deep mourning veil, and supported and followed by five or six women of good, (that is, of respectability,) dressed in the same melancholy attire. One of her attendants held an infant in her arms, the last pledge of poor Oliver's nuptial affections. Another led a little tottering creature of two years or thereabouts, which looked with wonder and fear, sometimes on the black dress in which they had muffled him, and sometimes on the scene around him.

The assembly rose to receive the melancholy group, and saluted them with an expression of the deepest sympathy, which Magdalen, though the mate of poor Oliver, returned with an air of dignity, which she borrowed, perhaps, from the extremity of her distress. Sir Patrick Charteris then stepped forwards with the courtesy of a knight to a female, and of a protector to an oppressed and injured widow, took the poor woman's hand, and explained to her briefly by what course the city had resolved to follow out the vengeance due for her husband's slaughter.

Having, with a softness and gentleness which did not belong to his general manner, ascertained that the unfortunate woman perfectly understood what was meant, he said aloud to the assembly, "Good citizens of Perth, and free-born men of guild and craft, attend to what is about to pass, for it concerns your rights and privileges. Here stands Magdalen Proudfute, desirous to follow forth the revenge due for the death of her husband, foully murdered, as she sayeth, by Sir John Ramorny, Knight, of that Ilk, and which she offers to prove, by the evidence of bier-right, or by the body of a man. Therefore, I, Patrick Charteris, being a belted knight and free-born gentleman, offer myself to do battle in her just quarrel, whilst man and horse may endure, if any one of my degree will lift my glove.—How say you, Magdalen Proudfute, will you accept me for your champion?"

The widow answered with difficulty,—"I can desire none nobler."

Sir Patrick then took her right hand in his, and, kissing her forehead, for such was the ceremony, said solemnly,—"So may God and St John prosper me at my need, as I will do my devoir as your champion, knightly, truly, and manfully. Go now, Magdalen, and choose at your will among the burgesses of this Fair City, present or absent, any one upon whom you desire to rest your challenge, if he against whom you bring plaint shall prove to be beneath my degree."

All eyes were turned to Henry Smith, whom the general voice had already pointed out as in every respect the fittest to act as champion on the occasion. But the widow waited not for the general prompting of their looks. As soon as Sir Patrick had spoken, she crossed the floor to the place where, near the bottom of the table, the armourer stood among the men of his degree, and took him by the hand:—

"Henry Gow, or Smith," she said, "good burgher and craftsman, my—my—" husband, she would have said, but the word would not come forth; she was obliged to change the expression.

"He who is gone, loved and prized you over all men; therefore meet it is that thou shouldst follow out the quarrel of his widow and orphans."

If there had been a possibility, which in that age there was not, of Henry's rejecting or escaping from a trust for which all men seemed to destine him, every wish and idea of retreat was cut off, when the widow began to address him; and a command from Heaven could hardly have made a stronger impression than did the appeal of the unfortunate Magdalen. Her allusion to his intimacy with the deceased moved him to the soul. During Oliver's life, doubtless, there had been a strain of absurdity in his excessive predilection for Henry, which, considering how very different they were in character, had in it something ludicrous. But all this was now forgotten, and Henry, giving way to his natural ardour, only remembered that Oliver had been his friend and intimate; a man who had loved and honoured him as much as he was capable of doing; and above all, that there was much reason to suspect that he had fallen victim to a blow meant for Henry himself.

It was, therefore, with an alacrity which, the minute before, he could scarce have commanded, and which seemed to express a stern pleasure, that, having pressed his lips to the cold brow of the unhappy Magdalen, the armourer replied—

"I, Henry the Smith, dwelling in the Wynd of Perth, good man and true, and freely born, accept the office of champion to this widow Magdalen, and these orphans, and will do battle in their quarrel to the death, with any man whomsoever of my own degree, and that so long as I shall draw breath. So help me at my need God and good St John!"

There rose from the audience a half-suppressed cry, expressing the interest which the persons present took in the prosecution of the quarrel, and their confidence in the issue.

Sir Patrick Charteris then took measures for repairing to the King's presence, and demanding leave to proceed with inquiry into the murder of Oliver Proudfute, according to the custom of bier-right, and, if necessary, by combat.

He performed this duty after the Town-Council had dissolved, in a private interview between himself and the King, who heard of this new trouble with much vexation, and appointed next morning, after mass, for Sir Patrick and the parties interested, to attend his pleasure in council. In the meantime, a royal pursuivant was dispatched to the Constable's lodgings, to call over the roll of Sir John Ramorny's attendants, and charge him, with his whole retinue, under high penalties, to abide within Perth, until the King's pleasure was farther known.

Chapter Nine

In God's name, see the lists and all things fit;
There let them end it—God defend the right!
Henry VI. Part II

IN THE SAME Council-room of the conventual palace of the Dominicans, King Robert was seated with his brother Albany, whose affected austerity of virtue, and real art and dissimulation, maintained so high an influence over the feeble-minded monarch. It was indeed natural, that one who seldom saw things according to their real forms and outlines, should view them according to the light in which they were presented to him by a bold astucious man, possessing the claim of such near relationship.

Ever anxious on account of his misguided and unfortunate son, the King was now endeavouring to make Albany coincide in opinion with him, in exculpating Rothsay from any part in the death of the Bonnet-maker, the precognition concerning which had been left by Sir Patrick Charteris for his Majesty's consideration.

"This is an unhappy matter, brother Robin," he said, "a most unhappy occurrence; and goes nigh to put strife and quarrel betwixt the nobility and the commons here, as they have been at war together in so many distant lands. I see but one cause of comfort in the matter; and that is, that Sir John Ramorny having received his dismissal from the Duke of Rothsay's family, it cannot be said that he or any of his people, who may have done this bloody deed, (if it has truly been done by them,) have been encouraged or hounded out upon such an errand by my poor David. I am sure, brother, you and I can bear witness, how readily, upon my entreaties, he agreed to dismiss Ramorny from his service, on account of that brawl in Couvrefew Street."

"I remember his doing so," said Albany; "and well do I hope that the connexion betwixt the Prince and Ramorny has not been renewed since he seemed to comply with your Grace's wishes."

"Seemed to comply?—the connexion renewed?" said the King; "what mean you by these expressions, brother? Surely, when David promised to me, that if that unhappy matter of Couvrefew Street were but smothered up and concealed, he would part with Ramorny, as he was a counsellor thought capable of involving him in similar fooleries, and would acquiesce in our inflicting on him either exile, or such punishment as it should please us to impose—surely you cannot doubt that he was sincere in his professions, and would keep his word? Remember you not, that when you advised that a heavy fine should be levied upon his estate in Fife in lieu of banishment, the Prince himself seemed to say, that exile would be better for Ramorny, and even for himself?"

"I remember it well, my royal brother. Nor truly could I have suspected Ramorny of having so much influence over the Prince, after having been accessary to placing him in a situation so perilous, had it not been for my royal kinsman's own confession, alluded to by your Grace, that, if suffered to remain at court, he might still continue to direct his conduct. I then regretted I had advised a fine in place of exile. But that time is passed, and now new mischief has occurred, fraught with much peril to your Majesty, as well as to your royal heir, and to the whole kingdom."

"What mean you, Robin?" said the weak-minded King. "By the tomb of our parents! by the soul of Bruce, our immortal ancestor! I entreat thee, my dearest brother, to take compassion on me. Tell me what evil threatens my son, or my kingdom?"

The features of the King, trembling with anxiety, and his eyes brimful of tears, were bent upon his brother, who seemed to assume time for consideration ere he replied.

"My lord, the danger lies here. Your Grace believes that the Prince had no accession to this second aggression upon the citizens of Perth —the slaughter of this bonnet-making fellow, about whose death they clamour, as a set of gulls about their comrade, when one of the noisy brood is struck down by a boy's shaft."

"Their lives," said the King, "are dear to themselves and their friends, Robin."

"Truly, ay, my liege; and they make them dear to us too, ere we can settle with the knaves for the least blood-witt.—But, as I said, your Majesty thinks the Prince had no share in this last slaughter: I will not attempt to shake your belief in that delicate point, but will endeavour to believe along with you. What you think is rule for me. Robin of Albany will never think otherwise than Robin of broad Scotland."

"Thank you, thank you," said the King, taking his brother's hand. "I knew I might rely that your affection would do justice to poor heedless Rothsay, who exposes himself to so much misconstruction that he scarcely deserves the sentiments you feel for him."

Albany had such an immovable constancy of purpose, that he was able to return the fraternal pressure of the King's hand, while tearing up by the very roots the hopes of the indulgent, fond old man.

"But, alas!" the Duke continued, with a sigh, "this burly intractable Knight of Kinfauns, and his brawling herd of burghers, will not view the matter as we do. They have the boldness to say, that this dead fellow had been misused by Rothsay and his fellows, who were in the street in mask and revel, stopping men and women, compelling them to dance, or to drink huge quantities of wine, with other follies needless to recount; and they say, that the whole party repaired to Sir John Ramorny's, and broke their way into the house, in order to conclude their revel there; thus affording good reason to judge, that the dismissal of Sir John from the Prince's service was but a feigned stratagem to deceive the public. And hence, they urge, that if ill were done that night, by Sir John Ramorny or his followers, much it is to be thought that the Duke of Rothsay must have at least been privy to, if he did not authorize it."

"Albany, this is dreadful!" said the King; "would they make a murderer of my boy? would they pretend my son would soil his hands in Scottish blood, without having either provocation or purpose? No, no—they will not invent calumnies so broad as these, for they are flagrant and incredible."

"Pardon, my liege," resumed the Duke of Albany; "they say the cause of quarrel which occasioned the riot in Couvrefew Street, and the consequences, was more proper to the Prince than to Sir John; since none suspects, far less believes, that that hopeful enterprise was conducted for the gratification of the Knight of Ramorny.".

"Thou drivest me mad, Robin!" said the King.

"I am dumb," answered his brother; "I did but speak my poor mind according to your royal order."

"Thou meanest well, I know," said the King; "but instead of tearing me to pieces with the display of inevitable calamities, were it not kinder, Robin, to point me out some mode to escape from them?"

"True, my liege; but as the only road of extrication is rough and difficult, it is necessary your Grace should be first possessed with the absolute necessity of using it, ere you hear it even described. The chirurgeon must first convince his patient of the incurable condition of a shattered member, ere he venture to name amputation, though it be the only remedy."

Robert, at these words, was roused to a degree of alarm and indignation, greater than his brother had deemed he could be awakened to.

"Shattered and mortified member! my Lord of Albany? amputation the only remedy?—These are unintelligible words, my lord.—If thou appliest them to our son Rothsay, thou must make them good to the letter, else mayst thou have bitter cause to rue the consequence."

"You construe me too literally, my royal liege," said Albany. "I spoke not of the Prince in such unbeseeming terms; for I call Heaven to witness, that he is dearer to me as the son of a well-beloved brother, than had he been son of my own. But I spoke in regard to separating him from the follies and vanities, which holy men say are like to mortified members, and ought, like them, to be cut off and thrown from us, as things which interrupt our progress in better things."

"I understand—thou wouldst have this Ramorny, who hath been thought the instrument of my son's follies, exiled from court," said the relieved Monarch, "until these unhappy scandals are forgotten, and our subjects are disposed to look upon our son with different and more confiding eyes."

"That were good counsel, my liege; but mine went a little—a very little—further. I would have the Prince himself remove for some brief period from court."

"How, Albany! part with my child, my first-born, the light of my eyes, and—wilful as he is—the darling of my heart!—Oh, Robin! I cannot, and I will not."

"Nay, I did but suggest, my lord—I am sensible of the wound such proceeding must inflict on a parent's heart, for am not I myself a father?" And he hung his head, as if in hopeless despondency.

"I could not survive it, Albany. When I think that even our own influence over him, which, sometimes forgotten in our absence, is ever effectual whilst he is with us, is by your plan to be entirely removed, what perils might he not rush upon? I could not sleep in his absence—I should hear his death-groan in every breeze; and you, Albany, though you conceal it better, would be nearly as anxious."

Thus spoke the facile monarch, willing to conciliate his brother and cheat himself, by taking it for granted that an affection, of which there were no traces, subsisted betwixt the uncle and nephew.

"Your paternal apprehensions are too easily alarmed, my lord," said Albany. "I do not propose to leave the disposal of the Prince's motions to his own wild pleasure. I understand that the Prince is to be placed for a short time under some becoming restraint—that he should be subjected to the charge of some grave counsellor, who must be responsible both for his conduct and his safety, as a tutor for his pupil."

"How! a tutor? and at Rothsay's age?" exclaimed the King; "he is two years beyond the space to which our laws limit the term of nonage."

"The wiser Romans," said Albany, "extended it for four years after the period we assign; and, in common sense, the right of control ought to last till it be no longer necessary, and so the time ought to vary with the disposition. Here is young Lindsay, the Earl of Crawford, who they say gives patronage to Ramorny on this appeal—He is a lad of fifteen, with the deep passions and fixed purpose of a man of thirty;

while my royal nephew, with much more amiable and noble qualities both of head and heart, sometimes shows, at twenty-three years of age, the wanton humours of a boy, towards whom restraint may be kindness.—And do not be discouraged that it is so, my liege, or angry with your brother for telling the truth; since the best fruits are those that are slowest in ripening, and the best horses those which give most trouble to the grooms who train them for the field or lists."

The Duke stopped, and after suffering King Robert to indulge for two or three minutes in a reverie which he did not attempt to interrupt, he added, in a more lively tone,—"But, cheer up, my noble liege; perhaps the feud may be made up without farther fighting or cumbers. The widow is poor, for her husband, though he was much employed, had idle and costly habits. The matter may be therefore redeemed for money, and the amount of an assythment* may be recovered out of Ramorny's estate."

"Nay, that we will ourselves discharge," said King Robert, eagerly catching at the hope of a pacific termination of this unpleasing debate. "Ramorny's prospects will be destroyed by his being sent from court, and deprived of his charge in Rothsay's household; and it would be ungenerous to load a falling man.—But here comes our secretary, the Prior, to tell us the hour of council approaches.—Good morrow, my worthy father."

"Benedicite, my royal liege," answered the Abbot.

"Now, good father," continued the King, "without waiting for Rothsay, whose accession to our counsels we will ourselves guarantee, proceed we to the business of our kingdom. What advices have you from the Douglas?"

"He has arrived at his Castle of Tantallon, my liege, and has sent a post to say, that though the Earl of March remains in sullen seclusion in his fortress of Dunbar, his friends and followers are gathering and forming an encampment near Coldingham, where it is supposed they intend to await the arrival of a large force of English, which Hotspur and Sir Ralph Percy are assembling on the English frontier."

"That is cold news," said the King; "and may God forgive George of Dunbar!"—The Prince entered as he spoke, and he continued—"Ha! thou art here at length, Rothsay;—I saw thee not at mass."

"I was an idler this morning," said the Prince, "having spent a restless and feverish night."

"Ah, foolish boy!" answered the King; "hadst thou not been over restless on Fastern's Even, thou hadst not been feverish on the night of Ash Wednesday."

"Let me not interrupt your prayers, my liege," said the Prince

* A mulct, in atonement for bloodshed, due to the nearest relations of the deceased.

lightly. "Your Grace was invoking Heaven in behalf of some one—an enemy doubtless, for these have the frequent advantage of your orisons."

"Sit down and be at peace, foolish youth!" said his father, his eye resting at the same time on the handsome face and graceful figure of his favourite son. Rothsay drew a cushion near to his father's feet, and threw himself carelessly down upon it, while the King resumed.

"I was regretting that the Earl of March, having separated warm from my hand with full assurance that he should receive compensation for everything which he could complain of as injurious, should have been capable of caballing with Northumberland against his own country—Is it possible he could doubt our intentions to make good our word?"

"That I will answer for him," said the Prince; "March never doubted your Highness's word. Marry, he may well have made question whether your learned councillors had left your Majesty the power of keeping it."

Robert the Third had adopted to a great extent the timid policy of not seeming to hear that which, being heard, required, even in his own eyes, some display of displeasure. He passed on, therefore, without observing his son's speech; but in private, Rothsay's rashness augmented the displeasure which his father began to entertain against him.

"It is well the Douglas is on the Marches," said the King. "His breast, like those of his ancestors, has ever been the best bulwark of Scotland."

"Then woe betide us if he should turn his back," said the incorrigible Rothsay.

"Dare you impeach the courage of Douglas?" replied the King, extremely chafed.

"No man dare question the Earl's courage," said Rothsay; "it is as certain as his pride—but his luck may be something doubted."

"By Saint Andrew, David!" exclaimed his father, "thou art like a screech-owl—every word thou sayest betokens strife and calamity."

"I am silent, father," answered the youth.

"And what news of our Highland disturbances?" continued the King, addressing the Prior.

"I trust they have assumed a favourable aspect," answered the clergyman. "The fire which threatened the whole country is likely to be drenched out by the blood of some forty or fifty kerne; for the two great confederacies have agreed, by solemn indenture of arms, to decide their quarrel with such weapons as your Highness may name, and in your royal presence, in such place as shall be appointed, upon the 30th of March next to come, being Palm Sunday; the number of combatants being limited to thirty on each side, and the fight to be maintained to extremity, since they affectionately make humble suit and petition to your Majesty, that you will parentally condescend to waive for the day your royal privilege of interrupting the combat, by flinging down of truncheon, or crying of Ho! until the battle shall be utterly fought to an end."

"The wild savages!" exclaimed the King; "would they limit our best and dearest royal privilege, to put a stop to slaughter, and cry truce to battle?—Will they remove the only motive which could bring me to the butcherly spectacle of their combat?—Would they fight like men, or like their own mountain wolves?"

"My lord," said Albany, "the Earl of Crawford and I had presumed, without consulting you, to ratify that preliminary, for the adoption of which we saw much and pressing reason."

"How! the Earl of Crawford!" said the King. "Methinks he is a young counsellor on such grave occurrents."

"He is," replied Albany, "notwithstanding his early years, of such esteem amongst his Highland neighbours, that I could have done little with them but for his aid and influence."

"Hear this, young Rothsay!" said the King reproachfully to his heir.

"I pity Crawford, Sire," replied the Prince. "He has too early lost a father, whose councils would have better become such a season as this."

The King turned next towards Albany with a look of triumph, in the affection which his son displayed.

Albany proceeded without emotion. "It is not the life of these Highlandmen, but their death, which is to be profitable to this commonwealth of Scotland; and truly it seemed to the Earl of Crawford and myself most desirable that the combat should be a strife of extermination."

"Marry," said the Prince, "if such be the juvenile policy of Lindsay, he will be a merciful ruler some ten or twelve years hence! Out upon a boy, that is hard of heart before he has hair upon his lip! Better he had contented himself with fighting cocks on Fastern's Even, than laying schemes for massacring men on Palm Sunday, as if he were backing a Welsh main, where all must fight to death."

"Rothsay is right, Albany," said the King; "it were unlike a Christian Monarch to give way in this point. I cannot consent to see men battle until they are all hewn down like cattle in a shambles. It would sicken me to look at it, and the warder would drop from my hand for mere lack of strength to hold it."

"It would drop unheeded," said Albany. "Let me entreat your

Grace to recollect, that you only give up a royal privilege, which, exercised, would win you no respect, since it would receive no obedience. Were your Majesty to throw down your warder when the war is high, and these men's blood is hot, it would meet no more regard than if a sparrow should drop among a herd of battling wolves the straw which he was carrying to his nest. Nothing will separate them but the exhaustion of slaughter; and better they sustain it at the hands of each other, than from the swords of such troops as might act upon your Majesty's commands. An attempt to keep the peace by violence would be construed into an ambush laid for them; both parties would unite to resist it,—the slaughter would be the same, and the hoped-for results of future peace would be utterly disappointed."

"There is e'en too much truth in what you say, brother Robin," replied the flexible King. "To little purpose is it to command what I cannot enforce; and, although I have the unhappiness to do so each day of my life, it were needless to give such a public example of royal impotency, before the crowds who may assemble to behold this spectacle. Let these savage men, therefore, work their bloody will to the uttermost upon each other; I will not attempt to forbid what I cannot prevent them from executing.—Heaven help this wretched country! I will to my oratory and pray for her, since to help her by hand and head is alike denied to me. Father Prior, I pray the aid of your arm."

"Nay, but, brother," said Albany, "forgive me if I remind you we must hear the matter between the citizens of Perth and Ramorny, about the death of a townsman"——

"True, true—" said the Monarch, reseating himself; "more violence—more battle—Oh, Scotland! Scotland! if the best blood of thy bravest children could enrich thy barren soil, what land on earth would excel thee in fertility! When is it that a white hair is seen on the beard of a Scottish man, unless he be some wretch like thy sovereign, protected from murder by impotence, to witness the scenes of slaughter to which he cannot put a period?—Let them come in—delay them not. They are in haste to kill, and grudge each other each fresh breath of their Creator's blessed air. The demon of strife and slaughter hath possessed the whole land!"

As the mild Prince threw himself back on his seat, with an air of impatience and anger not very usual with him, the door at the lower end of the room was unclosed, and, advancing from the gallery into which it led, (where in perspective was seen a guard of the Bute-men, or Brandanes, under arms,) came, in mournful procession, the widow of poor Oliver, led by Sir Patrick Charteris, with as much respect as if she had been a lady of the first rank. Behind them came two women of good, the wives of magistrates of the city, both in mourning garments, one bearing the infant, and the other leading the elder child. The Smith followed in his best attire, and wearing over his buff-coat a scarf of crape. Bailie Craigdallie, and a brother magistrate, closed the mournful procession, exhibiting similar marks of mourning.

The good King's transitory passion was gone the instant he looked on the pallid countenance of the sorrowing widow, and beheld the unconsciousness of the innocent orphans who had sustained so great a loss; and when Sir Patrick Charteris had assisted Magdalen Proudfute to kneel down, and, still holding her hand, kneeled himself on one knee, it was with a sympathetic tone that King Robert asked her name and business. She made no answer, but muttered something, looking towards her conductor.

"Speak for the poor woman, Sir Patrick Charteris," said the King, "and tell us the cause of her seeking our presence."

"So please you, my liege," answered Sir Patrick, rising up, "this woman, and these unhappy orphans, make plaint to your Highness upon Sir John Ramorny of Ramorny, Knight, that by him, or some of his household, her umquhile husband, Oliver Proudfute, freeman and burgess of Perth, was slain upon the streets of the city on the Eve of Shrove Tuesday, or the morning of Ash Wednesday."

"Woman," replied the King, with much kindness, "thou art gentle by sex, and should'st be pitiful even by thy affliction; for our own calamity ought to make us—nay, I think it doth make us—merciful to others. Thy husband hath only trodden the path appointed to us all."

"In his case," said the widow, "my liege must remember it has been a brief and a bloody one."

"I agree he hath had foul measure. But since I have been unable to protect him, as I confess was my royal duty, I am willing, in atonement, to support thee and these orphans, as well, or better, than you lived in the days of your husband; only do thou pass from this charge, and be not the occasion of spilling more life. Remember, I put before you the choice betwixt practising mercy and pursuing vengeance, and that betwixt plenty and penury."

"It is true, my liege, we are poor," answered the widow, with unshaken firmness; "but I and my children will feed with the beasts of the field, ere we live on the price of my husband's blood. I demand the combat by my champion, as you are belted knight and crowned King."

"I knew it would be so!" said the King, aside to Albany. "In Scotland, the first words stammered by an infant, and the last uttered by a dying grey-beard, are—'combat—blood—revenge.'—It skills not arguing further. Admit the defendants."

Sir John Ramorny entered the apartment. He was dressed in a long furred robe, such as men of quality wore when they were unarmed.

Concealed by the folds of drapery, his wounded arm was supported by
a scarf, or sling of crimson silk, and with the left arm he leaned on a
youth, who, scarcely beyond the years of boyhood, bore on his brow
the deep impression of early thought, and premature passion. This
was that celebrated Lindsay, Earl of Crawford, who, in his afterdays,
was known by the epithet of the Tiger Earl, and who ruled the great
and rich valley of Strathmore with the absolute power and unrelenting
cruelty of a feudal tyrant. Two or three gentlemen, friends of the Earl,
or of his own, countenanced Sir John Ramorny by their presence on
this occasion. The charge was again stated, and met by a broad denial
on the part of the accused; and in reply, the challengers offered to
prove their charge by an appeal to the ordeal of bier-right.

"I am not bound," answered Sir John Ramorny, "to submit to an
ordeal, since I can prove, by the evidence of my late royal master, that I
was in my own lodgings, lying on my bed, ill at ease, while this Provost
and these Bailies pretend I was committing a crime to which I had
neither will nor temptation. I can therefore be no just object of suspicion."

"I can aver," said the Prince, "that I saw and conversed with Sir
John Ramorny about some matters concerning my own household, on
the very night when this murder was a-doing. I therefore know that he
was ill at ease, and could not in person commit the deed in question.
But I know nothing of the employment of his attendants, and will not
take it upon me to say that one of them may not have been guilty of the
crime now charged on them."

Sir John Ramorny had, during the beginning of this speech,
looked round with an air of defiance, which was somewhat disconcerted by the concluding sentence of Rothsay's speech. "I thank
your Highness," he said, with a smile, "for your cautious and limited
testimony in my behalf. He was wise who wrote, 'Put not your faith
in Princes.'"

"If you have no other evidence of your innocence, Sir John Ramorny," said the King, "we may not, in respect to your followers, refuse
to the injured widow and orphans, the complainers, the grant of a
proof by ordeal of bier-right, unless any of them should prefer that of
combat. For yourself, you are, by the Prince's evidence, freed from the
attaint."

"My liege," answered Sir John, "I can take warrant upon myself for
the innocence of my household and followers."

"Why so a monk or a woman might speak," said Sir Patrick Charteris. "In knightly language, wilt thou, Sir John de Ramorny, do battle
with me in the behalf of thy followers?"

"The Provost of Perth had not obtained time to speak his duelling," said Ramorny, "ere I would have accepted it. But I am not at present fit to hold a lance."

"I am glad of it, under your favour, Sir John—There will be the less bloodshed," said the King. "You must therefore produce your followers according to your steward's household book, in the great church of St John's, that, in presence of all whom it may concern, they may purge themselves of this accusation. See that every man of them do appear at the time of High Mass, otherwise your honour may be sorely tainted."

"They shall attend to a man," said Sir John Ramorny. Then bowing low to the King, he directed himself to the young Duke of Rothsay, and making a deep obeisance, spoke so as to be heard by him alone. "You have used me generously, my lord!—one word of your lips could have ended this controversy, and you have refused to speak it!—"

"On my life," whispered the Prince, "I spake as far as the extreme verge of truth and conscience would permit. I think thou could'st not expect I should frame lies for thee.—After all, John, in my broken recollections of that night, I do bethink me of a butcherly-looking mute, with a curtal-axe, pretty much like such a one as may have done yonder night-job.—Ha! have I touched you, Sir Knight?"

Ramorny made no answer, but turned away as precipitately as if some one had pressed suddenly on his wounded arm, and regained his lodgings with the Earl of Crawford; to whom, though disposed for anything rather than revelry, he was obliged to offer a splendid collation, to acknowledge in some degree his sense of the countenance which the young noble had afforded him.

Chapter Ten

WHEN, after an entertainment, the prolonging of which was like torture to the wounded knight, the Earl of Crawford at length took horse, to go to his distant quarters in the Castle of Dupplin, where he resided as a guest, the Knight of Ramorny retired into his sleeping apartment, agonized by pains of body and anxiety of mind. Here he found Henbane Dwining, on whom it was his hard fate to depend for consolation in both respects. The physician, with his affectation of extreme humility, hoped he saw his exalted patient merry and happy.

"Merry as a mad dog!" said Ramorny, "and happy as the wretch whom the cur hath bitten, and who begins to feel the approach of the ravening madness. That ruthless boy saw my agony, and spared not a single carouse. I must do him *justice*, forsooth! If I had done justice to him and to the world, I had thrown him out of window, and cut short a career, which, if he grow up as he has begun, will prove a source of misery to all Scotland, but especially to Tayside.—Take heed as thou undoest the ligatures, chirurgeon; the touch of a fly's wing on that raw glowing stump were like a dagger to me."

"Fear not, my noble patron," said the leech, with a chuckling laugh of enjoyment, which he vainly endeavoured to disguise under a tone of affected sensibility. "We will apply some fresh balsam, and—he, he, he!—relieve your knightly honour of the irritation which you sustain so firmly."

"Firmly, man?" said Ramorny, grinning with pain; "I sustain it as I would the scorching flames of purgatory—the bone seems made of red-hot iron—thy greasy ointment will hiss as it drops upon the wound—And yet it is December's ice, compared to the fever-fit of my mind!"

"We will first use our art to the body, my noble patron," said Dwining; "and then, with your knighthood's permission, your servant will try his art on the troubled mind—though I fain hope even the mental pain also may in some degree depend on the irritation of the wound, and that, abated as I trust the corporeal pangs will soon be, perhaps the stormy feelings of the mind may subside of themselves."

"Henbane Dwining," said the patient, as he felt the pain of his wound assuaged, "thou art a precious and invaluable leech, but some things are beyond thy power. Thou canst stupify my bodily sense of this raging agony, but thou canst not teach me to bear the scorn of the boy whom I have brought up, whom I loved, Dwining—for I did love him,—dearly love him! The worst of my ill deeds have been done to flatter his vices—and he grudged me a word of his mouth, when a word would have allayed this cumber. He smiled, too—I saw him smile when yonder paltry Provost, the companion and patron of wretched burghers, defied me, whom this heartless Prince knew to be unable to bear arms.—Ere I forget or forgive it, thou thyself shalt preach up the pardoning of injuries!—And then the care for to-morrow.—Think'st thou, Henbane Dwining, that, in very reality, the wounds of the slaughtered corpse will gape, and shed tears of fresh blood at the murderer's approach?"

"I cannot tell, my lord, save by report," said Dwining, "which avouches the fact."

"The brute Bonthron," said Ramorny, "is startled at the apprehension of such a thing, and speaks of standing the combat. What think'st thou?—he is a fellow of steel."

"It is the armourer's trade to deal with steel," replied Dwining.

"Were Bonthron to fall it would little grieve me," said Ramorny; "though I should miss an useful hand."

"I well believe your lordship will not sorrow as for that you lost last
—Excuse my pleasantry—he, he, he!—But what are the useful properties of this fellow Bonthron?"

"Those of a bull-dog," answered the knight; "he worries without
barking."

"You have no fear of his confessing?" said the physician.

"Who can tell what the dread of approaching death may do?"
replied the patient. "He has already shown a timorousness entirely
alien from his ordinary sullenness of nature—he that would scarce
wash his hands after he had slain a man, is now afraid to see a dead
body bleed."

"Well," said the leech, "I must do somewhat for him if I can, since it
was to further my revenge that he struck yonder downright blow,
though by ill luck it lighted not where it was intended."

"And whose fault was that, timid villain," said Ramorny, "save thine
own, who marked a rascal deer for a buck of the first head?"

"Benedicite, noble sir," replied the mediciner; "would you have
me, who know little save of chamber practice, be as skilful of wood-
craft as your noble self, or tell hart from hind, doe from roe, in a glade
at midnight? I misdoubted me somewhat when I saw the figure run
past us to the smith's habitation in the wynd, habited like a morrice-
dancer; and my mind partly misgave me that it was our man—
methought he seemed less of stature. But when he came out again,
after so much time as to change his dress, and swaggered onwards
with buff-coat and steel-cap, whistling after the armourer's wonted
fashion, I do own I was mistaken, and loosed your knighthood's bull-
dog upon him, who did his devoir most duly, though he pulled down
the wrong deer. Therefore, unless the accursed Smith kills our poor
friend stone-dead on the spot, I am determined, if art may do it, that
ban-dog Bonthron shall not miscarry."

"It will put thine art to the test, man of medicine," said Ramorny;
"for know, that having the worst of the combat, if our champion be not
killed stone-dead in the lists, he will be drawn forth of them by the
heels, and without further ceremony knitted up to the gallows, as
convicted of the murder; and when he hath swung there like a loose
tassel for an hour or so, I think thou wilt hardly take it in hand to cure
his broken neck."

"I am of a different opinion, may it please your knighthood,"
answered Dwining, gently. "I will carry him off from the very foot of
the gallows into the land of faery, like King Arthur, or Sir Huon of
Bourdeaux, or Ugero the Dane; or I will, if I please, suffer him to
dangle on the gibbet for a certain number of minutes or hours, and
then whisk him away from the sight of all, with as much ease as the

wind wafts away the withered leaf."

"This is idle boasting, Sir Leech," replied Ramorny. "The whole mob of Perth will attend him to the gallows, each more eager than another to see the retainer of a nobleman die, for the slaughter of a cuckoldly citizen. There will be a thousand of them round the gibbet's foot."

"And were there ten thousand," said Dwining, "shall I, who am a high clerk, and have studied in Spain, and Araby itself, not be able to deceive the eyes of this hoggish herd of citizens, when the pettiest juggler that ever dealt in legerdemain can gull even the sharp observation of your most intelligent knighthood? I tell you, I will put the change on them as if I were possessed of Keddie's ring."

"If thou speakest truth," answered the knight, "and I think thou darest not palter with me on such a theme, thou must have the aid of Satan, and I will have nought to do with him.—I disown and defy him."

Dwining indulged in his internal chuckling laugh when he heard his patron testify his defiance of the foul fiend, and saw him second it by crossing himself. He composed himself, however, upon observing Ramorny's aspect become very stern, and said, with tolerable gravity, though a little interrupted by the effort necessary to suppress his mirthful mood, "Confederacy, most devout sir; confederacy is the soul of jugglery. But—he, he, he!—I have not the honour to be—he, he!—an ally of the gentleman of whom you speak—in whose existence I am—he, he!—no very profound believer, though your knightship, doubtless, hath better opportunities of acquaintance."

"Proceed, rascal, and without that sneer, which may otherwise cost thee dear."

"I will, most undaunted," replied Dwining. "Know that I have my confederate too, else my skill were little worth."

"And who may that be, pray you?"

"Stephen Smotherwell, if it like your honour, lockman* of this Fair City. I marvel your knighthood knows him not."

"And I marvel thy knaveship knows him not on professional acquaintance," replied Ramorny; "but I see thy nose is unslit, thy ears yet uncropped, and if thy shoulders are seared or branded, thou art wise for using a high-collared jerkin."

"He, he! your honour is pleasant," said the mediciner. "It is not by personal circumstances that I have acquired the intimacy of Stephen Smotherwell, but on account of a certain traffic betwixt us, in which, an't please you, I exchange certain sums of silver for the bodies, heads,

*Executioner. So called because one of his dues consisted in taking a small ladlefull (Scottice, *lock*) of meal, out of every caskful exposed in the market.

and limbs, of those who die by aid of friend Stephen."

"Wretch!" exclaimed the knight, with horror, "is it to compose charms and forward works of witchcraft, that you trade for these miserable relics of mortality?"

"He, he, he!—No, an it please your knighthood," answered the mediciner, much amused with the ignorance of his patron; "but we who are knights of the scalpel, are accustomed to practise careful carving of the limbs of defunct persons, which we call dissection, whereby we discover, by examination of a dead member, how to deal with one belonging to a living man, which hath become diseased through injury or otherwise. Ah! if your honour saw my poor laboratory, I could show you heads and hands, feet and lungs, which have been long supposed to be rotting in the mould. The skull of Wallace, stolen from London Bridge; the heart of Sir Simon Fraser, that never feared man; the lovely skull of the fair Margaret Logie. Oh, had I but had the fortune to have preserved the chivalrous hand of mine honoured patron!"

"Out upon thee, slave!—Thinkest thou to disgust me with thy catalogue of horrors?—Tell me at once where thy discourse drives. How can thy traffic with the hang-dog executioner be of avail to serve me, or to save my servant Bonthron?"

"Why, I do not recommend it to your knighthood, 'save in an extremity," replied Dwining. "But we will suppose the battle fought, and our cock beaten. Now we must first possess him with the certainty, that, if unable to gain the day, we will at least save him from the hangman, provided he confess nothing which can prejudice your knighthood's honour."

"Ha!—ay, a thought strikes me," said Ramorny. "We can do more than this—we can place a word in Bonthron's mouth that will be troublesome enough to him whom I am bound to curse, for being the cause of my misfortune. Let us to the ban-dog's kennel, and explain to him what is to be done in every view of the question. If we can persuade him to stand the bier-ordeal, it may be a mere bugbear, and in that case we are safe. If he take the combat, he is fierce as a baited bear, and may, perchance, master his opponent; then we are more than safe—we are revenged. If Bonthron himself is vanquished, we will put thy device in exercise; and if thou canst manage it cleanly, we shall dictate his confession, take the advantage of it, as I will show thee in further conference, and make a giant stride towards satisfaction for my wrongs.—Still there remains one hazard. Suppose our mastiff mortally wounded in the lists, who shall prevent his growling out some species of confession different from what we would recommend?"

"Marry, that can his mediciner," said Dwining. "Let me wait on him, and lay but a finger on his wound, and trust me he shall betray no confidence."

"Why, there's a willing fiend, that needs neither pushing nor prompting!" said Ramorny.

"As I trust I shall need neither in your knighthood's service."

"We will go indoctrinate our agent," continued the Knight. "We shall find him pliant; for hound as he is, he knows those who feed from those who brow-beat him; and he holds a late royal master of mine in deep hate for some injurious treatment and base terms which he received at his hand. I must also farther concert with thee the particulars of thy practice, for saving the ban-dog from the hands of the herd of citizens."

We leave this worthy pair of friends to their secret practices, of which we shall afterwards see the results. They were, although of different qualities, as well matched for device and execution of criminal projects, as the grey-hound is to destroy the game which the slow-hound raises, or the slow-hound to track the prey which the gaze-hound discovers by the eye. Pride and selfishness were the characteristics of both; but from the difference of rank, education, and talents, they had assumed the most different appearance in the two individuals.

Nothing could less resemble the high-blown ambition of the favourite courtier, the successful gallant, and the bold warrior, than the submissive unassuming mediciner, who seemed even to court and delight in insult; whilst, in his secret soul, he felt himself possessed of a superiority of knowledge,—a power, both of science and of mind, which placed the rude nobles of the day infinitely beneath him. So conscious was Henbane Dwining of this elevation, that, like a keeper of wild beasts, he sometimes adventured, for his own amusement, to rouse the stormy passions of such men as Ramorny, trusting, with his humble manner, to elude the turmoil he had excited, as an Indian boy will launch his light canoe, secure from its very fragility, upon a broken surf, in which the boat of an argosy would be assuredly dashed to pieces. That the feudal baron should despise the humble practitioner in medicine, was a matter of course; but Ramorny felt not the less the influence which Dwining exercised over him, and was in the encounter of their wits often mastered by him, as the most eccentric efforts of a fiery horse are overcome by a boy of twelve years old, if he has been bred to the arts of the manege. But the contempt of Dwining for Ramorny was far less qualified. He regarded the knight, in comparison with himself, as scarcely rising above the brute creation; capable indeed of working destruction, as the bull with his horns, or the wolf with his fangs, but mastered by mean prejudices, and a slave to priestcraft, in which phrase Dwining included religion of every kind. On the whole, he considered Ramorny as one whom nature had assigned to him as a serf, to mine for the gold which he worshipped, and the avaricious love of which was his greatest failing, though by no means his worst vice. He vindicated this sordid tendency in his own eyes, by persuading himself that it had its source in the love of power.

"Henbane Dwining," he said, as he gazed in delight upon the hoards which he had secretly amassed, and which he visited from time to time, "is no silly miser, that doats on those pieces for their golden lustre; it is the power with which they endow the possessor, which makes him thus adore them. What is there that these put not within your command? Do you love beauty, and are mean, deformed, infirm, and old?—here is a lure the fairest hawk of them all will stoop to. Are you feeble, weak, subject to the oppression of the powerful?—here is that will arm in your defence those more mighty than the petty tyrant whom you fear. Are you splendid in your wishes, and desire the outward show of opulence?—this dark chest contains many a wide range of hill and dale, many a fair forest full of game; the allegiance of a thousand vassals. Wish you for favour in courts, temporal or spiritual?—the smiles of kings, the pardon of popes and priests for old crimes, and the indulgence which encourages priest-ridden fools to venture on new ones,—all these holy incentives to vice may be purchased for gold. Revenge itself, which the gods are said to reserve to themselves, doubtless because they envy humanity so sweet a morsel—revenge itself is to be bought by it. But it is also to be won by superior skill, and that is the nobler mode of reaching it. I will spare, then, my treasure for other uses, and accomplish my revenge gratis; or rather I will add the luxury of augmented wealth to the triumph of requited wrongs."

Thus thought Dwining, as, returned from his visit to Sir John Ramorny, he added the gold he had received for his various services to the mass of his treasure; and having gloated over the whole for a minute or two, turned the key on his concealed treasure-house, and walked forth on his visits to his patients, yielding the wall to every man whom he met, and bowing and doffing his bonnet to the poorest burgher that owned a petty booth, nay, to the artificers who gained their precarious bread by the labour of their welked hands.

"Caitiffs," was the thought of his heart, while he did such obeisance, "base, sodden-witted mechanics! did you know what this key could disclose, what foul weather from Heaven would prevent your unbonneting? what putrid kennel in your wretched hamlet would be disgusting enough to make you scruple to fall down and worship the owner of such wealth? But I will make you feel my power, though it suits my humour to hide it. I will be an incubus to your city, since you have rejected me as a magistrate. Like the night-mare, I will hag-ride ye, yet remain invisible myself.—This miserable Ramorny too, he who, in losing his hand, has, like a poor artizan, lost the only valuable part of his frame, *he* heaps insulting language on me, as if anything which *he* can say has power to chafe a constant mind like mine! Yet while he calls me rogue, villain, and slave, he acts as wisely as if he should amuse himself by pulling hairs out of my head, while my hand has hold of his heart-strings. Every insult I can pay back instantly by a pang of bodily pain or mental agony—and—he! he!—I run no long accounts with his knighthood, that must be allowed."

While the mediciner was thus indulging his diabolical musing, and passing, in his creeping manner, along the street, the cry of females was heard behind him.

"Ay, there he is, Our Lady be praised!—there is the most helpful man in Perth," said one voice.

"They may speak of knights and kings for redressing wrongs, as they call it—but give me worthy Master Dwining the pottercarrier, cummers," replied another.

At the same moment, the leech was surrounded, and taken hold of by the speakers, good women of the Fair City.

"How now—what's the matter?" said Dwining, "whose cow has calved?"

"There is no calving in the case," said one of the women, "but a poor fatherless wean dying—so come awa' wi' you, for our trust is constant in you, as Bruce said to Donald of the Isles."

"*Opiferque per orbem dicor*," said Henbane Dwining. "What is the child dying of?"

"The croup—the croup," screamed one of the gossips; "the innocent is rouping like a corbie."

"*Cynanche trachealis*—that disease makes brief work. Show me the house instantly," continued the mediciner, who was in the habit of exercising his profession liberally, notwithstanding his natural avarice, and humanely, in spite of his natural malignity. As we can suspect him of no better principle, his motive was probably vanity and the love of his art.

He would nevertheless have declined giving his attendance in the present case, had he known whither the kind gossips were conducting him, in time sufficient to frame an apology. But ere he knew where he was going, the leech was hurried into the house of the late Oliver Proudfute, from which he heard the chant of the women, as they swathed and dressed the corpse of the umquhile Bonnet-maker, for the ceremony of next morning; of which chant, the following verses may be received as a modern imitation.

1.
Viewless Essence, thin and bare,
Well nigh melted into air;
Still with fondness hovering near
The earthly form thou once didst wear;

2.
Pause upon thy pinion's flight,
Be thy course to left or right;
Be thou doom'd to soar or sink,
Pause upon the awful brink.

3.
To avenge the deed expelling
Thee untimely from thy dwelling,
Mystic force thou shalt retain
O'er the blood and o'er the brain.

4.
When the form thou shalt espy
That darken'd on thy closing eye;
When the footstep thou shalt hear,
That thrill'd upon thy dying ear;

5.
Then strange sympathies shall wake,
The flesh shall thrill, the nerves shall quake;
The wounds renew their clotter'd flood,
And every drop cry blood for blood!

Hardened as he was, the physician felt reluctance to pass the threshold of the man to whose death he had been so directly, though mistakingly accessory.

"Let me pass on, women," he said, "my art can only help the living—the dead are past our power."

"Nay, but your patient is upstairs—the youngest orphan"——

Dwining was compelled to go into the house. But he was surprised, when, the instant he stepped over the threshold, the gossips, who were busied with the dead body, stinted suddenly in their song, while one said to the others, "In God's name, who entered?—that was a large gout of blood!"

"Not so," said another voice, "it is a drop of liquid balm."

"Nay, cummer, it was blood—Again I say, who entered the house even now?"

One looked out from the apartment into the little entrance, where Dwining, under pretence of not distinctly seeing the trap-ladder by which he was to ascend into the upper part of this house of lamentation, was delaying his progress purposely, disconcerted with what had reached him of the conversation.

"Nay, it is only worthy Master Henbane Dwining," answered one of the sibyls.

"Only Master Dwining?" replied the one who had first spoken, in a tone of acquiescence; "our best helper in need—then it must have been balm sure enough."

"Nay," said the other, "it may have been blood nevertheless—for the leech, look you, when the body was found, was commanded by the magistrates to probe the wound with his instruments, and how could the poor dead corpse know that that was done with good purpose?"

"Ay, truly, cummer; and as poor gossip Oliver often mistook friends for enemies while he was in life, his judgment cannot be thought to have mended now."

Dwining heard no more, being now forced up stairs into a species of garret, where Magdalen sat on her widowed bed, clasping to her bosom her infant, which, already black in the face, and uttering the gasping crowing sound which gives the popular name to the complaint, seemed on the point of rendering up its brief existence. A Dominican monk sat near the bed, holding the other child in his arms, and seeming from time to time to speak a word or two of spiritual consolation, or intermingle some observation on the child's disorder.

The mediciner cast upon the good father a single glance, filled with that ineffable disdain which men of science entertain against interlopers. His own aid was instant and efficacious; he snatched the child from the despairing mother, stripped its throat, and opened a vein, which, as it bled freely, relieved the little patient instantaneously. In a brief space every dangerous symptom disappeared, and Dwining, having bound up the wound, replaced the infant in the arms of the half distracted mother.

The poor woman's distress for her husband's loss, which had been suspended during the extremity of the child's danger, now returned on Magdalen with the force of an augmented torrent, which has borne down the dam-dike that for a while interrupted its waves.

"Oh, learned sir," she said, "you see a poor woman of her that you once knew a richer—But the hands that restored this bairn to my arms must not leave this house empty. Generous, kind Master Dwining, accept of his beads—they are made of ebony and silver—he aye liked to have his things as handsome as any gentleman—and liker he was in all his ways to a gentleman than any one of us, and even so came of it."

With these words, in a mute passion of grief, she pressed to her breast and to her lips the chaplet of her deceased husband, and proceeded to thrust it into Dwining's hands.

"Take it," she said, "for the love of one who loved you well.—Ah! he used ever to say, if ever man could be brought back from the brink of the grave, it must be by Master Dwining's guidance.—And his ain bairn is brought back this blessed day, and he is lying there stark and stiff, and kens naething of its health and sickness! O, woe is me, and wala wa!—But take the beads, and think on his puir saul, as you put them through your fingers—he will be freed from purgatory the sooner that good people pray to assoilzie him."

"Take back your beads, cummer—I know no legerdemain—can do no conjuring tricks," said the mediciner, who, more moved than perhaps his rugged nature had anticipated, endeavoured to avoid receiving the ill-omened gift. But his last words gave offence to the churchman, whose presence he had not recollected when he uttered them.

"How now, sir leech!" said the Dominican; "do you call prayers for the dead juggling tricks? I know that Chaucer, the Inglish Makar, says of you mediciners, that your study is but little on the Bible. Our Mother, the Church, hath nodded of late, but her eyes are now opened to discern friends from foes; and be well assured"—

"Nay, reverend father," said Dwining, "you take me at too great advantage. I said I could do no miracles, and was about to add, that as the Church certainly could work such conclusions, those rich beads should be deposited in your hands, to be applied as they may best benefit the soul of the deceased."

He dropped the beads into the Dominican's hand, and escaped from the house of mourning.

"This was a strangely timed visit," he said to himself, when he got safe out of doors. "I hold such things cheap as any can; yet, though it is but a silly fancy, I am glad I saved the squalling child's life.—But I must to my friend Smotherwell, whom I have no doubt to bring to my purpose in the matter of Bonthron; and thus I shall save two lives, and have destroyed only one."

Chapter Eleven

THE HIGH CHURCH of St John's in Perth, being that of the patron saint of the burgh, had been selected by the Magistrates as that in which the community was likely to have most fair play for the display of the ordeal. The churches and convents of the Dominicans, Carthusians, and others of the regular clergy, had been highly endowed by the kings and nobles, and therefore it was the universal cry of the city-council, that "their ain gude auld St John," of whose good graces they thought themselves sure, ought to be fully confided in, and preferred to the new patrons, for whom the Dominicans, Carthusians, Carmelites, and others, had founded newer seats around the Fair City. The disputes between the regular and secular clergy added to the jealousy which dictated this choice of the spot in which Heaven was to display a species of miracle, upon a direct appeal to the divine decision in a case of doubtful guilt; and the town-clerk was as anxious that the church of St John should be preferred, as if there had been a faction in the body of saints for and against the interests of that beautiful town.

Many, therefore, were the petty intrigues entered into and disconcerted, for the purpose of fixing on the church. But the Magistrates, considering it as a matter touching in a close degree the honour of the city, determined, with judicious confidence in the justice and impartiality of their patron, to confide the issue to the influence of St John.

It was, therefore, after High Mass had been performed, with the greatest solemnity of which circumstances rendered the ceremony capable, and after the most repeated and fervent prayers had been offered to Heaven by the crowded assembly, that preparations were made for appealing to the direct judgment of Heaven on the mysterious murder of the unfortunate Bonnet-maker.

The scene presented that effect of imposing solemnity, which the rites of the Catholic Church are so well qualified to produce. The eastern window, richly and variously painted, streamed down a torrent of chequered light upon the high altar. On the bier placed before it were stretched the mortal remains of the murdered man, his arms folded on his breast, and his palms joined together, with the fingers pointed upwards, as if the senseless clay was itself appealing to Heaven for vengeance against those who had violently divorced the immortal spirit from its mangled tenement.

Close to the bier was placed the throne, which supported Robert of Scotland, and his brother Albany. The Prince sat upon a lower stool, beside his father; an arrangement which occasioned some observation, as Albany's seat being little distinguished from that of the King, the heir-apparent, though of full age, seemed to be degraded beneath his uncle in the sight of the assembled people of Perth. The bier was so placed, as to leave the view of the body it sustained open to the greater part of the multitude assembled in the church.

At the head of the bier stood the Knight of Kinfauns, as the challenger, and at the foot the young Earl of Crawford, as representing the defendant. The evidence of the Duke of Rothsay in expurgation, as it was termed, of Sir John Ramorny, had exempted him from the necessity of attendance as a party subjected to the ordeal; and his illness served as a reason for his remaining at home. His household, including those who, though immediately in waiting upon Sir John, were accounted the Prince's domestics, and had not yet received their dismissal, amounted to eight or ten persons, most of them esteemed men of profligate habits, and who might therefore be deemed capable, in the riot of a festival evening, of committing the slaughter of the Bonnet-maker. They were drawn up in a row on the left side of the church, and wore a species of white cassock, resembling the dress of a penitentiary. All eyes being bent on them, several of this band seemed so much disconcerted, as to excite among the spectators strong prepossessions of their guilt. The real murderer had a countenance incapable of betraying him,—a sullen, dark look, which neither the feast nor wine-cup could enliven, and which the peril of discovery and death could not render dejected.

We have already noticed the posture of the dead body. The face was bare, as were the breast and arms. The rest of the corpse was shrouded in a winding-sheet of the finest linen, so that, if blood should flow from any place which was covered, it could not fail to be instantly manifest.

High Mass having been performed, followed by a solemn invocation to the Deity, that he would be pleased to protect the innocent, and make known the guilty, Eviot, Sir John Ramorny's page, was summoned to undergo the ordeal. He advanced with an ill-assured step. Perhaps he thought his internal consciousness that Bonthron must have been the assassin, might be sufficient to implicate him in the murder, though he was not directly accessary to it. He paused before the bier; and his voice faltered, as he swore by all that was created in seven days and seven nights, by heaven, by hell, by his part of paradise, and by the God and author of all, that he was free and sackless of the bloody deed done upon the corpse before which he stood, and on whose breast he made the sign of the cross, in evidence of the appeal. No consequences ensued. The body remained stiff as before; the curdled wounds gave no sign of blood.

The citizens looked on each other with faces of blank disappointment. They had persuaded themselves of Eviot's guilt; and their suspicions had been confirmed by his irresolute manner. Their surprise at his escape was therefore extreme. The other followers of Ramorny took heart, and advanced to take the oath, with a boldness which increased, as one by one they performed the ordeal, and were declared, by the voice of the judges, free and innocent of every suspicion attaching to them on account of the death of Oliver Proudfute.

But there was one individual, who did not partake that increasing confidence. The name of "Bonthron—Bonthron!" sounded three times through the aisles of the church; but he who owned it acknowledged the call no otherwise than by a sort of shuffling motion with his feet, as if he had been suddenly affected by a fit of palsy.

"Speak, dog," whispered Eviot, "or prepare for a dog's death!"

But the murderer's brain was so much disturbed by the sight before him, that the judges, beholding his deportment, doubted whether to ordain him to be dragged before the bier, or to pronounce judgment in default; and it was not, until he was asked for the last time, whether he would submit to the ordeal, that he answered, with his usual brevity, "I will not;—what do I know what juggling tricks may be practised to take a poor man's life?—I offer the combat to any man who says I harmed that dead body."

And, according to usual form, he threw his glove upon the floor of the church.

Henry Smith stepped forwards, amidst the murmured applauses of his fellow-citizens, which even the august presence could not entirely suppress; and lifting the ruffian's glove, which he placed in his bonnet, laid down his own in the usual form, as a gage of battle. But Bonthron raised it not.

"He is no match for me," growled the savage, "nor fit to lift my glove. I follow the Prince of Scotland, in attending on his Master of Horse. This fellow is a wretched mechanic."

Here the Prince interrupted. "Thou follow *me*, caitiff? I discharge thee from my service on the spot.—Take him in hand, Smith, and beat him as thou didst never thump anvil!—The villain is both guilty and recreant. It sickens me even to look at him; and if my royal father will be ruled by me, he will give the parties two handsome Scottish axes, and we will see which of them turns out the best fellow before the day is half an hour older."

This was readily assented to by the Earl of Crawford and Sir Patrick Charteris, the god-fathers of the parties, who, as the combatants were men of inferior rank, agreed that they should fight in steel caps, buff jackets, and with axes; and that as soon as they could be prepared for the combat.

The lists were appointed in the Skinners' Yards, a neighbouring space of ground, occupied by the corporation from which it had the name, and who quickly cleared a space of about thirty feet by twenty-five for the combatants. Thither thronged the nobles, priests, and commons,—all excepting the old King, who, detesting such scenes of blood, retired to his residence, and devolved the charge of the field upon the Earl of Errol, Lord High Constable, to whose office it more particularly belonged. The Duke of Albany watched the whole proceedings with a close and wary eye. His nephew gave the scene the heedless degree of notice which corresponded with his character.

When the combatants appeared in the lists, nothing could be more striking than the contrast betwixt the manly, cheerful countenance of the Smith, whose sparkling bright eye seemed already beaming with the victory he hoped for, and the sullen, downcast aspect of the brutal Bonthron, who looked as if he were some obscene bird, driven into sunshine out of the shelter of its darksome haunts. They made oath severally, each to the truth of his quarrel; a ceremony which Henry Gow performed with serene and manly confidence—Bonthron with a dogged resolution, which induced the Duke of Rothsay to say to the High Constable, "Didst thou ever, my dear Errol, behold such a mixture of malignity, cruelty, and I think fear, as in that fellow's countenance?"

"He is not comely," said the Earl, "but a powerful knave as I have seen."

"I'll gage a hogshead of wine with you, my good lord, that he loses the day. Henry the armourer is as strong as he, and much more active. And then look at his bold bearing! There is something in that other fellow that is loathsome to look upon. Let them yoke presently, my dear Constable, for I am sick of beholding him."

The High-Constable then addressed the widow, who, in her deep weeds, and having her children still beside her, occupied a chair within the lists:—"Woman, do you willingly accept of this man, Henry the Smith, to do battle as your champion in this cause?"

"I do. I do, most willingly," answered Magdalen Proudfute; "and may the blessing of God and St John give him strength and fortune, since he strikes for the orphan and fatherless!"

"Then I pronounce this a fenced field of battle," said the Constable aloud. "Let no one dare, upon peril of his life, to interrupt this combat by word, speech, or look.—Sound trumpets, and fight, combatants!"

The trumpets flourished, and the combatants, advancing from the opposite ends of the lists, with a steady and even pace, looked at each other attentively, well skilled in judging from the motion of the eye, the direction in which a blow was meditated. They halted opposite to, and within reach of, each other, and in turn made more than one feint to strike, in order to ascertain the activity and vigilance of the opponent. At length, whether weary of these manœuvres, or fearing lest in a contest so conducted his unwieldy strength would be foiled by the activity of the Smith, Bonthron heaved up his axe for a downright blow, adding the whole strength of his sturdy arms to the weight of the weapon in its descent. The Smith, however, avoided the stroke by stepping aside; for it was too forceful to be controlled by any guard which he could have interposed. Ere Bonthron recovered guard, Henry struck him a sideling blow on the steel head-piece, which prostrated him on the ground.

"Confess, or die," said the victor, placing his foot on the body of the vanquished, and holding to his throat the point of the axe, which terminated in a spike or poniard.

"I will confess," said the villain, glaring wildly upward on the sky. "Let me rise."

"Not till you have yielded," said Henry Smith.

"I do yield," again murmured Bonthron, and Henry proclaimed aloud that his antagonist was defeated.

The Dukes of Rothsay and Albany, the High Constable, and the Dominican Prior, now entered the lists, and addressing Bonthron, demanded if he acknowledged himself vanquished.

"I do," answered the miscreant.

"And guilty of the murder of Oliver Proudfute?"

"I am—but I mistook him for another."

"And for whom?" said the Prior. "Confess, my son, and merit thy pardon in another world; for with this thou hast little more to do."

"I took him for the man whose hand has struck me down, whose foot now presses me."

"Blessed be the saints!" said the Prior; "now all those who doubt the virtue of the holy ordeal, may have their eyes opened to their error. Lo, he is trapped in the snare which he laid for the guiltless."

"I scarce ever saw the man before," said the Smith. "I never did wrong to him or his.—Ask him, an it please your reverence, why he should have thought of slaying me treacherously."

"It is a fitting question," answered the Prior.—"Give glory where it is due, my son, even though it is manifested by thy shame. For what reason would'st thou have waylaid this armourer, who says he never wronged thee?"

"He had wronged him whom I served," answered Bonthron; "and I meditated the deed by his command."

"By whose command?" asked the Prior.

Bonthron was silent for an instant, then growled out,—"He is too mighty for me to name."

"Hearken, my son," said the churchman; "tarry but a brief hour, and the mighty and the mean of this earth shall to thee alike be empty sounds. The sledge is even now preparing to drag thee to the place of execution. Therefore, son, once more I charge thee to consult thy soul's weal by glorifying Heaven, and speaking the truth. Was it thy master, Sir John Ramorny, that stirred thee to so foul a deed?"

"No," answered the prostrate villain, "it was a greater than he." And at the same time he pointed with his finger to the Prince.

"Wretch!" said the astonished Duke of Rothsay; "do you dare to hint that *I* was your instigator?"

"You yourself, my lord," answered the unblushing ruffian.

"Die in thy falsehood, accursed slave!" said the Prince; and, drawing his sword, he would have pierced his calumniator, had not the Lord High Constable interposed with word and action.

"Your Grace must forgive my discharging mine office—this caitiff must be delivered into the hands of the executioner. He is unfit to be dealt with by any other, much less by your Highness."

"What? noble Earl," said Albany, aloud, and with much real or affected emotion, "would you let the dog pass alive from hence, to poison the people's ears with false accusations against the Prince of Scotland?—I say, cut him to mammocks on the spot!"

"Your Highness will pardon me," said the Earl of Errol; "I must protect him till his doom is executed."

"Then let him be gagged instantly," said Albany.—"And you, my royal nephew, why stand you there fixed in astonishment? Call your resolution up—speak to the prisoner—swear—protest by all that is sacred that you knew not of this felon deed. See how the people look on each other, and whisper apart—My life on't that this lie spreads faster than any gospel truth. Speak to them, royal kinsman, no matter what you say, so you be constant in denial."

"What, sir," said Rothsay, starting from his pause of surprise and mortification, and turning haughtily towards his uncle; "would you have me gage my royal word against that of an abject recreant? Let those who *can* believe the son of their sovereign, the descendant of Bruce, capable of laying ambush for the life of a poor mechanic, enjoy the pleasure of believing it."

"That will not I for one," said the Smith, bluntly. "I never did aught but what was in honour toward his royal Grace the Duke of Rothsay, and never received unkindness from him, in word, look, or deed; and I cannot think he would have given aim to such base practice."

"Was it in honour that you threw his Highness from the ladder in Curfew Street, upon Fastern's Even?" said Bonthron; "or think you the favour was received kindly or unkindly?"

This was so boldly said, and seemed so plausible, that it shook the Smith's opinion of the Prince's innocence.

"Alas, my lord," said he, looking sorrowfully towards Rothsay, "could your Highness seek an innocent fellow's life for doing his duty by a helpless maiden?—I would rather have died in these lists, than live to hear it said of the Bruce's heir!"

"Thou art a good fellow, Smith," said the Prince; "but I cannot expect thee to judge more wisely than others.—Away with that convict to the gallows, and gibbet him alive an you will, that he may speak falsehood and spread scandal on us to the last prolonged moment of his existence!"

So saying, the Prince turned away from the lists, disdaining to notice the gloomy looks cast towards him, as the crowd made slow and reluctant way for him to pass, and expressing neither surprise nor displeasure at a deep hollow murmur, or groan, which accompanied his retreat. Only a few of his own immediate followers attended him from the field, though various persons of distinction had come there in his train. Even the lower class of citizens ceased to follow the unhappy Prince, whose former indifferent reputation had exposed him to so many charges of impropriety and levity, and around whom there seemed now darkening suspicions of the most atrocious nature.

He took his slow and thoughtful way to the church of the Dominicans; but the ill news, which fly proverbially fast, had reached his father's place of retirement, before he himself appeared. On entering the palace and inquiring for the King, the Duke of Rothsay was surprised to be informed that he was in deep consultation with the Duke of Albany, who, mounting on horseback as the Prince left the lists, had reached the convent before him. He was about to use the privilege of his rank and birth, to enter the royal apartment, when MacLewis, the commander of the guard of Brandanes, gave him to understand, in the most respectful terms, that he had special instructions which forbade his admittance.

"Go at least, MacLewis, and let them know that I await their pleasure," said the Prince. "If my uncle desires to have the credit of shutting the father's apartment against the son, it will gratify him to know that I am attending in the outer hall like a lackey."

"May it please you," said MacLewis, with hesitation, "if your Highness would consent to retire just now, and to wait a while in patience, I will send to acquaint you when the Duke of Albany goes; and I doubt not that his Majesty will then admit your Grace to his presence. At present—your Highness must forgive me—it is impossible you can have access."

"I understand you, MacLewis; but go, nevertheless, and obey my commands."

The officer went accordingly, and returned with a message, that the King was indisposed, and on the point of retiring to his private chamber; but that the Duke of Albany would presently wait upon the Prince of Scotland.

It was, however, a full half hour ere the Duke of Albany appeared, —a period of time which Rothsay spent partly in moody silence, and partly in idle talk with MacLewis and the Brandanes, as the levity or irritability of his temper obtained the ascendant.

At length the Duke came, and with him the Lord High Constable, whose countenance expressed much sorrow and embarrassment.

"Fair kinsman," said the Duke of Albany, "I grieve to say that it is my royal brother's opinion, that it will be best, for the honour of the royal family, that your Royal Highness do restrict yourself for a time to the seclusion of the High Constable's lodgings, and accept of the noble Earl here present for your principal, if not sole companion, until the scandals which have been this day set abroad, shall be refuted, or forgotten."

"How is this, my Lord of Errol?" said the Prince, in astonishment. "Is your house to be my jail, and is your lordship to be my jailor?"

"The saints forbid, my lord," said the Earl of Errol; "but it is my unhappy duty to obey the commands of your father, by considering your Royal Highness for some time as being under my ward."

"The Prince, Heir of Scotland, under the ward of the High Constable!—What reason can be given for this? Is the blighting speech of a convicted recreant of strength sufficient to tarnish my royal escutcheon?"

"While such accusations are not refuted and denied, my kinsman," said the Duke of Albany, "they will contaminate that of a monarch."

"Denied, my lord!" exclaimed the Prince; "by whom are they asserted? save by a wretch too infamous, even by his own confession, to be credited for a moment, though a beggar's character, not a prince's, were impeached.—Fetch him hither,—let the rack be shown to him; you will soon hear him retract the calumny which he dared to assert."

"The gibbet has done its work too surely to leave Bonthron sensible to the rack," said the Duke of Albany. "He has been executed an hour since."

"And why such haste, my lord?" said the Prince; "know you it looks as if there were practice in it, to bring a stain on my name."

"The custom is universal—the defeated combatant in the ordeal of battle is instantly transferred from the lists to the gallows.—And yet, fair kinsman," continued the Duke of Albany, "if you had boldly and strongly denied the imputation, I would have judged right to keep the wretch alive for further investigation; but as your Highness was silent, I deemed it best to stifle the scandal in the breath of him that uttered it."

"Saint Mary, my lord, but this is too insulting! Do you, my uncle and kinsman, suppose me guilty of prompting such an useless and unworthy action, as that which the slave confessed?"

"It is not for me to bandy questions with your Highness; otherwise I would ask, whether you also mean to deny the scarce less unworthy, though less bloody attack, upon the house in Couvrefew Street?—Be not angry with me, kinsman; but, indeed, your sequestering yourself for some brief space from the court, were it only during the King's residence in this city where so much offence has been given, is imperiously demanded."

Rothsay paused when he heard this exhortation; and looking at the Duke in a very marked manner, replied, "Uncle, you are a good huntsman. You pitched your toils with much skill; but you would have been foiled, notwithstanding, had not the stag rushed among the nets of free will. God speed you, and may you have the profit by this matter which your measures deserve. Say to my father, I obey his arrest.—My Lord High Constable, I wait only your pleasure to attend you to your lodgings. Since I am to lie in ward, I could not have desired a kinder and more courteous warden."

The interview between the uncle and nephew being thus concluded, the Prince retired with the Earl of Errol to his lodgings; the citizens whom they met in the streets passing to the further side, when they observed the Duke of Rothsay, to escape the necessity of saluting one whom they had been taught to consider as a ferocious as well as unprincipled libertine. The Constable's lodgings received the owner and his princely guest, both glad to leave the streets, yet neither feeling easy in the situation which they occupied with regard to each other within doors.

We must return to the lists after the combat had ceased, and when the nobles had withdrawn. The crowds were now separated into two distinct bodies. That which made the smallest in number, was at the same time the most distinguished for respectability, consisting of the better class of inhabitants of Perth, who were gratulating the successful champion, and each other, upon the triumphant conclusion to which they had brought their feud with the courtiers. The magistrates were so much elated on the occasion that they entreated Sir Patrick Charteris's acceptance of a collation in the Town-hall. To this, Henry, the hero of the day, was of course invited, or rather commanded to come. He listened to the summons with great embarrassment, for it may be readily believed his heart was with Catherine Glover. But the advice of Simon Glover decided him. That veteran citizen had a natural and becoming deference for the magistracy of the Fair City, and a high estimation of all honours which flowed from such a source.

"Thou must not think to absent thyself from such a solemn occasion, son Henry," was his advice. "Sir Patrick Charteris is to be there himself, and I think it will be a rare occasion for thee to gain his goodwill. It is like he may order of thee a new suit of harness; and I myself heard worthy Bailie Craigdallie say, there was a talk of furbishing up the city's armory.—Thou must not neglect the good trade, now that thou takest on thee an expensive family."

"Tush, father Glover," answered the embarrassed victor, "I lack no custom—and thou knowest there is Catherine, who may wonder at my absence, and have her ear abused once more by tales of glee-maidens, and I wot not what."

"Fear not for that," said the Glover, "but go, like an obedient burgess, where thy betters desire to have thee. I do not deny that it will cost some trouble to make thy peace with Catherine about this duel; for she thinks herself wiser in such matters than King and Council, Kirk and Canons, Provost and Bailies. But I will take up the quarrel with her myself, and will so work for thee, that though she may receive thee to-morrow with somewhat of a chiding, it shall melt into tears and smiles, like an April morning, that begins with a mild shower. Away with thee then, my son, and be constant to-morrow after morning mass."

The Smith, though reluctantly, was obliged to defer to the reasoning of his proposed father-in-law; and, once determined to accept the honour destined for him by the fathers of the city, he extricated himself from the crowd, and hastened home to put on his best apparel; in which he presently afterwards repaired to the Council-house, where the ponderous oak table seemed to bend under the massy dishes of choice Tay salmon, and delicious sea-fish from Dundee, being the dainties which the fasting season permitted, whilst neither wine, ale, nor metheglin were wanting to wash them down. The waits, or minstrels of the burgh, played during the repast, and in the intervals of the music, one of them recited with great emphasis a long poetical account of the battle of Black-earn-side, fought by Sir William Wallace, and his redoubted captain and friend, Thomas of Longueville, against the English general, Seward—a theme perfectly familiar to all the guests, who, nevertheless, more tolerant than their descendants, listened as if it had all the zest of novelty. It was complimentary to the ancestor of the Knight of Kinfauns doubtless, and to other Perthshire families, in passages which the audience applauded vociferously, whilst they pledged each other in mighty draughts, to the memory of the heroes who had fought by the side of the Champion of Scotland. The health of Henry Wynd was quaffed with repeated shouts, and the Provost announced publicly, that the magistrates were consulting how they might best invest him with some distinguished privilege, or honorary reward, to show how highly his fellow-citizens valued his courageous exertions.

"Nay, take it not thus, an it like your worships," said the Smith, with his usual blunt manner, "lest men say that valour be rare in Perth, when they reward a man for fighting for the right of a forlorn widow. I am sure there are many scores of stout burghers in Perth would have done this day's dargue, as well or better than I. For, in good sooth, I ought to have cracked yonder head-piece like an earthen pipkin—ay, and would have done it too, if it had not been one which I myself tempered for Sir John Ramorny. But an the Fair City think my service of any worth, I will conceive it far more than acquitted by any aid which you may afford from the Common Good,* to the support of widow Magdalen and her poor orphans."

"That may well be done," said Sir Patrick Charteris, "and yet leave the Fair City rich enough to pay her debts to Henry Wynd, of which every man of us is a better judge than himself, who is blinded with an unavailing nicety, which men call modesty—And if the burgh be too poor for this, the Provost will bear his share. The Rover's golden angels have not all taken flight yet."

The beakers were now circulated, under the name of a cup of comfort to the widow, and anon flowed around once more to the happy memory of the murdered Oliver, now so bravely avenged. In short, it was a feast so jovial, that all agreed nothing was wanting to render it perfect, but the presence of the Bonnet-maker himself, whose calamity had occasioned the meeting, and who had usually furnished the standing jest at such festive assemblies. Had his attendance been possible, it was drily observed by Bailie Craigdallie, he would certainly have claimed the success of the day, and vouched himself the avenger of his own murder.

At the sound of the vesper bell the company broke up, some of the graver sort going to evening prayers, where, with half-shut eyes and shining countenances, they made a most orthodox and edifying portion of a Lenten congregation; others to their own homes, to tell over the occurrences of the fight and feast, for the information of their family circle; and some, doubtless, to the licensed freedoms of some tavern, the door of which Lent did not keep so close shut as the forms of the Church required. Henry returned to the Wynd, warm with the good wine and applause of his fellow-citizens, and fell asleep to dream of perfect happiness and Catherine Glover.

We have said, that when the combat was decided, the spectators were divided into two bodies: Of these, when the more respectable portion attended the victor in joyous procession, much the greater number, or what might be termed the rabble, waited upon the subdued and sentenced Bonthron, who was travelling in a different direction, and for a very opposite purpose. Whatever may be thought of the comparative attractions of the house of mourning and of feasting under other circumstances, there can be little doubt which will draw

* The public property of the burgh.

most visitors, when the question is, whether we would witness miseries which we are not to share, or festivities of which we are not to partake. Accordingly, the tumbril in which the criminal was conveyed to execution, was attended by far the greater proportion of the inhabitants of Perth.

A friar was seated in the same car with the murderer, to whom he did not hesitate to communicate, under the seal of confession, the same false asseveration which he had made upon the place of combat, which charged the Duke of Rothsay with being director of the ambuscade by which the unfortunate Bonnet-maker had suffered. The same falsehood he disseminated among the crowd, averring, with unblushing effrontery, to those who were nighest to the car, that he owed his death to his having been willing to execute the Duke of Rothsay's pleasure. For a time he repeated these words, sullenly and doggedly, in the manner of one reciting a task, or a liar who endeavours by reiteration to obtain a credit for his words, which he is internally sensible they do not deserve. But when he lifted up his eyes, and beheld in the distance the black outline of a gallows, at least forty feet high, with its ladder and its fatal cord, rising against the horizon, he became suddenly silent, and the friar could observe that he trembled very much.

"Be comforted, my son," said the good priest, "you have confessed the truth, and received absolution. Your penitence will be accepted according to your sincerity; and though you have been a man of bloody hands and cruel heart, yet, by the Church's prayers, you shall be in due time assoilzied from the penal fires of purgatory."

These assurances were calculated rather to augment than to diminish the terrors of the culprit, who was agitated by doubts whether the mode suggested for his preservation from death would to a certainty be effectual, and some suspicion whether there was really any purpose of employing them in his favour; for he knew his master well enough to be aware of the indifference with which he would sacrifice one who might on some future occasion be a dangerous evidence against him.

His doom, however, was sealed, and there was no escaping from it. They slowly approached the fatal tree, which was erected on a bank by the river's side, about half a mile from the walls of the city; a site chosen that the body of the wretch, which was to remain food for the carrion crows, might be seen from a distance in every direction. Here the priest delivered Bonthron to the executioner, by whom he was assisted up the ladder, and to all appearance dispatched according to the usual forms of the law. He seemed to struggle for life for a minute, but soon after hung still and inanimate. The executioner, after remaining upon duty for more than half an hour, as if to permit the last spark of life to be extinguished, announced to the admirers of such spectacles, that the irons for the permanent suspension of the carcass not having been got ready, the concluding ceremony of disembowelling the dead body, and attaching it finally to the gibbet, would be deferred till the next morning at sunrise.

Notwithstanding the early hour which he had named, Master Smotherwell had a reasonable attendance of rabble at the place of execution, to see the final proceedings of justice with its victim. But great was the astonishment and resentment of these amateurs, to find that the dead body had been removed from the gibbet. They were not, however, long at a loss to guess the cause of its disappearance. Bonthron had been the follower of a Baron whose estates lay in Fife, and was himself a native of that province. What was more natural than that some of the Fife men, whose boats were frequently plying on the river, should have clandestinely removed the body of their countryman from the place of public shame? The crowd vented their rage against Smotherwell, for not completing his job on the preceding evening; and had not he and his assistant betaken themselves to a boat, and escaped across the Tay, they would have run some risk of being pelted to death. The event, however, was too much in the spirit of the times to be much wondered at. Its real cause we will explain in the next volume.

END OF VOLUME SECOND

SAINT VALENTINE'S DAY;

OR,

THE FAIR MAID OF PERTH

VOLUME III

Chapter One

THE INCIDENTS of a narrative of this kind must be adapted to each other, as the wards of a key must tally accurately with those of the lock to which it belongs. The reader, however gentle, will not hold himself obliged to rest satisfied with the mere fact, that such and such occurrences took place, which is, generally speaking, all that in ordinary life he can know of what is passing around him; but he is desirous, while reading for amusement, of knowing the interior movements occasioning the course of events. This is a legitimate and reasonable curiosity; for every man hath a right to open and examine the mechanism of his own watch, put together for his proper use, although he is not permitted to pry into the interior of the time-piece, which, for general information, is displayed on the town-steeple.

It would be, therefore, uncourteous to leave my readers under any doubt concerning the agency which removed the assassin Bonthron from the gallows; an event which some of the Perth citizens ascribed to the foul fiend himself, while others were content to lay it upon the natural dislike of Bonthron's countrymen of Fife, to see him hanging on the river side, as a spectacle dishonourable to their province.

About midnight after the day when the execution had taken place, when the inhabitants of Perth were deeply buried in slumber, three men, muffled in their cloaks, and bearing a dark lantern, descended the alleys of a garden which led from the house occupied by Sir John Ramorny, to the banks of the Tay, where a small boat lay moored to a landing place, or little projecting pier. The wind howled in a low and melancholy manner through the leafless shrubs and bushes; and a pale moon *waded*, as it is termed in Scotland, amongst drifted clouds, which seemed to threaten rain. The three individuals entered the boat with great precaution, to escape observation. One of them was a tall powerful man; another short and bent downwards; the third middle-sized, and apparently younger than his companions, and light and active. Thus much even the imperfect light could discover. They seated themselves in the boat, and unmoored it from the pier.

"We must let her drift with the current, till we pass the bridge, where the burghers still keep guard; and you know the proverb—a Perth arrow hath a perfect flight," said the most youthful of the party, who assumed the office of helmsman, and pushed the boat off from the pier, whilst the others took the oars, which were muffled, and rowed with all precaution till they attained the middle of the river; they then ceased their efforts, lay upon their oars, and trusted to the steersman for keeping her in mid-channel.

In this manner they passed unnoticed or disregarded beneath the stately Gothic arches of the old bridge, erected by the magnificent patronage of Robert Bruce in 1329, and carried away by an inundation in 1621. Although they heard the voices of a civic watch, which, since these disturbances commenced, had been nightly maintained in that important pass, no challenge was given; and when they were so far down the stream as to be out of hearing of those guardians of the night, they began to row, but still with precaution, and to converse, though in a low tone.

"You have found a new trade, comrade, since I left you," said one of the rowers to the other. "I left you engaged in tending a sick knight, and I find you employed in purloining a dead body from the gallows."

"A living body, so please your squirehood, Master Buncle; or else my craft hath failed of its purpose."

"So I am told, Master Pottercarrier; but saving your clerkship, unless you tell me your trick, I will take leave to doubt of its success."

"A simple toy, Master Buncle, not likely to please a genius so acute as that of your valiancie. Marry, thus it is. This suspension of the human body, which the vulgar call hanging, operates death by apoplexia,—that is, the blood being unable to return to the heart by the compression of the veins, it rushes to the brain, and the man dies. Also, and as an additional cause of dissolution, the lungs no longer receive the needful supply of the vital air, owing to the ligature of the cord around the thorax; and hence the patient perishes."

"I understand that well enough—But how is it to be prevented, Sir Mediciner?" said the third person, who was no other than Ramorny's page Eviot.

"Marry, then," replied Dwining, "hang me the patient up in such fashion that the carotid arteries shall not be compressed, and the blood will not determine to the brain, and apoplexia will not take place; and again, if there be no ligature around the thorax, the lungs will be supplied with air, whether the man be hanging in the middle heaven, or standing on the firm earth."

"All this I conceive," said Eviot; "but how these precautions can be reconciled with the execution of the sentence of hanging, is what my dull brain cannot comprehend."

"Ah! good youth, thy valiancie hath spoiled a fair wit. Hadst thou studied with me, thou should'st have learned things more difficult than these. But here is my trick. I get me certain bandages, made of the same substance with your young valiancie's horse-girths, having especial care that they are of a kind which will not stretch on being strained, since that would spoil my experiment. One loop of this substance is drawn under each foot, and returns up either side of the leg to a cincture, with which it is united; these cinctures are connected by divers straps down the breast and back, in order to divide the weight, and there are sundry other contrivances for easing the patient; but the chief is this. The straps, or ligatures, are attached to a broad steel collar, curving outwards, and having a hook or two for the better securing of the halter, which the friendly executioner passes around that part of the machine, instead of applying it to the bare throat of the patient. Thus, when thrown off from the ladder, the sufferer will find himself suspended, not by his neck, if it please you, but by a steel circle, which supports the loops in which his feet are placed, and on which his weight really rests, diminished a little by similar supports under each arm. Thus, neither vein nor wind-pipe being compressed, the man will breathe as free, and his blood, saving from fright and novelty of situation, will flow as temperately as your valiancie's, when you stand up in your stirrups to view a field of battle."

"By my faith, a quaint and rare device!" quoth Buncle.

"Is it not?" pursued the leech, "and well worth being known to such mounting spirits as your valiancies, since there is no knowing to what heights Sir John Ramorny's pupils may arrive; and if these be such, that it is necessary to descend from them by a rope, you may find my mode of management more convenient than the common practice. Marry you must be provided with a high-collared doublet, to conceal the ring of steel; and, above all, such a *bonus socius* as Smotherwell to adjust the noose."

"Base poison-vender," said Eviot, "men of our calling die on the field of battle!"

"I will save the lesson, however," replied Buncle, "in case of some pinching occasion—But what a night the hang-dog bloody Bonthron must have had of it, dancing a pavin in mid air to the music of his own shackles, as the night wind swings him that way and this!"

"It were an alms deed to leave him there," said Eviot; "for his descent from the gibbet will but encourage him to new murders. He knows but two elements—drunkenness and bloodshed."

"Perhaps Sir John Ramorny might have been of your opinion," said Dwining; "but it would first have been necessary to cut out the rogue's tongue, lest he had told strange tales from his airy height. And there are other reasons that it concerns not your valiancies to know. In truth, I myself have been generous in saving him, for the fellow is built as strong as Edinburgh Castle, and his anatomy would have matched any that is in the chirurgical hall of Padua.—But tell me, Master Buncle, what news bring you from the doughty Douglas?"

"They may tell that know," said Buncle. "I am the dull ass that bears the message, and kens naught of its purport. The safer for myself perhaps. I carried letters from the Duke of Albany and from Sir John Ramorny to the Douglas, and he looked black as a northern tempest when he opened them—I brought them answers from the Earl, at which they smiled like the sun when the harvest storm is closing over him. Go to your Ephemerides, leech, and conjure the meaning out of that."

"Methinks I can do so without much cost of wit," said the chirurgeon; "but yonder I see in the pale moon our dead-alive.—Should he have screamed out to any chance passenger, it were a curious interruption to a night-journey, to be hailed from the top of such a gallows as these.—Hark, methinks I do hear his groans amid the whistling of the wind and the creaking of the chains. So—fair and softly—make fast the boat with the grappling—and get out the casket with my matters—we would be better for a little fire, but the light might bring observation on us.—Come on, my men of valour, march warily, for we are bound for the gallows foot—Follow with the lantern—I trust the ladder has been left."

As they advanced to the gibbet, they could plainly hear groans, though uttered in a low tone. Dwining ventured to give a low cough once or twice, by way of signal; but receiving no answer, "We had best make haste," said he to his companions, "for our friend must be *in extremis*, as he gives no answer to the signal which announces the arrival of help.—Come, let us to the gear. I will go up the ladder first and cut the rope. Do you two follow, one after another, and take hold of the body, so that he fall not when the halter is unloosed. Keep fast hold, for which the bandages will afford you convenience. Bethink you, that though he plays an owl's part to-night, he hath no wings, and to fall out of a halter may be as dangerous as to fall into one."

While he spoke thus he ascended the ladder, and having ascertained that the men-at-arms who followed him had the body in their hold, he cut the rope, and then gave his aid to support the almost lifeless form of the criminal.

By a skilful exertion of strength and address, the body of Bonthron was placed safely on the ground, and the faint, yet certain existence of life having been ascertained, it was thence transported to the river side, where, shrouded by the bank, the party might be best concealed from observation, while the leech employed himself in the necessary means of recalling animation, with which he had taken care to provide himself.

For this purpose he first freed the recovered person from his shackles, which the executioner had left unlocked on purpose, and at the same time disengaged the complicated envelopes and bandages by which he had been suspended. It was some time ere Dwining's efforts succeeded; for in despite of the skill with which his machine had been constructed, the straps designed to support the body had stretched so considerably as to occasion the sense of suffocation becoming extremely overpowering. But the address of the surgeon triumphed over all obstacles; and after sneezing and stretching himself, with one or two brief convulsions, Bonthron gave decided proofs of reanimation, by arresting the hand of the operator as it was in the act of dripping strong waters on his breast and throat; and, diverting the bottle which contained them to his lips, he took, almost perforce, a considerable gulp of the contents.

"It is spiritual essence double distilled," said the astonished operator, "and would blister the throat, and burn the stomach of any other man. But this extraordinary beast is so unlike all other men, that I should not wonder if it brought him to the complete possession of his faculties."

Bonthron sat up, stared around, and indicated some consciousness of existence.

"Wine—wine," were the first words which he articulated.

The leech gave him a draught of medicated wine, mixed with water. He rejected it, under the dishonourable epithet of "kennel-washings," and again uttered the words—"Wine—wine."

"Nay, take it to thee, i' the devil's name," said the leech, "since none but he can judge of thy constitution."

A draught, long and deep enough to have discomposed the intellects of any other person, was found effectual in recalling those of Bonthron to a more perfect state; though he betrayed no recollection of where he was or what had befallen him, and in his brief and sullen manner, asked why he was brought to the river side at this time of night.

"Another frolic of the wild Prince, for ducking me as he did before —Nails and blood, but I would"—

"Hold thy peace," interrupted Eviot, "and be thankful, I pray you, if you have any thankfulness in you, that thy body is not crows' meat, and thy soul in a place where water is too scarce to duck thee."

"I begin to bethink me," said the ruffian; and raising the flask to his mouth, which saluted it with a long and hearty kiss, he set the empty bottle on the earth, dropped his head on his bosom, and seemed to muse for the purpose of arranging his confused recollections.

"We can abide the issue of his meditations no longer," said Dwining, "he will be better after he has slept.—Up, sir! you have been riding the air these some hours—try if the water be not an easier mode of conveyance.—Your valours must lend me a hand. I can no more lift this mass than I could raise in my arms a slaughtered bull."

"Stand upright on thine own feet, Bonthron, now we have placed thee upon them," said Eviot.

"I cannot," answered the patient. "Every drop of blood tingles in my veins as it had pin-points, and my knees refuse to bear their burden. What can be the meaning of all this? This is some practice of thine, thou dog leech!"

"Ay, ay, so it is, honest Bonthron," said Dwining, "a practice thou shalt thank me for, when thou comest to learn it. In the meanwhile, stretch down in the stern of that boat, and let me wrap this cloak about thee." Assisted into the boat accordingly, Bonthron was deposited there as conveniently as things admitted of. He answered their attentions with one or two snorts resembling the grunt of a boar, who has got some food particularly agreeable to him.

"And now, Buncle," said the chirurgeon, "your valiant squireship knows your charge. You are to convey this lively cargo by the river to Newburgh, where you are to dispose of him as you wot of; meantime, here are his shackles and bandages, the marks of his confinement and liberation. Bind them up together, and fling them into the deepest pool you pass over; for, found in your possession, they might tell tales against us all. This low, light breath of wind from the west will permit you to use a sail as soon as the light comes in, and you are tired of rowing.—Your other valiancy, Master Page Eviot, must be content to return to Perth with me a-foot, for here severs our fair company.— Take with thee the lantern, Buncle, for thou wilt require it more than we, and see thou send me back my flasket."

As the pedestrians returned to Perth, Eviot expressed his belief that

Bonthron's understanding would never recover the shock which terror had inflicted upon it, and which appeared to him to have disturbed all the faculties of his mind, and in particular his memory.

"It is not so, an it please your pagehood," said the leech. "Bonthron's intellect, such as it is, hath a solid character—it will but vacillate to and fro like a pendulum which hath been put in motion, and then will rest in its proper point of gravity. Our memory is, of all our powers of mind, that which is peculiarly liable to be suspended. Deep intoxication or sound sleep alike destroy it, and yet it returns when the drunkard becomes sober, or the sleeper is awakened. Terror sometimes produces the same effects. I knew at Paris a criminal condemned to die by the halter, who suffered the sentence accordingly, showing no particular degree of timidity upon the scaffold, and behaving and expressing himself as men in the same condition are wont to do. Accident did for him what a little ingenious practice hath done for our amiable friend from whom we but now parted. He was cut down, and given to his friends before life was extinct, and I had the good fortune to recover him. But though he recovered in other particulars, he remembered but little of his trial and sentence. Of his confession on the morning of his execution—he! he! he! (in his usual chuckling manner)—he remembered him not a word, nor of leaving the prison —nor of his passage to the Grève, where he suffered—nor of the devout speeches which—he, he!—edified—he, he, he!—so many good Christians—nor of ascending the fatal tree, nor of taking the fatal leap—my revenant had not the slightest recollection.—But here we reach the point where we must separate; for it were unfit, should we meet any of the watch, that we be found together, and it were also prudent that we enter the city by different gates. My profession forms an excuse for my going and coming at all times. Your valiant pagehood will make such explanation as may seem sufficing."

"I shall make my will a sufficient excuse if I am interrogated," said the haughty young man. "Yet I will avoid interruption, if possible. The moon is quite obscured, and the roads as black as a wolf's mouth."

"Tut," said the physicianer, "let not your valour care for that; we shall tread darker paths ere it be long."

Without inquiring into the meaning of these evil-boding sentences, and indeed hardly listening to them, in the pride and recklessness of his nature, the page of Ramorny parted from his ingenious and dangerous companion; and each took his own way.

Chapter Two

"The course of true love never did run smooth."

THE OMINOUS anxiety of our armourer had not played him false. When the good Glover parted with his intended son-in-law, after the judicial combat had been decided, he found, what he indeed had expected, his fair daughter in no favourable disposition to her lover. But although he perceived that Catherine was cold, restrained, collected, had cast away the appearance of mortal passion, and listened with a reserve, implying contempt, to the most splendid description he could give her of the combat in the Skinners' Yards, he was determined not to take the least notice of her estranged manner, but to speak of her marriage with his son Henry as a thing which must of course take place. At length, when she began, as on a former occasion, to intimate, that her attachment to the armourer did not exceed the bounds of friendship,—that she was resolved never to marry,—that the pretended judicial combat was a mockery of the divine will, and of human laws,—the Glover not unnaturally grew angry.

"I cannot read thy thoughts, wench; nor can I pretend to guess under what wicked delusion it is that you kiss a declared lover,—suffer him to kiss you,—run to his house when a report is spread of his death, and fling yourself into his arms when you find him alone.—All this shows very well in a girl prepared to obey her parents in a match sanctioned by her father; but such tokens of intimacy, bestowed on one whom a young woman cannot esteem, and is determined not to marry, are uncomely and unmaidenly. You have already been more bounteous of your favours to Henry Smith than your mother, whom God assoilzie, ever was to me before I married her. I tell thee, Catherine, this trifling with the love of an honest man is what I neither can, will, nor ought to endure. I have given my consent to the match, and I insist it shall take place without delay; and that you receive Henry Wynd to-morrow, as a man whose bride you are to be with all dispatch."

"A power more potent than yours, father, will say no," replied Catherine.

"I will risk it; my power is a lawful one, that of a father over a child, and an erring child," answered her father. "God and man allow of my influence."

"Then, may Heaven help us!" said Catherine; "for if you are obstinate in your purpose, we are all lost."

"We can expect no help from Heaven," said the Glover, "when we act with indirection. I am clerk enough myself to know that; and that your causeless resistance to my will is sinful, every priest will inform you. Ay, and more than that, you have spoken degradingly of the blessed appeal to God in the combat of ordeal. Take heed! for the Holy Church is awakened to watch her sheepfold, and to extirpate heresy by fire and steel; so much I warn thee of."

Catherine uttered a suppressed exclamation; and, with difficulty compelling herself to assume an appearance of composure, promised her father, that if he would spare her farther discussion of this subject till to-morrow morning, she would then meet him, determined to make a full discovery of her sentiments.

With this promise, Simon Glover was obliged to remain contented, though extremely anxious for the postponed explanation. It could not be levity or fickleness of character which induced his daughter to act with so much apparent inconsistency towards the man of his choice, whom she had so lately unequivocally owned was also the man of her own. What external force there could exist, of a kind powerful enough to change the resolutions she had so decidedly expressed within twenty-four hours, was a matter of complete mystery.

"But I will be as obstinate as she can be," thought the Glover, "and she shall either marry Henry Smith without farther delay, or old Simon Glover will know an excellent reason to the contrary."

The subject was not renewed during the evening; but early on the next morning, just at sunrising, Catherine knelt before the bed in which her parent still slumbered. Her heart sobbed as if it would burst, and her tears fell thick upon her father's face. The good old man awoke, looked up, crossed his child's forehead, and kissed her affectionately.

"I understand thee, Kate," he said; "thou art come to confession, and, I trust, art desirous to escape a heavy penance by being sincere."

Catherine was silent for an instant.

"I need not ask, my father, if you remember the Carthusian monk, Clement, and his preachings and lessons; at which indeed you assisted so often, that you cannot be ignorant men called you one of his convertists, and with greater justice termed me so likewise?"

"I am aware of both," said the old man, raising himself on his elbow; "but I defy foul fame to show that I ever owned him in any heretical proposition, though I loved well to hear him talk of the corruptions of the Church, the misgovernment of the nobles, and the wild ignorance of the poor, proving, as it seemed to me, that the sole virtue of our commonweal, its strength, and its estimation, lay among the burgher craft of the better class, which I received as comfortable doctrine, and creditable to the town. And if he preached other than right doctrine, wherefore did his superiors in the Carthusian convent permit it? If the shepherds turn a wolf in sheep's clothing into the flock, they should not blame the sheep for being worried."

"They endured his preaching, nay, they encouraged it," said Catherine, "while the vices of the laity, the contentions of the nobles, and the oppression of the poor, were the subject of his censure, and they rejoiced in the crowds, who, attracted to the Carthusian church, forsook those of the other convents. But the hypocrites—for such they are—joined with the other fraternities in accusing him, when, passing from censuring the crimes of the state, he began to display the pride, ignorance, and luxury of the churchmen themselves; their thirst of power, their usurpation over men's consciences, and their desire to augment their worldly wealth."

"For God's sake, Catherine," said her father, "speak within doors; your voice rises in tone, and your speech in bitterness,—your eyes sparkle. It is owing to this especial zeal in what concerns you no more than others, that malicious persons fix upon you the odious and dangerous name of a heretic."

"You know I speak no more than what is truth," said Catherine, "and what you yourself have avouched often."

"By needle and buckskin, no!" answered the Glover, hastily—"would'st thou have me avouch what might cost me life and limb, land and goods? For a full commission hath been granted for taking and trying heretics, upon whom is laid the cause of all late tumults and miscarriages; wherefore, few words are best, wench. I am ever of mind with the old makar,—

> Since word is thrall, and thought is free,
> Keep well thy tongue, I counsel thee."

"The counsel comes too late, father," answered Catherine, sinking down on a chair by her father's bedside. "The words have been spoken and heard; and it is indited against Simon Glover, burgess in Perth, that he hath spoken irreverend discourses of the doctrines of Holy Church"—

"As I live by knife and needle," interrupted Simon, "it is a lie! I never was so silly as to speak of what I understood not."

"And hath slandered the anointed of the Church, both regular and secular," continued Catherine.

"Nay, I will never deny the truth," said the Glover; "an idle word I may have spoken at the ale-bench, or over a pottle pot of wine, or in right sure company; but else, my tongue is not one to run my head into peril."

"So you think, my dearest father; but your slightest language has been espied, your best-meaning phrases have been perverted, and you are in dittay as a gross railer against Church and churchmen, and for holding discourse against them with loose and profligate persons, such as the deceased Oliver Proudfute, the Smith Henry of the Wynd, and others, set forth as commending the doctrines of Father Clement, whom they charge with seven rank heresies, and seek for with staff and spear, to try him to the death.—But that," said Catherine, smiling, and looking upwards with the aspect of one of those beauteous saints whom the Catholics have given to the fine arts,—"that they shall never do. He hath escaped from the net of the fowler; and, I thank Heaven, it was by my means."

"Thy means, girl—art thou mad?" said the amazed Glover.

"I will not deny what I glory in," answered Catherine; "it was by my means that Conachar was led to come hither with a party of men, and carry off the old man, who is now far beyond the Highland line."

"O my rash—my unlucky child!" said the Glover; "hast thou dared to aid the escape of one accused of heresy, and to invite Highlanders in arms to interfere with the administration of justice within burgh? Alas! thou hast offended both against the laws of the Church and those of the realm. What—what would become of us, were this known!"

"It *is* known, my dear father," said the maiden, firmly; "known even to those who will be the most willing avengers of the deed."

"This must be some idle notion, Catherine, or some trick of those cogging priests and nuns; it accords not with thy late cheerful willingness to wed Henry Smith."

"Alas! dearest father, remember the dismal surprise occasioned by his reported death, and the joyful amazement at finding him alive; and deem it not wonder if I permitted myself, under your protection, to say more than my reflection justified. But then, I knew not the worst, and thought the danger exaggerated. Alas! I was yesterday fearfully undeceived, when the Abbess herself came hither, and with her the Dominican. They showed me the commission, under the broad seal of Scotland, for inquiring into and punishing heresy; they showed me your name, and my own, in a list of suspected persons; and it was with tears, real tears, that the Abbess conjured me to avert a dreadful fate by a speedy retreat into the cloister; and the monk pledged his word that you should not be molested, if I complied."

"The foul fiend take them both for crocodiles!" said the Glover.

"Alas!" replied Catherine, "complaint or anger will little help us; but you see I have had real cause for this present alarm."

"Alarm! call it utter ruin.—Alas! my reckless child, where was your prudence when you ran headlong into such a snare?"

"Hear me, father," said Catherine; "there is still one mode of safety held out; it is one which I have often proposed, and for which I have in vain supplicated your permission."

"I understand you—the convent," said her father. "But, Catherine, what abbess or prioress would dare"——

"That I will explain to you, father, and it will also show the circumstances which have made me seem unsteady of resolution to a degree which has brought censure upon me from yourself and others. Our confessor, old Father Francis, whom I chose from the Dominican convent at your command"——

"Ay, truly," interrupted the Glover; "and I so counselled and commanded thee, in order to take off the report that thy conscience was altogether under the direction of Father Clement."

"Well, this Father Francis has at different times urged me and provoked me to converse on such matters as he judged I was like to learn from the Carthusian Clement. Heaven forgive me my blindness! I fell into the snare, spoke freely, and, as he argued gently, as one who would fain be convinced, I even argued warmly in defence of what I believed devoutly. The confessor assumed not his real aspect, and betrayed not his secret purpose, until he had learned all that I had to tell him. It was then that he threatened me with temporal punishment, and with eternal condemnation. Had his threats reached me alone, I could have stood firm; for their cruelty on earth I could have endured, and their power beyond this life I have no belief in."

"For Heaven's sake!" said the Glover, who was wellnigh beside himself at perceiving at every new word the increasing extremity of his daughter's danger, "beware of blaspheming the Holy Church—whose arms are as prompt to strike as her ears are sharp to hear."

"To me," said the Maid of Perth, again looking up, "the terrors of the threatened denunciations would have been of little avail; but when they spoke of involving thee, my father, in the charge against me, I own I trembled, and desired to compromise. The Abbess Martha, of Elcho nunnery, being my mother's kinswoman, I told her my distresses, and obtained her promise that she would receive me, if, renouncing worldly love and thoughts of wedlock, I would take the veil in her sisterhood. She had conversation on the topic, I doubt not, with the Dominican Francis, and both joined in singing the same song. 'Remain in the world,' said they, 'and thy father and thou shall be brought to trial as heretics—assume the veil, and the errors of both shall be forgiven and cancelled.' They spoke not even of recantation of errors of doctrine; all should be peace if I would but enter the convent."

"I doubt not—I doubt not," said Simon; "the old Glover is thought rich, and his wealth would follow his daughter to the convent of Elcho, unless what the Dominicans might claim as their own share. So this was thy call to the veil—these thy objections to Henry Wynd?"

"Indeed, father, the course was urged on all hands, nor did my own mind recoil from it. Sir John Ramorny threatened me with the powerful vengeance of the young Prince, if I continued to repel his master's wicked suit—and as for poor Henry, it is but of late that I have discovered, to my own surprise—that—that I love his virtues more than I dislike his faults. Alas! the discovery has only been made to make my quitting the world more difficult than when I thought I had thee only to regret."

She rested her head on her hand, and wept bitterly.

"All this is folly," said the Glover. "Never was there an extremity so pinching, but what a wise man might find counsel if he was daring enough to act upon it. This has never been the land or the people over whom priests could rule in the name of Rome, without their usurpation being controlled. If they are to punish each honest burgher who says the monks love gold, and that the lives of some of them cry shame upon the doctrines they teach, why truly, Stephen Smotherwell will not lack employment—and if all foolish maidens are to be secluded from the world, because they follow the erring doctrines of a popular preaching friar, they must enlarge the nunneries, and receive their inmates on slighter composition. Our privileges have been often defended against the Pope himself, by our good monarchs of yore, and when he pretended to interfere with the temporal government of the kingdom, there wanted not a Scottish Parliament, who told him his duty in a letter that should have been written in letters of gold. I have seen the epistle myself, and though I could not read it, the very sight of the seals of the right reverend prelates, and noble and true barons, which hung at it, made my heart leap for joy. Thou should'st not have kept this secret, my child; but it is no time to tax thee with thy fault. Go down, get me some food—I will mount instantly, and go to our Lord Provost, and have his advice, and, as I trust, his protection and that of other true-hearted Scottish nobles, who will not see a true man trodden down for an idle word."

"Alas, my father," said Catherine, "it was even this impetuosity which I dreaded. I knew if I made my plaint to you there would soon be fire and feud, as if religion, though sent to us by the Father of peace, were fit only to be the mother of discord—and hence I could now— even now—give up the world, and retire with my sorrow among the sisters of Elcho, would you but let me be the sacrifice. Only, father— comfort poor Henry when we are parted for ever—and do not—do not let him think of me too harshly—Say Catherine will never vex him more by her remonstrances, but that she will never forget him in her prayers."

"The girl hath a tongue would make a Saracen weep," said her father, his own eyes sympathizing with those of his daughter. "But I will not yield way to this combination between the nun and the priest, to rob me of my only child.—Away with you, girl, and let me don my clothes; and prepare yourself to obey me in what I may have to recommend for your safety. Get a few clothes together, and what valuables thou hast—also, take the keys of my iron box, which poor Henry Smith gave me, and divide what gold you find into two portions,—put the one into a purse for thyself, and the other into the quilted girdle which I made on purpose to wear on journeys. Thus both shall be provided, in case fate should sunder us; in which event, God send the whirlwind may take the withered leaf, and spare the green one! Let them make ready my horse instantly, and the white jennet that I bought for thee but a day since, hoping to see thee ride to St John's Kirk with maids and matrons, as blithe a bride as ever crossed the holy threshold. But it skills not talking—Away, and remember that the saints help those who are willing to help themselves. Not a word in answer—begone, I say,—no wilfulness now. The pilot, in calm weather, will let a sea-boy trifle with the rudder; but, by my soul, when winds howl and waves arise, he stands by the helm himself. Away; no reply."

Catherine left the room to execute, as well as she might, the commands of her father, who, gentle in disposition, and devotedly attached to his child, suffered her often, as it seemed, to guide and rule both herself and him; yet who, as she knew, was wont to claim filial obedience, and exercise parental authority, with sufficient strictness, when the occasion seemed to require an enforcement of domestic discipline.

While the fair Catherine was engaged in executing her father's behests, and the good old Glover was hastily attiring himself, as one who was about to take a journey, a horse's tramp was heard in the narrow street. The horseman was wrapped in his riding cloak, having the cape of it drawn up, as if to hide the under part of his face, while his bonnet was pulled over his brows, and a broad plume obscured his upper features. He sprung from the saddle, and Dorothy had scarce time to reply to his inquiries that the Glover was in his bedroom, ere the stranger had ascended the stair and entered the sleeping apartment. Simon, astonished and alarmed, and disposed to see in this early visitant an apparitor or sumner, come to attach him and his daughter, was much relieved, when, as the stranger doffed the bonnet, and threw the skirt of the mantle from his face, he recognised the knightly Provost of the Fair City, a visit from whom, at any time, was a favour of no ordinary degree; but being made at such an hour, had something marvellous, and, connected with the circumstances of the times, even alarming.

"Sir Patrick Charteris?"—said the Glover—"this high honour done to your poor beadsman"—

"Hush!" said the Knight, "there is no time for idle civilities—I came hither, because a man is, in trying occasions, his own safest page, and I can remain no longer than to bid thee fly, good Glover, since warrants are to be granted this day in council for the arrest of thy daughter and thee, under charge of heresy; and delay will cost you both your liberty for certain, and perhaps your lives."

"I have heard something of such a matter," said the Glover, "and was this instant setting forth to Kinfauns, to plead my innocence of this scandalous charge, to ask your lordship's counsel, and to implore your protection."

"Thy innocence, friend Simon, will avail thee but little before prejudiced judges; my advice is, in one word, to fly, and wait for happier times. As for my protection, we must tarry till the tide turns ere it will in any sort avail thee. But if thou canst lie concealed for a few days or weeks, I have little doubt that the churchmen, who, by siding with the Duke of Albany in court intrigue, and by alleging the decay of the purity of Catholic doctrine as the sole cause of the present national misfortunes, have, at least for the present hour, an irresistible authority over the King, will receive a check. In the meanwhile, however, know that King Robert hath not only given way to this general warrant for inquisition after heresy, but hath confirmed the Pope's nomination of Henry Wardlaw, to be Archbishop of St Andrews, and Primate of Scotland; thus yielding to Rome those freedoms and immunities of the Scottish Church, which his ancestors, from the time of Malcolm Canmore, have so boldly defended. His brave fathers would have rather subscribed a covenant with the devil, than yielded in such a matter to the pretensions of Rome."

"Alas, and what remedy?"

"None, old man, save in some sudden court change," said Sir Patrick. "The King is but like a mirror, which, having no light itself, reflects back with equal readiness any which is placed near to it for the time. Now, although the Douglas is banded with Albany, yet the Earl is unfavourable to the high claims of those domineering priests, having quarrelled with them about the exactions which his retinue hath raised on the Abbot of Arbroath. He will come back again with a high hand, for report says, the Earl of March hath fled before him. When he comes we shall have a changed world, for his presence will control

Albany; especially, as many nobles, and I myself, as I tell you in confidence, are resolved to league with him to defend the general right. Thy exile, therefore, will end with his return to our court. Thou hast but to seek thee some temporary hiding place."

"For that, my lord," said the Glover, "I can be at no loss, since I have just title to the protection of the high Highland Chief, Gilchrist MacIan, Chief of the Clan Quhele."

"Nay, if thou canst take hold of his mantle thou needst no help of any one else—neither lowland churchman nor layman finds a free course of justice beyond the Highland frontier."

"But then my child, noble sir—my Catherine?" said the Glover.

"Let her go with thee, man. The graddan cake will keep her white teeth in order, the goat's whey will make the blood spring to her cheek again, which these alarms have banished; and even the Fair Maiden of Perth may sleep soft enough on a bed of Highland breckan."

"It is not from such idle respects, my lord, that I hesitate," said the Glover. "Catherine is the daughter of a plain burgher, and knows not nicety of food or lodging. But the son of MacIan hath been for many years a guest in my house, and I am obliged to say, that I have observed him looking at my daughter (who is as good as a betrothed bride) in a manner that, though I cared not for it in this lodging in Couvrefew Street, would give me some fear of consequences in a Highland glen, where I have no friends, and Conachar many."

The knightly Provost replied by a long "Whew! whew!—Nay, in that case I advise to send her to the nunnery at Elcho, where the Abbess, if I forget not, is some relation of yours. Indeed she said so herself, adding, that she loved her kinswoman well, together with all that belongs to thee, Simon."

"Truly, my lord, I do believe that the Abbess hath so much regard for me, that she would willingly receive the trust of my daughter, and my whole goods and gear into her sisterhood—Marry, her affection is something of a tenacious character, and would be loath to unloose its hold, either upon the wench or her tocher."

"Whew—whew!" again whistled the knightly Provost. "By the Thane's Cross, man, but this is an ill-favoured pirn to wind. Yet it shall never be said the fairest maid in the Fair City was cooped up in a convent, like a kain-hen in a cavey, and she about to be married to the bold burgess Henry Wynd. It shall never be while I wear belt and spurs, and am called Provost of Perth."

"But what remede, my lord?" asked the Glover.

"We must all take our share of the risk. Come, get you and your daughter presently to horse. You shall ride with me, and will see who dare gloom at you. The summons is not yet served on thee, and if they send an apparitor to Kinfauns, without a warrant under the King's own hand, I make mine avow, by the Red Rover's soul! that he shall eat his writ, both wax and wether-skin. To horse, to horse! and," addressing Catherine, as she entered at the moment, "you too, my pretty maid,

> To horse, and fear not for your quarters;
> They thrive in law that trust in Charters."

In a minute or two the father and daughter were on horseback, both keeping an arrow's flight before the Provost, by his direction, that they might not seem to be of the same company. They passed the eastern gate in some haste and rode forward roundly until they were out of sight. Sir Patrick followed leisurely; but when he was lost to the view of the warders, he spurred his mettled horse, and soon came up with the Glover and Catherine, when a conversation ensued which throws light upon some previous passages of this history.

Chapter Three

"I HAVE BEEN devising a mode," said the well-meaning Provost, "by which I may make you both secure from the malice of your enemies, for a week or two, when I have little doubt I may see a changed world at court. But that I may the better judge what is to be done, tell me frankly, Simon, the nature of your connexion with old Gilchrist MacIan, which leads you to repose such implicit confidence in him. You are a close observer of the rules of the city, and you are aware of the severe penalties which they denounce against such burghers as have covine and alliance with the Highland clans."

"True, my lord; but it is also known to you, that our craft, working in skins of cattle, stags, and every other description of hides, have a privilege, and are allowed to transact with those Highlanders, as with the men who can most readily supply us with the means of conducting our trade, to the great profit of the burgh. Thus it hath chanced me to have great dealings with these men; and I can take it on my salvation, that you nowhere find more just and honourable traffickers, or by whom a man may more easily make an honest penny. I have made in my day several distant journeys into the far Highlands, upon the faith of their chiefs; nor did I ever meet with a people more true to their word, when you can once prevail upon them to plight it in your behalf. And as for the Highland Chief, Gilchrist MacIan, saving that he is hasty in homicide and fire-raising towards those with whom he hath deadly feud, I have nowhere seen a man who walketh a more just and upright path."

"It is more than ever I heard before," said Sir Patrick Charteris. "Yet I have known something of the Highland runagates too."

"They show another favour, and a very different one, to their friends than to their enemies, as your lordship shall understand," said the Glover. "However, be that as it may, it chanced me to serve Gilchrist MacIan in a high matter. It is now about eighteen years since, that it chanced, the Clan Quhele and Clan Chattan being at feud, as indeed they are seldom at peace, the former sustained such a defeat, as wellnigh extirpated the family of their chief, MacIan. Seven of his sons were slain in battle and after it, himself put to flight, and his castle taken and given to the flames. His wife, then near the time of giving birth to an infant, fled into the forest, attended by one faithful servant and his daughter. Here, in sorrow and care enough, she gave birth to a boy; and as the misery of the mother's condition rendered her little able to suckle the infant, he was nursed with the milk of a doe, which the forester who attended her contrived to take alive in a snare. It was not many months afterwards, that, in a second encounter of these fierce clans, MacIan defeated his enemies in his turn, and regained possession of the district which he had lost. It was with unexpected rapture, that he found his wife and child were in existence, having never expected to see more of them than the bleached bones, from which the wolves and wild-cats had eaten the flesh.

"But a strong and prevailing prejudice, such as is often entertained by these wild people, prevented their Chief from enjoying the full happiness arising from having thus regained his only son in safety. An ancient prophecy was current among them, that the power of the tribe should fall by means of a boy born under a bush of holly, and suckled by a white doe. The circumstance, unfortunately for the Chief, tallied exactly with the birth of the only child which remained to him, and it was demanded of him by the elders of the clan, that the boy should be either put to death, or at least removed from the dominions of the tribe, and brought up in obscurity. Gilchrist MacIan was obliged to consent; and having made choice of the latter proposal, the child, under the name of Conachar, was brought up in my family, with the purpose, as was at first intended, of concealing from him all knowledge who or what he was, or of his pretensions to authority over a numerous and warlike people. But as years rolled on, the elders of the tribe, who had exerted so much authority, were removed by death, or rendered incapable of interfering in the public affairs by age; while, on the other hand, the influence of Gilchrist MacIan was increased by his successful struggles against the Clan Chattan, in which he restored the equality betwixt the two contending confederacies, which had existed before the calamitous defeat of which I told your honour.

Feeling himself thus firmly seated, he naturally became desirous to bring home his only son to his bosom and family; and for that purpose, caused me to send the young Conachar, as he was called, more than once to the Highlands. He was a youth expressly made, by his form and gallantry of bearing, to gain a father's heart. At length, I suppose the lad either guessed the secret of his birth, or something of it was communicated to him; and the disgust which the paughty Highland varlet had always shown for my honest trade, became more manifest; so that I dared not so much as lay my staff over his costard, for fear of receiving a stab with a dirk, as an answer in Gaelic to a Saxon remark. It was then I wished to be well rid of him, the rather that he showed so much devotion to Catherine, who, forsooth, set herself up to wash the Ethiopian, and teach a wild Highlandman mercy and morals. She knows herself how it ended."

"Nay, my father," said Catherine, "it was surely but a point of charity to snatch the brand from the burning."

"But a small point of wisdom," said her father, "to risk the burning of your own fingers for such an end.—What says my lord to the matter?"

"My lord would not offend the Fair Maid of Perth," said Sir Patrick; "and he knows well the purity and truth of her mind. And yet I must needs say, that had this nursling of the doe been shrivelled, haggard, cross-made, and red-haired, like some Highlanders I have known, I question if the Fair Maiden of Perth would have bestowed so much zeal upon his conversion; and if Catherine had been as aged, wrinkled, and bent by years, as the old woman that opened the door to me this morning, I would wager my gold spurs against a pair of Highland brogues, that this wild roe-buck would never have listened to a second lecture.—You laugh, Glover, and Catherine blushes a blush of anger. Let it pass, it is the way of the world."

"The way in which the men of the world esteem their neighbours, my lord," answered Catherine, with some spirit.

"Nay, fair saint, forgive a jest," said the knight; "and thou, Simon, tell us how this tale ended—with Conachar's escape to the Highlands, I suppose?"

"With his return thither," said the Glover. "There was, for some two or three years, a fellow about Perth, a sort of messenger, who came and went under divers pretences, but was in fact the means of communication between Gilchrist MacIan and his son, young Conachar, or, as he is now called, Hector. From this gillie, I learned, in general, that the banishment of the Dault an Neigh Dheil, or foster child of the White Doe, was again brought under consideration of the tribe. His foster father, Torquil of the Oak, the old forester, appeared with eight sons, the finest men of the clan, and demanded that the doom of banishment should be revoked. He spoke with the greater authority, as he was himself Taishatar, or a Seer, and supposed to have communication with the invisible world. He affirmed that he had performed a magical ceremony, termed Tin-Egan, by which he evoked a fiend, from whom he extorted a confession that Conachar, now called Eachin, or Hector MacIan, was the only man in the approaching combat between the two hostile clans, who should come off without blood or blemish. Hence, Torquil of the Oak argued that the presence of the fated person was necessary to insure the victory. 'So much I am possessed of this,' said the forester, 'that unless Eachin fight in his place in the ranks of the Clan Quhele, neither I, his foster-father, nor any of my eight sons, will lift a weapon in the quarrel.'

"This speech was received with much alarm; for the defection of nine men, the stoutest of their tribe, would be a serious blow, more especially if the combat, as begins to be rumoured, should be decided by a small number from each side. The ancient superstition concerning the foster son of the White Doe was counterbalanced by a new and later prejudice, and the father took the opportunity of presenting to the clan his long-hidden son, whose youthful, but handsome and animated countenance, haughty carriage, and active limbs, excited the admiration of the clansmen, who joyfully received him as the heir and descendant of their Chief, notwithstanding the ominous presage attending his birth and nurture.

"From this tale, my lord," continued Simon Glover, "your lordship may easily conceive why I myself should be secure of a good reception among the Clan Quhele; and you may also have reason to judge that it would be very rash in me to carry Catherine thither. And this, noble lord, is the heaviest of my troubles."

"We will lighten the load, then," said Sir Patrick; "and, good Glover, I will take risk for thee and this damsel. My alliance with the Douglas gives me some interest with Marjory, Duchess of Roth-say, his daughter, the neglected wife of our wilful Prince. Rely on it, good Glover, that in her retinue thy daughter will be as secure as in a fenced castle. The Duchess keeps house now at Falkland, a castle which the Duke of Albany, to whom it belongs, has lent to her for her accommodation. I cannot promise you pleasure, Fair Maiden; for the Duchess Marjory of Rothsay is unfortunate, and therefore splenetic, haughty, and overbearing; conscious of the want of attractive qualities, therefore jealous of those women who possess them. But she is firm in faith, and noble in spirit, and would fling Pope or prelate into the ditch of her castle, who should come to arrest any one under her protection. You will therefore have absolute safety, though you may lack comfort."

"I have no title to more," said Catherine; "and deeply do I feel the kindness that is willing to secure me such honourable protection. If she be haughty, I will remember she is a Douglas, and hath right to entertain as much pride as may become a mortal—if she be fretful, I will recollect that she is unfortunate—and if she be unreasonably captious, I will not forget that she is my protectress. Care not for me, my lord, when you have placed me under the noble lady's charge.— But my poor father, to be exposed amongst these wild and dangerous people!"

"Care not for me, Catherine," said the Glover; "I am as familiar with brogue and bracken as if I had worn them myself. I have only to fear that the decisive battle may be fought before I can leave their country; and if the Clan Quhele lose the combat, I may suffer by the ruin of my protectors."

"We must have that cared for," said Sir Patrick; "rely on my looking out for your safety.—But which party will carry the day, think you?"

"Frankly, my Lord Provost, I believe the Clan Chattan will have the worse; these nine children of the forest form a third nearly of the band surrounding the Chief of Clan Quhele, and are redoubted champions."

"And your apprentice, will he stand to it?"

"He is hot as fire, Sir Patrick," answered the Glover; "but he is also unstable as water. Nevertheless, if he is spared, he will be one day a brave man."

"But, as now, he has some of the White Doe's milk still lurking about his liver, ha, Simon?"

"He has little experience, my lord," said the Glover, "and I need not tell an honoured warrior like you, that danger must be familiar to us ere we can dally with it like a mistress."

This conversation brought them speedily to the Castle of Kinfauns, where, after a short refreshment, it was necessary that the father and the daughter should part, in order to seek their respective places of refuge. It was then first, as she saw that her father's anxiety on her account had drowned all recollections of his friend, that Catherine dropped, as if in a dream, the name of "Henry Gow."

"True, most true," continued her father; "we must possess him of our purposes."

"Leave that to me," said Sir Patrick. "I will not trust to a messenger, nor will I send a letter, because, if I could write one, I think he could not read it. He will suffer anxiety in the meanwhile, but I will ride to Perth to-morrow by times, and acquaint him with your designs."

The time of separation now approached. It was a bitter moment;

but the manly character of the old burgher, and the devout resignation of Catherine to the will of Providence, made it lighter than might have been expected. The good knight hurried the departure of the burgess, but in the kindest manner; and even went so far as to offer him some gold pieces in loan, which might, where specie was so scarce, be considered as the *ne plus ultra* of regard. The Glover, however, assured him he was amply provided, and departed on his journey in a north-westerly direction. The hospitable protection of Sir Patrick Charteris was no less manifested towards his fair guest. She was placed under the charge of a duenna, who managed the good Knight's household, and was compelled to remain several days in Kinfauns, owing to the obstacles and delays interposed by a Tay boatman, named Kitt Stenshaw, to whose charge she was to be committed, and whom the Provost highly trusted.

Thus severed the child and parent in a moment of great danger and difficulty, much augmented by circumstances of which they were then ignorant, and which seemed greatly to diminish any chance of safety that remained for them.

Chapter Four

"This Austin humbly did."—"Did he?" quoth he.
"Austin may do the same again for me."
POPE'S *Prologue to Canterbury Tales from Chaucer*

THE COURSE of our story will be best pursued by attending the course of Simon Glover. It is not our purpose to indicate the exact local boundaries of the two contending clans, especially since they are not clearly pointed out by the historians who have transmitted accounts of this memorable feud. It is sufficient to say, that the territory of the Clan Chattan extended far and wide, comprehending Caithness and Sutherland, and having for their paramount chief the powerful Earl of the latter shire, thence called Mohr ar chat. In this general sense, the Keiths, the Sinclairs, the Guns, and other families and clans of great power, were included in the confederacy. These, however, were not engaged in the present quarrel, which was limited to that part of the Clan Chattan occupying the extensive mountainous districts of Perthshire and Inverness-shire, which form a large portion of what is called the north-eastern Highlands. It is well known that two large clans, unquestionably known to belong to the Clan Chattan, the MacPhersons and the MacIntoshes, dispute to this day which of their chieftains was at the head of this Badenoch branch of the great confederacy, and both have of later times assumed the title of Captain of Clan Chattan. *Non nostrum est*—But, at all events, Badenoch must have been the centre of the confederacy, so far as involved in the feud of which we treat.

Of the rival league of Clan Quhele, or, as it is called by later authorities, Clan Kay, we have a still less distinct account, for reasons which will appear in the sequel. Buchanan and later authors have since identified them with the numerous and powerful sept of Mac-Kay. If this is done on good authority, which is to be doubted, the MacKays must have shifted their settlements greatly since the reign of Robert III., since they are now to be found (as a clan) in the extreme northern parts of Scotland, in the counties of Ross and Sutherland. We cannot, therefore, be so clear as we would wish in the geography of the story. Suffice it, that directing his course in a northwesterly direction, the Glover travelled for a day's journey in the direction of the Breadalbane country, from which he hoped to reach the Castle where Gilchrist MacIan, the captain of the Clan Quhele, and the father of his pupil Conachar, usually held his residence, with a barbarous pomp of attendance and ceremonial, suited to his lofty pretensions.

We need not stop to describe the toil and terrors of such a journey, where the path was to be traced among wastes and mountains, now ascending precipitous ravines, now plunging into inextricable bogs, and often intersected with large brooks, and even rivers. But all these perils Simon Glover had before encountered, in quest of honest gain; and it was not to be supposed that he shunned or feared them where liberty, and life itself, were at stake.

The danger from the warlike and uncivilized inhabitants of these wilds would have appeared to another at least as formidable as the perils of the journey. But Simon's knowledge of the manners and language of the people assured him on this point also. An appeal to the hospitality of the wildest Gael was never unsuccessful; and the kern, that in other circumstances would have taken a man's life for the silver button of his cloak, would deprive himself of a meal to relieve the traveller who implored hospitality at the door of his bothy. The art of travelling was to appear as confident and defenceless as possible; and accordingly the Glover carried no arms whatever, journeyed without the least appearance of precaution, and took good care to exhibit nothing which might excite cupidity. Another rule which he deemed it prudent to observe, was to avoid communication with any of the passengers whom he might chance to meet, except in the interchange of the common civilities of salutation, which the Highlanders rarely omit. Few opportunities occurred of exchanging even such passing greetings. The country, always lonely, seemed now entirely forsaken;

and even in the little straths or valleys which he had occasion to pass or traverse, the hamlets were deserted, and the inhabitants had betaken themselves to woods and caves. This was easily accounted for, considering the imminent dangers of a feud, which all expected would become one of the most general signals for plunder and ravage that had ever distracted that unhappy country.

Simon began to be alarmed at this state of desolation. He had made a halt since he left Kinfauns, to allow his nag some rest; and now he began to be anxious how he was to pass the night. He had reckoned upon spending it at the cottage of an old acquaintance, called Niel Booshalloch, (or the Cow-herd,) because he had charge of numerous herds of cattle belonging to the Captain of Clan Quhele, for which purpose he had a settlement on the banks of the Tay, not far from the spot where it leaves the lake of the same name. From this his old host and friend, with whom he had transacted many bargains for hides and furs, the old Glover hoped to learn the present state of the country, the prospect of peace or war, and the best measures to be taken for his own safety. It will be remembered, that the news of the indentures of battle entered into for diminishing the extent of the feud, had only been communicated to King Robert the day before the Glover left Perth, and did not become public till some time afterwards.

"If Niel Booshalloch hath left his dwelling like the rest of them, I shall be finely holped up," thought Simon, "since I want not only the advantage of his good advice, but also his interest with Gilchrist MacIan; and, moreover, a night's quarters and a supper."

Thus reflecting, he reached the top of a swelling green hill, and saw the splendid vision of Loch Tay lying beneath him, an immense plate of polished silver, its dark heathy mountains and leafless thickets of oak serving as an arabesque frame to a magnificent mirror.

Indifferent to natural beauty at any time, Simon Glover was now particularly so; and the only part of the splendid landscape on which he turned his eye was the angle or loop of meadow land, where the river Tay, rushing in full-swoln dignity from its parent lake, and wheeling around a beautiful valley of about a mile in breadth, begins his broad course to the south-eastward, like a conqueror and a legis-lator, to subdue and to enrich remote districts. Upon the sequestered spot, which is so beautifully situated between lake, mountain, and river, arose afterwards the feudal castle of Ballough, which in our time has been succeeded by the splendid palace of the Earl of Breadalbane.

But the Campbells, though they had already attained very great power in Argyleshire, had not yet extended themselves so far eastward as Loch Tay, the banks of which were, either by right, or in mere occupancy, possessed for the present by the Clan Quhele, whose choicest herds were fattened on the margin of the lake. In this valley, therefore, between the river and the lake, amid extensive forests of oak-wood, hazel, rowan-tree, and larches, arose the humble cottage of Niel Booshalloch, a village Eumæus, whose hospitable chimneys were seen to smoke plentifully, to the great encouragement of Simon Glover, who might otherwise have been obliged to spend the night in the open air, to his no small discomfort.

He reached the door of the cottage, whistled, shouted, and made his approach known. There was a baying of hounds and collies, and presently the master of the hut came forth. There was much care on his brow, and he seemed surprised at the sight of Simon Glover, though the herdsman covered both as well as he might; for nothing in that region could be reckoned more uncivil than for the landlord to suffer anything to escape him, in look or gesture, which might induce the visitor to think that his arrival was an unpleasing, or even an unexpected incident. The traveller's horse was conducted to a stable, which was almost too low to receive him, and the Glover himself was led into the mansion of the Booshalloch, where, according to the custom of the country, bread and cheese was placed before the traveller, while more solid food was preparing. Simon, who understood all their habits, took no notice of the obvious marks of sadness on the brow of his entertainer, and on those of the family, until he had eaten somewhat for form's sake; after which he asked the general question, Was there any news in the country?

"Bad news as ever were told," said the herdsman; "our father is no more."

"How?" said Simon, greatly alarmed, "is the Captain of the Clan Quhele dead?"

"The Captain of the Clan Quhele never dies," answered the Booshalloch; "but Gilchrist MacIan died twenty hours since, and his son, Eachin MacIan, is now Captain."

"What, Eachin—that is Conachar—my apprentice?"

"As little of that subject as you list, brother Simon," said the herdsman. "It is to be remembered, friend, that your craft, which doth very well for a living in the douce city of Perth, is something too mechanical to be much esteemed at the foot of Ben Lawers, and on the banks of Loch Tay. We have not a Gaelic word by which we can even name a maker of gloves."

"It would be strange if you had, friend Niel," said Simon, drily, "having so few gloves to wear. I think there be none in the whole Clan Quhele, save those which I myself gave to Gilchrist MacIan, whom God assoilzie, who esteemed them a choice propine. Most deeply do I regret his death, for I was coming to him on express business."

"You had better turn the nag's head southward with morning light," said the herdsman. "The funeral is instantly to take place, and it must be with short ceremony; for there is a battle to be fought by the Clan Quhele and the Clan Chattan, thirty champions on a side, as soon as Palm Sunday next, and we have brief time either to lament the dead or honour the living."

"Yet are my affairs so pressing, that I must needs see the young Chief, were it but for a quarter of an hour," said the Glover.

"Hark thee, friend," replied his host, "I think thy business must be either to gather money or to make traffic. Now, if the Chief owe thee anything for upbringing or otherwise, ask him not to pay it when all the treasures of the tribe are called in for making gallant preparation of arms and equipment for their combatants, that we may meet these proud hill-cats in a fashion to show ourselves their superiors. But if thou comest to practise commerce with us, thy time is still worse chosen. Thou knowest that thou art already envied of many of our tribe, for having had the fosterage of the young Chief, which is a thing usually given to the best of the clan."

"But, St Mary, man!" exclaimed the Glover, "men should remember the office was not conferred on me as a favour which I courted, but that it was accepted by me on importunity and entreaty, to my no small prejudice. This Conachar, or Hector of yours, or whatever you call him, has destroyed me doe-skins to the amount of many pounds Scots."

"There again, now," said the Booshalloch, "you have spoken a word to cost your life;—any allusion to skins or hides, or especially to deer and does, may incur no less a forfeit. The Chief is young, and jealous of his rank—none knows the reason better than thou, friend Glover. He will naturally wish that everything concerning the opposition to his succession, and having reference to his exile, should be totally forgotten; and he will not hold him in affection who shall recall the recollection of his people, or force back his own, upon what they must both remember with pain. Think how, at such a moment, they will look on the old Glover of Perth, to whom the Chief was so long apprentice!—Come, come, old friend, you have erred in this. You are in over great haste to worship the rising sun, while his beams are yet level with the horizon. Come thou when he has climbed higher in the heavens, and thou shalt have thy share of the warmth of his noonday height."

"Niel Booshalloch," said the Glover, "we have been old friends, as thou say'st; and as I think thee a true one, I will speak to thee freely, though what I say might be perilous if spoken to others of thy clan. Thou think'st I come hither to make my own profit of thy young Chief, and it is natural thou should'st think so. But I would not, at my years, quit my own chimney corner in Curfew Street, to bask me in the beams of the brightest sun that ever shone upon Highland heather. The very truth is, I come hither in extremity—my foes have the advantage of me, and have laid things to my charge whereof I am incapable, even in thought. Nevertheless, doom is like to go forth against me, and there is no remedy but that I must up and fly, or remain and perish. I come to your young Chief, as one who had refuge with me in his distress; who ate of my bread and drank of my cup. I ask of him refuge, which, as I trust, I shall need but a short time."

"That makes a different case," replied the herdsman. "So different, that if you came at midnight to the gate of MacIan, having the King of Scotland's head in your hand, and a thousand men in pursuit for the avenging of his blood, I could not think it for his honour to refuse you protection. And for your innocence or guilt, it concerns not the case, —or rather, he ought the more to shelter you if guilty, seeing your necessity and his risk are both in that case the greater. I must straightway to him, that no hasty tongue tell him of your arriving hither without saying the cause."

"A pity of your trouble," said the Glover; "but where lies the Chief?"

"He is quartered about ten miles hence, busied with the affairs of the funeral, and with preparations for the combat—the dead to the grave, and the living to battle."

"It is a long way, and will take you all night to go and come," said the Glover; "and I am very sure that Conachar, when he knows it is I who"——

"Forget Conachar," said the herdsman, placing his finger on his lips. "And as for the ten miles, they are but a Highland leap, when one bears a message between his friend and his Chief."

So saying, and committing the traveller to the charge of his eldest son and his daughter, the active herdsman left his house two hours before midnight, to which he returned long before sunrise. He did not disturb his wearied guest, but on arising in the morning, he acquainted him that the funeral of the late Chieftain was to take place the same day, and that, although Eachin MacIan could not invite a Saxon to the funeral, he would be glad to receive him at the entertainment which was to follow.

"His will must be obeyed," said the Glover, half smiling at the change of relation between himself and his late apprentice. "The man is the master now, and I trust he will remember, that, when matters were otherwise between us, I did not use my authority ungraciously."

"Traut shoe, friend!" exclaimed the Booshalloch, "the less of that you say the better. You will find yourself a right welcome guest to Eachin, and the deil a man dares stir you within his bounds. But fare you well, for I must go, as beseems me, to the burial of the best Chief the clan ever had, and the wisest Captain that ever cocked the sweet gale (bog-myrtle) in his bonnet. Farewell to you for a while, and if you will go to the top of the Tom-an-Lonach behind the house, you will see a gallant sight, and hear such a coronach as will reach the top of Ben Lawers. A boat will wait for you, three hours hence, at a wee bit creek about half a mile westward from the head of the Tay."

With these words he took his departure, followed by his three sons, to man the boat in which he was to join the rest of the mourners, and two daughters, whose voices were wanted to join in the Lament, which was chanted, or rather screamed, on such occasions of general affliction.

Simon Glover, finding himself alone, resorted to the stable to look after his nag, who, he found, had been well served with graddan, or bread made of scorched barley. Of this kindness he was fully sensible, knowing that, probably, the family had little of this delicacy left to themselves, until the next harvest should bring them a scanty supply. In animal food they were well provided, and the lake found them abundance of fish for their lenten diet, which they did not observe very strictly; but bread was a delicacy very scanty in the Highlands. The bogs afforded a soft species of hay, none of the best to be sure, but Scottish horses, like their riders, were then accustomed to hard fare. Gauntlet, for this was the name of the palfrey, had his stall crammed full of dried fern for litter, and was otherwise as well provided for as Highland hospitality could contrive.

Simon Glover being thus left to his own painful reflections, nothing better remained, after having seen after the comforts of the dumb companion of his journey, than to follow the herdsman's advice; and ascending towards the top of an eminence called Tom-an-Lonach, or the Knoll of Yew Trees, after a walk of half an hour he reached the summit, and could look down on the broad expanse of the lake, of which the height commanded a noble view. A few aged and scattered yew trees, of great size, still vindicated for the beautiful green hill the name attached to it. But a far greater number had fallen a sacrifice to the general demand for bow-staves in that warlike age, the bow being a weapon much used by the mountaineers, though those which they employed, as well as their arrows, were, in shape and form, and especially in efficacy, far inferior to the archery of merry England. The dark and shattered individual yews which remained were like the veterans of a broken host, occupying in disorder some post of advantage, with the stern purpose of resisting to the last. Behind this eminence, but detached from it, arose a higher hill, partly covered with copse-wood, partly opening into glades of pasture, where the cattle strayed, finding a scanty sustenance among the spring-heads and marshy places, where the fresh grass began first to arise.

The opposite, or northern shore of the lake, presented a far more Alpine prospect than that upon which the Glover was stationed. Woods and thickets ran up the sides of the mountains, and disappeared among the sinuosities formed by the winding ravines which separated them from each other; but far above these specimens of a tolerable natural soil arose the swart and bare mountains themselves, in the dark grey desolation proper to the season.

Some were peaked, some broad-crested, some rocky and precipitous, others of a tamer outline; and the clan of Titans seemed to be commanded by their appropriate chieftains—the frowning mountain of Ben Lawers, and the still more lofty eminence of Ben Mohr, arising high above the rest, whose peaks retain a dazzling helmet of snow far into the summer season, and sometimes during the whole year. Yet the borders of this wild and sylvan region, where the mountains descended upon the lake, intimated, even at this early period, many traces of human habitation. Hamlets were seen, especially on the northern margin of the lake, or half hid among the little glens that poured their tributary streams into Loch Tay, which, like many earthly things, made a fair show at a distance, but, when more closely approached, were disgustful and repulsive, from their squalid want of the conveniences which attend even Indian wigwams. They were inhabited by a race who neither cultivated the earth, nor cared for the enjoyments which industry procures. The women, although otherwise treated with affection, and even delicacy of respect, discharged all the absolutely necessary domestic labour. The men, excepting some reluctant use of an ill-formed plough, or more frequently a spade, grudgingly gone through, as a task infinitely beneath them, took no other employment than the charge of the herds of black cattle, in which their wealth consisted. At all other times, they hunted, fished, or marauded, during the brief intervals of peace, by way of pastime; plundering with bolder license, and fighting with embittered animosity, in time of war, which, public or private, upon a broader or a more restricted scale, formed the proper business of their lives, and the only one which they esteemed worthy of them.

The magnificent bosom of the lake itself was a scene to gaze on with delight. Its noble breadth, with its termination in a full and beautiful river, was rendered yet more picturesque by one of those islets which are often happily situated in Scottish lakes, and on which are usually castles or religious houses which the fear or the piety of the ancient inhabitants have caused to be founded there. The ruins upon that which adorns the foot of Loch Tay, now almost overgrown with wood, rose, at the time we speak of, into the towers and pinnacles of a priory where slumbered the remains of Sibilla, daughter of Henry I. of England, and consort of Alexander the First of Scotland. This holy place had been deemed of dignity sufficient to be the deposit of the remains of the Captain of the Clan Quhele, at least till times when the removal of the danger, now so imminently pressing, should permit of his body being conveyed to a distinguished convent in the north, where he was destined ultimately to repose with all his ancestry.

A number of boats pushed off from various points of the near and more distant shore, many displaying sable banners, and others having their several pipers in the bow, who from time to time poured forth a few notes of a shrill, plaintive, and wailing character, and intimated to the Glover that the ceremony was about to take place. These sounds of lamentation were but the tuning as it were of the instruments, compared with the general wail which was speedily to be raised.

A distant sound was heard from far up the lake, even as it seemed from the remote and dusky glens, out of which the Dochart and the Lochy pour their streams into Loch Tay. It was in a wild inaccessible spot, where the Campbells at a subsequent period founded their strong fortress of Finlayrigg, that the redoubted commander of the Clan Quhele drew his last breath; and, to give due pomp to his funeral, his corpse was now to be brought down the Loch to the island assigned for his temporary place of rest. The funeral fleet, led by the Chieftain's barge, from which a huge black banner was displayed, had made more than two thirds of its voyage ere it was visible from the eminence on which Simon Glover stood to overlook the ceremony. The instant the distant wail of the coronach was heard proceeding from the attendants on the funeral barge, all the subordinate sounds of lamentation were hushed at once, as the raven ceases to croak and the hawk to whistle, whenever the scream of the eagle is heard. The boats, which had floated hither and thither upon the lake, like a flock of water-fowl disporting themselves on its surface, now drew together with an appearance of order, that the funeral flotilla might pass onwards, and they themselves fall into their proper place in the rear. In the meanwhile the piercing din of the war-pipes became louder and louder, and the cry from the numberless boats which followed that from which the black banner of the Chief was displayed, rose in wild unison up to the Tom-na-Lonach, from which the Glover viewed the spectacle. The galley which headed the procession, bore on its poop a species of scaffold, upon which, arrayed in white linen, and with the face bare, was displayed the corpse of the deceased Chieftain. His son, and the nearest relatives, filled the vessel, while a great number of boats, of every description that could be assembled, either on Loch Tay itself, or brought by land carriage from Loch Earn and otherwise, followed in the rear, some of them of very frail materials. There were even curraghs, composed of ox-hides stretched over hoops of willow, in the manner of the ancient British; and some committed themselves to rafts formed for the occasion, from the readiest materials that occurred, and united in such a precarious manner as to render it probable, that, before the accomplishment of the voyage, some of the clansmen of the deceased might be sent to attend their Chieftain in the world of spirits.

When the principal flotilla came in sight of the smaller group of boats collected towards the foot of the lake, and bearing off from the little island, they hailed each other with a shout so loud and general, and terminating in a cadence so wildly prolonged, that not only the deer fled from their cover for miles around, and sought the distant recesses of the mountains, but even the domestic cattle, accustomed to the voice of man, felt the full panic which the human shout strikes into the wilder tribes, and like them fled from their pasture into morasses and dingles.

Summoned forth from their convent by those sounds, the monks who inhabited the little islet began to issue from its lowly portal, with cross and banner, and as much of ecclesiastical state as they had the means of displaying; their bells at the same time, of which the edifice possessed three, pealing the death-toll over the long lake, which came to the ears of the now silent multitude, mingled with the solemn chant of the Catholic Church, raised by the monks in their procession. Various ceremonies were gone through, while the kindred of the deceased brought the body ashore, and, placing it on a bank long consecrated to the purpose, made the Deasil* around the departed. When the corpse was uplifted to be carried into the church, another united yell burst from the assembled multitude, in which the deep shout of warriors, and the shrill wail of females, joined their notes with the tremulous voice of age, and the babbling cry of childhood. The coronach was again, and for the last time, shrieked, as the body was borne into the interior of the church, where only the nearest relations of the deceased, and the most distinguished of the leaders of the clan, were permitted to enter. The last yell of woe was so terribly loud,

---

* A very ancient custom, which consists in going three times round the body of a dead or living person, imploring blessings upon him. The Deasil must be performed sunways, that is, by moving from right to left. If misfortune is imprecated, the party moves withershins, (German, WIDDERSINS,) that is, from left to right.

and answered by so many hundred echoes, that the citizen of Perth instinctively raised his hands to his ears, to shut out, or deaden at least, a sound so piercing. He kept this attitude, while the hawks, owls, and other birds, scared by the wild scream, had begun to settle in their retreats, when, as he withdrew his hands, a voice said close by him, "Think you this, Simon Glover, the hymn of penitence and praise, with which it becomes poor forlorn man, cast out from his tenement of clay, to be wafted into the presence of his Maker?"

The Glover turned, and in the old man, with a long white beard, who stood close beside him, had no difficulty, from the clear mild eye, and the benevolent cast of features, to recognise the Carthusian monk Father Clement, no longer wearing his monastic habiliments, but wrapped in a frieze mantle, and having a Highland cap on his head.

It may be recollected that the Glover regarded this man with a combined feeling of respect and dislike—respect, which his judgment could not deny to the monk's person and character, and dislike, which arose from Father Clement's peculiar doctrines being the cause of his daughter's exile and his own distress. It was not, therefore, with sentiments of unmixed satisfaction, that he returned the greeting of the Father, and replied to the reiterated question, What he thought of the funeral rites, which were discharged in so wild a manner,—"I know not, my good Father; but these men do their duty to their deceased Chief according to the fashion of their ancestors; they mean it to express their regret for their friend's loss, and their prayers to Heaven in his behalf; and that which is done of good will, must, to my thinking, be accepted favourably. Had it been otherwise, methinks they had ere now been enlightened to do better."

"Thou art deceived," answered the Monk. "God has sent his light amongst us all, though in various proportions; but man wilfully shuts his eyes and prefers darkness. This benighted people mingle with the ritual of the Roman Church, the old heathen ceremonies of their own fathers, and thus unite with the abominations of a Church corrupted by wealth and power, the cruel and bloody ritual of savage Paynims."

"Father," said Simon, abruptly, "methinks your presence were more useful in yonder chapel, aiding your brethren in the discharge of their clerical duties, than in troubling and unsettling the belief of an humble, though ignorant Christian, like myself."

"And wherefore say, good brother, that I would unfix thy principles of belief?" answered Clement. "So Heaven deal with me, as, were my life-blood necessary to cement the mind of any man to the holy religion he professeth, it should be freely poured out for the purpose."

"Your speech is fair, Father, I grant you," said the Glover; "but if I am to judge the doctrine by the fruits, Heaven has punished me by the hand of the Church, for having ever hearkened thereto. Ere I heard you, my confessor was little moved, though I might have owned to have told a merry tale upon the ale-bench, even if a friar or a nun were the subject. If at a time I had called Father Hubert a better hunter of hares than of souls, I confessed me to the Vicar Vinesauf, who laughed and made me pay a reckoning for penance—or if I had said that the Vicar Vinesauf was more constant to his cup than to his breviary, I confessed me to Father Hubert, and a new hawking-glove made all well again; and thus I, my conscience, and Mother Church, lived together on terms of peace, friendship, and mutual forbearance. But since I have listened to you, Father Clement, this goodly union is broke to pieces, and nothing is thundered in my ear but purgatory in the next world, and fire and faggot in this. Therefore, avoid you, Father Clement, or speak to those who can understand your doctrine. I have no heart to be a martyr; I have never in my whole life had courage enough so much as to snuff a candle with my fingers; and, to speak the truth, I am minded to go back to Perth, sue out my pardon in the spiritual court, carry my faggot to the gallows' foot, in token of recantation, and purchase myself once more the name of a good Catholic, were it at the price of all the worldly wealth that remains to me."

"You are angry, my dearest brother," said Clement; "and repent you on the pinch of a little worldly danger, and a little worldly loss, for the good thoughts which you once entertained."

"You speak at ease, Father Clement, since I think you have long forsworn the wealth and goods of the world, and are prepared to yield up your life, when it is demanded, in exchange for the doctrine you preach and believe. You are as ready to put on your pitched shirt and brimstone head-gear, as a naked man is to go to his bed, and it would seem you have not much more reluctance to the ceremony. But I still wear that which clings to me. My wealth is still my own, and I thank Heaven it is a decent pittance whereon to live—my life, too, is that of a hale old man of sixty, who is in no haste to bring it to a close—and if I were poor as Job, and on the edge of the grave, must I not still cling to my daughter, whom your doctrines have already cost so dear?"

"Thy daughter, friend Simon," said the Carthusian, "may be truly called an angel upon earth."

"Ay; and by listening to your doctrines, Father, she is now like to be called on to be an angel in heaven, and to be transported thither in a chariot of fire."

"Nay, my good brother," said Clement, "desist, I pray you, to speak of what you little understand. Since it is wasting time to show thee the light that thou chafest against, yet listen to that which I have to say touching thy daughter, whose temporal felicity, though I weigh it not even for an instant in the scale against that which is spiritual, is, nevertheless, in its order, as dear to Clement Blair as to her own father."

The tears stood in the old man's eyes as he spoke, and Simon Glover was in some degree mollified as he again addressed him.

"One would think thee, Father Clement, the kindest and most amiable of men; how comes it then that thy steps are haunted by general ill-will, wherever thou chancest to turn them? I could lay my life thou hast contrived already to offend yonder half score of poor friars in their water-girdled cage, and that you have been prohibited from attendance on the funeral?"

"Even so, my son," said the Carthusian, "and I doubt whether their malice will suffer me to remain in this country. I did but speak a few sentences about the superstition and folly of frequenting St Fillan's church, to detect theft by means of his bell—of bathing mad patients in his pool, to cure their infirmity of mind—and lo! the persecutors have cast me forth of their communion, as they will speedily cast me out of this life."

"Lo you there now," said the Glover, "see what it is for a man that cannot take a warning! Well, Father Clement, men will not cast me forth unless it were as a companion of yours. I pray you, therefore, tell me what you have to say of my daughter, and let us be less neighbours than we have been."

"This then, brother Simon, I have to acquaint you with. This young Chief, who is swoln with contemplation of his own power and glory, loves one thing better than it all, and that is thy daughter."

"He, Conachar!" exclaimed Simon. "My runagate apprentice look up to my daughter!"

"Alas!" said Clement, "how close sits our worldly pride, even as ivy clings to the wall, and cannot be separated!—Look *up* to thy daughter, good Simon? Alas, no! The Captain of Clan Quhele, great as he is, and greater as he soon expects to be, looks *down* to the daughter of the Perth burgess, and considers himself demeaned in doing so. But, to use his own profane expression, Catherine is dearer to him than life here, and Heaven hereafter—he cannot live without her."

"Then he may die, if he lists," said Simon Glover, "for she is betrothed to an honest burgess of Perth; and I would not break my word to make my daughter bride to the Prince of Scotland."

"I thought it would be your answer," replied the Monk; "I would, worthy friend, thou could'st carry into thy spiritual concerns some part of that daring and resolved spirit with which thou canst direct thy temporal affairs."

"Hush thee—hush, Father Clement!" answered the Glover; "when thou fallest into that vein of argument, thy words savour of blazing tar, and that is a scent I like not. As to Catherine, I must manage as I can, so as not to displease the young dignitary; but well is it for me that she is far beyond his reach."

"She must then be distant indeed," said the Carthusian. "And now, brother Simon, since you think it perilous to own me and my opinions, I must walk alone with my own doctrines, and the dangers they draw on me. But should your eye, less blinded than it now is by worldly hopes and fears, ever turn a glance back on him who soon may be snatched from you, remember, that by nought, save a deep sense of the truth and importance of the doctrine which he taught, could Clement Blair have learned to encounter, nay, to provoke, the animosity of the powerful and inveterate, to alarm the fears of the jealous and timid, to walk in the world as he belonged not to it, and to be accounted mad of men, that he might, if possible, win souls to God. Heaven be my witness, that I would comply in all lawful things, to conciliate the love and sympathy of my fellow-creatures! It is no light thing to be shunned by the worthy as an infected patient; to be persecuted by the Pharisees of the day as an unbelieving heretic; to be regarded with horror at once and contempt by the multitude, who consider me as a madman, who may be expected to turn mischievous. But were all those evils multiplied an hundred fold, the fire within must not be stifled, the voice which says within me—Speak, must receive obedience. Woe unto me if I preach not the Gospel, even should I at length preach it from amidst the pile of flames!"

So spoke this bold witness; one of those whom Heaven raised up from time to time, to preserve amidst the most ignorant ages, and to carry down to those which succeed them, a manifestation of unadulterated Christianity, from the time of the Apostles to the age when, favoured by the invention of printing, the Reformation broke out in full splendour. The selfish policy of the Glover was exposed in his own eyes; and he felt himself contemptible as he saw the Carthusian turn from him in all the hallowedness of resignation. He was even conscious of a momentary inclination to follow the example of the preacher's philanthropy and disinterested zeal; but it glanced like a flash of lightning through a dark vault, where there lies nothing to catch the blaze; and he slowly descended the hill, in a direction different from that of the Carthusian, forgetting him and his doctrines, and buried in anxious thoughts about his child's fate and his own.

Chapter Five

THE FUNERAL OBSEQUIES being over, the same flotilla which had proceeded in solemn and sad array down the lake, prepared to return with displayed banners, and every demonstration of mirth and joy; for there was but brief time to celebrate festivities, when the awful conflict betwixt the Clan Quhele and their most formidable rivals so nearly approached. It had been agreed, therefore, that the funeral feast should be blended with that usually given at the inauguration of the young Chief.

Some objections were made to this arrangement, as containing an evil omen. But, on the other hand, it had a species of recommendation, from the habits and feelings of the Highlanders, who, to this day, are wont to mingle a degree of solemn mirth with their mourning, and something resembling melancholy with their mirth. The usual aversion to speak or think of those who have been beloved and lost, is less known to this grave and enthusiastic race than it is to others. You hear not only the young mention (as is everywhere usual) the merits and the character of parents, who have, in the course of nature, predeceased them; but the widowed partner speaks, in ordinary conversation, of the lost spouse, and, what is still stranger, the parents allude frequently to the beauty or valour of the child whom they have interred. The Scottish Highlanders appear to regard the separation of friends by death, as something less absolute and complete than it is generally esteemed in other countries, and converse of the dear connexions who have sought the grave before them, as if they had gone upon a long journey in which they themselves must soon follow. The funeral feast, therefore, being a general custom throughout Scotland, was not, in the opinion of those who were to share it, unseemingly mingled, on the present occasion, with the festivities which hailed the succession to the Chieftainship.

The barge which had lately borne the dead to the grave, now conveyed the young MacIan to his new command; and the minstrels sounded their gayest notes to gratulate Eachin's succession, as they had lately sounded their most doleful dirges when carrying Gilchrist to his grave. From the attendant flotilla rang notes of triumph and jubilee, instead of those yells of lamentation which had so lately disturbed the echoes of Loch Tay; and a thousand voices hailed the youthful Chieftain as he stood on the poop, armed at all points, in the flower of early youth, beauty and activity, on the very spot where his father's corpse had so lately been extended, and surrounded by tri-

umphant friends, as that had been by desolate mourners. One boat
kept closest of the flotilla to the honoured galley. Torquil of the Oak, a
grizzled giant, was steersman; and his eight sons, each exceeding the
ordinary stature of mankind, pulled the oars. Like some powerful
and favourite wolf-hound, unloosed from his couples, and frolicking
around a beloved master, the boat of the foster brethren passed the
Chieftain's barge, now on one side, and now on another, and even
rowed around it, as if in extravagance of joy; while, at the same time,
with the jealous vigilance of the animal we have compared it to, they
made it dangerous for any other of the flotilla to approach so near as
themselves, from the risk of being run down by their impetuous and
reckless manœuvres. Raised to an eminent rank in the clan by the
succession of their foster brother to the command of the Clan Quhele,
this was the tumultuous and almost terrible mode in which they testified their peculiar share in their Chief's triumph.

Far behind, and with different feelings, on the part of one at least of
the company, came the small boat, in which, manned by the Booshalloch and one of his sons, Simon Glover was a passenger.

"If we are bound for the head of the lake," said Simon to his friend,
"we shall hardly be there for hours."

But as he spoke, the crew of the boat of the foster brethren, or
Leichtach, on a signal from the Chief's galley, lay on their oars until
the Booshalloch's boat came up, and throwing on board a rope of
hides, which Niel made fast to the head of his skiff, they stretched to
their oars once more; and notwithstanding they had the small boat in
tow, swept through the lake with almost the same rapidity as before.
The skiff was tugged on with a velocity which seemed to hazard the
pulling her under water, or the separation of her slender timbers.

Simon Glover saw with anxiety the reckless fury of their course, and
the bows of the boat occasionally brought within an inch or two of the
level of the water; and although his friend Niel Booshalloch assured
him it was all done in especial honour, he heartily wished his voyage
might have a speedy and safe termination. It had so, and much sooner
than he apprehended; for the place of festivity was not four miles
distant from the sepulchral island, being chosen to suit the Chieftain's
course, which lay to the south-east, so soon as the banquet was concluded.

A bay on the southern side of Loch Tay presented a beautiful beach
of sparkling sand, on which the boats might land with ease, and a dry
meadow, covered with turf, verdant considering the season, behind
and around which rose high banks, fringed with copsewood, and
displaying the lavish preparation which had been made for the entertainment.

The Highlanders, well known for ready hatchet-men, had constructed a long arbour or sylvan banquetting-room, capable of receiving two hundred men, while a number of smaller huts around seemed intended for sleeping apartments. The uprights, the couples, and rooftree of the temporary hall, were composed of mountain-pine, still covered with its bark. The framework of the sides was of planks or spars of the same material, closely interwoven with the leafy boughs of the fir and other evergreens, which the neighbouring woods afforded, while the hills had furnished plenty of heath to form the roof. Within this sylvan palace the most important personages present were invited to hold high festival. Others of less note were to feast in various long sheds, constructed with less care; and tables of sod, or rough planks, placed in the open air, were allotted to the nameless multitude. At a distance were to be seen piles of glowing charcoal or blazing wood, around which countless cooks toiled, bustled, and fretted, like so many demons working in their native element. Pits, wrought in the hill-side and lined with heated stones, served for stewing immense quantities of beef, mutton, and venison—wooden spits supported sheep and goats, which were roasted entire; others were cut into joints and seathed in cauldrons made of the animal's own skins, sewed hastily together and filled with water; while huge quantities of pike, trout, salmon, and char, were broiled with more ceremony on glowing embers. The Glover had seen many a Highland banquet, but never one the preparations for which were on such a scale of barbarous profusion.

He had little time, however, to admire the scene around him; for, as soon as they landed on the beach, the Booshalloch observed with some embarrassment, that as they had not been bidden to the table of dais, to which he seemed to have expected an invitation, they had best secure a place in one of the inferior bothies or booths; and was leading the way in that direction, when he was stopped by one of the body-guards, seeming to act as master of ceremonies, who whispered something in his ear.

"I thought so," said the herdsman, much relieved, "I thought neither the stranger, nor the man that has my charge, would be left out of the high table."

They were conducted accordingly into the ample lodge, within which were long ranges of tables already mostly occupied by the guests, while those who acted as domestics were placing upon them the abundant though rude materials of the festival. The young Chief, although he certainly saw the Glover and the herdsman enter, did not address any personal salute to either, and their places were assigned them in a distant corner, far beneath the Salt, (a huge piece of antique silver-plate,) the only article of value that the table displayed, and which was regarded by the Clan as a species of palladium, only produced and used on the most solemn occasions, such as the present.

The Booshalloch, somewhat discontented, muttered to Simon as he took his place—"These are changed days, friend. His father, rest his soul, would have spoken to us both; but these are bad manners which he has learned among you Sassenachs in the Low Country."

To this remark the Glover did not think it necessary to reply, instead of which he adverted to the evergreens, and particularly the skins and other ornaments with which the interior of the bower was decorated. The most remarkable part of these ornaments was a number of Highland shirts of mail, with steel bonnets, battle-axes, and two-handed swords to match, which hung around the upper part of the room, together with targets highly and richly embossed. Each mail shirt was hung over a well-dressed stag's hide, which at once displayed the armour to advantage, and saved it from suffering by damp.

"These," whispered the Booshalloch, "are the arms of the chosen champions of the Clan Quhele. They are twenty-nine in number, as you see, Eachin himself being the thirtieth, who wears his armour today, else had there been thirty. And he has not got such a good hauberk after all, as he should wear on Palm Sunday. These nine suits of harness, of such large size, are for the Leichtach, from whom so much is expected."

"And these goodly deer-hides," said Simon, the spirit of his profession awakening at the sight of the goods in which he traded,—"think you the Chief will be disposed to chaffer for them?—they are in demand for the doublets which knights wear under their armour."

"Did I not pray you," said Niel Booshalloch, "to say nothing on that subject?"

"It is the mail shirts I speak of," said Simon,—"may I ask if any of them were made by our celebrated Perth armourer, called Henry of the Wynd?"

"Thou art more unlucky than before," said Niel; "that man's name is to Eachin's temper a whirlwind upon the lake; yet no man knows for what cause."

I can guess, thought our Glover, but gave no utterance to the thought; and, having twice lighted on unpleasing subjects of conversation, he prepared to apply himself, like those around him, to his food, without starting another topic.

We have said as much of the preparations as may lead the reader to conclude that the festivity, in respect of the quality of the food, was of the most rude description, consisting chiefly of huge joints of meat, which were consumed with little respect to the fasting season, although several of the friars of the Island Convent graced and hallowed the board by their presence. The platters were of wood, and so were the hooped cogues or cups, out of which the guests quaffed their liquor, and also the broth or juice of the meat, which was held a delicacy. There were also various preparations of milk which were highly esteemed, and were eaten out of similar vessels. Bread was the scarcest article at the banquet, but the Glover and his patron Niel were served with two small loaves expressly for their own use. In eating, as indeed was then the case all over Britain, the guests used their knives called skenes, or the large poniards named dirks, without troubling themselves by the reflection that they had occasionally served different or more fatal purposes.

At the upper end of the table stood a vacant seat, elevated a step or two above the floor. It was covered with a canopy of holly boughs and ivy, and there rested against it a sheathed sword and a folded banner. This had been the seat of the deceased Chieftain, and was left vacant in honour of him. Eachin occupied a lower chair on the right hand of the place of honour.

The reader would be greatly mistaken who should follow out this description, by supposing that the guests behaved like a herd of hungry wolves, rushing upon a feast rarely offered to them. On the contrary, the Clan Quhele conducted themselves with that species of courteous reserve and attention to the wants of others, which is often found in primitive nations, especially such as are always in arms; because a general observance of the rules of courtesy is necessary to prevent quarrels, bloodshed, and death. The guests took the places assigned them by Torquil of the Oak, who, acting as Marischal *Taeh*, i.e. sewer of the mess, touched with a white wand, without speaking a word, the place where each was to sit. Thus placed in order, the company patiently waited for the portion assigned them, which was distributed among them by the Leichtach; the bravest men, or more distinguished warriors of the tribe, being accommodated with a double mess, emphatically called *bieyfir*, or the portion of a man. When the sewers themselves had seen every one served, they resumed their places at the festival, and were each served with one of these larger messes of food. Water was placed within each man's reach, and a handful of soft moss served the purposes of a table-napkin, so that, as at an Eastern banquet, the hands were washed as often as the mess was changed. For amusement, the bard recited the praises of the deceased Chief, and expressed the clan's confidence in the blossoming virtues of his successor. The Seanachie recited the genealogy of the tribe, which they traced to the race of the Dalriads; the harpers played within, while the war-pipes cheered the multitude without.

The conversation among the guests was grave, subdued, and civil—
no jest was attempted beyond the bounds of a very gentle pleasantry,
calculated only to excite a passing smile. There were no raised voices,
no contentious arguments; and Simon Glover had heard a hundred
times more noise at a guild-feast, than was made on this occasion by
two hundred wild mountaineers.

Even the liquor itself did not seem to raise the festive party above
the same tone of decorous gravity. It was of various kinds—wine
appeared in very small quantity, and was served out only to the
principal guests, among which honoured number Simon Glover was
again included. The wine and the two wheaten loaves were indeed the
only marks of notice which he received during the feast; but Niel
Booshalloch, jealous of his master's reputation for hospitality, failed
not to enlarge on them as proofs of high distinction. Distilled liquors,
since so generally used in the Highlands, were then comparatively
unknown. The usquebaugh was circulated in small quantities, and
was highly flavoured with a decoction of saffron and other herbs, so as
to resemble a medicinal potion, rather than a festive cordial. Cider
and mead were seen at the entertainment, but ale, brewed in great
quantities for the purpose, and flowing round without restriction, was
the liquor generally used, and that was drunk with a moderation much
less known among the more modern Highlanders. A cup to the
memory of the deceased Chieftain was the first pledge solemnly
proclaimed after the banquet was finished; and a low murmur of
benedictions was heard from the company, while the monks alone,
uplifting their united voices, sung *Requiem eternam dona.* An unusual
silence followed, as if something extraordinary was expected, when
Eachin arose, with a bold and manly yet modest grace, and ascended
the vacant seat or throne, saying with dignity and firmness—

"This seat, and my father's inheritance, I claim as my right—so
prosper me God and St Barr!"

"How will you rule your father's children?" said an old man, the
uncle of the deceased.

"I will defend them with my father's sword, and distribute justice to
them under my father's banner."

The old man, with a trembling hand, unsheathed the ponderous
weapon, and holding it by the blade, offered the hilt to the young
Chieftain's grasp; at the same time Torquil of the Oak unfurled the
pennon of the tribe, and swung it repeatedly over Eachin's head, who,
with singular grace and dexterity, brandished the huge claymore as in
its defence. The guests raised a yelling shout, to testify their acceptance of the patriarchal Chief who claimed their allegiance, nor was
there any who, in the graceful and agile youth before them, was

disposed to recollect the subject of sinister vaticinations. As he stood in glittering mail, resting on the long sword, and acknowledging by gracious gestures the acclamations which rent the air within, without, and around, Simon Glover was tempted to doubt whether this majestic figure was that of the same lad whom he had often treated with little ceremony, and began to have some apprehension of the consequences of having done so. A general burst of minstrelsy succeeded to the acclamations, and rock and greenwood rang to harp and pipes, as lately to shout and yell of woe.

It would be tedious to pursue the progress of the inaugural feast, or detail the pledges that were quaffed to former heroes of the clan, and above all to the twenty-nine brave Gallowglasses who were to fight in the approaching conflict, under the eye and leading of their young Chief. The bards, assuming the prophetic character in old times combined with their own, ventured to assure them of the most distinguished victory, and to predict the fury with which the Blue Falcon, the emblem of the Clan Quhele, should rend to pieces the Mountain-cat, the well-known badge of the Clan Chattan.

It was approaching sunset, when a bowl, called the grace-cup, made of oak, hooped with silver, was handed around the table as the signal of dispersion, although it was left free to any who chose a longer carouse to retreat to any of the outer bothies. As for Simon Glover, the Booshalloch conducted him to a small hut, contrived, it would seem, for the use of a single individual, where a bed of heath and moss was arranged as well as the season would permit, and an ample supply of such delicates as the late feast afforded, showed that all care had been taken for the inhabitant's accommodation.

"Do not leave this hut," said the Booshalloch, taking leave of his friend and protegé; "this is your place of rest. But apartments are lost on such a night of confusion, and if the badger leaves his hole the tod* will creep into it."

To Simon Glover this arrangement was by no means disagreeable. He had been wearied by the noise of the day, and felt desirous of repose. After eating, therefore, a morsel, which his appetite scarce required, and drinking a cup of wine to expel the cold,—he muttered his evening prayer, wrapt himself in his cloak, and lay down on a couch which old acquaintance had made familiar and easy to him. The hum and murmur, and even the occasional shouts, of some of the festive multitude who continued revelling without, did not long interrupt his repose; and in about ten minutes he was as fast asleep as if he had lain in his own bed in Curfew Street.

---

*Tod, *Scottice* for fox.

Chapter Six

Polonius. Still harping on my daughter.
Hamlet

TWO HOURS before the black-cock crew, Simon Glover was
wakened by a well-known voice, which called him by name.

"What, Conachar!" he replied, as he started from sleep, "is the
morning so far advanced?" and raising his eyes, the person of whom
he was dreaming stood before him; and at the same moment, the
events of yesterday rushing on his recollection, he saw with surprise
that the vision retained the form which sleep had assigned it, and it
was not the mail-clad Highland Chief, with claymore in hand, as he
had seen him the preceding night, but Conachar of Curfew Street, in
his humble apprentice's garb, holding in his hand a switch of oak. An
apparition would not more have surprised our Perth burgher. As he
gaped with wonder, the youth turned upon him a piece of lighted bog-
wood which he carried in a lantern, and to his waking exclamation
replied, "Even so, father Simon; it is Conachar, come to renew our
old acquaintance, when our intercourse will attract least notice."

So saying, he sat down on a tressel which answered the purpose of a
chair, and placing the lantern beside him, proceeded in the most
friendly tone.

"I have tasted of thy good cheer many a day, father Simon—I trust
thou hast found no lack in my family?"

"None whatever, Eachin MacIan," answered the Glover,—for the
simplicity of the Celtic language and manners rejects all honorary
titles; "it was even too good for this fasting season, and much too good
for me, since I must be ashamed to think how hard you fared in
Curfew Street."

"Even too good, to use your own word," said Conachar, "for the
deserts of an idle apprentice, and for the wants of a young Highlander.
But yesterday, if there was, as I trust, enough of food, found you not,
good Glover, some lack of courteous welcome? Excuse it not,—I
know you did so. But I am young in authority with my people, and I
must not too early draw their attention to the period of my residence in
the Lowlands, which, however, I can never forget."

"I understand the cause entirely," said Simon; "and therefore it is
unwillingly, and as it were by force, that I have made so early a visit
hither."

"Hush, father, hush! It is well you are come to see some of my
Highland splendour while it yet sparkles—return after Palm-Sunday,

and who knows whom or what you may find in the territories we now possess. The Wild-cat may have made his lodge where the banquetting bower of MacIan now stands."

The young Chief was silent, and pressed the top of the rod to his lips, as if to guard against uttering more.

"There is no fear of that, Eachin," said Simon, in that vague way in which luke-warm comforters endeavour to turn the reflection of their friends from the consideration of inevitable danger.

"There *is* fear, and there is peril of utter ruin," answered Eachin; "and there is positive certainty of great loss. I marvel my father consented to this wily proposal of Albany. I would MacGillie Chattachan would take with me, and then, instead of wasting our best blood against each other, we would go down together to Strathmore, and kill and take possession. I would rule at Perth, and he at Dundee, and all the Great Strath should be our own to the banks of the Frith of Tay. Such is the policy I have caught from your old grey head, father Simon, when holding a trencher at thy back, and listening to thy evening talk with Bailie Craigdallie."

The tongue is well called an unruly member, thought the Glover. Here have I been holding a candle to the devil, to show him the way to mischief.

But he only said aloud, "These plans come too late."

"Too late, indeed," answered Eachin. "The indentures of battle are signed by our marks and seals; the burning hate of the Clan Quhele and Clan Chattan is blown up to an inextinguishable flame by mutual insults and boasts. Yes, the time is passed by.—But to thine own affairs, father Glover. It is religion that has brought thee hither, as I learn from Niel Booshalloch. Surely, my experience of thy prudence did not lead me to suspect thee of any quarrel with Mother Church. As for my old acquaintance, Father Clement, he is one of those who hunt after the crown of martyrdom, and think a stake, surrounded with blazing faggots, better worth embracing than a willing bride. He is a very knight-errant, in defence of his religious notions, and does battle wherever he comes. He hath already a quarrel with the monks of Sibyl's Isle yonder, about some point of doctrine—Hast seen him?"

"I have," answered Simon; "but we spoke little together, the time pressing."

"He may have said that there is a third person,—one more like, I think, to be a true fugitive for religion than either you, a shrewd citizen, or he, a wrangling preacher,—who would be right heartily welcome to share our protection?—Thou art dull, man, and wilt not guess my meaning—Thy daughter, Catherine?"

These last words the young Chief spoke in English; and he continued the conversation in that language, as if apprehensive of being overheard; and, indeed, as if under the sense of some involuntary hesitation.

"My daughter Catherine," said the Glover, remembering what the Carthusian had told him, "is well and safe."

"But where, or with whom?" said the young Chief. "And wherefore came she not with you? Think you the Clan Quhele have no cailliachs, as active as old Dorothy, whose hand has warmed my haffits before now, to wait upon the daughter of their Chieftain's master?"

"Again I thank you," said the Glover, "and doubt neither your power nor your will to protect my daughter, as well as myself. But an honourable lady, the friend of Sir Patrick Charteris, hath offered her a safe place of refuge, without the risk of a toilsome journey through a desolate and distracted country."

"Oh, ay,—Sir Patrick Charteris," said Eachin, in a more reserved and distant tone—"he must be preferred to all men, without doubt; he was your Provost, I think?"

Simon Glover longed to punish this affectation of a boy, who had been scolded four times a-day for running into the street to see Sir Patrick Charteris ride past; but he checked his spirit of repartee, and simply replied, "Sir Patrick Charteris has been Provost of Perth for seven years; and it is likely is so still, since the magistrates are elected, not in Lent, but at St Martinmas."

"Ah, father Glover," said the youth, in his kinder and more familiar mode of address, "you are so used to see the sumptuous shows and pageants of Perth, that you would but little relish our barbarous ritual in comparison. What didst thou think of our ceremonial of yesterday?"

"It was noble and touching," said the Glover; "and to me, who knew your father, most especially so. When you rested on the sword, and looked around you, methought I saw mine old friend Gilchrist MacIan arisen from the dead, and renewed in years and in strength."

"I played my part there boldly, I trust; and showed little of that paltry apprentice boy, whom you used to—use just as he deserved."

"Eachin resembles Conachar," said the Glover, "no more than a salmon resembles a par, though men say they are the same fish in a different state; or than a butterfly resembles a grub."

"Thinkest thou that while I was taking upon me the power which all women love, I would have been myself an object for a maiden's eye to rest upon?—To speak plain, what would Catherine have thought of me in the ceremonial?"

We approach the shallows now, thought Simon Glover; and without nice pilotage, we drive right on shore.

"Most women like show, Eachin; but I think my daughter Catherine be an exception. She would rejoice in the good fortune of her household friend and playmate; but she would not value the splendid MacIan, Captain of Clan Quhele, more than the orphan Conachar."

"She is ever generous and disinterested," replied the young Chief. "But yourself, father, have seen the world for many more years than she has done, and can better form a judgment what power and wealth do for those who enjoy them. Think, and speak sincerely, what would be your own thoughts, if you saw your Catherine standing under yonder canopy, with the command over an hundred hills, and the devoted obedience of ten thousand vassals; and as the price of these advantages, her hand in that of the man who loves her the best in the world?"

"Meaning in your own, Conachar?" said Simon.

"Ay, Conachar call me—I love the name, since it was by that I have been known to Catherine."

"Sincerely, then," said the Glover, endeavouring to give the least offensive turn to his reply, "my inmost thought would be the earnest wish that Catherine and I were safe in our humble booth in Curfew Street, with Dorothy for our only vassal."

"And with poor Conachar also, I trust? You would not leave him to pine away in solitary grandeur?"

"I would not," answered the Glover, "wish so ill to the Clan Quhele, mine ancient friends, as to deprive them, at a moment of emergency, of a brave young Chief, and that Chief of the fame which he is about to acquire at their head in the approaching conflict."

Eachin bit his lip to suppress his irritated feelings, as he replied,— "Words—words,—empty words, father Simon. You fear the Clan Quhele more than you love them, and you suppose their indignation would be formidable, should their Chief marry the daughter of a burgess of Perth."

"And if I do fear such an issue, Hector MacIan, have I not reason? How have ill-assorted marriages had issue in the House of MacCallanmore, in that of the powerful MacLeans, nay, of the Lords of the Isles themselves? What has ever come of them but divorce and exheredation—sometimes worse fate, to the ambitious intruder? You could not marry my child before a priest, and you could only wed her with your left hand; and I"—he checked the strain of impetuosity which the subject inspired, and concluded,—"And I am an honest, though humble burgher of Perth, who would rather my child were the lawful and undoubted spouse of a citizen in my own rank, than the licensed concubine of a monarch."

"I will wed Catherine before the priest and before the world,—

before the altar and before the black stones of Iona," said the impetuous young man. "She is the love of my youth, and there is not a tie in
religion or honour but I will bind myself by them! I have sounded my
people. If we do but win this combat—and, with the hope of gaining
Catherine, we *shall* win it—my heart tells me so—I shall be so much
lord over their affections, that were I to take a bride from the alms-
house, so it was my pleasure, they would hail her as if she were a
daughter of MacCallanmore.—But you reject my suit?" said Eachin,
sternly.

"You put words of offence in my mouth," said the old man, "and
may next punish me for them, since I am wholly in your power. But
with my consent my daughter shall never wed, save in her own degree.
Her heart would break amid the constant wars and scenes of bloodshed which connect themselves with your lot. If you really love her,
and recollect her dread of strife and combat, you would not wish her to
be subjected to the train of military horrors in which you, like your
father, must needs be inevitably and eternally engaged. Choose a
bride amongst the daughters of the mountain chiefs, my son, or fiery
Lowland nobles. You are fair, young, rich, high-born, and powerful,
and will not woo in vain. You will readily find one who will rejoice in
your conquests, and cheer you under defeat. To Catherine, the one
would be as frightful as the other. A warrior must wear a steel gauntlet
—a glove of kid-skin would be torn to pieces in an hour."

A dark cloud passed over the face of the young Chief, lately animated with so much fire.

"Farewell," he said, "the only hope which could have lighted me to
fame or victory!"—He remained for a space silent, and intensely
thoughtful, with down-cast eyes, a darkened brow, and folded arms.
At length he raised his eyes, and said, "Father,—for such you have
been to me,—I am about to tell you a secret. Reason and Pride both
advise me to be silent, but Fate urges me, and must be obeyed. I am
about to lodge in you the deepest and dearest secret that man ever
confided to man. But beware—end this conference how it will—
beware how you ever breathe a syllable of what I am now to trust to
you; for know, that were you to do so in the most remote corner of
Scotland, I have ears to hear it even there, and a hand and poniard to
reach a traitor's bosom.—I am—but the word will not out!"

"Do not speak it then," said the prudent Glover; "a secret is no
longer safe when it crosses the lips of him who owns it; and I desire
not a confidence so dangerous as you menace me with."

"Ay, but I must speak, and you must hear," said the youth. "In this
age of battle, father, you have yourself been a combatant?"

"Once only," replied Simon, "when the Southron assaulted the

Fair City. I was summoned to take my part in the defence, as my tenure required, like that of other craftsmen, who are bound to keep watch and ward."

"And how felt you upon that matter?" inquired the young Chief.

"What can that import to the present business?" said Simon, in some surprise.

"Much, else had I not asked the question," answered Eachin, in the tone of haughtiness which from time to time he assumed.

"An old man is easily brought to speak of olden times," said Simon, not unwilling, on an instant's reflection, to lead the conversation away from the subject of his daughter, "and I must needs confess, my feelings were much short of the high cheerful confidence, nay, the pleasure, with which I have seen other men go to battle. My life and profession were peaceful, and though I have not wanted the spirit of a man, when the time demanded it, yet I have seldom slept worse than the night before that onslaught. My ideas were harrowed by the tales we were told (nothing short of the truth) about the Saxon archers— how they drew shafts of a cloth-yard length, and used bows a third longer than ours. When I fell into a broken slumber, if but a straw in the mattress pricked my side, I started and waked, thinking an English arrow was quivering in my body. In the morning, as I began for very weariness to sink into some repose, I was waked by the tolling of the common bell, which called us burghers to the walls—I never heard its peal sound so like a passing knell before or since."

"Go on—what further chanced?" demanded Eachin.

"I did on my harness," said Simon, "such as it was—took my mother's blessing, a high-spirited woman, who spoke of my father's actions for the honour of the Fair Town. This heartened me, and I felt still bolder when I found myself ranked among the other crafts, all bowmen, for thou knowest the Perth citizens have good skill of archer-craft. We were disposed on the walls, several knights and squires in armour of proof being mingled amongst us, who kept a bold countenance, confident perhaps in their harness, and informed us, for our encouragement, that they would cut down with their swords and axes, any of those who should attempt to quit their post. I was kindly assured of this myself by the old Kempe of Kinfauns, as he was called, this good Sir Patrick's father, then our Provost. He was a grandson of the Red Rover, Tom of Longueville, and a likely man to keep his word, which he addressed to me in especial, because a night of much discomfort may have made me look paler than usual; and besides, I was but a lad."

"And did his exhortation add to your fear or your resolution?" said Eachin, who seemed very attentive.

"To my resolution," answered Simon; "for I think nothing can make a man so bold to face one danger at some distance in his front, as the knowledge of another close behind him, to push him forward. Well—I mounted the walls in tolerable heart, and was placed with others on the Spey Tower, being accounted a good bowman. But a very cold fit seized me as I saw the English, in great order, with their archers in front, and their men-at-arms behind, marching forwards to the attack in strong columns, three in number. They came on steadily, and some of us would fain have shot at them; but it was strictly forbidden, and we were obliged to remain motionless, sheltering ourselves behind the battlement as we best might. As the Southron formed their long ranks into lines, each man occupying his place as by magic, and preparing to cover themselves by large shields, called pavoises, which they planted before them, I again felt a strange breathlessness, and some desire to go home for a glass of distilled waters. But as I looked aside, I saw the worthy Kempe of Kinfauns bending a large cross-bow, and I thought it pity he should waste the bolt on a true-hearted Scotsman, when so many English were in presence; so I e'en staid where I was, being in a comfortable angle, formed by two battlements. The English then strode forward, and drew their bowstrings,—not to the breast, as your Highland kerne do, but to the ear,—and sent off their volleys of swallow-tails before we could call on St Andrew. I winked when I saw them haul up their tackle, and I believe I started as the shafts began to rattle against the parapet. But looking round me, and seeing none hurt but John Squallit, the town-crier, whose jaws were pierced through with a cloth-yard shaft, I took heart of grace, and shot in my turn with good will and good aim. A little man I shot at, who had just hopped out from behind his target, dropt with a shaft through his shoulder. The Provost cried—'Well stitched, Simon!'—'Saint John, for his own town, my fellow-craftsmen!'—shouted I,—though I was then but an apprentice,—for the honour of our guild. And if you will believe me, in the rest of the skirmish, which was ended by the foes drawing off, I drew bow-string and loosed shaft as calmly as if I had been shooting at butts instead of men's breasts. I gained some credit, and I have ever afterwards thought, that in case of necessity, (for with me it had never been matter of choice,) I should not have lost it again. And this is all I can tell of warlike experience in battle. Other dangers I have had, which I have endeavoured to avoid like a wise man, or, where they were inevitable, I have faced them like a true one. Upon other terms a man cannot live or hold his head up in Scotland."

"I understand your tale," said Eachin; "but I will find it difficult to make you credit mine, knowing the race of which I am descended, and especially him whom we have laid this day in the tomb—well that he lies where he will never learn what you are now to hear. Look, my father—the light which I bear grows short and pale, a few minutes will extinguish it—but before it expires, the hideous tale shall be told.— Father, I am—a *coward*!——It is said at last, and the secret of my disgrace is in keeping of another!"

The young man sunk back in a species of syncope, produced by the agony of his mind as he made the fatal communication. The Glover, moved as well by fear as by compassion, applied himself to recall him to life, and succeeded in doing so, but not in restoring him to composure. He hid his face with his hands, and his tears flowed plentifully and bitterly.

"For Our Lady's sake, be comforted," said the old man, "and recall the vile word! I know you better than yourself—you are *no* coward, but only too young and inexperienced, ay, and somewhat too quick of fancy, to have the steady valour of a bearded man. I would hear no other man say that of you, Conachar, without giving him the lie—You are no coward—I have seen high sparks of spirit fly from you even on slight enough provocation."

"High sparks of pride and passion!" said the unfortunate youth, "but when saw you them supported by the resolution that should have backed them?—the sparks you speak of fell on my dastardly heart as on a piece of ice which could catch fire from nothing—if my offended pride urged me to strike, my weakness of mind prompted me the next moment to fly."

"Want of habit," said Simon; "it is by clambering over walls that youths learn to scale precipices. Begin with slight feuds—exercise daily the arms of your country in tourney with your followers."

"And what leisure is there for this?" exclaimed the young Chief, starting as if something horrid had occurred to his imagination. "How many days are there betwixt this hour and Palm Sunday, and what is to chance then?—A list enclosed, from which no man can stir, more than the poor bear who is chained to his stake. Sixty living men, the best and fiercest, (one alone excepted!) which Albyn can send down from her mountains, all athirst for each other's blood, while a King and his nobles, and shouting thousands besides, attend, as at a theatre, to encourage their demoniac fury! Blows clang, and blood flows— thicker, faster, redder—they rush on each other like madmen—they tear each other like wild beasts—the wounded are trodden to death amid the feet of their companions! Blood ebbs, arms become weak— but there must be no parley, no truce, no interruption, while any of the maimed wretches remain alive! Here is no crouching behind battlements, no fighting with missile weapons,—all is hand to hand, till hands can no longer be raised to maintain the ghastly conflict.—If such a field is so horrible in idea, what think you it will be in reality?"

The Glover remained silent.

"I say again, what think you?"

"I can only pity you, Conachar," said Simon. "It is hard to be the descendant of a lofty line—the son of a noble father—the leader by birth of a gallant array—and yet to want, or think you want (for still I trust the fault lies much in a quick fancy that over-estimates danger,) to want that dogged quality, which is possessed by every game-cock that is worth a handful of corn, every hound that is worth a mess of offal. But how chanced it, that with such a consciousness of inability to fight in this battle, you proffered even now to share your chiefdom with my daughter? Your power must depend on your fighting this combat, and in that Catherine cannot help you."

"You mistake, old man," replied Eachin; "were Catherine to look kindly on the earnest love I bear her, it would carry me against the front of the enemies with the mettle of a war-horse. Overwhelming as my sense of weakness is, the feeling that Catherine looked on would give me strength. Say yet—oh, say yet—she shall be mine if we gain the combat, and not the *Gow Chrom* himself, whose heart is a piece of his anvil, ever went to battle so light as I shall do! One strong passion is conquered by another."

"This is folly, Conachar. Cannot the recollections of your interest, your honour, your kindred, do as much to stir your courage, as the thoughts of a brent-browed lass? Fie upon you, man!"

"You tell me but what I have told myself—but it is in vain," replied Eachin, with a sigh. "It is only whilst the timid stag is paired with the doe, that he is desperate and dangerous. Be it from constitution—be it, as our Highland cailliachs will say, from the milk of the White Doe —be it from my peaceful education, and the experience of your strict restraint—be it, as you think, from an over-heated fancy, which paints danger yet more dangerous and ghastly than it is in reality, I cannot tell. But I know my failing, and—yes, it must be said!—so sorely dread that I cannot conquer it, that, could I have your consent to my wishes, I would even here make a pause, renounce the rank I have assumed, and retire into humble life."

"What, turn glover at last, Conachar?" said Simon; "this beats the legend of St Crispin. Nay, nay, your hand was not framed for that; you shall spoil me no more doe-skins."

"Jest not," said Eachin, "I am serious. If I cannot labour, I will bring wealth enough to live without it. They will proclaim me recreant with horn and war-pipe—Let them do so—Catherine will love me the better that I have preferred the paths of peace to those of bloodshed, and Father Clement shall teach us to pity and forgive the world, which will load us with reproaches that wound not. I will be the happiest of men—Catherine will enjoy all that unbounded affection can confer upon her, and will be freed from apprehension of the sights and sounds of horror, which your ill-assorted match would have prepared for her; and you, father Glover, shall occupy your chimney-corner, the happiest and most honoured man that ever"——

"Hold, Eachin—I prithee, hold," said the Glover; "the fir light, with which this discourse must terminate, burns very low, and I would speak a word in my turn, and plain dealing is best. Though it may vex, or perhaps incense you, let me end these visions by saying at once— Catherine can never be yours. A glove is the emblem of faith, and a man of my craft should therefore less than any other break his own. Catherine's hand is promised—promised to a man whom you may hate, but whom you must honour—to Henry the Armourer. The match is fitting by degree, agreeable to their mutual wishes, and I have given my promise. It is best be plain at once—resent my refusal as you will—I am wholly in your power—But nothing shall make me break my word."

The Glover spoke thus decidedly, because he was aware from experience that the very irritable disposition of his former apprentice yielded in most cases to stern and decided resolution. Yet recollecting where he was, it was with some feelings of fear that he saw the dying flame leap up, and spread a flash of light on the visage of Eachin, which seemed pale as the grave, while his eye rolled like that of a maniac in his fever fit. The light instantly sunk down and died, and Simon felt a momentary terror, lest he should have to dispute for his life with the youth, whom he knew to be capable of violent actions when highly excited, however short a period his nature could support the measures which his passion commenced. He was relieved by the voice of Eachin, who muttered in a hoarse and altered tone, "Let what we have spoken this night rest in silence for ever—If thou bring'st it to light, thou wert better dig thine own grave."

Thus speaking, the door of the hut opened, admitting a gleam of moonshine. The form of the retiring Chief crossed it for an instant, the hurdle door was then closed, and the hut left in darkness.

Simon Glover felt relieved, when a conversation, fraught with offence and danger, was thus peaceably terminated. But he remained deeply affected by the condition of Hector MacIan, whom he had himself bred up.

"The poor child," said he, "to be called up to a place of eminence, only to be hurled from it with contempt! What he told me I partly knew, having often remarked that Conachar was more prone to quarrel than to fight. But this overpowering faint-heartedness, which neither shame nor necessity can overcome, I, though no Sir William Wallace, cannot conceive. And to propose himself for a husband to my daughter, as if a bride were to find courage for herself and the bridegroom! No, no—Catherine must wed a man to whom she may say— 'Husband, spare your enemy'—not one in whose behalf she must cry —'Generous enemy, spare my husband.'"

Tired out with these reflections, the old man at length fell asleep. In the morning, he was awakened by his friend the Booshalloch, who, with something of a blank visage, proposed to him to return to his abode on the meadow at the Ballough, that is, the discharge of the lake into the river. He apologized, that the Chief could not see Simon Glover that morning, being busied with things about the expected combat; and that Eachin MacIan thought the residence at the Ballough would be safest for Simon Glover's health, and had given charge that every care should be taken for his protection and accommodation.

Niel Booshalloch dilated on these circumstances, to gloss over the neglect implied in the Chief's dismissing his visitor without a particular audience.

"His father knew better," said the herdsman. "But where should he have learned manners, poor thing, and bred up among your Perth burghers, who, excepting yourself, neighbour Glover, who speak Gaelic as well as I do, are a race incapable of civility?"

Simon Glover, it may be well believed, felt none of the want of respect which his friend resented on his account. On the contrary, he greatly preferred the quiet residence of the good herdsman, to the tumultuous hospitality of the daily festival of the Chief, even if there had not just passed an interview with Eachin upon a subject which it would be most painful to revive.

To the Ballough, therefore, he quietly retreated, where, could he have been secure of Catherine's safety, his leisure was spent pleasantly enough. His amusement was sailing on the lake, in a little skiff, which a Highland boy managed, while the old man angled. He frequently landed on the little island, where he mused over the tomb of his old friend Gilchrist MacIan, and made friends with the monks, presenting the prior with gloves of martin's fur, and the superior officers with each of them a pair made from the skin of the wild-cat. The cutting and stitching of these little presents, served to beguile the time after sunset, while the family of the herdsman crowded around, admiring his address, and listening to the tales and songs with which the old man had skill to pass away a heavy evening.

It must be confessed that the cautious Glover avoided the conversation of Father Clement, whom he erroneously considered as rather the author of his misfortunes, than the guiltless sharer of them. I will not, he thought, to please his whims, lose the good-will of these kind monks, which may be one day useful to me. I have suffered enough by his preachments already, I trow. Little the wiser and much the poorer have they made me. No, no, Catherine and Clement may think as they will; but I will take the first opportunity to sneak back like a rated hound at the call of his master, submit to a plentiful course of hair-cloth and whip-cord, disburse a lusty mulct, and become whole with the Church again.

More than a fortnight had passed since the Glover had arrived at Ballough, and he began to wonder that he had not heard news of Catherine or of Henry Wynd, to whom he concluded the Provost had communicated the plan and place of his retreat. He knew the stout Smith dared not come up into the Clan Quhele country, on account of various feuds with the inhabitants, and with Eachin himself, while bearing the name of Conachar. But yet the Glover thought Henry might have found means to send him a message, or a token, by some one of the various couriers who passed and repassed between the court and the head-quarters of the Clan Quhele, in order to concert the terms of the impending combat, the march of the parties to Perth, and other particulars requiring previous adjustment. It was now the middle of March, and the fatal Palm Sunday was fast approaching.

Whilst time was thus creeping on, the exiled Glover had not even once set eyes upon his former apprentice. The care that was taken to attend to his wants and convenience in every respect, showed that he was not forgotten; but yet when he heard the Chieftain's horn ringing through the woods, he usually made it a point to choose his walk in a different direction. One morning, however, he found himself unexpectedly in Eachin's close neighbourhood, with scarce leisure to avoid him; and thus it happened.

As Simon strolled pensively through a little sylvan glade, surrounded on either side with tall forest trees, mixed with underwood, a white doe broke from the thicket, closely pursued by two deer grey-hounds, one of which griped her haunch, the other her throat, and pulled her down within half a furlong of the Glover, who was something startled at the suddenness of the incident. The near and piercing blast of a horn, and the baying of a slow-hound, made Simon aware that the hunters were close behind, and on the trace of the deer. Hallowing and the sound of men running through the copse, were heard close at hand. A moment's recollection would have satisfied Simon, that his best way was to stand fast, or retire slowly, and leave it to Eachin to acknowledge his presence or not, as he should see cause. But his desire of shunning the young man had grown into a kind of instinct, and in the alarm of finding him so near, Simon hid himself in a bush of hazels mixed with holly, which altogether concealed him. He had hardly done so, ere Eachin, rosy with exercise, dashed from the thicket into the open glade, accompanied by his foster-father, Torquil of the Oak. The latter, with equal strength and address, turned the struggling hind on her back, and holding her fore feet in his right hand, while he knelt on her body, offered his skene with the left to the young Chief, that he might cut the animal's throat.

"It may not be, Torquil; do thine office, and take the assay thyself. I must not kill the likeness of my foster-mother."

This was spoken with a melancholy smile, while a tear at the same time stood in the speaker's eye. Torquil stared at his young Chief for an instant, then drew his sharp wood-knife across the creature's throat, with a cut so swift and steady, that the weapon reached the back bone. Then rising on his feet, and again fixing a long piercing look on his chief, he said,—"As much as I have done to that hind, would I do to any living man whose ears could have heard my dault (foster-son) so much as name a white doe, and couple the word with Hector's name!"

If Simon had no reason before to keep himself concealed, this speech of Torquil furnished him with a pressing one.

"It cannot be concealed, father Torquil," said Eachin; "it will all out to the broad day."

"What will out? What will to broad day?" asked Torquil in surprise.

It is the fatal secret, thought Simon, and now, if this huge privy councillor cannot keep silence, I will, I suppose, be made answerable for Eachin's disgrace having been blown abroad.

Thinking thus anxiously, he availed himself, at the same time, of his position to see as much as he could of what passed between the afflicted Chieftain and his confident, impelled by that spirit of curiosity which prompts us in the most momentous, as well as the most trivial occasions of life, and which is sometimes found to subsist in company with great personal fear.

As Torquil listened to what Eachin communicated, the young man sank into his arms, and supporting himself on his shoulder, concluded his confession by a whisper into his ear. Torquil seemed to listen with such amazement as to make him incapable of crediting his ears. As if to be certain that it was Eachin who spoke, he gradually roused the youth from his reclining posture, and holding him up in some measure by a grasp on his shoulder, fixed on him an eye that seemed enlarged, and at the same time turned to stone, by the marvels he listened to.

And so wild waxed the old man's visage after he had heard the murmured communication, that Simon Glover apprehended he would
cast the youth from him as a dishonoured thing, in which case he
might have lighted on the very copse in which he lay concealed, and
occasioned his discovery in a manner equally painful and dangerous.
But the passions of Torquil, who entertained for his foster-child even
a double portion of that passionate fondness which always attends that
connexion in the Highlands, took a different turn.

"I believe it not!"—he exclaimed; "it is false of thy father's child—
false of thy mother's son—falsest of my *dault!* I offer my gage to
heaven and hell, and will maintain the combat with him that shall call it
true. Thou hast been spell-bound by an evil eye, my darling, and the
fainting which you call cowardice is the work of magic—I remember
the bat that struck the torch out on the hour that thou wert born—that
hour of grief and of joy. Cheer up, my beloved! Thou shalt with me to
Iona, and the good St Columbus, with the whole choir of blessed
saints and angels, who ever favoured thy race, shall take from thee the
heart of the white doe, and return that which they have stolen from
thee."

Eachin listened, with a look as if he would fain have believed the
words of the comforter.

"But, Torquil," he said, "supposing this might avail us, the fatal day
approaches, and if I go to the lists, I dread me we shall be shamed."

"It cannot be—it shall not be!" said Torquil—"Hell shall not prevail so far—we will steep thy sword in holy water—place vervain, St
John's-wort, and rowan-tree in thy crest. We will surround thee, I and
thy eight brethren—thou shalt be safe as in a castle."

Again the youth helplessly muttered something, which, from the
dejected tone in which it was spoken, Simon could not understand,
while Torquil's deep tones in reply fell full and distinct upon his ear.

"Yes, there may be a chance of withdrawing thee from the conflict.
Thou art the youngest who is to draw blade—Now, hear me, and thou
shalt know what it is to have a foster-father's love, and how far it
exceeds the love even of kind. The youngest on the indenture of Clan
Chattan is Ferquhard Day. His father slew mine, and the red blood is
seething hot between us—I looked to Palm Sunday as the term that
should cool it—But mark!—Thou would'st have thought that the
blood in the veins of this Ferquhard Day and in mine would not have
mingled, had they been put into the same vessel, yet hath he cast
the eyes of his love upon my only daughter Eva—the fairest of our
maidens. Think with what feelings I heard the news. It was as if a wolf
from the skirts of Ferragon had said, 'Give me thy child in wedlock,
Torquil.' My child thought not thus, she loves Ferquhard, and weeps

away her colour and strength in dread of the approaching battle. Let her give him but a sign of favour, and well I know he will forget kith and kin, forsake the field, and fly with her to the desert."

"He, the youngest of the champions of Clan Chattan being absent, I, the youngest of Clan Quhele, may be excused from combat," said Eachin, blushing at the mean chance of safety thus opened to him.

"See now, my Chief," said Torquil, "and judge my thoughts towards thee—others might give thee their own lives and that of their sons—I sacrifice to thee the honour of my house."

"My friend, my father," repeated the Chief, folding Torquil to his bosom, "what a base wretch am I that have a spirit dastardly enough to avail myself of your sacrifice!"

"Speak not of that—Greenwoods have ears. Let us back to the camp, and send our gillies for the venison.—Back, dogs, and follow at heel."

The slow-hound, or lyme-dog, luckily for Simon, had drenched his nose in the blood of the deer, else he might have found the Glover's lair in the thicket; but its more acute properties of scent being lost, it followed tranquilly with the gaze-hounds.

When the hunters were out of sight and hearing, the Glover arose, greatly relieved by their departure, and began to move off, in the opposite direction, as fast as his age permitted. His first reflection was on the fidelity of the foster-father.

"The wild mountain heart is faithful and true. Yonder man is more like the giants in romaunts, than a man of mould like ourselves, and yet Christians might take an example from him for his lealty. A simple contrivance this though, to finger a man off their enemies' chequer, as if there would not be twenty of the Wild-cats ready to supply his place."

Thus thought the Glover, not aware that the strictest proclamations were issued, prohibiting any of the two contending clans, their friends, allies, and dependents, from coming within fifty miles of Perth, during a week before and a week after the combat, which regulation was to be enforced by armed men.

So soon as our friend Simon arrived at the habitation of the herdsman, he found other news awaiting him. They were brought by Father Clement, who came in a pilgrim's cloak, or dalmatic, ready to commence his return to the southwards, and desirous to take leave of his companion in exile, or to accept him as a travelling companion.

"But what," said the citizen, "has so suddenly induced you to return within the reach of danger?"

"Have you not heard," said Father Clement, "that March and his

English allies having retired into England before the Earl of Douglas, the good Earl has applied himself to redress the evils of the common-wealth, and hath written to the Court letters, desiring that the warrant for the High Court of Commission against heresy be withdrawn, as a trouble to men's consciences—that the nomination of Wardlaw to be Prelate of St Andrews, be referred to the Parliament, with sundry other things pleasing to the commons? Now, most of the nobles that are with the King at Perth, and with them Sir Patrick Charteris, your worthy Provost, have declared for the proposals of the Douglas. The Duke of Albany hath agreed to them; whether from good-will or policy I know not. The good King is easily persuaded to mild and gentle courses. And thus are the jaw-teeth of the oppressors dashed to pieces in their sockets, and the prey snatched from their ravening talons. Will you with me to the Lowlands, or do you abide here a little space?"

Niel Booshalloch saved his friend the trouble of reply.

"He had the Chief's authority," he said, "for saying that Simon Glover should abide until the champions went down to the battle." In this answer the citizen saw something not quite consistent with his own perfect freedom of volition; but he cared little for it at the time, as it furnished a good apology for not travelling along with the clergy-man.

"An exemplary man," he said to his friend, Niel Booshalloch, as soon as Father Clement had taken leave, "a great scholar, and a great saint. It is pity almost he is not in danger to be burned, as his sermon at the stake would convert thousands. O, Niel Booshalloch! Father Clement's pile would be a sweet savouring sacrifice, and a beacon to all devout Christians. But what would the burning of a borrell ignorant burgess like me serve? Men offer not up old glove leather for incense, nor are beacons fed with undressed hides, I trow. Sooth to speak, I have too little learning and too much fear to get credit by the affair, and, therefore, I should, in our homely phrase, have both the scathe and the scorn."

"True for you," answered the herdsman.

Chapter Seven

WE MUST RETURN to the characters of our dramatic narrative, whom we left at Perth, when we accompanied the Glover and his fair daughter to Kinfauns, and from that hospitable mansion traced the course of Simon to Loch Tay; and the Prince, as the highest person-age, claims our immediate attention. This rash and inconsiderate young man endured with some impatience his sequestered residence with the Lord High Constable, with whose company, otherwise in every respect satisfactory, he became dissatisfied, from no other reason than that he held in some degree the character of his warder. Incensed against his uncle, and displeased with his father, he longed not unnaturally for the society of Sir John Ramorny, on whom he had been so long accustomed to throw himself for amusement, and, though he would have resented the imputation as an insult, for guidance and direction. He, therefore, sent him a summons to attend him, providing his health permitted; and directed him to come by water to a little pavilion in the High Constable's garden, which, like that of Sir John's own lodgings, ran down to the Tay. In renewing an intimacy so dangerous, Rothsay only remembered that he had been Sir John Ramorny's munificent friend; while Sir John, on receiving the invitation, only numbered up, on his part, the capricious insults he had sustained from his patron, the loss of his hand, and the lightness with which he had treated the subject, and the readiness with which Rothsay had abandoned his cause in the matter of the Bonnet-maker's slaughter. He laughed bitterly when he read the Prince's billet.

"Eviot," he said, "man a stout boat with six trusty men,—trusty men, mark me—lose not a moment; and bid Dwining instantly come hither.—Heaven smiles on us, my trusty friend," he said to the mediciner. "I was but beating my brains how to get access to this fickle boy, and here he writes to invite me."

"Hem!—I see the matter very clearly," said Dwining. "Heaven smiles on some untoward consequences—he! he! he!"

"No matter, the trap is ready; and it is baited, too, my friend, with what would lure the boy from a sanctuary, though a troop with drawn weapons waited him in the churchyard. Yet is it scarce necessary. His own weariness of himself would have done the job. Get thy matters ready—thou goest with us. Write to him, as I cannot, that we come instantly to attend his commands, and do it clerkly. He reads well, and that he owes to me."

"He will be your valiancy's debtor for more knowledge before he dies—he! he! he! But is your bargain sure with the Duke of Albany?"

"Enough to gratify my ambition, thy avarice, and the revenge of both. Aboard, aboard, and speedily; let Eviot throw in a few flasks of the choicest wine, and some cold baked meats."

"But your arm, my lord, Sir John? Does it not pain you?"

"The throbbing of my heart silences the pain of my wound. It beats as it would burst my bosom."

"Heaven forbid!"—said Dwining; adding, in a low voice, "It would be a strange sight if it should. I should like to dissect it, save that its stony case would spoil my best instruments."

In a few minutes they were in the boat, while a speedy messenger carried the note to the Prince.

Rothsay was seated with the Constable, after their noontide repast. He was sullen and silent; and the Earl had just asked whether it was his pleasure that the table should be drawn, when a note, delivered to the Prince, changed at once his aspect.

"As you will," he said. "I go to the pavilion in the garden (always with permission of my Lord Constable) to receive my late Master of the Horse."

"My lord?" said Lord Errol.

"Ay, my lord; must I ask permission twice?"

"No, surely, my lord," answered the Constable; "but has your royal Highness recollected that Sir John Ramorny"—

"Has not the plague, I hope?" replied the Duke of Rothsay. "Come, Errol, you would play the surly turnkey; but it is not in your nature,— farewell for half an hour."

"A new folly!" said Errol, as the Prince, flinging open a lattice of the ground-parlour in which they sate, stept out into the garden. "A new folly, to call back that villain to his councils. But he is infatuated."

The Prince, in the meantime, looked back, and said hastily, "Your lordship's good housekeeping will afford us a flask or two, and a slight collation in the pavilion? I love the al fresco of the river."

The Constable bowed, and gave the necessary orders; so that Sir John found the materials of good cheer ready displayed, when, landing from his barge, he entered the pavilion.

"It grieves my heart to see your Highness under restraint," said Ramorny, with a well-executed appearance of sympathy.

"That grief of thine will grieve mine," said the Prince. "I am sure here has Errol, and a right true-hearted lord he is, so tired me with grave looks, and something like grave lessons, that he has driven me back to thee, thou reprobate, from whom, as I expect nothing good, I may perhaps obtain something entertaining. Yet ere we say more, it was foul work, that upon the Fastern's Even, Ramorny. I well hope thou gavest not aim to it."

"On my honour, my lord, a simple mistake of the brute Bonthron. I did but hint to him that a dry beating would be due to the fellow by whom I had lost a hand; and lo you, my knave makes a double mistake —he takes one man for another, and instead of the batton he uses the axe."

"It is well if it went no farther. Small matter for the Bonnet-maker; but I had never forgiven you had the Armourer fallen—there is not his match in Britain.—But I hope they hanged the villain high enough?"

"If thirty feet might serve," replied Ramorny.

"Pah! no more of him," said Rothsay; "his wretched name makes the good wine taste of blood.—And what are the news in Perth, Ramorny?—How stands it with the bona robas and the galliards?"

"Little goliardise stirring, my lord," answered the Knight. "All eyes are turned to the motions of the Black Douglas, who comes with five thousand chosen men to put us all to rights, as if he were bound for another Otterburn. It is said he is to be Lieutenant again. It is certain many have declared for his faction."

"It is time, then, my feet were free," said Rothsay, "otherwise I may find a worse warder than Errol."

"Ah, my lord! were you once away from this place, you might make as bold a head as Douglas."

"Ramorny," said the Prince, gravely, "I have but a confused remembrance of your once having proposed something horrible to me. Beware of such counsel. I would be free—I would have my person at my own disposal. But I will never levy arms against my father, nor those it pleases him to trust."

"It was only for your Royal Highness's personal freedom that I was presuming to speak," answered Ramorny. "Were I in your Grace's place, I would get me into that good boat which hovers on the Tay, and drop quietly down to Fife, where you have many friends, and make free to take possession of Falkland. It is a royal castle; and though the King has bestowed it in gift on your uncle, yet surely even if the grant were not subject to challenge, your Grace might make free with the residence of so near a relation."

"He hath made free with mine," said the Duke, "as the Stewartry of Renfrew can tell. But stay, Ramorny—hold—Did I not hear Errol say that the Lady Marjory Douglas, whom they call Duchess of Rothsay, is at Falkland? I would neither dwell with that lady, nor insult her by dislodging her."

"The lady was there, my lord," replied Ramorny; "but I have sure advice that she is gone to meet her father."

"Ha! to animate the Douglas against me? or perhaps to beg him to spare me, providing I come on my knees to her bed, as pilgrims say the Emirs and Amirals, upon whom a Saracen Soldan bestows a daughter in marriage, are bound to do? Ramorny, I will act by the Douglas's own saying, 'It is better to hear the lark sing than the mouse squeak.' I will keep both foot and hand from fetters."

"No place fitter than Falkland," replied Ramorny. "I have enough of good yeomen to keep the place; and should your Highness wish to leave it, a brief ride reaches the sea in three directions."

"You speak well. But we shall die of gloom yonder. Neither mirth, music, nor maidens—Ha!" said the heedless Prince.

"Pardon me, noble Duke; but though the Lady Marjory Douglas be departed, like an errant dame in romance, to implore succour of her doughty sire, there is, I may say, a lovelier, I am sure a younger maiden, either presently at Falkland, or who will soon be on the road thither. Your Highness has not forgot the Fair Maid of Perth?"

"Forget the prettiest wench in Scotland!—No—any more than thou hast forgot the hand that thou hadst in the Curfew Street onslaught on St Valentine's Eve."

"The hand that I *had?*—Your Highness would say, the hand that I lost. As certain as I shall never regain it, Catherine Glover is, or will soon be, at Falkland. I will not flatter your Highness by saying she expects to meet you—in truth, she proposes to place herself under the protection of the Lady Marjory."

"The little traitress," said the Prince—"she too to turn against me? She deserves punishment, Ramorny."

"I trust your Grace will make her penance a gentle one," replied the knight.

"Faith, I would have been her Father Confessor long ago, but I have ever found her coy."

"Opportunity was lacking, my lord," replied Ramorny; "and time presses even now."

"Nay, I am but too apt for a frolic; but my father"——

"He is personally safe," said Ramorny, "and as much at freedom as ever he can be; while your Highness"——

"Must brook fetters, conjugal or literal—I know it.—Yonder comes Douglas, with his daughter in his hand, as haughty, and as harsh-featured as himself, bating the lack of an eye."

"And at Falkland sits in solitude the fairest wench in Scotland," said Ramorny. "Here is penance and restraint, yonder is joy and freedom."

"Thou hast prevailed, most sage counsellor," replied Rothsay; "but mark you, it shall be the last of my frolics."

"I trust so," replied Ramorny; "for, when at liberty, you may make a good accommodation with your royal father."

"I will write to him, Ramorny—Get the writing-materials—No, I cannot put my thoughts in words—do thou write."

"Your Royal Highness forgets," said Ramorny, pointing to his mutilated arm.

"Ah! that cursed hand of yours. What can we do?"

"So please your Highness," answered his counsellor, "if you would use the hand of the mediciner, Dwining—He writes like a clerk."

"Hath he a hint of the circumstances? Is he possessed of them?"

"Fully," said Ramorny; and stepping to the window called Dwining from the boat.

He entered the presence of the Prince of Scotland, creeping as if he trode upon eggs, with downcast eyes, and a frame that seemed shrunk up by a sense of awe produced by the occasion.

"There, fellow, are writing-materials. I will make trial of you—thou know'st the case—place my conduct to my father in a fair light."

Dwining sat down, and in a few minutes wrote a letter, which he handed to Sir John Ramorny.

"Why, the devil has aided thee, Dwining," said the knight. "Listen, my dear lord.—'Respected father and liege Sovereign,—Know that important considerations induce me to take my departure from this your court, purposing to make my abode at Falkland, both as the seat of my dearest uncle Albany, with whom I know your Majesty would desire me to use all familiarity, and as the residence of one from whom I have been too long estranged, and with whom I haste to exchange vows of the closest affection from henceforward.'"

The Duke of Rothsay and Ramorny laughed aloud; and the physician, who had listened to his own scroll as if it were a sentence of death, encouraged by their applause, raised his eyes, uttered faintly his chuckling note of He! he! and was again grave and silent, as if afraid he had transgressed the bounds of reverend respect.

"Admirable!" said the Prince—"Admirable! The old man will apply all this to the Duchess, as they call her, of Rothsay.—Dwining, thou should'st be *a secretis* to his Holiness the Pope, who sometimes, it is said, wants a scribe that can make one word cover two meanings. I will subscribe it, and have the praise of the device."

"And now, my lord," said Ramorny, sealing the letter, and leaving it behind, "will you not to boat?"

"Not till my chamberlain attends, with some clothes and necessaries—and you may call my sewer also."

"My lord," said Ramorny, "time presses, and preparation will but excite suspicion. Your officers will follow with the mails to-morrow. For to-night, I trust my poor service may suffice to wait on you at table and chamber."

"Nay, this time it is thou who forgets," said the Prince, touching the wounded arm with his walking-rod. "Recollect, man, thou canst neither carve a capon, nor tie a point—a goodly sewer, or valet of the chamber!"

Ramorny grinned with rage and pain; for his wound, though in a way of healing, was still highly sensitive, and even the pointing a finger towards it made him tremble.

"Will your Highness now be pleased to take boat?"

"Not till I take leave of the Lord Constable. Rothsay must not slip away, like a thief from a prison, from the house of Errol. Summon him hither."

"My Lord Duke," said Ramorny, "it may be dangerous to our plan."

"To the devil with danger, thy plan and thyself!—I must and will act to Errol as becomes us both."

The Earl entered, agreeable to the Prince's summons.

"I gave you this trouble, my lord," said Rothsay, with the dignified courtesy which he knew so well how to assume, "to thank you for your hospitality and your good company. I can enjoy them no longer, as pressing affairs call me to Falkland."

"My lord," said the Lord High Constable, "I trust your Grace remembers that you are under ward."

"How!—under ward? If I am a prisoner, speak plainly—if not, I will take my freedom to depart."

"I would, my lord, your Highness would request his Majesty's permission for this journey. There will be much displeasure."

"Mean you displeasure against yourself, my lord, or against me?"

"I have already said your Highness lies in ward here; but if you determine to break it, I have no warrant—God forbid—to put force on your inclinations. I can but entreat your Highness, for your own sake——"

"Of my own interests I am the best judge—Good evening to you, my lord."

The wilful Prince stepped into the boat with Dwining and Ramorny, and, waiting for no other attendance, Eviot pushed off the vessel, which descended the Tay rapidly by the assistance of sail and oar, and of the ebb-tide.

For some space the Duke of Rothsay appeared silent and moody, nor did his companions interrupt his reflections. He raised his head at length, and said, "My father loves a jest, and when all is over, he will take this frolic at no more serious rate than it deserves—a fit of youth, with which he will deal as he has with others.—Yonder, my masters, shows the old Hold of Kinfauns, frowning above the Tay. Now, tell me, John Ramorny, how thou hast dealt to get the Fair Maid of Perth out of the hands of yonder bull-headed Provost; for Errol told me it was rumoured that she was under his protection."

"Truly she was, my lord, with the purpose of being transferred to the patronage of the Duchess,—I mean of the Lady Marjory of Douglas. Now, this beetle-headed Provost, who is after all but a piece of blundering valiancy, has, like most such, a retainer of some slyness and cunning, whom he uses in all his dealings, and whose suggestions he generally considers as his own ideas. Whenever I would possess myself of a landward baron, I address myself to his factotum, who, in the present case, is called Kitt Henshaw, an old skipper upon the Tay, and who, having in his time sailed as far as Campvere, holds with Sir Patrick Charteris the respect due to one who has seen foreign countries. This his agent I have made my own, and by his means have insinuated various apologies, in order to postpone the departure of Catherine for Falkland."

"But to what good purpose?"

"I know not if it is wise to tell your Highness, lest you should disapprove of my views—I meant the officers of the Commission for inquiry into heretical opinions should have found the Fair Maid at Kinfauns, for our beauty is a peevish, self-willed swerver from the Church; and certes, I designed that the Knight should have come in for his share of the fines and confiscations that were about to be inflicted. The monks were eager enough to be at him, seeing he hath had frequent disputes with them about the salmon-tythe."

"But wherefore would'st thou have ruined the Knight's fortunes, and brought the beautiful young woman to the stake, perchance?"

"Pshaw, my Lord Duke!—monks never burn pretty maidens—an old woman might have been in some danger. And as for my Lord Provost, as they call him, if they had clipped off some of his fat acres, it would have been some atonement for the brave he put on me in Saint John's church."

"Methinks, John, it was but a base revenge," said Rothsay.

"Rest ye contented, my lord. He that cannot right himself by the hand must use his head.—Well, that chance was over by the tender-hearted Douglas's declaring in favour of tender consciences; and then, my lord, old Henshaw found no further objections to carrying the Fair Maid of Perth to Falkland,—not to share the dulness of the Lady Marjory's society, as Sir Patrick Charteris and she herself doth opine, but to keep your Highness from tiring when we return from hunting in the park."

There was again a long pause, in which the Prince seemed to muse deeply. At length he spoke.—"Ramorny, I have a scruple in this matter; but if I name it to thee, the devil of sophistry, with which thou art possessed, will argue it out of me, as it has done many others. This girl is the most beautiful, one excepted, whom I ever saw or knew; and I like her the more that she bears some features of—Elizabeth of Dunbar. But she, I mean Catherine Glover, is contracted, and presently to be wedded, to Henry the Armourer, a craftsman unequalled for skill, and a man-at-arms yet unmatched in the barrace. To follow out this intrigue would do a good fellow too much wrong."

"Your Highness will not expect me to be very solicitous of Henry Smith's interest," said Ramorny, looking at his wounded arm.

"By Saint Andrew with his shored cross, this disaster of thine is too much harped upon, John Ramorny. Others are content with putting a finger into every man's pie, but thou must thrust in thy whole gory hand. It is done, and cannot be undone—let it be forgotten."

"Nay, my lord, you allude to it more frequently than I," answered the Knight,—"in derision, it is true; while I—but I can be silent on the subject if I cannot forget it."

"Well, then, I tell thee that I have scruple about this intrigue. Dost thou remember, when we went in a frolic to hear Father Clement preach, or rather to see this fair heretic, that he spoke as touchingly as a minstrel about the rich man taking away the poor man's only ewe lamb?"

"A great matter, indeed," answered Sir John, "that this churl's wife's eldest son should be fathered by the Prince of Scotland! How many earls would covet the like fate for their fair countesses? and how many that have had such good luck sleep not a grain the worse for it?"

"And if I might presume to speak," said the mediciner, "the ancient laws of Scotland assigned such a privilege to every feudal lord over his female vassals, though lack of spirit and love of money hath made many exchange it for gold."

"I require no argument to urge me to be kind to a pretty woman: but this Catherine has been ever cold to me," said the Prince.

"Nay, my lord," said Ramorny, "if, young, handsome, and a Prince, you know not how to make yourself acceptable to a fine woman, it is not for me to say more."

"And if it were not far too great audacity in me to speak again, I would say," quoth the leech, "that all Perth knows that the *Gow Chrom* never was the maiden's choice, but fairly forced upon her by her father. I know for certain that she refused him repeatedly."

"Nay, if thou canst assure us of that, the case is much altered," said Rothsay. "Vulcan was a smith as well as Harry Wynd; he would needs wed Venus, and our Chronicles tell us what came of it."

"Then long may Lady Venus live and be worshipped," said Sir John Ramorny; "and success to the gallant knight Mars, who goes a-wooing to her goddess-ship!"

The discourse took a gay and idle turn for a few minutes; but the Duke of Rothsay soon dropped it. "I have left," he said, "yonder air of the prison-house behind me, and yet my spirits scarce revive. I feel that drowsy, not unpleasing, yet melancholy mood, that comes over us when exhausted by exercise, or satiated with pleasure. Some music now, stealing on the ear, yet not loud enough to make us lift the eye, were a treat for the gods."

"Your Grace has but to speak your wishes, and the nymphs of the Tay are as favourable as the fair ones upon the shore.—Hark—it is a lute."

"A lute!" said the Duke of Rothsay, listening; "it is, and rarely touched. I should remember that dying fall. Steer towards the boat from whence the music comes."

"It is old Henshaw," said Ramorny, "working up the stream.— How, skipper!"

The boatmen answered the hail, and drew up alongside of the Prince's barge.

"Oh ho! my old friend!" said the Prince, recognising the figure as well as the appointments of the French glee-woman, Louise. "I think I owe thee something for being the means of thy having a fright, at least, upon St Valentine's Day. Into this boat with thee, lute, puppy dog, scrip and all—I will prefer thee to a lady's service, who shall feed thy very cur on capons and canary."

"I trust your Highness will consider—" said Ramorny.

"I will consider nothing but my pleasure, John—pray, do thou be so complying as to consider it also."

"Is it indeed to a lady's service you would promote me?" said the glee-maiden. "And where does she dwell?"

"At Falkland," answered the Prince.

"Oh, I have heard of that great lady!" said Louise; "and will you indeed prefer me to your right royal consort's service?"

"I will, by my honour—whenever I receive her as such—Mark that reservation, John," said he aside to Ramorny.

The persons who were in the boat caught up the tidings, and concluding a reconciliation was about to take place betwixt the royal couple, hastily exhorted Louise to profit by her good fortune, and add herself to the Duchess of Rothsay's train. Several offered her some acknowledgment for the exercise of her talents.

During this moment of delay, Ramorny whispered to Dwining, "Make in, knave, with some objection. This addition is one too many. Rouse thy wits, while I speak a word with Henshaw."

"If I might presume to speak," said Dwining, "as one who have made my studies both in Spain and Arabia, I would say, my lord, that the sickness has appeared in Edinburgh, and that there may be risk in admitting this young wanderer into your Highness's vicinity."

"And what is it to thee," said Rothsay, "whether I choose to be poisoned by the pestilence or the pothecary? Must thou, too, needs thwart my humour?"

While the Prince thus silenced the remonstrances of Dwining, Sir John Ramorny had snatched a moment to learn from Henshaw that the removal of the Duchess of Rothsay from Falkland was still kept profoundly secret, and that Catherine Glover would arrive there that evening or the next morning, in expectation of being taken under the noble lady's protection.

The Duke of Rothsay, deeply plunged in thought, received this intimation so coldly, that Ramorny took the liberty of remonstrating. "This, my lord," he said, "is playing the spoiled child of fortune. You wish for liberty—it comes. You wish for beauty—it awaits you, with just so much delay as to render the boon more precious. Even your slightest desires seem a law to the Fates; for you desire music when it seems most distant, and the lute and song are at your hand. These things, so sent, should be enjoyed, else we are but like petted children, who break and throw from them the toys they have wept themselves sick for."

"To enjoy pleasure, Ramorny," said the Prince, "a man should have suffered pain, as it requires fasting to gain a good appetite. We, who can have all for a wish, little enjoy that all when we have possessed it. Seest thou yonder thick cloud, which is about to burst to rain? It seems to stifle me—the waters look dark and lurid—the shores have lost their beautiful form"——

"My lord, forgive your servant," said Ramorny. "You indulge a powerful imagination, as an unskilful horseman permits a fiery steed to rear, until he falls back on his master and crushes him. I pray you shake off this lethargy. Shall the glee-maiden make some music?"

"Let her—but it must be melancholy; all mirth would at this moment jar on my ear."

The maiden sung a melancholy dirge in Norman French; the words, of which the following is an imitation, were united to a tune as doleful as they are themselves.

I.
Yes, thou may'st sigh,
And look once more at all around,
At stream and bank, and sky and ground.
Thy life its final course has found,
And thou must die.

2.
Yes, lay thee down,
And while thy struggling pulses flutter,
Bid the gray monk his soul-mass mutter,
And the deep bell its death-tone utter—
Thy life is gone.

3.
Be not afraid.
'Tis but a pang, and then a thrill,
A fever fit, and then a chill;
And then an end of human ill,
For thou art dead.

The Prince made no observation on the music; and the maiden, at Ramorny's beck, went on from time to time with her minstrel craft, until the evening sunk down into rain, first soft and gentle, at length in great quantities, and accompanied by a cold wind. There was neither cloak nor covering for the Prince, and he sullenly rejected that which Ramorny offered.

"It is not for Rothsay to wear your cast garments, Sir John—this melted snow, which I feel pierce me to the very marrow, I am encountering by your fault. Why did you presume to put off the boat without my servants and apparel?"

Ramorny did not attempt an exculpation; for he knew the Prince was in one of those humours, when, to enlarge upon a grievance was more pleasing to him than to have his mouth stopped by any reasonable apology. In sullen silence, or amid unsuppressed chiding, the boat arrived at the fishing village of Newburgh. The party landed, and found horses in readiness, which indeed Ramorny had long since provided for the occasion. Their quality underwent the Prince's bitter sarcasm, expressed to Ramorny sometimes by direct words, oftener by bitter gibes. At length they were mounted, and rode on through the closing night and the falling rain, the Prince leading the way with reckless haste. The glee-maiden, mounted by his express order, attended them; and well for her that, accustomed to severe weather, and exercise both on foot and horseback, she supported as firmly as the men the fatigues of the nocturnal ride. Ramorny was compelled to keep at the Prince's rein, being under no small anxiety lest, in his wayward fit, he should ride off from him entirely, and, taking refuge in the house of some loyal baron, escape the snare which was spread for him. He therefore suffered inexpressibly during the ride, both in mind and in body.

At length the forest of Falkland received them, and a glimpse of the moon showed the dark and huge tower, an appanage of royalty itself, though granted for a season to the Duke of Albany. On a signal given the drawbridge fell. Torches glared in the court-yard, menials attended, and the Prince, assisted from horseback, was ushered into an apartment, where Ramorny waited on him, together with Dwining, and entreated him to take the leech's advice. The Duke of Rothsay repulsed the proposal, haughtily ordered his bed to be prepared, and having stood for some time shivering in his dank garments beside a large blazing fire, he retired to his apartment without taking leave of any one.

"You see the peevish humour of this childish boy, now," said Ramorny to Dwining; "can you wonder a servant, who has done so much for him as I have, should be tired of such a master?"

"No, truly," said Dwining, "that and the promised Earldom of Lindores would shake any man's fidelity. But shall we commence with him this evening? He has, if eye and cheek speak true, the foundation of a fever within him, which will make our work easy, while it will seem the effect of nature."

"It is an opportunity lost," said Ramorny; "but we must delay our blow till he has seen this beauty, Catherine Glover. She may be hereafter a witness that she saw him in good health, and master of his own motions, a brief space before—you understand me?"

Dwining nodded assent, and added, "There is no time lost; for there is little difficulty in blighting a flower, exhausted from having been made to bloom too soon."

Chapter Eight

WITH THE NEXT MORNING the humour of the Duke of Rothsay was changed. He complained, indeed, of pain and fever, but they rather seemed to stimulate than to overwhelm him. He was familiar with Ramorny, and though he said nothing on the subject of the preceding night, it was plain he remembered what he desired to obliterate from the memory of his followers—the ill-humour he had then displayed. He was civil to every one, and jested with Ramorny on the subject of Catherine's arrival.

"How surprised will the pretty prude be at seeing herself in a family of men, when she expects to be admitted amongst the hoods and pinners of Dame Marjory's waiting-women! Thou hast not many of the tender sex in thy household, I take it, Ramorny?"

"Faith, none but a household drudge or two whom we may not dispense with—except the minstrel wench. By the way, she is anxiously inquiring after the mistress your Highness promised to prefer her to—Shall I dismiss her, to hunt for her at leisure?"

"By no means, she will serve to amuse Catherine—And, hark you, were it not well to receive that coy jillet with something of a mumming?"

"How mean you, my lord?"

"Thou art dull, man—We will not disappoint her, since she expects

to find the Duchess of Rothsay—I will be Duke and Duchess in my
own person."

"Still I do not comprehend."

"No one so dull as a wit," said the Prince, "when he does not hit off
the scent at once. My Duchess, as they call her, has been in as great a
hurry to run away from Falkland, as I to come hither. We have both
left our apparel behind. There is as much female trumpery in the
wardrobe adjoining to my sleeping-room as would equip a whole
carnival. Look you, I will play Dame Marjory, disposed on this day-
bed here with a mourning veil and a wreath of willow, to show her
forsaken plight; thou, John, wilt look starched and stiff enough for her
Galwegian maid of honour, the Countess Hermigild; and Dwining
shall present the old Hecate, her nurse,—only she hath more beard on
her upper lip than Dwining on his whole face, and skull to boot. He
should have the commodity of a beard to set her forth conformably.
Get thy kitchen drudges, and what passable pages thou hast with
thee, to make my women of the bedroom. Hearest thou?—about it
instantly."

Ramorny hasted into the anteroom, and told Dwining the Prince's
device.

"Do thou look to humour the fool," he said; "I care not how little I
see him, knowing what is to be done."

"Trust all to me," said the physician, shrugging his shoulders.
"What sort of a butcher is he that can cut the lamb's throat, yet is
afraid to hear it bleat?"

"Tush, fear not my constancy—I cannot forget that he would have
cast me into the cloister with as little regard as if he threw away the
truncheon of a broken lance. Begone—yet stay—ere you go to arrange
this silly pageant, something must be settled to impose on the thick-
witted Charteris. He is like enough, should he be left in the belief that
the Duchess of Rothsay is still here, and Catherine Glover in attendance on her, to come down with offers of service, and the like, when,
as I need scarce tell thee, his presence would be inconvenient. Indeed,
this is the more likely, that some folks have given a warmer name to the
iron-headed Knight's great and tender patronage of this damsel."

"With that hint, let me alone to deal with him. I will send him such a
letter, that for this month he shall hold himself as ready for a journey
to hell as to Falkland.—Can you tell me the name of the Duchess's
confessor?"

"Waltheof, a grey friar."

"Enough—then here I start."

In a few minutes, for he was a clerk of rare celerity, Dwining
finished a letter, which he placed in Ramorny's hands.

"This is admirable, and would have made thy fortune with Rothsay —I think I should have been too jealous to trust thee in his household, save that his day is closed."

"Read it aloud," said Dwining, "that we may judge if it goes trippingly off." And Ramorny read as follows:—"By command of our high and mighty Princess Marjory, Duchess of Rothsay, and so forth, we Waltheof, unworthy brother of the order of St Francis, do thee, Sir Patrick Charteris, Knight, of Kinfauns, to know, that her Highness marvels much at the temerity with which you have sent to her presence a woman of whose fame she can judge but lightly, seeing she hath made her abode, without any necessity, for more than a week in thine own castle, without company of any other female, saving menials; of which foul cohabitation the savour is gone up through Fife, Angus, and Perthshire. Nevertheless, her Highness, considering the case as one of human frailty, hath not caused this wanton one to be scourged with nettles, or otherwise to dree penance; but as two good brethren of the convent of Lindores, the Fathers Thickscull and Dundermore, have been summoned up to the Highlands upon an especial call, her Highness hath committed to their care this maiden Catherine, with charge to convey her to her father, whom she states to be residing beside Loch Tay, under whose protection she will find a situation more fitting her qualities and habits, than the Castle of Falkland, while her Highness the Duchess of Rothsay abides there. She hath charged the said reverend brothers so to deal with thy young woman, as may give her a sense of the sin of incontinence, and she commendeth thee to confession and penitence.—Signed, Waltheof, by command of an high and mighty Princess—and so forth."

When he had finished, "Excellent—excellent!" Ramorny exclaimed. "This will drive Charteris mad! He hath been long making a sort of homage to this lady, and to find himself suspected of incontinence, when he was expecting the full credit of a charitable action, will altogether confound him; and, as thou say'st, it will be long enough ere he come hither to look after the damsel, or do honour to the dame.—But away to thy pageant, while I prepare that which shall close the pageant for ever."

It was an hour before noon, when Catherine, escorted by old Henshaw and a groom of the Knight of Kinfauns, arrived before the lordly tower of Falkland. The broad banner which was displayed from it bore the arms of Rothsay, the servants who appeared wore the colours of the Prince's household, all confirming the general belief that the Duchess still resided there. Catherine's heart throbbed, for she had heard that the Duchess had the pride as well as the high courage of the House of Douglas, and felt uncertain touching the reception she was to experience. On entering the Castle, she observed that the train was smaller than she had expected, but as the Duchess lived in close retirement, she was little surprised at this. In a species of anteroom she was met by a little old woman, who seemed bent double with age, and propped herself upon an ebony staff.

"Truly thou art welcome, fair daughter," said she, saluting Catherine, "and, as I may say, to an afflicted house; and I trust (once more saluting her) thou wilt be a consolation to my precious and right royal daughter the Duchess. Sit thee down, my child, till I see whether my lady be at leisure to receive thee. Ah, my child, thou art very lovely indeed, if Our Lady hath given thee a soul to match with so fair a body."

With that the counterfeit old woman crept into the next apartment, where she found Rothsay in the masquerading habit he had prepared, and Ramorny, who had evaded taking part in the pageant, in his ordinary attire.

"Thou art a precious rascal, Sir Doctor," said the Prince; "by my honour I think thou could'st find in thy heart to play out the whole play thyself, lover's part and all."

"If it were to save your Highness trouble," said the leech, with his usual subdued laugh.

"No, no," said Rothsay, "I'll never need thy help, man—and tell me now, how look I, thus disposed on the couch—languishing and lady-like, ha?"

"Something too fine-complexioned and soft-featured for the Lady Marjory of Douglas, if I may presume to say so," said the leech.

"Away, villain, and marshal in this fair frost-piece—fear not she will complain of my effeminacy—and thou, Ramorny, away also."

As the knight left the apartment by one door, the fictitious old woman ushered in Catherine Glover by another. The room had been carefully darkened to twilight, so that Catherine saw the apparently female figure stretched on the couch without the least suspicion.

"Is that the maiden?" asked Rothsay, in a voice naturally sweet, and now carefully modulated to a whispering tone—"Let her approach, Griselda, and kiss our hand."

The supposed nurse led the trembling maiden forward to the side of the couch, and signed to her to kneel. Catherine did so, and kissed with much devotion and simplicity the gloved hand which the counterfeit Duchess extended to her.

"Be not afraid," said the same musical voice; "in me you only see a melancholy example of the vanity of human greatness—happy those, my child, whose rank places them beneath the storms of state."

While she spoke, she put her arms around Catherine's neck and drew her towards her, as if to salute her in token of welcome. But the kiss was bestowed with an earnestness which so much overacted the part of the fair patroness, that Catherine, concluding the Duchess had lost her senses, screamed aloud.

"Peace, fool! it is I—David of Rothsay," said the Prince.

Catherine looked around her—the nurse was gone, and the Duke tearing off his veil, she saw herself in the power of a daring young libertine.

"Now be present with me, Heaven!" she said; "and thou wilt, if I forsake not myself."

As this resolution darted through her mind, she repressed her disposition to scream, and, as far as she might, strove to conceal her fear.

"The jest hath been played," she said, with as much firmness as she could assume; "may I entreat that your Highness will now unhand me," for he still kept hold of her arm.

"Nay, my pretty captive, struggle not—why should you fear?"

"I do not struggle, my lord. As you are pleased to detain me, I will not, by struggling, provoke you to use me ill, and give pain to yourself, when you have time to think."

"Why, thou traitress, thou hast held me captive for months," said the Prince; "and wilt thou not let me hold thee for a moment?"

"This were gallantry, my lord, were it in the streets of Perth, where I might listen or escape as I listed—it is tyranny here."

"And if I did let thee go, whither would'st thou fly?" said Rothsay. "The bridges are up—the portcullis down—and the men who follow me are strangely deaf to a peevish maiden's squalls. Be kind, therefore, and you shall know what it is to oblige a Prince."

"Unloose me, then, my lord, and hear me appeal from thyself to thyself—from Rothsay to the Prince of Scotland.—I am the daughter of an humble but honest citizen. I am, I may wellnigh say, the spouse of a brave and honest man. If I have given your Highness any encouragement for what you have done, it has been unintentional. Thus forewarned, I entreat you to forego your power over me, and suffer me depart. Your Highness can obtain nothing from me, save by means equally unworthy knighthood or manhood."

"You are bold, Catherine," said the Prince; "but neither as a knight nor a man can I avoid accepting a defiance—I must teach you the risk of such challenges."

While he spoke, he attempted to throw his arms again around her; but she eluded his grasp, and proceeded in the same tone of firm decision.

"My strength, my lord, is as great to defend myself in an honourable strife, as yours can be to assail me with a most dishonourable purpose. Do not shame yourself and me by putting it to the combat. You may stun me with blows, or you may call aid to overpower me—but otherwise you will fail of your purpose."

"What a brute would you make me!" said the Prince. "The force I would use is no more than excuses women in yielding to their own weakness."

He sat down in some emotion.

"Then keep it," said Catherine, "for those women who desire such an excuse. My resistance is that of the most determined mind, which love of honour and fear of shame ever inspired. Alas! my lord, could you succeed, you would but break every bond between me and life— between yourself and honour. I have been trained fraudulently here, by what decoys I know not. But were I to go dishonoured hence, it would be to denounce the destroyer of my happiness to every quarter of Europe. I would take the palmer's staff in my hand, and wherever chivalry is honoured, or the word Scotland has been heard, I would proclaim the heir of a hundred kings, the son of the godly Robert Stewart, the Heir of the heroic Bruce—a truthless, faithless man, unworthy of the crown he expects, and of the spurs he wears. Every lady in wide Europe would hold your name too foul for her lips—every worthy knight would hold you a baffled, forsworn caitiff, false to the first vow of arms, the protection of woman, and the defence of the feeble."

Rothsay resumed his seat, and looked at her with a countenance in which resentment was mingled with admiration. "You forget to whom you speak, maiden. Know, the distinction I have offered you is one for which hundreds, whose trains you are born to bear, would feel gratitude."

"Once more, my lord," resumed Catherine, "reserve these favours for those by whom they are prized—Or rather reserve your time and your health for other and nobler pursuits—for the defence of your country and the happiness of your subjects. Alas, my lord! how willingly would an exulting people receive you for their chief!—how gladly would they close around you, did you show desire to head them against the oppression of the mighty, the violence of the lawless, the seduction of the vicious, and the tyranny of the hypocrite!"

The Duke of Rothsay, whose virtuous feelings were as easily excited as they were evanescent, was affected by the enthusiasm with which she spoke. "Forgive me if I have alarmed you, maiden," he said; "thou art too noble-minded to be the toy of passing pleasure, for which my mistake destined thee; and I, even were thy birth worthy of thy noble spirit and transcendent beauty, have no heart to give thee;

for by the homage of the heart only should such as thou be wooed. But my hopes have been blighted, Catherine—the only woman I ever loved has been torn from me in the very wantonness of policy, and a wife imposed on me whom I must ever detest, even had she the loveliness and softness which alone can render a woman amiable in my eyes. My health is fading even in early youth; and all that is left for me is to snatch such flowers as the short passage from life to the grave will now present. Look at my hectic cheek—feel, if you will, my intermitting pulse; and pity me, and excuse me, if I, whose rights as a prince and as a man have been trampled upon and usurped, feel occasional indifference towards the rights of others, and indulge a selfish desire to gratify the wish of the passing moment."

"Oh, my lord!" exclaimed Catherine, with the enthusiasm which belonged to her character—"I will call you my dear lord,—for dear must the Heir of Bruce be to every child of Scotland,—let me not, I pray, hear you speak thus! Your glorious ancestor endured exile, persecution, the night of famine, and the day of unequal combat, to free his country,—do you practise the like self-denial to free yourself. Tear yourself from those who find their own way to greatness smoothed by feeding your follies. Distrust yon dark Ramorny!— you know it not, I am sure—you could not know; but the wretch who could urge the daughter to courses of shame by threatening the life of the aged father, is capable of all that is vile—all that is treacherous!"

"Did Ramorny do this?" said the Prince.

"He did indeed, my lord, and he dares not deny it."

"It shall be looked into," answered the Duke of Rothsay. "I have ceased to love him; but he has suffered much for my sake, and I must see his services honourably requited."

"*His* services? Oh, my lord, if chronicles speak true, such services brought Troy to ruins, and gave the infidels possession of Spain."

"Hush, maiden; speak within door, I pray you," said the Prince, rising up; "our conference ends here."

"Yet one word, my Lord Duke of Rothsay," said Catherine, with animation, while her beautiful countenance resembled that of an admonishing angel—"I cannot tell what impels me to speak thus boldly; but the fire burns within me, and will break out. Leave this castle without an hour's delay! the air is unwholesome for you. Dismiss this Ramorny, before the day is ten minutes older! his company is most dangerous."

"What reason have you for saying this?"

"None in especial," answered Catherine, abashed at her own eagerness,—"excepting my fears for your safety."

"To vague fears, the Heir of Bruce must not listen.—What, ho! who waits without?"

Ramorny entered, and bowed low to the Duke and to the maiden, whom, perhaps, he considered as preferred to the post of favourite Sultana, and therefore entitled to a courteous obeisance.

"Ramorny," said the Prince, "is there in the household any female of reputation, who is fit to wait on this young woman, till we can send her where she may desire to go?"

"I fear," replied Ramorny, "if it displease not your Highness to hear the truth, your household is indifferently provided in that way; and that, to speak the very truth, the glee-maiden is the most decorous amongst us."

"Let her wait upon this maiden, then, since better may not be.— And take patience, maiden, for a few hours."

Catherine retired.

"So, my lord,—part you so soon from the Fair Maid of Perth? This is, indeed, the very wantonness of victory."

"There is neither victory nor defeat in the case," returned the Prince, drily. "The girl loves me not; nor do I love her well enough to torment myself concerning her scruples."

"The chaste Malcolm the Maiden revived in one of his descendants!" said Ramorny.

"Favour me, sir, by a truce to your wit, or by choosing a different subject for its career. It is noon, I believe, and you will oblige me by commanding them to serve up dinner."

Ramorny left the room, but Rothsay thought he discerned a smile upon his countenance; and to be the subject of this man's satire, gave him no ordinary degree of pain. He summoned, however, the Knight to his table, and even admitted Dwining to the same honour. The conversation was of a lively and dissolute cast, a tone encouraged by the Prince, as if designing to counterbalance the gravity of his morals in the morning, which Ramorny, who was read in old chronicles, had the boldness to liken to the continence of Scipio.

The banquet, notwithstanding the Duke's indifferent health, was protracted in idle wantonness far beyond the rules of temperance; and, whether owing simply to the strength of the wine which he drank, or the weakness of his constitution, or, probably, that the last wine which he quaffed had been adulterated by Dwining, it so happened that the Prince, towards the end of the repast, fell into a lethargic sleep, from which it seemed impossible to rouse him. Sir John Ramorny and Dwining carried him to his chamber, accepting no other assistance than that of another person, whom we will afterwards give name to.

Next morning, it was announced that the Prince was taken ill of an infectious disorder; and, to prevent its spreading through the household, no one was admitted to wait on him save his late Master of Horse, the physician Dwining, and the domestic already mentioned; one of whom seemed always to remain in the apartment, while the others observed a degree of precaution respecting their intercourse with the rest of the family, so strict as to maintain the belief that he was dangerously ill with an infectious disorder.

Chapter Nine

FAR DIFFERENT had been the fate of the misguided Heir of Scotland, from that which was publicly given out in the town of Falkland. His ambitious uncle had determined on his death, as the means of removing the first and most formidable barrier betwixt his own family and the throne. James, the younger son of the King, was a mere boy, who might at more leisure be easily set aside. Ramorny's views of aggrandizement, and the resentment which he had latterly entertained against his master, made him a willing agent in young Rothsay's destruction. Dwining's love of gold, and his native malignity of disposition, made him equally forward. It had been resolved, with the most calculating cruelty, that all means which might leave behind marks of violence were to be carefully avoided, and the extinction of life suffered to take place of itself, by privation of every kind acting upon a frail and impaired constitution. The Prince of Scotland was not to be murdered, as Ramorny had expressed himself on another occasion,—he was only to cease to exist.

Rothsay's bedchamber in the Tower of Falkland was well adapted for the execution of such a horrible project. A small narrow staircase, scarce known to exist, opened from thence by a trap-door to the subterranean dungeons of the castle, through a passage by which the feudal lord was wont to visit, in private, and in disguise, the inhabitants of those miserable regions. By this staircase the villains conveyed the insensible Prince to the lowest dungeon of the Castle, so deep in the bowels of the earth that no cries or groans, it was supposed, could possibly be heard, while the strength of its door and fastenings must for a long time have defied force, even if the entrance could have been discovered. Bonthron, who had been saved from the gallows for the purpose, was the willing agent of Ramorny's unparalleled cruelty to his misled and betrayed patron.

This wretch revisited the dungeon at the time when the Prince's lethargy began to wear off, and when, awaking to sensation, he felt himself deadly cold, unable to move, and oppressed with fetters, which scarce permitted him to stir from the dank straw on which he was laid. His first idea was that he was in a fearful dream—his next brought a confused augury of the truth. He called, shouted, yelled at length in frenzy—but no assistance came, and he was only answered by the vaulted roof of the dungeon. The agent of Hell heard these agonizing screams, and deliberately reckoned them against the taunts and reproaches with which Rothsay had expressed his instinctive aversion to him. When, exhausted and hopeless, the unhappy youth remained silent, the savage resolved to present himself before the eyes of his prisoner. The locks were drawn, the chain fell; the Prince raised himself as high as his fetters permitted—a red glare, against which he was fain to shut his eyes, streamed through the vault; and when he opened them again, it was on the ghastly form of one whom he had reason to think dead. He sunk back in horror. "I am judged and condemned!" he exclaimed; "and the most abhorred fiend in the infernal regions is sent to torment me!"

"I live, my lord," said Bonthron; "and that you may live and enjoy life, be pleased to sit up and eat your victuals."

"Free me from these irons," said the Prince,—"release me from this dungeon,—and, dog as thou art, thou shalt be the richest man in Scotland."

"If you would give me the weight of your shackles in gold," said Bonthron, "I would rather see the iron on you than have the treasure myself!—But look up—you were wont to love delicate fare—behold how I have catered for you." The wretch, with fiendish glee, unfolded a piece of raw hide covering a bundle which he bore under his arm, and, passing the light to and fro before it, showed the unhappy Prince a bull's head recently hewn from the trunk, and known in Scotland as the certain signal of death. He placed it at the foot of the bed, or rather lair, on which the Prince lay. "Be moderate in your food," he said; "it is like to be long ere thou getst another meal."

"Tell me but one thing, wretch," said the Prince. "Does Ramorny know of this practice?"

"How else hadst thou been decoyed hither? Poor woodcock, thou art snared!" answered the murderer.

With these words the door shut, the bolts resounded, and the unhappy Prince was left to darkness, solitude, and despair. "Oh my father!—my prophetic father!—The staff I leaned on has indeed proved a spear!"—We will not dwell on the subsequent hours, nay days, of bodily agony and mental despair.

But it was not the pleasure of Heaven that so great a crime should be perpetrated with impunity.

Catherine Glover and the glee-woman, neglected by the other inmates, who seemed to be engaged with the tidings of the Prince's illness, were, however, refused permission to leave the Castle, until it should be seen how this alarming disease was to terminate, and whether it was actually an infectious sickness. Forced on each other's society, the two desolate women became companions, if not friends; and the union drew somewhat closer, when Catherine discovered that this was the minstrel on whose account Henry Wynd had fallen under her displeasure. She now heard his complete vindication, and listened with ardour to the praises which Louise heaped on her gallant protector. On the other hand, the minstrel, who felt the superiority of Catherine's station and character, willingly dwelt upon a theme which seemed to please her, and recorded her gratitude to the stout Smith in the little song of "Bold and True," which was long a favourite in Scotland.

> Oh, Bold and True,
> In bonnet blue,
> That fear or falsehood never knew;
> Whose heart was loyal to his word,
> Whose hand was faithful to his sword—
> Seek Europe wide from sea to sea,
> But bonny Blue-cap still for me!
>
> I've seen Almain's proud champions prance—
> Have seen the gallant knights of France,
> Unrivall'd with the sword and lance—
> Have seen the sons of England true,
> Wield the brown bill and bend the yew.
> Search France the fair, and England free,
> But bonny Blue-cap still for me!

In short, though Louise's disreputable occupation would have been in other circumstances an objection to Catherine's voluntarily frequenting her company, yet, forced together as they now were, she found her a humble and accommodating associate.

They lived in this manner for four or five days, and, in order to avoid as much as possible the gaze, and perhaps the incivility, of the menials in the offices, they prepared their food in their own apartment. In the absolutely necessary intercourse with domestics, Louise, more accustomed to expedients, bolder by habit, and desirous to please Catherine, willingly took on herself the trouble of getting from the pantler the materials of their slender meal, and of arranging it with the dexterity of her country.

The glee-woman had been abroad for this purpose upon the sixth day, a little before noon; and the desire of fresh air, or the hope to find some sallad or pot-herbs, or at least an early flower or two, with which to deck their board, had carried her into the small garden appertaining to the castle. She re-entered her apartment in the tower with a countenance pale as ashes, and a frame which trembled like an aspen-leaf. Her terror instantly extended itself to Catherine, who could hardly find words to ask what new misfortune had occurred.

"Is the Duke of Rothsay dead?"

"Worse! they are starving him alive."

"Madness, woman!"

"No, no, no, no!" said Louise, speaking under her breath, and huddling her words so thick upon each other, that Catherine could hardly catch the sense. "I was seeking for flowers to dress your potage, because you said you loved them yesterday—my poor little dog, thrusting himself into a thicket of yew and holly bushes that grow out of some old ruins close to the castle-wall, came back whining and howling.—I crept forward to see what might be the cause—and, oh! I heard a groaning as of one in extreme pain, but so faint, that it seemed to arise out of the very depth of the earth. At length, I found it proceeded from a small rent in the wall, covered with ivy; and when I laid my ear close to the opening, I could hear the Prince's voice distinctly say,—'It cannot now last long;' and then it sunk away in something like a prayer."

"Gracious Heaven!—did you speak to him?"

"I said, 'Is it you, my lord?' and the answer was, 'Who mocks me with that name?'—I asked him if I could help him, and he answered with a voice I shall never forget,—'Food!—food!—I die of famine!' So I came hither to tell you.—What is to be done?—Shall we alarm the house?"——

"Alas! that were more like to destroy than to aid him," said Catherine.

"And what then shall we do?" said Louise.

"I know not yet," said Catherine, prompt and bold on occasions of moment, though yielding to her companion in ingenuity of resource on ordinary occasions. "I know not yet—but something we will do—the blood of Bruce shall not die unaided."

So saying, she seized the small cruise which contained their soup, and the meat of which it was made, wrapped some thin cakes which she had baked, into the fold of her plaid, and, beckoning her companion to follow with a vessel of milk, also part of their provisions, she hastened towards the garden.

"So, our fair vestal is stirring abroad?" said the only man she met, who was one of the menials; but Catherine passed on without notice or reply, and gained the little garden without farther interruption.

Louise indicated to her a heap of ruins, which, covered with underwood, was close to the castle-wall. It had probably been originally a projection from the building; and the small fissure, which communicated with the dungeon, contrived for air, had terminated within it. But the aperture had been a little enlarged by decay, and admitted a dim ray of light to its recesses, although it could not be observed by those who visited the place with torches.

"Here is dead silence," said Catherine, after she had listened attentively for a moment.—"Heaven and earth, he is gone!"

"We must risk something," said her companion, and ran her fingers over the strings of her guitar.

A sigh was the only answer from the depth of the dungeon. Catherine then ventured to speak. "I am here, my lord—I am here, with food and drink."

"Ha! Ramorny?—The jest comes too late—I am dying," was the answer.

His brain is turned, and no wonder, thought Catherine; but whilst there is life, there is hope.

"It is I, my lord, Catherine Glover—I have food, if I could pass it safely to you."

"Heaven bless thee! I thought the pain was over, but it glows again within me at the name of food."

"The food is here, but how, ah how, can I pass it to you? the chink is so narrow, the wall is so thick—I have it. Quick, Louise; cut me a willow bough, the tallest you can find."

The glee-maiden obeyed, and by means of a cleft in the top of the wand, Catherine transmitted several morsels of the soft cakes, soaked in broth, which served at once for food, and for drink.

The unfortunate young man ate little, and with difficulty, but prayed for a thousand blessings on the head of his comforter. "I had destined thee to be the slave of my vices," he said, "and yet thou triest to become the preserver of my life! But away, and save thyself."

"I will return with food as I shall see opportunity," said Catherine, just as the glee-maiden plucked her sleeve, and desired her to be silent, and stand close.

Both couched among the ruins, and they heard the voices of Ramorny and the physician in close conversation.

"He is stronger than I thought," said the former, in a low croaking tone. "How long held out Dalwolsey, when the Knight of Liddesdale prisoned him in his Castle of Hermitage?"

"For a fortnight," answered Dwining; "but he was a strong man, and had some assistance by grain which fell from a granary above his prison-house."

"Were it not better end the matter more speedily? The Black

Douglas comes this way. He is not in Albany's secret. He will demand to see the Prince, and all *must* be over ere he comes."

They passed on in their dark and fatal conversation.

"Now gain we the tower," said Catherine to her companion, when she saw they had left the garden. "I had a plan of escape for myself—I will turn it into one of rescue for the Prince. The dey-woman enters the Castle about vespers time, and usually leaves her cloak in the passage as she goes into the pantler's office with the milk. Take thou the cloak, muffle thyself close, and pass the warder boldly; he is usually drunken at that hour, and thou wilt go, as the dey-woman, unchallenged through gate and along bridge, if thou bear thyself with confidence. Then away to meet the Black Douglas; he is our nearest and only aid."

"But," said Louise, "is he not that terrible lord who threatened me with shame and punishment?"

"Believe it," said Catherine, "such as thou and I never dwelt an hour in the Douglas's memory, either for good or evil. Tell him that his son-in-law, the Prince of Scotland, dies,—treacherously famished,—in Falkland Castle, and thou wilt merit not pardon only, but reward."

"I care not for reward," said Louise; "the deed will reward itself. But methinks to stay is more dangerous than to go—Let me stay, then, and nourish the unhappy Prince; and do you post to bring help. If they kill me before you return, I leave you my poor lute, and pray you to be kind to my poor Charlot."

"No, Louise," replied Catherine, "you are a more privileged and experienced wanderer than I—do you go—and if you find me dead on your return, as may well chance, give my poor father this ring, and a lock of my hair, and say, Catherine died in striving to save the blood of Bruce. And give this other lock to Henry; say, Catherine thought of him to the last; and that if he has judged her too scrupulous touching the blood of others, he will then know it was not because she valued her own."

They sobbed in each other's arms, and the intervening hours till evening were spent in endeavouring to devise some better mode of supplying the captive with nourishment, and in the construction of a tube, composed of hollow reeds, slipping into each other, by which liquids might be conveyed to him. The bell of the village church of Falkland tolled to vespers. The dey,* or farm-woman, entered with her pitchers, to deliver the milk for the family, and to hear and tell the news stirring. She had scarce entered the kitchen, when the female minstrel, again throwing herself in Catherine's arms, and assuring her

* Hence, perhaps, dairy-woman and dairy.

of her unalterable fidelity, crept in silence down stairs, the little dog under her arm. A moment after, she was seen by the breathless Catherine, wrapt in the dey-woman's cloak, and walking composedly over the draw-bridge.

"So," said the warder, "you return early to-night, May Bridget? Small mirth towards in the hall—Ha, wench!—Sick times are sad times!"

"I have forgotten my tallies," said the ready-witted Frenchwoman, "and will return in the skimming of a bowie."

She went onward, avoiding the village of Falkland, and took a foot-path which led through the park. Catherine breathed freely, and blessed God when she saw her safe out of sight. It was another anxious hour for Catherine, which occurred before the escape of the fugitive was discovered. This happened so soon as the dey-girl, having taken an hour to perform a task which ten minutes might have accomplished, was about to return, and discovered that some one had taken away her grey frieze cloak. A strict search was set on foot; at length the women of the house remembered the glee-maiden, and ventured to suggest her as one not unlikely to exchange an old cloak for a new one. The warder, strictly questioned, averred he saw the dey-woman depart presently after vespers; and on this being contradicted by the party herself, he could suggest, as the only alternative, that it must needs have been the devil.

As, however, the glee-woman could not be found, the real circumstances of the case were easily guessed at; and the steward went to inform Sir John Ramorny and Dwining, who were now scarcely ever separate, of the disappearance of Louise. Everything awakens the suspicions of the guilty. They looked on each other with faces of dismay, and then went together to the humble apartment of Catherine, that they might take her as much as possible by surprise, while they inquired into the facts attending Louise's disappearance.

"Where is your companion, young woman?" said Ramorny, in a tone of austere gravity.

"I have no companion here," answered Catherine.

"Trifle not," replied the knight; "I mean the glee-maiden, who lately dwelt in this chamber with you."

"She is gone, they tell me—" said Catherine, "gone about an hour since."

"And whither?" said Dwining.

"How," answered Catherine, "should I know which way a professed wanderer may choose to travel? She was assigned to me only to wait on me, and tired no doubt of the solitary life, so different from the scenes of feasting and dancing which her trade leads her to frequent.

She is gone, and the only wonder is that she should have stayed so long."

"This, then, is all you have to tell us?"

"All that I have to tell you, Sir John," answered Catherine, firmly; "and if the Prince himself inquire, I can tell him no more."

"There is little danger of his again doing you the honour to speak to you in person," said Ramorny, "even if Scotland should escape being rendered miserable by the sad event of his decease."

"Is the Duke of Rothsay so very ill?" asked Catherine.

"No help, save in Heaven," answered Ramorny, looking upward.

"Then may there yet be help there," said Catherine, "if human aid prove unavailing!"

"Amen!" said Ramorny, with the most determined gravity; while Dwining adopted a face fit to echo the feeling, though it seemed to cost him a painful struggle to suppress his sneering yet soft laugh of triumph, which was peculiarly excited by anything having a religious tendency.

"And it is men—earthly men, and not incarnate devils, who thus appeal to heaven, while they are devouring by inches the life-blood of their hapless master!" muttered Catherine, as her two baffled inquisitors left the apartment.—"Why sleeps the thunder?—But it will roll ere long, and oh! may it be to preserve as well as to punish."

The hour of dinner alone afforded a space, when, all in the Castle being occupied with that meal, Catherine thought she had the best opportunity of venturing to the breach in the wall, with the least chance of being observed. In waiting for the hour, she observed some stir in the Castle, which had been silent as the grave ever since the seclusion of the Duke of Rothsay. The portcullis was lowered and raised, and the creaking of the machinery was intermingled with the tramp of horse, as men-at-arms went out and returned with steeds hard ridden and covered with foam. She observed, too, that such domestics as she casually saw from her window were in arms. All this made her heart throb high, for it augured the approach of rescue; and besides, the bustle left the little garden more lonely than ever. At length, the hour of noon arrived. She had taken care to provide, under pretence of her own wishes, which the pantler seemed disposed to indulge, such articles of food as could be the most easily conveyed to the unhappy captive. She whispered to intimate her presence—there was no answer—she spoke louder— still there was silence.

"He sleeps"—she muttered these words half aloud, and with a shuddering which was succeeded by a start and a scream, when a voice replied behind her, "Yes, he sleeps—but it is for ever."

She looked round—Sir John Ramorny stood behind her in complete armour, but the visor of his helmet was up, and displayed a countenance more resembling one about to die than to fight. He spoke with a grave tone, something between that of a calm observer of an interesting event, and that of an agent and partaker in it.

"Catherine," he said, "all is true which I tell you. He is dead—you have done your best for him—you can do no more."

"I will not—I cannot believe it," said Catherine. "Heaven be merciful to me! it would make one doubt of Providence, to think so great a crime has been accomplished."

"Doubt not of Providence, Catherine, though it has suffered the profligate to fall by his own devices. Follow me—I have that to say which concerns you. I say follow, (for she hesitated) unless you prefer being left to the mercies of the brute Bonthron, and the mediciner Henbane Dwining."

"I will follow you," said Catherine. "You cannot do more to me than you are permitted."

He led the way into the tower, and mounted staircase after staircase, and ladder after ladder.

Catherine's resolution failed her. "I will follow no farther," said she. "Whither would you lead me?—If to my death, I can die here."

"Only to the battlements of the castle, fool," said Ramorny, throwing wide a barred door which opened upon the vaulted roof of the castle, where men were bending mangonels, as they called them, (that is military engines for throwing arrows or stones,) getting ready crossbows, and piling stones together. But the defenders did not exceed twenty in number, and Catherine thought she could observe doubt and irresolution amongst them.

"Catherine," said Ramorny, "I must not quit this station, which is necessary for my defence; but I can speak with you here as well as elsewhere."

"Say on," answered Catherine. "I am prepared to hear you."

"You have thrust yourself, Catherine, into a bloody secret. Have you firmness to keep it?"

"I do not understand you, Sir John," answered the maiden.

"Look you. I have slain—murdered, if you will—my late master, the Duke of Rothsay. The spark of life which your kindness would have fed was easily smothered. His last words called on his father. You are faint—bear up—you have more to hear. You know the crime, but you know not the provocation. See! this gauntlet is empty—I lost my right hand in his cause; and when I was no longer fit to serve him, I was cast off like a worn-out hound, my loss ridiculed, and a cloister recommended, instead of the halls and palaces in which I had my natural sphere. Think on this—pity and assist me."

"In what manner can you require my assistance?" said the trembling maiden; "I can neither repair your loss, nor cancel your crime."

"Thou canst be silent, Catherine, on what thou hast seen and heard in yonder thicket. It is but a brief oblivion I ask of you, whose word will, I know, be listened to—that of your mountebank companion, the foreigner, none will hold it of a pin-point's value. If you grant me this, I will take your promise for my security, and throw the gate open to those who now approach it. If you will not, I defend this castle till every one perishes, and I fling you headlong from these battlements. Ay, look at them—it is not a leap to be rashly braved. Seven courses of stairs brought you up hither with fatigue and shortened breath; but you shall go from the top to the bottom in briefer time than you can breathe a sigh! Speak the word, fair maid; for you speak to one unwilling to harm you, but determined in his purpose."

Catherine stood terrified, and without power of answering a man who seemed so desperate; but she was saved the necessity of reply by the approach of Dwining. He spoke with the same humble congés which at all times distinguished his manner, and with his usual suppressed ironical sneer, which gave that manner the lie.

"I do you wrong, noble sir, to intrude on your valiancy when engaged with a fair damsel. But I come to ask a trifling question."

"Speak, tormentor!" said Ramorny; "ill news is sport to thee even when they affect thyself, so they concern others also."

"Hem!—he, he!—I only desired to know if your knighthood proposed the chivalrous task of defending the Castle with your single hand—I crave pardon—I meant your single arm? The question is worth asking, for I am good for little to aid the defence, unless you could prevail on the besiegers to take physic—he, he, he!—and Bonthron is as drunk as ale and strong waters can make him—and you, he, and I, make up the whole garrison who are disposed for resistance."

"How!—Will the dogs not fight?" said Ramorny.

"Never saw men who showed less stomach"—Here come a brace of them.—*Venit extrema dies*—he, he, he!"

Eviot and his companion Buncle now approached, with sullen resolution in their faces, like men who had made their minds up to deny that authority which they had so long obeyed.

"How now!" said Ramorny, stepping forward to meet them. "Why from your posts?—Why have you left the barbican, Eviot?—And you, other fellow, did I not charge you to look to the mangonels?"

"We have something to tell you, Sir John Ramorny," answered Eviot. "We will not fight in this quarrel."

"How—my own squires control me?" said Ramorny.

"We were your squires and pages, my lord, while you were master of the Duke of Rothsay's household—It is bruited about the Duke no longer lives—we desire to know the truth."

"What traitor dares spread such falsehoods?" said Ramorny.

"All who have gone out to skirt the forest, my lord, and I myself among others, bring back the same news. The minstrel woman who left the Castle yesterday has spread the report everywhere, that the Duke of Rothsay is murdered, or at death's door. The Douglas comes on us with a strong force"——

"And you, cowards, take advantage of an idle report to forsake your master?" said Ramorny, indignantly.

"My lord," said Eviot, "let Buncle and myself see the Duke of Rothsay, and receive his personal orders, and if we do not fight to the death in defence of the Castle, I will consent to be hanged on its highest turret. But if he be gone by natural disease, we will yield up the Castle to the Earl of Douglas, who is, they say, the King's Lieutenant—Or if,—which Heaven forefend!—the noble Prince has had foul play, we will not involve ourselves in the guilt of using arms in defence of the murderers, be they who they will."

"Eviot," said Ramorny, raising his mutilated arm, "had not that glove been empty, thou hadst not lived to utter two words of this insolence."

"It is as it is—" answered Eviot, "and we do but our duty. I have followed you long, my lord, but here I draw bridle."

"Farewell, then, and a curse light on all of you!" exclaimed the incensed Baron. "Let my horse be brought forth!"

"Our Valiancy is about to run away," said the mediciner, who had crept close to Catherine's side before she was aware. "Catherine, thou art a superstitious fool, like most women; nevertheless thou hast a mind, and I speak to thee as one of more understanding than the buffaloes which are herding about us. These haughty barons who overstride the world, what are they in the day of adversity?—Chaff before the wind. Let their sledge-hammer hands, or their column-resembling legs, have injury, and bah!—the men-at-arms are gone—heart and courage is nothing to them, lithe and limb everything—give them animal strength, what are they better than furious bulls—take that away, and your hero of chivalry lies grovelling like the brute when he is hamstrung. Not so the sage; while a grain of sense remains in a crushed or mutilated frame, his mind shall be strong as ever.—Catherine, this morning I was practising your death; but methinks I now rejoice that you may survive, to tell how the poor mediciner, the pill-gilder, the mortar-pounder, the poison-vender, met his fate, in company with the gallant Knight of Ramorny, Baron in possession, and

Earl of Lindores in expectation—God save his lordship!"

"Old man," said Catherine, "if thou be indeed so near the day of thy deserved doom, other thoughts were far wholesomer than the vainglorious ravings of a vain philosophy.—Ask to see a holy man——"

"Yes," said Dwining, scornfully, "refer myself to a greasy monk, who does not—he! he! he!—understand the barbarous Latin he repeats by rote. Such would be a fitting counsellor to one who has studied both in Spain and Arabia! No, Catherine, I will choose a confessor that is pleasant to look upon, and you shall be honoured with the office.—Now, look yonder at his Valiancy—his eyebrow drops with moisture, his lip trembles with agony; for his Valiancy,—he! he! he!—is pleading for his life with his late domestics, and has not eloquence enough to persuade them to let him slip. See how the fibres of his face work as he implores the ungrateful brutes, whom he has heaped with obligations, to permit him to get such a start for his life as the hare has from the greyhounds when men course her fairly. Look also at the sullen, downcast, dogged faces with which, fluctuating between fear and shame, the domestic traitors deny their lord this poor chance for his life. These things thought themselves the superior of a man like me—And you, foolish wench, think so meanly of your Deity, as to suppose wretches like these are the work of Omnipotence!"

"No!—man of evil—no!" said Catherine, warmly; "the God I worship made these men with the attributes to know and adore him, to guard and defend their fellow-creatures, to practise holiness and virtue. Their own vices, and the temptations of the Evil One, have made them such as they now are. Oh, take the lesson home to thine own heart of adamant! Heaven made thee wiser than thy fellows, gave thee eyes to look into the secrets of nature, a sagacious head and a skilful hand; but thy pride has poisoned all these fair gifts, and made an ungodly Atheist of one who might have been a Christian Sage!"

"Atheist, say'st thou?" answered Dwining; "perhaps I have doubts on that matter—But they will be soon solved—yonder comes one who will send me, as he has done thousands, to the place where all mysteries shall be cleared."

Catherine followed the mediciner's eye up one of the forest glades, and beheld it occupied by a body of horsemen advancing at full gallop. In the midst was a pennon displayed, which, though its bearings were not visible to Catherine, was, by a murmur around, acknowledged as that of the Black Douglas. They halted within arrow-shot of the Castle, and a herald with two trumpets advanced up to the main portal, where, after a loud flourish, he demanded admittance for the high and dreaded Archibald Earl of Douglas, Lord Lieutenant of the

King, and acting for the time with the plenary authority of his Majesty; commanding, at the same time, that the inmates of the Castle should lay down their arms, all under penalty of high treason.

"You hear?" said Eviot to Ramorny, who stood sullen and undecided. "Will you give orders to render the Castle, or must I"——

"No, villain!" interrupted the knight, "to the last I will command you. Open the gates, drop the bridge, and render the castle to the Douglas."

"Now, that's what may be called a gallant exertion of free will," said Dwining. "Just as if the pieces of brass that were screaming a minute since, should pretend to call those notes their own, which are breathed through them by a frowsy trumpeter."

"Wretched man," said Catherine, "either be silent, or turn thy thoughts to the eternity on the brink of which thou art standing."

"And what is that to thee?" answered Dwining. "Thou canst not, wench, help hearing what I say to thee, and thou wilt tell it again, for thy sex cannot help that either. Perth and all Scotland shall know what a man they have lost in Henbane Dwining!"

The clash of armour now announced that the new comers had dismounted and entered the Castle, and were in the act of disarming the small garrison. Earl Douglas himself appeared on the battlements, with a few of his followers, and signed to them to take Ramorny and Dwining into custody. Others dragged from some nook the stupified Bonthron.

"It was to these three that the custody of the Prince was solely committed, during his alleged illness?" said the Douglas, prosecuting an inquiry which he had commenced in the hall of the Castle.

"No other saw him," said Eviot, "though I offered my services."

"Conduct us to the Duke's apartment, and bring the prisoners with us—Also there should be a female in the Castle, if she hath not been murdered or spirited away—the companion of the glee-maiden who brought the first alarm."

"She is here, my lord," said Eviot, bringing Catherine forward.

Her beauty and her agitation made some impression even upon the impassible Earl.

"Fear nothing, maiden," he said; "thou hast deserved both praise and reward. Tell to me, as thou would'st confess to Heaven, the things thou hast witnessed in this Castle."

Few words served Catherine to unfold the dreadful story.

"It agrees," said the Douglas, "with the tale of the glee-maiden, from point to point.—Now show us the Prince's apartment."

They passed to the room which the unhappy Duke of Rothsay had been supposed to inhabit; but the key was not to be found, and the

Earl could only obtain entrance by forcing the door. On entering, the wasted and squalid remains of the unhappy Prince were discovered, flung on the bed as if in haste. The intention of the murderers had apparently been to arrange the dead body, so as to resemble a timely parted corpse, but they had been disconcerted by the alarm occasioned by the escape of Louise. Douglas looked on the body of the misguided youth, whose wild passions and caprices had brought him to this fatal and premature catastrophe.

"I had wrongs to be redressed," he said; "but to see such a sight as this banishes all remembrance of injury."

"He! he!—It should have been arranged," said Dwining, "more to your omnipotence's pleasure; but you came suddenly on us, and hasty masters make slovenly service."

Douglas seemed not to hear what his prisoner said, so closely did he examine the wan and wasted features, and stiffened limbs, of the dead body before him. Catherine, overcome by sickness and fainting, at length obtained permission to retire from the dreadful scene, and, through confusion of every description, found her way to her former apartment, where she was locked in the arms of Louise, who had returned in the interval.

The investigations of Douglas proceeded. The dying hand of the Prince was found to be clenched upon a lock of hair, resembling, in colour and texture, the coal-black bristles of Bonthron. Thus, though famine had begun the work, it would seem that Rothsay's death had been finally accomplished by violence. The private stair to the dungeon, the keys of which were found at the subaltern assassin's belt,— the situation of the vault, its communication with the external air by the fissure in the walls, and the wretched lair of straw, with the fetters which remained there,—fully confirmed the story of Catherine and of the glee-woman.

"We will not hesitate an instant," said the Douglas to his near kinsman, the Lord Balveny, as soon as they returned from the dungeon. "Away with the murderers! hang them over the battlements."

"But, my lord, some trial may be fitting," answered Balveny.

"To what purpose?" answered Douglas. "I have taken them redhand; my authority will stretch to instant execution. Yet stay—have we not some Jedwood men in our troop?"

"Plenty of Turnbulls, Rutherfords, Ainslies, and so forth," said Balveny.

"Call me an inquest of these together; they are all good men and true, saving a little shifting for their living. Do thou see to the execution of these felons, while I hold a court in the great hall, and we'll try whether the jury or the provost-marshal do their work first; we will have Jedwood justice,—hang in haste, and try at leisure."

"Yet stay, my lord," said Ramorny, "you may rue your haste—Will you grant me a word out of ear-shot?"

"Not for worlds!" said Douglas; "speak out what thou hast to say before all that are here present."

"Know all, then," said Ramorny, aloud, "that this noble Earl had letters from the Duke of Albany and myself, sent him by the hand of yon cowardly deserter, Buncle—let him deny it if he dare,—counselling the removal of the Duke for a space from court, and his seclusion in this Castle of Falkland."

"But not a word," replied Douglas, sternly smiling, "of his being flung into a dungeon—famished—strangled.—Away with the wretches, Balveny, they pollute God's air too long!"

The prisoners were dragged off to the battlements. But while the means of execution were in the act of being prepared, the apothecary expressed so ardent a desire to see Catherine once more, and, as he said, for the good of his soul, that the maiden, in hopes his obduracy might have undergone some change even at the last hour, consented again to go to the battlements, and face a scene which her heart recoiled from. A single glance showed her Bonthron, sunk in total and drunken insensibility; Ramorny, stripped of his armour, endeavouring in vain to conceal fear, while he spoke with a priest, whose good offices he had solicited; and Dwining, the same humble, obsequious-looking, crouching individual she had always known him. He held in his hand a little silver pen, with which he had been writing on a scrap of parchment.

"Catherine," he said,—"he, he, he!—I wish to speak to thee on the nature of my religious faith."

"If such be thy intention, why lose time with me?—Speak with this good father."

"The good father," said Dwining, "is—he, he!—already a worshipper of the Deity whom I have served. I therefore prefer to give the altar of mine idol a new worshipper in thee, Catherine. This scrap of parchment will tell thee how to make your way into my chapel, where I have worshipped so often in safety. I leave the images which it contains to thee as a legacy, simply because I hate and contemn thee something less than any of the absurd wretches whom I have hitherto been obliged to call fellow-creatures. And now away, or remain and see if the end of the quacksalver belies his life."

"Our Lady forbid!" said Catherine.

"Nay," said the mediciner, "I have but a single word to say, and yonder nobleman's valiancy may hear it if he will."

Lord Balveny approached, with some curiosity; for the undaunted resolution of a man who never wielded sword or bore armour, and was in person a poor dwindled dwarf, had to him an air of something resembling sorcery.

"You see this trifling implement," said the criminal, showing the silver pen. "By means of this I can escape the power even of the Black Douglas."

"Give him no ink nor paper," said Balveny, hastily, "he will draw a spell."

"Not so, please your wisdom and valiancy,—he, he, he!"—said Dwining, with his usual chuckle, as he unscrewed the top of the pen, within which was a piece of sponge, or some such substance, no bigger than a pea. "Now, mark this——" said the prisoner, and drew it between his lips. The effect was instantaneous. He lay a dead corpse before them, the contemptuous sneer still on his countenance.

Catherine shrieked and fled, seeking, by a hasty descent, an escape from a sight so appalling. Lord Balveny was for a moment stupified, and then exclaimed, "This may be glamour! hang him over the battlements, quick or dead. If his foul spirit hath only withdrawn for a space, it shall return to a body with a dislocated neck."

His commands were obeyed. Ramorny and Bonthron were then ordered for execution. The last was hanged before he seemed quite to comprehend what was designed to be done with him. Ramorny, pale as death, yet with the same spirit of pride which had occasioned his ruin, pled his knighthood, and demanded the privilege of dying by the sword, and not by the noose.

"The Douglas never alters his doom," said Balveny. "But thou shalt have all thy rights.—Send the cook hither with a cleaver." The menial whom he called appeared at his summons. "What shakest thou for, fellow?" said Balveny; "here, strike me this man's gilt spurs from his heels with thy cleaver—And now, John Ramorny, thou art no longer a knight, but a knave—To the halter with him, provost-marshal! hang him betwixt his companions, and higher than them if it may be."

In a quarter of an hour afterwards, Balveny descended to tell the Douglas that the criminals were executed.

"Then there is no further use in the trial," said the Earl. "How say you, good men of inquest, were these men guilty of high-treason—ay or no?"

"Guilty," exclaimed the obsequious inquest, with edifying unanimity, "we need no farther evidence."

"Sound trumpets, and to horse then, with our own train only; and let each man keep silence on what has chanced here, until the proceedings shall be laid before the King, which cannot conveniently be till the battle of Palm Sunday shall be fought and ended. Select our attendants, and tell each man who either goes with us or remains behind, that he who prates dies."

In a few minutes the Douglas was on horseback, with the followers selected to attend his person. Expresses were sent to his daughter, the widowed Duchess of Rothsay, directing her to take her course to Perth, by the shores of Lochleven, without approaching Falkland, and committing to her charge Catherine Glover and the glee-woman, as persons whose safety he tendered.

As they rode through the forest, they looked back, and beheld the three bodies hanging, like specks darkening the walls of the old castle.

"The hand is punished," said Douglas; "but who shall arraign the head by whose direction the act was done!"

"You mean the Duke of Albany?" said Balveny.

"I do, kinsman; and were I to listen to the dictates of my heart, I would charge him with the deed, which I am certain he has authorized. But there is no proof of it beyond strong suspicion, and Albany has attached to himself the numerous friends of the House of Stewart, to whom, indeed, the imbecility of the King, and the ill-regulated habits of Rothsay, left no other choice of a leader. Were I, therefore, to break the band which I have so lately formed with Albany, the consequence must be civil war, an event ruinous to poor Scotland, while threatened by invasion from the activity of the Percy, backed by the treachery of March. No, Balveny—the punishment of Albany must rest with Heaven, which, in its own good time, will execute judgment on him and on his house."

Chapter Ten

WE ARE NOW to recall to our reader's recollection, that Simon Glover and his fair daughter had been hurried from their residence without having time to announce to Henry Smith, either their departure or the alarming cause of it. When, therefore, the lover appeared in Curfew Street, on the morning of their flight, instead of the hearty welcome of the honest burgher, and the April reception, half joy half censure, which he had been promised on the part of his lovely daughter, he received only the astounding intelligence that her father and she had set off early, on the summons of a stranger, who had kept himself carefully muffled from observation. To this, Dorothy, whose talents for forestalling evil, and communicating her views of it, are known to the reader, chose to add, that she had no doubt her master and young mistress were bound for the Highlands, to avoid a visit which had been made since their departure, by two or three apparitors, who, in the name of a Commission appointed by the King, had searched the house, put seals upon such places as were supposed to contain papers, and left citations for father and daughter to appear before the Court of Commission on a day certain, under pain of outlawry. All these alarming particulars Dorothy took care to state in the gloomiest colours, and the only consolation which she afforded the alarmed lover was, that her master had charged her to tell him to reside quietly at Perth, and that he should soon hear news of them. This checked the Smith's first resolve, which was to follow them instantly to the Highlands, and partake the fate which they might encounter.

But when he recollected his repeated feuds with divers of the Clan Quhele, and particularly his personal quarrel with Conachar, who was now raised to be a high chief, he could not but think, on reflection, that his intrusion on their place of retirement was more likely to disturb the safety which they might otherwise enjoy there, than be of any service to them. He was well acquainted with Simon's habitual intimacy with the Chief of the Clan Quhele, and justly augured that the Glover would obtain protection, which his own arrival might be likely to disturb, while his personal prowess could little avail him in a quarrel with a whole tribe of vindictive mountaineers. At the same time his heart throbbed with indignation, when he thought of Catherine being within the absolute power of young Conachar, whose rivalry he could not doubt, and who had now so many means of urging his suit. What if the young Chief should make the safety of the father depend on the favour of the daughter? He distrusted not Catherine's affections; but then her mode of thinking was so disinterested, and her affection to her father so tender, that, if the love she bore her suitor was weighed against his security, or perhaps his life, it was matter of deep and awful doubt, whether it might not be found light in the balance. Tormented by thoughts on which we need not dwell, he resolved nevertheless to remain at home, stifle his anxiety as he might, and await the promised intelligence from the old man. It came, but it did not relieve his concern.

Sir Patrick Charteris had not forgotten his promise to communicate to the Smith the plans of the fugitives. But amid the bustle occasioned by the movement of troops, he could not himself convey the intelligence. He therefore intrusted to his agent, Kitt Henshaw, the task of making it known. But this worthy person, as the reader knows, was in the interest of Ramorny, whose business it was to conceal from every one, but especially from a lover so active and daring as Henry, the real place of Catherine's residence. Henshaw therefore announced to the anxious Smith, that his friend the Glover was secure in the

Highlands; and though he affected to be more reserved on the subject of Catherine, he said little to contradict the belief, that she as well as Simon shared the protection of the Clan Quhele. But he reiterated, in the name of Sir Patrick, assurances that father and daughter were both well, and that Henry would best consult his own interest and their safety, by remaining quiet, and waiting the course of events.

With an agonized heart, therefore, Henry Gow determined to remain quiet till he had more certain intelligence, and employed himself in finishing a shirt of mail, which he intended should be the best tempered, and the most finely polished, that his skilful hands had ever executed. This exercise of his craft pleased him better than any other occupation which he could have adopted, and served as an apology for secluding himself in his work-shop, and shunning society, where the idle reports which were daily circulated served only to perplex and disturb him. He resolved to trust in the warm regard of Simon, the faith of his daughter, and the friendship of the Provost, who, having so highly commended his valour in the combat with Bonthron, would never, he thought, desert him at this extremity of his fortunes. Time, however, passed on day by day; and it was not till Palm Sunday was near approaching, that Sir Patrick Charteris, having entered the city to make some arrangements for the ensuing combat, bethought himself of making a visit to the Smith of the Wynd.

He entered his work-shop with an air of sympathy unusual to him, and which made Henry instantly augur that he brought bad news. The Smith caught the alarm, and the uplifted hammer was arrested in its descent upon the heated iron, while the agitated arm that wielded it, strong before as that of a giant, became so powerless, that it was with difficulty Henry was able to place the weapon on the ground, instead of dropping it from his hand.

"My poor Henry," said Sir Patrick, "I bring you but cold news— they are uncertain, however; and, if true, they are such as a brave man like you should not take too deeply to heart."

"In God's name, my lord," said Henry, "I trust you bring no evil news of Simon Glover or his daughter?"

"Touching themselves," said Sir Patrick, "no; they are safe and well. But as to thee, Henry, my tidings are more cold. Kitt Henshaw has, I think, apprised thee that I had endeavoured to provide Catherine Glover with a safe protection in the house of an honourable lady, the Duchess of Rothsay. But she hath declined the charge; and Catherine hath been sent to her father in the Highlands. What is worst is to come. Thou mayest have heard that Gilchrist MacIan is dead, and that his son Eachin, who was known in Perth as the apprentice of old Simon, by the name of Conachar, is now the Chief of Clan Quhele;

and I heard from one of my domestics, that there is a strong rumour
among the MacIans, that the young Chief seeks the hand of Catherine
in marriage. My domestic learned this (as a secret, however) while in
the Breadalbane country, on some arrangements touching the ensuing combat. The thing is uncertain; but, Henry, it wears a face of
likelihood."

"Did your lordship's servant see Simon Glover and his daughter?"
said Henry, struggling for breath, and coughing, to conceal from the
Provost the excess of his agitation.

"He did not," said Sir Patrick; "the Highlanders seemed jealous,
and refused to permit him to speak to the old man, and he feared to
alarm them by asking to see Catherine. Besides he talks no Gaelic, nor
had his informer much English, so there may be some mistake in the
matter. Nevertheless there *is* such a report, and I thought it best to tell
it you. But you may be well assured, that the wedding cannot go on till
the affair of Palm Sunday be over; and I advise you to take no step till
we learn the circumstances of the matter, for certainty is most desirable, even when it is.a painful one.—Go you to the Council-House,"
he added, after a pause, "to speak about the preparations for the lists
in the North Inch? You will be welcome there."

"No, my good lord."

"Well, Smith, I judge by your brief answer, that you are discomposed with this matter; but after all, women are weather-cocks, that is
the truth on't. Solomon and others have proved it before you."

And so Sir Patrick Charteris retired, fully convinced he had discharged the office of a comforter in the most satisfactory manner.

With very different impressions did the unfortunate lover regard
the tidings, and listen to the consoling commentary.

"The Provost," he said bitterly to himself, "is an excellent man;
marry, he holds his knighthood so high, that if he speaks nonsense, a
poor man must hold it sense, as he must praise dead ale if it be handed
to him in his lordship's silver flaggon. How would all this sound in
another situation? Suppose I were rolling down the steep descent of
the Corrichie Dhu, and before I came to the edge of the rock, comes
my Lord Provost, and cries, 'Henry, there is a deep precipice, and I
grieve to say you are in the fair way of rolling over it. But be not
downcast, for Heaven may send a stone or a bush to stop your progress. However, I thought it would be comfort to you to know the
worst, which you will be presently aware of. I do not know how many
hundred feet deep the precipice descends, but you may form a judgment when you are at the bottom, for certainty is certainty. And hark
ye, when come you to take a game at bowls?' And this gossip is to serve
instead of any friendly attempt to save the poor wight's neck! When I

think of this, I could go mad, seize my hammer, and break and destroy all around me. But I will be calm; and if this Highland kite, who calls himself a falcon, should stoop at my turtle dove, he shall know whether a burgess of Perth can draw a bow or not."

It was now the Thursday before the fated Palm Sunday, and the champions on either side were expected to arrive the next day, that they might have the interval of Saturday to rest, refresh themselves, and prepare for the combat. Two or three of each of the contending parties were detached to receive directions about the encampment of their little band, and such other instructions as might be necessary to the proper ordering of the field. Henry was not, therefore, surprised at seeing a tall and powerful Highlander peering anxiously about the wynd in which he lived, in the manner in which the natives of a wild country examine the curiosities of one that is more civilized. The Smith's heart rose against the man, on account of his country, to which our Perth burgher bore a natural prejudice, and more especially as he observed the individual wear the plaid peculiar to the Clan Quhele. The sprig of oak-leaves, worked in silk, intimated also that the individual was one of those personal guards of young Eachin, upon whose exertions in the future battle so much reliance was placed.

Having observed so much, Henry withdrew into his smithy, for the sight of the man raised his passion; and knowing that the Highlander came plighted to a solemn combat, and could not be the subject of any inferior quarrel, he was resolved at least to avoid friendly intercourse with him. In a few minutes, however, the door of the smithy flew open, and, fluttering in his tartans, which greatly magnified his actual size, the Gael entered with the haughty step of a man conscious of a personal dignity superior to anything which he is likely to meet with. He stood looking around him, and seemed to expect to be received with courtesy, and regarded with wonder. But Henry had no sort of inclination to indulge his vanity, and kept hammering away at a breast-plate, which was lying upon his anvil, as if he were not aware of his visitor's presence.

"You are the *Gow Chrom?*" (the bandy-legged smith,) said the Highlander.

"Those that wish to be crook-backed call me so," answered Henry.

"No offence meant," said the Highlander; "but her own self comes to buy an armour."

"Her own self's bare shanks may trot hence with her," answered Henry,—"I have none to sell."

"If it was not within two days of Palm Sunday, herself would make you sing another song," retorted the Gael.

"And being the day it is," said Henry, with the same contemptuous indifference, "I pray you to stand out of my light."

"You are an uncivil person; but her own self is *fir nan ord* too; and she knows the smith is fiery when the iron is hot."

"If her nainsell be hammer-man hersell, her nainsell may make her nain harness," replied Henry.

"And so her nainsell would, and never fash you for the matter; but it is said, *Gow Chrom*, that you sing and whistle tunes over the swords and harnishes that you work, that have power to make the blades cut steel-links as if they were paper, and the plate and mail turn back steel-lances as if they were boddle-prins?"

"They tell your ignorance any nonsense that Christian men refuse to believe," said Henry. "I whistle at my work whatever comes uppermost, like an honest craftsman, and commonly it is the Highlandman's 'Och hone for Houghmanstairs!' My hammer goes naturally to that tune."

"Friend, it is but idle to spur a horse when his legs are hamshackled," said the Highlander, haughtily. "Her own self cannot fight even now, and there is little gallantry in taunting her thus."

"By nails and hammer, you are right there," said the Smith, altering his tone. "But speak out at once, friend, what is it thou would'st have of me? I am in no humour for dallying."

"A hauberk for her Chief, Eachin MacIan," said the Highlander.

"You are a hammerman, you say? Are you a judge of this?" said our Smith, producing from a chest the mail shirt on which he had been lately employed.

The Gael handled it with a degree of admiration which had something of envy in it. He looked curiously at every part of its texture, and at length declared it the very best piece of armour that he had seen.

"A hundred cows and bullocks, and a good drift of sheep, would be e'en ower cheap an offer," said the Highlandman, by way of tentative; "but her nainsell will never bid thee less, come by them how she can."

"It is a fair proffer," replied Henry; "but gold nor gear will never buy that harness. I want to try my own sword on my own armour; and I will not give that mail-coat to any one but who will face me for the best of three blows and a thrust in the fair field; and it is your Chief's upon these terms."

"Hut, prut, man—take a drink, and go to bed," said the Highlander, in great scorn. "Are ye mad? Think ye the Captain of the Clan Quhele will be brawling and battling with a bit Perth burgess body like you? Whisht, man, and hearken. Her nainsell will do ye mair credit than ever belonged to your kin. She will fight you for the fair harness hersell."

"She must first show that she is my match," said Henry, with a grim smile.

"How! I, one of Eachin's Leichtach, and not your match!"

"You may try me, if you will. You say you are a *fir nan ord*—Do you know how to cast a sledge-hammer?"

"Ay, truly—ask the eagle if he can fly over Ferragon."

"But before you strive with me, you must first try a cast with one of *my* Leichtach.—Here, Dunter, stand forth for the honour of Perth!— And now, Highlandman, there stands a row of hammers—choose which you will, and let us to the garden."

The Highlander, whose name was Norman nan Ord, or Norman of the Hammer, showed his title to the epithet by selecting the largest hammer of the set, at which Henry smiled. Dunter, the stout journeyman of the Smith, made what was called a prodigious cast; but the Highlander, making a desperate effort, threw beyond it by two or three feet, and looked with an air of triumph to Henry, who again smiled in reply.

"Will you mend that?" said the Gael, offering our Smith the hammer.

"Not with that child's toy," said Henry, "which has scarce weight to fly against the wind.—Janniken, fetch me Sampson; or one of you help the boy, for Sampson is somewhat ponderous."

The hammer now produced was half as heavy again as that which the Highlander had selected as one of unusual weight. Norman stood astonished; but he was still more so when Henry, taking his position, swung the ponderous implement far behind his right haunch joint, and dismissed it from his hand as if it had flown from a warlike engine. The air groaned and whistled as the mass flew through it. Down at length it came, and the iron head sunk a foot into the earth, a full yard beyond the cast of Norman.

The Highlander, defeated and mortified, went to the spot where the weapon lay, lifted it, poised it in his hand with great wonder, and examined it closely, as if he expected to discover more in it than a common hammer. He at length returned it to the owner with a melancholy smile, shrugging his shoulders and shaking his head, as the Smith asked him whether he would not mend his cast.

"Norman has lost too much at the sport already," he replied. "She has lost her own name of the Hammerer. But does her ownself, the *Gow Chrom*, work at the anvil with that horse's load of iron?"

"You shall see, brother," said Henry, leading the way to the smithy. "Dunter," he said, "rax me that bar from the furnace;" and uplifting Sampson, as he called the monstrous hammer, he plied the metal with a hundred strokes from right to left—now with the right hand, now with the left, now with both, with so much strength at once and dexterity, that he worked off a small but beautifully proportioned horse-shoe in half the time that an ordinary smith would have taken for the same purpose with a more manageable implement.

"Oigh, oigh!" said the Highlander, "and what for would you be fighting with our young Chief, who is far above your standard, though you were the best smith ever wrought with wind and fire?"

"Hark you!" said Henry—"You seem a good fellow, and I'll tell you the truth. Your master has wronged me, and I give him this harness freely for the chance of fighting him myself."

"Nay, if he hath wronged you, he must meet you," said the life-guardsman. "To do a man wrong takes the eagle's feather out of the Chief's bonnet; and were he the first in the Highlands, and to be sure so is Eachin, he must fight the man he has wronged, or else a rose falls from his chaplet."

"Will you move him to this," said Henry, "after the fight on Sunday?"

"Oh, her nainsell will do her best, if the hawks have not got her bones to pick; for you must know, brother, that Clan Chattan's claws pierce rather deep."

"The armour is your Chief's on that condition," said Henry; "but I will disgrace him before King and Court if he does not pay me the price."

"Deil a fear, deil a fear; I will bring him in to the barrace myself," said Norman, "assuredly."

"You will do me a pleasure," replied Henry; "and that you may remember your promise, I will bestow on you this dirk. Look—If you hold it truly, and can strike between the mail-hood and the collar of your enemy, the surgeon will be needless."

The Highlander was lavish in his expressions of gratitude, and took his leave.

"I have given him the best mail harness I ever wrought," said the Smith to himself, rather repenting his liberality, "for the poor chance that he will bring his Chief into a fair field with me; and then let Catherine be his who can win her fairly. But much I dread the youth will find some evasion, unless he have such luck on Palm Sunday as may induce him to try another combat. That is some hope, however; for I have often, ere now, seen a raw young fellow, shoot up after his first fight, from a dwarf into a giant-queller."

Thus, with little hope, but with the most determined resolution, Henry Smith awaited the time that should decide his fate. What made him augur the worst was the silence both of the Glover and of his daughter. They are ashamed, he said, to confess the truth to me, and therefore they are silent.

Upon the Friday at noon, the two bands representing the contending Clans arrived at the several points where they were to halt for refreshments.

The Clan Quhele was entertained hospitably at the rich Abbey of Scone, while the Provost regaled their rivals at his Castle of Kinfauns; the utmost care being taken to treat both parties with the most punctilious attention, and to afford neither an opportunity of complaining of partiality. All points of etiquette were, in the meanwhile, discussed and settled by the Lord High Constable Errol, and the young Earl of Crawford, the former acting on the part of the Clan Chattan, and the latter patronising the Clan Quhele. Messengers were passing continually from the one Earl to the other, and they held more than six meetings within thirty hours, before the ceremonial of the field could be exactly arranged.

Meanwhile, in case of revival of ancient quarrel, many seeds of which existed betwixt the burghers and their mountain neighbours, a proclamation commanded the citizens not to approach within half a mile of the place where the Highlanders were quartered; while on their part the intended combatants were prohibited from approaching Perth without special license. Troops were stationed to enforce this order, who did their charge so scrupulously, as to prevent Simon Glover himself, burgess and citizen of Perth, from approaching the town, because he owned having come thither at the same time with the champions of Eachin MacIan, and wore a plaid around him of their check or pattern. This interruption prevented Simon from seeking out Henry Wynd, and possessing him with a true knowledge of all that had happened since their separation, which intercourse, had it taken place, must have materially altered the catastrophe of our narrative.

On Saturday afternoon another arrival took place, which interested the city almost as much as the preparations for the expected combat. This was the approach of the Earl Douglas, who rode through the town with a troop of only thirty horse, but all of whom were knights and gentlemen of the first consequence. Men's eyes followed this dreaded peer as they pursue the flight of an eagle through the clouds, unable to ken the course of the bird of Jove, yet silent, attentive, and as earnest in observing him, as if they could guess the object for which he sweeps through the firmament. He rode slowly through the city, and passed out at the northern gate. He next alighted at the Dominican Convent, and desired to see the Duke of Albany. The Earl was introduced instantly, and received by the Duke with a manner which was meant to be graceful and conciliatory, but which could not conceal both art and inquietude. When the first greetings were over, the Earl said with great gravity, "I bring you melancholy news. Your Grace's royal nephew, the Duke of Rothsay, is no more, and I fear hath perished by some foul practices."

"Practices!" said the Duke, in confusion, "what practices?—who dared practise on the heir of the Scottish throne?"

"'Tis not for me to state how these doubts arise," said Douglas— "but men say the eagle was killed with an arrow fledged from his own wing, and the oak trunk rent by a wedge of the same wood."

"Earl of Douglas," said the Duke of Albany, "I am no reader of riddles."

"Nor am I a propounder of them," said Douglas, haughtily. "Your Grace will find particulars in these papers worthy of perusal. I will go for half an hour to the cloister garden, and then rejoin you."

"You go not to the King, my lord?" said Albany.

"No," answered Douglas; "I trust your Grace will agree with me that we should conceal this great family misfortune from our Sovereign till the business of to-morrow be decided."

"I willingly agree," said Albany. "If the King heard of this loss, he could not witness the combat; and if he appear not in person, these men are likely to refuse to fight, and the whole work is cast loose. But I pray you sit down, my lord, while I read these melancholy papers respecting poor Rothsay."

He passed the papers through his hands, turning some over with a hasty glance, and dwelling on others as if their contents had been of the last importance. When he had spent nearly a quarter of an hour in this manner, he raised his eyes, and said very gravely, "My lord, in these most melancholy documents, it is yet a comfort to see nothing which can renew the divisions in the King's councils, which were settled by the last solemn agreement between your lordship and myself. My unhappy nephew was by that agreement to be set aside, until Time should send him a graver judgment. He is now removed by Fate, and our purpose in that matter is anticipated and rendered unnecessary."

"If your Grace," replied the Earl, "sees nothing to disturb the good understanding which the tranquillity and safety of Scotland require should exist between us, I am not so ill a friend of my country as to look closely for such."

"I understand you, my Lord of Douglas," said Albany, eagerly. "You hastily judged that I would be offended with your lordship for exercising your powers of Lieutenancy, and punishing the detestable murderers within my territory of Falkland. Credit me, on the contrary, I am obliged to your lordship for taking out of my hands the punishment of these wretches, as it would have broken my heart even to have looked on them. The Scottish Parliament will inquire, doubtless, into this sacrilegious deed; and happy am I that the avenging sword has been in the hand of a man so important as your lordship. Our communication together, as your lordship must well recollect, bore only concerning a proposed restraint of my unfortunate nephew, until the advance of a year or two had taught him discretion?"

"Such was certainly your Grace's purpose, as expressed to me," said the Earl; "I can safely avouch it."

"Why, then, noble Earl, we cannot be censured; because villains, for their own revengeful purposes, appear to have engrafted a bloody termination on our honest purpose?"

"The Parliament will judge it after their wisdom," said Douglas. "For my part, my conscience acquits me."

"And mine assoilzies *me*," said the Duke, with solemnity. "Now, my lord, touching the custody of the boy James* who succeeds to his brother's claims of inheritance?"

"The King must decide it," said Douglas, impatient of the conference. "I will consent to his residence anywhere save at Stirling, Doune, or Falkland."

With that he left the apartment abruptly.

"He is gone," muttered the crafty Albany, "and he must be my ally —yet feels himself disposed to be my mortal foe. No matter—Rothsay sleeps with his fathers—James may follow in time, and then—a crown is the recompense of my perplexities."

Chapter Eleven

PALM SUNDAY now dawned. At an earlier period of the Christian Church, the use of any of the days of Passion Week for the purpose of combat would have been accounted a profanity worthy of excommunication. The Church of Rome, to her infinite honour, had decided that during the holy season of Easter, when the redemption of man from his fallen state was accomplished, the sword of war should be sheathed, and angry monarchs should respect the season termed the Truce of God. The ferocious violence of the latter wars betwixt Scotland and England had destroyed all observance of this decent and religious ordinance. Very often the most solemn occasions were chosen by one party for an attack, because they hoped to find the other engaged in religious duties, and unprovided for defence. Thus the

---

* Second son of Robert III., brother of the unfortunate Duke of Rothsay, and afterwards King James I. of Scotland.

truce, once considered as proper to the season, had been discontinued; and it became not unusual even to select the sacred festivals of the Church for decision of the trial by combat, to which this intended contest bore a considerable resemblance.

On the present occasion, however, the duties of the day were observed with the usual solemnity, and the combatants themselves took share in them. Bearing branches of yew in their hands, as the readiest substitute for palm boughs, they marched respectively to the Dominican and Carthusian convents to hear High Mass, and, by a show at least of devotion, to prepare themselves for the bloody strife of the day. Great care had of course been taken, that, during this march, they should not even come within the sound of each other's bagpipes; for it was certain that, like game-cocks exchanging mutual notes of defiance, they would have sought out and attacked each other before they arrived at the place of combat.

The citizens of Perth crowded to see the unusual procession on the streets, and thronged the churches where the two clans attended their devotions, to witness their behaviour, and to form a judgment from their appearance which was most likely to obtain the advantage in the approaching conflict. Their demeanour in the church, although not habitual frequenters of places of devotion, was perfectly decorous; and, notwithstanding their wild and untamed dispositions, there were few of the mountaineers who seemed affected either with curiosity or wonder. They appeared to think it beneath their dignity of character to testify either curiosity or surprise at many things which were probably then presented to them for the first time.

On the issue of the combat, few even of the most competent judges dared venture a prediction; although the great size of Torquil and his eight stalwart sons induced some who professed themselves judges of the thews and sinews of men, to incline to ascribe the advantage to the party of the Clan Quhele. The opinion of the female sex was much decided by the handsome form, noble countenance, and gallant demeanour of Eachin MacIan. There were more than one who imagined they had recollection of his features; but his splendid military attire rendered the humble Glover's apprentice unrecognisable in the young Highland Chief, saving by one person.

That person, as may well be supposed, was the Smith of the Wynd, who had been the foremost in the crowd that thronged to see the gallant champions of Clan Quhele. It was with mingled feelings of dislike, jealousy, and something approaching to admiration, that he saw the Glover's apprentice stripped of his mean slough, and blazing forth as a chieftain, who, by his quick eye and gallant demeanour, the noble shape of his brow and throat, his splendid arms and well-proportioned limbs, seemed well worthy to hold the foremost rank among men selected to live or die for the honour of their race. The Smith could hardly think that he looked upon the same passionate boy, whom he had brushed off as he might a wasp that stung him, and, in mere compassion, forbore to dispatch by treading on him.

"He looks it gallantly with my noble hauberk," thus muttered Henry to himself, "the best I ever wrought. Yet if he and I stood together where there was neither hand to help nor eye to see, by all that is blessed in this holy church, the good harness should return to its owner! All that I am worth would I give for three fair blows on his shoulders to undo my own best work; but such happiness will never be mine. If he escape from the conflict, it will be with so high a character for courage, that he may well disdain to put his fortune, in its freshness, to the risk of an encounter with a poor burgess like myself. He will fight by his champion, and turn me over to my fellow-craftsman the Hammerer, when all I can reap will be the knocking a Highland bullock on the head. If I could but see Simon Glover!—I will to the other church in quest of him, since for sure he must have come down from the Highlands."

The congregation was moving from the church of the Dominicans, when the Smith formed this determination, which he endeavoured to carry into speedy execution, by thrusting through the crowd as hastily as the solemnity of the place and occasion would permit. In making his way through the press, he was at one instant carried so close to Eachin that their eyes encountered. The Smith's hardy and embrowned countenance coloured up like the heated iron on which he wrought, and retained its dark red hue for several minutes. Eachin's features glowed with a brighter blush of indignation, and a glance of fiery hatred was shot from his eyes. But the sudden flash died away in ashy paleness, and his gaze instantly avoided the unfriendly and steady look with which it was encountered.

Torquil, whose eye never quitted his foster-son, saw his emotion, and looked anxiously around to discover the cause. But Henry was already at a distance, and hastening on his way to the Carthusian convent. Here also the religious service of the day was ended; and those who had so lately borne palms in honour of the great event which brought peace on earth, and good-will to the children of men, were now streaming to the place of combat; some prepared to take the lives of their fellow-creatures, or to lose their own; others to view the deadly strife with the savage delight which the heathens took in the contests of their gladiators.

The crowd was so great that any other person might well have despaired of making way through it. But the general deference entertained for Henry of the Wynd, as the Champion of Perth, and the universal sense of his ability to force a passage, induced all to unite in yielding room for him, so that he was presently quite close to the warriors of the Clan Chattan. Their pipers marched at the head of their column. Next followed the well-known banner, displaying a mountain cat rampant, with the appropriate caution,—"Touch not the cat but (*i. e.* without) the glove." The Chief followed with his two-handed sword advanced, as if to protect the emblem of the tribe. He was a man of middle stature, more than fifty years old, but betraying, neither in features nor form, any decay of strength, or symptoms of age. His dark-red close-curled locks were in part chequered by a few grizzled hairs, but his step and gesture were as light in the dance, in the chase, or in the battle, as if he had not passed his thirtieth year. His grey eye gleamed with a wild light expressive of valour and ferocity mingled; but wisdom and experience dwelt on the expression of his forehead, eyebrows, and lips. The chosen champions followed by two and two. There was a cast of anxiety on several of their faces, for they had that morning discovered the absence of one of their appointed number; and, in a contest so desperate as was expected, the loss seemed a matter of importance to all save to their high-mettled Chief, MacGillie Chattanach.

"Say nothing to the Saxons of his absence," said this bold leader, when the diminution of his force was reported to him. "The false Lowland tongues might say that one of Clan Chattan was a coward, and perhaps that the rest favoured his escape, in order to have a pretence to avoid the battle. I am sure that Ferquhard Day will be found in the ranks ere we are ready for battle; or, if he should not, am I not man enough for two of the Clan Quhele? or would we not fight them fifteen to thirty, rather than lose the renown that this day will bring us?"

The tribe received the brave speech of their leader with applause, yet there were anxious looks thrown out in hopes of espying the return of the deserter; and perhaps the Chief himself was the only one of the determined band who was totally indifferent on the subject.

They marched on through the streets without seeing anything of Ferquhard Day, who, many a mile beyond the mountains, was busied in receiving such indemnification as successful love could bestow for the loss of honour. MacGillie Chattanach marched on without seeming to observe the absence of the deserter, and entered upon the North Inch, a beautiful and level plain, closely adjacent to the city, and appropriated to the martial exercises of the inhabitants.

The plain is washed on one side by the deep and swelling Tay. There was erected within it a strong palisade, inclosing on three sides a space of one hundred and fifty yards in length, and seventy-four yards in width. The fourth side of the lists was considered as sufficiently fenced by the river. An amphitheatre for the accommodation of spectators surrounded the palisade, leaving a large space free to be occupied by armed men on foot and horseback, and for the more ordinary class of spectators. At the extremity of the lists, which was nearest to the city, there was a range of elevated balconies for the King and his courtiers, so highly decorated with rustic treillage, intermingled with gilded ornaments, that the spot retains to this day the name of the Golden, or Gilded Arbour.

The mountain minstrelsy, which sounded the appropriate pibrochs or battle-tunes of the rival confederacies, was silent when they entered on the Inch, for such was the order which had been given. Two stately, but aged warriors, each bearing the banner of his tribe, advanced to the opposite extremities of the lists, and pitching their standards into the earth, prepared to be spectators of a fight in which they were not to join. The pipers, who were also to be neutral in the strife, took their places by their respective *brattachs*.

The multitude received both bands with the same general shout, with which on similar occasions they welcome those from whose exertion they expect amusement, or what they term sport. The destined combatants returned no answer to this greeting, but each party advanced to the opposite extremities of the lists, where were entrances by which they were to be admitted to the interior. A strong body of men-at-arms guarded either access; and the Earl Marshal at the one, and the Lord High Constable at the other, carefully examined each individual, to see whether he had the appropriate arms, being steel-cap, mail-shirt, two-handed sword, and dagger. They also examined the numbers of each party; and great was the alarm among the multitude when the Earl of Errol held up his hand and cried,—"Ho!—The combat cannot proceed, for the Clan Chattan lack one of their number."

"What reck of that?" said the young Earl of Crawford; "they should have counted better ere they left home."

The Earl Marshal, however, agreed with the Constable, that the fight could not proceed until the inequality should be removed; and a general apprehension was excited in the assembled multitude, that after all the preparation there would be no battle.

Of all present, there were only two perhaps who rejoiced at the prospect of the combat being adjourned; and these were, the Captain of the Clan Quhele, and the tender-hearted King Robert. Meanwhile the two Chiefs, each attended by a special friend and adviser, met in the midst of the lists, having, to assist them in determining what was to be done, the Earl Marshal, the Lord High Constable, the Earl of Crawford, and Sir Patrick Charteris. The Chief of the Clan Chattan declared himself willing and desirous of fighting upon the spot, without regard to the disparity of numbers.

"That," said Torquil of the Oak, "Clan Quhele will never consent to. You can never win honour from us with the sword, and you seek but a subterfuge, that you may say when you are defeated, as you know you will be, that it was for want of the number of your band fully counted out. But I make a proposal—Ferquhard Day was the youngest of your band, Eachin MacIan is the youngest of ours—we will set him aside in place of the man who has fled from the combat."

"A most unjust and unequal proposal," exclaimed Toshach Beg, the second, as he might be termed, of MacGillie Chattanach. "The life of the Chief is to the clan the breath of our nostrils, nor will we ever consent that our Chief shall be exposed to dangers which the Captain of Clan Quhele does not share."

Torquil saw with deep anxiety that his plan was about to fail, when the objection was made to Hector's being withdrawn from the battle; and he was meditating how to support his proposal, when Eachin himself interfered. His timidity, it must be observed, was not of that sordid and selfish nature which induces those who are infected by it calmly to submit to dishonour rather than risk danger. On the contrary, he was morally brave, though constitutionally timid, and the shame of avoiding the combat became at the moment more powerful than the fear of facing it.

"I will not hear," he said, "of a scheme which will leave my sword sheathed during this day's glorious combat. If I am young in arms, there are enough of brave men around me, whom I may imitate if I cannot equal."

He spoke these words in a spirit which imposed on Torquil, and perhaps on the young Chief himself.

"Now, God bless his noble heart!" said the foster-father to himself. "I was sure the foul spell would be broken through, and that the tardy spirit which besieged him would fly at the sound of the pipe, and the first flutter of the Brattach!"

"Hear me, Lord Marshal," said the Constable. "The hour of combat may not be much longer postponed, for the day approaches to high noon. Let the Chief of Clan Chattan take the half hour which remains, to find, if he can, a substitute for this deserter; if he cannot, let them fight as they stand."

"Content I am," said the Marshal, "though, as none of his own clan are nearer than fifty miles, I see not how MacGillie Chattanach is to find an auxiliary."

"That is his business," said the High Constable; "but if he offers a high reward, there are enough of stout yeomen surrounding the lists, who will be glad enough to stretch their limbs in such a game as is expected. I myself, did my quality and charge permit, would blithely take a turn of work amongst these wild fellows, and think it fame won."

They communicated their decision to the Highlanders, and the Chief of the Clan Chattan replied,—"You have judged impartially and nobly, my lords, and I deem myself obliged to follow your direction.—So make proclamation, heralds, that if any one will take his share with Clan Chattan of the honours and chances of this day, he shall have present payment of a gold crown, and liberty to fight to the death in my ranks."

"You are something chary of your treasure, Chief," said the Earl Marshal; "a gold crown is poor payment for such a campaign as is before you."

"If there be any man willing to fight for honour," replied MacGillie Chattanach, "the price will be enough; and I want not the service of a fellow who draws his sword for gold alone."

The heralds had made their progress, moving half way round the lists, stopping from time to time to make proclamation as they had been directed, without the least apparent disposition on the part of any one to accept of the proffered enlistment. Some sneered at the poverty of the Highlanders, who set so mean a price upon such a desperate service. Others affected resentment, that they should esteem the blood of citizens so lightly. None showed the slightest intention to undertake the task proposed, until the sound of the proclamation reached Henry of the Wynd, as he stood without the barrier, speaking from time to time with Bailie Craigdallie, or rather listening vaguely to what the magistrate was saying to him.

"Ha! what proclaim they?" he cried out.

"A liberal offer on the part of MacGillie Chattanach," said the Host of the Griffin, "who proposes a gold crown to any one who will turn wild cat for the day, and be killed a little in his service. That's all."

"How!" exclaimed the Smith, eagerly, "do they make proclamation for a man to fight against the Clan Quhele?"

"Ay, marry do they," said Griffin; "but I think they will find no such fools in Perth."

He had hardly said the word, when he beheld the Smith clear the barriers at a single bound, and alight in the lists, saying, "Here am I, Sir Herald, Henry of the Wynd, willing to do battle with the Clan Quhele."

A cry of admiration ran through the multitude, while the grave burghers, not being able to conceive the slightest reason for Henry's behaviour, concluded that his head must be absolutely turned with the love of fighting. The Provost was especially shocked.

"Thou art mad," he said, "Henry! Thou hast neither two-handed sword nor shirt of mail."

"Truly, no," said Henry, "for I parted with a mail-shirt, which I had made for myself, to yonder gay Chief of the Clan Quhele, who will soon find on his shoulders with what sort of blows I clink my rivets! As for two-handed sword, why this boy's brand will serve my turn till I can master a heavier one."

"This must not be," said Errol. "Hark thee, armourer, by Saint Mary, thou shalt have my Milan hauberk and good Spanish sword."

"I thank your noble earlship, Sir Gilbert Hay; but the yoke with which your brave ancestor turned the battle at Loncarty would serve my turn well enough. I am little used to sword or harness that I have not wrought myself, because I do not well know what blows the one will bear out without being cracked, or the other lay on without snapping."

The cry had in the meanwhile run through the multitude, and passed into the town, that the dauntless Smith was about to fight without armour, when, just as the fated hour was approaching, the shrill voice of a female was heard screaming for passage through the crowd. The multitude gave place to her importunity, and she advanced, breathless with haste, under the burden of a mail hauberk and a large two-handed sword. The widow of Oliver Proudfute was soon recognised, and the arms which she bore were those of the Smith himself, which, occupied by her husband on the fatal evening when he was murdered, had been naturally conveyed to his house with the dead body, and were now, by the exertions of his grateful widow, brought to the lists at a moment when such proved weapons were of the last consequence to their owner. Henry joyfully received the well-known arms, and the widow with trembling haste assisted in putting them on, and then took leave of him, saying, "God for the orphans' champion, and ill luck to all who come before him!"

Confident at feeling himself in his well-proved armour, Henry shook himself as if to settle the steel shirt around him, and, unsheathing the two-handed sword, made it flourish over his head, cutting the air through which it whistled in the form of the figure eight, with an ease and sleight of hand that proved how powerfully and skilfully he could wield the ponderous weapon. The champions were now ordered to march in their turns around the lists, crossing so as to avoid meeting each other, and making obeisance as they passed the Golden Arbour where the King was seated.

While this course was performing, most of the spectators were again curiously comparing the stature, limbs, and sinews of the two parties, and endeavouring to form a conjecture as to the probable issue of the combat. The feud of a hundred years, with all its acts of aggression and retaliation, was concentrated in the bosom of each combatant. Their countenances seemed fiercely writhen into the wildest expression of pride, hate, and a desperate purpose of fighting to the very last.

The spectators murmured a joyful applause, in high-wrought expectation of the bloody game. Wagers were offered and accepted both on the general issue of the conflict, and on the feats of particular champions. The clear, frank, and elated look of Henry Smith, rendered him a general favourite among the spectators, and odds, to use the modern expression, were taken, that he would kill three of his opponents before he himself fell. Scarcely was the Smith equipped for the combat, when the commands of the Chiefs ordered the champions into their places; and at the same moment Henry heard the voice of Simon Glover issuing from the crowd, who were now silent with expectation, and calling on him, "Harry Smith, Harry Smith, what madness hath possessed thee?"

"Ay, he wishes to save his hopeful son-in-law, that is, or is to be, from the Smith's handling," was Henry's first thought—his second, was to turn and speak with him—and his third, that hè could on no pretext desert the band which he had joined, or even seem desirous to delay the fight, consistently with honour.

He turned himself, therefore, to the business of the hour. Both parties were disposed by the respective Chiefs in three lines, each containing ten men. They were arranged with such intervals between each individual, as offered him scope to wield his sword, the blade of which was five feet long, not including the handle. The second and third lines were to come up as reserves, in case the first experienced disaster. On the right of the array of Clan Quhele, the Chief, Eachin MacIan, placed himself in the second line betwixt two of his foster-brothers. Four of them occupied the right of the first line, whilst the father and two others protected the rear of the beloved chieftain. Torquil, in particular, kept close behind, for the purpose of covering him. Thus Eachin stood in the centre of nine of the strongest men of his band, having four especial defenders in front, one on each hand, and three in his rear.

The line of the Clan Chattan was arranged in precisely the same order, only that the Chief occupied the centre of the middle rank, instead of being on the extreme right. This induced Henry Smith, who saw in the opposing bands only one enemy, and that was the unhappy Eachin, to propose placing himself on the left of the front rank of the Clan Chattan. But the leader disapproved of this arrangement; and having reminded Henry that he owed him obedience, as having taken wages at his hand, he commanded him to occupy the space in the third line, immediately behind himself,—a post of honour, certainly, which Henry could not decline, though he accepted of it with reluctance.

When the clans were thus drawn up opposed to each other, they intimated their feudal animosity, and their eagerness to engage, by a wild scream, which, uttered by the Clan Quhele, was answered and echoed back by the Clan Chattan, the whole at the same time shaking their swords, and menacing each other, as if they meant to conquer the imagination of their opponents ere they mingled in the actual strife.

At this trying moment, Torquil, who had never feared for himself, was agitated with alarm on the part of his Dault, yet consoled by observing that he kept a determined posture; and that the few words which he spoke to his clan were delivered boldly, and well calculated to animate them to combat, as expressing his resolution to partake their fate in death or victory. But there was no time for further observation. The trumpets of the king sounded a charge, the bagpipes blew up their screaming and maddening notes, and the combatants, starting forward in regular order, and increasing their pace till they came to a smart run, met together in the centre of the ground, as a furious torrent encounters an advancing tide.

For an instant or two the front lines, hewing at each other with their long swords, seemed engaged in a succession of single combats; but the second and third ranks soon came up on either side, actuated alike by the eagerness of hatred and the thirst of honour, pressed through the intervals, and rendered the scene a tumultuous chaos, over which the huge swords rose and sunk, some still glittering, others streaming with blood, appearing, from the wild rapidity with which they were swayed, rather to be put in motion by some complicated machinery, than to be wielded by human hands. Some of the combatants, too much crowded together to use those long weapons, had already betaken themselves to their poniards, and endeavoured to get within the sword-sweep of those opposed to them. In the meantime, blood flowed fast, and the groans of those who fell began to mingle with the cries of those who fought; for, according to the manner of the Highlanders at all times, they could hardly be said to shout, but to yell. Those of the spectators, whose eyes were best accustomed to such scenes of blood and confusion, could nevertheless discover no advantage yet acquired by either party. The conflict swayed, indeed, at different intervals forwards or backwards, but it was only in momentary superiority, which the party who acquired it almost instantly lost by a corresponding exertion on the other side. The wild notes of the pipers were still heard above the tumult, and stimulated to farther exertions the fury of the combatants.

At once, however, and as if by mutual agreement, the instruments sounded a retreat; it was expressed in wailing notes, which seemed to imply a dirge for the fallen. The two parties disengaged themselves from each other, to take breath for a few minutes. The eyes of the spectators greedily surveyed the shattered array of the combatants as they drew off from the contest, but found it still impossible to decide which had sustained the greater loss. It seemed as if the Clan Chattan had lost rather fewer men than their antagonists; but in compensation, the bloody plaids and shirts of their party (for several on both sides had thrown their mantles away) showed more wounded men than the Clan Quhele. About twenty of both sides lay on the field dead or dying; and arms and legs lopped off, heads cleft to the chine, slashes deep through the shoulder into the breast, showed at once the fury of the combat, the ghastly character of the weapons used, and the fatal strength of the arms which wielded them. The Chief of the Clan Chattan had behaved himself with the most determined courage, and was slightly wounded. Eachin also had fought with spirit, surrounded by his body-guard. His sword was bloody; his bearing bold and warlike; and he smiled when old Torquil, folding him in his arms, loaded him with praises and with blessings.

The two Chiefs, after allowing their followers to breathe for the space of about ten minutes, again drew up in their files, diminished by nearly one-third of their original number. They now chose their ground nearer to the river than that on which they had formerly encountered, which was encumbered with the wounded and the slain. Some of the former were observed, from time to time, to raise themselves to gain a glimpse of the field, and sink back, most of them to die from the effusion of blood which poured from terrific gashes inflicted by the claymore.

Harry Smith was easily distinguished by his Lowland habit, as well as his remaining on the spot where they had first encountered, where he stood, leaning on his sword beside a corpse, whose bonneted head, carried to ten yards distance from the body by the force of the blow which had swept it off, exhibited the oak-leaf, the appropriate ornament of the body-guard of Eachin MacIan. Since he slew this man, Henry had not struck a blow, but had contented himself with warding off many that were dealt at himself, and some which were aimed at the Chief. MacGillie Chattanach became alarmed, when, having given the signal that his men should again draw together, he observed that his powerful recruit remained at a distance from the ranks, and showed little disposition to join them.

"What ails thee, man?" said the Chief. "Can so strong a body have a mean and cowardly spirit? Come, and make in to the combat."

"You as good as called me hireling but now," replied Henry—"If I am such," pointing to the headless corpse, "I have done enough for my day's wage."

"He that serves me without counting his hours," replied the Chief, "I reward him without reckoning wages."

"Then," said the Smith, "I fight as a volunteer, and in the post which best likes me."

"All that is at your own discretion," replied MacGillie Chattanach, who saw the prudence of humouring an auxiliary of such promise.

"It is enough," said Henry; and shouldering his heavy weapon, he joined the rest of the combatants with alacrity, and placed himself opposite to the Chief of the Clan Quhele.

It was then, for the first time, that Eachin showed some uncertainty. He had long looked up to Henry as the best combatant which Perth and its neighbourhood could bring into the lists. His hatred to him as a rival was mingled with recollection of the ease with which he had once, though unarmed, foiled his own sudden and desperate attack; and when he beheld him with his eyes fixed in his direction, the dripping sword in his hand, and obviously meditating an attack on him individually, his courage fell, and he gave symptoms of wavering, which did not escape his foster-father.

It was lucky for Eachin, that Torquil was incapable, from the formation of his own temper, and that of those with whom he had lived, to conceive the idea of one of his own tribe, much less of his Chief and foster-son, being deficient in animal courage. Could he have imagined this, his grief and rage might have driven him to the fierce extremity of taking Eachin's life, to save him from staining his honour. But his mind rejected the idea that his Dault was a personal coward, as something which was monstrous and unnatural. That he was under the influence of enchantment, was a solution which superstition had suggested, and he now anxiously, but in a whisper, demanded of Hector, "Does the spell now darken thy spirit, Eachin?"

"Yes, wretch that I am," answered the unhappy youth; "and yonder stands the fell enchanter!"

"What!" exclaimed Torquil, "and you wear harness of his making? —Norman, miserable boy, why brought you that accursed mail?"

"If my arrow has flown astray, I can but shoot my life after it," answered Norman-nan-Ord. "Stand firm, you shall see me break the spell."

"Yes, stand firm," said Torquil. "He may be a fell enchanter; but my own ear has heard, and my own tongue has told, that Eachin shall leave the battle whole, free, and unwounded—let us see the Saxon wizard who can gainsay that. He may be a strong man, but the fair forest of the oak shall fall, stock and bough, ere he lay a finger on my Dault. Ring around him, my sons,—*Bas air son Eachin!*"

The sons of Torquil shouted back the words, which signify, "Death for Hector."

Encouraged by their devotion, Eachin renewed his spirit, and called boldly to the minstrels of his clan, "*Seid suas,*" that is, Strike up.

The wild pibroch again sounded the onset; but the two parties approached each other more slowly than at first, as men who knew and respected each other's valour. Henry Wynd, in his impatience to begin the contest, advanced before the Clan Chattan, and signed to Eachin to come on. Norman, however, sprang forward to cover his foster-brother, and there was a general, though momentary pause, as if both parties were willing to obtain an omen of the fate of the day, from the event of this duel. The Highlander advanced, with his large sword uplifted, as in act to strike; but just as he came within sword's length, he dropt the long and cumbrous weapon, leapt lightly over the Smith's sword, as he fetched a cut at him, drew his dagger, and being thus within Henry's guard, struck him with the weapon (his own gift) on the side of the throat, directing the blow downwards into the chest, and calling aloud, at the same time, "You taught me the stab!"

But Henry Wynd wore his own good hauberk, doubly defended with a lining of tempered steel. Had he been less surely armed, his combats had been ended for ever. Even as it was, he was slightly wounded.

"Fool!" he replied, striking Norman a blow with the pommel of his long sword, which made him stagger backwards, "you were taught the thrust, but not the parry;" and fetching a blow at his antagonist, which cleft his skull through the steel-cap, he strode over the lifeless body to engage the young Chief, who now stood open before him.

But the sonorous voice of Torquil thundered out, "*Far eil air son Eachin!*" (Another for Hector!) and the two brethren who flanked their Chief on each side, thrust forward upon Henry, and, striking both at once, compelled him to keep the defensive.

"Forward, race of the Tiger Cat!" cried MacGillie Chattanach; "save the brave Saxon! let these kites feel your talons!"

Already much wounded, the Chief dragged himself up to the Smith's assistance, and cut down one of the *Leichtach*, by whom he was assailed. Henry's own good sword rid him of the other.

"*Reist air son Eachin!*" (Again for Hector,) shouted the faithful foster-father.

"*Bas air son Eachin!*" (Death for Hector,) answered two more of his devoted sons, and opposed themselves to the fury of the Smith and those who had come to his aid; while Eachin, moving towards the left wing of the battle, sought less formidable adversaries, and again, by some show of valour, revived the sinking hopes of his followers. The two children of the Oak, who had covered this movement, shared the fate of their brethren; for the cry of the Clan Chattan Chief had drawn to that part of the field some of his bravest warriors. The sons of Torquil did not fall unavenged, but left dreadful marks of their swords on the persons of the dead and living. But the necessity of keeping their most distinguished soldiers around the person of their Chief told to disadvantage on the general event of the combat; and so few were now the number who remained fighting, that it was easy to see that the Clan Chattan had fifteen of their number left, though most of them wounded; and that of the Clan Quhele, only about ten remained, of whom there were four of the Chief's body-guard, including Torquil himself.

They fought and struggled on, however, and as their strength decayed, their fury seemed to increase. Henry Wynd, now wounded in many places, was still bent on breaking through, or exterminating, the band of bold hearts who continued to fight around the object of his animosity. But still the father's shout of, "Another for Hector!" was cheerfully answered by the fatal countersign, "Death for Hector!" and though the Clan Quhele were now outnumbered, the combat seemed still dubious. It was bodily lassitude alone that again compelled them to another pause.

The Clan Chattan were then observed to be twelve in number, but two or three were scarce able to stand without leaning on their swords. Five were left of the Clan Quhele; Torquil and his youngest son were of the number, both slightly wounded. Eachin alone had, from the vigilance used to intercept all blows levelled against his person, escaped without injury. The rage of both parties had sunk, through exhaustion, into sullen desperation. They walked staggering, as if in their sleep, through the carcasses of the slain, and gazed on them, as if again to animate their hatred towards their surviving enemies, by viewing the friends they had lost.

The multitude soon after beheld the survivors of the desperate conflict drawing together to renew the exterminating feud on the banks of the river, as the spot least slippery with blood, and less encumbered with the bodies of the slain.

"For God's sake—for the sake of the mercy which we daily pray for," said the kind-hearted old King to the Duke of Albany, "let this be ended! Wherefore should these wretched rags and remnants of humanity be suffered to complete their butchery?—Surely they will now be ruled, and accept of peace on moderate terms?"

"Compose yourself, my liege," said his brother. "These men are the pest of the Lowlands. Both Chiefs are still living—if they go back unharmed, the whole day's work is cast away. Remember your promise to the council, that you would not cry hold."

"You compel me to a great crime, Albany, both as a King, who should protect his subjects, and as a Christian man, who respects the brother of his faith."

"You judge wrong, my lord," said the Duke; "these are not loving subjects, but disobedient rebels, as my Lord of Crawford can bear witness; and they are still less Christian men, for the Prior of the Dominicans will vouch for me, that they are more than half heathen."

The King sighed deeply. "You must work your pleasure, and are too wise for me to contend with. I can but turn away, and shut my eyes from the sights and sounds of a carnage which makes me sicken. But well I know that God will punish me even for witnessing this waste of human life."

"Sound, trumpets," said Albany; "their wounds will stiffen if they dally longer."

While this was passing, Torquil was embracing and encouraging his young Chief.

"Resist the witchcraft but a few minutes longer! Be of good cheer— you will come off without either scar or scratch, wem or wound. Be of good cheer!"

"How can I be of good cheer," said Eachin, "while my brave kinsmen have one by one died at my feet?—died all for me, who could never deserve the least of their kindness!"

"And for what were they born, save to die for their Chief?" said Torquil, composedly. "Why lament that the arrow returns not to the quiver, providing it hit the mark? Cheer up yet—Here are Tormot and I but little hurt, while the wild-cats drag themselves through the plain as if they were half throttled by the terriers—Yet one brave stand, and the day shall be your own, though it may well be that you alone remain alive.—Minstrels, sound the gathering!"

The pipers on both sides blew their charge, and the combatants again mingled in battle, not indeed with the same strength, but with unabated inveteracy. They were joined by those whose duty it was to have remained neuter, but who now found themselves unable to do so. The two old champions who bore the standards had gradually advanced from the extremity of the lists, and now approached close to the immediate scene of action. When they beheld the carnage more nearly, they were mutually impelled by the desire to revenge their brethren, or not to survive them. They attacked each other furiously with the lances to which the standards were attached, closed after exchanging several deadly thrusts, then grappled in close strife, still holding their banners, until at length, in the eagerness of their conflict, they fell together into the Tay, and were found drowned after the combat, closely locked in each other's arms. The fury of battle, the frenzy of rage and despair, infected next the minstrels. The two pipers, who, during the conflict, had done their utmost to keep up the spirits of their brethren, now saw the dispute wellnigh terminated for want of men to support it. They threw down their instruments, rushed desperately upon each other with their daggers, and each being more intent on dispatching his opponent than in defending himself, the piper of Clan Quhele was almost instantly slain, and he of Clan Chattan mortally wounded. The last, nevertheless, again grasped his instrument, and the pibroch of the clan yet poured its expiring notes over the Clan Chattan, while the dying minstrel had breath to inspire it. The instrument which he used, or at least that part of it called the chanter, is preserved in the family of a Highland Chief to this day, and is much honoured under the name of the *Federan Dhu*, or Black Chanter.*

Meanwhile, in the final charge, young Tormot, devoted, like his brethren, by his father Torquil to the protection of his Chief, had been mortally wounded by the unsparing sword of the Smith. The other two remaining of the Clan Quhele had also fallen, and Torquil, with his foster son, and the wounded Tormot, forced to retreat before eight or ten of the Clan Chattan, made a stand on the bank of the river, while their enemies were making such exertions as their wounds would permit to come up with them. Torquil had just reached the spot where he had resolved to make the stand, when the youth Tormot dropped and expired. His death drew from his father the first and only sigh which he had breathed throughout the eventful day.

"My son Tormot!" he said, "my youngest and dearest! But if I save Hector, I save all.—Now, my darling Dault, I have done for thee all that man may, excepting the last. Let me undo the clasps of that ill-omened armour, and do thou put on that of Tormot; it is light, and

---

*The present Clunie MacPherson, Chief of his Clan, is in possession of this ancient trophy of their presence at the North Inch. Another account of it is given by a tradition, which says, that an aerial minstrel appeared over the heads of the Clan Chattan, and having played some wild strains, let the instrument drop from his hand. Being made of glass, it was broken by the fall, excepting only the chanter, which, as usual, was of lignum vitæ. The MacPherson piper secured this enchanted pipe, and the possession of it is still considered as ensuring the prosperity of the clan.

will fit thee well. While you do so, I will rush on these crippled men, and make what play with them I can. I trust I shall have but little to do, for they are following each other like disabled steers. At least, darling of my soul, if I am unable to save thee, I can show thee how a man should die."

While Torquil thus spoke, he unloosed the clasps of the young Chief's hauberk, in the simple belief that he could thus break the meshes which fear and necromancy had twined about his heart.

"My father, my father, my more than parent!" said the unhappy Eachin—"Stay with me!—with you by my side, I feel I can fight to the last."

"It is impossible," said Torquil. "I will stop them coming up, while you put on the hauberk. God eternally bless thee, beloved of my soul!"

And then, brandishing his sword, Torquil of the Oak rushed forward with the same fatal war-cry, which had so often sounded over that bloody field, *Bas air son Eachin!*—The words rung three times in a voice of thunder; and each time that he cried his war-shout, he struck down one of the Clan Chattan, as he met them successively straggling towards him.—"Brave battle, hawk—well flown, falcon!" exclaimed the multitude, as they witnessed exertions which seemed, even at this last hour, to threaten a change of the fortunes of the day. Suddenly these cries were hushed into silence, and succeeded by a clashing of swords so dreadful, as if the whole conflict had recommenced in the person of Henry Wynd and Torquil of the Oak. They cut, foined, hewed and thrust, as if they had drawn their blades for the first time that day; and their inveteracy was mutual, for Torquil recognised the foul wizard, who, as he supposed, had cast a spell over his child; and Henry saw before him the giant, who, during the whole conflict, had interrupted the purpose for which alone he had joined the combatants. They fought with an equality which, perhaps, would not have existed, had not Henry, more wounded than his antagonist, been somewhat deprived of his usual agility.

Meanwhile Eachin, finding himself alone, after a disorderly and vain attempt to put on his foster brother's harness, became animated by an emotion of shame and despair, and hurried forward to support his foster-father in the terrible struggle, ere some other of the Clan Chattan should come up. When he was within five yards, and sternly determined to take his share in the death-fight, his foster-father fell, cleft from the collar-bone wellnigh to the heart, and murmuring with his last breath, *Bas air son Eachin!*—The unfortunate youth saw the fall of his last friend, and at the same moment beheld the deadly enemy who had hunted him through the whole field, standing within sword's point of him, and brandishing the huge weapon which had hewed its way to his life through so many obstacles. Perhaps this was enough to bring his constitutional timidity to its highest point; or perhaps he recollected at the same moment that he was without defensive armour, and that a line of enemies, halting indeed and crippled, but eager for revenge and blood, were closely approaching. It is enough to say, that his heart sickened, his eyes darkened, his ears tingled, his brain turned giddy—all other considerations were lost in the apprehension of instant death; and drawing one ineffectual blow at the Smith, he avoided that which was aimed at him in return, by bounding backward; and ere the former could recover his weapon, Eachin had plunged into the stream. A roar of contumely pursued him as he swam across the river, although, perhaps, not a dozen of those who joined in it would have behaved otherwise in the like circumstances. Henry looked after the fugitive in silence and surprise, but could not speculate on the consequences of his flight, on account of the faintness which seemed to overpower him as soon as the animation of the contest had subsided. He sat down on the grassy bank, and endeavoured to stanch such of his wounds as were pouring fastest.

The victors had the general meed of gratulation. The Duke of Albany and others went down to survey the field; and Henry Wynd was honoured with particular notice.

"If thou wilt follow me, good fellow," said Douglas, "I will change thy leathern apron for a knight's girdle, and thy burgage tenement for an hundred-pound-land to maintain thy rank withal."

"I thank you humbly, my lord," said the Smith, dejectedly, "but I have shed blood enough already; and Heaven has punished me, by foiling the only purpose for which I entered the combat."

"How, friend?" said Douglas. "Didst thou not fight for the Clan Chattan, and have they not gained a glorious conquest?"

"*I fought for my own hand,*" said the Smith, indifferently; and the expression is still proverbial in Scotland.

The good King Robert now came up on an ambling palfrey, having entered the barriers for the purpose of causing the wounded to be looked after.

"My Lord of Douglas," he said, "you vex the poor man with temporal matters, when it seems he may have short time to consider those that are spiritual. Has he no friends here who will bear him where his bodily wounds, and the health of his soul, may be both cared for?"

"He hath as many friends as there are good men in Perth," said Sir Patrick Charteris; "and I esteem myself one of the closest."

"A churl will savour of churl's kind—" said the haughty Douglas, turning his horse aside; "the proffer of knighthood from the sword of

Douglas had recalled him from death's door, had there been a drop of gentle blood in his body."

Disregarding the taunt of the mighty Earl, the Knight of Kinfauns dismounted to take Henry in his arms, as he now sunk back from very faintness. But he was prevented by Simon Glover, who, with other burgesses of consideration, had now entered the barrace.

"Henry, my beloved son Henry!" said the old man. "O, what tempted you to this fatal affray!—Dying—speechless?"

"No—not speechless," said Henry.—"Catherine——"

He could utter no more.

"Catherine is well, I trust: and shall be thine—that is, if——"

"If she be safe, thou would'st say, old man," said the Douglas, who, though something affronted at Henry's rejection of his offer, was too magnanimous not to interest himself in what was passing,—"She is safe, if Douglas's banner can protect her—safe, and shall be rich. Douglas can give wealth to those who value it more than honour."

"For her safety, my lord, let the heartfelt thanks and blessings of a father go with the noble Douglas. For wealth, we are rich enough— Gold cannot restore my beloved son."

"A marvel!" said the Earl,—"a churl refuses nobility—a citizen despises gold."

"Under your lordship's favour," said Sir Patrick, "I, who am knight and noble, take license to say, that such a brave man as Henry Wynd may reject honourable titles—such an honest man as this reverend citizen may dispense with gold."

"You do well, Sir Patrick, to speak for your town, and I take no offence," said the Douglas. "I force my bounty on no one.—But," he added, in a whisper to Albany, "your Grace must withdraw the King from this bloody sight, for he must know *that* to-night which will ring over broad Scotland when to-morrow dawns. This feud is ended. Yet even *I* grieve that so many brave Scottish men lie here slain, whose brands might have decided a pitched field in their country's cause."

With difficulty King Robert was withdrawn from the field; the tears running down his aged cheeks and white beard, as he conjured all around him, nobles and priests, that care should be taken for the bodies and souls of the few wounded survivors, and honourable burial rendered to the slain. The priests who were present answered zealously for both services, and redeemed their pledge faithfully and nobly.

Thus ended this celebrated conflict. Of sixty-four brave men (the minstrels and standard-bearers included) who strode manfully to the fatal field, seven alone survived, who were conveyed from thence in litters, in a case little different from the dead and dying around them, and mingled with them in the sad procession which carried them from the scene of their strife. Eachin alone had left it void of wounds, and void of honour.

It remains but to say, that not a man of the Clan Quhele survived the bloody combat, except the fugitive Chief; and the consequence of the defeat was the dissolution of their confederacy. The clans of which it consisted are now only matter of conjecture to the antiquary, for, after this eventful contest, they never assembled under the same banner. The Clan Chattan, on the other hand, continued to increase and flourish; and the best families of the Northern Highlands boast their descent from the race of the Cat-a-Mountain.

Chapter Twelve

WHILE THE KING rode slowly back to the convent which he then occupied, Albany, with a discomposed aspect and faltering voice, asked the Earl of Douglas, "Will not your lordship, who saw this most melancholy scene at Falkland, communicate the tidings to my unhappy brother?"

"Not for broad Scotland," said the Douglas. "I would sooner bare my breast, within flight-shot, as a butt to an hundred Tynedale bowmen. No, by St Bride of Douglas! I could but say I saw the ill-fated youth dead. How he came by his death, your Grace can perhaps better explain. Were it not for the rebellion of March, and the English war, I would speak my own mind of it." So saying, and making his obeisance to the King, the Earl rode off to his own lodgings, leaving Albany to tell his tale as he best could.

"The rebellion and the English war?" said the Duke to himself,— "Ay, and thine own interest, haughty Earl, which, imperious as thou art, thou darest not separate from mine. Well, since the task falls on me, I must and will discharge it."

He followed the King into his apartment. The King looked at him with surprise after he had assumed his usual seat.

"Thy countenance is ghastly, Robin," said the King. "I would thou would'st think more deeply when blood is to be spilled, since its consequences affect thee so powerfully. And yet, Robin, I love thee the better that thy kind nature will sometimes show itself, even through thy reflecting policy."

"I would to Heaven, my royal brother," said Albany, with a voice half choked, "that the bloody field we have seen were the worst we had to see or hear of this day. I should waste little sorrow on the wild kerne who lie piled on it like carrion. But—" he paused.

"How!" exclaimed the King, in terror,—"What new evil?—Rothsay?—It must be—it is Rothsay!—Speak out!—What new folly has been done?—What fresh mischance?"

"My lord—my liege—folly and mischance are now ended with my hapless nephew."

"He is dead!—he is dead!" screamed the agonized parent. "Albany, as thy brother, I conjure thee—But no—I am thy brother no longer! As thy King, dark and subtle man, I charge thee to tell the worst!"

Albany faltered out,—"The details are but imperfectly known to me—but the certainty is, that my unhappy nephew was found dead in his apartment last night from sudden illness—as I have heard."

"O, Rothsay!—O, my beloved David!—Would to God I had died for thee, my son—my son!"

So spoke, in the emphatic words of Scripture, the helpless and bereft father, tearing his grey beard and hoary hair, while Albany, speechless and conscience-struck, did not venture to interrupt the tempest of his grief. But the agony of the King's sorrow almost instantly changed to fury,—a mood so contrary to the gentleness and timidity of his nature, that the remorse of Albany was drowned in his fear.

"And this is the end," said the King, "of thy moral saws and religious punishments!—But the besotted father, who gave the son into thy hands, who gave the innocent lamb to the butcher, is a King! and thou shalt know it to thy cost. Shall the murderer stand in presence of his brother—stained with the blood of that brother's son? No!—What ho, without there!—MacLouis!—Brandanes!—Treachery!—Murder!—Take arms, if you love the Stewart!"

MacLouis, with several of the guards, rushed into the apartment.

"Murder and treason!" exclaimed the miserable King. "Brandanes —your noble Prince—" here his grief and agitation interrupted for a moment the fatal information it was his object to convey. At length he resumed his broken speech,—"An axe and a block instantly into the court-yard!—Arrest—" The word choked his utterance.

"Arrest whom, my noble liege?" said MacLouis, who, observing the King influenced by a tide of passion so different from the gentleness of his ordinary demeanour, almost conjectured that his brain had been disturbed by the unusual horrors of the combat he had witnessed,—"Whom shall I arrest, my liege?" he replied. "Here is none but your Grace's royal brother of Albany?"

"Most true," said the King, his brief fit of vindictive passion soon dying away. "Most true—none but Albany—none but my parents' child—none but my brother. O God! enable me to quell the sinful passion which glows in this bosom—*Sancta Maria, ora pro nobis!*"

MacLouis cast a look of wonder towards the Duke of Albany, who endeavoured to hide his confusion under an affectation of deep sympathy, and muttered to the officer, "The great misfortune has been too much for his understanding."

"What misfortune, please your Grace?" replied MacLouis. "I have heard of none."

"How!—Not heard of the death of my nephew Rothsay?"

"The Duke of Rothsay dead, my Lord of Albany!" exclaimed the faithful Brandane, with the utmost horror and astonishment,—"When, how, and where?"

"Two days since—the manner as yet unknown—at Falkland."

MacLouis gazed at the Duke for an instant; then, with a kindling eye and determined look, said to the King, who seemed deeply engaged in his mental devotion,—"My liege! a minute or two since you left a word—one word—unspoken. Let it pass your lips, and your pleasure is law to your Brandanes!"

"I was praying against temptation, MacLouis," said the heart-broken King, "and you bring it to me. Would you arm a madman with a drawn weapon?—But oh, Albany! my friend, my brother, my bosom counsellor!—how—how camest thou by the heart to do this!"

Albany, seeing that the King's mood was softening, replied with more firmness than before,—"My castle is no barrier against the power of death—I have not deserved the foul suspicions which your Majesty's words imply. I pardon them, from the distraction of a bereaved father. But I am willing to swear by cross and altar—by my share in salvation—by the souls of our royal parents——"

"Be silent, Robert!" said the King; "add not perjury to murder.— And was this all done to gain a step nearer to a crown and sceptre? Take them to thee at once, man; and may'st thou feel, as I have done, that they are both of red-hot iron!—Oh Rothsay, Rothsay! thou hast at least escaped being a king!"

"My liege," said MacLouis, "let me remind you, that the crown and sceptre of Scotland are, when your Majesty ceases to bear them, the right of Prince James, who succeeds to his brother's rights."

"True, MacLouis," said the King, eagerly, "and will succeed, poor child, to his brother's perils! Thanks, MacLouis, thanks—You have reminded me that I have still work upon earth. Get thy Brandanes under arms with what speed thou canst. Let no man go with us whose truth is not known to thee. None in especial who has trafficked with the Duke of Albany—that man, I mean, who calls himself my brother! —and order my litter to be instantly prepared. We will to Dunbarton, MacLouis, or to Bute. Precipices, and tides, and my Brandanes' hearts, shall defend the child till we can put oceans betwixt him and his cruel uncle's ambition.—Farewell, Robert of Albany—farewell for ever, thou hard-hearted bloody man! Enjoy such share of power as the Douglas may permit thee—But seek not to see my face again, far less to approach my remaining child! for, that hour thou dost, my guards shall have orders to stab thee down with their partizans!—MacLouis, look it be so directed."

The Duke of Albany left the presence without attempting further justification or reply.

What followed is matter of history. In the ensuing Parliament, the Duke of Albany prevailed on that body to declare him innocent of the death of Rothsay, while, at the same time, he showed his own sense of guilt by taking out a remission or pardon for the offence. The unhappy and aged monarch secluded himself in his Castle of Rothsay, in Bute, to mourn over the son he had lost, and watch with feverish anxiety over the life of him who remained. As the best step for the youthful James's security, he sent him to France to receive his education at the court of the reigning sovereign. But the vessel in which the Prince of Scotland sailed was taken by an English cruizer, and although there was a truce for the moment betwixt the kingdoms, Henry IV. ungenerously detained him a prisoner. This last blow completely broke the heart of the unhappy King Robert III. Vengeance followed, though with a slow pace, the treachery and cruelty of his brother. Robert of Albany's own grey hairs went, indeed, in peace to the grave, and he transferred the regency which he had so foully acquired to his son Murdoch. But nineteen years after the death of the old King, James I. returned to Scotland, and Duke Murdoch of Albany, with his sons, was brought to the scaffold, in expiation of his father's guilt and his own.

Chapter Thirteen

WE NOW RETURN to the Fair Maid of Perth, who had been sent from the horrible scene at Falkland, by order of the Douglas, to be placed under the protection of his daughter, the now widowed Duchess of Rothsay. That lady's temporary residence was a religious house called Campsie, the ruins of which still occupy a striking situation on the Tay. It arose on the summit of a precipitous rock, which descends on the princely river, there rendered peculiarly remarkable by the cataract called Campsie Linn, where its waters rush tumultuously over a range of basaltic rock, which intercepts the current, like a dike erected by human hands. Delighted with a site so romantic, the monks of the Abbey of Cupar reared a structure there, dedicated to an obscure Saint, named St Hunnand, and hither they were wont themselves to retire for pleasure or devotion. It had readily opened its gates to admit the noble lady who was its present inmate, as the country was under the influence of the powerful Lord Drummond, the ally of the Douglas. There the Earl's letters were presented to the Duchess by the leader of the escort which conducted Catherine and the glee-maiden to Campsie. Whatever reason she might have to complain of Rothsay, his horrible and unexpected end greatly shocked the noble lady, and she spent the greater part of the night in indulging her grief, and in devotional exercises.

On the next morning, which was that of the memorable Palm Sunday, she ordered Catherine Glover and the minstrel into her presence. The spirits of both the young women had been much sunk and shaken by the dreadful scenes in which they had so lately been engaged; and the outward appearance of the Duchess Marjory was, like that of her father, more calculated to inspire awe than confidence. She spoke with kindness, however, though apparently in deep affliction, and learned from them all which they had to tell concerning the fate of her erring and inconsiderate husband. She appeared grateful for the efforts which Catherine and the glee-maiden had made, at their own extreme peril, to save Rothsay from his horrible fate. She invited them to join in her devotions; and at the hour of dinner gave them her hand to kiss, and dismissed them to their own refection, assuring both, and Catherine in particular, of her efficient protection, which should include, she said, her father's, and be a wall around them both, so long as she herself lived.

They retired from the presence of the widowed Princess, and partook of a repast with her duennas and ladies, all of whom, amid their profound sorrow, showed a character of stateliness, which chilled the light heart of the Frenchwoman, and imposed constraint even on the more serious character of Catherine Glover. The friends, for so we may term them, were fain, therefore, to escape from the society of these persons, all of them born gentlewomen, who thought themselves but ill-assorted with a burgher's daughter and a strolling glee-maiden, and saw them with pleasure go out to walk in the neighbourhood of the convent. A little garden, with its bushes and fruit-trees, advanced on one side of the convent, so as to skirt the precipice, from which it was only separated by a parapet built on the ledge of the rock, so low that the eye might easily measure the depth of the crag, and gaze on the conflicting waters which foamed, struggled, and chafed over the reef below.

The Fair Maiden of Perth and her companion walked slowly on a path that ran within this parapet, looked at the romantic prospect, and judged what it must be when the advancing summer should clothe the grove with leaves. They observed for some time a deep silence. At length the gay and bold spirit of the glee-maiden rose above the circumstances in which she had been and was now placed.

"Do the horrors of Falkland, fair May, still weigh down your spirits? Strive to forget them as I do; we cannot tread life's path lightly, if we shake not from our mantles the rain-drops as they fall."

"These horrors are not to be forgotten," answered Catherine. "Yet my mind is at present anxious respecting my father's safety; and I cannot but think how many brave men may be at this instant leaving the world, even within six miles of us, or little farther."

"You mean the combat betwixt sixty champions, of which the Douglas's equerry told us yesterday? It were a sight for a minstrel to witness. But out upon these womanish eyes of mine—they could never see swords cross each other, without being dazzled. But see,— look yonder, May Catherine, look yonder! That flying messenger certainly brings news of the battle."

"Methinks I should know him who runs so wildly," said Catherine —"But if it be he I think of, some wild thoughts are urging his speed."

As she spoke, the runner directed his course to the garden. Louise's little dog ran to meet him, barking furiously, but came back, to cower, creep, and growl behind its mistress; for even dumb animals can distinguish when men are driven on by the furious energy of irresistible passion, and dread to cross or encounter them in their career. The fugitive rushed into the garden at the same reckless pace. His head was bare, his hair dishevelled; his rich acton, and all his other vestments, looked as if they had been lately drenched in water. His leathern buskins were cut and torn, and his feet marked the sod with blood. His countenance was wild, haggard, and highly excited, or, as the Scottish phrase expresses it, much *raised*.

"Conachar!" said Catherine, as he advanced, apparently without seeing what was before him, as hares are said to do when severely pressed by the greyhounds. But he stopped short when he heard his own name.

"Conachar," said Catherine, "or rather Eachin MacIan—what means all this?—Have the Clan Quhele sustained a defeat?"

"I *have* borne such names as this maiden gives me," said the fugitive, after a moment's recollection. "Yes, I was called Conachar when I was happy, and Eachin when I was powerful. But now I have no name, and there is no such clan as thou speak'st of; and thou art a foolish maid to speak of that which is not, to one who has no existence."

"Alas! unfortunate"——

"And why unfortunate, I pray you?" exclaimed the youth. "If I am coward and villain, have not villainy and cowardice command over the elements?—Have I not braved the water without its choking me, and trod the firm earth without its opening to devour me? And shall a mortal oppose my purpose?"

"He raves, alas!" said Catherine. "Haste to call some help. He will not harm me; but I fear he will do evil to himself. See how he stares down on the roaring waterfall!"

The glee-woman hastened to do as she was ordered; and Conachar's half-frenzied spirit seemed relieved by her absence. "Catherine," he said, "now she is gone, I will say I know thee—I know thy love of peace and hatred of war. But hearken—I have, rather than strike a blow at my enemy, given up all that a man calls dearest—I have lost honour, fame, and friends; and such friends! (he placed his hands before his face,)—Oh! their love surpassed the love of woman! Why should I hide my tears?—All know my shame—all should see my sorrow. Yes, all might see, but who would pity it?—Catherine, as I ran like a madman down the strath, man and woman called shame on me! —The beggar to whom I flung an alms that I might purchase one blessing, threw it back in disgust, and with a curse upon the coward! Each bell that tolled rung out, Shame on the recreant caitiff! The brute beasts in their lowing and bleating—the wild winds in their rustling and howling—the hoarse waters in their dash and roar, cried, Out upon the dastard!—The faithful nine are still pursuing me; they cry with feeble voice, 'Strike but one blow in our revenge, we all died for you!'"

While the unhappy youth thus raved, a rustling was heard in the bushes. "There is but one way," he exclaimed, springing upon the parapet, but with a terrified glance towards the thicket, through which one or two attendants were stealing, with the purpose of surprising him. But the instant he saw a human form emerge from the cover of the thicket, he waved his hands wildly over his head, and shrieking out, "*Bas air Eachin!*" plunged down the precipice into the raging cataract beneath.

It is needless to say, that aught save thistle-down must have been dashed to pieces in such a fall. But the river was swelled, and the remains of the unhappy youth were never seen. A varying tradition has assigned more than one supplement to the history. It is said by one account, that the young Captain of Clan Quhele swam safe to shore, far below the Linns of Campsie; and that, wandering disconsolately in the deserts of Rannoch, he met with Father Clement, who had taken up his abode in the wilderness as a hermit, on the principle of the old Culdees. He converted, it is said, the heart-broken and penitent

Conachar, who lived with him in his cell, sharing his devotion and privations, till death removed them in succession.

Another wilder legend supposes that he was snatched from death by the *Daione-Shie*, or fairy-folk; and that he continues to wander through wood and wild, armed like an ancient Highlander, but carrying his sword in his left hand. The phantom appears always in deep grief. Sometimes he seems about to attack the traveller, but, when resisted with courage, always flies. These legends are founded on two peculiar points in his story—his evincing timidity, and his committing suicide; both of them circumstances unexampled in the history of a Mountain Chief.

When Simon Glover, having seen his friend Henry duly taken care of in his own house in Curfew Street, arrived that evening at the Place of Campsie, he found his daughter extremely ill of a fever, in consequence of the scenes to which she had lately been a witness, and particularly the catastrophe of her late play-mate. The affection of the glee-maiden rendered her so attentive and careful a nurse, that the Glover said it should not be his fault if she ever touched lute again, save for her own amusement.

It was some time ere Simon ventured to tell his daughter of Henry's late exploits, and his severe wounds; and he took care to make the most of the encouraging circumstance, that her faithful lover had refused both honour and wealth, rather than become a professed soldier, and follow the Douglas. Catherine sighed deeply, and shook her head at the history of bloody Palm Sunday on the North Inch. But apparently she had reflected that men rarely advance in civilization or refinement beyond the ideas of their own age, and that a headlong and exuberant courage, like that of Henry Smith, was, in the iron days in which they lived, preferable to the deficiency which had led to Conachar's catastrophe. If she had any doubts on the subject, they were removed in due time by Henry's protestations, so soon as restored health enabled him to plead his own cause.

"I should blush to say, Catherine, that I am even sick of the thoughts of doing battle. Yonder last field showed carnage enough to glut a tiger. I am therefore resolved to hang up my broad-sword, never to be drawn more unless against the enemies of Scotland."

"And should Scotland call for it," said Catherine, "I will buckle it round you."

"And, Catherine," said the joyful Glover, "we will pay largely for soul masses for those who have fallen by Henry's sword; and that will not only cure spiritual flaws, but make us friends with the Church again."

"For that purpose, father," said Catherine, "the hoards of the wretched Dwining may be applied. He bequeathed them to me, but I think you would not mix his base blood-money with your honest gains!"

"I would bring the plague into my house as soon," said the resolute Glover.

The treasures of the wicked apothecary were distributed accordingly among the four monasteries; nor was there ever after a breath of suspicion concerning the orthodoxy of old Simon or his daughter.

Henry and Catherine were married within four months after the battle of the North Inch, and never did the corporations of the glovers and hammermen trip their sword-dance so featly as at the wedding of the boldest burgess and brightest maiden in Perth. Ten months after, a gallant infant filled the well-spread cradle, and was rocked by Louise, to the tune of

> Bold and True,
> In bonnet blue.

The names of the boy's sponsors are recorded, as "Ane Hie and Michty Lord, Archibald Erl of Douglas, ane Honorabil and gude Knicht, Schir Patrick Charteris of Kinfauns, and ane Gracious Princess, Marjory Dowaire of his Serene Highness David, umquhile Duke of Rothsay." Under such patronage a family rises fast; and several of the most respected houses in Scotland, but especially in Perthshire, and many individuals, distinguished both in arts and arms, record with pride their descent from the *Gow Chrom* and the Fair Maid of Perth.

THE END

ESSAY ON THE TEXT

1. THE GENESIS OF *SAINT VALENTINE'S DAY*   2. THE COM-
POSITION OF *SAINT VALENTINE'S DAY*: the Manuscript; Manu-
script to First Edition   3. THE LATER EDITIONS: Second Edition; the
Interleaved Copy and the Magnum   4. THE PRESENT TEXT OF *SAINT
VALENTINE'S DAY*: Emendations consequent upon the disclosure
of Scott's authorship in 1827; Verbal emendations; Capitalisation and
Punctuation; Emendations from the Interleaved Copy and the Magnum;
Conclusion.

The following conventions are used in transcriptions from Scott's
manuscript and proofs: deletions are enclosed ⟨thus⟩ and insertions
↑thus↓; superscript letters are lowered without comment. The same
conventions are used as appropriate for indicating variants between the
printed editions.

1. THE GENESIS OF *SAINT VALENTINE'S DAY*

Saint Valentine's Day; or, The Fair Maid of Perth was written and published between December 1827 and May 1828. However, Scott had
long been familiar with the core material out of which much of the
novel's plot, action, and characterisation grew. Towards the end of
Volume 2 of *Rob Roy* (1818), Bailie Nicol Jarvie, in conversation with
Frank Osbaldistone, explains that Rob Roy's allegiance, in the event of a
Jacobite rising, would be uncertain. 'The truth is', he concludes, 'that
Rob is for his ain hand, as Henry Wynd feught—He'll take the side that
suits him best'.[1] Henry Wynd is of course the Smith of the Wynd of the
later novel; Henry Adamson in *The Muses Threnodie* (1638)—one of
Scott's major sources for the novel—has Henry say 'I'm for mine owne
hand' (The First Muse),[2] and by the nineteenth century the phrase had
become proverbial. What is significant is that Scott could remember and
call upon such a detail as a colourful way of defining Rob Roy's attitude
and stance. Such recall suggests that Scott was well acquainted with the
traditional account of the clan battle on the Perth Inch in 1396—and
with the stories and legends that had quickly developed around it (see
the Historical Note, 454). However, it was a winding path that eventually led to the creation of a novel centred on Henry Smith and the clan
battle.

The earliest discussions of a work to follow *Chronicles of the Canongate*, First Series, seem to have been on 2 August 1827 in a meeting
between Robert Cadell and James Ballantyne. Cadell, formerly a partner in the business of Archibald Constable and Co. whose failure in
1826 was the proximate cause of Scott's own, was attempting to re-
establish himself as a publisher, and specifically as Scott's publisher.

James Ballantyne had been Scott's partner in the printing business of James Ballantyne and Co.; it too failed in 1826 but had been continued by Scott and Ballantyne's trustees because it was considered a viable business, and because, as is explained in the General Introduction, it was an essential part of the system that had evolved for the creation and production of Scott's novels. On 2 August Cadell recorded in his diary that Ballantyne thought that Scott's next work should be 'a continuation of Quentin Durward'; he remarked 'I approve of this',[3] and wrote the same day to Scott:

> I have just had a conversation with Mr Ballantyne as to your future plans after the Chronicles [First Series] and the above little book [Tales of a Grandfather], and have no hesitation in stating that a three volume Novel would be well received after these, and I think were you to continue so popular a theme as Lewis eleventh, and Quentin Durward, it could not fail to be popular. . . . After Quentin No. 2, or let me say Lewis XIth, a second Series of the Chronicles might follow if the good public like the first two volumes.[4]

Scott's immediate response was to ask for books on Switzerland; in other words Cadell's letter starts off ideas which were later to issue in *Anne of Geierstein*.[5] Later in August Cadell proposed a third volume for the two-volume *Chronicles* that Scott was just finishing.[6] But Scott, and John Gibson, the chairman of Scott's trustees, objected on the grounds that it could be held that a three-volume work belonged to the creditors of Archibald Constable and Co., as before his insolvency Scott had been under contract to write future works for Constable, and until that issue had been resolved by Lord Newton, the arbiter appointed for the task, nothing should be done which would allow Alexander Cowan, Constable's trustee, to claim the profits of *Chronicles*.[7] Scott instead suggested a second series of *Chronicles of the Canongate*, writing:

> I have as many small pieces as I think would make one or even two volumes of the Chronicles. Should it be thought advisable they may be printed as Second Series of the Chronicles & place such an interval betwixt them and the first series as would make them inaccessible to the Cormorant Cowan.[8]

Scott repeated the suggestion to Cadell in a letter of 10 September.[9] On 19 October he was writing 'We must now think of the Continuation of the Chronicles as I am ready to go on directly'[10] and on 26 October said 'I will begin the Chronicles immediately'.[11] By 28 November four sheets (64 pages) were in type.[12]

The crucial event which released Scott's creative energies was Lord Newton's decision on 27 October that the profits from the novel *Woodstock* which had been published in 1826, and from *The Life of Napoleon Buonaparte* which had been published earlier in 1827, belonged to Scott's trustees, and not to Constable's. Scott was now free to write three-volume novels once more without fear of their being claimed by

Alexander Cowan. By 19 November he informed Gibson that he was 'ready to go to press with 2d Series of Chronicles',[13] and suggested that he, Gibson, make a bargain with Cadell for the publication of a three-volume work. He also proposed that the profits from the new work be applied to the purchase of a half-share of the copyrights of earlier Waverley Novels which were owned by Constable's trustees, and which were to be auctioned on 20 December on behalf of Constable's creditors. Thus what would eventually be *Saint Valentine's Day* became the means of securing all the copyrights, and facilitated the production of the Magnum Opus. On 29 November Gibson and Cadell agreed on £4200 for 8500 copies.[14]

Although the contract was an agreement for a three-volume work, Scott was still thinking of a miscellany, a group of stories rather than a single work. The material which he had 'ready to go to press' and which probably consisted of a long introduction in the style of the Croftangry narrative which opens the *Chronicles of the Canongate*, First Series, went to James Ballantyne on 22 November.[15] And in the *Journal* entry for 3 December Scott records 'Finishd my tale of the Mirror'.[16] (Entitled 'My Aunt Margaret's Mirror' the story would eventually be published in *The Keepsake*.)

What was to come next, however, still remained uncertain, as the entry for the following day, 4 December, makes clear: 'I feel a little puzzled about the character and stile of the next tale. The world has had so much of chivalry.'[17] Does he mean from himself? The notion that the reading public had been exposed to a surfeit of works on the theme of chivalry was one that had been concerning Scott for quite some time. In fact his most recent work, the First Series of *Chronicles*, had not been about chivalry. But a *Journal* entry for 17 October 1826 had recognised Harrison Ainsworth's *Sir John Chiverton* (1826) as a tale of chivalry and, like Horace Smith's *Brambletye House* (1826) about the English Civil War, a work written in clear imitation of his own historical novels.[18] Scott could equally have in mind a work such as Kenelm Digby's *The Broadstone of Honour*, first published in 1822, but reissued in an expanded form in 1826–27, a kind of handbook on the rules of chivalry for English gentlemen. In any event, he leaves the topic with a final enigmatic comment: 'yet scarce a good sum yet'—which might seem to imply that there is room for more consideration of chivalry in some aspects at least. Next morning, 5 December, Scott resolved that his 'new tale'—the use of the term 'tale' probably indicates that he is still thinking in terms of a short story—would concern Harry Wynd.[19]

What is equally clear is that on that December morning Scott was aware his decision to work on the story of Harry Wynd might not please his associates Ballantyne and Cadell. Ballantyne's criticisms of his recent work were certainly in his mind, and he may even have known that Ballantyne was unhappy about the material already written for the

Second Series. Within a week, on 11 December, he would receive a letter from Cadell, passed on by Ballantyne, which, according to the *Journal*, pointed to the only moderate success of the first series of *Chronicles of the Canongate*, and confirmed that the material already written for the Second Series was in their view unsatisfactory. Ballantyne seems always to have urged the view that Scott would be best advised to go on giving the public more of what it had already so clearly liked: as Scott put it in the *Journal* on 8 July 1826, when he was writing the first series of *Chronicles*, 'J. B. roars for chivalry'.[20] But Scott himself disagreed. As the same *Journal* entry says, he felt that Ballantyne 'does not quite understand that everything may be overdone in this world or sufficiently estimate the necessity of novelty'. Hence whatever Ballantyne's view, Scott is confident he has done well with 'The Highland Widow', particularly since—as he puts it—'The highlanders have been off the field now for some time'.[21]

Ballantyne, chivalry, Highlanders—all of these may well have been floating in and out of Scott's consciousness as he sat at his desk that morning in early December 1827. And resolving that the way forward was 'to make some thing out of the story of Harry Wynd', he was certainly imagining a story whose themes would include both Highlanders and chivalry—even if in other respects he was not prepared to accommodate Ballantyne's views. His first thought was that the work might be entitled 'The North Inch of Perth' (where the clan battle took place) and that the material would enable him 'to take a difference betwixt the old highlander and him of modern date'.[22] But in fact no theme of contrasting old and new Highlanders would appear in *Saint Valentine's Day*. What does appear is the topic to which that morning Scott's attention swiftly moved. It is 'the fellow that swam the Tay and escaped' who intrigues him. Such a figure 'would be a good ludicrous character', but that is not the way he sees it. Rather, he writes, 'I have a mind to try him in the serious line of tragedy'. For Scott a possible picture is already becoming clear: 'Suppose a man's nerves supported by feelings of honour or say by the spur of jealousy supporting him against constitutional timidity to a certain point then suddenly giving way—I think some thing tragic might be produced'. Conachar of the novel is already instantly recognisable in this description—down to the moment of the sudden failure of nerve, though it is fear of his jealous rival that finally precipitates his flight. None the less, at this time Scott is still all too aware of Ballantyne's potential disagreement: 'James Ballantyne's criticism is too much moulded upon the general tast[e] of novels to admit (I fear) this species of reasoning'. Ballantyne, Scott is sure, will not be happy about a story with a tragic action—but he decides to go ahead all the same: 'But what can one do? I am hard up as far as imagination is concernd yet the world calls for Novelty. Well—I'll try my brave coward or cowardly brave man.'[23]

Scott is struggling here to balance his need to attend to the demands of the reading-public—as mediated by James Ballantyne—and the direction in which his own creative imagination appears to be leading. But significantly it is the latter that seems to be taking control. The *Journal* tells us he remained at home that morning 'adjusting my ideas on this point untill one o'clock'; but further consideration clearly served only to confirm his original decision. *Saint Valentine's Day* will concern the 'brave coward or cowardly brave man' and will move towards 'the serious line of tragedy'.

2. THE COMPOSITION OF *SAINT VALENTINE'S DAY*

Two days later, Friday 7 December 1827, Scott wrote four leaves of his new tale but, as he put it, 'not very freely or happily. I was not in the vein.' He reminds himself that he does his best work when he has more than one book in his mind at the same time so as to prevent his 'thoughts from wandering and so give the deeper current the power to flow undisturbd'.[24] But on Sunday the 9th he had a good day: 'I set hard to work and had a long day with my new tale. I did about twelve leaves.'[25] Two days later, Tuesday 11 December, he reports writing a little, 'and seemd to myself to get on'.[26] But it was later that day, after returning from court, that he received the bombshell letter from Cadell and Ballantyne expressing dissatisfaction both with the sales of the first series of *Chronicles* and with the material proposed for the second.

Scott had completed two stories for the new *Chronicles* (probably 'The Tapestried Chamber', and 'My Aunt Margaret's Mirror' which he finished on 3 December, in addition to Croftangry's Narrative of four sheets, 64 pages). On 3 December Cadell had a 'long talk'[27] with Ballantyne about *Chronicles*, Second Series; it is probable that by then they had read and were considering the proofs of the four sheets which had been sent to the printers on 22 November and had been set by the 28th. They met again on 10 December,[28] after which they seem to have written to Scott who received the letter on his return from court on the 11th. Scott wrote in his *Journal*: 'It seems Mr. Cadell is dissatisfied with the moderate success of the 1st Series of *Chronicles* and disapproving of about half the volume already written of the second Series'. Scott responded by return. In one sense he seems to have accepted their judgement, seeing in Ballantyne and Cadell 'tolerable good representatives of the popular taste'. But in his reply he argued that he had never imagined his 'favour with the public could last for ever', insisting that he was 'neither shockd nor alarmd to find that it had ceased now as cease it must one day soon'. He offered to discontinue the arrangement for a Second Series of *Chronicles of the Canongate*, and proposed that he should take a rest from writing, 'lying lea for a little while taking a fallow-break to reli[e]ve my Imagination which may be esteemd nearly cropd out'.[29] Scott sounds robust and resilient here, and in a letter to

Ballantyne next day (12 December) he appears to repeat both notions of abandoning his current commitment to a Second Series, and of taking a break from writing.[30] But the next *Journal* entry makes it clear just how worried and concerned he is. He tells himself that he is largely indifferent to the 'probable downfal[l]' of his 'literary reputation'—having '*had the crown*', he does not much care losing it.[31] On the other hand, given the state of his financial affairs, this would be a bad time to give up writing. The answer he seems to be contemplating is to give up 'the losing game of novel writing', and to move in new (undefined) directions 'which may promise novelty at the least'.[32]

This would appear to be the proposal Scott put to Ballantyne and Cadell later that day. They were horrified. Clearly they had never imagined that Scott would consider, even temporarily, abandoning the writing of fiction. Cadell and Ballantyne conferred again on 12 December, and in the evening, according to Cadell's diary, they went to see Scott: 'Ballantyne called about 7 in his gig, drove to W Scotts & had a long conversation about leaving out the two short Tales in Chron: 2d Series'.[33] Or, as Scott puts it in the *Journal* these 'two learned Thebans are arrived and departed after a long consultation'.[34] In fact Scott had out-manoeuvred them: the critics clearly found themselves begging the writer to continue his work.

Both Cadell and Ballantyne were in a weak position. Cadell was an undischarged bankrupt, and the publishing business he was re-establishing and which bore his name was nominally owned by his brother-in-law, George William Mylne. Mylne had advertised in the *Edinburgh Evening Courant* of 2 November 1826 that he had purchased Constable's stock and that the business, to be known as Cadell and Co., was to be managed by Robert Cadell. In fact the business was four-fifths owned by his brother, Hew Francis Cadell. Robert Cadell wished to bid in concert with Scott's trustees for the Scott copyrights at the auction later in the month, using the anticipated profits from the new novel to fund the purchase. Thus Scott's productive capacity was essential to the rehabilitation of Robert Cadell. James Ballantyne was now less dependent on Scott's success, but even so the business which he now only managed needed Scott and his works. A Scott sabbatical would have wrecked the hopes of both. By now Ballantyne and Cadell had read the opening leaves of *Saint Valentine's Day*, and Scott agreed to continue with it, while attending in turn to their criticisms: 'we resolved the present work should go on, leaving out some parts of the introduction which they object to'.[35]

Next day, 13 December, Scott was sure they had made the right decision: 'Having turnd over my thoughts with some anxiety about the important subject of yesterday I think we have done for the best.'[36] He recalls what happened with the *Tales of the Crusaders* (1825), when the relative failure of *The Betrothed* had been more than compensated for by the success of *The Talisman*, and decides that the Second Series of *Chronicles* (which now would consist only of the 'present work',[37] i.e. Croftangry's Narrative and *Saint Valentine's Day*) gives him the chance to pull it off again. Two days later Scott is back at work on the opening section of the new novel, to parts of which Ballantyne and Cadell had objected, and has got as far as the opening of what he calls 'the Tale of *Saint Valentine's Eve*'—'a good title by the way', he adds.[38] By Monday 17 December he is in a position to send off to Ballantyne what he calls 'the beginning of the *Chronicles*'—the revised, and no doubt abbreviated, Chrystal Croftangry chapter with which the novel begins.[39]

With Christmas at Abbotsford fast approaching, Scott seems at this point to have set the new work aside. In the next three weeks the *Journal* suggests that his professional activities were confined to planning the buying up of copyrights so that the Magnum Opus edition could go forward, and to working on several other literary projects. He also had company at Abbotsford, and had a good time; as he puts it in a letter, 'The *daft days* have occupied more of my time than usual'.[40] Scott returned to Edinburgh on 13 January and work resumed on the *Chronicles*. For a time all went smoothly: within three weeks the first volume was complete, the only hiccup occurring early in February when Scott notes a day on which he 'did not get two pages finishd' because there was a 'mist on my mind which my exertions could not dispel'.[41] As to the quality of his work, he is less than sanguine. On 5 February, the day the first volume was completed, he announces himself 'but indifferently pleased', adding 'Either the kind of thing is worn out or I am worn out myself or, lastly, I am stupid for the time'.[42] 'Stupid' or not, however, Scott was not prepared to entertain misguided criticism from the Ballantyne-Cadell quarter. A letter to James Ballantyne on 7 February rejects out of hand criticism of the chronology of events towards the end of Volume I involving Louise the glee-woman, and her sleeping arrangements: 'I think you are hypercritical in your commentary. I counted the time with accuracy.'[43] (Once again it appears that Scott did not write quite so casually as he was self-deprecatingly inclined to pretend.) On 12 February he wrote in his *Journal*: 'Ballantyne blames the Ossianick monotony of my principal characters', but, significantly, he added: 'Now they are not Ossianick'.[44] What is in question is the language of Chivalry—which may indeed be monotonous. Scott clearly enjoys turning the tables on poor Ballantyne: Ballantyne it is who has called for more in the chivalry vein, while Scott has warned of the dangers of repetition. He repeats the point in his letter: 'There are some subjects which will not bear repeated painting & these of chivalry though brilliant for once are of this kind'.[45] Scott is clearly unwilling to allow either Ballantyne or Cadell to dictate to him in aesthetic areas. On the same day Ballantyne did receive a kind of apology for the dismissal of his opinion, 'Remember I never mean to repress criticism though I may not always comply where you boggle',[46] but even the apology registers disagreement between the artist and the men he saw as 'good specimens of the public taste'.[47]

Volume 2 was underway by Thursday 7 February.[48] Once again the writing appears to have moved forward with extraordinary speed. On one day, Monday 11 February, Scott completed six pages, the equivalent, he calculated, of 25 pages of print 'or about the 13th part of a volume'. Such output would mean 'a volume in a fortnight with a holiday to boot'.[49] On the next day he completed four pages, despite having to spend part of the day in court. Then on Tuesday 19 February, he hit an all-time high: after a day 'of hard and continued work', no fewer than eight manuscript pages, 'equal to forty printed pages of the Novels'.[50] But even Scott concedes that such a performance 'may be accounted the maximum of my literary labour'. By Wednesday 20 February, Volume 2 was almost complete: it 'may be concluded with the week or run over to Sunday at most'.[51]

In fact it took exactly one week longer. Scott suddenly found himself in trouble. There were too many plot lines in his story; he needed to find a way of bringing them together, but for a day or two none suggested itself. On Thursday 21 February he wrote in the *Journal*: 'I am watching and waiting till I hit on some quaint and clever mode of extricating but do not see a glimpse of any one'.[52] On Friday and Saturday he worked on 'proof sheets galore', and remained unmoved by Ballantyne's 'outrageous' reaction to the death of Oliver Proudfute; 'I have a humour to be cruel', he notes.[53] But no progress was made with *Saint Valentine's Day*. No progress, that is, until the morning of Sunday 24 February, when inspiration (Scott's word) struck. 'For this two or three days', he tells us, 'I have been at what the *Critic* calls a deadlock—all my incidents and personages run into a gordian knot of confusion to which I could devize no possible extrication.'[54] Scott is underlining again that his problem is with the lack of links between the different strands of his story. As we have seen, the *donnée* of the novel involved Henry Smith, the clan battle, and the hero who turns out to be a coward; the romantic involvement of the Fair Maid with both Henry and Conachar has also been there from the beginning. So the chances are that the problem lay with the involvement of the historical characters: King Robert III, Albany, Douglas, and Rothsay. How were the lives of the 'historical' characters to become integrated with the lives of the 'romantic' ones? Overnight— and probably helped, Scott tells us, by an extra glass of wine the evening before—he has come up, as he implies he has done on previous occasions, with the way 'in which the plot might be extricated'. His conscious mind that is, has struggled unavailingly to solve the problem, but his subconscious has come to the rescue:

> I had thought on the subject several days with some[thing] like the
> despair which seized the fair princess commanded by her ugly

step-mother to assort a whole garret full of tangled silk threads of every kind and colour when in comes prince Percinet with wand, whisks it over the miscellaneous mass, and lo! all the threads are as nicely arranged as in a seamstresses housewife.[55]

Scott's *Journal* entry does not even hint at the nature of the magical solution to his problem conjured up by prince Percinet, but the temptation to speculate is irresistible. All of Scott's comments imply that some major decision is in question here: he does not seem to be talking about a minor piece of plotting such as, say, planting a Ramorny spy in Kinfauns Castle. His repeated resort to imagery of a gordian knot and tangled silk threads (they will subsequently become 'strands of rope') makes it certain that his difficulty did indeed lie with combining what we have seen are the three separate interests of the developing novel: the clan fight and Conachar's cowardice; the love story of Henry and Catherine; and the involvement of Rothsay and other historical characters. Our proposal is that it is only at this late stage that Scott realises that what he must do to bring together these different story lines is to abandon strict historical chronology and make Rothsay's murder coincide with the clan battle. This gives an effective double climax to the novel; provides an active role for Catherine and Louise; strengthens the symmetry between the stories of Conachar and Rothsay; and reinforces Rothsay's role as central to the narrative action. The rescue of Bonthron from the gallows, which has no other plot necessity than that he should be the character to confront Rothsay with his doom, might reasonably be seen as a 'quaint and clever mode of extricating'. Again it may be significant that the first chapter of Volume 3, which presents this scene, opens (257) with the elaborated, Fieldingesque images of narrative as key and lock, watch and town-clock, while the first sentence of the chapter that marks the novel's final movement (314) signals with some emphasis the switch of focus to the fate of Rothsay.

In any event, the solution Scott had come up with—whatever it was— pleased him greatly. The final sentence of the *Journal* entry for Sunday 24 February goes as follows: 'So now this hitch bein[g] over I fold my paper, lock up my Journal and proceed to labour with good hope.'[56] In the week that followed, working to what he described as 'the new model',[57] Scott made steady progress with Volume 2, which was finally completed on Sunday 2 March. The relevant *Journal* entry does not, however, express any sense of satisfaction: 'I am not much pleased with it', he writes; 'It wants what I desire it to have, and that is passion'.[58] None the less, by 8 March in the middle of the following week the writing of Volume 3 is underway. This time there appear to be no serious hitches, and progress is made at a more or less steady rate. On Sunday 16 March he records three days of writing interrupted only by meals, exercise and rest: if such a pattern could be maintained, then, as he had noted earlier, a volume could be completed in twelve days, though as he says, 'no brain could hold it out longer'.[59] By Thursday 20 March the end is in sight: less than a quarter of the final volume remains to be written—about four days' work. On the question of the quality of what he is producing, Scott appears to remain uneasy. (The responses from Ballantyne and Cadell were apparently contradictory. Ballantyne unimpressed, but Cadell 'equall[y] uppish'.)[60] On Thursday 27 March, working on the closing pages, he returns to the notion that the different strands of his story are not sufficiently interwoven: 'My story has unhappily a divided interest. There are three distinct strands of the rope and they are not well twisted together.'[61] Many readers will probably feel that Scott is being unduly severe on himself here: at the level of image, theme, and even action, the parallels and connections between the Henry-Catherine, Conachar, and Rothsay, plot-lines, and what they involve, may well emerge as aesthetically and imaginatively satisfying. The different 'interests' enhance rather than divide. Of course one recalls that, throughout his career, Scott had accused himself of being poor at plots and plotting—most famously, perhaps, in the Introductory Epistle to *The Fortunes of Nigel*;[62] so the issue becomes one of definition: what did he understand by the term 'plot'? One suspects he took the term in the narrowest of possible meanings, that suggested perhaps by Coleridge's recognition of the plot of *Tom Jones* as one of the three most perfect in the world.[63] Clearly *Saint Valentine's Day* lacks any such Fielding-like interconnectedness of every detail of action and event, and this might then explain Scott's own reservations. In any event, Volume 3 was completed on the morning of Saturday 29 March, and given that a three-volume novel had been written in a little over three months, one can hardly disagree with Scott when he comes to the conclusion: 'I have let no grass grow beneath my heels this bout'.[64]

In fact Scott's brief note of self-congratulation seriously understates his achievement in the sense that, in the three months in question, the writing of the novel, as has been indicated, in no way received his undivided attention. Scott was simultaneously engaged in producing two extremely long reviews for the *Quarterly Review* and the *Foreign Quarterly Review*—his review of Sir Henry Steuart's *The Planter's Guide* for the *Quarterly* of March 1828 runs to 74 pages in Volume 21 of his *Prose Works*, while the review article on a *Life of Molière* for the 1828 *Foreign Quarterly* fills 78 pages in Volume 17 of the same edition. Another major task undertaken in the same period was the revision and expansion of *Tales of My Grandfather*. The *Journal* entry for 7 January 1828, tells us that 'great additions'[65] have been made to Volumes 1 and 2, and the completion of this process of revision seems to have more or less coincided with the writing of the concluding section of *Saint Valentine's Day*. On Sunday 23 March he writes:

> With my usual delight in catching an apology for escaping the regular task of the day I threw by the novel of *Saint Valentine's Eve*

and began to run through and correct the Grandfather's tales for the press.[66]

Then again odd hours in January 1828, and later, were occupied by consideration of revisions of the *Life of Napoleon*, correcting the proofs of two sermons which he had reluctantly allowed his young friend George Huntly Gordon to publish in order to pay off his debts, writing a memoir of George Bannatyne for Bannatyne Club publication number 33, and supplying Cadell with notes on *Guy Mannering* for the Magnum Opus edition. The relentlessness of such literary activity is almost beyond belief: it comes almost as a surprise that on 13 December 1827 Scott turned down an offer to write a life of Garrick,[67] and that the volume on landscape gardening he is considering never got written.[68] Amazingly, in these three months, *Saint Valentine's Day; or, The Fair Maid of Perth*, did.

The Manuscript. Much of the manuscript of *Chronicles of the Canongate*, Second Series, exists in a volume in the National Library of Scotland[69] bound in with the first series of *Chronicles of the Canongate*. At the beginning of the volume, on a binder's leaf, is written:

> This, the Original Manuscript of Chronicles of the Canongate, FIRST and SECOND Series. I received as a gift from Sir Walter Scott at Abbotsford on 9th April 1831. Rob Cadell 1834

The portion containing *Saint Valentine's Day*, however, is not complete. The surviving manuscript begins at folio 9 (p. 26 in this edition). The rest of Volume 1 is complete except that folio 54 (101–02) is missing. Volume 2 is complete except for folio 57 (237–39). Volume 3, however, has large gaps: folios 10–15 (273–85) are missing from the NLS volume though in fact folio 12 (277–78) survives in two sections, one held in the Houghton Library of Harvard University, the other in the Kelvingrove Art Gallery in Glasgow. The manuscript ends with folio 47 which means that the final four and a half chapters of the novel are missing.

Manuscript to First Edition. In February 1827 Scott had publicly acknowledged his authorship of the Waverley Novels. The announcement had a significant impact upon the means of production of the subsequent novels. Secrecy being no longer an issue, the need to copy Scott's manuscripts before their delivery to the printer ceased. Thus much of the *Chronicles of the Canongate*, First Series, and all of the Second Series, went direct to Ballantyne's Printing Office, and was used as printer's copy. The manuscripts of all the novels written before *Chronicles of the Canongate* are clean; there are a few copy-editing insertions in manuscripts of *Guy Mannering* and *The Antiquary*, but it is obvious from their condition that none had previously been used in the

Printing Office. However, most of the manuscript of *Chronicles of the Canongate*, from folio 21 of 'The Highland Widow' and through the whole of *Saint Valentine's Day*, was used as printer's copy; all the leaves are marked by dirty and inky finger prints and many have been much handled. As some look as though they have been handled by several people, it is possible that the compositors collectively deciphered the difficult bits.

The import of this change is clear. Scott, his copyists, his amanuenses and his printer were well known to each other; John and James Ballantyne, George Huntly Gordon and William Laidlaw could all check with Scott what he had written. The compositors in the Printing Office were not in such a happy position. Less familiar with Scott's handwriting, and not personally close to Scott, they had to do the best they could, without the aid of any kind of copy-editing, with the pages of manuscript that were delivered to them. After their primary task was complete, the processes followed the established pattern. The first proofs were read in-house, but against the manuscript rather than the transcripts. The type was corrected, and new proofs pulled. These were read and probably annotated as before by James Ballantyne; references to Ballantyne's interventions in both the *Journal* and the letters already cited make this clear. The annotated proofs went to Scott. It is probable that when they were returned Ballantyne saw no need to transcribe corrections on to a clean set of proofs, and so proofs with both Scott's and Ballantyne's corrections, and their comments to each other, were, very likely, returned to the compositors. Cadell, however, constitutes a new factor; his diaries confirm that he too was reading the sheets of *Saint Valentine's Day* as they were printed, but the dates on which he records this activity imply that he was reading post-authorial proofs.[70] There was thus a new layer of 'correcting'.

However, the key point is that the initial transfer of Scott's handwriting to print must have been done by men with only limited experience of his hand. Their task was a difficult one. The manuscript of *Saint Valentine's Day* is not an easy read. Each page is very closely written with about fifty lines squeezed in. Except on the left hand margin the writing runs right up to the edge of the page. Indeed Scott often seems to squeeze and reduce a final word rather than begin a new line. The writing is fluent and many lines run on without any corrections, or only of the most minor kind. Most of these corrections were made as Scott wrote, but some were made a little later, perhaps when he resumed writing after a break, and read over what he had last written. Most involve no more than a single word or phrase: changes of mind about word choice, to avoid repetition, or to modify an initial thought or intention. Occasional longer additions or re-writings are entered on the preceding verso and their place in the text indicated by a caret. There is no evidence that Scott looked at or consulted the manuscript after he had passed over the latest batch to Ballantyne for entry into the printing process.

Paragraphing, and punctuation in general, are at a minimum in the manuscript pages. Occasionally Scott writes NL (new line) to indicate the start of a new paragraph; but direct speech or dialogue is never indicated by the indentation customary in print. Full-stops or tiny dashes appear at the end of most sentences but the use of a capital letter is sometimes the only indication that the previous sentence has ended and a new one begun. Easily the most common punctuation mark is the dash (used with a range of meanings), though direct speech is usually indicated by inverted commas. Commas themselves appear only on the rarest of occasions. Spelling is in line with Scott's normal practice with, for example, the 'e' being elided from the 'ed' verb ending unless required for pronunciation in words like 'defended' or 'retired'. The cramped script frequently makes it extremely difficult to distinguish individual letters: often it is the requirements of sense alone that allow one to distinguish between 'm', 'n', 'i', and 'e', or a double 'ee' and 'u'. All in all, the reading and setting of this manuscript must have been a difficult and demanding task for the compositors in Ballantyne's Printing Office.

The manuscripts also provide some evidence about procedures, and about the syncopation of authorial and printing composition, for the printers put large marks (like square parentheses) in ink on the manuscript to indicate precise page-breaks, and numbers either in left margin or in the text to identify the first page of a new gathering. These must have been inserted after the compositors had set the type (no one estimating extents could have regularly got the exact word on which a gathering would end), and must have signalled where the compositor was to resume, or where the proof-reader was to start.

Over the first volume of the novel the marks in the text correspond *exactly* with page breaks except on three occasions when the marks are a short phrase out. The second volume is more informative both about the author's and compositors' practice. Page 33 is marked on folio 7, and it corresponds exactly with the division between pages 32 and 33 in the first edition; thereafter there is a slight divergence as Scott inserted extra material in the proofs until the marked break for page 145 (f. 28) which actually comes at 146.10 in the first edition. There is neither number nor mark for page 161, but the mark on folio 35 indicating page 177 coincides exactly with the break between 176 and 177 of the first edition. For the next four gatherings the marked breaks more or less correspond to the breaks between the gatherings in the first edition, but thereafter the breaks indicated in the manuscript get increasingly far away from the actual division between gatherings in the first edition: the break indicating page 321 (f. 63) comes at 324.4 in the first edition. It appears, then, that the compositors incorporated Scott's proof corrections for the first half of Volume 2 before setting the second half of the volume, thus saving themselves the need to repaginate the whole novel, and at the same time allowing themselves to be guided by the authorial corrections in the first half of the volume as to how they should prepare Scott's text for print in the second.

Scott finished the third volume of *Saint Valentine's Day* on the morning of 29 March, and he left for London on 3 April. Proofs followed him there, and by 18 April things had moved forward so far that Cadell was able to hazard 15 May as the publication day,[71] a date he confirmed in his diary on 26 April.[72] One thousand copies were sent to Simpkin and Marshall in London on 3 May, and a further 5000 by steam-boat on the 9th.[73] The date of publication was 15 May 1828 (although copies may have been available the day before), and the price £1 11s. 6d.; among those who received presentation copies were George IV and the Duke of Wellington.

3 . THE LATER EDITIONS

Only two later editions were prepared in Scott's lifetime, a 'second edition' which came out in June 1828, and Volumes 42 and 43 of the Magnum Opus which appeared in November and December 1832.

The Second Edition. When *Chronicles of the Canongate*, Second Series, was published on 15 May 1828 Scott was in London. He returned to Edinburgh at the beginning of June, and had breakfast with Cadell on 5 June. On 6 June Cadell wrote to Simpkin and Marshall apparently instructing that they take orders for a 'second edition' from the trade on 18 June (and not before), and issue this 'new edition' on 20 June.[74] He advertised the second edition of *Saint Valentine's Day* in the *Edinburgh Evening Courant* on 7 June. He wrote again to Simpkin and Marshall on 10 June, sent them 1500 new title pages, and instructed that if the trade complained about the too rapid publication of a second edition 'you will not hesitate to take back the first, and give second editions'.[75] In fact this was not a new edition at all but a reissue; Cadell's purpose was to give the novel a new identity, a purpose which Simpkin and Marshall did not seem to understand, for on 13 June he wrote once more explaining (with some irritation) 'it is the name of the Novel which is wished to be more prominent . . . all cry out make St Valentine's Day the prominent title'.[76] Who 'all' were, whether author, publishers, reviewers, or purchasers, is not stated, but Cadell clearly wanted to retitle the novel, and to force Simpkin and Marshall into compliance with his instructions (which they did only on 30 June). The sole difference between the first edition and the so-called second is in the new title page which effectively renames the novel; whereas the title page of the first edition reads 'CHRONICLES OF THE CANONGATE. 𝕾𝖊𝖈𝖔𝖓𝖉 𝕾𝖊𝖗𝖎𝖊𝖘. BY THE AUTHOR OF "WAVERLEY," &C.', the title-page of the second reads 'ST VALENTINE'S DAY; OR, THE FAIR MAID

OF PERTH. BY THE AUTHOR OF "WAVERLEY," &C. forming the
𝕾𝖊𝖈𝖔𝖓𝖉 𝕾𝖊𝖗𝖎𝖊𝖘 OF CHRONICLES OF THE CANONGATE.'. The
rest of the 'second' edition consists of sheets from the same settings of
type as the first.

The Interleaved Copy and the Magnum. To facilitate the preparation of the Magnum Opus (1829–33), Scott's publishers took down
sets of the octavo versions of the collected editions, and interleaved
them with blank paper.[77] However, the four works of fiction published
between 1827 and 1831 did not appear in collected editions during
Scott's lifetime, and so when in a letter of 23 April 1830 Scott asked
Cadell for interleaved copies of 'Anne of Geierstein and Chronicles of
Canongate',[78] Cadell used first editions for the purpose. In fact for *Saint
Valentine's Day* it was the three volumes of the nominal second edition
which were interleaved, and sent to Scott on 6 May.[79] Probably because
they were not uniform with the other volumes, they do not form part of
the Interleaved Set in the National Library of Scotland, but, according
to a pencilled note in the first volume, were sold by Cadell's widow
'about the year 1850', and are now in the University of Texas Library in
Austin.[80]

Although the provenance is different, Scott's procedures were essentially the same: as he went through his novel he used the interleaves, and
the margins surrounding the text, for correcting errors, revising the text,
and adding notes. But *Saint Valentine's Day* differs from the works in the
Interleaved Set in that most of the annotation was done by Scott's son-
in-law, John Gibson Lockhart. On 17 or 18 April 1831 Scott had
suffered a stroke. After a week he had begun to write up his *Journal* once
more, but it is clear that there was some paralysis which affected his
handwriting, and that he continued to be very ill. In July he agreed to
winter in the Mediterranean for the sake of his health, but he had first to
complete his work on the Magnum Opus: the corrections, notes and
introduction to *Saint Valentine's Day* were probably written in July or
August 1831. 'Aug. 1831' is the date attached to Lockhart's rewritten
version of the personal note in which Scott hopes to make good the
implied boast in the opening motto of the story, 'But where's the Scot
that would the vaunt repay,/ And hail the puny Tiber for the Tay?':

> Such is the authors opinion founded perhaps on national pride of
> the relative importance of the Roman & the classical stream If he
> should again be a blotter of paper the Editor hopes to be able to
> speak on this subject the surer language of personal conviction
> (ICopy, 1.23)

In August 1831 Lockhart went over Scott's work. He deleted some of
what Scott had written, and at times refashioned Scott's material. He
added most of the notes and all the new mottoes, and he also made a
number of textual changes. There are also some additions in other

hands which for the most part have not been identified, although it was James Ballantyne who took out of the text 'as both words equally indicated his profession', to form a new footnote: '*Gow* is Gaelic for *Smith*.' (ICopy, 1.49), and some of the examples of the word 'Note' at the head of a note seem to have been added by Daniel McCorkindale, Ballantyne's foreman (e.g. see ICopy, 3.106).

There are thus two main layers of correction and annotation: Scott's and Lockhart's. In all there are about 370 interventions in the Interleaved Copy: the addition of a comma or the addition of a note are alike counted as single interventions, and a Scott intervention deleted by Lockhart is reckoned as two, one Scott's and the other Lockhart's. Of the total of about 370, 146 are Scott's, 190 are Lockhart's (including 30 occasions on which he deletes or rewrites what Scott had written) and in 34 cases the hand is either another's or cannot be identified. However, Lockhart supplied the overwhelming bulk of new material for it was he who did the long notes and the mottoes.

The most important category of Scott's own changes in the Interleaved Copy is the correction of historical error. The first time the Duke of Rothsay is mentioned Scott alters 'Robin of Rothsay' to 'David of Rothsay' (ICopy, 1.298; EEWN, 113.43), and on 10 of the 20 times the change has to be made, Scott does it. He must have considered the correction of historical error to be necessary, for he carried it through even when it diminished rhetorical impact, as in his removing of the Christian name from the King's affectionate declaration 'Now are we three Robin Stewarts' (ICopy, 2.186; 198.38). Scott also deletes the misleading term the 'Black Douglas', and the first edition's confusion of the third and fourth earls of Douglas (see Historical Note, 465) is partly rectified, with the novel's Douglas being specified as 'Archibald earl of Douglas calld THE GRIM' (ICopy, 1.284; 108.29), although the nickname *Tine-Man* (which belonged to the fourth earl) was probably deleted by someone else (ICopy, 2.262; 227.32). The corrections extend to quotations: the second line of the couplet (ICopy, 1.21; 10.16–17) on geographers in Croftangry's Narrative is amended, but the lines are still attributed to Prior instead of Swift.

Scott adds little to the text, but much of what he does is distinctly effective. In Chrystal Croftangry's chapter the English businessman who tries to scrub away the mark left by Rizzio's blood is restrained from doing so, 'as two or three inhabitants appeard who like me threatend to bring main force to the housekeepers side of the question. He therefore took his leave'(ICopy, 1.9; 5.29). (Unfortunately the comic idea of an ancient stain provoking violence is lost for Lockhart deletes 'bring main force to' and substitutes 'maintain', and it is the Lockhart version that goes into the Magnum.) The insertion of 'connecting the highlands with the lowlands' (ICopy, 1.24; 11.23) helps indicate where the citation of Lady Mary Wortley Montagu has ended, although full clarification has to wait for the Magnum version. Catherine is a 'princess of *white* doe-skin' to balance 'blue silk' (ICopy, 1.42; 17.40); and, perhaps most effectively, when Douglas envisages firing Perth its 'insolent churls' are to be 'stifled . . . like *malicious* fox-cubs in a burning brake of furze' (ICopy, 2.10; 132.8). To the description of Oliver on horseback is added 'and as it is termd and as it is termd [*sic*] duck-leggd' (ICopy, 1.191; 74.10); but this did not make the Magnum, for Lockhart's sensitivity to anything coarse made him change the phrase to 'and what is vulgarly called duck-legged'. The address 'Sir Smith' in Rothsay's exchange with Henry neatly picks up the latter's rejection of the role of 'Sir Pandarus of Troy' (ICopy, 2.296; 113.20). The insertion of 'Grace's' may heighten Albany's courtly decorum (ICopy, 2.6; 130.29). Dwining adds a Latin tag-phrase *Super totam materiem* (ICopy, 2.281; 234.26) after 'mistaken'; Simon's estimation of honours bestowed by the city magistrates (ICopy, 2.326; 251.36–37) is expanded; and Scott writes in a song for Dwining as they approach Bonthron's gallows (ICopy, 3.12; 260.34).

In spite of his infirmities, Scott's eye was still observant, and he could deftly convert the weak word or phrase into something more telling. Catherine decides not to let a 'childish bashfullness' rather than 'childish fear' (ICopy, 1.126; 49.37) prevent her from kissing the sleeping Henry. March's treacherous irritation is more strongly voiced: 'My counsels here avail not—nay are so unfavourably received' as against the first edition's 'and those of others are so favourably received' (ICopy, 2.13; 133.3–4). Rothsay's casual 'how can I tell the men' is reworded as a more blatant denial: 'how can I, of all men, tell' (ICopy, 2.41; 143.38–39). Simon now thinks that Conachar 'seems likely to be' rather than 'will be' a brave man one day (ICopy, 3.58; 277.24–25). The priests who promise to care for the survivors and bury the slain of the combat 'redeemed their pledge faithfully and piously' rather than the first edition's vaguer 'faithfully and nobly' (ICopy, 3.325; 378.38–39). A few changes avoid either potential infelicities as when the hand 'you lost last' becomes 'you lost in Curfew Street' (ICopy, 2.279; 234.1), or correct first-edition absurdities—most strikingly when the deer who 'fled from their caves' (a misreading of the manuscript 'cover') now flee their 'glens' (ICopy, 3.84; 287.17), and again when the 'little man' who, in the first edition (by virtue of a misreading of the manuscript 'hopped') 'popped out from behind his target', now 'peeped out' (ICopy, 3.133; 305.28).

Of course, not all Scott's verbal changes succeed. A few insertions of the 'said so-and-so' variety, such as 'said Catharine' (ICopy, 1.40; 17.17), and 'replied the prince' (ICopy, 1.292; 111.39), although characteristic of Scott's practice in the Magnum, do not assist comprehension. Some alterations generate repetition, without there being clear rhetorical purpose as with the change of 'direct' to 'influence' (ICopy,

2.251; 223.11), or when Dwining binds up the infant's 'vein' rather than 'wound' (ICopy, 2.298; 241.27)—there is greater precision, but also a repetition. Some changes—predictably—seem neither for the better nor the worse: 'finding that they contained' for 'seeing' (ICopy, 1.6; 6.17); 'ban' for 'brand' (ICopy, 1.310; 118.18); and if 'flitted about' is arguably more vivid than 'fled' (ICopy, 2.16; 134.13), 'conveyed' for 'carried' is not only indifferent but also repetitious (ICopy, 3.325; 378.42).

Scott's changes mainly affect the text. He wrote only 14 notes in the Interleaved Copy, all of them brief as they mainly explicate phrases used in the novel: for instance in Volume 1 he defines the 'skene-occle' (ICopy, 1.62), 'jackmen' (ICopy, 1.78), 'horse and hattock' (ICopy, 1.179), 'cogan na schie' (ICopy, 1.197), 'thiggers and sorners' (ICopy, 1.193); and there is only one brief topographical, one historical and one personal note (quoted above).

Lockhart continues where Scott left off, but his input was considerably more extensive, and can significantly modify the text. He corrects the misnumbering caused by the two fourth chapters in Volume 1. He carries through the renaming of Rothsay. In the night-scene with Ramorny the text is finely amended to preserve the rhetorical run of the Prince's self-defining speech. Scott intended replacing 'Robert, fourth of his name' by 'David, third of his name'. Lockhart cancels the latter and between 'Should I ever fill the throne' and 'every Scots lad' he inserts 'I suppose like my father before me I must dropt my own name, & dubbed Robert in honour of the Bruce—well an' if it be so—' (ICopy, 2.160; 188.40); the historical correction is achieved without damaging the rhythm of the speech. Robert or Robert de Wardlaw becomes Henry Wardlaw (271.28), a change completed in the Magnum (92.13; 314.5); Clan Kay as an alternative to Clan Quhele disappears (134.6; 136.23; 279.4–5). The monks are summoned from their island convent, not convents (287.22). The slip which includes Rothsay among the illiterate nobility (130.13–14), and which is contradicted by Ramorny's later comment (315. 33–34), is gracefully adjusted.

Minor changes are made to existing epigraphs: 'Never to man shall Catharine give her hand' (53) is now assigned to *The Taming of the Shrew*, instead of '*Taming of a Shrew*'; 'The course of true love never did run smooth' (264) to Shakespeare. The misattribution of the epigraph for Volume 2, Chapter 9, to the Second Part of *Henry IV* rather than *Henry VI* (222) goes uncorrected; and the epigraph for the first chapter of *Saint Valentine's Day* (11) is not assigned to Anonymous until the Magnum. Twenty-one new epigraphs are added and provide the most pointed examples of Lockhart's shaping of Scott's text. An *Old Ballad* epigraph proposed by Scott for the second chapter is cancelled by Lockhart in favour of one from Dryden (13). The lines of the distracted Regent York in *Richard II* are shifted from Volume 1, Chapter 10 (95), to Chapter 9, highlighting the helplessness of Robert III on our first introduction to him; while a new epigraph to Chapter 10 signals Louise as its focal figure ('Gentle friend!/ Chide not her mirth, who was sad yesterday,/ And may be so tomorrow'). The jaunty *Old Ballad* heading ('Will you go the Hielands, Lizzy Lyndesay') to Volume 2, Chapter 2 (145), provides a sardonic counterpoint to Conachar's wooing. Pistol's 'Let gallows gape for dogs, let men go free' preludes Bonthron's taking down in Volume 3, Chapter 1 at 257 (the Interleaved Copy entry has 'dog' for 'dogs', corrected in the Magnum). *Childe Harold* supplies several of the new epigraphs. For the Highland feast in Volume 3, Chapter 5 (292), Lockhart first took a single line 'Kinder than polished slaves though not so bland' from the account of Albanian hospitality in the second Canto (stanza 68), then cancelled and replaced it with lines from Canto 3 on the medieval robber barons of the Rhine, which comment caustically on the valuations of history: 'What want these outlaws conquerors should have,/ But History's purchased page to call them great,/ A wider space, an ornamented grave?' (stanza 48). A new epigraph from *Richard II* for Rothsay's fate (Volume 3, Chapter 9; 334) strengthens the working of that play as one of the sub-texts for the novel. The penultimate chapter has a compassionate epigraph from Burns, 'Who made the heart, 'tis *He* alone/ Decidedly can try us', ('Address to the Unco Guid', stanza 8) which is then cancelled, leaving it without heading in the Magnum, while the cheerful Burns lines 'The honest heart that's free frae a'/ Intended fraud or guile,/ However Fortune kick the ba',/ Has aye some cause to smile.' ('Epistle to Davie', lines 35–38) that point up the happiness of Henry and Catherine rather than the tragedy of Conachar head the final chapter in the Magnum (382)

Lockhart's notes substantially expand Scott's own editorial activity. In all there are 94 notes in the Magnum version of *Saint Valentine's Day*: 21 appeared in the first edition, and two of these are expanded by Lockhart in the Interleaved Copy; 15 were written by Scott and of these five were rewritten by Lockhart; 36 were written by Lockhart himself; 21 appeared in the Magnum for the first time, and one was written by James Ballantyne.

Volume 1, Chapter 2, supplies a range of typical examples of footnoting. The glossing of Gow (20.27–29) on Henry's introduction is clarified slightly and removed by Ballantyne from text to footnote for the Magnum. Scott's first-edition footnote gloss on *Maker* (he had correctly written 'Makar' in the original manuscript) as 'Old Scottish for *Poet*' is swelled by Lockhart's addition of: '& indeed the literal translation of the original Greek Ποιητης' (ICopy, 1.53; 22.43). *Burn-the-wind* is glossed as 'an old cant term for Blacksmith' (ICopy, 1.57; 23.34) with a quotation from Burns; *skene-occle* is first defined by Scott as 'Knife of the armpit a species of dirk so calld used among highlanders', then redefined by Lockhart as 'knife of the armpit—the highlanders' stiletto'

(ICopy, 1.62; 26.1); and the glossing of *cateran* as 'robber' prompts the information that the 'beautiful Lake of the Trossachs [Loch Katrine] is supposed to have taken its name from the habits of its frequenters' (ICopy, 1.62; 25.35). Sir Magnus Redman is first identified by Scott in a footnote as 'Governor of Berwick and afterwards slain at the battle of Sark[?] in which the English were defeated'. This is cancelled by Lockhart for what becomes the Magnum footnote: 'Sir Magnus Redman, sometime Governor of Berwick, fell in one of the Battles on the border which followed on the Treason of the Earl of March, alluded to herafter' (ICopy, 1.54; 22.28).

Most of Lockhart's own notes are historical or quasi-historical: e.g. on royal mistresses (ICopy, 1.32); on Bruce and the spider (inaccurately ascribed to Barbour: ICopy, 1.65); on Jamie Keddie's ring (ICopy, 1.128); on the Charteris of Amisfield (ICopy, 1.188); on the Dukedom of Albany (ICopy, 1.230), the Galilee of a Catholic Cathedral (ICopy, 1.245), and so on. At the end of Volume 3, Chapter 1, Lockhart supplies a modern parallel to Bonthron's delivery in the case of a girl hanged for child-murder at Oxford but acknowledges he cannot find the reference for 'the learned Professor of that University' who conversed with her after her recovery, an admission understandably omitted in the Magnum. And in the third volume there are also substantial extracts from Wyntoun, Boece, Bower, and Fordun in illustration of historical events such as the murder of Rothsay and the clan battle. All in all these additions constitute a substantial armature for the narrative, the original sources grounding its fiction in history.

Lockhart's correction of the text is less happy. Some changes certainly remove repetition: 'the boy Darnley' is now 'in the plight of a mischievous lad', as against the first edition's 'in the plight of a mischievous boy' (8.36); and Scott's inserted 'boyish' describing his step is cancelled. The King receives his council 'with a mixture of courtesy and loftiness' (129.25) where the substitution of 'loftiness' for 'dignity' avoids a repetition of 'dignity' in the previous sentence and plays against 'each haughty peer' in the following clause. The clumsy repetition of 'course' (278. 23–24) yields to a simple 'that'. But a large number of the changes, although apparently generated by a desire to clarify, generate a fussy precision, and at times sheer fustian. When Rizzio has been dispatched 'at the door of the ante-room' we hardly need to be told that it was 'the ill-fated minion's blood' that was spilled (ICopy, 1.12; 7.2). The same might hold for the insertion of 'weeping' before 'crocodiles' (ICopy, 2.32; 267.38) or of 'by decapitation' (ICopy, 3.249; 349.24) into Ramorny's demand for 'the privilege of dying by the sword, and not by the noose' (349.24–25). Such changes as 'a look' to 'an aspect' (130.1), and 'give' to 'afford' (108.20) look very like verbal inflation.

The new material in the Interleaved Copy mostly appears with minor variations in the Magnum. Sometimes the variations may be worth noting, as with the footnote to Rothsay's carnival claim (182.20–21) to be 'the real King over all in Scotland that is worth commanding', where the Magnum's 'mumming dignitaries' replaces the original 'mumming monarchs' of the Interleaved Copy (Magnum, 42.359). The additional changes that occur in the Magnum for the most part tidy up the text. The opening paragraph of Volume 1, Chapter 1, is finally made perspicuous, and the unspecified 'citizen' at 43.6 becomes 'another citizen'. There are a number of alterations to regularise grammar. The eliminating of repetitions is pursued: sometimes deftly, but sometimes so mechanically as to be fatuous, as when the 'severed fingers' are changed to 'several fingers' (Magnum, 42.326; 165.18–19). Small stylistic changes can tighten the first edition text: 'as much variety as beauty, as much of historical interest as of natural sublimity' (3.15–16) becomes 'as much of historical interest as of natural beauty' (Magnum, 42.3). But some other changes are probably errors: 'divan' to 'divine' (Magnum, 42.378; 192.15) suggests misunderstanding of Scott's original antithesis; and the alteration of 'flash' to 'flush' (Magnum, 43.338; 362.29) looks like a straightforward misreading.

In addition the Magnum extends the annotation on a large scale, for Lockhart includes a series of notes on the topography and traditional history of Perth 'furnished by a gentleman well versed in the antiquities of bonny St Johnston' (Magnum, 42.89), later identified as 'Mr Morison of Perth' (Magnum, 1.176).

What relation did Scott have to all this? Lockhart was in Chiefswood less than two miles from Abbotsford for much of the summer, and Scott might have told him of the notes he wanted put in. Alternatively he might have handed over his corrections and revisions and asked Lockhart to complete the work for him; or yet again Lockhart may have been asked by Cadell to complete the work of editing since Scott was too ill to be capable of finishing the task. The manuscript of the Magnum Introduction has not survived and no answer has been found to the question whether it was written by Lockhart or Scott. Whichever it was, it is clear that Lockhart interpreted his brief with much greater licence than any normal intermediary would have done. On 30 occasions he went beyond adjusting what Scott wrote to normalise spelling and punctuation, or to fit its context in the text, and rewrote Scott's notes and corrections, or deleted them. His annotation can be held to continue Scott's own practice for the Magnum; his sometimes brilliant use of epigraph shows a real appreciation of Scott's mastery of this device. But the overall effect of Lockhart's interventions is to create a new layer of meaning which is emphatically his and not Scott's. In this we may see, if we wish, a transfer of power from the ailing author to the man who was to become the guardian of the public image of Sir Walter Scott.

4. THE PRESENT TEXT OF *SAINT VALENTINE'S DAY*

In editing *Saint Valentine's Day* the policy and procedures have been those of the Edinburgh Edition of the Waverley Novels. Essentially what is here published is a first-edition text, but emended by manuscript readings which had been lost through error or misunderstanding in the process of converting the holograph text into a printed book. In all some two thousand emendations have been made.

Emendations consequent upon the disclosure of Scott's authorship in 1827. Although this edition follows the general textual policy of the EEWN, textual practice has to accommodate the specific circumstances of composition and production. Three factors distinguish the novels published from 1827, including *Saint Valentine's Day*, from their predecessors. First, as explained previously, the manuscripts of these novels were used as printers' copy. The compositors were presented with difficult and imperfect copy, and did not have immediate access to the author. Secondly, while in the past James Ballantyne had been a trusted editor, not only correcting obvious errors but prompting Scott to explain issues that were not clear to his commonplace intelligence, he now seems to be less in harmony with Scott's literary purposes. With Cadell he had confronted Scott on 12 December 1827 about the opening of the new *Chronicles*. Scott in his letter of that day[81] was reassuring about their relationship, but on 7 February 1828 he objected to further criticism ('I think you are hypercritical in your commentary'),[82] and yet again on the 12th.[83] Thirdly, Cadell appears to have begun the procedure which he followed for the Magnum, i.e. he normalised aspects of Scott's corrected text before publication. Thus the input from Scott's assistants was probably less sympathetic and less effective than it had been, and the movement from manuscript to print created rather more problems than in the past.

The manuscript itself exhibits more mistakes than earlier ones. Scott now more frequently omits words, writes wrong words, lets word-ends get lost, and leaves sentences with incomplete meanings. As a result there is much here for the intermediaries to put right. On the whole they do an excellent job. But infallible they are not, and on occasion their corrections of the manuscript can be clumsy and heavy-handed. Consider these examples. In the manuscript Scott wrote:

> We play for our lives now thou silly wench and not for the bread supports them—for that part those who are strong take those who are weak yield and happy is the man ⟨whil⟩ who like my worthy son has means of obtaining his living otherwise than by the point of the sword which he makes— (30.24–28; MS 23048, *Saint Valentine's Day*, Volume 1, f. 12)

There are obvious problems here, particularly in the absence of punctuation. But it is surprising, none the less, to read the version printed in the first edition:

> We want swords to protect ourselves every moment now, thou silly wench, and not ploughs to dress the ground for the grain we may never see rise. As for the matter of our daily bread, those who are strong seize it, and live; those who are weak yield it, and die of hunger. Happy is the man who, like my worthy son, has means of obtaining his living otherwise than by the point of the sword which he makes. (1.74.20–75.4)

This elaboration is not without some rhetorical vigour of its own. But the recasting of the first sentence, the vacuous 'as for the matter of', and the padding in 'yield it, and die of hunger' all render the first edition much inferior to the speed and terseness of the manuscript version. None of the changes is an improvement, and none is necessary: once the required punctuation has been added the manuscript makes perfect sense. It cannot be proved that Scott is *not* responsible for the first edition reading; but given the new, post-anonymity situation, and the unnecessary inflation involved, we would argue that the manuscript reading should prevail, as truer to Scott's dominant style in this novel.

The superior economy and greater dramatic effectiveness of the manuscript version is equally evident in the following example. After the Smith has overcome Bonthron in the trial by combat, the Prior asks him whom he had intended to slay. In the manuscript Bonthron replies:

> "I took him for the man ⟨whose⟩ whose hand has struck me down whose foot now presses me"— (247.16–17; Volume 2, f. 62)

In the first edition, this becomes:

> "I took the slain man," answered the discomfited combatant, "for him whose hand has struck me down, whose foot now presses me." (2.314.16–18)

This is exactly the kind of unnecessary inflation and pedantic overkill that has given Scott's prose a bad name.

A similar clumsiness of intervention is apparent in this example from Volume 1, Chapter 10. When the King is afraid that Douglas and Rothsay are about to come to blows, the manuscript reads: 'go my Good father Abbot call Rothsay here instantly—go good cousin of March' (103.31–33; f. 55). In the first edition this becomes:

> Go, my good Father Abbot, call the Prince here instantly—Go, my dearest brother——"—And when they had both left the room, the King continued, "Go, good cousin of March— (1.270.5–9)

Here 'the Prince' is substituted for 'Rothsay' because 'Rothsay' appears a line or two above: the intermediaries are at their most inflexible in always removing what they regard as damaging repetitions of the same word. In terms of verisimilitude it was necessary to get Albany out of the room, so the addition of 'Go, my dearest brother' is understandable. But there is no need whatsoever to insert the phrase 'And when they had both left the room, the King continued'. Its only effect is to diminish the dramatic movement of the scene. And it is also clumsily inserted: a long dash followed by inverted commas, followed by a short dash occurs nowhere else in the first edition.

Our view is that the intermediaries are, generally speaking, rather too ready to change Scott's text by inserting clumsy and unnecessary indicators of who is speaking (as in the example just cited), by providing other redundant explanations of what is already clear, and by substituting inflation and periphrasis for Scott's simplicity and directness. Thus, for example, 'pace' becomes 'celerity of movement' (121.35); 'for Wallace' becomes 'for Wight Wallace' (189.18); 'bad news' becomes 'sinister intelligence' (199.13); 'as much as he was capable of doing' becomes 'as much as he was capable of entertaining such sentiments for anyone' (221.19); and 'men' becomes 'human creatures' (261.30). These and all similar changes work to weaken the impact of what Scott originally wrote.

For EEWN editors, the most important test of whether a change is likely to be authorial is to consider whether the new reading is an enhancement. If a reading is strengthened as a result of an alteration, if a more vivid word, or a fuller passage is substituted for what was previously there, the change is probably authorial; however, the verbal inflation of many of the changes made at the proof stages of *Saint Valentine's Day* is at odds with the directness of what are unquestionably Scott's own words in the manuscript. Whether or not the new situation created by the ending of anonymity is responsible, the intermediaries' changes in this context often work to diminish rather than enhance the effectiveness of what Scott actually wrote. Ballantyne, said Scott in the *Journal*, 'blames the Ossianick monotony of my principal characters. Now they are not Ossianick.'[84] In other words, Scott felt that Ballantyne did not understand the predominant mode and style of the novel—another reason for our decision often to prefer the authority of manuscript to first edition readings.

The adjustment from 1827 onwards in the practices for processing Scott's text also affected punctuation. In the discussion of the punctuation of the Waverley Novels it has been assumed that there is a first-edition style of punctuation, and that there is a Magnum style of punctuation. The distinction has some argumentative purpose, but is less absolute than might appear. First-edition punctuation is not a constant, but something which evolves. Partly this is a question of changes in Scott's own manuscript practice over eighteen years of novel-writing: as we have seen commas are few and far between in the manuscript of *Saint Valentine's Day*, but the manuscripts of earlier novels such as *Guy Mannering* and *The Antiquary* contain quite a number. In other words, with the passage of time Scott left more and more punctuation to be supplied by the intermediaries. One result is an overall increase in the quantity of punctuation. For example, whereas there are 15,487 first-edition commas in *Guy Mannering* and 15,949 in *The Antiquary*, there are 18,147 in *Ivanhoe*, and 18,255 in *Saint Valentine's Day*; the latter novels are longer than the former, but the incidence of commas rises from 97 per 1000 words in the first pair to 101 per 1000 words in the second.

There is no doubt that *Saint Valentine's Day* is more heavily punctuated than some earlier novels, but one of the basic policies of the EEWN is that the punctuation of the base-text should be accepted unless it is manifest that the intermediaries misinterpreted Scott's purpose as expressed in the words and signs of the manuscript, and even then only very limited, local change is envisaged. Thus the punctuation of this edition is essentially that of the first edition. Yet there are peculiarities in the punctuation of *Saint Valentine's Day*. The most odd is the apparent insistence that new speech must *always* start a new line, even if the speech indicator comes first. Thus at 186.6–9, the first edition reads:

> As they approached the calabash to this ungainly and truculent-looking savage, and as he extended a hand soiled, as it seemed, with blood, to grasp it, the Prince called out,—
> 'Down stairs with him! let not the wretch drink in our presence; find him some other vessel than our holy calabash, the emblem of our revels—a swine's trough were best, if it could be come by.
> (2.153.6–14)

On nineteen occasions in this edition paragraphs have been reformed so that the direct speech runs on after the speech indicator. In the first edition, commas are often inserted mechanically: they separate noun phrases and clauses from their verb; they invariably precede comparisons introduced by 'like', 'as', or 'than'; they always precede relative clauses with no distinction being made between the defining and the descriptive; they precede infinitives, as at 31.27 where the first edition reads: 'some other day I will tell you how, and also how long these bottles were concealed under ground, to save them from the reiving Southron'. All of these features can be found in other Waverley Novels, but the provision of commas in such contexts is nowhere else so unthinking. The system of punctuation employed in the early printed versions of Scott's fiction follows Joseph Robertson's *An Essay on Punctuation* (1785), but Robertson insists that commas should not be used when the noun clauses or the comparative phrases are short, and he proposes that defining relatives should not be separated from the words they qualify.[85] It is also significant that Scott in the Interleaved Copy of the novel deletes some of the commas to be found in these contexts, and that the Magnum does likewise. This edition of *Saint Valentine's Day* follows Scott's example. The vast majority of the marks of punctuation supplied by the intermediaries are respected: emendations have only

been made when the punctuational practice does not accord with the
norms of the period as formulated by Robertson, and where the punctuation supplied has been insensitive to Scott's meaning in the manuscript, or, in its proliferation, has made the process of reading and
understanding the text more rather than less difficult.

Verbal emendations. In addition to the two special categories described above, the text of *Saint Valentine's Day* has been emended to
correct the usual straightforward mistakes in reading the manuscript.
These involve misinterpreting Scott's hand so that one word was read
for another, omitting terminal letters, misunderstanding what Scott had
written, wrong omissions and wrong additions.

1] *Misreadings*. As usual, small words were misread: 'their' as 'these'
(e.g. 137.16), or 'this' as 'the' (e.g. 52.18), or 'in' as 'on' or vice versa
(e.g. 32.23). Sometimes the substitution makes little difference, but at
others it certainly does, as when the first edition reads 'the juice of this
Indian gum will bring sleep on the healthy man' (166.20–21), rather
than 'in the healthy man', thus creating a phrase that is not idiomatic.
Letters at the ends of words can be omitted; for instance the first edition
has 'lattice window' instead of 'latticed window' (40.34) and 'Eve' instead of 'Even' (226.40). And words can quite simply be misread: Ramorny mocks Dwining for his 'professional acquaintance' with the Perth
hangman, and says that 'if thy shoulders are seared or branded, thou art
wise for using a high-collared jerkin' (235.35–36); but the first edition
printed 'scared or branded'. And, ludicrously, the shouts at the funeral
of Conachar's father are so loud that, in the first edition, 'the deer fled
from their caves for miles around' (287.17) instead of 'from their cover'.

2] *Wrong substitutions*. It has been previously argued that there is a
discernible tendency to substitute inflated terms for the direct ones used
by Scott in manuscript, but there are also other categories of substitution. For instance, the replacement of 'remote and dusky glens' by
'remote and distant glens' (286.19) suggests a compositor proceeding
by mechanical association rather than accurate decipherment. At times
it seems the intermediaries did not appreciate what they were reading;
for Scott's manuscript description of Chaucer as the 'Inglish Makar'
(242.14) they substituted 'English Maker', thus revealing that they
understood neither middle Scots spelling nor its vocabulary. The
replacement of 'cat-a-mountain' at 61.30 by 'wild-cat' suggests a
misguided zeal to make things easily understood. And making explicit
whom a pronoun refers to may imply that the intermediaries had little
trust in the reader's common sense. At 79.2–3, 'when he saw his
adversary bestride him' was changed into 'when the Bonnet-maker's
adversary was seen to bestride him'; the antecedent of 'he' is, strictly
speaking, not Henry Smith, but no reader could possibly be confused by
the construction.

3] *Wrong omissions and insertions*. There are many omissions of single letters and of the odd word: at 38.33 Scott wrote of a 'small purse made of links of the finest work in steel as if it had been designed for a hauberk to King Oberon', but in the first edition the sentence ends with 'to a king'. The omission destroys the sense. On the other hand fewer passages (in comparison with earlier novels) were lost, and this is one of the direct benefits of using the manuscript as printer's copy, for it is probable that the work of the copyists was never independently proof-read, whereas the unusual inclusiveness of the text of *Saint Valentine's Day* suggests that Ballantyne's readers did their work well. Nonetheless, a complete clause was lost at 285.42–286.1 ('and on which are usually situated castles or religious houses which the fear or the piety of the ancient inhabitants have causd to be founded there'); the missing matter disrupted the sense, and enforced further revision. However, the manuscript makes good and effective sense, and the original reading needs only light editing to assimilate it to the printed text.

4] *Proper names*. Throughout the manuscript of *Saint Valentine's Day* the heroine is called 'Catherine', but is consistently 'Catharine' in print. The spelling 'Catharine' may have been Ballantyne's (he uses this form in the one extant gathering of proofs of *The Abbot*),[86] and it is likely that Scott accepted it rather than require systematic correction to the print —even Scott could limit his profligate use of compositors' time. (The most important instance of Scott's accepting a compositorial blunder was when Ballantyne and his staff consistently called Bonaparte 'Buonaparte' in Scott's *Life of Napoleon Buonaparte*, published in 1827, and although Scott criticised Ballantyne for the error,[87] and apologised for it in the Advertisement to the first edition,[88] it was not corrected). 'St Johnstoun' is accepted as the dominant manuscript form. The other error in naming is Scott's own, but proper copy-editing ought to have cured the problem. In the early stages of the novel Scott identified the bonnet-maker as Deacon Caw. Thereafter, Deacon Caw was transformed into Oliver Proudfute. But in the first edition and in the Magnum Oliver is twice still referred to as 'the deacon', an error corrected in this edition (64.1; 64.33).

Capitalisation and Punctuation. The system of capitalisation in the manuscript, and that of the first edition are not the same, and, inevitably, Scott was not wholly consistent about what he did. It was up to the intermediaries to convert Scott into print in a consistent way. This they did well, but they did not always understand the force of certain manuscript capitals. Scott nearly always capitalises 'the Church', or 'Holy Church' when he refers to the institution, but writes 'the church' when he refers to a building. The distinction was lost in the first edition and is here restored, and those occasions when Scott inconsistently gave the institution a lower case initial letter are normalised. Similarly, the 'Royal

Burghs' individually and as a group deserve their capitals (70.10; 70.28). The Fair City, an alternative title for Perth, is usually capitalised in manuscript and print, but on three occasions (65.33; 67.36; 69.38) inconsistency is editorially rectified.

As has been explained the punctuation of this edition is largely that of the first; the removal of 500 commas from the 50,000 marks of punctuation supplied does not even modify that judgment. Elsewhere little is changed. Scott's own marks of punctuation are rare, but when provided have more force than if the manuscript text had been conventionally punctuated. The intermediaries did not recognise Scott's clear distinction between "——— as the sign for interrupted speech and ———" as the sign for speech which trails off; that distinction is restored on the basis of manuscript evidence. And they did not perceive that Scott punctuates narrative differently from speech; while narrative sentences have very little internal punctuation, the dash is used to indicate the rhetorical shaping of speech. When Scott's purpose in speech is clearly frustrated by the punctuation supplied, it is restored in this edition. For instance, in the first edition Dorothy's speech at 201.13–18 reads:

> "Indeed, and I daresay you have lighted on the very man, Catharine. They quarrelled, as you saw, on the St Valentine's Even, and had a warstle. A Highlandman has a long memory for the like of that. Gie him a cuff at Martinmas, and his cheek will be tingling at Whitsunday. But what could have brought down the lang-legged loons to do their bloody wark within burgh?" (2.192.22–193.6)

This edition restores Scott's dashes, thus retaining the unity of Dorothy's commentary on Highland memory, while using the full-stop to signal a change of subject:

> "Indeed, and I daresay you have lighted on the very man, Catherine. They quarrelled, as you saw, on the St Valentine's Even, and had a warstle—a Highlandman has a long memory for the like of that—gie him a cuff at Martinmas, and his cheek will be tingling at Whitsunday. But wha could have brought down the lang-legged loons to do their bloody wark within burgh?"

Punctuation added in the first edition is also rejected when it seems to alter Scott's sense, as when Simon says 'fie,—now, you are jealous' (34.8) where it seems that 'now' is intended as an adverb and not an interjection, or Henry's 'No doubt, his notions of skin-cutting are rather different' (34.41).

Emendations from the Interleaved Copy and the Magnum. Twenty-seven emendations arising from changes in the Interleaved Copy of *Saint Valentine's Day* and nineteen from the Magnum have been made.

It is clear that Scott set out to correct the most obvious historical error, the name of the heir to the throne. On 20 occasions Rothsay's name had to be changed from Robert or Robin to David. The initial alterations, ten in all, were effected by Scott; Lockhart made eight, and a further two occur in the Magnum. On the basis of Scott's original decision to make the correction, all of these have been adopted in this edition. Rectifying other mistakes in the naming of historical characters follows perforce. Scott changed two misleading references to the Earl of Douglas (108.29; 227.32); Lockhart gave Wardlaw his proper Christian name, Henry, at 271.28, and the Magnum caught the instance Lockhart missed (92.13)—each of these is adopted in this edition. Following the EEWN's rule on consistent naming, we have accepted the Magnum's correction of 'Carmelite' to 'Carthusian' (289.36; 291.6), as well as two alterations of 'Kay' to 'Quhele' made by an unidentified hand in the Interleaved Copy (134.6; 136.23), on the grounds that Scott was initially uncertain about the name to use but always calls the clan 'Quhele' in the later stages of the novel. We have also restored the correct name to David II's mistress, Margaret Logie. In the first edition she appears once as 'Catherine' (151.11), once as 'Jean' (236.15). In the Interleaved Copy 'Jean' is turned into 'Katie' by a hand which has not been identified (ICopy, 2.285), and while this standardises the name, it is still wrong. To complicate the position further Lockhart quoted the historical source, John Bellenden's translation of Boece's *History of Scotland*, but in calling her 'Catharine Logie' in the quotation (ICopy, 1.32; see Magnum, 42.59) Lockhart cheats: Bellenden has 'Margaret Logy'.[89] Given that it was not Scott who corrected 'Jean' to 'Katie', there is much to be said for giving Margaret Logie her own name.

All of these emendations concern historical names, and although the mistakes would not be noticed by most modern readers it is proper to accept Scott's self-correcting in the Interleaved Copy, and the consequent tidying up by Lockhart and the proof-readers of the printing house. Other changes are not accepted, unless they repair obvious faults. Perhaps the most notable of these is the homophone in the manuscript and first edition in Dorothy's expostulation: 'You made such a peace of work about his companying with a glee woman as if he had companied with a Jewess!' (200.19–20). It was the Magnum which changed 'peace' to 'piece'. Other changes are minor but necessary, for example following the Magnum in converting a single inverted comma to a double at 282.39, and at 359.5 (in a portion of the novel for which the manuscript is missing) altering 'practice' to 'practices' to agree with the plural verb.

Conclusion. *Saint Valentine's Day* is a remarkable novel. It is remarkable in part because late in his career Scott has a new subject, 'my brave coward or cowardly brave man',[90] in part because he employs a spare narrative style that is without parallel in the rest of his *oeuvre*. The process which produced the novel is also remarkable, for, coexisting with Scott's strategy of securing the copyrights of his earlier fiction by the profits from *Saint Valentine's Day*, we see a luminous creative intelligence working at high pressure to produce a tightly organised and deeply moving novel. Far too many critics, from his son-in-law J. G. Lockhart to the present day, have written off late Scott, and seen his last works as evidence of failing powers. The readers of this edition of *Saint Valentine's Day* will see that these critics are wrong.

NOTES

All manuscripts referred to are in the National Library of Scotland unless otherwise stated.

1 *Rob Roy* (1818), 2.296.19–21.
2 Henry Adamson, *The Muses Threnodie*, ed. James Cant (Perth, 1774); originally published 1638; *CLA*, 17.
3 MS 21017, f. 34r.
4 MS 794, f. 187v–186r [*sic*: the letter has been misbound]. A few days later, on 6 August, Cadell is suggesting subjects from Scottish history such as 'Lord James of Douglas' (MS 794, f. 192r).
5 MS 744, f. 195.
6 MS 21017, f. 37r; MS 3904, f. 237.
7 MS 3904, f. 242; MS 3904, ff. 244v, 245r.
8 *The Letters of Sir Walter Scott*, ed. H. J. C. Grierson and others, 12 vols (London, 1932–37), 10.272; hereafter cited as *Letters*.
9 *Letters*, 10.275.
10 *Letters*, 10.291.
11 *Letters*, 10.294.
12 MS 21017, ff. 50v, 51r
13 *Letters*, 10.314.
14 MS 21017, ff. 50v, 51r.
15 *The Journal of Sir Walter Scott*, ed. W. E. K. Anderson (Oxford, 1972), 383; hereafter cited as *Journal*.
16 *Journal*, 388.
17 *Journal*, 389.
18 *Journal*, 213.
19 *Journal*, 389.
20 *Journal*, 169. The *Journal* entry for 8 July 1826 also indicates that Ballantyne had not been enthusiastic about the Highland material in the first series of *Chronicles of the Canongate*: *Journal*, 168–69.
21 *Journal*, 169. In insisting that the Highlanders have been 'off the field now for some time' Scott may be seeking to reassure himself. Towards the end of Chrystal Croftangry's narrative in the first volume of the first series of *Chronicles*, he allows Mrs Baliol to suggest that 'The Highlands *were* indeed a rich mine; but they have, I think, been fairly wrought out' (*Chronicles of the Canongate*, ed. Claire Lamont, EEWN 20, 67.7–8), while at the beginning of Volume 2 Croftangry himself concedes that the theme of the Highlands 'is becoming a little exhausted' (154.38).
22 *Journal*, 389–90.

23 *Journal*, 390.
24 *Journal*, 391.
25 *Journal*, 392.
26 *Journal*, 393.
27 MS 21017, f. 51v.
28 MS 21017, f. 52v.
29 *Journal*, 393.
30 *Letters*, 10.329.
31 *Journal*, 393. There is an echo here of the exchanges between Captain Clutterbuck and the Author of Waverley in the Introductory Epistle to *The Fortunes of Nigel*. The Author accepts that he will one day fall out of public favour but adds 'They cannot say but what you *had* the crown' (*The Fortunes of Nigel* (1822), ed. Frank Jordan, EEWN 13, 15.38–39.).
32 *Journal*, 394.
33 MS 21017, f. 52v.
34 *Journal*, 394.
35 *Journal*, 394.
36 *Journal*, 395.
37 *Journal*, 394.
38 *Journal*, 396.
39 *Journal*, 397.
40 *Letters*, 10.351.
41 *Journal*, 422.
42 *Journal*, 423.
43 *Letters*, 10.376. A note signed J. B. indicates that the criticism originated with Cadell. J. B. writes: 'You may keep this, if you like. The tone of it determines me, in future, to send no criticisms to the Author, *but my own*; and these only when they are positively demanded. He hates trouble; and as, after all, the matter is his, not mine, I am resolvd to give him no more than I can help.'
44 *Journal*, 426.
45 *Letters*, 10.382.
46 *Letters*, 10.381.
47 *Journal*, 394–95.
48 *Journal*, 424.
49 *Journal*, 426.
50 *Journal*, 429.
51 *Journal*, 429.
52 *Journal*, 431.
53 *Journal*, 432.
54 *Journal*, 433.
55 *Journal*, 433.
56 *Journal*, 433.
57 *Journal*, 434.
58 *Journal*, 436.
59 *Journal*, 444.
60 *Journal*, 446.
61 *Journal*, 448.
62 *The Fortunes of Nigel* (1822), ed. Frank Jordan, EEWN 13, 6–7, 10–11.

63 Samuel Taylor Coleridge, *Table Talk*, ed. Carl Woodring (Princeton, 1990), in *The Collected Works of Samuel Taylor Coleridge*, ed. Kathleen Coburn, 16 vols, Vol. 14:2, 295.

64 *Journal*, 448.

65 *Journal*, 411. Scott was pleased with his work on the *Tales of a Grandfather*; so much so that the notion of abandoning fiction for history resurfaces in his mind: 'Nay—I will hash History with anybody, be he who he will. I do not know but it would be wise to let romantic composition rest and turn my mind to the History of England, France and Ireland to be *da capo rota'd* as well as that of Scotland.'

66 *Journal*, 447.

67 *Journal*, 395.

68 In fact in an unpublished manuscript ('Sylvae') in the Abbotsford Library, Scott did describe the development of the landscape gardening of Abbotsford itself.

69 MS 23048.

70 MS 21018. Entries for 14 February, 27 February, 3 March, 6 March, 12 March, 26 March, 28 March, 21 April, 22 April, 23 April, 25 April, all refer to such readings. Several times Cadell uses the word 'revising' to describe his activities.

71 MS 794, f. 274r.

72 MS 21018, f. 20r.

73 MS 794, ff. 281r, 288r.

74 MS 797, f. 25r.

75 MS 797, f. 26r.

76 MS 797, f. 27r.

77 The standard modern accounts of Scott's preparation of the Magnum Opus are in Jane Millgate, *Scott's Last Edition* (Edinburgh, 1987) and *Scott's Interleaved Waverley Novels*, ed. Iain G. Brown (Aberdeen, 1987).

78 *Letters*, 11.340.

79 MS 794, f. 366; MS 21043, f. 40v.

80 Harry Ransom Humanities Research Centre, University of Texas at Austin, Wn Sco86 828Cb.

81 *Letters*, 10.329–30.

82 *Letters*, 10.376.

83 *Journal*, 426; *Letters*, 10.382.

84 *Journal*, 426.

85 [Joseph Robertson], *An Essay on Punctuation* (London, 1785), 23, 34, 59, 70–71, 72–73.

86 MS 3401, *The Abbot*, 1.20.8.

87 *Letters*, 10.224.

88 *The Prose Works of Sir Walter Scott, Bart.*, [ed. J. G. Lockhart], 12 vols (Edinburgh, 1833–36), 8.viii.

89 Hector Boece, *The History and Chronicles of Scotland*, trans. John Bellenden, 3 vols (Edinburgh, 1821), 2.449.

90 *Journal*, 390.

EMENDATION LIST

The base-text for this edition of *Saint Valentine's Day* is a specific copy of the first edition, owned by the Edinburgh Edition of the Waverley Novels. All emendations to this base-text, whether verbal, orthographic, or punctuational, are listed below, with the exception of certain general categories of emendation described in the next paragraph, and of those errors which result from accidents of printing such as a letter dropping out, provided always that evidence for the 'correct' reading has been found in at least one other copy of the first edition.

The following proper names have been standardised throughout on the authority of Scott's preferred usage as deduced from the manuscript (see Essay on the Text, 415): Catherine and St Johnstoun. Inverted commas are sometimes found in the first edition for displayed verse quotations, sometimes not; the present text has standardised the inconsistent practices of the base-text by eliminating such inverted commas, except when they occur at the beginning or end of speeches. Chapter numbering has been normalised. The typographic presentation of volume and chapter headings, of the opening words of volumes and chapters, and of letters quoted in the primary text, has been standardised. Ambiguous end-of-line hyphens in the base-text have been interpreted in accordance with the following authorities (in descending order of priority): predominant first-edition usage; Magnum; MS.

Each entry in the list below is keyed to the text by page and line number; the reference is followed by the new, EEWN reading, then in brackets the reason for the emendation, and after the slash the base-text reading that has been replaced. Occasionally, some explanation of the editorial thinking behind an emendation is required, and this is provided in a brief note.

The great majority of emendations are derived from the manuscript. Most merely involve the replacement of one reading by another, and these are listed with the simple explanation '(MS)'. The spelling and punctuation of some emendations from the manuscript have been normalised in accordance with the prevailing conventions of the base-text, and although as far as possible emendations have been fitted into the existing base-text punctuation, at times it has been necessary to provide emendations with a base-text style of punctuation. Where the manuscript reading adopted by the EEWN has required editorial intervention to normalise spelling or punctuation, the exact manuscript reading is given in the form: '(MS actual reading)'. Where the new reading has required editorial interpretation of the manuscript, e.g. when interpreting a homophone, or supplying a missing word, the explanation is given in the form '(MS derived: actual reading)'. In transcriptions from Scott's manuscript, deletions are enclosed ⟨thus⟩ and insertions

421

↑ thus ↓ ; superscript letters are lowered without comment.

In spite of the care taken by the intermediaries, some local confusions in the manuscript persisted into the first edition. When straightening these, the editors have studied the manuscript context so as to determine Scott's original intention, but sometimes problems cannot be rectified in this way. In these circumstances, Scott's own corrections and revisions in the Interleaved Copy may be adopted; Lockhart's corrections in the Interleaved Copy are adopted only when they continue what Scott had left incomplete or as the neatest means of rectifying a fault. Readings from the Magnum are adopted only in identical circumstances. Readings from the Interleaved Copy are indicated by 'ICopy' when the hand making the correction cannot be identified, by 'Scott in ICopy', or by 'Lockhart in ICopy'; readings from the Magnum are indicated by 'Magnum'. Emendations which have not been anticipated by a contemporaneous version are indicated by 'Editorial'.

3.7	Chrystal Croftangry's Narrative (Editorial) / CHAPTER I.

In Ed1 'Chapter I' appears twice, here and at the beginning of *Saint Valentine's Day*. The Magnum relables this chapter 'Introductory', but 'Chrystal Croftangry's Narrative' is the name used of Croftangry material in *Chronicles of the Canongate*, First Series.

4.14	chanced that (Editorial) / chanced, that
4.17	*umph* to (Editorial) / *umph*, to
7.11	says that (Editorial) / says, that
7.24	purpose as (Editorial) / purpose, as
9.42	to the (Magnum) / tothe
11.24	soil is (Editorial) / soil, is
11.26	profusion clothe (Editorial) / profusion, clothe
17.21	low that (Editorial) / low, that
17.29	Highness (Editorial) / highness

'Highness' is used 75 times in Ed1 and on all but two occasions there is an initial capital.

18.43	how many (Magnum) / how, man
21.1	gallant. [new paragraph] Her (Editorial) / gallant. Her

A new paragraph should have been opened here rather than immediately before the direct speech (see the next emendation).

21.3	hesitation, "Her (Editorial) / hesitation,— [new paragraph] "Her
21.20	head-ache (Editorial) / headach

This emendation follows those at 59.6 and 59.7.

22.17	Makar (Editorial) / Maker

On the two other occasions (242.14, 266.26) on which Scott uses this word his MS 'makar' was wrongly changed to 'maker'.

26.6	lint to (Editorial) / lint, to
26.19	where (MS) / what
26.23	is that (MS) / is, that
26.25	absence?—my (MS) / absence? My
26.25	say?—nay (MS) / say? nay
26.31	enough to (MS) / enough, to
26.31	assailant or (MS) / assailant, or
27.6	was (MS) / were
27.7	Robert of (MS) / Robert, of
27.8	butchers to (MS) / butchers, to
27.28	glorious that (MS) / glorious, that

28.6   duty in (MS) / duty, in
28.28   thy (MS) / Thy
28.36   anger which (MS) / anger, which
28.36   Fling (MS) / fling
28.36   cursed (MS) / accursed
29.6   sword and (MS) / sword, and
29.32   industry"——(MS) / industry——"
29.43   it entered into none of (MS it enterd into none of) / her arguments
           interfered with
30.3   Perth in (MS) / Perth, in
30.5   Henry Smith (MS) / Henry the Smith
30.15   that (MS) / the
30.22   days men (MS) / days, men
30.24   play for our lives (MS) / want swords to protect ourselves every moment
30.25   for the bread supports them—for that part those who are strong take,
           those (MS for the bread supports them—for that part those who are
           strong take those) / ploughs to dress the ground for the grain we may
           never see rise. As for the matter of our daily bread, those who are strong
           seize it, and live; those
30.26   yield, and happy (MS yield and happy) / yield it, and die of hunger.
           Happy
30.33   Henry Smith (MS) / Henry the Smith
30.36   a year (MS) / a-year
30.38   and without (MS) / and, without
31.3   seemed it (MS) / seemed as if it
           The 'as if' was inserted above the line in a different hand.
31.13   Stay then, (MS) / Stay, then,
31.27   ground to (MS) / ground, to
31.28   the health (MS) / the soul's health
31.34   apartment according (MS) / apartment, according
31.38   grieves me from my soul that (MS) / grieves me, from my soul, that
31.39   idle (MS) / silly
32.1   them (MS) / these
32.3   thou last left (MS) / thy last departure from
32.4   burgesses (MS) / burghers
32.6   arm at (MS) / arm, at
32.12   So I (MS) / So, I
32.19   man's. So (MS) / man's;—so
32.23   on (MS) / in
32.25   no. Otherwise (MS) / no; otherwise
32.28   mislikes (MS) / dislikes
32.28   much—although (MS) / much. Although
33.6   Henry (MS) / Harry
33.12   worthy (MS) / deserving
33.15   persons. (MS) / persons, even though windows be down and doors
           shut.
33.16   named, though windows be down and doors shut—Ay (MS) / named,
           —ay
33.34   cumbered (MS cumberd) / troubled
33.41   kindred!—what (MS) / kindred! What
33.42   him (MS) / he
34.7   for schoolmistress. (MS) / for a schoolmistress.
34.8   now you (MS) / now, you
34.9   here because (MS) / here, because
34.11   father (MS) / Father

34.20   skins (MS) / hides
34.21   man by (MS) / man, by
34.30   Burn-the-wind (MS burn the wind) / Gow
         The form follows that used at 23.34.
34.41   doubt his (MS) / doubt, his
35.3   furnace like (MS) / furnace, like
35.8   thee with (MS) / thee, with
35.12   wert a witch going (MS) / wert going
35.12   but a (MS) / but like a
35.12   fellow who (MS) / fellow, who
35.21   anvil?—why (MS) / anvil? why
35.26   Ever (MS) / ever
35.28   pshaw (MS) / Pshaw
35.33   certainty," said (MS) / certainty,"—said
35.38   but she hath . . . taken the young catheran in hand (MS but she hath . . .
         taken the you Catheran in hand) / but Catharine," replied the Glover,
         "hath . . . taken the young reiver in hand
         When the intermediaries substituted the proper name 'Catharine' for
         'she' they created a near-repetition (Catharine / Catheran), and 'reiver'
         was probably substituted to avoid this; however, 'reiver' is not used of
         Conachar elsewhere in the novel.
35.41   Clement?" (MS) / Clement!"
35.42   Pray who (MS) / Pray, who
35.43   trains (MS) / is trained
36.4   Church (Editorial) / church
36.7   Eve to (MS) / Eve, to
36.12   neither one (MS) / neither the one
36.16   cumber (MS) / abide in
36.22   cumber (MS) / difficulty
36.32   fiend (MS) / Fiend
36.33   Vennel when (MS) / Vennel, when
37.7   him. And (MS him And) / him; and
37.9   pleases; marry (MS) / pleases. Marry
37.13   Henry. Be (MS) / Henry; be
37.16   at window (MS) / at the window
37.20   left thee (MS) / left on thee
37.25   and moved (MS) / and, though completely undaunted, moved
37.26   guard though completely undaunted, to (MS) / guard, to
37.30   be well believed (MS) / be believed
37.36   of some of (MS) / of many of
37.39   chain-mail, so (MS) / chain-mail, made so
38.6   Cordovan (MS) / cordovan
38.14   assuming in (MS) / assuming, in
38.15   dress as (MS) / dress, as
38.16   encroaching that (MS) / encroaching on that
38.21   upon consciousness (MS) / upon a consciousness
38.29   now (MS) / presently
38.33   to King Oberon. (MS) / to a king.
39.2   Couvrefew (MS) / Curfew
39.5   nearer (MS) / near
39.6   himself about (MS) / himself, about
39.7   well as (MS) / well, as
39.9   father (MS) / Father
39.9   bloody (MS) / stain
39.10   with the (MS) / with the blood of the

39.10	worth (MS) / worthy
39.10	notice? (MS) / notice since they are so much less fortunate than myself?
39.19	on which slight (MS) / in which no slight
39.20	flicker, but too faintly and indistinctly to (MS) / flicker, to
39.20	the certain approach (MS) / the approach
39.21	dawn which (MS) / dawn, however, distant, which
39.28	armourer, standing and looking (MS) / armourer, looking
39.35	neglected—Saint (MS) / neglected. Saint
40.9	The first of them thrust (MS) / The nearest made a thrust
40.11	time gave (MS) / time, gave
40.12	in (MS) / at
40.13	applied that (MS) / applied, that
40.15	forwards (MS) / forward
40.20	held (MS) / kept
40.22	windows (MS) / window
40.24	Why (MS) / why
40.32	further (MS) / farther
40.32	forwards (MS) / forward
40.34	latticed (MS) / lattice
40.41	Henry to (MS) / Henry, to
41.17	up and (MS) / up, and
41.24	bribes (MS) / promises
41.34	noise and (MS) / noise; and
41.38	here as (MS) / here, as
41.40	private and (MS) / private, and
41.41	thee that (MS) / thee, that
41.42	shall (MS) / will
42.3	me—there (MS) / me. There
42.12	behind (MS) / betwixt
42.12	buttress (MS) / buttresses
42.34	gate to (MS) / gate of the sanctuary to
42.36	Ay (MS Aye) / Yes
42.36	poor soul (MS) / poor hunted soul
43.6	citizens, shaking their heads. (MS) / citizen, shaking his head.
43.13	large indeed, (MS) / large, indeed,
43.28	hand-habend and back-bearand, (MS) / hand-habend, our back-bear-and
43.28	blood-suits and (MS) / blood-suits, and
43.29	escheats and (MS) / escheats, and
43.32	such an injustice (MS) / such injustice
43.35	you of (MS) / you, of
44.1	burgher (MS) / burgess
44.3	friends—the (MS) / friends, the
44.25	dressed—Come on, man—She (MS) / dressed.—Come on, man. She
44.35	as (MS) / when
45.3	"Now go thy ways for (MS) / "Now, go thy ways, for
45.12	safety—but (MS) / safety; but
45.13	relief—and (MS) / relief, and
45.18	saint till (MS) / saint, till
45.25	shall again intrude (MS) / shall intrude
45.27	further (MS) / farther
45.27	to-night—but (MS) / to-night, but
45.29	meet that (MS) / meet, that
45.34	love (MS) / like
45.40	Ay (MS) / ay

46.2	is (MS) / be
46.9	was still on (MS) / was on
46.30	earthly can (MS) / earthly thing can
47.5	is (MS) / has
47.7	other all (MS) / other, all
47.12	Tay than (MS) / Tay, than
47.13	you choose (MS) / you can but choose
47.20	shrine if (MS) / shrine, if
47.21	man (MS) / one
47.24	Only (MS) / only
47.26	Church (MS) / church
47.27	as duly as (MS) / as justly, I say, as
47.28	means; but (MS) / means doth; but
47.28	Church (MS) / church
47.33	Master (MS) / friend
47.41	and more (MS) / or more
48.9	do? Will (MS) / do? will
48.19	burly (MS) / bodily
48.34	them. At (MS) / them; at
48.35	Squire (MS) / squire
49.4	for her and (MS) / for and
49.7	upon was (MS) / upon, was
49.11	suit. I (MS) / suit; I
49.13	myself—I (MS) / myself. I
49.14	bold when (MS) / bold, when
49.19	chamber in (MS) / chamber, in
49.21	her own purpose (MS) / her purpose
49.24	omen if (MS) / omen, if
49.27	tie than (MS) / tie, than
49.30	Catherine, who saw them generally fluctuating (MS Catherine who saw them generally fluctuating) / Catharine had thought, who having generally seen them fluctuating
49.32	them. (MS) / them some idea of imbecility.
49.34	awakes we (MS) / awakes—we
49.35	But no!—it (MS) / but no! it
49.36	honour—I (MS) / honour. I
50.9	Valentine to (MS) / Valentine, to
50.23	ashamed thou (MS) / ashamed that thou
50.26	darling, look up and (MS) / darling! look up, and
50.33	eyes my (MS) / eyes, my
50.35	little it (MS) / little, it
51.3	Perth with (MS) / Perth, with
51.13	once—enough (MS) / once; enough
51.16	further (MS) / farther
51.17	bravely—excellently (MS) / bravely, excellently
51.17	and now (MS) / And now
51.18	sluggard. We (MS) / sluggard; we
51.20	cakes which (MS) / cakes, which
51.29	him began (MS) / him, began
51.36	you that (MS) / you, that
51.38	blithe (MS blythe) / lively
51.40	brow which (MS) / brow, which
52.1	What the (MS) / What, the
52.10	lips! Now I (MS) / lips! I
52.18	this matter (MS) / the matter

52.21	up on and (MS) / upon, and
52.31	mind (MS) / observe
52.39	in bringing such (MS) / in the trick of bringing about such
52.40	purpose." (MS) / purpose for the occasion."
52.43	man wins (MS) / man, wins
52.43	booth—thou (MS) / booth; thou
53.1	kid, (MS) / kid-skin,
53.5	beauties in (MS) / beauties of
53.5	art (MS) / shalt be
53.6	tongue, providing (MS) / tongue upon, providing
53.18	much if (MS) / much, if
53.19	period would (MS) / period, would
53.23	conversation, and (MS) / conversation,—and
53.24	reflections, that (MS) / reflections,—that
53.29	followed— "There (MS followed "There) / followed,— [new paragraph] "There
53.31	fast—I (MS) / fast. I
53.31	them myself for that matter of it." (MS) / them do so myself, for the matter of that."
53.33	"And (MS) / "—And
54.6	making like (MS) / making, like
54.8	mail—and that as (MS mail and that as) / mail as
54.8	*brattach** and but (MS) / *brattach;** and that is but
54.9	the clan-smith (MS) / the clumsy clan-smith
54.20	handed to him (MS) / offered him
54.35	reveller (MS) / revellers
54.41	thee which (MS) / thee, which
55.13	justly (MS) / exactly
55.26	you take up (MS) / in taking up
55.26	of the time as (MS) / of your time at your pleasure, as
55.34	sporran that (MS) / sporran, that
55.34	free of (MS) / free to you of
55.35	in that (MS) / in, that
55.35	to come down from (MS) / to be sent down to you from
56.6	churl-blood (MS churle-blood) / churl's blood
56.10	be to come (MS) / be that thou shouldst come
56.25	blended, hesitated (MS blended hesitated) / blended. He hesitated
56.35	hand (MS) / fingers
56.42	yet bound (MS) / yet he hath bound
56.43	would (MS) / should
57.8	craft, in (MS) / craft of the two, in
57.20	through (MS) / over
57.23	for one (MS) / avow myself to
57.43	proposal that (MS) / proposal, that
58.3	Glover as (MS) / Glover, as
58.9	upon (MS) / on
58.22	beside to (MS) / beside it to
58.24	that (MS) / which
58.26	grasp (MS) / keeping
58.29	"surely (MS) / "and surely
58.29	(there (MS) / (and there
58.30	and my preserver (MS) / as well as my Valentine and preserver
59.6	head-ache (MS) / head-ach
59.7	head-ache (MS headache) / head-ach
59.7	fair Catherine (MS derived: fair Chirine) / dearest maiden

It appears that Scott began to write 'Child', and then remembered that Henry was speaking and switched to 'Catherine', thus generating a hybrid.

59.8   heart-ache (MS) / heart-ach
The MS may read 'heart ache'.

59.8   shall not (MS) / will not

59.8   Catherine with (MS) / Catharine, with

59.17   upon"———— (MS) / upon————"

59.27   thy spirit (MS) / your spirit

59.27   anger and (MS) / anger, and

59.27   thy hand (MS) / your hand

59.28   have thee (MS) / have you

59.28   persuade thee (MS) / persuade you

59.29   thyself (MS) / yourself

59.29   which thou (MS) / which you

59.30   conscience than (MS) / conscience, than

59.32   days the (MS) / days, the

59.34   causes; the taking of deadly (MS) / causes; of the taking deadly

59.36   know that (MS) / know, that

59.41   henceforwards (MS) / henceforward

59.41   much indeed, (MS) / much, indeed,

60.4   quarrel,—I, (MS) / quarrel,—and suppose that I,

60.12   hollowing (MS) / hallooing

60.15   fling aside (MS derived: fling) / despise

60.16   they be (MS) / they may be

60.24   seriousness that (MS) / seriousness, that

60.31   could recollect (MS) / could have cause to recollect

60.32   whisper—'Henry, (MS) / whisper, 'Henry,

60.35   mood than (MS) / mood, than

60.36   call (MS) / cry

60.39   "think that (MS) / "do think, that

60.39   striking you (MS) / striking, you

60.40   hand, in (MS) / hand, that in

60.40   wounds you (MS) / wounds, you

61.1   you're (MS) / you are

61.8   commands were (MS) / commands, were

61.10   but a (MS) / but for a

61.11   love (MS) / wish

61.14   give and (MS) / give, and

61.16   work (MS) / daily toil

61.18   strife as (MS) / strife, as

61.22   me (MS) / I am

61.30   cat-a-mountain Conachar (MS) / wild-cat, Conachar

61.31   looks"———— (MS) / looks————"

61.35   passions—and (MS) / passions, and

61.41   who (MS) / which

61.42   painted, perfumed (MS painted perfumed) / painted and perfumed

61.43   crafts (MS) / craft

62.6   opinion than (MS) / opinion, than

62.7   utters in (MS) / utters, in

62.11   know (MS) / be aware

62.12   desire as (MS) / desire, as

62.18   to tell— (MS) / to tell;—

62.20   some (MS) / an

62.22   recollected was (MS) / recollected, was

63.11   whisper than (MS) / whisper, than
63.26   affray (MS) / scuffle
63.34   bad (MS) / evil usage
63.36   is (MS) / was
63.37   Is it (MS) / Was it
64.1   him (Editorial) / the deacon
       See Essay on the Text, 415, for a discussion of this emendation.
64.10   be that (MS) / be, that
64.9   masquing (MS) / masking
64.18   matter as (MS) / matter, as
64.20   say that (MS) / say, that
64.33   Oliver. "There (Editorial and MS) / deacon. [new paragraph] "There
       For the Editorial emendation 'Oliver' for 'deacon' see Essay on the
       Text, 415. Secondly, a verso insert was not recognised as a continuation
       of Craigdallie's speech, and a new paragraph was mistakenly opened.
64.33   here; but (Editorial) / here," said the Bailie; "but
       The sentence 'There . . . secret' was added in proof, and having
       wrongly opened a new paragraph (see above), a speaker had then to be
       identified.
64.35   wrong than (MS) / wrong, than
65.23   main (MS) / power
65.26   it's (MS) / it is
65.26   we'll (MS) / we will
65.29   citizens unanimously. (MS) / citizens, unanimously.
65.33   Fair City (Editorial) / fair city
65.37   broke (MS) / broken
65.37   body that (MS) / body, that
66.9   better?" (MS) / better to deal with?"
66.10   answer. (MS) / answer for a minute.
66.13   to—"The (MS) / to—[new paragraph] "The
66.15   father (MS) / Father
66.18   by Craigdallie, (MS) / by Bailie Craigdallie,
66.18   looking significantly (MS) / looking very significantly
66.20   speak (MS) / talk
66.26   Bloody Heart (Magnum) / bloody heart
67.10   morn that (MS) / morn, that
67.11   may (in (MS) / may—in
67.11   mean) become (MS) / mean—become
67.20   forward and (MS) / forward, and
67.25   brimeston, (MS) / brimstone,
67.28   Glover in (MS) / Glover, in
67.32   prove we (MS) / prove that we
67.33   by lightness (MS) / by any lightness
67.36   consult and (MS) / consult, and
67.36   Fair City (Editorial) / fair city
67.40   me that (MS) / I that
68.2   Provost—Are (MS) / Provost, are
68.7   Bailie—"and God (MS) / Bailie. "God
68.9   years"—— (MS) / years——"
68.18   leader; (MS) / leader against them;
68.23   least, and with thanks to Harry Smith." (MS derived: least and wi
       thanks to Harry Smith"—) / least, thanks to Harry Smith——"
68.30   honour and (MS) / honour, and
68.31   up and (MS) / up, and
68.38   his downright way. (MS) / his usual downright manner.

68.43 and hands (MS) / and man's hand
69.2 myself if (MS) / myself, if
69.2 me. He (MS me He) / me; he
69.5 is Provost (MS) / is the Provost
69.16 Charteris in (MS) / Charteris, in
69.22 sword than (MS) / sword, than
69.38 Fair City (Editorial) / fair city
69.41 Privy Council (MS) / privy council
70.2 future against (MS) / future, against
70.5 necessary for some readers to learn in (MS) / necessary, for the information of some readers, to state in
70.10 Royal Burghs (MS) / royal burghs
70.12 artizans (MS) / citizens
70.15 neighbourhood, who (MS) / neighbourhood of the burgh, who
70.25 benevolence as (MS) / benevolence, as
70.28 Royal Burgh (MS) / royal burgh
70.30 Council (MS) / council
70.32 protector of (MS) / protector and Provost of
70.33 the family (MS) / the knightly family
70.38 alien in (MS) / alien, in
71.12 him that (MS) / him, that
71.18 it. (MS) / that element.
71.21 added that (MS) / added, that
71.37 orders (MS) / instructions
71.38 steer as, while (MS steer as while) / steer, as that, while
71.40 deck that (MS) / deck, that
71.43 Wallace (MS) / the Champion
71.43 pirate captain (MS) / Red Rover
72.2 shout as (MS) / shout, as
72.7 began with (MS) / began betwixt them with
72.7 fury that (MS) / fury, that
72.13 the Champion of Scotland (MS) / the Scottish Champion
72.20 Wallace (MS) / The victor
72.26 in (MS) / on
72.27 announced the (MS) / announced that the
72.33 victor that (MS) / victor, that
73.22 murmuring, upon (MS) / murmuring, the citizens, upon
73.23 alarm the citizens were (MS) / alarm, were
73.30 complaints at (MS) / complaints, at
73.33 fairer as (MS) / fairer person as
74.16 each foot (MS) / every hoof
74.17 extraordinary that (MS) / extraordinary, that
74.23 opinion that (MS) / opinion, that
74.29 true the (MS) / true, the
74.33 hallowing (MS) / hallooing
75.1 seat without (MS) / seat, without
75.2 ay! I (MS) / ay; I
75.3 mine—But (MS) / mine; but
75.4 perilous—so (MS) / perilous; so
75.8 Isabel or Jezabel,—'tis the (MS) / Isabel, or Jezabel,—all the
75.28 like (MS) / likely
75.29 spoke (MS) / talked
75.30 once in (MS) / once, in
76.7 gloves filled full (MS) / gloves full
76.20 deeds till (MS) / deeds, till

76.22   reckon up (MS) / count
76.25   burgh—an (MS Borough an) / burgh as an
76.25   and his (MS) / and one which, his
76.26   excepted, neither (MS) / excepted, is neither
76.28   hand the (MS) / hand, the
76.34   chief (MS) / prime
76.40   horseman—if (MS) / horseman. If
77.3   hobbiler (MS) / hobbler
77.4   Southland (MS) / southland
77.5   Southron that (MS) / Southron, that
77.14   tremble in (MS) / tremble, in
77.24   considerably by (MS) / considerably, by
77.33   discourse by (MS) / discourse, by
78.4   harangue had (MS) / harangue, had
78.6   thought fitting (MS) / thought most fitting
78.9   menacing (MS) / repulsive
78.11   Hellgarth-hill (MS) / Hellgarth
78.20   head when (MS) / head, when
78.20   added, "And (MS added "And) / added,— [new paragraph] "And
78.22   any who (MS) / any one who
78.29   whisper (MS) / whimper
78.33   oaths that (MS) / oaths, that
78.40   hobbiler (MS hobiler) / hobbler
79.2   he saw his (MS) / the Bonnet maker's
79.2   adversary bestride (MS) / adversary was seen to bestride
79.5   rifled and (MS) / rifled, and
79.22   toward (MS) / towards
79.23   altogether so (MS) / altogether exhibiting an aspect so
79.24   appearance that (MS) / appearance, that
79.33   war-saddle as (MS) / war-saddle, as
79.42   honour if (MS) / honour, if
79.43   of your (MS) / of you, your
80.35   friend, that (MS) / friend, Henry Smith, that
81.10   the armourer. (MS) / the stout armourer.
81.20   bewrays"—— (MS) / bewrays——"
81.27   yard. It is carved (MS yard It is carved) / yard, and had it painted and carved
81.33   one most (MS) / one, most
81.34   blow that, (MS) / blow, that,
81.41   evil—Besides (MS) / evil;—besides
82.11   Bonnet-maker and (MS) / Bonnet-maker, and
82.40   clapper as (MS) / clapper, as
83.1   him (MS) / his
83.10   Harry (MS) / Henry
83.10   looks and (MS) / looks, and
83.13   is to (MS) / is, to
83.22   armourer, again (MS) / armourer," again
83.27   undone (MS) / opened
83.31   intimation with (MS) / intimation, with
83.38   casks and (MS) / casks, and
83.41   reverendly (MS) / reverently
83.43   sword or (MS) / sword, or
85.8   length—fill (MS) / length. Fill
85.9   cup—Prosperity (MS) / cup. Prosperity
85.11   up and (MS) / up, and

85.24	riving (MS) / reiving
85.24	courtiers and (MS) / courtiers, and
85.26	night, stood (MS) / night; they stood
85.31	Longueville I (MS) / Longueville, I
85.33	Do (MS) / do
85.40	said that (MS) / said, that
86.10	chamber the (MS) / chamber, the
86.12	man and (MS) / man, and
86.28	flaming (MS) / flashing
87.8	claimed if the owner or his (MS) / claimed of the owner, if his
87.9	Here (MS) / Hark
87.11	are to (MS) / must
87.29	paid than (MS) / paid, than
87.32	intrusion or (MS) / intrusion, or
87.36	pearls of (MS) / pearls, of
87.39	an embroidered (MS) / the embroidered
88.1	moved ungracefully, (MS) / moved, lame and ungracefully,
88.4	and second (MS) / and the second
88.9	were ought (MS) / were, ought
88.12	beloved. Robert (MS) / beloved. The qualities of Robert
88.12	was (MS) / were
88.12	this (MS) / all these
88.15	achievement (MS) / achievements
88.20	which he (MS) / which, he
88.31	his fond father (MS) / in fondness he
88.37	amours and (MS) / amours, and
88.37	revels practised (MS) / revels, practised
88.43	temper had (MS) / temper, had
89.5	sovereign so (MS) / sovereign, so
89.7	machinations the (MS) / machinations, the
89.9	would (MS) / should
89.9	daughter might (MS) / daughter, might
89.11	competition (MS) / contest for preference
89.31	to a (MS) / to Marjory Douglas, a
89.35	ratification the (MS) / ratification, the
89.38	like (MS) / likely
90.7	House (MS) / house
90.8	Drummond, and gifted (MS) / Drummond, gifted
90.19	complicated that (MS) / complicated, that
90.24	cham..leon (MS) / cameleon
90.31	course that (MS) / course, that
90.33	excellent, and his resolutions so (MS) / excellent, but whose resolutions were so
90.36	scarce (MS) / scarcely
90.36	add that (MS) / add, that
90.38	facile (MS) / easy-tempered
90.38	indeed theirs (MS) / indeed, theirs
91.14	view were (MS) / view, were
91.15	Church (MS) / church
91.17	belief and the (MS) / belief, and by the
91.22	mentioned secured (MS) / mentioned, secured
91.24	Church as (MS) / Church, as
92.9	Church (MS) / church
92.11	Keys both (MS) / keys, both
92.13	Henry (Magnum) / Robert

92.13   nominated (MS) / recommended
92.14   lips of (MS) / lips, of
92.15   pravity (MS) / depravity
92.40   rein (MS) / reins
92.40   much—more (MS) / much; more
92.42   sovereign—but (Editorial) / sovereign; but
        There is no punctuation in the MS here. Scott opened a parenthetical
        comment with a dash (see the preceding emendation); a second dash is
        required.
92.42   Grace (MS) / grace
93.9   good (MS) / holy
93.17   title (MS) / reason
93.30   sorners than (MS) / sorners, than
93.34   in (MS) / of
93.42   hospitality (MS) / generous kindness
93.43   House (MS) / house
94.16   seek (MS) / ask
94.26   Monarch. "But (MS Monarch "But) / Monarch; "but
94.27   alas (MS) / Alas
94.43   known. The (MS) / known to us. The
95.6   his (MS) / this temporary
95.10   executed must (MS) / executed, must
95.18   now to (MS) / now, to
95.28   housewife who (MS) / housewife, who
95.39   John until (MS) / John, until
96.2   agreed that (MS) / agreed, that
96.4   this to (MS) / this, to
96.15   attain while (MS) / attain, while
96.17   a very different (MS) / a different
96.20   brother in (MS) / brother, in
96.24   whether sword were worn or no (MS) / in absence of a sword
96.29   mention that (MS) / mention, that
96.30   buildings called (MS) / buildings, called
96.31   in fact (MS) / unless on such occasions
96.35   building containing (MS) / building, containing
96.40   *hospitium* for (MS) / *hospitium*, for
96.42   accommodation for (MS) / accommodation, for
97.8   brothers (MS) / relatives
97.9   Albany as (MS) / Albany, as
97.11   Steward (MS) / Stewart
97.12   Muir (MS) / More
97.14   forget (MS) / omit
97.43   Rothsay as you (MS) / Rothsay you
99.12   March with (MS) / March, with
99.21   glee-woman with (MS) / glee-woman, with
99.27   want (MS) / wants
99.37   poniard: he (MS) / poniard. He
99.37   anteroom (MS) / antiroom
100.16 charge as (MS) / charge, as
100.30 kerne than (MS) / kerne, than
100.33 arms when (MS) / arms, when
101.14 by (MS) / beside
101.18 'tis (MS) / so
101.19 glee-woman (MS) / glee-maiden
101.24 Prior like (MS) / Prior, like

101.25 implied. The (MS) / implied, as an attempt to prevent the dispute betwixt Albany and himself. The
103.1 finished than (MS) / finished, than
103.12 as by her (MS) / as her
103.22 that of (MS) / that, of
103.24 as every (MS) / as of every
103.27 gay science (MS) / Gay Science
103.32 brother—Go (MS) / brother——"—And when they had both left the room, the King continued, "Go
The MS reads: 'go my Good Father Abbot call Rothsay here instantly—go good cousin of March'. For a repeated 'Rothsay' 'the Prince' was substituted; it was also necessary to get Albany out of the room, and so the addition of 'Go, my dearest brother' is appropriate. But the phrase 'And when they had both left the room, the King continued' is unnecessary, and has been clumsily inserted: a long dash followed by inverted commas, followed by a short dash has no parallel in Ed1.
103.33 it—I (MS) / it. I
103.42 ground in such a manner that (MS) / ground, in such a manner, that
104.3 monarch (MS) / Monarch
104.14 Majesty (MS) / royal person
104.16 redress"——(Magnum) / redress—"
104.27 Edinburgh ere (MS) / Edinburgh, ere
104.38 Oh my (MS) / Oh, my
105.1 Even the deep-vaulted (MS) / The deep-vaulted
105.6 broil. Humbly (MS) / broil—Humbly
105.11 distinctly (MS) / correctly
105.17 amongst (MS) / of
105.21 lay (MS) / sat
105.22 them as (MS) / them, as
105.26 round (MS) / worn around
105.26 neck involved (MS) / neck, involved
105.28 them to (MS) / them, to
105.30 the gay or joyous science (MS) / Gay or Joyous Science
105.33 country which lay (MS derived: country lay) / country lying
105.40 suit which (MS) / suit, which
106.1 at least (MS) / about
106.2 had, anticipating the (MS had anticipating the) / had anticipated the
106.2 obliterated (MS) / in obliterating
106.6 assumed as (MS) / assumed, as
106.7 miseries that (MS) / miseries, that
106.13 joyous science (MS) / Joyous Science
106.15 jest or (MS) / jest, or
106.18 It was (MS) / It may be here remarked, that it was
106.18 women could (MS) / women, very numerous in that age, could
106.20 age (MS) / time
106.21 these (MS) / such
106.22 safely where (MS) / safely, where
106.25 other (MS) / similar
106.26 public pleasure, itinerant musicians and (MS) / public amusement, the itinerant musicians, for instance, and
106.27 our day (MS) / our own day
106.27 precarious to (MS) / precarious, to
106.31 forward and (MS) / forward to the bystanders, and
106.34 Aymer; and now she prayed (MS) / Aymer; who now prayed
106.39 affected whether (MS) / affected, whether

106.41 by-standers thought (MS) / by-standers, thought
107.13 horseman the (MS) / horseman, the
107.14 bearing forwards thus gracefully (MS) / thus gracefully bearing forward
107.18 low and (MS) / low, and
107.26 to in (MS) / to, in
107.29 unbonneted and (MS) / unbonneted, and
107.37 on all hands (MS) / by all around
107.39 She sung (MS) / She recommenced her lay, and sung
107.39 accordingly and (MS) / accordingly, while
107.42 melancholy song (MS) / plaintive ditty
108.6   and presence, circumstances of which (MS and presence circumstances
        of which) / and circumstances, a discrepancy to which
108.27 he (MS) / the Duke of Rothsay
108.27 had remained (MS) / now remained
108.28 anger. Even (MS) / anger, at this unseemly spectacle. Even
108.29 Archibald Earl of Douglas, called THE GRIM (Scott in ICopy Archi-
        bald earl of Douglas, calld THE GRIM) / the Black Douglas
108.36 step-father was (MS) / step-father, was
108.42 respectful or (MS) / respectful, or
109.2   said. "I put one (MS) / said, "I give thee one
109.2   piece in thy little purse for (MS) / piece for
109.3   me, and another (MS) / me, another
109.5   lips make music (MS) / lips (and thine for fault of better may be called
        so) make sweet music
109.31 dared"——— (MS) / dared———"
109.41 The Prior had (MS) / The Prior, dispatched by the King, as we have
        seen in the last chapter, had
110.2   beardless (MS) / childish
110.4   Douglas— (MS) / Douglas,—
110.21 thrust (MS) / rush
110.21 fighting, but (MS) / fighting with each other, but
111.2   overset (MS) / upset
111.4   endanger your (MS) / endanger the dissolution of your
111.12 dismounted and (MS) / dismounted, and
111.24 few." (MS) / few for resistance."
112.10 lord, between (MS) / lord," answered our acquaintance the Smith,
        "between
112.17 smith (MS) / Smith
112.19 spoke (MS) / spoken
112.21 Duke, my Lord (MS) / Duke!—My Lord
112.23 his ear." (MS) / his royal ear."
112.42 canst (MS) / Canst
113.5   Smith, must (MS) / Smith, she must
113.13 service and (MS) / service, and
113.15 find among (MS) / find, among
113.15 retinue knights (MS) / retinue, knights
113.19 true—I (MS) / true, I
113.20 craft and (MS) / craft, and
113.20 general to (MS) / general, to
113.25 serve (MS) / obey
113.26 weapon or (MS) / weapon, or
113.26 wielding (MS) / welding
113.31 thee if (MS) / thee, if
113.34 bowstring with (MS) / bowstring, with
113.42 take her safe (MS) / place her in safety

113.43 David (Scott in ICopy David of) / Robin
114.2 rather take (MS) / rather give
114.9 Boniface"——(MS) / Boniface——"
114.24 hurried (MS) / hastened
114.31 Galwegians and (MS) / Galwegians, and
114.39 priest had left (MS) / priest left
114.40 them both followed (MS) / them followed
115.8 Monk and (MS) / Monk, and
115.11 looks (MS) / aspect
115.29 chapel and (MS) / chapel, and
115.31 time the (MS) / time, the
116.20 bones (MS) / relics
116.23 tone. "The (MS) / tone; "the
116.36 which held (MS) / which had before held
116.37 clothes (MS) / attire
117.3 But"——(MS) / But——"
117.11 can—And (MS) / can; and
117.18 his (MS) / its
117.19 feet to (MS) / feet, to
117.31 goliard (MS) / *galliard*
118.3 Henry roughly, (MS) / Henry, roughly,
118.4 pinning (MS) / palming
118.8 Achter (MS) / Auchter
118.22 incumbrance—there (MS) / incumbrance. There
118.28 thither; good friend, is there (MS thither; good friend is there) /
       thither, good friend! Is there
118.34 like (MS) / lack
119.2 grief and (MS) / grief, and
119.8 see (MS) / observe
119.12 trade, I'll be sworn by (MS trade Ill be sworn by) / trade—I'll be sworn,
       by
119.28 custom I (MS) / custom, I
119.35 make disturbance (MS) / make a disturbance
119.38 and find (MS) / and will find
119.39 country in (MS) / country, in
120.3 standard like (MS) / standard, like
120.25 and put (MS) / and would put
120.32 seven (MS) / six
120.32 morning when (MS) / morning, when
121.11 Catherine were (MS) / Catharine, were
121.16 added that (MS) / added, that
121.26 and in (MS) / and moreover in
121.33 Dominicans' (MS Dominicans) / Dominican's
121.35 pace (MS) / celerity of movement
121.37 of hard walking (MS) / of walking
122.8 beheld he (MS) / beheld, he
122.10 gently as (MS) / gently, as
122.17 carry it (MS) / take it up
122.24 voice requested (MS) / voice, requested
122.29 struck (MS) / touched
122.30 S'nails (MS) / 'Snails
123.16 peculiar (MS) / particular
123.27 me if (MS) / me, if
123.31 fantasy work (MS) / fantastic vanity
124.2 begin the very holiday (MS) / begins with the holiday

124.5   one (MS) / tooth
124.15 here be (MS) / here are
124.18 Bonnet-maker—"but (MS) / Bonnet-maker; "but
124.23 tale-bearer with my heels." (MS) / tale-bearer."
124.34 upon (MS) / on
125.3   considerable (MS) / large
125.4   behind, it (MS behind it) / behind it, it
125.8   house introduced (MS) / house, introduced
125.33 the delusions (MS) / the wicked delusions
125.37 it—but (MS) / it! But
125.38 fiend (MS) / Fiend
125.42 forty (MS) / thirty
126.23 sae (MS) / so
126.26 forward (MS) / forwards
127.9   ganging (MS) / going
127.9   Douglas for (MS) / Douglas, for
127.10 Henry, Henry, there (MS Henry Henry there) / Henry Gow, there
127.13 who's (MS whose) / who is
127.15 bride that (MS) / bride, that
127.21 want (MS) / wish
127.22 safely cared for. I (MS) / safely taken care of; and I
127.27 her, and (MS her and) / her during the night, and
127.28 call her (MS) / call on her
127.33 matter is (MS) / matter, is
127.43 morning and (MS) / morning, and
128.1   kindly if (MS) / kindly, if
128.11 the hard and sinewy fingers in (MS) / the sinewy fingers, in
128.19 home she (MS) / home, she
128.21 hail (MS) / whole
129.7   drama to (MS) / drama, to
129.10 armourer to (MS) / armourer, to
129.20 exterior dignity of his (MS) / exterior appearance of dignity becoming
      his
129.22 his external composure (MS) / his apparent composure
129.29 command when (MS) / commands, when
130.2   making (Editorial) / made
      There is a MS lacuna; the intermediaries supplied an appropriate word,
      but not the correct form.
130.3   reproof, laid (MS) / reproof, as he laid
130.3   head, as he said (MS) / head, and said
130.12 Dominic's (MS) / Dominic
130.14 company (MS) / subjects present
130.15 meeting by (MS) / meeting, by
130.21 more near (MS) / nearer
130.41 see (MS) / of course know
131.1   here a goodly train of witnesses (MS) / here goodly witnesses
131.9   retreat when (MS) / retreat, when
131.13 lords, and (Editorial) / lords," said the King, "and
      The phrase 'when the king interrupted him' is not in the MS; when it
      was added the speech marker 'said the King' became redundant and
      should have been deleted.
131.23 buff-coat a (MS) / buff-coat, a
131.36 Knight (MS) / knight
131.37 barrace. Or, (MS) / barrace; or,
132.2   hoot at and (MS) / hoot and

132.5   rascaille (MS) / rascally
132.8   churls like (MS) / churls, like
132.11   father—"Since (MS) / father—[new paragraph] "Since
132.20   Law (MS) / law
132.26   stand prepared (MS) / stand well prepared
132.29   Charteris's (MS) / Charteris'
132.33   Rover when (MS) / Rover, when
132.41   Crown (MS) / crown
133.1   command while (MS) / command, while
133.1   earldom of the Crown (MS) / my Earldom of the crown
133.2   Douglas it (MS) / Douglas, it
133.10   tiger. (MS) / tiger!—
133.21   Nevertheless (MS) / nevertheless
133.22   but 'Arrest (MS) / but, 'Arrest
133.25   other than (MS) / other, than
134.6   Quhele," (ICopy) / Quhele, or Kay,"
134.11   man claiming (MS) / man, claiming
134.11   kindred but (MS) / kindred, but
134.15   Firth. May Heaven (MS) / Firth—may Heaven
134.16   wide and (MS) / wide, and
134.17   Church in (MS) / Church must in
134.19   Heaven as (MS) / Heaven, as
134.25   me than (MS) / me, than
134.27   will (MS) / shall
134.30   honourable (MS) / venerable
134.32   will (MS) / must
134.34   layman in (MS) / layman, in
134.39   perceive it (MS) / perceive that it
134.42   pinafore or (MS) / pinafore, or
135.7   weather that (MS) / weather, that
135.10   battles like (MS) / battles, like
135.12   vengeance if (MS) / vengeance, if
135.13   grants (MS) / largesses
135.14   Catherans (MS) / Highlanders
135.15   to defend the (MS) / to maintain the Church in possession of the
135.16   to the Church, (MS) / to her,
135.16   he still (MS) / he himself still
135.18   David (Scott in ICopy) / Robert
135.28   masquers (MS) / maskers
135.34   neighbours than (MS) / neighbours, than
136.9   Irish (MS) / Earish
136.18   interfered to (MS) / interfered, to
136.18   Earl giving (MS) / Earl from giving
136.23   Chattan and (MS) / Chattan, and
136.23   Quhele are (ICopy and MS) / Kay, are
          There is no comma in the MS. 'Quhele' in an unidentified hand is
          substituted for 'Kay' in the ICopy.
136.24   tribes who (MS) / tribes, who
136.31   will (MS) / shall
136.37   frontier to (MS) / frontier, to
136.39   ferocity (MS) / fury
136.41   pleasure than (MS) / pleasure, than
137.5   me that (MS) / me, that
137.6   thee?'—it tells me (Editorial) / thee?' it tells me
          The phrase 'it tells me' is not in the MS; when it was added the interme-

diaries failed to provide adequate punctuation.

137.6　me that (MS) / me, that
137.16　their (MS) / these
137.21　they (MS) / both
137.23　attained—and (MS) / attained, and
137.23　would (MS) / should
137.27　David (Lockhart in ICopy) / son Robert
137.30　think that (MS) / think, that
137.37　it requires (MS) / these require
137.41　dispatch (MS) / destruction
137.42　they (MS) / these Gael
137.43　sand-bags like (MS) / sand-bags, like
138.2　skeans in (MS) / skeans, in
138.5　court will (MS) / court, will
138.16　say that (MS) / say, that
138.24　chivalry as (MS) / chivalry, as
138.28　blood but what I (MS) / blood, but I
138.41　reason and (MS) / reason or
139.20　limbs without (MS) / limbs, without
139.28　seek wool (MS) / seek such wool
139.30　prince who (MS) / prince, who
139.31　bonnet by (MS) / bonnet, by
139.33　they who (MS) / men who
139.39　mute (MS) / dumb
140.4　understand that (MS) / understand, that
140.5　settlement"——(MS) / settlement——"
140.6　Robert?" (MS) / Robert!"
140.11　warfare (MS) / battle
140.17　pieces than (MS) / pieces, than
140.18　finished so (MS) / finished, so
140.21　mournfully because (MS) / mournfully, because
140.33　him when (MS) / him, when
140.36　congregation as (MS) / congregation, as
141.10　monastery (MS) / Monastery
141.12　plenty were (MS) / plenty, were
141.22　desire is (MS) / desire, is
142.3　assurance that (MS) / assurance, that
142.6　crown we (MS) / crown, we
142.10　delusions." (MS) / delusions.'
142.25　We sit (MS) / We shall sit
142.41　ours. Yet (MS) / ours; yet
142.42　council too, that (MS to) / council, that
143.18　Prince which (MS) / Prince, which
143.34　David (Magnum) / Robert
144.4　man carelessly. (MS) / man, carelessly.
144.7　David (Lockhart in ICopy) / Robert
144.25　David (Scott in ICopy) / Robin
144.34　tools rather (MS) / tools, rather
144.37　David (Scott in ICopy) / Robin
145.6　David (Scott in ICopy) / Robin
145.15　two that (MS) / two, that
145.24　service to (MS) / service, to
145.32　direction sat (MS) / direction, sat
146.2　my dearest daughter (MS) / my daughter
146.12　duties—their (Editorial) / duties;—their

Here and in the next emendation the intermediaries inserted different rather than parallel punctuation marks.

146.15 Heaven—all (MS) / Heaven,—all
146.16 duties (MS) / claims
146.18 Surely (MS) / Verily
146.20 world when (MS) / world, when
146.27 persons as (MS) / persons, as
146.29 Church which (Magnum and MS) / church, which
146.42 light (MS) / lightly
147.4 heathenesse (MS) / Heathenesse
147.8 since (MS) / that
147.10 cruelty as (MS) / cruelty, as
147.24 customs to (MS) / customs, to
147.28 is that (MS) / is, that
148.6 you than (MS) / you, than
148.7 inform (MS) / reform
148.12 and a looking (MS) / and some wishful regards looking
148.20 affirmed concerning (MS) / affirmed, concerning
148.30 changed hastily from (MS) / changed from
148.31 she replied (MS) / she hastily replied
148.35 "*Your* Valentine (MS) / "Your Valentine
148.39 bishop as (MS) / bishop, as
149.4 misconstructions (MS) / misconstruction
149.9 to misconstruction (MS) / to worse misconstruction
149.12 do—and (MS) / do; and
149.16 Day is (MS) / Day, is
149.18 sound (MS) / prove
149.29 wooer (MS) / lover
149.37 Know that (MS) / Know, that
150.2 party by your (MS) / party as I passed your
150.3 Bailie Craigdallie's (MS) / the civil power in order
150.6 view that (MS) / view, that
150.11 may gratify (MS) / may promise to gratify
150.14 man to (MS) / man, to
150.17 threats from (MS) / threats, from
150.18 ought to (MS) / ought as much to
150.19 would prevent (MS) / should prohibit
150.29 nay I (MS) / nay, I
150.29 convinced, his (MS) / convinced, that his
150.31 Church and (Editorial and MS) / church, and
150.32 sink more deeply (MS) / sink deeply
150.33 fruits for (MS) / fruits, for
150.34 said that (MS) / said, that
150.36 things to (MS) / things, to
150.37 on (MS) / at
150.40 prospect (MS) / prospects
150.42 display it. But my (MS) / display them; but my
151.11 Margaret (Editorial) / Catharine
This emendation is discussed in the Essay on the Text, 417.
151.15 alliance from temporal and (MS) / alliance, from temporal, and
151.21 among those sovereigns (MS) / and those heroines
151.25 calm yet (MS) / calm, yet
151.31 world affect (MS) / world, affect
151.34 Clement who (MS) / Clement, who
151.37 Church (MS) / church

151.40 much to (MS) / much, to
151.42 her father's (MS) / my father's
152.1 you that (MS) / you, that
152.12 Heaven that (MS) / Heaven, that
152.14 Yes! Catherine (MS) / Yes, Catharine,
152.15 exclaim when (MS) / exclaim, when
152.16 harshly struggling (MS) / harshly, struggling
152.18 lips rather (MS) / lips, rather
152.23 their place (MS) / this place
152.24 contiguity that (MS) / contiguity, that
152.26 breadth betwixt (MS) / breadth, betwixt
152.34 were fixed (MS) / were visible among them, fixed
152.35 speaking pointed (MS) / speaking, pointed
152.36 attention could (MS) / attention, could
153.2 head and (MS) / head, and
153.9 Perth to (MS) / Perth, to
153.12 monk (MS) / Monk
153.18 monk (MS) / Monk
153.27 monk (MS) / Monk
153.36 Conachar to (MS) / Conachar, to
153.39 roebuck from (MS) / roebuck, from
153.43 person was (MS) / person, was
154.1 burnished that (MS) / burnished, that
154.4 clasp adorned (MS) / clasp, adorned
154.7 stick with (MS) / stick, with
154.28 autumn (MS) / Autumn
154.34 servitude to (MS) / servitude, to
155.26 mantle (MS) / plaid
155.29 eye seems (MS) / eye, seems
155.32 forests extend (MS) / forests, extend
155.36 also to (MS) / also, to
155.36 them right glad (MS) / them glad
155.43 mean Hector. (MS) / mean, Hector.
156.9 prayest (MS) / shalt pray
156.19 where (MS) / when
156.23 suspected that (MS) / suspected, that
156.29 lips by (MS) / lips, by
156.34 anxiety as (MS) / anxiety, as
156.37 Perth from (MS) / Perth, from
156.40 appearance than (MS) / appearance, than
157.6 now avowed (MS) / seemed now to avow
157.9 died (MS) / had fallen
157.11 in behalf (MS) / on behalf
157.13 to while (MS) / to, while
157.24 bosom when (MS) / bosom, when
158.1 ills by (MS) / ills, by
158.5 them—well (MS) / them; well
158.20 in things (MS) / in some things
158.23 shoulders instead (MS) / shoulders, instead
158.32 them too (MS) / them, too
158.36 dresses (MS) / dressings
159.12 drips (MS) / drops
159.13 practises though (MS) / practises, though
159.17 stillest are (MS) / stillest, are
159.19 men-at-arms go (MS) / men-at-arms, go

159.20 We who are clerks win (MS) / We, who are clerks, win
159.29 lessons—why wouldst (MS) / lessons? Why wouldst
159.29 me further (MS) / me faster or further
159.30 vengeance than (MS) / vengeance, than
159.33 such as I am (MS) / men like me
159.42 suffered has (MS) / suffered, has
160.5 too much below me in degree to be either (MS too much below me
        degree to be either) / too low in degree, to be to me either
160.6 fear to me. Yet (MS) / fear. Yet
160.7 wound and (MS) / wound, and
160.12 prince should (MS) / prince, should
160.13 sapling by (MS) / sapling, by
160.39 one chance more (MS) / one more chance
160.43 hand that (MS) / hand, that
161.1 word?—is (Editorial and MS: word—is) / word! is
161.5 Stand (MS) / stand
161.7 itself requires (MS) / itself, requires
161.13 ease while (MS) / ease, while
161.18 Wynd or (MS) / Wynd, or
161.19 action assuage (MS) / action, assuage
161.27 house were (MS) / house, were
161.31 forced the (MS) / forced, the
161.36 street like (MS) / street, like
161.38 citizens to (MS) / citizens, to
161.42 peace or (MS) / peace, or
162.9 Pottercarrier (MS) / Leech
162.13 townsfolks (MS) / townsfolk
162.23 would (MS) / should
162.24 a smith (Editorial) / a Smith
162.32 keenly that (MS) / keenly, that
162.38 brotherly"—— (MS brotherly ⟨vow⟩"——) / brotherly league,
        which——"
163.4 him after (MS) / him, after
163.8 entered whose (MS) / entered, whose
163.14 circumstance as (MS) / circumstance, as
163.29 sure—I (MS) / sure. I
163.30 you—and (MS) / you, and
163.35 man (MS) / party
164.7 insinuated (MS) / insinuating
164.12 swordman (MS) / swordsman
164.16 ordinance (MS) / ordinances
165.7 say that (MS) / say, that
165.12 mentionest (MS) / mentioned
165.27 lion as (MS) / lion, as
165.28 remember that (MS) / remember, that
165.41 coolness instead (MS) / coolness, instead
165.42 patient that (MS) / patient, that
166.9 scoffs to (MS) / scoffs, to
166.19 him with (MS) / him, with
166.19 will (MS) / would
166.20 sleep in (MS) / sleep on
166.27 him—yet, (MS) / him. Yet,
166.29 balm as (MS) / balm, as
166.32 essences before (MS) / essences, before
166.33 dimly till (MS) / dimly, till

166.35   power if (MS) / power, if
167.2   conscience acknowledge (MS) / conscience, acknowledge
167.4   room, his (Editorial) / room; his
167.17   commands (MS) / command
167.19   intoxicated see (MS) / intoxicated, see
167.21   fellow before (MS) / fellow, before
167.23   crosses (MS) / has crossed
167.38   is that (MS) / is, that
167.39   head were (MS) / head, were
167.40   powers—to (MS) / powers to
168.2   Ramorny was (MS) / Ramorny, was
168.11   minstrel; the (MS) / minstrel; while the
168.13   that is the fat broth (MS) / the fat broth, that is,
168.14   highly-toasted (MS) / highly-roasted
168.17   evening that (MS) / evening, that
168.20   Perth as (MS) / Perth, as
168.29   nobility to (MS) / nobility, to
168.31   deaths and (MS) / deaths, and
168.38   persons habited (MS) / persons, habited
168.40   slashed and (MS) / slashed, and
169.4   weapons and (MS) / weapons, and
169.9   habitation to (MS) / habitation, to
169.12   father (MS) / Father
169.15   bloods than (MS) / bloods, than
169.22   ring in (MS) / ring-in
169.25   flagon or (MS) / flagon, or
169.25   merry in (MS) / merry, in
169.31   cruize (MS) / progress
169.40   and owe (MS) / and you owe
170.15   not of my (MS) / not my
170.17   Douglas-man whom (MS) / Douglas-man, whom
170.19   conscience and (MS) / conscience, and
170.20   father (MS) / Father
170.20   choler have (MS) / choler, have
170.30   man. Henry (MS man Henry) / man that Henry
170.31   struck him at the (MS) / struck at in the
170.38   charges with (MS) / charges, with
170.40   sword they (MS) / sword, they
170.41   father (MS) / Father
170.43   patient: thou (MS) / patient; thou
171.1   turn an (MS) / turn, an
171.13   that hath (MS) / that shall win
171.14   regret"——(MS) / regret——"
171.15   Prithee (MS) / Pr'ythee
171.19   hold (MS) / held
171.26   hasty (MS) / rash
171.37   her"——(MS) / her—"
         The dash is short in Ed1 because it comes at the end of a line.
172.1   swear he (MS) / swear that he
172.3   therefore in (MS) / therefore, in
172.8   three-year (MS) / four-years
172.10   petticoat and (MS) / petticoat, and
172.13   streets"——(MS) / streets——"
172.15   house with (MS) / house, with
172.22   catheran than (MS) / catheran, than

172.35 himself would (MS) / himself, would
172.36 But"——(MS) / But——"
172.38 like (MS) / likely
172.42 Confession (MS) / confession
172.43 thee that (MS) / thee, that
173.1   myself——" (MS) / myself"——
173.5   thee—as (MS) / thee, as
173.8   door if (MS) / door, if
173.9   old who (MS) / old, who
173.11 trouble to (MS) / trouble, to
173.21 youth and (MS) / youth, and
173.26 can (MS) / should
173.30 I that (MS) / I, that
173.33 should (MS) / would
173.35 maintained though (MS) / maintained, though
173.39 wrath (MS) / unrestrained anger
174.2   rampage (MS) / rampauge
174.3   return—But this (MS) / return, and this
174.9   slip (MS) / step
174.18 high (MS) / High
174.19 street (MS) / Street
174.43 masquers (MS) / maskers
175.9   dominions without (MS) / dominions, without
175.20 silk so (MS) / silk, so
175.23 feathers assembled (MS) / feathers, assembled
175.32 him, "Crack (MS him "Crack) / him,—[new paragraph] "Crack
175.42 twinge (MS) / touch
176.15 door (MS) / house
176.27 masquers (MS) / maskers
176.29 hurried though (MS) / hurried, though
176.35 I see (MS) / I will see
176.43 voice the (MS) / voice, the
177.1   exclaimed, "For (MS exclaimed "For) / exclaimed,—[new paragraph] "For
177.5   be shame (MS) / be a shame
177.13 lane and (MS) / lane, and
177.17 apprehensions which (MS) / apprehensions, which
177.26 house. I (MS) / house—I
177.28 evening for (MS) / evening, for
177.31 cup (MS) / draught
177.42 table he (MS) / table, he
178.9   afflicted (MS) / affected
178.10 David (Scott in ICopy) / Robin
178.24 is she (MS) / is, she
178.29 thee of moment," (MS) / thee about of moment,"
178.34 waive (MS) / wave
178.42 called from (MS) / called, from
178.43 carried in (MS) / carried, in
178.43 duty to (MS) / duty, to
179.16 truth at (MS) / truth, at
179.17 the quarrel (MS) / thy quarrel
179.19 afraid—But (MS) / afraid. But
179.19 ruffian—and (MS) / ruffian; and
179.20 family—And (MS) / family, and
179.21 thou"——(MS) / thou——"

179.22   Henry hastily (MS) / Henry, hastily
179.22   will (MS) / shall
179.32   breakfast and (MS) / breakfast, and
179.33   Soldan as (MS) / Soldan, as
179.40   humour and (MS) / humour, and
179.43   gold for (MS) / gold, for
180.4   thus Sir (MS) / thus, Sir
180.6   Provost is (MS) / Provost, is
180.19   not him (MS) / him not
180.21   all saints (MS) / all the saints
180.22   and"—— (MS) / and——"
181.2   voice—"And what (MS) / voice, "and if thou hast, what
181.5   close if (MS) / close, if
181.8   glee-woman in (MS) / glee-woman, in
181.13   father (MS) / Father
181.14   us in (MS) / us, in
181.15   now he (MS) / now, he
181.20   mire an (MS) / mire, an
181.21   head to (MS) / head, to
181.24   Come you—out, (MS) / Come, get you out,
181.28   me as far as my own house in (MS) / me to my own house, in
181.33   of 'Broken (MS) / of, 'Broken
182.2   innocent though (MS) / innocent, though
182.2   fellow stepped (MS) / fellow, stepped
182.4   behind against (MS) / behind, against
182.15   path in (MS) / path, in
182.17   injury either (MS) / injury, either
182.18   person (MS) / persons
182.21   command (MS) / sway
182.22   circulates and beauty (MS) / circulates, and when beauty
182.23   awake and (MS) / awake, and
182.27   forces to (MS) / forces, to
183.6   streets, since he had (MS) / streets, he having had
183.6   burghers (MS) / burgesses
183.11   called than (MS) / called, than
183.15   mutiny and (MS) / mutiny, and
183.20   who bear these firkins which (MS) / who carry these firkins, which
183.34   recusants who (MS) / recusants, who
183.39   best (MS) / better
183.40   all in (MS) / all, in
184.10   proper to (MS) / characteristic of
184.11   period. [new paragraph] (MS) / period [new paragraph]
184.14   force that (MS) / force, that
184.22   and the (MS) / and to the
184.25   saying he (MS) / saying, he
184.25   spoke (MS) / spoken
184.32   body and (MS) / body, and
185.6   terrific that (MS) / terrific, that
185.10   himself, "It (MS himself— "It) / himself,— [new paragraph] "It
185.12   external but (MS) / external, but
185.12   at—my (MS) / at my
185.16   knees implored (MS) / knees, implored
185.23   him—he (Editorial) / him, he
185.38   butcher?—and (MS) / butcher—and
185.39   E'en (MS e'en) / Eve

185.42 house where (MS) / house, where
185.43 wine which (MS) / wine, which
186.8 out, "Down (MS out— "Down) / out,— [new paragraph] "Down
186.10 best if (MS) / best, if
186.33 Highness's service (MS highnesses) / Highness' service
186.35 Prince. "I (Magnum) / Prince "I
The space for punctuation is evident in Ed1, but which mark should be there cannot be determined from the context, and there is no punctuation in the MS.
186.38 "It (MS) / 'It
187.9 awakened summoned (MS) / awakened, summoned
187.17 snake from (MS) / snake, from
187.36 furnace.—I (MS) / furnace. I
187.41 trifle were (MS) / trifle, were
187.43 artizan by (MS) / artizan, by
188.4 opposites, (MS) / opposites as you have,
188.5 *but*—You (MS) / *but*—you
188.15 nay more (MS) / nay, more
188.16 must"——(MS) / must——"
188.17 Ramorny?" said (MS) / Ramorny?"—said
188.20 truly—but (MS) / truly; but
188.21 might (MS) / may
188.27 stump told (MS) / stump, told
188.29 am (MS) / may be
188.32 butterfly on (MS) / butterfly, on
188.40 in the one hand and (MS) / in one hand, and
188.43 David, third (Scott in ICopy David third) / Robert, fourth
Lockhart deleted Scott's ICopy change and inserted after 'throne' at 188.40 ', throne, I suppose like my father before me I must dropt my own name, & dubbed Robert in honour of ↑ the ↓ Bruce—well an' if it be so—'.
189.8 you that (MS) / you, that
189.10 two (MS) / too
189.12 steel-coat to (MS) / steel-coat, to
189.12 night-gown (MS) / gown
189.12 night-brawl"——(MS) / night-brawl——"
189.15 how (MS) / How
189.18 for Wallace (MS) / for wight Wallace
189.23 that a hand of flesh and blood might do in (MS) / that might be done by a hand of flesh and blood, in
189.31 truth of (MS) / truth touching the legend of
189.31 Steelhand better (MS) / Steelhand of Carselogie better
189.32 time that (MS) / time, that
190.1 glove as (MS) / glove, as
190.2 you though (MS) / you, though
190.9 presently (MS) / immediately
190.11 interior to (MS) / interior, to
190.13 privilege (MS) / privileges
190.16 take yonder (MS) / takes back yonder
190.17 bed at (MS) / bed, at
190.21 presses and (MS) / presses, and
190.28 Robert and (MS) / Robert, and
190.29 measure the King (MS) / measure which the good King
190.35 me to (MS) / me, to
190.38 life?—I (MS) / life? I

190.39 kingdom?—it (MS) / kingdom? It
191.1   temptations is (MS) / temptations, is
191.1   believe so (MS) / believe, so
191.6   house a (MS) / house, a
191.8   fie (MS) / Fie
191.9   saw that (MS) / saw, that
191.10 —it is (MS) / —It is
191.13 Highness (MS) / highness
191.21 court till (MS) / court, till
191.26 shed. Life (MS shed Life) / shed; life
191.27 itself—for (MS) / itself. For
191.29 socket—to (MS) / socket. To
191.34 David (Lockhart in ICopy) / Robert
191.37 David the Third (Lockhart in ICopy) / Robert the Fourth
192.4   cell where (MS) / cell, where
192.9   guilt mixed (MS) / guilt, mixed
192.12 will (MS) / would
192.17 example for (MS) / example, for
192.23 me on (MS) / me, on
192.25 land shall (MS) / land, shall
192.27 Scotland. Well (MS) / Scotland!—Well
192.27 indeed, the (MS) / indeed, that the
192.41 it (Editorial) / It
193.3   colloquy than (MS) / colloquy, than
193.9   attendance (MS) / attendants
193.14 will"——— (MS) / will———"
193.15 brute (MS) / beast
193.15 is (MS) / are
193.23 revelry and (MS) / revelry, and
193.24 expended and (MS) / expended, and
193.27 sobriety endeavoured (MS) / sobriety, endeavoured
193.34 thither, wellnigh (MS) / thither, had wellnigh
193.36 said he (MS) / he said
193.43 apartments in (MS) / apartments, in
194.11 mind and (MS) / mind, and
194.15 that your (MS) / that the residue of your
194.16 sober to (MS) / sober, to
194.20 household as (MS) / household, as
194.43 hope that (MS) / hope, that
195.4   excuse. But (MS) / excuse; but
195.16 fast (MS) / frost
195.20 Perth. The ... morning. It therefore was (MS Perth The rich or rather those who had spent money on the preceding day slept off the remains of their unusual revelry—the poor lay in bed to enjoy the unusual indulgences of the morning. It therefore was) / Perth so that it was
195.26 fallen under (MS) / fallen, under
195.27 pleasure of (MS) / pleasure, of
195.32 buff-coat and (MS) / buff-coat, and
195.34 Smith lay (MS) / Smith that lay
195.39 Perth who (MS) / Perth, who
196.2   Scottish (MS) / Scotch
196.2   simple (MS) / semple
196.6   people who (MS) / people, who
196.8   convent (MS) / Convent
196.16 Albany that (MS) / Albany, that

196.33 priests or (MS) / priests, or
196.37 man with (MS) / man, with
196.39 back and (MS) / back, and
197.1 rioters or (MS) / rioters, or
197.1 King's (MS) / king's
197.2 ay and (MS) / ay, and
197.11 man (MS) / one
197.13 useless. Cut (MS useless. ↓ cut) / useless—cut
197.13 yeomen—lame (MS) / yeomen; lame
197.14 maim, stab (MS) / maim, and stab
197.14 horses—kill (Editorial) / horses; kill
        There is no MS punctuation here, but as there is a MS dash earlier in the
        sentence the intermediaries should have supplied a dash rather than a
        semicolon.
197.26 people whose (MS) / people, whose
197.39 time so (MS) / time, so
197.40 citizens, but (MS) / citizens; but
198.18 alarm, spread (MS) / alarm bells, spread
198.20 rendezvous where (MS) / rendezvous, where
198.27 nature as (MS) / nature, as
198.31 armour and (MS) / armour, and
198.38 three Stewarts," (Scott in ICopy) / three Robin Stewarts,"
199.5 bells (MS) / bell
199.8 practised under (MS) / practised, under
199.11 even an affectionate (MS) / even affectionate
199.13 bad news which (MS) / sinister intelligence, which
199.18 abroad than (MS) / abroad, than
199.22 lies—his (MS) / lies; his
199.23 born that (MS) / born, that
199.29 bed"—(MS) / bed—"
199.33 am (MS) / *am*
199.37 cause—Here (MS) / cause. Here
199.38 points—(MS) / points.—
199.38 Fortingall—(MS) / Fortingall.—
199.43 wilful that (MS) / wilful, that
200.10 She therefore hollowed (MS) / She, therefore, hollowed
200.11 hear (MS) / have been at
200.13 word—But (MS) / word, but
200.19 You (MS) / you
200.19 piece (Magnum) / peace
200.20 woman as (MS) / woman, as
200.23 doting (MS) / dotage
200.23 fool—no (MS) / fool. No
200.24 catching (MS) / snatching
200.31 Impossible!—Does (MS) / Impossible! Does
201.5 tirrivie and (MS) / tirrivie, and
201.10 Highlandmen (MS) / Highlanders
201.13 Catherine—they (MS) / Catharine. They
201.15 warstle—a (MS) / warstle. A
201.15 that—gie (MS) / that. Gie
201.17 wha (MS) / what
201.20 down to the—I (MS) / down—I
201.25 wad na (MS) / would not
201.31 amang (MS) / among
201.32 I were (MS) / am I

201.33 Catherine, why she's out (MS derived: Catherine whi shes out) / Catharine, who ere this is out
201.33 am—So (MS) / am?—so
201.36 manner which (MS) / manner, which
201.38 one who (MS) / one, who
201.40 pace (MS) / step
201.41 normally (MS derived: nomaly) / universally
201.42 them when (MS) / them, when
202.3 attracting any more (MS) / attracting more
202.6 general, or, it (MS general or it) / general—it
202.6 be, to (MS be to) / be to
202.6 friends for (MS) / friends, for
202.15 dearer than (MS) / dearer, than
202.24 spot which (MS) / spot, which
202.31 lover who (MS) / lover, who
202.32 her as (MS) / her, as
202.35 lanes and vennels on (MS) / lanes on
202.39 them, while (MS) / them, however, while
203.1 alarm which (MS) / alarm, which
203.17 and a buckler (MS) / and buckler
203.19 service as (MS) / service, as
203.22 Perth that (MS) / Perth, that
203.26 peevish peat Catherine (MS) / peevish Catharine
203.32 anxiety did (MS) / anxiety, did
203.42 someone (MS some one) / one
204.3 upon (MS) / on
204.8 thou that (MS) / thou, that
204.8 mayst (MS) / may
204.23 "Me (MS) / "*I*
204.24 fore-hammer as (MS) / fore-hammer, as
204.32 advantage by (MS) / advantage, by
204.34 dawning (MS) / colouring
204.35 regular for (MS) / regular, for
205.5 lover than (MS) / lover, than
205.10 is probable (MS) / would seem
205.12 scarce (MS) / scarcely
205.13 posture than (MS) / posture, than
205.30 amongst (MS) / among
205.36 woman who (MS) / woman, who
206.9 relief?—Did (MS) / relief? Did
206.39 measure (MS) / fortune
206.42 smith (MS) / Smith
207.8 ordained it that (MS ordaind it that) / ordered it, that
207.13 fellow who (MS) / fellow, who
207.26 both hands (MS) / both her hands
207.27 that (MS) / this
208.15 pleased stop (MS) / pleased to stop
208.18 father—and (MS) / father, and
208.20 unless"— (MS) / unless—"
208.28 witness"— (MS) / witness—"
208.29 "wherefore (MS) / "but wherefore
208.29 differences which should be (MS) / differences, which should all be
209.15 Ringan! None (MS) / Ringan! Let none
209.21 father (MS) / Father
210.13 habit—seemed (MS) / habit; seemed

210.15 danger—but (MS) / danger; but
210.15 man—I (MS) / man; I
210.17 liquor—and (MS) / liquor; and
210.17 me!—I (MS) / me! I
210.18 wrong—Holy (MS) / wrong. Holy
210.27 rid his (MS) / rid of his
211.15 Simon. "But (MS) / Simon; "but
211.16 have (MS) / Have
211.39 again. Had (MS) / again! Had
212.38 description (MS) / descriptions
213.18 its (MS) / the
214.3   reverend (MS) / Reverend
214.5   entry (MS) / Entry
214.6   Couvrefew (MS Couvrfew) / Curfew
214.7   pageant—That (MS) / pageant. It is also manifested, that
214.30 Street; by (MS) / Street, by
214.30 intreated (MS) / treated
214.40 masquing (MS) / masking
215.6   articles have (MS) / articles, have
215.7   masque (MS) / mask
215.15 masquers (MS) / maskers
215.35 masquing (MS) / masking
216.3   masquing (MS) / masking
216.11 conjecture (MS) / supposition
216.13 For whom think you the blow was meant (MS) / For whom, think you,
        was the blow meant
216.35 a face, friend Smith (MS) / a likely front, Smith
216.36 lie (MS) / are
216.37 masquers (MS) / maskers
217.10 Ramorny—How (MS) / Ramorny. How
217.13 Craigdallie. (MS) / Craigdallie,—
217.14 Provost—We (MS) / Provost,—we
217.26 are Ramorny's (MS) / are in Ramorny's
218.5   me (MS) / us
218.11 will (MS) / shall
218.36 upon wall and at gate, (MS) / upon the wall,
218.43 their (MS) / the
219.2   the ordeal (MS) / that
219.16 but (MS) / be
219.42 under contending (MS) / under these contending
220.1   supported and followed (MS) / followed and supported
220.5   years or (MS) / years, or
220.12 forwards with (MS) / forward, and with
220.14 briefly by (MS) / briefly,
220.28 will (MS) / shall
220.35 of this Fair (MS) / of the Fair
221.1   my—" husband (MS) / my—" [new paragraph] Husband
221.19 doing; (MS) / entertaining such sentiments for any one;
221.20 he (MS) / the deceased
221.24 —[new paragraph] (MS derived) / ,—[new paragraph]
222.2   was (MS) / should be
222.6   *VI* (MS) / *IV*
222.28 David (Scott in ICopy) / Robin
        Lockhart deleted Scott's change in the ICopy and substituted 'boy'
        instead.

222.30 Couvrefew (MS) / Curfew
222.33 Grace's (MS) / grace's
222.34 the (MS) / The
222.35 David (Lockhart in ICopy) / Robin
222.36 Couvrefew (MS) / Curfew
224.18 resumed (MS) / answered
224.19 Couvrefew (MS) / Curfew
224.38 remedy? (MS) / remedy!
225.2 vanities, which (MS) / vanities of life, which
225.11 further (MS) / farther
225.11 remove (MS) / removed
225.16 such proceeding (MS) / such a proceeding
225.17 am not I (MS) / am I not
226.6 those which (MS) / such as
226.11 cumbers (MS) / difficulty
226.40 Even (MS) / Eve
227.14 "That I (MS) / "I
227.14 him," said (MS) / him, No," said
227.16 had left (MS) / would leave
227.18 policy of (MS) / policy, of
227.19 that which (MS) / expressions, which
227.20 therefore, without (MS) / therefore, in his discourse, without
227.24 Marches (MS) / marches
227.31 is as certain (MS) / is certain
227.32 pride—but (MS) / pride;—But
227.32 doubted." (ICopy) / doubted, else have the annals of his house given
       him the name of Tine-man* for nothing."
       The footnote '*Tine-man, i. e. Lose-man.' was also deleted. It is not
       possible to tell who made the deletions, but Scott's is the only recognis-
       able hand on the page, and the change is in line with that at 108.29.
227.33 David (Scott in ICopy) / Robin
227.43 upon (MS) / on
228.5 waive (MS) / wave
228.9 to put (MS) / that of putting
228.9 slaughter (MS) / strife
228.9 cry (MS) / crying
228.13 Albany, "the (MS Albany "the) / Albany; "the
228.19 amongst (MS) / among
228.25 in the affection (MS) / at the filial affection
228.26 displayed. (MS) / displayed in his reply.
228.38 Rothsay is (Magnum) / Robin says
228.40 a (MS) / the
229.8 act upon (MS) / attempt to separate them at
229.9 violence would (MS) / violence, would
229.13 e'en (MS) / even
229.21 help (MS) / aid
229.22 aid (MS) / support
229.23 you we (MS) / you, that we
229.25 townsman"—— (MS) / townsman——"
230.17 or some (MS) / or by some
230.20 or the morning (MS) / or morning
231.12 charge (MS) / assertion
231.13 an (MS) / this
231.24 that one (MS) / that some one
231.43 speak his duelling (MS) / name the word combat

232.13 one (MS) / One
232.17 thee.—After (MS thee—After) / thee;—and after
232.19 curtal-axe, pretty much (MS) / curtal-axe, much
233.15 art to (MS) / emollients upon
233.29 yonder (MS) / yon
233.39 standing (MS) / being rather willing to stand
234.9   nature—he (MS) / nature; he
234.20 somewhat (MS) / little
234.22 and my (MS) / and yet my
234.22 that (MS) / whether
234.22 man—methought (MS) / man, for methought
234.29 that ban-dog (MS) / that the ban-dog
235.12 possessed (MS) / in possession
235.18 fiend (MS) / Fiend
235.22 mirthful mood, "Confederacy (MS mirthful mood "Confederacy) / mirthful mood,— [new paragraph] "Confederacy
235.27 may otherwise cost thee dear (MS) / thou mayest otherwise dearly pay for
235.36 seared (MS) / scared
236.15 Margaret (Editorial) / Jean
        This emendation is discussed in the Essay on the Text, 417.
236.21 save (MS) / help
236.22 Why (MS) / Nay
236.38 shall (MS) / may
236.39 in (MS) / on
238.41 hamlet would (MS) / hamlet, would
239.6   has (MS) / had
239.9   has (MS) / had
239.25 dying—so (MS) / dying; so
239.39 knew where (MS) / guessed whither
240.28 though mistakingly (MS) / though, so far as the individual was concerned, mistakingly
240.32 upstairs (MS) / up stairs
240.32 orphan"——(MS) / orphan——"
240.36 others, "In (MS theres "In) / others,— [new paragraph] "In
240.38 of liquid (MS) / of the liquid
241.4   need— (MS) / need?—
241.16 sound which (MS) / sound, which
241.32 a (MS) / the
242.4   saul (MS) / soul
242.5   fingers—he (MS) / fingers; he
242.14 Inglish Makar (MS) / English Maker
242.16 Mother (MS) / mother
242.17 assured"—(MS) / assured—"
242.20 Church (Editorial) / church
242.37 kings (MS) / king
242.38 gude (MS) / good
243.13 High Mass (MS) / high mass
243.20 Church (Editorial) / church
243.36 Kinfauns, as the (MS) / Kinfauns, the
244.17 Mass (MS) / mass
244.43 by (MS) / with
244.43 of palsy (MS) / of the palsy
245.6   brevity, "I (MS brevity "I) / brevity,— [new paragraph] "I
245.12 forwards (MS) / forward

245.20 interrupted. (MS) / interrupted him.
245.20 caitiff? (MS) / caitiff!
245.34 twenty-five for (MS) / twenty-five, for
245.39 proceedings (MS) / proceeding
246.22 do. I (MS) / do—I
246.29 ends (MS derived: end⟨d⟩) / end
246.35 conducted his (MS) / conducted, his
246.39 forceful (MS) / forcible
247.5 Henry (MS) / Harry
247.14 for whom (MS) / whom didst thou intend to slay
247.16 took him for the man whose (MS) / took the slain man," answered the
         discomfited combatant, "for him whose
248.10 on (MS) / upon
248.16 deed. See (MS) / deed.—See
248.17 apart—My (MS) / apart! My
248.18 truth. Speak (MS) / truth.—Speak
248.25 believing it." (MS) / thinking the villain's tale true."
249.22 await (MS) / wait
249.30 present—your (MS) / present, your
249.30 me—it (MS) / me,—it
250.6 set (MS) / spread
250.13 Prince, Heir (MS Prince Heir) / Prince—the heir
250.29 name." (MS) / name?"
251.5 replied, "Uncle (MS replied "Uncle) / replied,— [new paragraph]
         "Uncle
251.6 you pitched (MS) / you have pitched
251.12 and (MS) / or
251.29 occasion that (MS) / occasion, that
251.31 or rather (MS) / or he was rather
251.32 come (MS) / attend
252.24 metheglin were (MS) / metheglin, were
252.26 emphasis a (MS) / emphasis, a
252.42 valour be (MS) / valour must be
253.3 head-piece like (MS) / head-piece, like
253.7 of widow (MS) / of the widow
253.21 assemblies. Had (MS) / assemblies Had
253.29 their (MS) / the
253.33 and applause (MS) / and the applause
254.32 one who (MS) / one, who
255.21 will (MS) / shall
257.22 fiend (Editorial) / Fiend
         This word appears in MS with a lower-case 'f' on each of the other 7
         occasions on which it is used.
258.7 much even the (MS) / much the
258.10 a (MS) / A
258.13 pier, whilst (Editorial) / pier; whilst
258.14 precaution till (MS) / precaution, till
259.14 stretch (Editorial) / shrink
         The wrong word was supplied by the intermediaries in filling a MS
         lacuna.
259.19 contrivances (MS) / conveniences
259.21 two for (MS) / two, for
259.22 securing (MS) / security
259.35 heights (MS) / height
259.38 Marry, you (MS) / Marry, but you

260.2   pavin (MS) / pavise
260.11   saving (MS) / serving
260.17   naught (MS) / nought
260.28   these (MS) / that
260.38   *in extremis* (Lockhart in ICopy) / in extremes
        The MS probably also reads 'in extremis', but the phrase is not under-
        lined.
260.41   take hold (MS) / take fast hold
260.42   fast hold (MS) / sure gripe
261.19   body had (MS) / body, had
261.25   dripping (MS) / dropping
261.25   diverting (MS) / directing
261.30   men (MS) / human creatures
262.4   ducking (MS) / drenching
262.5   would"—(MS) / would—"
262.10   saluted it (MS) / he saluted
262.17   mass than (MS) / mass, than
262.21   as it (MS) / as if it
262.32   convey (MS) / carry
262.37   west will (MS) / west, will
263.20   he! (in (MS) / he!—(in
263.21   word, nor of (MS) / word. Neither of
263.23   Grève (Editorial) / Greve
263.23   speeches which—(MS) / speeches with which he—
263.25   leap—my (MS) / leap, had my
263.25   revenant had not the (MS) / revenant the
263.33   roads (MS) / road
264.6   expected, his (MS) / expected, that his
264.6   daughter in (MS) / daughter was in
264.11   estranged (MS) / altered
264.26   Smith than (MS) / Smith, than
264.28   man is (MS) / man, is
265.1   indirection (MS) / indiscretion
265.5   Holy (MS) / holy
265.9   her farther (MS) / her any farther
265.9   this (MS) / the
265.15   choice, whom (MS) / choice, and whom
265.16   was (MS) / to be
265.35   convertists (MS) / converts
265.38   loved well to (MS) / loved to
265.39   Church (Editorial) / church
266.9   him (MS) / their preacher Clement
266.16   this especial zeal (MS) / this zeal
266.20   what (MS) / which
266.21   hastily—"would'st (MS) / hastily; "would'st
266.26   makar (MS) / Maker
266.32   irreverend (MS) / irreverent
266.33   Holy (MS) / holy
266.33   Church"—(MS) / Church—"
267.1   Church (MS) / church
267.6   smiling (MS) / kneeling
267.18   Church (Editorial) / church
267.35   fate by (MS) / fate, by
267.36   and the (MS) / and that the
268.4   dare"——(MS) / dare——"

268.9 command"——(ms) / command——"
268.13 urged me and (ms) / urged and
268.14 like (ms) / likely
268.15 learn from (ms) / learn something of from
268.15 Clement (ms) / preacher
268.26 Holy (ms) / holy
269.6 his master's wicked (ms) / his wicked
269.32 food—I (ms) / food. I
270.3 tongue would (ms) / tongue that would
270.22 howl and (ms) / howl, and
271.6 beadsman"——(ms) / beadsman—"
271.7 civilities—I (ms) / civilities. I
271.28 Henry (Lockhart in ICopy) / Robert
271.30 Church (Editorial) / church
271.43 comes (ms) / returns
272.8 needst (ms) / needs
272.21 manner that (ms) / manner, that
272.21 Couvrefew (ms) / Curfew
272.23 friends (ms) / friend
272.24 long "Whew! (ms) / long whistle.—"Whew!
272.25 advise to (ms) / advise thee to
272.38 It shall never be while (ms) / That tale shall not be told while
272.42 will (ms) / we'll
273.18 secure from (ms) / secure for a week or two, from
273.18 enemies, for a week or two, when (ms) / enemies, when
273.21 with old Gilchrist (ms) / with Gilchrist
273.23 and you are (ms) / and are
275.7 Highland (Editorial) / Hieland
     Two earlier instances of 'Hieland', in Vol. 3, ff. 9 and 10 of the ms,
     appear as 'Highland' in print; that this and the following emendation
     were not also converted is a mistake given that the Glover's speech is
     standard written English, not Scots.
275.13 Highlandman (Editorial) / Hielandman
276.30 will (ms) / shall
277.7 Care not (ms) / Heed no longer
277.11 Care not for me (ms) / Think not of that
277.12 brogue (ms) / brogues
277.13 their (ms) / this
277.22 it? (ms) / it, thinkest thou?
277.29 you (ms) / yourself
278.15 Thus severed (ms) / thus were severed
279.10 III (Lockhart in ICopy) / II
279.28 wilds would (Editorial) / wilds, would
279.31 Gael was (Magnum) / Gael, was
280.32 eye was (Magnum) / eye, was
281.13 uncivil than (Editorial) / uncivil, than
282.39 height." (Magnum) / height.'
283.15 or guilt (Magnum) / and guilt
283.27 who"——(Editorial) / who——"
     This is the normal ms convention for indicating interrupted speech,
     and is adopted here even although the ms is not extant at this point.
284.41 remained were (Editorial) / remained, were
285.10 soil arose (Editorial) / soil, arose
285.19 this (ms) / that
285.21 lake, or half (ms) / lake, half

285.31　through, as (ICopy) / through, and as
　　　　　The deletion mark is probably but not certainly in Scott's hand.
285.41　river (MS) / run
285.42　lakes, and on which are usually castles or religious houses which the fear
　　　　　or the piety of the ancient inhabitants have caused to be founded there.
　　　　　The ruins upon that which adorns the foot of Loch Tay, now almost
　　　　　overgrown (MS lakes and on which are usually situated castles or reli-
　　　　　gious houses which the fear or the piety of the ancient inhabitants have
　　　　　causd to be founded there. The ruins upon that which adorns the foot of
　　　　　Loch Tay now almost overgrown) / lakes. The ruins upon that isle, now
　　　　　almost shapeless, being overgrown
　　　　　Apart from a normalisation and the insertion of two commas, only one
　　　　　editorial intervention (preventing the close repetition of 'situated') is
　　　　　required to restore the omitted passage.
286.19　dusky (MS) / distant
286.35　disporting (MS) / dispersing
286.37　onwards (MS) / onward
286.37　and they (MS) / and that they
286.37　themselves fall (MS) / themselves might fall
286.37　place in the rear (MS) / places
286.41　Tom-na-Lonach (MS) / Tom-an-Lonach
287.17　cover (MS) / caves
287.22　convent (MS) / convents
287.23　islet began (MS) / islet, began
287.28　Church (Editorial) / church
287.30　brought (MS) / carried
287.32　carried (MS) / borne
287.37　borne (MS) / carried
287.37　relations (MS) / relatives
288.5　　voice said close by him, "Think (MS voice said close by him "Think) /
　　　　　voice, close by him, said,— [new paragraph] "Think
288.19　greeting (MS) / greetings
288.32　Church (Editorial) / church
289.1　　having ever hearkened (MS) / having hearkened
289.36　Carthusian (Magnum) / Carmelite
291.6　　Carthusian (Magnum) / Carmelite
291.10　him who (MS) / him, who
291.33　Carthusian (MS) / Carmelite
292.5　　festivities (MS) / festivals
292.16　race than (MS) / race, than
292.33　sounded (MS) / sent forth
292.36　lamentation which (MS) / lamentation, which
293.6　　beloved (MS) / liberal
293.28　slender (MS) / head from her other
293.31　although (MS) / though
293.33　a speedy and safe (MS) / a safe
293.36　was (MS) / should be
293.42　preparation (MS) / preparations
294.13　nameless (MS) / numberless
294.28　of dais (MS) / of the dais
294.35　of (MS) / at
295.9　　particularly the (MS) / particularly to the
295.34　temper a (MS) / temper like a
295.37　unpleasing (MS) / unpleasant
295.41　festivity (MS) / festival

296.4 and (MS) / as
296.11 they had occasionally served (MS) / they might occasionally have served
296.42 race of the (MS) / race [space] the
297.9 quantity (MS) / quantities
298.14 assuming the (MS) / assuming, in old times, the
298.14 character in old times combined (MS) / character combined
298.20 around (MS) / round
298.26 delicates (MS) / delicacies
299.15 gaped (MS) / gazed
299.17 replied, "Even (MS replied— "Even) / replied,— [new paragraph] "Even
299.40 return (MS) / Return
300.2 possess. (MS) / possess!
300.36 time pressing." (MS) / time being pressing."
300.38 like (MS) / likely
300.39 religion than (MS) / religion, than
301.17 was your Provost (MS was your provost) / is your friend
301.21 simply replied, "Sir (MS derived: simply re "Sir) / simply said,— [new paragraph] "Sir
301.26 ritual (MS) / festival
302.27 lip to (MS) / lip, to
303.3 honour but (MS) / honour, but
303.5 *shall* (MS) / SHALL
303.26 hope which (MS) / hope, which
303.28 darkened (MS darkend) / lowering
303.29 eyes (MS) / hands
304.17 archers—how (MS) / archers; how
304.23 walls—I (MS) / walls;—I
304.24 peal sound (MS) / sound peal
304.30 of archer-craft (MS) / in archery
304.31 disposed (MS) / dispersed
305.7 forwards (MS) / forward
305.14 pavoises (MS) / pavesses
305.28 hopped (MS) / popped
305.30 Simon! (MS) / Simon Glover!
305.40 where (MS) / when
305.41 his head up (MS) / up his head
305.43 will (MS) / shall
306.2 laid this day (MS) / this day laid
306.3 hear. (MS) / hear!
306.5 shall (MS) / will
306.6 *coward* (MS) / COWARD
306.14 comforted (MS) / composed
306.15 *no* (MS) / NO
306.23 them?—the (MS) / them? the
306.23 of fell (MS) / of, fell
306.38 flows—thicker (MS) / flows, thicker
307.9 fancy that (MS) / fancy, that
307.21 is a (MS) / is of a
307.21 of (MS) / with
307.35 wishes, I (MS) / wishes on such terms, I
308.3 will (MS) / shall
308.7 father (MS) / Father
308.8 man that (MS) / man, that
308.8 ever"—— (MS) / ever——"

308.9   prithee (MS) / pr'ythee
308.12   incense (MS) / enrage
308.18   best be (MS) / best to be
308.32   tone, "Let (MS tone "Let) / tone,— [new paragraph] "Let
309.6   say— (MS) / say,—
309.7   cry— (MS) / cry,—
310.4   whims (MS) / fancies
310.11   Church (Editorial) / church
310.18   Conachar. But (MS Conachar But) / Conachar; but
310.41   Hallowing (MS) / Hallooing
311.9   left to (MS) / left, to
311.26   out? What (MS) / out? what
311.28   will, I suppose, be (MS will I suppose be) / shall be
311.28   answerable for (MS) / answerable, I suppose, for
312.9   child— (MS) / child;—
312.10   son— (MS) / son;—
312.13   magic—I (MS) / magic. I
312.14   born— (MS) / born,—
312.24   not be! (MS) / not!
312.24   Torquil— (MS) / Torquil,—
312.25   water— (MS) / water,—
312.32   blade—Now (MS) / blade. Now
313.5   of Clan (MS) / of the Clan
313.14   Greenwoods (MS) / Green woods
314.3   Court (MS) / court
314.5   of Wardlaw (ICopy) / of Robert de Wardlaw
314.25   is pity (MS) / is a pity
315.15   numbered up (MS) / recollected
315.25   writes (MS) / sends
316.7   drawn (MS) / cleared
316.9   garden (always . . . Constable) to (MS) / garden,—always . . . Constable,—to
316.15   Ramorny"— (MS) / Ramorny—"
316.22   hastily, "Your (MS hastily— "Your) / hastily,— [new paragraph] "Your
316.39   mistake—he (MS) / mistake. He
316.42   if (MS) / that
317.6   goliardise (MS) / galliardise
317.18   disposal. But (MS) / disposal; but
317.27   relation (MS) / relative
318.7   forgot (MS) / forgotten
318.9   forgot (MS) / forgotten
318.24   father"—— (MS) / father——"
318.26   Highness"—— (MS) / Highness——"
318.29   the lack of an eye (MS) / touches of age
318.30   Falkland sits (MS) / Falkland, sits
319.2   window called (MS) / window, he called
319.23   reverend (MS) / reverent
319.27   cover (MS) / record
319.40   chamber (MS) / mouth
321.3   his factotum (MS his fac totum) / such a confident
321.21   monks (MS) / Monks
321.21   maidens—an (MS) / maidens. An
321.22   danger. And (MS) / danger; and
321.28   hand must (MS) / hand, must

321.29 consciences (MS) / conscience
322.24 but (MS) / But
323.20 John—pray (MS) / John. Pray
323.31 couple, hastily exhorted (MS) / couple, exhorted
323.41 "And (MS) / "Ah! and
324.22 form"——(MS) / form——"
325.14 am encountering (MS) / am now encountering
325.32 should (MS) / might
325.37 appanage (MS) / appendage
326.4   wonder a (MS) / wonder that a
326.15 added, "There (MS) / added, [new paragraph] "There
326.31 none but (MS) / none except the minstrel wench, but
326.32 with—except the minstrel wench. (MS) / with.
327.8   sleeping-room as (MS) / sleeping-room, as
327.11 starched (MS) / starch
327.33 inconvenient. Indeed (MS) / inconvenient—Indeed
328.24 thy (MS) / the
328.29 This will (MS) / This unexpected rebuff will
328.43 House (MS) / house
329.5   propped (MS) / supported
329.11 given thee (MS) / given to thee
330.5   David (Lockhart in ICopy) / Robert
330.19 struggling (MS) / striving
330.34 me depart (MS) / me to depart
330.36 unworthy knighthood (MS) / unworthy of knighthood
330.38 defiance—I (MS) / defiance. I
331.3   me—but (MS) / me; but
331.14 not. But (MS not—But) / not; but
331.30 reserve (MS) / keep
331.31 prized—Or (MS) / prized; or
331.32 pursuits—for (MS) / pursuits,—for
331.34 how (MS) / How
332.10 prince (MS) / Prince
332.27 into (MS) / to
332.30 services? (MS) / services!
332.32 door (MS) / compass
332.36 admonishing (MS) / admonitory
332.43 "excepting (MS) / "none, perhaps, excepting
333.4   as preferred (MS) / as likely to be preferred
333.11 truth (MS) / verity
333.13 maiden (MS) / young person
333.26 discerned (MS) / discovered
333.35 wantonness far (MS) / wantonness, far
333.37 or, probably, that the (MS or as it probably that the) / or, as it is
        probable, because the
        It appears that Scott started one construction and then moved to an-
        other without deleting the redundant phrase.
334.8   ill with (MS) / ill of
334.19 made (MS) / rendered
334.33 earth that (MS) / earth, that
335.3   was that (MS) / was, that
335.4   shouted, yelled (MS shouted yelled) / shouted,—yelled
335.5   frenzy—but (MS) / frenzy,—but
335.12 permitted—a (MS) / permitted,—a
335.27 a bundle (MS) / the bundle

336.8　　the minstrel (MS) / the same female minstrel
337.27　　house?"——(MS) / house?——"
337.28　　like (MS) / likely
338.17　　is (MS) / may be
338.23　　thick—I (MS) / thick. Yet there is a remedy—I
339.7　　vespers (MS) / vesper
339.16　　and (MS) / or
339.23　　post (MS) / depart
339.29　　striving (MS) / endeavouring
339.41　　scarce (MS) / scarcely
340.3　　over (MS) / across
340.12　　safe out of sight (MS) / lost in the distance
340.21　　presently (MS) / immediately
340.27　　disappearance (MS) / escape
340.27　　Louise (MS) / one of their female captives
340.41　　was assigned to me only to wait on me, and tired (MS was assigned to me
　　　　　only to wait on me and tired) / was tired
340.42　　the solitary (MS) / a solitary
341.22　　punish." (MS) / punish!"
341.35　　arrived. She (MS arrived She) / arrived; she
341.39　　louder—still (Editorial) / louder, still
　　　　　This completes the sequence of dashes.
341.43　　her, "Yes (MS her "Yes) / her,— [new paragraph] "Yes
342.5　　and that of an (MS) / and of one who is an
342.20　　said she (MS) / she said
342.24　　that is military engines (MS) / military engines, that is,
342.32　　Catherine. "I (MS) / Catharine,—"I
342.34　　you firmness (MS) / you the firmness
343.1　　sphere. Think (MS) / sphere! Think
343.6　　to—that (MS) / to, whether you say such things were or were not. That
343.7　　it (MS) / to be
343.9　　not, I (MS) / not promise silence, I
343.9　　castle (MS) / Castle
343.17　　reply by (MS) / reply, by
343.23　　is (MS) / are
343.24　　so they (MS) / so that they
343.29　　physic—he (MS) / physic—He
343.32　　the dogs (MS) / the other dogs
343.33　　stomach"—Here (MS) / stomach to the work," answered Dwining,
　　　　　"never. But here
343.34　　*dies*—he! he! he! (MS) / *dies*.—He, he, he!
343.38　　Why (MS) / Wherefore
344.9　　force"——(MS) / force——"
344.29　　a mind (MS) / some mind
344.32　　Chaff (MS) / chaff
344.38　　sage (MS) / Sage
345.20　　me—And (MS) / me! and
345.21　　these (MS) / them
345.23　　No!—man of evil—no! (MS) / No! man of evil, no!
345.24　　made (MS) / created
345.29　　head (MS) / heart
345.31　　Sage (MS) / sage
345.33　　But (MS) / but
345.33　　solved—yonder (MS) / solved. Yonder
346.5　　I"——(Magnum) / I——"

346.17 know what (Editorial) / know, what
346.38 Castle." (Editorial) / Castle?"
350.34 intelligence that (Editorial) / intelligence, that
352.14 circulated served (Editorial) / circulated, served
357.43 worst was (Editorial) / worst, was
358.4   Clans arrived (Editorial) / Clans, arrived
359.5   what practices (Magnum) / what practice
360.16 James* (Editorial) / James,*
360.17 brother's (Editorial) / father's
        This emendation accords with historical fact, and is in line with Scott's
        footnote below.
360.29 combat would (Editorial) / combat, would
360.30 decided that (Editorial) / decided, that
361.3   Church (Editorial) / church
361.9   convents to (Editorial) / convents, to
361.29 sons induced (Editorial) / sons, induced
362.40 strife with (Editorial) / strife, with
362.42 great that (Editorial) / great, that
364.29 multitude when (Editorial) / multitude, when
366.20 time to (Editorial) / time, to
367.13 Loncarty would (Editorial) / Loncarty, would
367.38 hand that (Editorial) / hand, that
374.1   King to (Editorial) / King, to
374.42 standards had (Editorial) / standards, had
380.13 David (Lockhart in ICopy) / Robert
381.4   officer, "The (Editorial) / officer,— [new paragraph] "The
        This emendation is modelled on 18 others based upon the MS reading.
382.19 sailed was (Editorial) / sailed, was
382.25 acquired to (Editorial) / acquired, to
384.43 unfortunate"—— (Magnum) / unfortunate——"
387.20 David (Lockhart in ICopy) / Robert

END-OF-LINE HYPHENS

All end-of-line hyphens in the present text are soft unless included in the list below. The hyphens listed are hard and should be retained when quoting.

4.43	all-deterging		189.13	night-brawl
5.23	broad-cloth		193.37	horse-trough
12.38	foot-path		206.38	fellow-citizen
15.16	to-morrow		211.21	ill-willers
17.24	to-morrow		213.7	town-clerk
18.35	night-walkers		215.9	feather-dresser
23.5	six-weeks'		215.17	fellow-citizen
27.21	tourney-ground		215.28	well-meaning
30.1	son-in-law		222.17	Bonnet-maker
34.11	narrow-minded		233.32	to-morrow
41.40	iron-fisted		234.26	bull-dog
42.26	burial-ground		237.16	slow-hound
52.27	half-an-hour		237.17	gaze-hound
52.29	bed-side		242.37	city-council
56.6	churl-blood		245.34	twenty-five
77.30	ill-favoured		251.40	good-will
78.24	riding-rod		252.4	glee-maidens
106.41	by-standers		252.20	Council-house
108.30	buff-coat		258.5	middle-sized
111.13	well-armed		276.12	foster-father
112.17	men-at-arms		295.19	to-day
116.18	glee-maiden		298.17	Mountain-cat
118.29	cow-house		299.15	bog-wood
120.9	men-at-arms		303.6	alms-house
120.40	to-morrow		310.9	hair-cloth
120.42	to-morrow		315.18	Bonnet-maker
121.23	newly-acquired		318.28	harsh-featured
123.1	spindle-shanks		321.28	tender-hearted
148.2	light-footed		327.9	day-bed
148.26	prize-fighter		327.29	thick-witted
152.42	green-checked		340.10	foot-path
153.22	pole-axes		340.20	dey-woman
155.4	bandy-legged		342.25	cross-bows
159.11	fiery-souled		344.33	column-resembling
164.42	barber-chirurgeon		344.41	pill-gilder
168.19	morrice-dancers		345.3	vain-glorious
171.18	glee-women		347.35	red-hand
172.25	Bonnet-maker		348.23	obsequious-looking
176.41	Bonnet-maker		354.31	breast-plate
177.20	Bonnet-maker		355.16	ham-shackled
179.30	Lack-a-day		357.12	life-guardsman
183.21	life-blood		363.7	two-handed
186.6	truculent-looking		364.27	steel-cap
187.1	bed-clothes		367.30	well-known

368.32 foster-brothers
375.36 ill-omened

381.18 heart-broken
383.7 glee-maiden

HISTORICAL NOTE

In Chrystal Croftangry's Narrative, which opens *Saint Valentine's Day*, the Second Series of *Chronicles of the Canongate*, Scott alludes to the kinds of problem involved in writing historical novels. As a writer of fiction he enjoys a freedom of invention denied the historian; yet he cannot completely ignore the historical record. Urged by Mrs Baliol to write a story involving Mary Queen of Scots and the murder of Rizzio, Chrystal Croftangry refuses because 'the events are too well known in Mary's days to be used as vehicles of romantic fiction'. It is much better, he tells Mrs Baliol, to avoid all such 'well known paths of history'— because then readers will be less likely to accuse the author of historical inaccuracy. Thus this story will not be set in the 'certain path' of Edinburgh in the sixteenth century but rather in the historical 'wilderness' which is Perth at the turn of the fifteenth. Writing about a period so remote that the historical record itself is far from complete or clear— and tradition and legend are therefore alternative sources of information—Scott is insisting on his right as novelist to use the historical past with a freedom not available to the historian.

Scott's Version of the Historical Events. *Saint Valentine's Day* originates in the well-authenticated episode of a battle between two sets of champions of powerful Highland clans which took place, in the presence of King Robert III and his court, on the North Inch of Perth in 1396—though significantly Scott does not specify that year in the novel. The political context of this episode inevitably involves the king, his powerful brother the Duke of Albany, and the king's son and heir apparent, the Duke of Rothsay. Two legends attached to the clan battle from an early date supply the other characters whose stories figure prominently in the novel: first, the idea of one of the clan champions proving a coward and fleeing either before or during the conflict, and second, the suggestion that a Perth artisan makes up the numbers of one of the sides. The *donnée* of the novel then—as Henry James would have called it—already involved both history and legend.

Scott, however, chooses to manipulate the historical record, particularly in relation to the chronology of the action. The novel's chronology runs from 13 February (the day before St Valentine's Day) to Palm Sunday in Holy Week. But the year in question remains deliberately unspecified because into it Scott fits both the clan battle in Perth and Rothsay's death in Falkland Palace—soon followed, he implies, by the capture by the English of the future James I, and the death of Robert III. Historically, however, these events spanned a ten year period, the clan battle occurring in September, 1396, the murder of Rothsay in March, 1402, the capture of the young Prince James and the death of his father in March–April, 1406. Given the text's emphasis on St Valentine's

Day, the period of Lent, Palm Sunday, and Easter Week, it is the death of Rothsay in March, 1402, which seems to focus Scott's fictional chronology. Collapsing ten years' history into a period of about six weeks, however, inevitably creates some minor chronological problems: Archibald, the 3rd Earl of Douglas, for example, actually died in 1400—thus it was a different Douglas, the 4th Earl, who was subsequently involved in Rothsay's death. The Explanatory Notes draw attention to some other examples of similar anachronisms.

In the broad outlines of his characterisation of the historical figures in the novel, Scott does not depart from what was available to him in the early and later sources. Thus Robert III had come generally to be seen as a weak and ineffectual king, too easily led by those around him. His brother Albany, too, had normally been portrayed very much as Scott presents him: scheming and devious, but resolute in pursuing his selfish aims. Rothsay, Robert's son and heir, was described in the early accounts as a licentious and irresponsible young man, while the Earl of Douglas, Archibald the Grim, was always seen as a warrior of imposing presence and power. But the historical record, limited as it is, cannot be regarded as of unimpeachable objectivity or neutrality. As always, the early chronicles and accounts reflect the particular circumstances of their writing—which usually means they present the views of the apparent winners. Thus a modern historian might complain that Scott has done rather less than justice to Robert III and his son. The evidence is strong that while Earl of Carrick and heir apparent, the future Robert III had been an active and vigorous figure successfully building a power-base for himself, particularly in Scotland south of the Forth, with the aim of ensuring that when he became king he would be strong enough to dominate powerful nobles such as the Earls of Douglas and March. It is true that when he did become king in 1390 his control soon began to weaken—perhaps as a result of the physical injury he seems to have sustained about 1388. However his son Rothsay seems to have been equally active and successful in the 1390s in beginning to build up a strong position for himself within the kingdom; Rothsay may well have been a fun-loving young man, but he was certainly not lacking in political energy, ambition or understanding. It was because Albany realised that his own position as the most powerful man in Scotland was under threat from Rothsay's growing strength that he seems to have gambled —successfully as it turned out—on being able to dispose of him.[1]

Scott's sources. Scott's sources for the period of history in which *Saint Valentine's Day* takes place are largely cited in the text itself or in the notes subsequently supplied by Scott for the Magnum Opus edition. They include the two medieval narrative poems: *The Bruce* by John Barbour (c. 1325–95), and *The Wallace* by Blind Hary (c. 1440–92); the *Original Chronicle of Scotland* by Andrew of Wyntoun (c. 1350–1422); the Latin *Chronica gentis scotorum* by John of Fordun (c. 1320–c. 1384), and the continuation of that work by Walter Bower (1385–1449) known as *Scotichronicon*; and the Latin *Scotorum historiae* by Hector Boece (c. 1465–1536) translated by John Bellenden (c.

1495–*c*. 1547). Scott also used the *History of the Houses of Douglas and Angus* (Edinburgh, 1648), by David Hume of Godscroft, and he found many useful details about Perth and its history in *The Muses Threnodie*, a long poem by Henry Adamson, first published in Edinburgh in 1638. Scott certainly possessed a copy of Adamson's poem edited by James Cant and published in Perth in 1774 (*CLA*, 17); Cant's commentary and notes on the poem were so detailed that his edition became known as 'The History of Perth'. Scott also read such relevant eighteenth-century Scottish historians as John Pinkerton whose *History of Scotland under the House of Stuart* was published in 1797. Indeed Pinkerton's work seems to have been a primary source for Scott: his accounts of Robert III—including his physical appearance—of Albany, Rothsay, and Ramorny, all seem to derive largely from Pinkerton; similarly, main events in the action of the novel—the clan battle, the murder of Rothsay —seem to develop what is contained in Pinkerton's history.[2]

However, soon after completing *Saint Valentine's Day*, Scott made it clear that he was deeply sceptical about the reliability of most traditional accounts of early Scottish history. Writing on Joseph Ritson's *Annals of the Caledonians, Picts, and Scots* (2 vols, 1828) in the *Quarterly Review* for July 1829, he is dismissive of Boece, Buchanan and the rest as little more than shameless mythologisers; only with Father Innes and Lord Hailes, he suggests, does early Scottish history begin to be written with a degree of scholarly accuracy. John Pinkerton's *An Inquiry into the History of Scotland Preceding the Reign of Malcolm III* (1789)—though not his book on the Stuarts—is seen as exhibiting all that is most unacceptable in the study of early Scottish history.

The Clan Battle. Beyond the fact that a bloody contest took place on the North Inch of Perth in September 1396, between representatives of two feuding Highland clans, little or nothing is known about the battle which provides the novel with its violent climax. Even the identity of the two clans is disputed, as Scott acknowledges in the Preface to the Magnum. The near-contemporary lowland chroniclers, Wyntoun and Bower, differ in their accounts: Wyntoun makes no mention of one side lacking a man, nor of a Perth artisan supplying his place; but both of these details appear in Bower. Clearly the passage of time encouraged the emergence of these and other colourful details.

Not in dispute is that the battle was organised and arranged by Robert III and his advisers—and that it took place in the presence of the king and his court. What it was meant to demonstrate was that the royal authority did extend into the turbulent Highland region of the Scottish realm. As one recent Scottish historian describes it, the clan battle was 'a public relations triumph' for Robert III.[3] In Scott's account, it is Rothsay who first proposes that the feud between the clans be resolved by a kind of parody of knightly combat, and historically this may well have been the case. The king's son had been in the north of the kingdom, visiting Montrose and Aberdeen on royal business in the summer of 1396; one of his companions had probably been Sir David Lindsay (later Earl of Crawford), outstanding among Scotland's chivalric knights, who, as

Scott indicates, was much involved in arranging the clan battle. Lindsay's involvement is all the more significant if, as appears likely, the so-called Clan Quhele had been involved in the threatening Glasclune raid in Angus in 1392 (see note to 157.7–8). The Highland 'cateran' forces had on that occasion proved unexpectedly formidable. In a pitched battle the Sheriff of Angus, Walter Ogilvie, was killed alongside several other Angus knights and lairds; Lindsay arrived in time to come to the assistance of Ogilvy's force, but was himself badly wounded in the struggle. Glasclune called into question the assumed military superiority of Lowland chivalry. In this context Lindsay's involvement with Rothsay in persuading the Highland clans to participate in a mutually self-destructive battle in Perth makes a great deal of sense. Scott, that is, is right to insist on the *realpolitik* dimension of the whole affair.[4]

Scotland at the end of the fourteenth century. The governance of fourteenth-century Scotland was much as Scott represents it in the novel. The king, with the royal household, remained at the head of national affairs, but royal business was not yet conducted from a fixed capital. The royal household, that is, was itinerant, moving between burghs such as Edinburgh, Stirling, Dunfermline, Dumbarton, Rothesay, Scone, as well as a range of other occasional locations. For Robert III, however, Perth seems to have been one of the court's most favoured residences. A Scottish Parliament did exist, largely comprised of earls and barons, bishops, abbots and priors—all of them great landowners and tenants-in-chief of the king—with the power to make decisions and advise the king concerning affairs of state and the well-being of the kingdom. In practice a less formal body, similarly composed, called the 'general council', frequently took over the parliamentary role. However, day-to-day policy and decision-making remained very much in the hands of the king and a small group of courtiers and magnates who constituted what would become known as the privy council. In the novel it is this kind of council—made up of Robert III, his brother Albany, his son Rothsay, the Earls of March and Douglas, and Prior Anselm—that we see in action.

The other level of government very relevant to the novel's themes is that of the town or burgh. Here again Scott's general account appears to be accurate. In the fourteenth century, Perth was one of over thirty royal burghs. Some burghs provided the monarch with revenues of various kinds including rents, tolls, and taxes. But a royal burgh also enjoyed a considerable degree of control over its own affairs. Of particular importance were the town's merchant guilds whose activities went considerably beyond the regulation of particular trades and the maintenance of trading rights and privileges. The guild burgesses were involved in the election of the burgh council, the Provost, the Bailies or magistrates, the Dean of Guild, other burgh officers, and in the organisation of the burgh courts. Town burgesses were thus a powerful élite, effectively in control of the administration and daily life of the burgh, making and enforcing its system of law and regulation. In the novel Scott is thus able to exploit the potential conflict between the civic polity of Perth and its values, and the traditional feudal values of the Scottish nobles who rival the king in exercising power over much of Scotland.

In his presentation of the third dimension of fourteenth-century Scottish life in the novel—the life of the Scottish Highlands north of Perth—Scott, as in his earlier Scottish novels, owes much to the social or sociological ideas of Scottish Enlightenment figures such as Adam Smith or Adam Ferguson. The Highlands are presented as possessing their own distinctive form of complex social organisation, while still being at an earlier stage of social development than Perth; but the two areas are closely linked. Just as Bailie Nicol Jarvie is a cousin of Rob Roy so Simon Glover is an old friend of the Chief of Clan Quhele; and the flourishing of Simon's business of glovemaking depends on the supply of raw materials from the Highlands.

Scott's portrayal of other aspects of life in late fourteenth-century Scotland are also in line with the historical record. Scottish knights and earls did continue to subscribe to the traditional values of chivalry. In the 1390s Anglo-Scottish chivalric contests were frequent; trials by combat also occurred. Through the character of Father Clement, Scott suggests that demands for the reformation of the excesses of orthodox Catholicism were arising in this period. Once again the historical record supports the view: in 1407 one James Resby was burnt in Perth for expressing Lollard beliefs. Finally Scott's constant emphasis in the novel on the absence in late fourteenth-century Scotland of a dependable system of law and order (and therefore of the need for any individual or group to be able to rely on self-defence) is one that contemporary chronicles also reflect. The Register of Moray describes the situation around 1398:

> In those days there was no law in Scotland, but he who was stronger oppressed him who was weaker and the whole realm was a den of thieves; murders, herschips and fireraising and all other misdeeds remained unpunished; and justice, as if outlawed, lay in exile outwith the bounds of the realm.[5]

NOTES

1   For a modern historical account of the period in which the novel is set see Stephen I. Boardman, *The Early Stewart Kings: Robert II and Robert III 1371–1406* (East Linton, 1996).

2   *The Prose Works of Sir Walter Scott, Bart.*, 28 vols (Edinburgh, 1834–36), 20.301–26.

3   Boardman, 203.

4   For a comprehensive account of the historiography of the clan battle, and of the ongoing debate over the identities of the participating clans, see Graeme M. Mackenzie, '*The Rarest Decision Recorded in History*: The Battle of the Clans in 1396', in *Transactions of the Gaelic Society of Inverness*, 59 (1994–96), 420–87.

5   *Registrum Episcopatus Moraviensis* (Edinburgh, 1837), 382; translated by Ranald Nicholson, in *Scotland: the Later Middle Ages* (Edinburgh, 1974), 210–11.

EXPLANATORY NOTES

In these notes a comprehensive attempt is made to identify Scott's sources, and all quotations, references, historical events, and historical personages, to explain proverbs, and to translate difficult or obscure language. (Phrases are explained in the notes while single words are treated in the glossary.) The notes are brief; they offer information rather than critical comment or exposition. Gaelic phrases are first transliterated into modern Gaelic, and then translated. When a quotation has not been recognised this is stated: any new information from readers will be welcomed. References are to standard editions, or to the editions Scott himself used. Books in the Abbotsford Library are identified by reference to the appropriate page of the *Catalogue of the Library at Abbotsford*. When quotations reproduce their sources accurately, the reference is given without comment. Verbal differences in the source are indicated by a prefatory 'see', while a general rather than a verbal indebtedness is indicated by 'compare'. Biblical references are to the Authorised Version. Plays by Shakespeare are cited without authorial ascription, and references are to *William Shakespeare: The Complete Works*, edited by Peter Alexander (London and Glasgow, 1951, frequently reprinted).

The following publications are distinguished by abbreviations, or are given without the names of their authors:

Cant   notes to Henry Adamson, *The Muses Threnodie*, ed. James Cant (Perth, 1774); *CLA*, 17.

CLA   [J. G. Cochrane], *Catalogue of the Library at Abbotsford* (Edinburgh, 1838).

The Canterbury Tales   Geoffrey Chaucer, *The Canterbury Tales* (written *c.* 1387–1400), in *The Riverside Chaucer*, 3rd edn, ed. Larry D. Benson (Oxford, 1988); see *CLA*, 42, 154, 155, 172, 239.

ICopy   The interleaved copy of *Saint Valentine's Day*, in the Harry Ransom Humanities Research Centre, University of Texas at Austin, shelf-mark Wn Sco86 828Cb.

Letters   *The Letters of Sir Walter Scott*, ed. H. J. C. Grierson and others, 12 vols (London, 1932–37).

Magnum   Walter Scott, *Waverley Novels*, 48 vols (Edinburgh, 1829–33).

Minstrelsy   Walter Scott, *Minstrelsy of the Scottish Border*, ed. T. F. Henderson, 4 vols (Edinburgh, 1902).

The Muses Threnodie   Henry Adamson, *The Muses Threnodie*, ed. James Cant (Perth, 1774): *CLA*, 17; originally published 1638.

OED   *The Oxford English Dictionary*, 12 vols (Oxford, 1933).

ODEP   *The Oxford Dictionary of English Proverbs*, 3rd edn, rev. F. P. Wilson (Oxford, 1970).

Poetical Works   *The Poetical Works of Sir Walter Scott, Bart.*, [ed. J. G. Lockhart], 12 vols (Edinburgh, 1833–34).

Prose Works   *The Prose Works of Sir Walter Scott, Bart.*, 28 vols (Edinburgh, 1834–36).

Ray   [John Ray], *A Compleat Collection of English Proverbs*, 3rd edn (London, 1737): *CLA*, 169.

Wallace   *Hary's Wallace*, ed. Matthew P. McDiarmid, Scottish Text Society,

New Series 4 and 5, 2 vols (Edinburgh and London, 1968, 1969); see *CLA*, 4, 8.

title-page   Chronicles of the Canongate Second Series   stories collected and retold by the fictional character Chrystal Croftangry, who is represented as residing in the Canongate. The First Series, containing the three stories 'The Highland Widow', 'The Two Drovers', and 'The Surgeon's Daughter', was published in 1827. The Canongate, now just the name of a street, was a burgh separate from Edinburgh until 1639 and not formally incorporated in the city until 1856; it stretched from Edinburgh's Netherbow Port, or Gate, near the modern St Mary's Street, to Holyrood.

title-page   sic itur ad astra   *Latin literally* thus it is gone to the stars, i.e. thus one attains to the stars: the motto on the coat of arms of the burgh of the Canongate.

3   motto   not identified; probably by Scott. The verse refers to Holyrood Abbey (Augustinian) and the adjoining Palace in Edinburgh; the Abbey was the burial place of the Stewart kings, several of whom were murdered, and the Palace the scene of the murder of David Rizzio, the favourite of Mary Queen of Scots (see note to 4.24).

3.17–18   The Castle may excel ... of site   Edinburgh Castle is built on a lofty outcrop of rock; its height and central position mean that it dominates the entire city.

3.18–20   the Calton ... triumphal arches   the Calton Hill, rising at the E end of Edinburgh's Princes Street, allows spectacular views of the city. In the early 19th century it was linked to Princes Street and North Bridge by the construction of Waterloo Bridge; a memorial tower to Lord Nelson was constructed on the Calton Hill, and Waterloo Place contains the fine Regent Arch. In the ICopy, Lockhart removes the 'bridges' and substitutes 'the pillars of its Parthenon'—a reference to the never-completed National Memorial to the Scottish soldiers killed in the Napoleonic wars. In 1831 the incomplete Parthenon was a much more prominent feature of the Calton Hill than its almost subterranean bridges. For Lockhart's involvement in the ICopy see Essay on the Text, 403–09.

3.20–21   The High Street   Edinburgh's High Street, the central axis of the medieval Old Town, ran from St Giles at its W end down to the Netherbow Port. Unlike the Canongate, the High Street was protected by a wall which lay between it and the Cowgate on the S side; this wall was superseded by the Flodden Wall in the 16th century and was entirely built over.

3.23–24   Old New Town   the original New Town as designed by James Craig. The plan for the development of the New Town of Edinburgh in Bearford's Parks to the N of the existing Old Town, had been approved in 1767; it consisted of three main thoroughfares running east-west (Princes, George and Queen Street), with two grand squares at either end (St Andrews and Charlotte Square), and with a series of shorter streets running north-south. Castle Street, in which Scott himself had lived from 1801–26, was part of Craig's New Town.

3.24   New New Town   the rapid expansion, mainly by private development in the early 19th century, of the original New Town, in areas to the N and W of Craig's scheme.

3.24–25   Moray Place   a circus, considered one of Edinburgh's finest 'squares'; construction began in 1824.

3.27–29   the Court end ... ancient Monarchs   Holyrood Palace, one of the residencies of the Scottish kings, is at the foot of the Canongate; the Abbey was one of their burial places.

4.1–5   ancient grandeur ... deserted halls ... present gracious sovereign   the Abbey was the occasional residence of Scottish monarchs from

David I to James IV, but became the principal residence of James V and Mary Queen of Scots in the 16th century. Charles I was the last reigning monarch to stay there (in 1633) until the visit of George IV (reigned 1820–30) to Scotland in August 1822. Scott was responsible for the arrangements for the visit in Edinburgh.

4.9 Queen Mary's Apartments   on the 3rd floor of the oldest extant part of the palace.

4.11 the exploit of Chatelet   Pierre de Boscosel de Chatelet (or Chastelard), a French poet executed in 1563 having admitted to a criminal passion for Mary Queen of Scots.

4.18 provincial cicerone   tour guide in an area outside London.

4.19 great house in the city   large business firm in the City of London.

4.20–21 putting off the goods ... account of commission   disposing of his goods and thus increasing his own financial return.

4.24 Rizzio's assassination   David Rizzio, or Riccio (*c.* 1533–66), an Italian musician of humble origins, had been appointed her French secretary by Queen Mary, and had become the Queen's confidante and companion. This intimacy with the Queen, his lack of social status, and his Catholic religion, made him the enemy of Darnley, the Queen's husband, and a group of Protestant Scottish nobles, who murdered him in Holyrood Palace, effectively in the presence of the pregnant Queen.

4.32 Scouring Drops   liquid cleansing agent.

5.3 the Abbess of St Bridget's   neither a literary nor historical source has been identified.

5.12 Harrow now out!   see Spenser, *The Faerie Queene*, Bks 1–3 (1590), 2.6.43, line 388; and compare Chaucer, 'The Nun's Priest's Tale', *The Canterbury Tales*, VII, 3380.

5.13–15 adjoining gallery ... the Kings of Scotland ... around me   a series of 111 portraits of Scottish kings listed in the history of Scotland by Hector Boece (*c.* 1465–1536). They were commissioned in 1671 by Charles II from the Dutch artist Jacob de Wet the Younger (1640–97) who was in Scotland 1682–88; 89 of the portraits remain and are in the picture gallery in the Palace of Holyrood House at the E end of the Canongate. Most of the ancient kings in Boece's *Scotorum historiae* (see *CLA*, 4) have no historical basis.

5.32 blood-boltered, like Banquo's ghost   see *Macbeth*, 4.1.123: 'For the blood-bolter'd Banquo smiles upon me'; blood-boltered means 'with clotted or blood-matted hair'.

6.3–4 old Irish ditty ... long enough ago   compare the 'Irish air' quoted by Scott in a letter to Maria Edgeworth, 22 September 1823: 'I went to the mill, but the miller was gone;/ I sate me down and cried ochone,/ To think on the days that are past and gone,/ Of Dickie Macphalion that's slain.' (*Letters*, 8.90).

6.5–6 editors of romantic narrative   in the 18th and early 19th centuries novelists frequently pretended, particularly if they were writing a Gothic tale, that they were no more than editors, making available to the public a 'true story' that had chanced to come into their possession. Compare Scott's citation of 'The Wardour Manuscript' in the Dedicatory Epistle to *Ivanhoe*, ed. Graham Tulloch, EEWN 8, 12.39.

6.10 Mrs Baliol   purportedly a cousin of Chrystal Croftangry, and source of the tales retold by Croftangry in the first series of *Chronicles of the Canongate*.

6.14 Automathes   protagonist of a work by John Kirkby, published in London in 1745 and entitled *Automathes, or the Capacity and Extent of the Human Understanding, exemplified in the Extraordinary Case of Automathes.*

6.19 the fairy tester   sixpenny coin left by the fairies. The reference is to the folk-belief that fairies expecting to undertake housework during the night (compare *A Midsummer Night's Dream*, 5.1.390–91, and Milton's 'L'Allegro',

105–14) leave a reward if they find the work already done.

6.24   the Age of Chivalry still exists   in his lament for Marie Antoinette in his *Reflections on the Revolution in France* (1790), Edmund Burke had famously written, 'the age of chivalry is gone.—That of sophisters, oeconomists, and calculators, has succeeded; and the glory of Europe is extinguished for ever': *The Writings and Speeches of Edmund Burke*, Vol. 8, *The French Revolution 1790–1794*, ed. L. G. Mitchell (Oxford 1989), 127. The early 19th century, however, had seen a widening interest in tales of chivalry, strongly fed by Scott's own narrative poems and prose romances of the Middle Ages, though his view of chivalry in novels such as *Ivanhoe* (1819) and in his 'Essay on Chivalry' (*Prose Works*, 6.1–126) is notably more nuanced than Burke's or that offered by some other romantic medievalists.

6.25   'London prentice bold'   *The Fortunes of Nigel*, ed. Frank Jordan, EEWN 13, 63.43. Although the phrase appears in *The Fortunes of Nigel*, there may be some further reference to Thomas Heywood, *The Four Prentices of London* (performed *c.* 1600; printed 1615), or to Francis Beaumont, *The Knight of the Burning Pestle* (performed 1607–08; printed 1613).

6.32   the statutes of the Order of Errantry   the code of medieval chivalry required the knight to protect women; 'to do ladyes, damesels, and jantilwomen and wydowes socour: strengthe hem in hir ryghtes, and never to enforce them, uppon payne of dethe': *The Works of Sir Thomas Malory*, ed. Eugène Vinaver, 2nd edn, 3 vols (Oxford, 1967), 1.120. See also *Prose Works*, 6.26–28.

6.33   take up the gauntlet   accept a challenge on one's own or someone else's behalf. The metaphor originates in the practice of the throwing down of his gauntlet by a knight as a chivalric act of challenge (compare *Richard II*, 4.1.25–90, or *Henry V*, 4.1.201–15).

7.31   Patent Drops   proprietary cleaning agent in liquid form.

7.40   supposititious stigmata   deliberately misleading evidence of suffering; 'stigmata' are traditionally bodily wounds identical to those suffered by the crucified Christ.

8.7   a credulous vulgar   common people ready to believe on little evidence.

8.8   a vulgar incredulity   a commonplace scepticism.

8.10   an esprit fort   *French* a bold spirit who rejects conventional views.

8.13   Open Sesamun   the magical words used by Ali Baba to open the door of the robbers' den in the *Arabian Nights*. See 'The Story of Ali Baba, and the forty thieves detroyed by a slave', in *Tales of the East*, ed. Henry Weber, 3 vols (Edinburgh, 1812), 1.402–14 (*CLA*, 43).

8.21   the Rose of Scotland   Mary Queen of Scots.

8.27   the fierce fanatic Ruthven   William, 4th Lord Ruthven, later Earl of Gowrie (*c.* 1541–84), was a determined Protestant. A leader of the conspiracy to murder Rizzio, he had himself been seriously ill in the preceding months.

8.32–33   the boy Darnley   Henry Stewart, Lord Darnley (1546–67), married Queen Mary in July 1565. He was himself murdered at Kirk o' Field, Edinburgh, in February 1567, only eleven months after the murder of Rizzio.

8.40   the Postulate, George Douglas   illegitimate son (d. *c.* 1590) of the 6th Earl of Angus; he persistently pursued a claim to the property of Arbroath Abbey (Tironensian: i.e. reformed Benedictine) and as a result became known as the 'Postulate', i.e. one who seeks a benefice in the Church.

9.3   Tantalus   in Greek mythology, Tantalus was punished in Hades for his misdeeds by having to stand in water that receded when he tried to drink it, and beneath fruits that moved away when he reached out for them.

9.13   Andrew Ker of Faldonside   Andrew Ker of Fawdonside was an active and enthusiastic Protestant; the widow of John Knox became his wife. During the murder of Rizzio he is supposed to have held a pistol to the stomach of the pregnant Queen Mary.

9.14   Sir David Ker of Cessford   probably Sir Walter Kerr of Cessford (d. *c.* 1582), known to have been an active opponent of Mary.

9.29   Robertson   William Robertson (1721–93) whose *History of Scotland* was published in 1759. Book IV of the *History* contains a full account of Rizzio's murder.

9.29–30   I awake...a dream   see the closing words of Part 1 of John Bunyan's *The Pilgrim's Progress* (1678).

9.41–43   Punch in the show-box...Master Noah   the puppet-show involving Punch and his wife developed in Italy in the 17th century and was already popular in England in the 18th. Richard Steele in *The Tatler* in 1709 refers to a Noah's Flood scene in which Punch and his wife are shown dancing in the Ark. The joke about the rainy weather which in fact turns out to be the biblical Flood exists in a variety of forms.

9.41   King Solomon in his glory   see Matthew 6.29 and Luke 12.17.

10.2–3   the mendacious Mr Fagg   character in R. B. Sheridan's play *The Rivals* (1775).

10.10–17   There are plenty of wildernesses...want of towns   compare Scott's article on the 'Ancient History of Scotland', in the *Quarterly Review*, July 1829, which includes the couplet as here quoted (see next note): *Prose Works*, 20.301–76.

10.16–17   Geographers...of towns   although Scott attributes these lines to Matthew Prior (1664–1721), they come from Jonathan Swift, 'On Poetry' (1733), lines 177–80: 'So geographers, in Africk maps/ With savage pictures fill their gaps,/ And o'er unhabitable downs/ Place elephants for want of towns': *The Life and Works of Jonathan Swift*, ed. Walter Scott, 19 vols (Edinburgh, 1814), 8.171.

10.22   Historical Romance   Scott called the second collection of his fiction (containing *Ivanhoe, The Monastery, The Abbot,* and *Kenilworth*) *Historical Romances* (1822). In his 'Essay on Romance' (1824) he distinguishes between the Novel, a narrative of a realistic kind, and the Romance, a narrative including the marvellous and uncommon, but says that some compositions 'partake of the nature of both' (*Prose Works*, 6.129–30).

10.26–27   Scottish of that day...Anglo-Saxon   see Lismahago in Tobias Smollett, *Humphry Clinker* (1771): 'He said, what we generally called the Scottish dialect was, in fact, true, genuine old English' (ed. Thomas R. Preston and O. M. Brack, Jr. (Athens and London, 1990), 193–94; J. Melford to Sir Watkin Phillips, 13 July). See also Scott's comments in his 1804 review of George Ellis, *Specimens of the Early English Poets*, in *Prose Works*, 17.9–10.

10.29   the Chronicles of Winton   Andrew of Wyntoun (*c.* 1355–1422) provides in octosyllabic couplets a history of Scotland from its mythical origins down to the achievement of independence under Robert the Bruce in the early 14th century.

10.29–30   History of Bruce...Barbour   John Barbour (*c.* 1320–95), author of *The Bruce* (written *c.* 1372–86), was Archdeacon of Aberdeen. His poem, written half a century after the events it describes, becomes a national epic celebration of Bruce's successful struggle for Scottish independence.

10.30–33   supposing my own skill...general reader   compare the fuller discussion of historical distance and how to deal with it in the Dedicatory Epistle to *Ivanhoe*, ed. Graham Tulloch, EEWN 8, 9.3–10.30.

11.1   Saint Valentine's Day   14 February. St Valentine was Bishop of Terni, a 3rd century martyr whose feast day by historical accident became associated with various courtship rituals such as the sending of gifts or messages of love, and the choosing of mates.

11   motto   not identified; probably by Scott.

11.5   Tiber   the river on which Rome is built: see note to 12.7–11.

11.6   **Tay**   one of Scotland's major rivers, flowing E into the North Sea; see also note to 12.7–11.

11.6   **Beglie's side**   see text 12.24–34, and note to 12.24.

11.11   **the county of Perth**   one of the larger Scottish counties, in the centre of the country, and containing both Highland and Lowland areas.

11.15   **Caledonia**   the traditional Latin name for Scotland.

11.16   **Lady Mary Wortley Montague**   1689–1762. Writer, intellectual, friend (and later enemy) of Pope, Montagu is now best known for her letters from Turkey (published posthumously in 1763) when her husband was ambassador there. Her grand-daughter, Lady Louisa Stuart, was a close friend of Scott's. The citation (as the ICopy revision makes clear: ICopy, 1.24; EEWN, 11.23) ends at 'more level land'. The passage to which Scott refers has not been identified.

11.28   **the poet Gray**   Thomas Gray (1716–71), poet, scholar, and traveller. He visited Scotland in 1765.

11.28–29   **Gray, or someone else... Terror**   Scott rightly hesitates over the attribution to Thomas Gray (1716–71), although kindred expressions can be found in Gray's letters; e.g. (after his Scottish tour) Gray writes: 'the Lowlands are worth seeing once, but the Mountains are extatic, & ought to be visited in pilgrimage once a year. none but those monstrous creatures of God know how to join so much beauty with so much horror.' (*Correspondence of Thomas Gray*, ed. Paget Toynbee and Leonard Whibley, 3 vols (Oxford, 1935), 2.899). The phrase 'Beauty lying in the lap of Horror' occurs in William Gilpin, *Observations Relative Chiefly to Picturesque Beauty Made in the Year 1772, on Several Parts of England; Particularly the Mountains and Lakes of Cumberland and Westmorland*, 2 vols (London, 1786), 1.183, where it is attributed to a Mr Avison. The same concept figures in various Romantic texts including Ann Radcliffe, *The Mysteries of Udolpho* (1794), where it appears as 'beauty sleeping in the lap of horror' (ed. Bonamy Dobrée (Oxford, 1970), 55), and P. B. Shelley, *Alastor* (1816), lines 577–78: 'It was a tranquil spot, that seemed to smile/ Even in the lap of horror'.

11.32   **the Highland tour**   the original Highland tour was restricted to the Trossachs area of Stirlingshire. The tour was already established before Scott popularised it in his own *The Lady of the Lake* (1810).

12.1   **the Saxons of the plain, and the Gael of the mountains**   Scott uses the terms 'Saxon' and 'Gael' to distinguish between the inhabitants of the Scottish Lowlands, whom he regards as being of Anglo-Saxon origin, and of the Scottish Highlands, whom he identifies as a Celtic people.

12.5–7   **Perth... Roman foundation**   Scott is almost certainly right in suggesting that the origins of Perth go back to the Roman occupation of lowland Scotland under Agricola *c*. AD 78–87. See *The Muses Threnodie* (Third Muse).

12.7–11   **That victorious nation... Campus Martius**   Henry Adamson in *The Muses Threnodie* (Third Muse) has the invading Romans compare Perth Inches with the Campus Martius: '... which when they did espy/ Incontinent they *campus Martius* cry'. Some lines later the Roman soldiers name the River Tay the 'New Tiber'. The Campus Martius was a large, level open space near Rome used in classical times for military exercises. Scott's description of the Tay as 'magnificent and navigable' reminds us that in the Middle Ages Perth was a considerable port, its merchant vessels trading with much of N Europe.

12.12   **the Cistercian Convent**   it was the Dominican, i.e. Blackfriars Monastery founded by Alexander II in 1231, at the N end of Perth's Blackfriars Wynd, in which the kings of Scotland frequently held court. Robert II and Robert III both made regular use of this location. See also note to 18.1.

12.13–15   **James the First... vengeful aristocracy**   King James I, second son of Robert III, reigned 1406–37. He was murdered in the Blackfriars

Monastery in Perth in February 1437, as the result of a conspiracy of nobles led by Walter Stewart, Earl of Atholl (the King's uncle), Sir Robert Stewart (the Earl's grandson), and Sir Robert Graham.

12.16 conspiracy of Gowrie John, 3rd Earl of Gowrie, and his brother Alexander, Master of Ruthven, probably conspired to murder King James VI of Scotland, but were overpowered and slain at Gowrie House in Perth on 5 August 1600. Gowrie, an accomplished scholar who had studied at Padua University, was also a popular Provost of Perth. The conspiracy is described as 'mysterious' because there have always been those who argue that it was King James who had conspired to kill Gowrie and his brother.

12.17 destruction of the ancient palace Gowrie House, demolished 1805.

12.18 Antiquarian Society of Perth the first and only published volume of the *Transactions of the Literary and Antiquarian Society of Perth* (1827) described in detail Gowrie House, its apartments, interior plans, and gardens.

12.24 the Wicks of Beglie pass in the Ochil Hills about 11 km S of Perth near the road to Edinburgh. See Magnum, 42.title-page for an engraving of the view, and for an alternative verbal representation see Magnum, 42.24–25.

12.25 stage from Kinross about 29 km. A *stage* was the distance between staging-posts where horses were hired for riding or for pulling a carriage.

12.30–31 hills of Moncrieff and Kinnoull Moncrieffe (221 m) and Kinnoull (222 m) are the two highest hills in the immediate vicinity of Perth.

13.2–3 Chrystal Croftangry ... the matchless scene although the fiction that Croftangry is the narrator is maintained (the speaker is more than 65), it was Scott himself who was so delighted by the view from the Wicks of Baiglie, when he travelled to Perthshire to visit legal clients of his father probably in the autumn of 1786.

13.25 remarkable historical transactions i.e. the murder of James I and the Gowrie Conspiracy.

13.28–29 John, who reigned under the title of Robert the Third Robert III, King of Scots 1390–1406, was born John Stewart. He was the eldest son of Robert II and was created Earl of Carrick by David II in 1368.

13.40–14.5 the love ... due to Heaven compare Scott's 1803 review of translations of *Amadis of Gaul*: 'the duty of obeying the hests, and fighting for the honour of a lady, was indispensable ... Even the zeal of devotion gave way to this all devouring sentiment; and very religious indeed must the knight have been, who had, as was predicted of Esplandian, God upon his *right* hand, and his lady upon his *left*' (*Prose Works*, 18.26–27).

14.8–10 the reign preceding that of Robert III. ... the Scottish throne Robert III's predecessor was Robert II (reigned 1371–90); after the issue of a papal dispensation in 1347 he married his mistress, Elizabeth Mure of Rowallan, and legitimised his children. As Elizabeth Mure died *c.* 1353 she was never queen. However Robert II's predecessor, David II, married his mistress, Margaret Logie or Drummond, in 1364 after the death of his first wife, Joanna. Scott's mistake in calling Elizabeth Mure 'queen' is derived from his source, John Bellenden's translation (1536) of Hector Boece's *Scotorum historiae*: see Hector Boece, *The History and Chronicles of Scotland*, trans. John Bellenden, 3 vols (Edinburgh, 1821), 2.449 (*CLA*, 4).

14.21 Couvrefew, or Curfew Street on this initial occasion, Scott indicates two acceptable versions of the street name; but in the rest of the novel one or other form appears with almost equal regularity, both in dialogue and narrative. The street was so-called because it contained the curfew bell rung as a warning of the nightly necessity to cover over or extinguish fires.

15.2–4 To-morrow is Saint Valentine's Day ... with the kite *Hamlet*, 4–5.46. See also Chaucer's 'The Parlement of Fowles' (*c.* 1382), in which the choice of mates on St Valentine's Day by different kinds of bird reflects allegorically the class structure of society.

15.7 shamoy leather 'shammy' leather, i.e. leather made from the skin of the chamois goat.

15.10 Provost principal magistrate of a Scottish burgh; equivalent to a mayor in England and other countries. In the medieval period the Provost was often of knightly rank.

15.26–27 mantilla still worn in Flanders lace or silk scarf covering the head and shoulders. Flanders was a medieval principality in the SW of the Low Countries; it was long controlled by Spain where the mantilla was originally worn.

16.3 barrets in *Ivanhoe*, 'basnet' was misread as 'barret', and 'basnet' would also be a better reading here, but as the manuscript is not extant for this part of the novel, there are no grounds for an emendation. A *basnet* is a hemispherical helmet without a visor, worn under the fighting helmet, while a *barret* is a small flat cap: see *Ivanhoe*, ed. Graham Tulloch, EEWN 8, 385.34 and note.

16.7–8 took the wall took the right or privilege of walking closest to the buildings, the wall side being regarded as the cleaner and safer section of a street.

16.19–24 What have we ... in my company compare Nicol Jarvie in *Rob Roy* (1818): 'I maun hear naething about honour—we ken naething here but about credit. Honour is a homicide and a bloodspiller, that gangs about making frays in the street' (2.271.2–5).

17.2 St Catherine Christian martyr who was executed in Alexandria in AD 307, having been tortured on a wheel.

17.25 sun first peeps over the eastern hill compare *Hamlet*, 1.1.166–67.

18.1 Dominican the Dominican order, an order specially devoted to preaching and study, hence their official title *Ordo Praedicatorum* (the Order of Preachers), was founded in 1215 by the Spaniard St Dominic (1170–1221). In Britain its members were called the Blackfriars, from the black mantle which was worn over a white habit.

19.21–22 a country where ... defend themselves in the course of the novel Scott frequently reiterates the idea that in 14th-century Scotland the rule of law hardly existed and that as a result individuals had to be ready to protect themselves.

19.31 show us thy shapes come into view.

19.37 curfew has not rung yet rung at 7 p.m.: see text, 168.4.

20.3–4 beauffet, popularly called the Bink a *beauffet*, or buffet, was a piece of furniture with cupboards and open shelves used to display plates etc.; a *bink* was a shelf, plate-rack, or dresser.

22.10 St Johnstoun another name for Perth. In the pre-Reformation period, John the Baptist was the tutelary saint of the town, of the bridge over the River Tay, and of St John's Church, also known as the Kirk of the Holy Cross of St Johnstoun.

22.14–15 like a Fairy Queen in romance see *A Midsummer Night's Dream*, 2.1.248–67; no medieval or contemporary romance in which a Fairy Queen is found asleep has been identified.

22.15 a wilderness of flowers James Thomson, *Spring*, edition of 1746, line 528, in *The Seasons*, ed. James Sambrook (Oxford, 1981).

22.23 mend my fortune ... verses compare *King Lear*, 1.1.93–94: 'Mend your speech a little,/ Lest you may mar your fortunes'.

22.27 four hundred marks £267 Scots, about £133 sterling. The Scots pound had roughly half the value of the English in this period. The sum of £133 sterling shows the value of good armour in the Middle Ages, but is so great that it is possible that Scott was thinking of the value of the mark at the time of the abolition of the Scots currency in 1707, when 400 marks were worth £22 sterling.

22.27–28 English Warden . . . Redman the Marches, East and West, comprised the border country between Scotland and England. The Wardens of the Marches, both English and Scottish, were responsible for the protection and defence of these areas. Scott's footnote in the Magnum (Magnum, 42.43) tells us that Sir Magnus Redman was a Governor of Berwick. Jean Froissart (*c.* 1337–*c.* 1410) in his *Chronicles* refers to Sir Mathew Redman as an English knight present at the Battle of Otterburn in 1388 (*Chroniques de J. Froissart*, 15 vols, 1869–1975, Vol. 15, ed. Albert Mirot, 161–64; see *CLA*, 28, 29, 51).

23.2–3 St Dunstan . . . of our craft Dunstan, Archbishop of Canterbury 960–88, was responsible for a revival of monasticism in England. In his pre-monastic days, his many skills included metal-work; as a result he subsequently became patron-saint of locksmiths.

23.21 your patient sufferance compare *The Merchant of Venice*, 1.3.104–05.

23.34 some Edinburgh Burn-the-wind some blacksmith or armourer from Edinburgh. Compare Robert Burns, 'Scotch Drink' (written 1785–86), lines 59–60: 'Then Burnewin comes on like Death,/ At every chap'.

23.36 St Leonard's Crags rocky area in the W of the King's Park below Arthur's Seat in Edinburgh; traditionally a site for the fighting of duels. Compare *The Heart of Mid-Lothian* (1818), 1.271.17–272.15.

23.43 the Hermit's Lodge not identified.

24.4 Berwick fortified town at the mouth of the River Tweed on the eastern border between Scotland and England. It changed hands frequently throughout the period of the Anglo-Scottish border wars.

24.4–5 the old question of the Supremacy the claim of the Kings of England to have feudal sovereignty over the Kings of Scotland, an issue central to the struggle for Scottish independence in the 13th and 14th centuries.

24.8 St Andrew patron saint of Scotland.

24.10 the Torwood ancient forest located between Falkirk and Stirling in the Scottish Lowlands.

24.22 presenting . . . Stirling Bridge in Henry Smith's eyes, by crossing over the bridge to the S side of the River Forth at Stirling, the Highlander has left his native region and is 'trespassing' in the Lowlands.

24.24 cans clink compare Iago's song in *Othello*, 2.3.64–68.

25.8 stowed the lugs out of the head cut off your ears.

27.6–7 as loath . . . King Robert Robert the Bruce's legendary encounter with the persevering spider is supposed to have led to his descendants' general reluctance to harm spiders: see *Tales of a Grandfather*, First Series, in *Prose Works*, 22.108–10. The legend itself is not recorded before the 17th century.

28.36 which most easily beset thee compare Hebrews 12.1.

29.26–28 the forging of swords . . . ploughshare see Isaiah 2.4; Micah 4.3.

30.19–20 grates . . . country the Glover implies that Catherine would turn Henry Smith into a tinker.

30.19 Culross girdles see Magnum, 42.57n: 'The *girdle* is the thin plate of iron used for the manufacture of the staple luxury of Scotland, the oaten cake. The town of Culross [on the Forth in W Fife] was long celebrated for its girdles.'

30.25–26 for that part those who are strong . . . weak yield compare Wordsworth's poem 'Rob Roy's Grave', which Scott knew well, for he had used these lines as a motto on the title-page of *Rob Roy* (1818): 'For why? Because the good old rule/ Sufficeth them; the simple plan,/ That they should take who have the power,/ And they should keep who can'.

31.22   Crabbe the Flemish engineer   John Crabb, a Flemish military engineer and naval captain, was an expert in siege warfare. Early in the 14th century he assisted the Scots in various encounters with the English, but, captured in 1332, he switched his allegiance to Edward III of England. He could have been involved in the siege of Perth in 1332 when it was occupied by Edward Balliol after his victory at the battle of Dupplin, a few miles outside the city.

32.39–33.2   more beautiful ... approach Catherine   compare John Milton, *Paradise Lost* (1667), 8.546–59.

33.8   a conceited ape   a fool who thinks too well of himself.

33.23   every sprig of chivalry   every offshoot of a noble or knightly family.

33.29   trick of defence   skill in self-defence.

33.30   great Minister-church   large church or cathedral.

34.10   on the other side of the hill   i.e. in the Highlands.

34.13   packing and peeling   trading of doubtful legality.

34.31   yonder cat-a-mountain   literally a leopard or panther or any species of tiger-cat (presumably including the wild cat once common in the Scottish Highlands). By extension a *cat-a-mountain* or catamountain comes to mean a wild man from the mountains.

34.32   the Shoe-gate   the Shoe-gate, or South High Street, was one of the two principal streets of medieval Perth.

35.24   sword-and-buckler player   competitor in games in which men armed with swords and small round shields fought each other.

35.26   the weapon-shawing   the 'wappenshaw' or 'weapon-showing' involved the mustering of any group of Scottish men to determine whether they were properly armed. Medieval wappenshaws normally occurred when the Scottish feudal host was being raised either to resist English cross-border invasions, or to attack the northern counties of England. Compare *The Tale of Old Mortality* (1816), ed. Douglas Mack, EEWN 4b, 14.29–16.24, for Scott's own account of the traditional wappenshaw.

35.30   the devil having his due ... Highlandmen   Simon suggests that Conachar, like all Highlanders, is in debt to the devil. For 'the devil having his due' see *ODEP*, 304.

35.35   Old Nick   the devil.

35.36   in the same element   i.e. in fire.

35.37   the devil will have the tartan   in any contest with Catherine over possession of Conachar, the devil will win.

35.42–43   devil's drubber   one who 'drubs' or beats the devil.

36.7   Fastern's Eve   the Tuesday evening prior to Ash Wednesday (40 days before Palm Sunday); Fastern's Eve is therefore the last opportunity for uninhibited eating and drinking before Lent, the period of fasting and penance leading up to the celebration of Easter.

36.8   has a pleasant in principio   compare Chaucer's Friar in the 'General Prologue' to *The Canterbury Tales* (1 (A), 253–55): 'So plesaunt was his "*In principio*"' that he could get a farthing even from a poor widow. The Latin phrase *In principio* means 'in the beginning', the opening words of Genesis 1.1, and John 1.1.

36.10   on the bow-hand   wide of the mark.

36.33   the Meal Vennel   an alley or lane in medieval Perth; 'vennels' and 'wynds' were common features of the old city's street topography.

36.35   a priest's scapular   part of the standard monastic dress, consisting of a cloth worn over the shoulders and hanging down in front and behind to the ankles.

36.36   when our stately bridge ... away   the bridge over the River Tay in the centre of Perth was swept away more than once in the Middle Ages. The first recorded occasion was in 1210, and a similar disaster occurred in 1328. See *The Muses Threnodie* (Third Muse), and note to 258.17–21.

37.10–11 Five nobles to our altar . . . with the donation of five gold coins to the Church gained the Smith absolution for what he did to the best man he injured.

37.19–20 for all thou be'st covered with the lion's hide . . . of the ass see the Aesop fable of the Ass in the Lion's Skin.

37.23–24 Sir Chanticleer the cock with the peerless crow best known from 'The Nun's Priest's Tale' in Chaucer's *The Canterbury Tales*; he reappears in 'The Taill of Schir Chantecleir and the Foxe' in Robert Henryson's *Morall Fabillis of Esope* (late 15th century).

37.27 the Mill Wynd alley or lane in medieval, and modern, Perth.

38.3 Flemish hose and doublet stockings and close-fitting jacket worn by men, especially when engaged in active pursuits. The special characteristics (if any) of *Flemish* hose and doublet are not known.

38.4 broad cloth plain, fine-wove, woollen cloth. Originally indicating width (two yards), the term came to be used to indicate quality rather than size. In the later 14th and 15th centuries England was the source of much of Europe's fine woollen cloth.

38.5 slashed out having vertical slits to show a contrasting fabric (here black satin).

38.6 Cordovan leather fine goat or horse-skin leather, from Córdoba in S Spain, used particularly in shoes for the higher classes.

38.7 Scottish grey grey, flecked or checked cloth from Scotland. It was generally used for outer garments and was fairly coarse.

38.8 couteau de chasse *French* hunting knife.

38.15–16 stepping beyond his own rank, and encroaching that of the gentry rank was usually regulated by dress, which was regulated by sumptuary laws (laws relating to expenditure). For an act of 1458 see P. Hume Brown, *History of Scotland to the Present Time*, 3 vols (Cambridge, 1911), 1.197.

38.18–19 bravoes or swash-bucklers hired killers or aggressive ruffians.

38.33 King Oberon king of the fairies: see e.g. *A Midsummer Night's Dream*, or the 13th-century French *chanson de geste*, *Huon of Bordeaux* and the 15th-century prose romance descended from it.

38.35–37 love's darts . . . mail-shirts not identified; probably by Scott.

39.1 Saint John's Church some form of church had existed on the site of St John's in Perth since the earliest days of Christianity in Scotland. David I refers to the church in 1126 and may have been responsible for rebuilding it. Only the choir added in 1440 survives from the medieval period.

39.24 Saint Anne's Chapel chapel dedicated to St Anne, mother of the Virgin Mary, on the S side of St John's Church in Perth.

40.26–27 die the death the phrase enters the language through Coverdale's translation (1535) of Judges 13.22. It is used by Shakespeare in e.g. *A Midsummer Night's Dream*, 1.1.65, and *Measure for Measure*, 2.4.165, where Samuel Johnson in his edition of Shakespeare (1765) glosses it as 'a solemn phrase for death inflicted by law'.

41.37 to prove godfather to act as the juryman condemning someone to the gallows. Compare *The Merchant of Venice*, 4.1.393–95.

42.19 my old two-handed Trojan like the heroes of epic or romance, Henry has given his favourite sword a proper name.

42.31 girth and sanctuary defined area round a church and the church building offering safety or asylum.

43.7 breaches in our walls in the course of the 14th century Perth underwent various sieges during or after which the city's walls and fortifications were frequently damaged or even levelled. See *The Muses Threnodie* (Fourth Muse).

Edinburgh and Perth were Scotland's only walled cities.

43.19 the Justiciar an officially-appointed legal officer who deputized for the King, and in his absence presided over the royal courts of law.

43.21 hard laws against mutilation a statute of Robert II, enacted in 1384, required that anyone who, with malice aforethought, mutilated another, and was pursued by the injured party, should be prosecuted as a manslayer before the justiciar; if convicted, his life was 'redeemable', that is, in the king's will: *The Acts of the Parliament of Scotland*, ed. T. Thomson and C. Innes, 12 vols (1814–75), 1.550b.

43.24 stout old Romans . . . could see note to 12.5–7.

43.25 charters from all our noble kings i.e. the royal charters granted to the town giving the kinds of privilege listed below.

43.27–29 rights . . . commodities in question here are the special privileges of jurisdiction granted to burgesses within a royal burgh (see note to 70.10) by various royal charters: 'outfang and infang' refer to the right to try a thief taken either outside the jurisdiction or inside the jurisdiction; both 'hand-habend' and 'back-bearand' describe thieves caught in the act of carrying off stolen property; 'blood-suits' refers to the right to hold courts and recover fines for a wrong or injury, such as the drawing of blood; 'amerciaments' are fines paid by offenders; 'escheats' refers to the forfeiture of the goods of a convicted person; 'commodities' are the benefits or advantages deriving from the possession or use of property.

43.31 the Tay shall flow back to Dunkeld i.e. will reverse its natural flow. Dunkeld is a town some 23 km N of Perth.

44.4 watch and ward i.e. the duties of watching and guarding the city from any form of attack, traditional responsibilities of the burgesses of Perth.

44.30 to boot in addition.

45.19 St Catherine the Second the original Catherine, after whom Catherine Glover is presumably named, was St Catherine of Alexandria (see note to 17.2); martyred in AD 307, she was much honoured in medieval England.

45.36 St Macgrider one of the many variants of St Medan or Modan, an obscure Celtic saint who also appears as Magridin and Macgidrin.

46.19 sack, or rhenish, or wine of Gascony 'sack' is dry white wine from any part of SW Europe; 'rhenish' is hock, a white wine from the Rhineland area; Gascony is an area of SW France.

46.39 and please ye if it please you.

46.40 that obedience to which law and gospel give me right both Old and New Testaments ('law and gospel') supply texts stressing children's duty of submission to their parents: compare Exodus 20.12; Ephesians 6.1–3.

47.27 tithes and alms, wine and wax the giving to the Church of one-tenth part of his income, as well as money for the poor and the purchase of communion wine and wax-candles.

47.28–29 my only and single ewe-lamb see 2 Samuel 12.1–3.

48.35–37 the squire of low degree . . . King of Hungary's daughter see the 15th-century romance 'The Squyr of Lowe Degre', which begins: 'It was a squire of low degré/ That loved the kings doughter of Hungré' (in *Ancient Engleish Metrical Romancëes*, ed. Joseph Ritson, 3 vols (London, 1802), 3.145; *CLA*, 174).

49.2–3 lady of romance . . . tame lion the most famous such lion is the one that accompanies and protects Una in Spenser's *The Faerie Queene*, Bk 1 (1590).

50.14–15 strike while the iron is hot proverbial: *ODEP*, 781; Ray, 125.

50.15 let sleeping dogs lie still proverbial: see *ODEP*, 456.

50.30 Jamie Keddie's ring in a Magnum note (42.102) Lockhart says that Keddie is supposed to have found a magic ring, able to make him invisible, in a cave in Kinnoull Hill near Perth. See *The Muses Threnodie* (Sixth Muse).

50.43 fool used as a term of endearment: compare *King Lear*, 5.3.305.

51.38 blithe as a lark proverbial: see *ODEP*, 527.

52.1 What the foul fiend what the devil.

52.8 St Macgrider see note to 45.36.

52.16–17 burgess' tenure in royal burghs (towns whose privileges were granted by the crown) burgesses had the privilege of holding their land on 'burgage' or burgess tenure; this meant that in effect their only feudal superior was the Crown. Burgage tenure was not abolished until the 19th century.

52.23 Tutti taitti *exclamation* expressing derision or impatience.

52.23–24 neither Rome nor Perth ... a day version of the proverb (originally French) that Rome was not built in a day: see *ODEP*, 683.

53.6 theme to wag thy tongue compare *Hamlet*, 3.4.39–40 ('What have I done that thou dar'st wag thy tongue/ In noise so rude against me?'), and 5.1.260–61 ('Why, I will fight with him upon this theme/ Until my eyelids will no longer wag.').

53 motto this line does not occur in either Shakespeare's *The Taming of the Shrew* or the anonymous Elizabethan play *The Taming of a Shrew*.

53.14 proof of ... pudding proverbial: see Ray, 149; *ODEP*, 650.

53.19 Seneca Lucius Annaeus Seneca (*c.* 4 BC–AD 65). Roman philosopher and dramatist whose writings inculcate Stoic attitudes to the vicissitudes of life.

53.31–32 for that matter of it for that matter.

53.33–34 King Arthur and his Round Table the legendary King Arthur and his company of knights were traditionally regarded as exemplary warriors.

54.6 Paladins the legendary twelve peers of the court of Charlemagne, King and Emperor, and hence knightly champions in general.

54.10 our honourable mystery the blacksmith trade, or the guild to which members of the blacksmith trade belonged.

54.39 the merry hunts up early morning clamour (or song) originally designed to awaken the huntsmen.

56.11 the Low Country the Lowlands as opposed to the Highlands of Scotland.

56.41 hath long hands ... reaches ... hears proverbial: see *ODEP*, 428 ('Kings have long arms').

56.43–57.1 the Gentle Craft ... of St Crispin Crispin is the patron saint of shoemakers; noble-born, he made shoes with his own hands, stealing the leather and giving the shoes away to the poor. Thus Henry argues that as the son of a Celtic chief ('some great Mac or O') shoe-making would have been the proper trade for Conachar.

57.32 these bare-breeched Dunniewassals these bare-arsed gentlemen. The term 'dunniewassal' is used to describe a Highland gentleman below the rank of chief.

59.24–25 worn ... spurs on his heels been of knightly rank.

59.29–30 the sins of vanity ... easily beset see note to 151.17.

59.36–37 for all these things ... judgment see Ecclesiastes 11.9.

60.20–21 Blind Harry the Minstrel Blind Harry or Hary (*c.* 1440–92), author of *Wallace* (*c.* 1478), a long narrative poem describing the heroic career of Sir William Wallace (see next note).

60.22–23 William Wallace Sir William Wallace, Scottish patriot (*c.* 1270–1305). He led the resistance to Edward I's attempt to subjugate Scotland, but was eventually betrayed, and then executed in London.

60.36–37 bell, book, and candle items used in the Catholic ritual of excommunication.

61.15 as large a daily alms as a deacon gives there is no reference here to a legal or religious duty; the Smith simply means that he is rich enough to be able to be as charitable as any head of a trade guild.

62.14 **Thorbiorn, the Danish armourer** possibly fictional, meaning 'son of Thor', the Norse god of thunder. There is a 'Thorbiorn' in 'The Abstract of the Eyrbiggia-Saga', in *Prose Works*, 5.357–413.

62.14–17 **spoke of a spell ... no proof against weapons** for the Norse belief in defensive incantations see e.g. the poem *Háva-Mál*, where Odin, reciting the wisdom he has learned, hanging sacrificed on the world-tree, says: 'I know songs, such as no king's daughter, nor son of man knows ... If I am in sore need of bonds for my enemies, I can deaden my enemies' swords, their swords will bite no more than staves' (*Corpus Poeticum Boreale*, ed. G. Vigfusson and F. York Powell (1883), 1.26). Runes are, properly, incised characters of an angular script. For the conception of them as charms see M. Mallet, *Northern Antiquities*, trans. Bishop Percy, with an Absract of the *Eyrbyggja Saga* by Sir Walter Scott, ed. I. A. Blackwell (London, 1847), 226: 'The *noxious*, or, as they called them, the *bitter runes*, were employed to bring various evils on their enemies; the *favourable* averted misfortunes; the *victorious* procured conquest to those who used them.... In the strict observance of these childish particulars consisted that obscure and ridiculous art, which acquired to so many weak and wicked persons the respectable name of priests and prophetesses.' Compare Norman on Henry at 355.6–10.

62.17 **Loncarty** or Luncarty; the site, some 7 km NW of Perth, of a battle in which the Scots defeated the Danes. The battle occurred during the reign of Kenneth III, probably around the year 990.

63 **motto** see *1 Henry VI*, 2.4.134: 'This quarrel will drink blood another day'.

63.9 **bailies and deacons** municipal magistrates and the presidents of the various trade guilds.

65.12 **I have heard ... but one eye** the Cyclops, who worked as smiths for Vulcan, god of fire: see Virgil, *Aeneid* (30–19 BC), 8.423–54.

65.40 **the Duke of Albany** Robert Stewart (1339–1420), Earl of Fife and Menteith, younger brother of Robert III, was created Duke of Albany in 1398. By then he was already proving himself the most ruthlessly successful politician of the Stewart family.

66.1 **Duke of Rothsay** David Stewart (1378–1402), Earl of Carrick and Atholl, son and heir of Robert III, was created Duke of Rothsay in 1398 on the same day as his uncle became Duke of Albany. They were the first Scottish dukes.

66.9 **the Black Douglas** Archibald Douglas (*c.* 1330–1400), 3rd Earl of Douglas, lord of Galloway; also known as Archibald the Grim. The style 'the Black Douglas' was most commonly used by English chroniclers. After the death of the 2nd Earl of Douglas, at Otterburn in 1388, without an heir, a dispute over the Douglas estates led to a bifurcation of the Douglas power. The inheritors of the Douglas lands in Galloway in SW Scotland became known as the 'Black' Douglases, while those who took possession of the Douglas territory in Angus in E Scotland became the 'Red' Douglases.

66.26 **the Bloody Heart** part of the coat of arms of the Douglas family commemorating the fame and honour of Sir James Douglas, 'the Good' (*c.* 1286–1330), killed in Spain by the Moors as he tried to carry Robert the Bruce's heart to the Holy Land.

66.28 **Short rede, good rede** *proverbial literally* short counsel, good counsel: see *ODEP*, 728.

66.42–43 **bred in Paris ... cursus medendi** been at university in Paris (already one of the great European centres of teaching and learning), studied the various branches of classical learning (humanities) and taken a course in medical study (*cursus medendi*).

67.9 fugitive essences volatile or fickle in their essential nature.

68.16–17 hawks will not pick hawks' eyes out proverbial: see *ODEP*, 359.

68.19 cloth of gold cloth of silk or fine wool interwoven with wires or ribbons of gold, and thus worn only by the most wealthy.

68.20 tartan and Irish frieze Scottish Highlanders wearing tartan and heavy woollen cloth; the term 'Irish' may refer to both the Scottish Highlands and Ireland.

68.21 Take a fool's advice take the advice of someone who is naive about such matters.

69.3–4 gentleman of ... amongst us for how Wallace settled Sir Patrick Charteris's great-grandfather in the area of Perth see text 70.31–73.25.

69.14 Kinfauns village and castle 3 km E of Perth on the road to Dundee.

69.18 belted knight knights and earls wore a distinctive belt as a mark of their rank.

69.27 horse and hattock in the ICopy Scott explains that this phrase is the 'cry of the fairies at taking their enchanted horses & hence a token of a mounting of any kind' (ICopy, 1.179); for Lockhart's version of the same note see Magnum, 42.140.

69.28 the East Port fortified gate at the E end of the High Street in Perth.

69.32 bell-the-cat undertake a dangerous enterprise. The phrase alludes to the traditional fable of the mice (or rats) who propose to hang a bell round the cat's neck so as to be warned of its approach; however, in Scottish history, the phrase is especially linked with the behaviour of Archibald Douglas, Earl of Angus, who in 1482 acquired the sobriquet 'Archibald, Bell-the-Cat' after agreeing to initiate the attack on the unpopular courtiers of James III.

69.41–42 privy council, or Lords of the Articles council of state or permanent committee of the Scottish Parliament.

70.8–30 It was the custom ... in the field compare the terser formulation of Louis XI in *Quentin Durward* (1823), 2.44.22–23: 'A plebeian mob ever desire an aristocratic leader'.

70.10 Royal Burghs of Scotland towns whose rights to some self government and to other privileges (see note to 43.27–29 for examples of these) were established by charters granted directly by the crown. Perth was made a royal burgh between 1124 and 1127.

70.16 common weal good of the community.

70.18 feudal retainers those who in return for the protection and maintenance provided by their lord were obliged to bear arms in his support.

70.21 tenements belonging to the common good holdings of land owned by the burgh in trust for its citizens.

70.30 Council i.e. the Privy Council of Scotland, which advised the king.

70.34 scarce a century for the story of de Longueville, the Red Rover, see *Wallace*, 9.182–554, but it is unlikely to be historical. For the connection with Kinfauns see Henrie Charteris's Preface to his 1594 edition of *Wallace* where he says that de Longueville married a Charteris heiress and took her name (*Wallace*, 9.229–41n), and *The Muses Threnodie* (Sixth Muse).

70.35–36 the strong castle the castle of Kinfauns which stands at the base of Kinnoull Hill on the N bank of the Tay, 3 km E of Perth.

71.8 The Scottish Champion a traditional way of referring to Sir William Wallace.

71.9 Dieppe seaport in Normandy on the NW coast of France.

71.16 Thomas de Longueville whether de Longueville is a historical character is not known. See note to 70.34.

71.19–20 Norse Sea-kings piratical Scandinavian chiefs who ravaged the coasts of Europe in the 9th and succeeding centuries.

71.33 Boyd, Kerlie, Seton Sir Robert Boyd (dates unknown) is the first of Wallace's companions to be introduced in *Wallace* (see note to 60.20–21); he also appears in John Barbour's *The Bruce* (written *c.* 1372–86; see *CLA*, 4, 8, 173) as one of Bruce's earliest followers. Kerle (Keirlie, Kerly, Kerlye) appears frequently in *Wallace* as one of the hero's closest friends. Historically he is probably the William Ker whose name appears with that of Robert Boyd in a document of 1292. Seton may be Sir Christopher Seton (*c.* 1278–1306); he does not feature in *Wallace* but does in *The Bruce*. He married Robert the Bruce's sister and was probably the person who actually murdered Sir John Comyn in 1306.

71.34 the breath of life see Genesis 2.7 etc.

72.26 The Scottish Lion in his shield of gold the Scottish flag, or, more properly, the arms of the Scottish monarch.

73.7–8 The estate ... Lord Gray in the 16th century the daughter of Alexander Blair of Balthyock in Perthshire married George Charteris of Kinfauns; the estate subsequently passed to the Blair family and in the 18th century the Blair heiress married John, Lord Gray, father of Francis, the 15th Baron Gray, to whom Scott refers.

73.32 pacing palfrey horse trained to walk by lifting both feet on the same side at the same time.

74.1 the old Galloway breed small but strong and hardy breed of horse originating in Galloway, the extreme SW of Scotland.

74.11 hawking pouch bag used for captured game worn by a falconer when hunting with hawks.

74.14 Flemish mare heavy horse used for carrying knights in full armour or for ploughing and other heavy work on farms.

75.3 hard set obstinate, determined.

75.5 I call her Jezabel, after the Princess of Castille as Henry Smith points out, Oliver confuses Jezebel, the wife of Ahab, King of Israel, with Isabella I, Queen of Castille (1451–1504). For Jezebel, see 1 Kings 18.17–20, 19.1–3, 21.1–29.

75.16 Bully Smith 'Bully' is used as a term of affection. Compare *A Midsummer Night's Dream*, 4.2.18: 'O sweet bully Bottom'.

75.39 Bourdeaux wine Bordeaux on the SW coast of France is the centre of one of the country's major wine-producing regions; its best red wine is the finest available.

75.43 curious comfits sweets, usually sugar-coated, containing nuts or seeds.

75.43 loaves of wastel bread bread of a fine, white quality.

76.1 cakes ... sugar sugar, which came in solid form, remained a rare and costly luxury throughout Europe until the 18th century. One of the earliest references to sugar in a British context occurs in the financial accounts of Robert the Bruce's chamberlain in 1319.

76.6 last year's snow compare François Villon's 'Ballade' with its famous refrain: 'Mais où sont les neiges d'antan?' ('where are the snows of yester-year?').

76.11 hawking glove thick leather glove used to protect the hand and lower arm from the talons of the perching falcon.

76.14 go to ... the less I lie *go to* expresses incredulity; *the less I lie* means *literally* 'I lie to a smaller extent'; i.e. 'really, then my point is correct'.

76.17–18 cogan na schie *Gaelic* 'Cogadh no sìth' ('war or peace'). 'Cogadh no sth' is usually part of a longer saying: 'Is coma leam cogadh no sìth' ('I care not whether it is war or peace').

76.22–23 to reckon up for wine and walnuts to make up an account of such minor matters as the accompaniments of a meal.

76.35 put him to the question interrogate or examine him in a threatening manner.

77.4–5 Southland lords i.e. lords from the Scottish Borders.

77.5 black jack jerkin of black leather, sometimes reinforced with plate or mail.

77.13–14 the old Spanish general not identified. He is also cited in *Redgauntlet*, ed. G. A. M. Wood with David Hewitt, EEWN 17, 15.12.

77.28 the Philistine was upon him see Judges 16.9.

77.32 Stand and deliver the traditional command of the highwayman to his intended victims.

77.34 The devil catch you for a cuckoo may you go to the devil for being a fool.

78.10–14 Devil's Dick of Hellgarth … Wamphray … Douglas the Johnstone family were powerful landowners in Annandale in Dumfriesshire; Wamphray is in Annandale, halfway between Moffat and Lockerbie. Scott probably invented Hellgarth as an appropriate base for the Devil's Dick. For Douglas see note to 66.9. 'Gentle' is a traditional sobriquet of the Johnstones, but they were a wild clan, in this period operating almost wholly independently of the Scottish crown.

78.23 the flying spur part of the coat of arms of the Johnstone of Annandale family, supposed to originate in a coded warning once sent to Robert the Bruce in the form of a spur with a feather attached.

79.2 their Oliver meet with a Rowland Roland and Oliver are the most famous of the twelve legendary peers of Charlemagne (reigned 768–814), equally matched in knightly prowess (on one occasion they are supposed to have fought in single combat for five days without either gaining any advantage), whence the proverbial phrase 'a Roland for an Oliver', i.e. tit for tat. They fell in the battle of Roncevalles, Charlemagne having arrived too late to save them.

79.37 spoken in sorrow more than anger compare *Hamlet*, 1.2.231.

80.4–5 like the King … a city was burning Nero the Roman emperor who is supposed to have played his fiddle while Rome was burning in AD 64.

80.18 moss-trooper term used in the 17th century to describe lawless men on the Borders; it derives from their frequenting the moss country of the wastes, through which troops of them passed on expeditions into England for plunder.

81.19–20 your speech bewrays see Matthew 26.73 where (as the parallel passage in Mark 14.70 makes clear) Peter is recognised by his Galilean accent.

81.26 St Andrew patron saint of Scotland.

81.28 Soldan or Saracen sultan (Muslim sovereign) or any Muslim Arab.

81.30–31 Lord of the Marches see note to 22.27–28.

82.31 winged spur for his cognizance see note to 78.23.

83.11 this wretched anatomy walking skeleton.

83.18 Elcho castle on the S side of the Tay, opposite Kinfauns. A km nearer Perth was the Cistercian nunnery founded by David Lindsay of Glenesk, 1st Earl of Crawford, and his mother, in the mid-13th century.

83.34–35 Mahound and Termagant Mohammed (*c.* 570–632), prophet of Islam, and Termagant were believed in the Middle Ages to be worshipped as gods by Muslims. Both occur as characters in the medieval mystery plays.

84.36–37 he that the rhymes and romances are made on … had been Robert Robert the Devil was Robert, 6th Duke of Normandy, father of William the Conqueror. Literary treatments of him include an anonymous French play of the 14th century; a metrical romance; and the prose romance by Thomas Lodge (1558–1625), *The Famous, True and Historical Life of Robert 2nd Duke of Normandy, surnamed for his monstrous Birth and Behaviour, Robin the Devil.*

85.18 **playing at football** football was a popular sport in the 14th century, so much so that in 1424 James I attempted to ban it: 'the King forbiddis that na man play at the fut ball' (*The Acts of the Parliaments of Scotland*, [ed. Thomas Thomson and C. Innes], 12 vols (1814–75), 2.5, c.18). Cant refers to this act (Cant, 21).

85.36 **Scottish pearls** mussels in the River Tay were long the most important source of pearls in Scotland. See *The Muses Threnodie* (Fourth Muse).

88.1 **chair of state** throne, chair with a canopy of some magnificence.

88.4–5 **the ill-fated family of Stewart** Robert III's father, Robert II (reigned 1370–90) was the first Scottish king of the House of Stewart. Scott calls the family 'ill-fated' because of the untimely deaths of the majority of the Stewart kings. Both Robert II and Robert III died natural deaths; but James I, son of Robert III, was murdered in Perth in 1437; James II was killed accidentally by the bursting of a cannon in 1460; James III was murdered after the Battle of Sauchieburn in 1488; James IV was killed at the battle of Flodden in 1513; James V died at the age of 30; and Mary Queen of Scots was executed in 1586. James VI of Scotland, after the Union of the Crowns in 1603, became James I of England and Scotland, but his son Charles I was executed in 1649.

88.12–13 **In youth he had indeed seen battles** the future Robert III was a much more active figure politically than Scott allows. The Earl of Carrick, as he then was, was declared heir to the throne in 1371. In the 1370s and 80s he built his own power base in Scotland particularly S of the River Forth. Appointed the King's 'Lieutenant for the Marches' in 1381, he was allied with the 2nd Earl of Douglas (compare note to 66.9) and other bellicose Scottish nobles who conducted a series of largely successful Border campaigns against the English. It was only after the death of Douglas at the battle of Otterburn in 1388 that his brother, the Earl of Fife (later Duke of Albany: see note to 65.40), replaced Carrick as the guardian of the kingdom and thus as the centre of political power in Scotland.

88.18–19 **the young Earl of Carrick... of Dalkeith** the story of Robert III's lameness (alleged to have resulted from a kick from a horse belonging to Sir James Douglas of Dalkeith, formerly a close friend and ally) only emerges around 1388 when his brother's growing power allowed him to replace the then Earl of Carrick as the kingdom's Guardian.

88.29 **Lieutenant-general of the kingdom** in the 14th century, members of the king's family, and powerful nobles such as Douglas, were sometimes appointed Lieutenant-general of the kingdom of Scotland with executive power over its affairs.

88.32 **the Duke of Rothsay** see note to 66.1.

89.11–12 **George, Earl of Dunbar and March** George Dunbar (*c.* 1340–*c.* 1420), 10th Earl of Dunbar and 3rd or 5th Earl of March. A powerful Scottish noble, he had been a favourite of David II and a supporter of Robert II. However when his daughter's marriage to Rothsay, Robert III's heir, was dissolved under pressure from the 3rd Earl of Douglas, Dunbar renounced his allegiance to the Scottish king and from 1400 joined the English side in border warfare.

89.21–23 **The Earl... reigning Monarch** it was the *son* of Archibald, 3rd Earl of Douglas, who married Margaret, eldest daughter of Robert III.

89.27 **entered the lists** engaged in the contest, became involved; the lists were originally the enclosed field of combat in which knightly tournaments were conducted.

89.34 **the States of Parliament** the Scottish parliament comprised three estates, bishops, nobles, and merchants.

90.7–9 **Queen Annabella... a son who respected her** the future Robert III had married Annabella Drummond, niece of David II's Queen Margaret, in

1367. Her death in 1401, according to some, led the Duke of Rothsay to return to a life of irresponsibility. In the 15th-century *Scotichronicon*, Walter Bower writes: 'on the death of... his noble mother, who used to curb him in many things, it was as if a noose had become worn: he hoped to free himself and ... gave himself up wholly once more to his previous frivolity' (*Scotichronicon*, ed. D. E. R. Watt, 9 vols, Vol 8 (Aberdeen, 1987), 39). However, one cannot assume that Bower is a neutral observer.

91.19 Prior Anselm the Scottish kings, like other medieval monarchs, regularly made use of the abilities and learning of senior churchmen in the administration of the kingdom; but there is no evidence of a Prior Anselm serving Robert III.

92.10–11 our Holy Father the Pope...to unloose in Catholic tradition, Christ conferred upon the Apostle Peter full ecclesiastical authority and spiritual power, including the punishment and absolution of sin, subsequently transmitted to the Popes as Peter's successors. Compare Matthew 16.17–19.

92.13 Henry of Wardlaw...to fill that See Henry Wardlaw (*c.* 1370–1440) was the nephew of Walter Wardlaw (*c.* 1317–90), Bishop of Glasgow, who in the 1380s had served as the future Robert III's chief diplomat in his period as Guardian of the kingdom. In 1402 Henry Wardlaw was the Pope's appointee to the see of St Andrews; but a problem arose over the Duke of Albany's support for another candidate, Gilbert Greenlaw, Bishop of Aberdeen, and Chancellor of the kingdom. In 1406 Henry Wardlaw protected James, son and heir of Robert III, in St Andrews castle; in 1411 he was responsible for the founding of St Andrews University.

92.16 Obedience is better than sacrifice see 1 Samuel 15.22.

92.19–20 the Estates of our Kingdom see note to 89.34.

92.26 the red levin-bolt bolt of lightning.

93.6 Saint David David I (*c.* 1084–1153; succeeded 1124). Of the early Scottish kings he was the most generous benefactor of the Church, but came into dispute with various popes over the status of the Scottish bishops. In the reign of Alexander I, John, the Bishop of Glasgow (who had been David's tutor) was directed by Pope Calixtus II to render canonical obedience to the Archbishop of York in 1119. He failed to do so. In 1125, by which time David had become King, Pope Honorius despatched a papal legate to enquire into the dispute; but in 1128 David was still resisting the suggestion that the Scottish bishops should be obedient to York. In 1131 Pope Innocent II wrote to Bishop John complaining of his failure to render obedience to the Archbishop of York as his Metropolitan. But by this point the situation had been complicated by David's support for the antipope in a dispute over Innocent's election. In 1135 another papal legate, Alberic, Bishop of Ostia, arrived in Britain to confirm Innocent's status as pope after the death of the antipope, and also to try to pacify the warring Scots and English. Prior Anselm argues that it was his defiance of the papacy that led to David's defeat at Northallerton in 1138 (see note to 93.11–13).

93.10–11 given to be a rout and a spoil to his enemies see 2 Kings 21.14.

93.11–13 the banners of St Peter and St Paul...of the Standard David I was defeated by the English at Northallerton in 1138 in what became known as the Battle of the Standard. The English warriors are supposed to have rallied around the standard of St Peter of York, raised on a cart or mast. Some accounts add the banners of St John of Beverley and St Wilfrid of Ripon.

93.14–15 the son of Jesse...punished upon earth see 2 Samuel 12.7–13.

93.24 the Monastery of Aberbrothock Arbroath Abbey (Tironensian, i.e. reformed Benedictine), on the E coast 60 km E of Perth. Founded in 1178 by King William I, among its benefactors were the Earls of Angus. By the 14th century the Earls of Angus were of the 'Red Douglas' family and so related to the 'Black Douglases' of whom Archibald the Grim was one.

93.30   thiggers and sorners   defined by Scott as 'sturdy [i.e. pretend] beggars' (ICopy, 1.243; for Lockhart's version of the note see Magnum, 42.190); while a *thigger* simply begged, a *sorner* exacted free board and lodgings by force or threats.

94.16   girth and sanctuary   see note to 42.31.

94.18   Lochaber axes   long-shafted pike or bill-like weapons with a hook above the blade.

94.21   the Galilee of the Church   a chapel or porch at the entrance to a church open to excommunicated persons and criminals claiming sanctuary; see Magnum, 42.191n.

95.1–2   the sanctuary of St Dominic   fugitives were entitled to immunity from arrest while they remained within the consecrated area of a religious house (see note to 42.31). For St Dominic see note to 18.1.

95   motto   see *Richard II*, 2.2.109–11.

95.41–96.1   misfortune in the lives and reigns . . . John Baliol of Scotland   in the reign of John (1199–1216) England lost most of its possessions in France; the country suffered a period under papal interdict; and in 1215 John was compelled by his barons to sign Magna Carta. John II of France (reigned 1350–64) was taken prisoner at the disastrous French defeat at Poitiers in 1356; he was released in 1360 under a settlement very unfavourable to France. John Balliol, King of Scots (reigned 1292–96) experienced an unhappy reign marked by military and political failure as he struggled to establish himself as king while owing allegiance to Edward I of England.

96.4   Robert Bruce   Robert I (reigned 1306–29) successfully asserted Scotland's independence from England at the battle of Bannockburn in 1314. Scott's explanation of the reasons behind John Stewart's decision to change his name to Robert on his accession to the Scottish throne in 1390 is almost certainly correct. One other motive might have been involved: the styling John II would have appeared to give credence to the Balliol family's claim to the throne, which it had already ceded to Edward III, King of England.

96.7   Albany, also an aged man   at the time around 1402 when the events of the novel are set, the Duke of Albany was 62 years old (see note to 65.40). After Robert III's death in 1406, Albany remained the effective ruler of Scotland until his own death in 1420. Despite what Scott says, Albany had been an effective military leader in his younger days.

96.30–31   the monastic buildings . . . Kings of Scotland   see note to 12.12.

97.11–12   sons of the same Steward of Scotland, and of the same Elizabeth Muir   both Robert III and the Duke of Albany were sons of Robert Stewart (later Robert II) and his first wife Elizabeth Mure. See note to 14.8–10.

97.36   my poor prodigal   see the parable of the prodigal son, Luke 15.11–32.

98.38   no mother now to plead his cause   Rothsay's mother, Queen Annabella, died in 1401: see note to 90.7–9.

99.16   Brandanes   Scott's footnote suggests that the origin of this term for natives of the island of Bute in the Firth of Clyde is uncertain. However the word probably derives from St. Brandan or Brendan of Clonfert in Ireland who had established a foundation in Bute.

100.16–17   Warden of the Eastern Marches   as the most powerful baron in Berwickshire and Lothian, the Earl of March was responsible for the defence of the E section of Scotland's border with England; see note to 22.27–28.

100.23–24 The descendant of Thomas Randolph ... grandson of Robert Bruce George Dunbar's mother, Isabella Randolph, was a daughter of Thomas Randolph, 1st Earl of Moray (d. 1332), and companion-in-arms of Robert the Bruce. Robert III was the great-grandson of Robert the Bruce.

100.25–26 the far-famed James of Douglas Archibald Douglas, 'the Grim', was the son of Sir James Douglas, 'the Good' (c. 1286–1330), knight companion of Robert the Bruce. This was the Douglas who, chosen to carry Bruce's heart to the Holy Land, died fighting the Moors in Spain.

100.31 Henry Hotspur Sir Henry Percy (1364–1403), son of the Earl of Northumberland, frequently involved in border warfare with the Scots, and famously defeated by the 2nd Earl of Douglas at the battle of Otterburn in 1388. In literature he appears in the ballad 'The Battle of Otterburn', included by Scott in *Minstrelsy* (1.276–301), and is a character in *Richard II* and *1 Henry IV*.

101.13 the gay science translation of *gai saber*, the old Provençal name for the art of poetry.

101.27–28 Troubadour music music associated with the troubadours, composers of lyrical love poetry mainly in Provence in S France between the 11th and 13th centuries.

101.36–39 desire of vengeance ... his betrothed daughter in 1395 Robert III's son David, Earl of Carrick (later Duke of Rothsay), entered into a marriage arrangement with Elizabeth Dunbar, daughter of the Earl of March. The King seems not to have approved, and moved to have the marriage declared invalid. His son resisted this pressure and appealed to Pope Benedict XIII to have his marriage to Elizabeth allowed (although after 1397 the couple do not appear to have lived together). When in 1400 it emerged that the heir apparent was about to set aside Elizabeth and marry Marjory, daughter of Archibald, 3rd Earl of Douglas, the Earl of March reacted with fury, and in the end did renounce his allegiance to Robert III and transferred it to Henry IV of England.

102.5 the Provençal dialect troubadour love poetry was normally written in the language of Provence in S France.

102.8 the Sirventes political and moral satires as written by the troubadour poets.

102.8–9 the lai of a Norman Minstrel short lyric or narrative poem sung by a minstrel; Normandy is in NW France. The poem that follows is Scott's own composition.

104.18 the Prince and Marjory Douglas are nearly related Rothsay's aunt, Isabella, sister of Robert III, had married the 2nd Earl of Douglas; Rothsay and Marjory Douglas were thus in five degrees of consanguinity (the steps measured up to and down from a common ancestor), and within the prohibited seven as defined by civil law. That Rothsay's sister Margaret had married Marjory's brother Archibald (who became 4th Earl of Douglas) was another factor.

104.21 in respect of the pre-contract with reference to the prior agreement for the marriage of Rothsay and Elizabeth Dunbar.

104.26–27 George of Dunbar ... Edinburgh the Earl of March and his followers were the main defenders of Scotland's E border with the N England (see notes to 22.27–28 and 100.16–17) and without them an English army could march unopposed through Berwickshire and Lothian to Edinburgh. This happened in the summer of 1400 when Henry IV led a huge English army to Leith and Edinburgh virtually unopposed. Cairntable is a mountain near Muirkirk in SW Scotland (where the Black Douglases had their strength) at a point where the counties of Lanarkshire, Ayrshire, and Dumfriesshire adjoin.

106.20–21 rights of chivalry chivalric ideals included the protection of widows and orphans, and all virtuous women. See note to 6.32.

106.28–29 life too irregular and precarious ... creditable part of

society   compare *Prose Works*, 17.36: 'Individual instances excepted, the player and the musician of modern days, the genuine successors of the minstrels, incur a certain degree of contempt from their situation, which they are too often driven to merit.'

106.33–34   a Court of Love and Music ... Count Aymer   Scott accepted the theory that Aix-en-Provence was the location of one of four permanent 'courts of love' held in the 12th and 13th centuries, at which nice issues of amorous conduct were debated and troubadours' songs judged, often by aristocratic ladies, though as early as 1825 the idea of such a formal court had been demolished as fanciful. The 'brief', or written qualiWcation referred to, seems to derive from the quasi-degrees awarded at an academy established in Toulouse in 1324 in an attempt to revive the 'gay science' (Provençal *gai saber*) of the troubadours. Count Aymer is probably not intended to be identified with a specific historical figure, though there was a celebrated troubadour of that name in the late 12th and early 13th centuries.

107.32   St Giles   popular 7th-century saint. Patron saint of beggars, cripples, and lepers, the centre of his cult was near Arles in Provence. His British cult developed mainly in the period of the Crusades; St Giles Cathedral in Edinburgh is the most famous of the many churches dedicated to him in Britain.

107.37   on all hands   on all sides.

107.42   nut-brown maid   girl of reddish-brown hair or complexion; in this context Scott has in mind the popular ballad concerning woman's constancy, 'The Not-Browne Mayd', published in *Reliques of Ancient English Poetry*, [ed. Thomas Percy], 3 vols (London, 1765), 2.26–42; see *CLA*, 172.

108.3   ma bella tenebrosa   *Italian* my beautiful dark-haired one.

108.20–21   poor wandering ape   Rothsay addresses Louise sympathetically here as one compelled by her profession to be constantly on the move; 'ape' suggests her role as a mimic or entertainer.

108.32   loss of an eye in battle   it was Archibald the Grim's son, Archibald, 4th Earl of Douglas, who lost an eye at the battle of Homildon Hill in 1402, when the Scots were defeated by Henry Percy (Hotspur) and the Earl of March. This was the Douglas who subsequently joined the Percys in their rebellion against Henry IV, and fought valiantly at the battle of Shrewsbury in 1403.

108.36   his terrible step-father   although questioning whether it is a conscious misuse, the *OED* does define step-father as meaning father-in-law.

109.28   St Bride of Douglas   St Bride or Bridget of Ireland, abbess of Kildare, died around 525. Her cult was widespread, and in Ireland itself second only to that of St Patrick. Douglas, a small town in Lanarkshire beside Douglas Water, was in the Middle Ages an important burgh, a trade and marketing centre. Its Kirk of St Bride, a prebend of Glasgow Cathedral, was founded in the 13th century; the choir of the church became the traditional burial-place of the Douglas family.

110.24   the Bloody Heart   see note to 66.26.

110.35   penalty of excommunication   punishment excluding a Roman Catholic from the communion of believers, participation in the sacraments, and all the privileges and prayers of the Church.

111.4–5   your family match ... authority from Rome   see notes to 101.36–39 and 104.18.

111.32   breach of contract   March refers to the previously-arranged marriage between his daughter Elizabeth Dunbar and the Duke of Rothsay. See note to 101.36–39.

112.11   the Southland loons who ride with the Douglas   Douglas's men who come from his lands in SW Scotland.

112.43 **Milan hauberk** coat of mail from Milan in N Italy; in the Middle Ages Milan was recognised as a centre of excellence in the making of armour.

113.14 **squire of dames** one who devotes himself to the service of ladies; see Edmund Spenser, *The Faerie Queene*, Bks 1–3 (1590), 3.7.51–61. As a generic term, the title can elide into meaning pimp or pandar; see e.g. Philip Massinger, *The Emperor of the East* (1631), 1.2.258–61: 'You are / The Squire of Dames, devoted to the service / Of gamesome Ladies . . . their close bawde' (in *The Plays and Poems of Philip Massinger*, ed. Philip Edwards and Colin Gibson, 5 vols (Oxford, 1976), Vol. 3).

113.16 **Sir Pandarus of Troy** compare *The Merry Wives of Windsor*, 1.3.72: 'Shall I Sir Pandarus of Troy become . . .?'. In Chaucer's *Troilus and Crysede*, and generally in medieval legend, Pandarus was the Trojan uncle of the beautiful Crysede whose love affair with Troilus, son of King Priam, he arranged.

113.21 **men lure not hawks with empty hands** proverbial: see *ODEP*, 219.

113.41 **ill at ease** ill, unwell, in discomfort.

115.22 **finely sped** *ironic* awkwardly placed.

115.32 **Chapel of Holy St Madox** *Madox* is a variant of Madoc or Maidoc, an Irish saint of the 7th century, the founder of three Irish monasteries. St Madoe's in the Carse of Gowrie between Perth and Dundee may be named after St Madoc.

116.30 **That He invites . . . to approach** compare Matthew 9.13; Mark 2.17; Luke 5.32: 'I came not to call the righteous, but sinners to repentance'.

117.13–14 **the wild Scot of Galloway . . . the Liddell** Archibald the Grim or, more probably, his men in general. Galloway in SW Scotland and Liddel Water, a river rising in Roxburghshire, and here standing for Liddesdale, were Douglas territory. The Smith's use of the phrases 'the wild Scot' and 'the Devil's legion' reflects the continuing evil reputation of the men of Galloway originally acquired in the early 12th century. The English chroniclers of David I's cross-border invasion of 1138 identify the Galwegians, wild Picts as they are sometimes called, as especially barbarous and responsible for the worst atrocities in the ravaging of northern England.

117.33 **a light o' love** one who is inconstant or wanton in love.

117.40–41 **free of my guild** having all the rights and privileges of my guild (*OED*, *free*, adjective, 29).

118.6 **the feast of St Madox, at Auchterarder** the festival of St Madox celebrated at Auchterarder, a village 22 km SW of Perth. As the saint's feast day falls on 31 January and this is 14 February the Smith's comment is less than accurate. For *St Madox* see note to 115.32.

118.16 **the hospital of the Convent** the section of the Blackfriars monastery used for the shelter of travellers

118.20 **Ramorny** Sir John Ramornie or Ramorgny (d. 1402), a Scottish courtier who served as Rothsay's personal chamberlain for a number of years. He seems also to have been closely allied to the Duke of Albany, and his role in Rothsay's fate was very much as Scott portrays it.

118.25–26 **Master of the Horse, and privado** in the English royal household the Master of the Horse was the title of the third most senior official. Here the title indicates Ramorny's important position in the Prince's retinue, an idea reinforced by his being described as the Prince's 'privado' or favourite.

119.12 **Ringan** variant of Ninian, traditionally identified as the first Christian missionary in Scotland; he lived in SW Scotland in the later 4th and early 5th centuries.

119.41 **Dundee** seaport between Arbroath where the Douglas is quartered and Perth, on the N side of the Firth of Tay, 32 km E of Perth.

120.3   like Highlandmen at the fiery cross   the fiery cross, traditionally used by the chiefs of the Highland clans to summon their clansmen in preparation for battle, was dipped in blood or charred, and carried through all parts of the clan's territory. Scott himself had boosted this legend by his description of the fiery cross in Canto 3 of *The Lady of the Lake* (1810).

120.6   Annandale   in Dumfriesshire.

120.14–15   All is fish that comes to their net   proverbial: see Ray, 190; *ODEP*, 264–65.

120.24   Our Lady's Stairs   landing stage on the Tay at Perth mentioned in *The Muses Threnodie* (Sixth Muse).

121.1–2   you know ... reproaches   in the Introduction to the *Minstrelsy* Scott quotes Spenser's *State of Ireland*: 'There is, among the Irish, a certaine kinde of people, called bardes, which are to them instead of poets; whose profession is to set forth the praises or dispraises of men in their poems or rhymes; the which are had in such high regard or esteem amongst them, that none dare displease them, for fear of running into reproach through their offence, and to be made infamous in the mouths of all men' (*Minstrelsy*, 1.158).

121.19   Vulcan   the Roman god of fire and metalwork.

121.21   Venus ... Mars   the Roman deities of love and war.

121.30   even-song time   the Church's evening service of prayers and readings; also known as vespers, and usually celebrated just before sunset.

122.30   S'nails   *oath* by God's nails (i.e. the nails on the Cross on which Christ was crucified).

122.35–36   from St Valentine's Day to next Candlemass   i.e. for the year from 14 February to the following 2 February.

123.2–3   the small dull eye   compare S. T. Coleridge, 'Christabel' (written 1797–1801, published 1816), line 583: 'A snake's small eye blinks dull and shy'.

123.16   salmon resembles a par   a parr is a salmon up to two years of age.

123.24   Save you   i.e. God save you.

123.27–28   swallow that pill ... be gilded   proverbial: see *ODEP*, 786. To 'gild the pill' means to soften or tone down something unpleasant; Henry's use of the metaphor is particularly appropriate given Dwining's occupation.

123.29   knows a wild-duck from a tame   proverbial: compare 'knows a hawk from a handsaw' (*ODEP*, 434), 'a cat from a cony' (*ODEP*, 436), 'a goose from a capon' (*ODEP*, 433).

123.35   St Dunstan!   see note to 23.2–3.

123.39   Thou art ... Tom   from an Elizabethan drinking song or round; see Francis Beaumont and John Fletcher, *The Coxcomb* (written 1608–10; published 1647), 1.6.108, in *The Dramatic Works in the Beaumont and Fletcher Canon*, ed. Fredson Bowers, Vol. 1 (Cambridge, 1966), 285.

123.40   had made no dry meal   i.e. had been drinking.

123.41   in the manner   in a way that reveals you.

123.40–124.1   Can Vulcan ... in her own coin?   Vulcan's wife was Venus who had an affair with Mars, which Vulcan discovered. He devised a net to capture the lovers in bed, and then exhibited them together to the other gods. Here, however, Oliver suggests that Henry is paying back his Venus (whom Rothsay was attempting to seduce) by taking home a lover of his own. The 'minstrel' has not been identified, but the story of Vulcan, Venus, and Mars (or Hephaestus, Aphrodite, and Ares in Greek myth) is found in Homer, *The Odyssey*, 8.266–369, and in Ovid (43 BC–AD 18), *Metamorphoses*, 4.167–89.

124.10   thy Dalilah   Samson's Philistine mistress who deprived him of his strength by cutting off his hair; hence any temptingly attractive woman: see Judges 16.4–21.

124.23–24   scorn ... with my heels   proverbial: see *The Merchant of Venice*, 2.2.8; *ODEP*, 705.

124.26   life and mettle into the heels   see Robert Burns, 'Tam o' Shanter' (1791), line 118.

124.30–31   fabliau of a daw with borrowed feathers   the most handsome of birds was to be appointed king, and so the jackdaw fitted himself out with feathers that had moulted from other birds; he was nearly successful but the other birds indignantly reclaimed their own feathers and reduced him to his native plainness. The fabliau (fable) is in Æsop.

124.33   as never hawk plumed a partridge   'plumed' in the sense of plucking the feathers from its prey: see *OED*, *plume*, verb, 1.

125.17   Shoolbred   the name of the housekeeper at Lochore, the family home of Scott's daughter-in-law, Jane Jobson; see *Letters*, 9.50.

126.33   fee and bountith   wages plus a gratuity paid at the end of employment.

127.19–20   chambering and wantonness   see Romans 13.13.

127.23   Carlisle Castle   a key stronghold on the English side of the W border with Scotland.

127.41–42   has dreed a sore weird   paid a severe penalty.

130.14–15   writing materials ... the churchman was alone able to use   in fact Rothsay could read and write, and Lockhart in a Magnum note observes: 'Mr Chrystal Croftangry had not, it must be confessed, when he indited this sentence, exactly recollected the character of Rothsay, as given by the Prior of Lochleven./ "A seemly person in stature,/ Cunnand into letterature."/ B. ix. cap. 23.' (Magnum, 42.260).

130.19   the waste and destruction of the country   in this period the Scottish kings found it extremely difficult to impose their authority in the Highland areas of their kingdom.

130.36   the Bloody Heart   see note to 66.26.

131.18–19   the Carthusian Convent   the Carthusian Monastery or Charterhouse, situated in the W end of Perth, founded in 1429.

131.20   the baser sort   compare Acts 17.5.

131.20–21   the Cross   in the middle of the High Street between the Kirkgate and the Skinnergate; it was the place from which all official proclamations were issued. Oliver Cromwell demolished the Cross in 1652.

132.20   the insurgents of the Jacquerie   peasant uprising in northern Fance in 1358.

132.21   Jack Straw, Hob Miller, and Parson John Ball   leading figures in the Peasants' Revolt, headed by Wat Tyler, in England in 1381.

132.30–31   lift Sir Patrick's gauntlet   take up Sir Patrick's challenge.

132.33   descendant of the Red Rover   Patrick Charteris of Kinfauns; see text 70.43–73.8.

132.34–35   heir of Thomas Randolph   George Dunbar, Earl of March: see note to 100.23–24.

132.36–37   asking the grace   being granted the favour of accepting the challenge.

133.1–2   while I continue to hold my Earldom of the crown of Scotland   March chooses his words carefully implying that the time could come when his feudal allegiance for his Earldom could be to other than the crown of Scotland, i.e. to the King of England.

133.19   that sea-worn Hold   March's castle on the E coast of Scotland at Dunbar.

133.22   the Earn   tributary to the River Tay just below the city of Perth.

133.32   it skills not   it avails not, there is no point in.

133.34   the South Port   the South Street gate, by which the main road S left the city.

134.7   our brethren at Dunkeld   the clergy at Dunkeld Cathedral, whose construction began in 1320; Dunkeld is a small town 22 km N of Perth.

134.9   sons of Belial   see Judges 19.22; 1 Samuel 2.12. Belial is a demon figure, sometimes identified with Satan; in the Old Testament the phrase 'the sons of Belial' is a general term for evil-doers.

134.11   tenth degree of kindred   10 steps measured up to and down from a common ancestor; i.e. distantly related.

134.12–13   fire and sword   *Scots law* burning the house and killing all its inhabitants; if authorised by a sheriff this was a legal mode of punishing recalcitrant followers.

134.13   fiery cross   see note to 120.3.

134.14–15   the distant Murray Firth   the Moray Firth, the largest arm of the sea indenting the NE coast of Scotland between Aberdeenshire and Caithness.

134.18   Amalekites   Old Testament people characterised as inveterate enemies of the children of Israel; see Exodus 17.8–16; 1 Samuel 15.1–33.

134.21   Mahound and Termagaunt   see note to 83.34–35.

134.33   army of martyrs   compare the invocation in the traditional *Te Deum* hymn to 'the noble army of martyrs'.

135.10   St George of England   England's patron saint.

135.14–15   bell, book, and candle   see note to 60.36–37.

135.15   make no speed   have no success.

135.43   the Sheriff, Lord Ruthven   Sir William Ruthven, Sheriff of Perth around the mid 15th century. In 1443 he was attacked near Perth by a band of Highlanders led by one Gormac or Cormac, but he won the day and subsequently hanged his attackers.

136.1   the Carse   the carse of Gowrie, a rich and fruitful area of low-lying country, along the N bank of the Tay, stretching for some 25 km between Kinnoull Hill and Dundee Law.

136.5–7   Donald Cormac ... Houghman Stairs   for Cormac, see note to 135.43. The Moor of Thorn, Rochinroy Wood and Houghman Stairs are all located between Perth and Dunkeld and are supposed to be the scene of the hanging of the band of Highlanders who had attacked Ruthven, Sheriff of Perth. Rochinroy Wood is said to be the remains of the ancient Birnam Wood: according to Cant it contained a large oak tree called 'the *Hanged mens-tree*' (Cant, xx).

136.9   Irish   the term 'Irish' may refer to both the Scottish Highlands and Ireland.

137.3   Achitophel   counsellor of David, and then of his son Absalom in the latter's rebellion: see 2 Samuel 15.12–17; 16.20–17.14; 17.23.

137.5   the awful day   the Day of Judgment.

137.12   you bear the sword ... sceptre   compare Romans 13.3–4.

137.43–138.1   with sand-bags, like the crestless churls of England   primitive weapons made out of a bag of sand tied to the end of a staff likely to be used by peasants ('churls') lacking the badges of knighthood ('crestless'). See the stage direction following *2 Henry VI*, 2.3.58, where Horner and his apprentice enter to combat with sandbags fastened to staves.

138.25   trial by combat   the determination of a person's guilt or innocence, or the righteousness of his cause, by a combat between the accuser and accused, or their champions. Such a form of trial was a recognised process in Scots law in both civil and criminal matters. However, such ordeals, open only to free men, were beginning to fall out of use by the 13th century.

139.4–7   Marked you ... King Robert's vassal   see note to 133.1–2.

139.10   the Percies   Percy was the family name of the Earls of Northumberland, the most powerful of the English barons with land adjoining the border with Scotland.

139.14 I have seen the backs ... ere now Scott here fuses the 3rd Earl of Douglas with his successor. It was Archibald, 4th Earl of Douglas, who in 1401 met and defeated near Dunbar an invading English force led by Henry Percy and the now exiled Earl of March.

139.28–29 he who goes forth ... back shorn version of the proverb 'Many go out for wool and come home shorn' (Ray, 170; *ODEP*, 913).

139.34–35 par amours *French* sexually, i.e. as a lover rather than as a husband.

140.3 the bards Highland chieftains traditionally included in their households poets who, with the sennachies, celebrated the history, legends, and achievements of the clan.

140.22 St Dominick see note to 18.1.

140.36–37 as wolves steal lambs from the sheepfold compare Acts 20.28–30.

140.39 four convents Perth's four monasteries were the Dominican (Blackfriars), founded by Alexander II in 1231; the Carmelite (Whitefriars) founded in the second half of the 13th century; the Carthusian, founded in 1425; and the Franciscan (Greyfriars) founded in 1460. Historical licence allows Rothsay to see all four.

140.40 secular clergy clergy living in the world, as opposed to living in monastic seclusion.

141.24–25 reverend official of the bounds officer appointed to determine the limits of lawful action.

141.38–40 I am a true Scotsman ... mitre and cowl Douglas is opposed to a policy which would make the Catholic Church in Scotland more subservient to the Pope in Rome, and the Scottish nobility obedient to the clergy.

142.1 the smell of a faggot execution by burning, the normal punishment for crimes of heresy.

142.36 Gascon wine see note to 46.19.

143.41 a man of Belial see note to 134.9.

144.3–4 man of mould i.e. man of substance or distinction; see *Henry V*, 3.2.21.

144.30 the false knight ... degradation the knight who has broken the laws of chivalry should be deprived of his knightly status. See also note to 349.30–31.

145.34 Carthusian monk monk of the Carthusian order, founded by St Bruno in 1084 at La Grande Chartreuse. The monks are vowed to silence and spend much time in solitary contemplation. The habit is white.

146.7–8 dens for robbers and ruffians compare Matthew 21.13: 'My house shall be called the house of prayer; but ye have made it a den of thieves'.

146.10–11 yonder four goodly convents see note to 140.39.

146.26 the love of many has waxed cold see Matthew 24.12.

146.34–35 a teacher in Israel see John 3.10.

147.2 a Lollard and a Wickliffite John Wycliffe (d. 1384) was a 14th-century English religious reformer; as one who attacked Church doctrines and abuses he was often seen as a precursor of the Reformation. His followers were called Lollards, a term which began to be used pejoratively in the 14th century for those with views labelled heretical. In 'The Epilogue to the Man of Law's Tale' (*The Canterbury Tales*, II (B1), 1170–77), the austere Parish Parson is accused of being a 'Lollere'.

147.4 the religion of heathenesse the false religion of the pagan world as opposed to Christendom.

147.7–9 in a more gracious ... presumption Highlanders are more favoured by God because their sins result from ignorance rather than human pride or arrogance.

148.17–19 Marriage is ... race of man see 'The Form of Solemnization of Matrimony', in *The Book of Common Prayer* (1662).

148.19–21 I read not ... of celibacy in the Western Church the position that all clergy should be celibate only prevailed gradually. The Council of Elvira (*c.* 306) had required continence of all clergy under pain of deposition, but concubinage was rife in some subsequent periods. The Second Lateran Council (1139) decreed the marriage of clergy unlawful and invalid. Scholastic theologians concluded that the requirement of clerical celibacy was a Church law, not part of divine revelation (Thomas Aquinas, *Summa Theologiae* (written 1265–74), 2.2 q.88a.11). Some Lollards favoured a married clergy; see Anne Hudson, *The Premature Reformation* (Oxford, 1988), 357–58.

148.41 the heathen worship of Flora or Venus in Roman mythology Flora is the goddess of flowers and fertility, Venus the goddess of love. For some of the rituals associated with the cult of Flora see Ovid (43 BC–AD 18), *Fasti*, 5.331.

150.33–34 Old prophecies ... speech of a woman not identified.

150.35 visions ... ordinary affairs of earth compare Scott's comment in his *Journal* entry for 19 April 1828: 'the adaptation of religious motives to earthly policy is apt—among the infinite delusions of the human heart—to be a snare' (*The Journal of Sir Walter Scott*, ed. W. E. K. Anderson (Oxford, 1972), 461).

151.2–3 Rome will dissolve the union see text, 104.17–21, and note to 104.18.

151.11–12 What did beauty do ... David Bruce David II's first wife Joanna died in England in 1362; in 1364 he married Margaret Logie or Drummond who had been his mistress for the preceding three years.

151.17 vanity and vexation of spirit see Ecclesiastes 1.14. David II's Queen Margaret had her reward in 'vexation of spirit' as she was divorced in 1370.

151.18–19 the believing wife ... husband compare 1 Corinthians 7.12–16.

151.20 Queen Margaret 1046–93. Grand-daughter of Edmund Ironside, King of England, she married Malcolm III, King of Scots, in 1068. Her devoted support of the Church led to her canonisation in 1250.

151.21–22 nursing mothers of the Church see Isaiah 49.23.

151.27–29 a cherub ... to rebuke compare Ithuriel in Milton's *Paradise Lost* (1667), 4.788–873.

152.11–12 By the mouths ... in their generation see Psalm 8.2; Luke 16.8.

153.4–5 Danish pole-axe ... lochaber axe see note to 94.18.

154.22 the children of my belt those who execute my will and pleasure.

154.28 braes of Lednoch hillsides near the river Almond, a few miles NW of Perth.

154.32–33 the truncheon of my tribe the clan's short staff or baton, a symbol of the chief's authority.

155.30 Bengoile Benygloe or Benglo, *Gaelic* Beinna' Ghlo, mountain 13 km NE of Blair Atholl in Perthshire.

156.19–20 Liddesdale and Annandale lancers mounted soldiers of the Earl of Douglas; Liddesdale and Annandale are both areas in Douglas territory in Roxburghshire and Dumfriesshire respectively.

156.21 throng upon the highway as the leaves at Hallowmass compare John Milton, *Paradise Lost* (1667), 1.302–03. *Hallowmass* is All Saints' Day, celebrated on 1 November.

156.24 casting his slough transforming his nature, as a serpent casts off its previous skin; compare *Twelfth Night*, 2.5.135.

156.38–39 rules of chivalry see note to 6.32.

157.7–8 repeated incursions... of their city there is little evidence for this statement, but in the 14th century the ongoing Anglo-Scottish border wars made the Highland-lowland border increasingly insecure, and at Glasclune in NE Perthshire in 1392 a marauding band of Highland 'caterans' met Sir Walter Ogilvy, Sheriff of Angus, leading a body of knights and men-at-arms. Ogilvy was killed along with his half-brother and other gentlemen in his household, and the Lowlanders were only saved from complete disaster by the arrival of David Lindsay, 1st Earl of Crawford, who was himself wounded. After this encounter the superiority of knightly forces over the semi-professional Highland warriors could not be taken for granted.

158.11 all the medicines of Arabia compare *Macbeth*, 5.1.48–49: 'All the perfumes of Arabia will not sweeten this little hand'.

159.11–12 Granada, where the fiery-souled Moor... dagger city in S Spain. Granada was long a centre of Moorish culture including the study of medicine. The Moors were an Islamic people, originally from N Africa, who ruled much of Spain in the earlier Middle Ages.

159.17–18 waters that are the stillest... the deepest *proverbial* see 'still waters run deep' (*ODEP*, 774).

160.23–24 the strength of Sampson Israelite champion, proverbial for his strength: see Judges Chs 13–16.

161.20–21 the balm of Mecca a soothing ointment from Mecca, the holy city of Saudi Arabia where the prophet Mohammed was born.

161.39 whose spurs should be hacked off from his heels i.e. who should be degraded from his status as a knight. See note to 349.30–31.

162.11 within compass within the bounds of moderation.

162.11 an outlier and a galliard one who does not remain decorously at home but like a gallant stays or 'lies' out all night.

162.23 a precisian instead of a galliard one who observes the rules (of morality) rather than behaving like a gallant.

162.32 opened on the scent *of hounds* begin to cry when taking up the scent.

162.40 priests say... common earth compare Genesis 2.7.

163.3 Eviot Ramorny's page is not strictly a historical character. However, Cant's notes to *The Muses Threnodie* (First Muse) alludes to the Eviots of Balhousie in the 15th century.

163.10 deal upon set to work upon.

164.22 Fife Scottish county on the S of the Firth of Tay.

164.42–43 barber-chirugeon until as late as the 18th century barbers regularly also acted as surgeons (and dentists).

165.12 worse-omened name henbane is the name of a poisonous plant.

166.5 four seas of Britain the seas on the four sides of the British Isles.

166.20 juice of this Indian gum probably a reference to opium, the sedative and narcotic drug which the *Medical Journal* defined in 1802 as 'composed of a gum'.

166.38 the breath of whose nostrils whose inspiration of life; see Genesis 2.7, 7.22.

168.6 Shrovetide the Sunday, Monday, Tuesday preceding Ash Wednesday, the first day in Lent (see note to 36.7) in the Christian calendar, but here specifically the Tuesday.

168.7 Fastern's E'en the evening of Shrove Tuesday.

168.10 foot-ball see note to 85.18.

168.19 dance at the ring i.e. dance in a ring.

168.19–20　morrice-dancers　dating from at least the 15th century, morris-dancers in fancy dress performed a type of grotesque, miming dance; traditionally the performers often represented characters from the legend of Robin Hood.

168.23　the long term of Lent　the period of 40 days culminating in Palm Sunday; see note to 36.7.

168.33　The Carnival　the season of revelry and indulgence immediately preceding Lent. This is the origin of the general meaning of 'carnival' as any festive occasion of merrymaking and entertainment.

168.37　The Entry　type of dance performed as an interlude between two parts of an entertainment; here the word must refer to those performing the dance.

169.17　ill at ease　ill, unwell, in discomfort.

169.22　ring in　a church service is rung in by a single bell as an indication that the service is about to begin. Here Lent is going to be rung in by the clinking of cans of drink.

169.24　have with you　I shall be with you.

169.33　Coryphæus　leader of the Chorus in classical Greek drama.

170.1–8　My dog and I ... my dog and I　stanzas 7 and 9 of a Gloucestershire song 'George Ridler's Oven'. It is in the Materials for the *Minstrelsy*, NLS MS 893, f. 43; for a printed text see Grantley F. Berkeley, *Berkeley Castle: an Historical Romance*, 3 vols (London, 1836), 3.161–62; Robert Bell, *Ancient Poems Ballads and Songs of the Peasantry of England* (London, 1857), 201–02; and Alfred Williams, *Folk Songs of the Upper Thames* (London, 1923), 291–92.

170.22　worsted thrums　loose ends of unwoven wool.

170.25　this bout　on this occasion, this time.

172.20　worship Mahound　see note to 83.34–35.

173.6　base lantern　dark lantern; i.e. one in which the light can be concealed by a slide.

173.19　Trust thy coxcomb no longer with me　do not entrust me with your foolish head any longer.

173.25–26　I am ashamed ... power to move me thus　compare *King Lear*, 1.4.296–97.

174.11　Ringan　version of Ninian. See note to 119.12.

174.33　resembling wild men　wearing the conventional costumes for representing savages in pageants or masques.

175.2　the bastinado　punishment or torture in which the soles of the feet are beaten with a stick.

175.3　puissant man of Ind　man of power from India.

175.25　mister wight　kind of person

175.40–43　Art thou in case ... in a gutter　compare Sir Toby Belch and Sir Andrew Aguecheek, *Twelfth Night*, 1.3.105–32.

176.6　the Douze peers　the twelve peers or paladins of Charlemagne. See note to 54.6.

176.36　dunghill cock　ordinary farmyard cock as distinct from a gamecock.

178.16　bodily oath　oath originally sworn on the consecrated host or 'body' of Christ.

178.17　Innocent's　Innocent's Day, 28 December in the Christian calendar. It commemorates the slaughter of children under two years of age around Bethlehem by order of King Herod: see Matthew 2.16.

178.17　of a quaint device　skilfully made so as to have a good appearance.

178.34　waive his gentry　waive or relinquish his rank as a gentleman.

179.12–14　So, having said so ... twenty duels　Oliver means that since he has sworn not to fight, he would be perjuring himself if he agreed to do so.

180.2   the Sleepless Isle   see *The Muses Threnodie* which refers to the gifting of this small island to the city of Perth: 'By Sleeplesse Isle we row; which our good Kings/ Gave to our town' (Sixth Muse). Cant's note says that the island belonged to the Kinfauns estate, but Perth was granted its fishing rights.

180.8–9   the Fair City . . . cumber   Perth is free of the Earl of Douglas and the trouble he has been creating.

181.27   in sadness   seriously.

181.33–34   thy pibroch of 'Broken Bones at Loncarty'   bagpipe tune celebrating the defeat of the Danes by the Scots at Loncarty, 7 km NW of Perth. See note to 62.17.

182   motto   see *1 Henry IV*, 2.4.429.

182.23   Gravity   *1 Henry IV*, 2.4.285.

184.31   Dan Bacchus   Roman god of wine and jollity; *Dan* is a version of 'Dominus', i.e. Sir or Master.

185.11–13   The fire is not external . . . work within   compare the climax of William Beckford's *Vathek* (1787), ed. Roger Lonsdale (Oxford, 1970), 118–20; also *Kenilworth*, ed. J. H. Alexander, EEWN 11, 287.39–41.

185.12–13   seven times heated   see Daniel 3.19.

185.39   Do butchers ply their craft on Fastern's Eve?   the Prince implies that as Lent, with its rule on abstinence from meat-eating is about to begin, butchers will not be active in their trade.

188.39–189.7   Should I ever fill . . . bowl   compare Prince Hal in *1 Henry IV*, 2.4.89–107.

188.42   dirks and dourlachs   Highland daggers and short swords.

189.1–3   from a count to a king like Robert the Second   Robert Stewart was High Steward of Scotland and Earl of Strathearn before his accession (on the death of his uncle David II) to the Scottish throne as Robert II.

189.2–3   He founded not churches like Robert the Third   Robert III was certainly a generous benefactor of the Blackfriars monastery in Perth, where his mother was entombed, but he does not appear to have been a founder of churches.

189.3   King of good fellows   *Henry V*, 5.2.240.

189.6   Old King Coul   legendary British king.

189.15–19   how canst thou . . . a hasty humour   in 1296 Wallace (see note to 60.22–23) is supposed to have fought with an English contingent at Elcho Park near Perth. Fighting in support of Wallace was a character called Fawdon. However Fawdon would not agree to continue the battle along the N side of the River Earn and in anger Wallace struck off his head. That night Fawdon's ghost appeared in the House of Gask and threw his severed head at Wallace. See *Wallace*, 5.170–223.

189.21   the steel hand of the old Knight of Carselogie   Carselogie is an estate near Cupar in Fife, the seat of the Clephane family. The family was long believed to have in its possession a steel hand supposedly given to a laird or baron of Carselogie by a Scottish king in whose service he had lost his own.

189.33   an hundred merks   £67 Scots, or about £33 sterling. A merk or mark was worth two thirds of a pound Scots, which at this period had about half the value of its English counterpart.

190.35–36   Albany . . . your Grace's life   in the sources available to Scott, Ramorny first proposes to Rothsay the murder of Albany—a suggestion that Rothsay strongly rejects. It is only subsequently that Ramorny plots with Albany to eliminate Rothsay. See *Scotichronicon*, ed. D. E. R. Watt, 9 vols, Vol 8 (Aberdeen, 1987), 41; David Hume of Godscroft, *The History of the House of Douglas*, ed. David Reid, Scottish Text Society, 2 vols (Edinburgh, 1996), 1.259.

191.9–10   evil doers are evil dreaders   see *ODEP*, 398.

191.35   alter ego   in the sense of a 'second self' the Latin phrase *alter ego* ('another I') has been used in English since the 16th century.

191.39–40　Ille, manu fortis,/ Anglis ludebit in hortis　*Latin* that man, brave in combat, will play in English gardens. The source has not been identified, but the rhyme and metre suggest that it is probably medieval.

191.43　laying his grey hairs in the grave　compare Genesis 42.38.

192.4–5　the wicked cease from troubling, and the weary are at rest see Job 3.17.

192.25–26　as many market crosses ... carcass　the public exhibition in towns and cities of severed portions of the bodies of those executed for treason was normal practice in the Middle Ages. Cant refers to the exhibiting of Wallace's limbs at Perth and Aberdeen (71).

192.36　the convent of Lindores　Abbey (Tironensian, i.e. reformed Benedictine), founded in the late 12th century by David, Earl of Huntingdon, grandson of David I in the village of Lindores near Newburgh in NW Fife. Edward I of England, John Balliol, Sir William Wallace, and David II, all visited Lindores Abbey.

192.38　Put not thy faith in princes　see Psalm 146.3.

194.1–2　called the Constable's lodgings ... Earls of Errol　a property of the Hay family which stood near the S end of the Watergate in Perth, adjacent to the River Tay. The earldom of Errol was created only in 1453 when William Hay, High Constable of Scotland, was elevated by James II, but the office of Constable (one of the three major offices in the King's household) was a hereditary position held by the Hays of Errol from *c.* 1306.

194.5–6　it was very familiar in me　I was taking liberties.

194.15　Under favour　by your leave.

194.36–37　Queen Annabella　see note to 90.7–9.

195.10　which moped, and chattered　compare *The Tempest*, 2.2.9.

195.14　Ash Wednesday　the first day of Lent; see note to 36.7.

195.27　boy of the belt　see note to 154.22.

196.1　ten Scottish miles　18 km. A Scots mile was 1⅛ English miles.

196.2　gentle or simple　gentry and commoners alike.

196.20　ring the bells backward　process in which the ordinary succession of chimes in a peel is reversed.

196.21　cry and spare not　see Isaiah 58.1.

196.21　St Johnstoun's hunt is up　the rallying slogan used by the people of Perth, quoted in *The Muses Threnodie* (Fifth Muse).

197.23–24　an official protocol, or ... precognition　a 'protocol' is an official record; a 'precognition' is the taking of evidence from witnesses to produce a written record which has legal significance.

198　motto　see *Othello*, 2.3.153–54.

198.38–39　the holy Trefoil　plant having triple or trifoliate leaves; *holy* because taken as an image of the Trinity.

199.4　the apostate Judas　at the moment of his betrayal of Jesus, the disciple Judas kissed him as a way of identifying who should be arrested. See Matthew 26.48–49; Mark 14.44–45; Luke 22.47–48.

199.38–39　Fortingall　village in the Highland area of Perthshire, on the N side of Loch Tay. Legend has it that Pontius Pilate was born there, his father being on a mission for the Roman army.

199.43　banging out　dashing or hurrying out.

200.1　be the cause what it like　whatever the cause.

200.19　such a piece of work　such a fuss.

200.34–35　figure like ... hair dishevelled　compare *Richard III*, 1.4.52–54.

201.16　Martinmas　11 November; a Scottish term or quarter day.

201.16　Whitsunday　15 May; a Scottish term or quarter day. It is also a church festival, falling on the 7th Sunday after Easter, and commemorates the descent of the Holy Spirit on the Apostles: see Acts Ch. 2.

201.26 kenn'd for known as.

201.29 will she nill she, flyte she fling she whether she wants to or not, whether she argues or kicks out.

201.41 women of good women of good standing, Scott's variation on the obsolete phrase 'man of good'.

202.26 evening of Shrove-tide the evening of Shrove-Tuesday, the day before the beginning of Lent; see note to 168.6.

203.16–19 in compliance with a summons ... as his tenure bound him Henry Smith is obliged to offer military assistance to the magistrates of the burgh as required, according to the terms on which he holds his land in the burgh.

204.41–42 like Portuguese Catholics ... their saints the reference has not been identified.

205.17 by the lug and the horn by the ear and the horn: the Smith will be dragged out by using a method for making recalcitrant sheep move. See *Letters*, 7.384, where Scott ascribes the phrase to James Hogg; see also *The Tale of Old Mortality*, ed. Douglas Mack, EEWN 4b, 58.4, and James Hogg, *The Brownie of Bodsbeck*, ed. Douglas S. Mack (Edinburgh and London, 1976), 157.

205.43–206.1 to lower his crest ... out of season the (implicit) image is of the cock, a traditional emblem of vainglorious boasting.

206.6 the deadly lot the chance of death.

206.38 Town-House the house or hall from which the affairs of the city were administered.

207.3 sick or sullen see *Antony and Cleopatra*, 1.3.13.

207.38 curl my cheek smile.

208.2 St Cupid Cupid is the Roman god of love. Simon is ironically awarding him a sainthood parallel to that of Valentine.

210.20–21 sat at the same board ... same cup compare 2 Samuel 12.3.

210.26–27 ill at ease ill, unwell.

211.6 war-horse ever heard the trumpet compare Job 39.25.

211.9 man of my hands man of my valour and fighting skill.

211.22 to owe me a shrewd turn feeling obliged to repay me with a violent action.

212.15 vengeance which Heaven ... will take see Romans 12.19.

212.33 bearing, like the regent York ... aged necks see *Richard II*, 2.2.74.

212.36 presidents, or deacons the appointed heads of individual trade guilds.

213.5 Sir Louis Lundin the surname Lundin is linked to the ownership of lands both in Fife and Forfar from the reign of Malcolm IV in 12th-century Scotland. Sir Louis Lundin, however, is probably not a historical figure.

215.23 ill talk ... a full man and a fasting *proverbial* a man who has eaten and a man who is fasting are likely to disagree: see *ODEP*, 293. For the most notorious use of the proverb, by a Douglas of a later generation, see *Tales of a Grandfather*, First Series, in *Prose Works*, 22.288–90.

215.32 found masses for his soul pay the clergy to say masses on behalf of the soul of the bonnet-maker.

216.2–3 garb of fence clothing for defence and protection.

216.13 burgher faith and oath on being admitted a burgess of Perth Henry Smith would have had to take an oath and promise to serve the town faithfully and to obey its officers.

216.22 Angus county on the E coast of Scotland.

216.35 It bears a face it seems plausible.

217.16–17   of that Ilk   of the place or estate of the same name, i.e. Ramorny, which is near Ladybank, in Fife.

217.23   find law for firing the lodging, and putting all within it to the sword   burning a house and killing all its inhabitants was a legal mode of punishing delinquents, but had to be authorised by a sheriff; in the Highlands legal nicety was less observed (see note to 134.12–13).

217.24   short rede, good rede   see note to 66.28.

217.41   proof by bier-right ... land of Scotland   rather than a specific legal procedure, what is in question here is the traditional belief that if a murderer should touch the corpse of the murdered person, the corpse will bleed. The appeal to mythic figures and to historic figures with mythic status is typical of the way in which chronicles presented the supposed legislation of early kings.

217.42   bulls and decretals   'bulls' are formal documents issued and sealed by the Pope; 'decretals' are legislative edicts on doctrine or church law issued by the Catholic Church. No bulls or decretals approving of bier-right have been identified.

217.43   Emperor Charlemagne   *c.* 742–814. He became Holy Roman Emperor in 800 and ruled over almost all of W Europe.

217.43   King Arthur   legendary king of the Britons in the 6th century who presided over the Knights of the Round Table.

218.1   Gregory the Great   Giric or Grig (d. 884), disputed King of Alba (the united kingdom of Picts and Scots N of the Forth-Clyde line), was a son of King Donald I (d. 863); for reasons unknown he became recognised as 'Liberator of the Scottish Church' and thus as a Scottish 'Gregory the Great'. Pope Gregory the Great (*c.* 540–604; Pope from 590) did much to strengthen the authority of the papacy.

218.1   the mighty Achaius   legendary king of Scotland. Boece (see note to 5.13–15), George Buchanan (1506–82) in his *Rerum scoticarum historia* (1582; *CLA*, 9, 10) and Walter Bower (1383–1437) in his *Scotichronicon* (*CLA*, 12, 14, 27) give his reign as 787–819 and stress his relations with Charlemagne.

218.4   our charters of the Fair City   see note to 43.25.

218.30   the Bruce's time   King Robert the Bruce, reigned 1306–29.

219.2   that of combat   see note to 138.25.

219.5   if he refuses both, he must be held as guilty   because he has refused to submit to either of the ordeals through which the judgment of God would be revealed.

219.11–12   this ancient form ... the seventeenth century   the last known trial by combat in Scotland was in 1597; there were subsequent instances where such a trial was considered but not used, or where, for some reason, the combat did not take place.

222   motto   see *2 Henry VI*, 2.3.54–55.

222.21–23   to put strife and quarrel ... distant lands   the King has in mind the various peasant revolts in England and France previously referred to. See notes to 132.20 and 132.21.

223.15–16   by the tomb ... immortal ancestor   the King and Albany were sons of Robert II and Elizabeth Mure; they were great-grandsons of Robert the Bruce.

225.2–4   the follies and vanities of life ... in better things   see Mark 9.43–48.

225.33–37   tutor ... nonage   in Scots law a *tutor* (i.e. a guardian) had complete responsibility for the upbringing and the property of a minor below the age of 14; a *curator* had responsibility for the property of a minor aged from 14 to 21. The age of majority in Scotland was 21, and Rothsay is 23.

225.38   wiser Romans ... four years   in Roman law the age of majority was 25.

225.41 young Lindsay, the Earl of Crawford historically the Lindsay involved with Albany, Rothsay, and Ramorny, was Sir David Lindsay of Glenesk, created 1st Earl of Crawford by his brother-in-law, Robert III, in 1398. Long a member of Rothsay's household, he seems at the last to have sided with Albany against him. As emerges at 231.4–8 Scott conflates this Lindsay with Sir Alexander Lindsay who became the 4th Earl of Crawford in 1446 and was known as the Tiger Earl.

226.20 ungenerous to load a falling man see *Henry VIII*, 5.3.76–77: ' 'tis a cruelty/ To load a falling man'.

226.28 his Castle of Tantallon Tantallon Castle, on the coast of East Lothian, near North Berwick, had been effectively occupied by the Douglases since around 1379.

226.30 his fortress of Dunbar Dunbar Castle is situated some 13 km further along the coast of East Lothian from Tantallon. Deemed impregnable to siege before the invention of artillery, it was demolished in 1567.

226.31 Coldingham small town 18 km N of Berwick-upon-Tweed.

226.32–33 Hotspur and Sir Ralph Percy Henry ('Hotspur') and Ralph Percy, sons of Henry Percy, Earl of Northumberland.

227.11 Northumberland Henry Percy (1342–1408), Earl of Northumberland, the most powerful nobleman in the N of England, and leader of the rebellion against Henry IV's seizure of the English crown.

227.34 like a screech-owl . . . calamity the screech-owl or barn owl, from its discordant cry supposed to be of evil omen.

227.41 indenture of arms written agreement to settle differences through battle. The deed, which also contained the rules of engagement, was drawn up in the Court and would have been executed in several copies, each of which would have borne the 'marks and seals' (300.23–24) of all parties.

228.1 Palm Sunday the Sunday before Easter commemorating Christ's entry into Jerusalem. As explained in the Historical Note Scott assimilates historical events which took place between 1396 and 1406 to the year of Rothsay's death, 1402. In the Gregorian calendar Palm Sunday would have been on 30 March in 1402, but was on 19 March according to the Julian calendar then in use.

228.12 their own mountain wolves there were wolves in the Scottish Highlands in the 14th and subsequent centuries; the last wolf in Scotland is supposed to have been killed in E Sutherland in 1743.

228.37 Welsh main particularly vicious form of cock-fighting in which, say, sixteen pairs of cocks fight; the winners then fight again leaving eight; and so on, until only one survives.

230.27 foul measure wicked treatment.

231.6 the Tiger earl see note to 225.41.

231.7 Strathmore large stretch of fertile country to the N of the Firth of Tay extending from Methven in Perthshire to Laurencekirk in the Mearns. The name means the 'great valley'.

231.15 ill at ease ill, unwell.

231.30–31 Put not your faith in Princes see Psalm 146.3.

231.38 take warrant guarantee.

232.5 your steward's household book all aspects of a nobleman's domestic arrangements were looked after by his steward; the steward's accounts book would include a list of all those employed by the household.

232.30 Dupplin village 8 km N of Perth.

234.16 marked a rascal deer for a buck of the first head mistook a young, lean or inferior deer for a full grown antlered stag.

234.40–41 like King Arthur . . . the Dane in some versions of his legend Arthur at the end of his life is said to have been carried away to the fairyland of

Avalon; in the 13th-century *chanson de geste*, *Huon of Bordeaux*, Huon's succession as King of Fairyland is predicted by Oberon while later versions of the story describe the event; Ugero or Ogier the Dane, one of Charlemagne's paladins, is said to have been taken to Avalon by Morgan le Fay (who sent him back two hundred years later to defend France against invasion).

235.4–5 a cuckoldly citizen the stereotype of the bourgeois husband whose natural fate is to be cuckcolded runs from Shakespeare and Jacobean city comedy to the literature of the Restoration.

235.7–8 I, who am . . . Araby itself Dwining implies that the Moors of Spain and their fellows in Arabia were the most advanced students of medicine. See the note to 159.11–12.

235.12 Keddie's ring see the note to 50.30.

235.13–14 thou darest not palter with me see *Macbeth*, 5.8.19–22.

235.22–23 confederacy is the soul of jugglery the most successful trickster requires an accomplice.

235.35–37 but I see thy nose . . . jerkin i.e. he has not suffered any of these judicial mutilations as a sentenced criminal.

236.7 we who are knights of the scalpel Dwining's metaphor for surgeons mockingly confers on them the status of the chivalry he despises.

236.13–15 the skull of Wallace . . . Margaret Logie after his execution at London in 1305, Wallace's head was exhibited above London bridge. Lockhart identifies Sir Simon Fraser as the 'famous ancestor of the Lovats, slain at Halidon Hill' (Magnum, 43.86). A Simon Fraser is said to have been at the battle of Halidon Hill near Berwick upon Tweed (1333) in which Edward III of England destroyed a Scottish army under Archibald Douglas (see Hector Boece, *The History and Chronicles of Scotland*, trans. John Bellenden, 3 vols (Edinburgh, 1821), 2.423; *CLA*, 4), but Dwining (given his interest in executions) may well be referring to the companion of Robert the Bruce, executed by Edward I in 1306. Margaret Logie was David II's mistress before becoming Queen Margaret.

237.31 as an Indian boy whether Scott has in mind a native American Indian or an inhabitant of the East or West Indies or India is not clear. The reference to the 'light canoe' suggests a native American; but the references to the sea's surf and an argosy suggest the Indies.

238.7–25 Henbane . . . bought by it compare Volpone's opening address to his gold in Ben Jonson's play *Volpone* (performed 1605–06; printed 1607), 1.1.1–22; also *Timon of Athens*, 4.3.25–41.

238.23–24 Revenge itself . . . to themselves see Romans 12.19.

239.2–3 like the night-mare . . . invisible myself the night-mare is an incubus which afflicts and oppresses; compare *2 Henry IV*, 2.1.74.

239.7 rogue, villain, and slave compare *Hamlet*, 2.2.543.

239.10–11 I run no long accounts with his knighthood i.e. he does not wait a long time to repay Ramorny.

239.25–26 our trust is constant . . . Donald of the Isles in *The Lord of the Isles* (1815) Scott has Robert the Bruce say during the battle of Bannockburn: 'One effort more, and Scotland's free!/ Lord of the Isles, my trust in thee/ Is firm as Ailsa Rock'. In a note to the stanza, he writes: 'It is traditionally said, that at this crisis, he [Bruce] addressed the Lord of the Isles in a phrase used as a motto by some of his descendants, "My trust is constant in thee."' (*The Lord of the Isles*, 6.28, in *Poetical Works*, 10.259).

239.27 Opiserque per orbem dicor *Latin* I am called Help-bringer throughout the world; said of himself by Apollo, as god of medicine, in Ovid (43 BC–AD 17), *Metamorphoses*, 1.521–22.

239.31 cynanche trachealis disease of the windpipe.

240.3–26 Viewless . . . blood probably by Scott.

241.38 and even so came of it Scott's meaning is not clear; Proudfute's wife may be suggesting that it was Oliver's pretensions to gentlemanly status that led to his death, or that despite all his pretensions he still ended up murdered in the street.

242.14–15 Chaucer ... on the Bible compare Chaucer, 'General Prologue' to *The Canterbury Tales*, 1 (A), 438. The avarice of Chaucer's Physician ('For gold in phisik is a cordial,/ Therefore he lovede gold in special': 1 (A), 443–44) may have been a starting point for Scott's creation of Dwining.

243.2 the regular and secular clergy regular clergy were bound by the vows of a monastic or other order; secular clergy were not so bound.

244.24–25 all that was created ... seven nights see Genesis Ch. 1, and 2.1–2.

245.22 as thou didst never thump anvil compare *2 Henry VI*, 2.3.83–84.

245.32 Skinners' Yards the working area in Perth for those employed in the animal skin trade.

245.38 the Earl of Erroll, Lord High Constable see note to 194.1–2.

246.25 fenced field of battle i.e. an area that has been enclosed or marked off for formal fighting.

246.27 Sound trumpets *Richard II*, 1.3.117.

247.20 trapped in the snare see e.g. Psalm 9.15.

249.12 ill news ... proverbially fast see Ray, 125; *ODEP*, 400.

249.42 the High Constable's lodgings see note to 194.1–2.

251.6 pitched your toils set out your snares or traps. Compare *Love's Labour's Lost*, 4.3.2.

252.9–10 King and Council ... Provost and Bailies i.e. Catherine thinks that she knows better than the King and his advisers, the Church and its clergy, and the civic authorities.

252.23 the dainties which the fasting season permitted in the period of Lent the consumption of meat was forbidden, but fish allowed.

252.26–29 a long poetical account ... Seward see *Wallace*, 9.779–1106.

253.13–14 The Rover's golden angels ... flight yet 'angels' are gold coins; Sir Patrick means that with his inheritance from the Red Rover (see text 70.43–73.8) he is a wealthy man.

253.41 comparative attractions ... feasting see Ecclesiastes 7.2.

257.27 dark lantern lantern with a slide or arrangement for concealing the light.

258.10–11 a Perth arrow hath a perfect flight Perth's traditional expertise in archery is described in *The Muses Threnodie* (First Muse).

258.17–21 the stately Gothic arches ... in 1621 a flood in 1328 swept away Perth's bridge over the Tay and the construction of a new one was authorised by King Robert I. However, inundations in 1573, 1582, and 1589 all appear to have damaged or destroyed the existing bridge. Hence the bridge swept away in 1621 was of relatively recent construction. See *The Muses Threnodie* (Third Muse) which contains an account of the Tay bridges, and note to 36.36.

258.34 your valiancie you man of valiance.

259.39 bonus socius *Latin* good friend or ally

260.1 pinching occasion *understatement* hanging.

260.13 the chirurgical hall of Padua hall for surgeons at the University of Padua, in N Italy, famous in the Middle Ages as a centre for medical studies.

260.22 Ephemerides almanacs containing tables of information on the positions of the planets, sun, moon, eclipses etc. in the course of a year.

260.38–39 in extremis *Latin* in difficulties, at his end.

260.40 let us to the gear i.e. let us get on with the business.

261.1 plays an owl's part i.e. floating in the air at night like an owl.

261.15 shackles those to be hanged had their hands and feet bound in chains.

261.28 spiritual essence double distilled i.e. extremely powerful alcoholic spirits.

261.37–38 kennel-washings liquid contents of an open sewer.

262.5 Nails and blood *oaths* abbreviated versions of 'by God's nails' and 'by God's blood'.

262.16 your valours i.e. you men of valour.

262.33 Newburgh town in NW Fife, on the Firth of Tay; its origins are linked to the creation of the nearby Abbey of Lindores in the 12th century.

263.22 the Grève the Place de la Grève, adjacent to the river Seine, a regular site of executions in Paris in the period 1310–1830.

264.2 motto *A Midsummer Night's Dream*, 1.1.134.

264.35 my power is a lawful one see e.g. Ephesians 6.1.

265.1 with indirection deviously.

265.5 to watch her sheepfold see John 10.1–16; Acts 20.28–30.

266.2 a wolf in sheep's clothing see Matthew 7.15; *ODEP*, 907.

266.14 speak within doors keep your voice down.

266.25 few words are best proverbial: Tobias Smollett, *Humphry Clinker* (1771), ed. Thomas R. Preston and O. M. Brack, Jr. (Athens and London, 1990), 64; Matt. Bramble to Dr. Lewis, 8 May. The phrase translates the Latin tag *pauca verba*: *Love's Labour's Lost*, 4.2.155.

266.26–28 old makar, . . . counsel thee see James I, 'Good Counsel', lines 15–16, in *The Kingis Quair*, ed. Walter W. Skeat, Scottish Text Society, New Series 1 (Edinburgh and London, 1911), 51–54: 'Sen word is thrall, and thocht is only free,/ Thow dant thi twnge, that power has and may'. Compare James 3.8. In the ICopy Scott says 'These lines are still extant in the ruinous house of an Abbot and are said to be allusive to the holy man having kept a mistress' (ICopy, 3.29; Magnum, 43.146).

266.36–37 regular and secular see note to 243.2.

267.1 in dittay *Scots law* indicted.

267.9 the net of the fowler see Psalm 124.7, in both prose and metrical versions.

267.14 the Highland line the cultural and geographical 'frontier' between the Highlands and the Lowlands.

267.31–32 the Abbess . . . the Dominican the identity of these characters is explained in the text below.

267.38 the foul fiend . . . crocodiles Simon believes that the concern shown by the two characters is self-serving and hypocritical; i.e. both are shedding crocodile tears. See *ODEP*, 155. Compare the account of the crocodile in Hakluyt's 'The Second Voyage of Sir John Hawkins': 'His nature is ever when hee would have his praie, to crie, and sobbe like a christian bodie, to provoke them to come to him, and then hee snatcheth at them' (Richard Haklyut, *The Principall Navigations, Voiages and Discoveries of The English Nation* (London, 1589), 535).

268.31–32 Elcho nunnery nunnery established in the 14th century on the S bank of the Tay near Elcho Castle some 8 km from Perth.

269.22–23 receive their inmates on slighter composition allow new entrants for smaller (financial) returns.

269.23–30 Our privileges . . . for joy Simon has mainly in mind the Declaration of Arbroath. Popes Clement V and John XXII had been reluctant to give formal recognition to Robert the Bruce's title to the Scottish crown; Bruce and his immediate supporters were excommunicated in 1318 and Scotland placed under papal interdict. The Scottish response was the Declaration of Arbroath of 1320, probably drawn up by the Abbot of Arbroath, and signed by 8 earls and 31 barons, in which they rejected papal interference with Scottish national freedom. See also text 271.27–33.

270.13–14 God send the whirlwind ... the green one the language and imagery suggest the biblical, though no individual passages from the Bible appear to be in question.

270.18 it skills not it makes no difference.

270.18–19 the saints help those ... themselves proverbial: see 'God (or Heaven) helps those who help themselves', *ODEP*, 310.

270.41 apparitor or sumner ... him summoning officer of the ecclesiastical court come to arrest him.

271.19 tarry till the tide turns proverbial: *ODEP*, 848.

271.28 Henry Wardlaw see notes to 92.13 and 269.23–30.

271.30–31 Malcolm Canmore Malcolm III, King of Scots, reigned 1057–93; his second wife was St Margaret of Scotland (see note to 151.20). For relations between Scotland and the papacy see the notes to 92.13, 93.6, 101.36–39, 141.38–40, 269.23–30.

271.41–42 with a high hand acting imperiously.

272.2–3 the general right the rights of the people as a whole.

272.12 graddam cake cake made of toasted corn.

272.34–35 the Thane's Cross not identified.

272.35 an ill-favoured pirn to wind *proverbial* a troublesome business to get clear of (*OED*, *pirn* 1b).

272.37 like a kain-hen in a cavey like a hen kept in a hen-coop to be payment of rent in kind.

272.38–39 belt and spurs the 'badges' of knighthood: see notes to 59.24–25 and 69.18.

273.3 both wax and wether-skin the sealing wax and the sheepskin parchment on which the summons is written. A *wether* is a castrated sheep.

273.6–7 To horse ... in charters most probably by Scott.

273.23 the rules of the city the Council's laws and regulations concerning the civic life of the city.

273.25 on my salvation by swearing on his hope of salvation.

273.33–34 a man who walketh ... path compare e.g. Proverbs 10.9.

275.12–13 to wash the Ethiopian proverbial image of futility originating in Jeremiah 13.23: 'can the Ethiopian change his skin?'. See *ODEP*, 868.

275.16 to snatch the brand from the burning save someone from imminent danger: proverbial image originating in Amos 4.11, 'ye were as a firebrand plucked out of the burning'. See also Zechariah 3.2.

275.41 Dault an Neigh Dheil *Gaelic* 'Dalta an Fhèidh Ghil' ('foster child of the White Deer').

276.3 Taishatar *Gaelic* 'Taibhsear' ('seer').

276.5 Tin-Egan *Gaelic* 'Teine èiginn' ('fire of necessity'). In a note Lockhart explains that the *tine-egan* ceremony involved two men producing fire by rubbing together pieces of wood (Magnum, 43.165).

276.35 Falkland Falkland Castle, a hunting lodge from the 12th century, near Cupar in Fife. The present palace was built between 1501–41 as a country residence for the Stewart kings. The town was made a royal burgh in 1458.

277.24 unstable as water see Genesis 49.4.

277.26–27 milk still lurking about his liver making him cowardly; compare 'lily-livered'. The liver was formerly thought to be the seat of the strong passions.

277.42 by times betimes, early.

278.6 ne plus ultra *Latin literally* nothing beyond; the highest possible.

278 motto from the modernised version of the 'General Prologue' to *The*

Canterbury Tales, by Thomas Betterton (d. 1710), actor and friend of Pope, which was published posthumously in Barnaby Lintot's *Miscellaneous Poems and Translations* (1712). Pope's assistance in having the version (perhaps revised by himself) published for the benefit of Betterton's widow gave rise to a story that he was actually the author: see Samuel Johnson, *Lives of the English Poets*, ed. George Birkbeck Hill, 3 vols (Oxford, 1905), 3.108; and Joseph Warton, *The Works of Alexander Pope*, 9 vols (London, 1797), 2.166.

278.29   Caithness and Sutherland   the two northernmost counties of the Scottish mainland.

278.30   Mohr ar chat   *Gaelic* 'Morair Chat' ('Lord of the Cats [or Cat people]'). Lockhart translates the phrase as 'The Great Cat' (Magnum, 43.170).

278.31   the Keiths, the Sinclairs, the Guns   these clans or septs (the spelling 'Gunn' is more common) are all associated with Caithness in particular.

278.39   Badenoch   wild and mountainous area in SE Inverness-shire.

279.1   non nostrum est   *Latin* it is not our business [to resolve this].

279.4   Clan Quhele, or, as it is called by later authorities, Clan Kay   'the actual identity of the two clans involved has never been satisfactorily established, despite much learned debate': Stephen Boardman, *The Early Stewart Kings: Robert II and Robert III 1371–1406* (East Linton, 1996), 202, and note 45, 219.

279.6   Buchanan   George Buchanan (1506–82), Scottish Renaissance scholar, author of a history of Scotland entitled *Rerum scoticarum historia* (1582).

279.15   Breadalbane   mountainous district in NW Perthshire.

280.10–11   Niel Booshalloch   *Gaelic* 'Niall Buachaille' ('Niel the Cowherd').

280.23   finely holped up   left in a difficult position, embarrassed.

280.33   parent lake   Tobias Smollett (1721–71), 'Ode to Leven Water', line 17, in *Humphry Clinker* (1771), ed. Thomas R. Preston and O. M. Brack, Jr. (Athens and London, 1990), 242, Matt. Bramble to Dr. Lewis, 28 August; Robert Fergusson (1750–74), 'The Author's Life', line 10; Ann Grant of Laggan (1755–1838), 'The Highlanders', Part 4, in *Poems on Various Subjects* (1803), p. 60.

280.38–39   the feudal castle of Ballough...Earl of Breadalbane   the old castle at Ballough or Balloch, built *c*. 1580, in Kenmore, beside Loch Tay, was replaced by the Marquis of Breadalbane's Taymouth Castle in the early 19th century.

280.40–41   the Campbells...Argyleshire   the Campbells were a powerful Highland clan whose territory included Argyllshire in the SW Highlands of Scotland.

281.4   Eumaeus   Odysseus's swineherd in Homer's *Odyssey*, Bk 14.

281.36   Ben Lawers   to the N of Loch Tay, Ben Lawers (1214 m) is the highest mountain in Perthshire.

282.10   make traffic   engage in trade.

283.23–24   pounds Scots   in this period the Scottish pound had about half the value of its English counterpart.

283.43   Traut shoe   *Gaelic* 'Trobhad an seo' ('come here a minute', 'look here'); the phrase is used when someone wishes to 'flag up' a point.

284.2   deil a   *emphatic* not a.

284.6   Tom-an-Lonach   *Gaelic* 'Toman Lònach' (*literally* 'meadowy hillock'); it is apparently translated below (284.32) as the 'Knoll of Yew Trees', but this could be an alternative name rather than a translation.

284.8   wee bit   small.

285.13   Titans   mythological giant gods, the sons and daughters of Uranus (sky) and Gaea (earth).

285.15 Ben Mohr in the SW corner of Perthshire, Ben More (1171 m) is marginally lower than Ben Lawers.

285.25–38 They were inhabited ... of them this passage repeats, in much abbreviated form, the sociological analysis of the Highland problem that Scott had provided in *Rob Roy* (1818), Vol. 2, Ch. 13. Analysis of the nature and structure of society in different historical periods is one of the major concerns of the Scottish Enlightenment.

286.4 Sibilla Sybilla, illegitimate daughter of Henry I of England, married Alexander I of Scotland (*c.* 1077–1124). She died in 1122 and was buried on the Isle of Tay where Alexander had founded a priory.

286.19–20 the Dochart and the Lochy the river Dochart flows from Loch Dochart in W Perthshire into the head of Loch Tay; the river Lochy flows into the Dochart near Killin, just before the latter enters Loch Tay.

286.22 fortress of Finlayrigg Finlarig Castle in Killin, at the head of Loch Tay in W Perthshire, the ancestral seat of the Campbells of Lochow.

287.5 Loch Earn a ten-km long loch in the Breadalbane district of Perthshire, SW of Loch Tay.

288.7–8 tenement of clay see John Dryden, *Absalom and Achitophel* (1681), line 158.

288.28–30 God has sent ... prefers darkness compare John 3.19–20.

289.4–5 Father Hubert a better hunter of hares Hubert is the name of the Friar in the 'General Prologue' to *The Canterbury Tales* (1 (A), 269); but it is Chaucer's Monk of whom we are told that 'huntyng for the hare / Was al his lust' (1 (A), 191–92).

289.5 Vicar Vinesauf a priest who drinks too much; 'Vinesauf' means 'wine-saver'.

289.18 carry my faggot ... gallow's foot this action (faggots were the bundles of wood in the midst of which heretics were burned) was performed by those who had formally renounced heresy.

289.28–29 pitched shirt and brimstone head-gear pitch (tar) and brimstone (sulphur) were regularly used in the burning of heretics. In Foxe's *Book of Martyrs* the account of the death of the Rev. George Marsh refers to 'a number of fagottes under him, and a thing made like a firkin, with pitch and tarre in the same, ouer his head' (John Foxe, *Ecclesiasticall Historie, conteining the Actes and Monuments of Martyrs*, 4th edn, 2 vols (London, 1583), 2.1507; see *CLA*, 235).

289.34 poor as Job in Job 1 the upright man loses all his worldly wealth.

289.39–40 transported thither in a chariot of fire see 2 Kings 2.11.

290.15–17 the superstition and folly ... of mind St Fillans, at the E end of Loch Earn in Perthshire, had been the site of a Priory since the early 14th century. The saint himself was believed to have miraculous powers: immersion in the nearby St Fillans Pool was supposed to be a cure for madness, while the chapel bell, used in the cure, also had miraculous properties. If stolen by a person undergoing the cure it was supposed to be able to extricate itself from the thief's hands and return home ringing all the way.

291.20 Pharisees one of the Jewish religious groupings in the time of Jesus; they taught strict observance of rabbinical tradition, and in the Gospels are presented as Jesus's main opponents.

291.23–24 the fire within must not be stifled compare Psalm 39.2–3; Jeremiah 20.7–9.

291.25 Woe unto me if I preach not the gospel see 1 Corinthians 9.16. Father Clement's speech, of which this is the conclusion, seems to echo various passages in this Pauline epistle.

291.31 the Reformation the religious (and political) movement in 16th-century Europe that began as an attempt to reform the existing Roman Catholic church and ended in the creation of the Protestant Churches. It was believed by later ages that the invention of printing in the 15th century had given all men access to scripture and thus had facilitated and promoted the Reformation.

292.38 at all points in every particular.

294.35 the man that has my charge the person in my care.

294.43 far beneath the Salt i.e. in a very lowly position. The principal salt-box stood at the centre of the table; those of rank sat above the salt, retainers below it.

295.2 species of palladium type of object believed to afford protection.

295.22 Leichtach possibly from the Gaelic 'laoch' ('hero'), thus 'Laoich-raidh' ('body of heroes') or 'Laoich taighe' ('heroes of the house [or house-hold]'); 'foster brethren' is here rather an alternative description than a translation.

296.27 Marischal Taeh, i.e. sewer of the mess *marischal* is an alternative form of 'marshal'; the *sewer* is the high-ranking servant in charge of the seating and serving arrangements for the meal.

296.33 bieyfir *Gaelic* 'biadh fir' ('food of a man').

296.42 the race of the Dalriads Dalriada was originally the name of a district in the N of Ireland. In the 5th or 6th centuries the Scots who lived there passed over to the adjacent area of W Scotland, approximating modern Argyll-shire. This area in turn became known as Dalriada.

297.26 Requiem eternam dona *Latin* grant eternal rest: from the final part of the Roman Catholic funeral liturgy.

297.31 St Barr Barr or Finbarr, a 6th-century Irish saint, first bishop of Cork.

299 motto *Hamlet*, 2.2.185.

300.12 would take with me would ally with me.

300.13–14 kill and take possession see 1 Kings 21.19.

300.15 the great Strath alternative version of Strathmore; see note to 231.7.

300.19 The tongue . . . member compare James 3.2–8.

300.21 holding a candle . . . the way to mischief proverbial: see Ray, 55; *ODEP*, 377 where this example is cited.

301.8 hand has warmed my haffits 'boxed my ears' (Scott in 1Copy, 3.122; Magnum, 43.215).

301.22–23 the magistrates are elected . . . St Martinmas Lent is the season before Easter, while Martinmas is celebrated on 11 November.

301.42–43 without nice pilotage without skilful guidance.

302.33–35 How have ill-assorted marriages . . . themselves 'ill-assorted marriages,' with unfortunate outcomes, in the three families mentioned by Simon have not been clearly identified. The most notorious marriage break-down in the history of the clan Campbell (of which *MacCallanmore* is the chief) did not occur until 1513 when Lachlan Cattanach Maclean, married to Lady Elizabeth Campbell, daughter of Archibald, 2nd Earl of Argyle, tried to get rid of his wife by exposing her on a rock that would be covered by the incoming tide. In fact she was rescued and, many years later, Maclean was killed by her brother. Joanna Baillie's play, *The Family Legend* (1809), for which Scott wrote a poetical prologue, was based on this story. Much earlier another Maclean had been involved in the rough wooing of Margaret, daughter of John Lord of the Isles. The Maclean chief had taken the Lord of the Isles prisoner, and an agreement to the marriage of his daughter to Maclean was the condition of his freedom. (A son of this forced marriage would be the Maclean chief killed at the Battle of Harlaw in 1411, fighting alongside Donald, Lord of the Isles.) Finally, the marriage of John Lord of the Isles to a daughter of the future Robert II had involved his setting aside a previous marriage whose legitimacy has sometimes been questioned.

302.37–38 wed her with your left hand in a marriage between a man of high (usually royal) rank and a woman of inferior status (a morganatic marriage), it was customary for the husband to pledge his troth with his left hand. The wife and the offspring had no claim to the husband's possessions or status. Compare *Kenilworth*, ed. J. H. Alexander, EEWN 11, 306.36–40.

303.1 the black stones of Iona Iona, a small island beside Mull, on the W coast of Scotland, became in the 6th century the base for St Columba's mission to bring Christianity to Scotland and other areas of northern Europe. The Black Rock of Iona seems to have been a sacred stone upon which vows were sworn. Subsequently the people of the Hebrides came to swear by the *black stones* of Iona, though no such stones have ever been found.

303.43–304.1 when the Southron assaulted the Fair City Perth was besieged by both Scottish and English forces several times in the 14th century.

304.2–3 tenure . . . watch and ward for *tenure* see note to 203.16–19; for *watch and ward* see note to 44.4.

304.26 did on put on.

304.32 of proof impenetrable.

304.36 old Kempe of Kinfauns according to the *OED kemp* is an obsolete word meaning 'brave warrior' or 'champion'. Hence Kempe of Kinfauns 'as he was called' may be no more than an honourable nickname for Sir Patrick's father.

305.5 the Spey Tower part of the medieval fortifications of Perth; it was built above the Spey or South gate, one of the three fortified entrances to the town.

305.23–24 haul up their tackle draw up their arrows.

307.21 Gow Chrom bandy-legged Smith.

307.39 legend of St Crispin see note to 56.43–57.1.

308.13 A glove is the emblem of faith the throwing down of the glove is the binding act in the ritual of knightly challenge: compare *Richard II*, 4.1.76 where Fitzwater refers to his gage as 'my bond of faith', and the text at 132.29–37. In the rituals of St Valentine the woman is given a pair of gloves in return for her kiss.

308.17 fitting by degree appropriate in terms of social status.

309.38 martin's fur the fur of the pine marten once common, now rare, in the Scottish Highlands.

310.9–11 submit to a . . . the Church again Simon means to be reconciled to the authority of the Church by doing penance (wearing a hair shirt and whipping himself) and by paying a large fine.

311.11 assay the process of killing a deer and establishing whether it is fat or lean. Cutting up a deer was 'an operation of great skill and nicety'. For an extended analysis, see Scott's edition of *Sir Tristrem*, in *Poetical Works*, 5.381–89, in which Scott quotes from *The Boke of St. Albans* from which the term 'assay' comes.

312.7 double portion 2 Kings 2.9.

312.16 Iona, and the good St Columbus see note to 303.1.

312.24–25 Hell shall not prevail so far compare Matthew 16.18.

312.25–26 place vervain . . . in thy crest vervain or verbena, St. John's-wort (a plant traditionally gathered on St John's Eve; also known as rose of Sharon), and rowan or mountain-ash, were all believed to have the power of warding-off witchcraft or evil spirits.

312.42 Ferragon or Farragon Hill (780 m), N of Aberfeldy at the E end of Loch Tay.

313.14 Greenwoods have ears proverbial: see *ODEP*, 255.

314.5–6   Wardlaw... of St Andrews   see note to 92.13.

314.12   the jaw-teeth of the oppressors   compare Psalms 3.7, and 58.6; Proverbs 30.14.

314.13–14   prey... ravening talons   compare Psalm 124.6–7.

314.27   a sweet savouring sacrifice   compare Ephesians 5.2.

314.33   the scathe and the scorn   *proverbial* the harm or injury and the scorn accompanying it: see *ODEP*, 705; compare Ray, 143, *ODEP*, 596.

316.1–2   its stony case   see e.g. Ezekiel 11.19, 36.26; *ODEP*, 352.

316.24   al fresco   *Italian* in the open air, but here 'the open air'.

316.36   thou gavest not aim for it   you did not instruct it.

316.38   dry beating   severe beating, but involving no loss of blood.

317.4   makes the good wine taste of blood   compare *Redgauntlet*, ed. G. A. M. Wood and David Hewitt, EEWN 17, 90.20–21, where Sir Robert Redgauntlet, in his death agonies calling for wine to cool his throat, cries out that he has been given 'blood instead of burgundy'.

317.5   bona robas   wenches. See *2 Henry IV*, 3.2.200.

317.9   another Otterburn   at the battle of Otterburn, in 1388, James Douglas, 2nd Earl of Douglas, gained a famous victory over the English led by Henry Percy (Hotspur). However, Douglas himself was killed in the course of the battle.

317.9   he is to be Lieutenant again   see note to 88.29.

317.24   Falkland   see note to 276.35.

317.28–29   the Stewartry of Renfrew   lands in the W of Scotland, S of the Clyde, traditionally belonging to the royal Stewart family. The term *stewartry* was applied to crown property administered by a steward rather than a sheriff.

317.37   Emirs and Amirals   Islamic chieftains and commanders. *Amiral* is a form of 'admiral', in use with this meaning and spelling from the 13th to 17th centuries.

317.39   better to hear the lark sing than the mouse squeak   'Implying that it was better to keep the forest than shut themselves up in fortified places' (Scott in ICopy, 3.167; see Magnum, 43.247).

317.43   a brief ride... in three directions   N to the Firth of Tay; S to the Firth of Forth; E to the North Sea.

318.29   the lack of an eye   see note to 108.32.

319.16   use all familiarity   conduct close and friendly relations.

319.26   a secretis   *Latin literally* on account of secrets; i.e. private secretary.

321.2–3   possess myself... baron   make use of or control a country nobleman.

321.5   Campvere   trading centre located near Flushing in Holland. In the later Middle Ages it became an important centre for Scotland's trade with northern Europe.

321.18   the salmon-tythe   the Church's share of the proceeds of salmon fishing in the River Tay.

321.29   tender consciences   sensitivities to religious scruples.

321.40–41   Elizabeth of Dunbar   daughter of the Earl of March to whom Rothsay had originally been attached. See note to 101.36–39.

322.4   Saint Andrew with his shored cross   *The Battle of Flodden Field; A Poem of the Sixteenth Century*, ed. Henry Weber (Edinburgh, 1808), line 510. The edition is dedicated to Scott, and appeared after the publication of *Marmion* (1808). 'Shored' carries the sense of being propped up.

322.5–6   putting a finger into every man's pie   see *ODEP*, 258. The proverbial meaning seems less relevant here than the reference to fingers and hands.

322.14–15   the rich man... only ewe lamb   see 2 Samuel 12.1–4.

322.20–23 the ancient laws of Scotland . . . for gold in fact such a feudal *droit de seigneur* never did exist in Scotland, though other types of feudal obligation were often remitted in exchange for money.

322.34–35 Vulcan was a smith . . . what came of it Vulcan, the lame god of metalwork, was cuckolded by his wife Venus, the goddess of love. For the story see note to 123.40–124.1. The 'Chronicles' may allude to John Lydgate's *Troy Book* version (Bk 2, lines 5803–25), which Scott quotes with relish in his review of George Ellis's *Specimens of the Early English Poets* in *Prose Works*, 17.11–12. For Henry's self-description at 35.1–4 compare Lydgate's 'This smotry [smoky] smyth, this swart[e] Vlcanus': *Lydgate's Troy Book* A.D. 1412–20, ed. Henry Bergen, 4 vols., Early English Text Society, Extra Series 97, 103, 106, 126 (1906–35), 1.310; Bk 2, line 5803.

322.43–323.1 Some music now . . . ear compare *Twelfth Night*, 1.1.1–15.

323.7 dying fall *Twelfth Night*, 1.1.4.

324.34–325.6 Yes, thou may'st sigh, . . . art dead probably by Scott.

325.21 Newburgh see note to 262.33.

326.7 Lindores see note to 192.36.

326.28–29 the hoods and pinners types of headgear. A 'pinner' is a close-fitting cap with long side-flaps.

327.10–11 wreath of willow . . . plight the willow tree is traditionally associated with death and loss: compare Desdemona's willow-song in *Othello*, 4.3.39–50.

327.13 old Hecate in classical mythology goddess of the moon in her sinister aspect, associated with witchcraft and the underworld: compare *A Midsummer Night's Dream*, 5.1.360–76, and Hecate's role as mistress of the witches in *Macbeth*, 3.5 and 4.1.

327.13–14 hath more beard . . . lip compare *Macbeth*, 1.3.45–47.

327.15 the commodity of a beard compare *Twelfth Night*, 3.1.42–43.

327.40 grey friar friar of the Franciscan Order.

328.4–5 goes trippingly off see *Hamlet*, 3.2.1–2.

329.23–24 disposed on the couch—languishing and ladylike compare Lady Wishfort in William Congreve, *The Way of the World* (1700), 4.1. Lydia Languish in R. B. Sheridan, *The Rivals* (1775) may also have been in Scott's mind.

331.16 the palmer's staff a palmer is a pilgrim who carried a palm-leaf as a sign of having visited the Holy Land.

331.19 Heir of the heroic Bruce Rothsay was great-great-grandson of Robert the Bruce.

331.32 baffled, forsworn caitiff semi-technical terms for a disgraced knight.

332.16–18 Your glorious ancestor . . . his country before his eventual victory over the English at Bannockburn in 1314, Robert the Bruce had had to survive in earlier years a series of setbacks and defeats which had often made Scottish independence seem impossible to achieve.

332.30–31 if chronicles speak true . . . of Spain the war with Greece that ended in the destruction of Troy was in Homer's account occasioned by Paris's abduction of Helen, wife of the Spartan king Menelaus. The original successful Moorish invasion of Spain was traditionally seen as having been caused by Roderick, the King of Spain's violation of the daughter of one of his nobles.

332.32 speak within door keep your voice down.

332.37 the fire burns within me compare Psalm 39.3.

333.4–5 favourite Sultana wife or mistress of an Islamic sovereign.

333.21 Malcolm the Maiden Malcolm IV, King of Scots (reigned

1153–65), called *maiden* because of his youthful and feminine appearance.

333.32–33   read in old chronicles . . . continence of Scipio   after his capture of New Carthage in Spain (209 BC) the Roman general Scipio (235–*c*. 183 BC) is said to have been made a present of an exceptionally beautiful native girl. According to the Greek historian Polybius (10.19), Scipio, though fond of women, refused to take advantage of her on account of his responsibilities as a general. In the more elaborate version of the Roman historian Livy (26.50) the girl is engaged to be married and Scipio with a feeling speech restores her to her fiancé.

334.14   James, the younger son of the King   born in 1394, James succeeded his father as James I in 1406. At that time, however, he was a prisoner in England at the court of Henry IV and his release was not negotiated until 1424. He was murdered in 1437.

335.29   bull's head . . . signal of death   the best known example of the use of this form of fatal symbolism occurred in 1440, when William, 6th Earl of Douglas, and his brother were invited to dine in Edinburgh Castle. At the close of the dinner a bull's head was placed on the table and the two Douglases were removed and executed. Scott tells the story in *Tales of a Grandfather*, First Series, in *Prose Works*, 22.280.

335.35–36   woodcock . . . snared   compare *ODEP*, 768; *Hamlet*, 1.3.115 and 5.2.298. The woodcock is proverbially easy to snare.

335.38–39   Oh my father . . . father!   compare *Hamlet*, 1.5.40–41.

335.39–40   the staff . . . a spear   compare 2 Kings 18.21.

336.16–29   Oh, Bold and True, . . . still for me!   the words are probably by Scott, but developed from the common folk tradition of declaring loyalty to a set of emblematic colours: compare 'A Ballad call'd Blew Cap for me', in *Antidote against Melancholy* (1661), 29; Hyder Rollins, *Cavalier and Puritan* (New York, 1923), 9; Walter Scott, 'March, march, Ettrick and Teviotdale', in *The Monastery*, ed. Penny Fielding, EEWN 12, 230.10–31, sung to 'the ancient air of "Blue Bonnets over the Border"'.

338.38–39   How long held out . . . of Hermitage   the Knight of Liddesdale was Sir William Douglas. Alexander Ramsay of Dalhousie was a rival knight whom he imprisoned and murdered in Hermitage Castle in the Scottish Borders. Lockhart cites the source of his information as the 1743 edition of David Hume of Godscroft's *History of the Houses of Douglas and Angus* (Magnum, 43.287).

339.7   vespers time   see note to 121.30.

340.9   in the skimming of a bowie   in the time it takes to skim a bowl of milk; i.e. very soon.

343.34   Venit extrema dies   *Latin* the last day has come. See Virgil, *Aeneid* (30–19 BC), 2.324: 'venit summa dies' (on the fall of Troy).

344.16   the Earl of Douglas . . . the King's Lieutenant   although prefigured in the narrative (317.9), Scott is not following the historical record at this point. Rothsay had a much more active role in the affairs of the kingdom than Scott allows, and in the years immediately prior to his death, Rothsay himself was Lieutenant-general of the kingdom (see note to 88.29).

344.24   draw bridle   come to a halt.

344.31–32   haughty barons who overstride the world   see *Julius Caesar*, 1.2.135–36.

344.32   day of adversity   Proverbs 24.10.

344.32–33   Chaff before the wind   Psalm 35.5.

344.33–34   their column-resembling legs   compare *Julius Caesar*, 1.2.135–37.

345.6   barbarous Latin   like a Renaissance humanist, Dwining scorns the non-classical Latin of the medieval Church.

345.28 heart of adamant see Zechariah 7.12; compare Job 41.24 and Ezekiel 36.36.

347.12–13 hasty masters make slovenly servants compare 'A bad master makes a bad servant' (*ODEP*, 517, 'like master, like man').

347.31–32 his near kinsman, the Lord Balveny James Douglas of Balvenie and Abercorn (d. 1443) was the second son of Archibald the Grim. In 1440 he became the 7th Earl of Douglas.

347.35–36 red-hand *Scots law* redhanded, in the very act of committing the crime. Someone caught red-hand could be subjected to summary justice, but otherwise had to be tried by due process of law.

347.37 Jedwood men men from the Jedforest or Jedburgh area of the Scottish Borders.

348.1 Jedwood justice,—hang in haste . . . leisure *ODEP*, 410, where this example is cited.

348.33 altar of mine idol compare Volpone's opening address to his gold in Ben Jonson's play: *Volpone* (performed 1605–06, printed 1607), 1.1.1–22.

349.30–31 no longer a knight, but a knave see 'An Essay on Chivalry', in *Prose Works*, 6.105–06, where Scott describes the processes involved in degrading a knight; his quotation from 'Stowe's *Chronicle*' includes the words: 'now art thou no knight, but a knave'.

350.6 Lochleven large loch near Kinross, to the S of Perth. Falkland is some 13 km E of Lochleven.

350.23–25 the punishment of Albany . . . on his house Albany only profited from the death of Rothsay. When James I, a prisoner in England, succeeded Robert III at the age of eleven, Albany was appointed Governor of Scotland, a post which he retained until his death in 1420. He ensured that his son Murdoch Stewart succeeded him as Governor, but the luck of the house ran out soon afterwards. When James I was released and returned to Scotland in 1424, one of his first actions was to arrange the execution not only of Albany's son Murdoch, but of Murdoch's two sons as well.

350.32 the April reception like the mixed weather traditionally associated with April.

353.23–24 women are weathercocks . . . before you there is no specific biblical allusion here, but compare the mordant sketches of the 'strange woman' in Proverbs 5.1–6, or Ecclesiastes 7.25–26. In 1 Kings 11.1–8, Solomon's many wives are held responsible for turning his heart away from God.

353.33–34 the steep descent of the Corrichie Dhu probably referring to the vale of Corrichie, a marshy hollow surrounded by the steep slopes of the Hill of Fare (471 m) 24 km W of Aberdeen. 'Dhu' is a version of the Gaelic 'dubh' meaning 'black'. The Corrichie brook is a head-stream of the Black Burn.

353.42 a game at bowls the game of bowls was played in England as early as the 13th century; both Edward III and Richard II in the 14th century included bowls in the sports they wished to ban (because of the threat to the practice of archery). However, the game is not recorded in Scotland before the 16th century.

354.2–3 Highland kite, who calls himself a falcon, should stoop at my turtle dove Henry images Conachar as a base bird of prey with pretensions to nobility swooping down ('stoop') on his 'turtle-dove', the traditional emblem of female innocence, vulnerability and constancy.

354.37 her own self I myself. Gender confusion when moving from Gaelic to English or Scots is a literary device for suggesting Highland speech and is found as early as Richard Holland's *The Buke of the Howlat* (*c.* 1450).

355.2 fir nan ord *Gaelic* a man of the hammer.

355.6–10 it is said . . . boddle-pins see note to 62.14–17.

355.14   Och hone   ochone, alas.

355.14   Houghmanstairs   see note to 136.5–7.

355.38   Hut, prut   *exclamation* come, come.

356.4   fir nan ord   see note to 355.2.

356.6   Ferragon   see note to 312.42.

356.8   Dunter   the name means 'hitter', or 'striker'.

356.21   Janniken   the name of the Wife of Bath's apprentice: 'The Wife of Bath's Prologue', in *The Canterbury Tales*, III (D), 303.

356.21   Sampson   named for the biblical giant of Judges Chs 13–16.

357.15–16   rose falls from his chaplet   see John Barbour, *The Bruce* (written *c.* 1372–86), ed. Matthew P. McDiarmid and James A. C. Stevenson, 3 vols, Scottish Text Society, 4th Series, 12, 13, 15 (1980–85), Vol. 3, 22; Bk 11, 552–54: 'ye king haid said him rudly/ Yat a rose of his chaplete/ Was fallyn'.

357.25   Deil a   *emphatic* not a.

358.6–7   Abbey of Scone   Augustinian, founded in 1115, 4 km NE of Perth on the banks of the Tay, and destroyed at the Reformation. Most Scottish kings were formally crowned at Scone sitting on the chair which had contained the Stone of Destiny before its removal to London by Edward I in 1296.

358.11–12   Lord High Constable Errol and the young Earl of Crawford   see notes to 245.38 and 225.41.

358.37   the bird of Jove   the eagle; in classical mythology usually linked with the king of the gods.

359.31   My unhappy nephew ... set aside   in the fiction this refers to the Council which made Rothsay the ward of the High Constable; in fact in 1399 Rothsay had been appointed Lieutenant-General of the kingdom, almost certainly with the agreement of Albany and Douglas. But unusually the council which appointed him also required him to take the advice of twenty-one wise men: the implication is that Albany and Douglas wished to remain in ultimate control. Before long, however, Rothsay was acting independently, and emerging as the principal focus of power in the kingdom. It was this development that made Albany determined to destroy him.

360.2   The Scottish Parliament ... deed   within two months of Rothsay's death a meeting of the general council in Edinburgh granted Albany and the 4th Earl of Douglas a royal pardon and indemnity for themselves and their followers over any involvement in the heir apparent's death.

360.24–25   James may follow in time ... my perplexities   in 1406 Rothsay's younger brother James escaped Albany's clutches, being moved first to St Andrews, then to the Bass Rock and the ship intended to spirit him to safety in France. When this ship was intercepted by the English and the young prince taken prisoner, the outcome was that for the rest of his life Albany did rule Scotland, king in all but name.

360.28   Passion Week   Holy week in which Christ's crucifixion and resurrection are commemorated and celebrated.

360.34   Truce of God   instituted at the Council of Elne in 1027, although the days of peace were not as described by Scott.

360.34–35   The ferocious violence ... religious ordinance   from the period of the Wars of Independence (1296–1328) Scottish history is very much a matter of wars, invasions, raids, battles, particularly in the S of Scotland and the N of England, occasionally interrupted by short periods of truce or peace-agreements. The reign of Robert III was in this respect entirely typical.

361.7–8   Bearing branches ... boughs   palm branches commemorate the triumphal entrance of Christ into Jerusalem: see John 12.12–13.

361.30   thews and sinews   muscles and tendons. This phrase seems to have been first used by Scott in *Guy Mannering* (1815), ed. P. D. Garside, EEWN 2, (Edinburgh, 1999), 133.5.

362.37 peace on earth ... of men   see Luke 2.8–14.

362.40–41 the savage delight ... their gladiators   in ancient Rome trained warriors fought each other, often to the death, in public arenas, as a form of mass entertainment.

364.10 Gilded Arbour   see *The Muses Threnodie* (First Muse), and Magnum, 43.332–33, note II.

364.25 the Earl Marshal   royal officer with particular responsibility for the organisation of royal processions and other ceremonial occasions. The office was hereditary and was held by the Keith family from the time of Robert I, but the Earldom was created only in 1458.

364.26 the Lord High Constable   see note to 245.38.

365.14 breath of our nostrils   common biblical phrase: see e.g. Genesis 2.7; Psalm 18.15.

366.4 my quality and charge   my noble status and responsibilities.

367.12 your noble earlship, Sir Gilbert Hay   the first Earl of Errol (see note to 194.1–2) was in fact Sir William Hay (d. *c.* 1462), but there are many Gilberts in the Hay family in this period. The Constable at the time of Rothsay's death was called Thomas.

367.12–13 the yoke with which ... Loncarty   Smith refers to the tradition that the Scots were able to defeat the Danes at the battle of Loncarty (see note to 62.17) by the intervention of a farmer called Hay and his sons who used their ploughshares as weapons. The noble Hay family traced their origins to this incident. See *The Muses Threnodie* (Second Muse).

370.15–19 About twenty ... wielded them   compare *Tales of a Grandfather*, First Series, in *Prose Works*, 22.244–45.

372.6 Bas air son Eachin   *Gaelic* 'Bàs airson Eachainn' ('death for [the sake of] Hector'). Scott's account of the behaviour of Torquil and his sons derives from a story he was told on 17 October 1827 about the Battle of Sheriffmuir (1715). The Macleans were commanded by a chief called Hector whose bodyguard consisted of his foster-father and his seven sons. When the chief was pressed the foster-father sent the sons forward as required. 'The signal he gave was "Another for Hector." The youths replied "Death for Hector" and were all successively killd.' (*The Journal of Sir Walter Scott*, ed. W. E. K. Anderson (Oxford, 1972), 365).

372.10 Seid suas   *Gaelic* 'Sèid suas' ('blow up [the pipes]').

372.31–32 the thrust, but not the parry   in fencing, the attacking move as opposed to the defensive one.

372.35–36 Far eil air son Eachin   *Gaelic* 'Fear eil' airson Eachainn' ('another man for Hector').

373.1 Reist air son Eachin   *Gaelic* 'Rìst airson Eachainn' ('again for Hector').

373.3 Bas air son Eachin   see note to 372.6.

374.8 cry hold   see *Macbeth*, 1.5.51, 5.8.34.

374.12–14 these are not loving subjects ... bear witness   in 1392 the Earl of Crawford had been unable to destroy an invading force of Highlanders at Gasclune. See note to 157.7–8.

374.21 Sound, trumpets   *Richard II*, 1.3.117.

375.21 Federan Dhu   *Gaelic* 'Feadaran Dubh' ('black chanter').

376.16 Bas air son Eachin   see note to 372.6.

376.40 Bas air son Eachin   see note to 372.6.

377.22–24 If thou wilt follow me ... rank withal   Douglas is offering the smith the opportunity to elevate his social status from that of an artisan armourer to that of a land-owning knight.

377.23 burgage tenement   burgage tenure, for which see note to 52.16–17.

377.30   I fought for my own hand   see *The Muses Threnodie* (First Muse): 'and ever since those dayes/ This proverb current goes, when any sayes,/ How came you here? this answer doth he finde,/ I'm for mine owne hand, as fought Henry Winde'. See *ODEP*, 256, but it is apparent that Scott's use of the saying here and in *Rob Roy* (2.296.19–20) gave it proverbial status.

377.32   ambling palfrey   horse that moves at a smooth and easy walking pace.

377.42   A churl will savour of churl's kind   not a recognised proverb, but is based on the 'cat after kind' idea (*ODEP*, 107).

379.19–20   Tynedale bowmen   archers from the valley of the River Tyne in NE England.

379.20   St Bride of Douglas   see note to 109.28.

380.13–14   Would to God ... my son—my son   see 2 Samuel 18.33.

381.1   Sancta Maria, ora pro nobis   *Latin* Holy Mary, pray for us: from the 'Hail Mary' one of the most familiar Catholic prayers.

381.36–37   poor child   at the time of Rothsay's death, James (b. 1394) was only 7 years old.

381.42–43   We will to Dumbarton ... or to Bute   Dumbarton is a royal burgh on the N side of the Firth of Clyde; Bute is an island in the Firth of Clyde. Both, that is, are in the area of Scotland in which the Stewart family held sway.

381.43   Precipices, and tides, ... uncle's ambition   the King believes that Dumbarton Castle, on top of lofty Dumbarton Rock, or Bute's island status, and his personal bodyguard from Bute, will protect his surviving son until he can be sent for safety to France.

382.10–13   In the ensuing Parliament ... for the offence   see note to 360.2.

382.14   Castle of Rothsay   Rothesay Castle on the island of Bute dates from the 11th century. Used occasionally by Robert III's predecessors Robert I and Robert II, it was largely destroyed in the 17th century.

382.20–21   Henry IV ungenerously detained him a prisoner   Prince James was captured in March 1406; Robert III died in Rothesay Castle a week or two later. James remained a prisoner in England until April 1424.

382.22–23   Vengeance followed ... slow pace   see Horace (65–8 BC), *Odes*, 3.2.31–32: 'rarely does vengeance, albeit with a hobbling gait, fail to overtake the guilty'. For history see note to 350.23–25.

382.23–24   Robert of Albany's own grey hairs ... the grave   see 1 Kings 2.5–6; Genesis 42.38.

382.26–29   But nineteen years after ... and his own   Scott here returns to an accurate historical chronology, but has created the impression that the clan battle in Perth, which actually took place in 1396, and the capture of Prince James, in 1406, more or less coincided with Rothsay's death in 1402.

382.35   a religious house called Campsie ... on the Tay   built, as Scott indicates below, on a rock rising high above the Campsie Linn, a cataract on the river Tay near Stanley village, 10 km N of Perth (see *The Muses Threnodie*: Second Muse). It is supposed to have been dependent on the Abbey of Coupar, a Cistercian foundation.

385.15   their love surpassed ... of woman   see 2 Samuel 1.26.

385.33   Bas air Eachin   *Gaelic* 'Bàs air Eachainn' ('death upon [or for] Hector').

385.41   the deserts of Rannoch   largely in NW Perthshire, Rannoch is a wild and desolate area of lochs, mountains, and moorlands.

385.42–43   old Culdees   the name derives ultimately from *Céli Dé* ('companions of God'), used in the 8th and 9th-century Irish Church for monks who sought a life of stricter devotion. The form 'Culdees' goes back to Boece who glossed it as *cultores dei* ('worshippers of God'). It came to be used loosely, as here, for any monks of the Celtic as opposed to Roman observance.

386.4   Daione Shie   *Gaelic* 'Daoine Sìthe' ('fairy people').

386.39–40   we will pay largely ... by Henry's sword   we shall give the Church a generous sum of money to pay for masses to be said for the souls of those Henry has killed.

387.2   base blood-money   money paid to a murderer.

387.7   the four monasteries   see the note to 140.39.

387.10-11   the corporations of the glovers and hammermen   the craft guilds to which Simon and Henry belong.

387.15   Bold ... blue   see note to 336.16–29.

GLOSSARY

This selective glossary defines single words; phrases are treated in the Explanatory Notes. It covers Scottish words, archaic and technical terms, and occurrences of familiar words in senses that are likely to be strange to the modern reader, which are unlikely to be in commonly-used one-volume dictionaries. For each word (or clearly distinguishable sense) glossed, up to four occurrences are normally noted; when a word occurs four or more times in the novel, only the first instance is normally given, followed by 'etc.'. Orthographical variants of single words are listed together, usually with the most common use first. Often the most economical and effective way of defining a word is to refer the reader to the appropriate explanatory note.

a' all 201.34
abide remain 24.40 etc.; wait 262.13
acton stuffed jerkin worn under mail 384.27
adamant impregnable stone 345.28
address skill 14.23 etc.
adjustment arranging one's dress 105.39
advanced lifted up, carried in front 363.8
ain own 200.19 etc.
Albyn Scotland 306.35
allay mix with something inferior 166.11
Almain Germany 336.23
almoner chaplain in a noble household 131.42
amang among 201.31
amateur one who follows something as a pastime 255.9
ambuscade group of armed men 150.5; ambush 254.9
amerciament see note to 43.27–29
amiral see note to 317.37
amour sexual affair 88.37, 202.32
an if 33.27 etc.
anatomy skeleton 75.15, 83.11, 260.12
ane one 201.5, 387.17, 387.18, 387.19
anent concerning 171.2
angel gold coin, worth 13s. 4d. (67p) 253.14
an't if it 235.41
appanage property designed for the maintenance or accommodation of

the younger children of kings, princes etc. 325.37
apparitor officer of a civil or ecclesiastical court 270.41, 273.1, 350.40
appointments accoutrements, outfit 323.14
arbitrement decision-making 138.7
argosy merchant vessel of the largest size 237.33
asperse slander 130.43
assay see note to 311.11
assoilzie absolve from sin or from purgatory 242.6 etc.
assythment fine for bloodshed, paid to nearest relatives of the slain person 226.14
astucious astute 222.13
athirst thirsty 142.38, 306.36
attaint imputation of crime or dishonour 231.37
auld old 200.2 etc.
ave *Latin* abbreviated form of 'ave maria' (hail Mary), a Catholic prayer 39.24
avoid take (oneself) away 289.13
aweel *exclamation* well, sometimes expressing resignation or submission 126.20, 200.10, 200.11
Bacchanalian *adjective* riotously drunken 107.24; *noun* drunken revellers 198.33
bachelor girl's valentine 27.29, 162.5
back-bearand see note to 43.27–29
backsliding lapsing into vices 151.33
baggage woman of loose sexual morals

115.25, 125.38, 172.6

bailie member of a town council who acted as a magistrate 43.35 etc.

bairn child 126.20 etc.

baldrick belt worn from the shoulder across the breast to support weapons 102.28, 212.34

ballet¹ ballad 22.18

ballet² group involved in theatrical representation consisting of dancing and pantomime 169.22

balsam aromatic ointment used for healing wounds or soothing pain 233.7

band bond, agreement 350.20

ban-dog dog tied up on account of its ferocity; bloodhound 234.30, 236.31, 237.11

bang see note to 199.43

barber-chirurgeon surgeon 164.42

barbican watchtower 39.23, 343.39

bard Highland minstrel or seer 140.3, 296.39, 298.14

bare-breeched without breeches, bare-arsed 57.32

barrace lists or enclosure where knightly encounters took place 138.21 etc.

barret small flat cap 16.3

bastinado for 175.2 see note

bating omitting, except for 318.29

batton stick, used as a weapon 316.40

beads small balls threaded on a string for keeping count of the number of prayers said 87.34 etc.

beadsman pensioner, bound to pray for the soul of his benefactor 191.42, 271.6

beauffet sideboard 20.3

beetle-headed dull and heavy 320.42

beeves cattle 141.9

belted see note to 69.18

benedicite *Latin* bless us 36.24 etc.

benefice church office with an income 9.7

benison pronouncing of a blessing, benediction 167.36

beshrew curse 19.36, 23.25

bespeak order (goods) 22.30

bestial cattle, beasts 34.21

bewrays betrays 81.20

bielded sheltered, helped 126.36

bier-right ordeal in which person accused of murder is required to

approach corpse and clear themselves on oath 217.41 (see note) etc.

biggen night-cap 189.12

bigging building 22.10

bill pike or halberd 94.17, 167.23, 336.27

billet note 315.20

bink range of shelves for holding dishes 20.4

bit small, insignificant 284.8, 355.40

black-cock male of the black grouse 299.4

blade sword 34.34 etc.; gallant fellow 76.22 etc.

blood-boltered see note to 5.32

blood-suit see note to 43.27–29

blood-witt penalty for bloodshed 223.30

board-end table-bottom 53.21

boddle-prins pins of small value 355.10

bodkin dagger 56.2; ornamental hair-pin 105.35

bog-wood oak or other wood found preserved in peat bogs 299.15

bolt arrow normally for a crossbow 130.32 etc.

bonny beautiful 21.6

boon benefit, gift or favour 6.31, 77.1, 324.11

boot for to boot 44.30 etc. see note to 44.30

bootless unavailing, without success 42.25

bo-peep hide-and-seek 19.29, 117.10

bordel bordello, brothel 85.23

bordeller frequenter of brothels 203.27

Borderman Borderer, person from the Scottish Borders 127.22

borrel, borrell rough, rude 47.16, 69.12; unlearned 314.29

bosket thicket 120.39

bothy hut 279.34, 294.30, 298.24

bountith something given over and above usual wages, a bounty 126.33 (see note), 126.35

bout for 170.25 and 201.7 see note to 170.25

bowie wooden milk bowl 340.9

brae hillside 154.28

braggadocio braggart 83.1

brake thicket 132.9

brand mark (made on criminals by hot iron) 118.18; instrument for cauterising a wound 188.28; piece of burning wood 275.16 (see note); sword 367.8, 378.32

brattach *Gaelic* standard 54.8 etc.

brave splendid, fine 83.22, 161.9, 201.29; affront 321.24

bravo daring villain, desperado 38.18

bray pound as in a mortar 67.13

breckan bracken 272.15

brent-browed with unwrinkled forehead 307.26

brewis brose; for 168.12 see text 168.12–14

brief letter establishing the bearer's credentials 106.32

brimeston, brimstone sulphur 67.25, 289.29 (see note to 289.28–29)

brimmer glass filled to the brim 35.9

broad-cloth for 5.23 see note to 38.4

brogue Highland shoe of untanned hide with leather thongs 43.13, 275.28, 277.12

broidered embroidered 68.19

broil disturbance, brawl 39.11, 105.6, 174.8

brook enjoy, hold 110.41, 188.14; endure 114.32, 166.8, 318.27

brose for 168.12 see text 168.12–14

bruited noised, rumoured 344.2

buckler small round shield 29.26 etc.

buff made of leather from the hides of oxen 17.20 etc.

bugbear imaginary being evoked to frighten children 236.33

bull see note to 217.42

bully good friend 75.16 (see note)

burgess citizen or freeman of a burgh 15.23 etc.

burgher respectable citizen; member of the mercantile class 15.5 etc.

burthensome burdensome 18.21

busk prepare, get ready 45.15

buskin sandal-like foot and leg covering 56.27, 105.38, 384.29

but without 27.12 etc.

buxom vigorous and attractive 35.17, 36.6, 162.15

by-street side-street 118.20, 121.36

caballing plotting 227.11

cailliachs *Gaelic* old women 301.7, 307.30

caitiff base, despicable wretch 165.28 etc.

calabash shell of ground pumpkin or

calabash-tree fruit, used as a vessel 175.31 etc.

can drinking vessel 19.39, 24.24, 36.7

canary light sweet wine from the Canary Islands 323.18

canna cannot 200.11

capon castrated cock 319.39, 323.18

career charge, gallop 333.24, 384.25

carle man, fellow 69.20

carouse toast drunk to the bottom 232.39; drinking bout 298.22

cartel written challenge 131.36, 132.14, 132.28

cateran, catheran *pejorative* Highland brigand or marauder 25.35 etc.

caudle warm drink or thin gruel, sweetened and spiced, given to sick persons 209.43

causeway paved part of a street or path 16.17, 40.11

cautery metal tool or medicine used to sterilise open wounds by burning the tissue 165.9

cavalier gallant or courtly gentleman 31.40 etc.

cavey hen-coop 272.37 (see note)

chafe fret, gall 158.15 etc.

chaffer bargain 295.26

chambering sexual indulgence 127.19

chamberlain household steward or manager 109.1 etc.

chaplet string of beads, one third the length of a rosary 241.40; wreath for the head 357.16

charnel skeleton 116.21

charnel-house building or vault for depositing corpses and bones 116.9, 146.5

chased embossed, engraved 146.32

chequer chess-board 313.28

chevron, cheveron kid-glove 45.38, 162.25

chine spine 370.16

chirurgeon surgeon 158.7 etc.

churl *disparaging* low-bred fellow 132.8 etc.

cicerone sightseers' guide 4.18

cincture belt, girdle, something which encircles 20.21 etc.

clanjamfray rabble, riff-raff 127.39

claymore two-edged Highland broadsword 157.10 etc.

clerk officer in charge of the records and correspondence of an institution 134.3 etc.; someone able to read and write 134.34 etc.; cleric 155.19 etc.

clotter'd clotted 240.25

clown boor, someone who is ignorant or ill-bred 41.41, 131.8, 162.22

cocked set jauntily 284.4

cock-loft small attic or garret 21.29, 31.30

cogging fawning, cheating 267.24

cognizance heraldic badge 82.31, 110.24, 156.40

cogue wooden drinking vessel 296.3

collation meal of cold foods 232.24, 251.30, 316.24

collie sheep-dog 281.9

comfit for 75.43 and 76.3 see note to 75.43

commonweal commonwealth, society 265.41; for **common weal** see note to 70.16

company keep company with 200.19, 200.20

concert arrange, contrive 145.21, 237.10, 310.21

condign *of punishment* appropriate 143.41

confident trusty adherent 311.32

congee, congé bow 84.17, 343.18

conjure implore 110.39, 111.33, 267.35, 378.34

contemn despise, treat with contempt 89.41, 348.36

convertist convert 265.35

convoy convey 115.25

corbie raven or carrion-crow 239.30

Cordovan fine leather principally made from horse-hide 38.6 (see note)

cordwainer shoemaker using cordovan leather 57.9, 57.12, 123.22

coronach Highland funeral song 284.7, 286.30, 287.36

coronal wreath for the head 215.11

coronet small crown 87.34 etc.

corslet armour for the top part of the body 29.3

costard *humorous* head 275.9

countenance *noun* the face 15.32 etc.; moral support 66.29 etc.; patronage 106.23; *verb* support morally 77.16 etc.

couples brace for holding two dogs together 293.5; pairs of rafters, meeting at the top, and fixed at the

bottom by a tie 294.4

covine private agreement 273.25

cowl hood or the hooded habit of a monk 114.9, 141.40

coy *verb* affect shyness or reserve 109.10

crape black gauze-like silk or other transparent fabric 230.3

cripple *Scots* hobble, limp 79.22

cross-made ugly 275.23

cruise earthen vessel used for liquids 337.35

cruize journey round a particular area without having a destination 169.31

cruizer warship sailing around to protect a country's own commercial vessels, and to harry those of an enemy 382.19

crutch-headed having a head like a crutch 87.40

cumber *noun and verb* trouble 25.36 etc.

cummer woman, term for female intimate 239.19 etc.

curious careful, accurate 63.28; exquisitely prepared or made 75.43, 152.32; observant, particular 123.7; ingenious 189.32; strange (perhaps with implications of the occult) 260.26

curiously intricately, subtly 117.5 etc.

curragh boat (of hide over a wickerwork frame) 287.6

curtal-axe cutlass 30.31, 232.19

dalmatic ecclesiastial dress with wide sleeves and two stripes 313.38

dargue day's-work, specific body of work 253.2

dark-lantern lantern with a shutter to shield or open the light 42.2

dault *Gaelic* foster-son 275.41 etc.

daw jackdaw 124.30

deacon president of a trade guild 63.9, 212.36

deboshed debauched 43.42

decretal see note to 217.42

defensible capable of defending 206.35

degradation loss of rank 144.30; see also note to 349.30–31

deil devil; for 284.2 and 357.25 see notes

delicate choice food, delicacy 298.26

devoir duty 76.19 etc.

devoted condemned 83.34; doomed

88.7, 375.23
dey, dey-woman, dey-girl dairy woman 339.6 etc.
dinging hammering, dealing heavy blows 200.33
dingle deep dell or hollow 287.21
dink haughty 205.40
dirk Highland dagger 16.15 etc.
disclamation repudiation 183.15
dittay see note to 267.1
divan Oriental council 192.15
divers several, sundry 214.3 etc.
don put on 45.13 etc.
doomed destined 168.3, 240.10
door-stane threshold 199.42
doting stupidity, imbecility 200.23
doublet close-fitting body garment 17.10 etc.
douce sedate 281.35
doughty formidable 46:12 etc.
dour stubborn, sullen 34.23
dourlach short sword, dagger 188.42
dowaire dowager, widow enjoying property or title from deceased husband 387.20
downright plain and direct 62.21, 68.38, 174.7
downs open elevated ground 10.16
dree suffer 328.16
dresses dressings, bandages 158.36
drift flock 355.30
dromond large sailing ship 81.22, 81.26, 179.33
drubber for 35.43 see note to 35.42–43
duenna elderly woman whose duty it is to watch over a young one 278.10
dunniewassal see note to 57.32
durst dared 201.7
earnest promise 161.15
e'en¹ even 47.22 etc.
e'en² even, day before a festival 168.7, 185.39
elixir preparation which changes one thing into another 4.37, 4.41, 5.34
eneugh enough 200.42
enthusiasm rapturous intensity, fervour 121.17
enthusiastic capable of passionate feeling or extravagant religious fervour 292.16
entry dance introduced between parts of an entertainment 168.37 (see note), 214.5
ephemerides astronomical almanac

260.22 (see note)
equerry officer charged with the care of a nobleman's or monarch's horses 384.14
errant wandering 106.21 etc.
escheat see note to 43.27–29
escutcheon shield on which a coat of arms is depicted 250.15
even evening, day before a festival 16.40 etc.
exheredation disinheritance 302.36
expurgation clearing 243.38
fabliau fable 124.30
facile easily-wrought upon 90.38, 225.25
factotum servant who has the entire management of his employer's affairs 321.3
faggot bundle of sticks 142.1
fain *adverb* gladly 35.29 etc.
fain *adjective* willing, eager 72.12 etc.; obliged 135.15
faitour impostor, scoundrel 80.3
fash trouble 355.6
Fastern for 36.7 etc. see note to 36.7
favour badge or ribbon bestowed on a knight by a lady 139.32; for 194.15, 232.3, and 378.22 see note to 194.15; face, countenance 194.21, 274.3
fealty loyalty sworn to one's lord, homage 132.41
feather-dresser worker in feathers 215.9
featly deftly 387.11
fee pay 126.33 (see note), 126.34
fell terrible 371.38, 372.1
fence defence, particularly self-defence 37.9, 82.3, 216.3
fenced enclosed 246.25, 276.35, 364.3
fey fated to die 170.14
fillet strip of ribbon or lace 87.34
finger-post sign pointing the direction to a place 10.6
fire-prongs fire-irons 30.19
firkin small cask, holding c. 8 gallons (36 litres) 178.11, 183.21
flagitious atrociously wicked, vicious 144.23
flasket long shallow basket 262.42
flight-speed the speed of a flight-arrow (light, well-feathered arrow for long-distance shooting) 133.33
foin lunge 376.24

fond foolishly tender 88.31, 223.41

fore-hammer large hammer which strikes first, sledge-hammer 35.2, 67.41, 204.24

fortalice small fortress 83.15

fraternities religious bodies 266.9

fraught attended, filled 157.6, 223.13, 308.38

frieze coarse woollen cloth (with a nap, usually on one side only) 68.20 etc.

frost-piece temperamentally, sexually cold person 329.27

frowsy frowsty, unkempt 346.12

furze gorse 132.9

gabbart sailing vessel for inland navigation 172.30

gaffer *affectionate* grandfather 169.41

gage *noun and verb* pledge, bet 57.21 etc.

galliard gallant 42.5 etc.

gallipot earthenware container for ointments 67.22, 171.41

gallo-glass, gallowglass heavy-armed Highlander 56.11, 298.12

gallow-lee where the gallows is set up 35.12

gallows-bird one who deserves to be hanged 25.7

Galwegian from or belonging to the district of Galloway in SW Scotland 114.31, 327.12

game-cock cock of the breed used in cock-fighting 307.10, 361.13

gang go 127.9, 201.25

garniture ornament or trimming 16.23

gate street 34.32, 201.34

gathering signal (by beat of drum etc.), 374.37

gaze-hound dog which follows its prey by sight, not scent 237.17, 313.20

gear goods, property 34.18, 272.31, 355.33; business, work 260.40

gentleman-usher gentleman acting as usher to someone of superior rank 6.2, 162.18

gie give 201.15

gillie attendant on a Highland chief 275.40, 313.15

girdle¹ circular metal plate on which cakes are cooked over a fire 30.19

girdle² belt 96.23, 270.11, 377.23

girnel granary, store-house 141.10

girth for 42.31 and 94.16 see note to 42.31

glamour magic 349.17

glee-maiden female minstrel 102.2 etc.

glee-woman female minstrel 99.21 etc.

glibb bushy head of hair 153.2

gloom *noun* scowl 21.31; *verb* scowl, look displeased 200.42, 272.43

Glune-amie, Glunami Celt or Gael 34.23, 54.30

godfather, god-father someone who will send another to God 41.37; sponsor 245.28

Godsend unexpected but welcome happening 6.11

goliard singer and jester 117.31

goliardise singers and jesters 317.6

goodman, good-man term of address between equals who are not on familiar terms 16.40; head of the household 199.43

goose-cap foolish person 51.42

gorget piece of armour protecting the throat 72.16, 212.33

gossip friend 172.11 etc.

gossipred friendship 177.2; gossiping 214.20

gouge wench 119.12

gouvernante housekeeper, duenna 126.25

graddan parched grain 272.12, 284.16

graith equipment, weapons 30.18, 48.13

gramercy thanks, God reward you 179.8

gratis without charge or pay 238.27

gratulate hail, salute 252.26, 292.33

gratulation expression of pleasure on someone's success 377.19

grey flecked or checked grey cloth 38.7 (see note)

gripe tight grasp 41.40; grasp or seize tightly 310.36

groom serving man, attendant 99.19 etc.; fellow 181.27

gude good 242.38, 387.18

guerdon reward 161.16

guild-feast feast arranged by a craft guild or association 297.5

gull easily fooled person 118.43; dupe 179.27, 235.10

habergeon light sleeveless coat of mail 22.26, 52.37

habiliments dress or attire 116.35, 288.12

habit apparel, dress 15.30 etc.

hae have 200.2, 200.18, 200.42

haffets, haffits temples 201.26, 301.8

hail, haill whole 128.21, 199.42, 200.33

halloo *verb* encourage by shouting 140.17; *noun* shouting 176.14

hallow shout 9.42, 74.33, 310.41; urge on by shouting 60.12

hallowedness holiness 291.34

Hallowmass All Saint's Day, 1 November 156.21

hamshackled fettered 355.16

hand-habend see note to 43.27–29

hank means of restraint or check 124.30

hap happen, come to pass 170.5

hards coarse ends of flax or wool 47.43

harlotry harlot, prostitute 122.31

harness body-armour 23.29 etc.

harnish harness, body armour 355.8

harrow cry of distress 5.12

hattock for 69.27 and 69.39 see note to 69.27

hauberk long coat of mail 38.33 etc.

heathenesse the pagan world 147.4

hinny honey, sweet one 200.42

hireling one who serves only for wages, a mercenary 371.5

hobbiler small or middle-sized horse 77.3, 78.40

hobbleshow hubbub, tumult 200.29

hogshead large cask holding 52½ gallons (239 litres) 183.36, 246.13

holds strongholds 196.23

holidame anything regarded as sacred 179.26

hollow shout 183.33, 200.10

holped see note to 280.23

holytide holy time, church feast-day 15.38

hone moan or grieve 52.9; for 355.14 see note

honest respectable 15.5 etc.; open, frank 38.26 etc.; chaste 67.9

horse-girth belt or band placed round the body of a horse and drawn tight so as to secure a saddle etc. on its back 259.13

hospital house for the reception and entertainment of travellers 118.16; institution for looking after the needy 166.9

hospitium *Latin* house for the reception and entertainment of travellers 96.40

hostelrie inn 99.23, 118.41, 169.21

hosting raising an army at the command of a chief or feudal superior 55.19

hurdle composed of crossing bars 308.37

hurry disturb 107.9

ilk for 217.17 and 220.24 see note to 217.16–17

impassible incapable of feeling, unimpressible 346.35

incognito anonymity, disguise 16.36

incontinence unchastity 328.25, 328.30

incubus demon or person that oppresses like a nightmare 239.1

indenture sealed agreement between two or more parties 227.41 (see note) etc.

index sun-dial pointer 95.16

indirection for 265.1 see note

indited set down in writing 266.31

infang see note to 43.27–29

Inglish English 242.14

intelligence news 350.34

intreat treat, deal with 214.30

Irish pertaining to Ireland or the Scottish Highlands 68.10, 136.9 (see note)

I'se I'll 201.3, 201.6

jack sleeveless leather tunic sometimes reinforced with plate or mail 77.5 (see note), 87.10, 212.39

jackanapes monkey 122.28

jackman man wearing a short sleeveless coat of mail 32.5, 85.17, 85.20

jennet small Spanish horse 270.15

jillet flighty young woman, wench 326.36

jilt woman who has lost her chastity, whore 172.17

jolter-headed block-headed, stupid 161.38

justiciar see note to 43.19

kain-hen hen paid as rent in kind 272.37 (see note)

ken know, identify 35.10 etc.; track 258.37

kennel surface drain, gutter 175.39 etc.

kerne, kern *derogatory* originally light-armed Irish foot-soldier then applied to Scottish Highlanders 100.30 etc.

kind kindred 312.34

kirstening christening 76.2

kirtle dress, skirt 15.20, 45.14, 123.29

knave base rogue 41.13 etc.; fellow 23.22, 123.28, 123.36; man, servant 84.14 etc.

lack *intransitive* be missing 135.37

lack-a-day shame or reproach to the day, alack 167.19, 172.7, 179.30

lai *French* lyric or narrative song 103.9

landlouper vagabond 34.29

land-louping roaming 43.8

landward pertaining to the country (as opposed to town) 209.38, 211.22, 321.3

lang-legged long-legged 201.17

lank limp 23.4

laps side-flaps 74.21

lassie (young) girl 201.24

lathy tall and thin 77.30

lawing reckoning 118.43

lay lyric or narrative song 22.22 etc.

leal loyal, honest 182.33

lealty loyalty 313.27

leech physician 62.18 etc.

legerdemain tricks performed by sleight of hand 242.8

leman lover, mistress 125.41, 126.1

liege one owed feudal allegiance 91.26

liegeman loyal subject 143.35

limmer rascal, scoundrel 41.36, 131.32

lipping making notches in 83.24

list please 281.33, 290.37, 330.24

lists enclosed space in which tournaments etc. are held 137.40; for 89.27 see note

lithe lith, joint 344.35

loaning lane 181.9

lockman executioner 235.32

long-breathed having a lot of breath, i.e. having much stamina 81.19

loon fellow 34.14 etc.; whore 15.14; lower-class person 76.26, 201.7

lower lour, scowl 129.13

luckie familiar name for an old woman 125.17

lug ear 25.8, 205.17 (see note)

lurdane rascal 34.37

lure bait used by falconers to recall their hawks 80.15 etc.; attract with bait 113.21, 315.29

lyme-dog bloodhound 313.17

mail luggage, baggage 122.20, 123.20, 319.34

main[1] strength, power 65.23

main[2] cock-fight 228.37 (see note)

mair[1] more 200.43, 355.41

mair[2] executive officer of the law 207.4

maist most 201.4

makar poet 22.17, 242.14, 266.26

maltalent ill-will 67.37, 127.7

malvoisie French dessert wine 84.15, 169.15, 178.11

mammocks shreds 248.10

manege riding school 237.39

mansworn false to an oath or promise 179.13, 204.43

mantilla lace or silk scarf 15.26 (see note to 15.26–27)

mantle cloak 39.43

mark[1] target 19.9, 374.33

mark[2] see merk

marry name of the Virgin Mary used as an exclamation 37.9 etc.

martialist military man 74.32 etc.

mask masque, drama involving dance and dumb-show in which participants wore masks 224.3

masker person in a mask or performing a masque 214.29

masking for performing a masque 174.33

masque drama involving dance and dumb-show in which particpants wore masks 215.7

masquer person in a mask or performing a masque 135.28 etc.

masquing wearing of masks or performing a masque 64.9, 64.12; for performing a masque 214.40, 215.35, 216.3

Mass *expletive* by the Mass 201.27, 205.15

massamore main dungeon 183.36

maun must 200.1, 200.14

May maiden 207.23, 340.5, 384.6, 384.17

mechanic skilled manual worker 117.40 etc.

mediciner medicine-man, quack

159.26 etc.

meed reward 377.19

meet *adjective* right, fitting 50.25 etc.

merk, mark 13*s*. 4*d*. Scots, about 33p sterling 22.27 (see note), 30.36, 189.33

mess food, meal, portion 296.28 etc.

messan lap-dog 162.15

metheglin spiced mead 252.24

minion favourite 115.20

mirk dark 181.9

miscarriages bad conduct 266.25

mislike dislike 32.28

mitre cap of a bishop or abbot 141.40

moss-trooper see note to 80.18

mould[1] for 144.4 and 313.26 see note to 144.3–4

mould[2] earth of the grave 236.13

mountebank itinerant performer, charlatan 343.6

mulct fine imposed for an offence, penalty 175.14, 226.43, 310.10

mummer actor in a dumb-show or play 174.38

mummery dumb-show, play 64.12

mumming play-acting 114.6, 193.23, 326.36

mumper beggar 122.33

muniments documents relating to the ownership of land 32.43, 73.5

muster calling together of men for military purposes 15.10

mystery trade-guild 54.10, 57.26

mystic religiously mysterious 49.26, 218.31, 240.15

na not 200.25

naething nothing 242.3

nainsell *Highland Scots* ownself 355.4 etc.

natheless nonetheless 77.42

nice discriminating, fastidious, careful 148.23, 301.43

nicety excessive refinement 116.17 etc.

night-walker, nightwalker person walking about at night possibly with criminal intent 18.35, 40.37, 85.24, 131.29

noble gold coin, worth 6*s*. 8*d*. (33p) sterling 37.10, 60.10

nonage period of legal minority 225.36 (see note to 225.33–37)

nook corner 15.8, 128.15, 346.23

nut-brown ale 24.25; reddish brown 107.42

occurrent narration of what has happened 172.3

ony any 200.43

orisons prayers 227.2

outfang see note to 43.27–29

outrance utmost (i.e. death) 219.22

overset overturn 111.2

own acknowledge 12.35 etc.; approve of 265.37

pacing see note to 73.32

packing see note to 34.13

palfrey horse for ordinary riding 73.32 (see note), 284.25, 377.32 (see note)

palladium see note to 295.2

palter equivocate 235.14

pantler officer in charge of the pantry 336.40, 339.8, 341.36

par parr, salmon up to two years of age 301.36

partizan long-handled spear whose blade has one or more lateral projections 75.10, 382.6

passage exchange of blows 75.4

passamented laced 38.5

passing extremely 142.23, 171.7

pate head 76.41, 123.34, 173.21

pattering mumbling or muttering prayer 125.35

paughty haughty, insolent 275.7

pavin stately dance 260.2

pavoise pavise, convex shield large enough to cover the whole body 305.14

paynim pagan (chiefly Moslem) 288.33

peat *disparaging* woman 190.16, 203.26

peccadillo petty sin 90.35

peeling see note to 34.13

pellach porpoise or dolphin 36.35

penitentiary penitent 244.6

perturbators disturbers 197.1

petronel large calibre pistol 9.13

physic medicine, drug 75.23, 343.29

pibroch variations for the bagpipe, chiefly martial 181.33 etc.

pinner close-fitting cap with long side-flaps 326.29

pin-points pins and needles 262.21

pipkin small earthenware pot 253.3

pirn see note to 272.35

pitched covered in pitch (tar) 289.28 (see note to 289.28–29)

plaid tartan outer garment or shawl

43.5 etc.

plaided plaid-wearing 12.4

plaint legal statement of wrong or grievance, complaint 220.37, 230.16, 269.37

pledge toast 31.30 etc.; promise 57.18 etc.; give an assurance of friendship by drinking 47.4, 252.34

plough-graith fittings and attachments of a plough 30.18

plume pluck 124.33 (see note)

points ties for fastening clothes 199.38, 200.5

pole-axe lochaber axe (see note to 94.18) 153.4, 153.22

poniard small dagger 20.20 etc.

port gate of a city 69.28 etc.

portal gateway 97.4 etc.

post hurry 339.23

postern at the side or back 8.24 etc.

postulate one who seeks a benefice in the church 8.40 (see note)

potage soup 337.12

potter-carrier apothecary 162.9 etc.

pottingar apothecary 68.5 etc.

pottle half gallon 266.9

pouncet-box small box with a perforated lid, used for holding perfumes 167.1

prank dress in a showy manner 27.41

prate talk, blab 350.2

pravity wickedness, depravity 92.15

preachment sermonising 28.12, 310.6

precisian strict observer of moral rules 162.23

precognition *Scots Law* statements gathered from those likely to have relevant evidence by the magistrate examining a case 65.19, 197.24, 222.18 (see note to 197.23–24)

prefer put forward, advance, promote 144.35 etc.

prentice apprentice 6.25

presence those present, company 108.6

present act 327.13

presently immediately 41.30 etc.

prick spur on 48.33, 76.35, 84.34

primitive original 147.1

privado favourite 118.26

proof tested power of resistance 62.16, 304.32

propine gift 75.36, 281.42

prorogation temporary discontinuance of a public meeting 63.40

provost principal magistrate of a Scottish burgh 15.10 (see note) etc.

provost-marshal officer charged with conduct of military trial 47.43, 349.31

ptisan barley-water, mixture of mildly medicinal character 186.25

puir poor 242.4

puissant mighty, powerful 174.15, 175.3

punctilio attention to points of etiquette 113.29

pursuivant messenger with power to execute warrants 222.41

quacksalver, quack salver quack, unqualified medical practitioner 67.24 etc.

quarter-staff iron-tipped wooden staff used as a weapon 19.31

quean woman, hussy, slut 110.4 etc.

rake-hell profligate 68.31

rampage scold, storm 174.2

rampant rearing, with forepaws in the air 363.6

ranter strolling minstrel 126.22

rascaille belonging to the rabble 132.5

rated scolded 310.8

rax reach out and get 356.42

rebeck medieval stringed instrument 122.28, 174.22

receipt recipe 53.12

reck care, heed 364.33

recreant *noun* cowardly, unfaithful or disloyal person 133.18 etc.

recreant *adjective* surrendering to an opponent, cowardly, false 176.39 etc.

recusant refusing to submit to authority 21.29; person so refusing 183.34

rede advice or counsel 66.27 etc.

red-hand *Scots law* redhanded, in the very act of committing the crime 347.35–36 (see note)

reiving stealing, plundering 31.28

remede remedy 272.40

revenant one who returns from the dead 263.25

ribband ribbon 105.31 etc.

ridge-bone back-bone, spine 74.14

riving violent 85.24

romaunt verse romance 60.18, 313.26

roof-tree, rooftree main beam of a roof 37.22, 294.5

rough-rider horse-breaker 179.7

round-about plump, rounded 123.31

roundel poem of three stanzas 22.18

roundly rapidly 273.11

rouping croaking 239.30

rouse glass filled to the brim 124.10, 169.23

roysterer reveller 45.37

roystering swaggering, revelling 76.22

rude rough, humble, unsophisticated, inelegant 16.5 etc.

ruffle disorder, struggle 45.34

rummer short-stemmed 31.18

run *Scots* ran 32.9, 127.25

runagate vagabond, runaway 274.2, 290.28

runic mysterious and magical 62.16

sable black 107.3, 286.12

sackless innocent 244.26

sae so 126.23, 200.1, 200.38

sair grievous 201.8

salvage wild, savage 127.34

salve healing ointment 25.28, 67.26, 157.28; apply healing ointment 62.19, 161.21

salver see quacksalver

Sassenach Saxon, lowlander 295.7

saul soul 242.4

saving excepting 38.40 etc.; not involving losses though not profitable 22.25; that makes an exception 95.24

saw saying, maxim 191.9, 380.22

Saxon for 12.1 etc. see note to 12.1

scapegrace man or boy of disorderly habits 74.30

scapular part of a monk's dress worn over the shoulders and hanging down in front and behind to the ankles 36.35, 145.34

scathe harm 200.28

screech-owl bearer of evil tidings 199.32, 227.34

screen veil or head-scarf 15.26

scrip small bag or wallet 105.30 etc.

seanachie chronicler or genealogist of a Highland clan 296.41

seathe seethe, boil 294.20

seneschal steward of a noble household 7.37

sept clan 279.7

serf bondman, slave 238.3

sewer attendant at a meal who supervises table and seating arrangements and the serving and tasting of dishes, steward of a high rank 83.36 etc.

shaft arrow 223.26 etc.

shambles slaughter-house 161.37, 228.40

shank leg 200.2, 354.39

shift change (clothing) 115.33

shifting living by fraud or theft 347.41

shog get on one's way 180.33

shored see note to 322.4

show-box box for a peepshow 9.41

shrift act of confession 18.30, 36.40, 87.38

Shrovetide, Shrove-tide Shrove Tuesday, the Tuesday before the beginning of Lent 168.6 (see note), 202.26, 208.23

sibyl old woman, woman endowed with powers of prophecy and divination 241.2

sideling oblique 246.41

signet ring used to impress seals 144.20, 161.35, 191.19

simple ordinary people 141.27, 196.2 (see note)

sirname surname 14.25

skene, skean Highland dagger 25.42 etc.

skene-occle Highland dagger carried under the armpit 26.1

skills for 133.32, 172.34, 173.34, 230.40, 270.18 see note to 133.32

slashed for 38.5 and 168.40 see note to 38.5

slashing spirited, dashing 74.27, 84.8, 169.28

slough outer covering, cast-off outer skin 156.24, 361.41

slow-hound species of bloodhound used in Scotland for tracking game 237.16 etc.

smaik rogue, rascal 84.37

smithy blacksmith's forge 52.17 etc.

smithy-dander cinder from a forge 34.30

S'nails *oath* by God's nails 122.30 (see note)

somedeal to some extent 182.32

sorner see note to 93.30

sound test 149.18; ascertain the views [of] 303.3

Southron *noun and adjective* southern,

i.e. English 31.28

spang-cockle game like marbles but played with shells 109.32

specie money, *specifically* coins 278.5

spindle-shank thin leg 123.1

sprig twig, offshoot 33.23 (see note), 354.18

squire well-born young man attendant on a knight 16.3 etc.

staid stayed 305.19

stark rigid in death 242.2

start *hunting* force (an animal) out of hiding into the open 42.27

state costly and imposing display 88.1 (see note); canopy 91.1

stay stop, arrest 178.8

step-father father-in-law 108.36 (see note)

stint desist 240.35

stithy anvil 124.42, 161.28, 200.33

stouthrief violent theft 29.30

strath tract of low-lying ground traversed by a river and bounded by hills 280.1, 300.15, 385.18

stroller vagrant, vagabond 112.2, 115.33, 122.29

styptic medicament used to stop a wound bleeding 165.9

subsist exist 7.32 etc.

sufferance endurance 23.21

sumner person employed to summon people to appear in court 270.41

supposititious intending to deceive 7.40

swallow-tail arrow with broad or barbed heads 305.22

swart swarthy 58.26, 108.30, 285.10

swash-buckler swaggering bully 38.19

swashing swaggering 181.33

swinge beat 112.12

switch lash, whip 74.34; long, thin shoot cut from a tree 299.13

sword-and-buckler see note to 35.24

sword-dint sword-blow 22.29

syncope failure of the heart's action 306.8

tabouring drumming 118.36

tallies sticks marked with notches representing the amount of debts or payments 340.8

target small round shield 15.8 etc.

tattling gossiping, tale-telling 164.20, 172.38

tauld told 199.41

tearer swaggerer, tear-away 124.17

temporalities secular matters 93.20

tender regard with solicitude 350.8

tenement block of flats under one roof and with a common stair 6.16; real property such as land or dwellings 70.21; the body as the abode of the soul 243.27, 288.7; tenure 377.23 (see note)

tent take care of 67.1

tester coin 6.19 (see note); canopy 42.20

thigger see note to 93.30

thraw oppose, thwart 127.9

thrum loose thread 170.22

tide time 38.4

tight lively 35.22

tirrivie fit of temper 201.5

tocher dowry 272.33

tod fox 298.30

toe-tripping dancing 118.36

tolbooth prison 25.37

toy mere talk, fanciful notion 111.7, 172.10

traffic dealing, communication 109.8 etc.

traverse temporary wall or screen 7.16 etc.

treillage lattice-work on which ornamental plants are trained 364.8

trencher plate, platter 20.1 etc.

troll sing loudly and merrily 123.38

troller one who sings loudly and merrily 35.23

trow suppose, think 84.38, 310.6, 314.30

trumpery worthless 126.6; worthless stuff 193.20, 327.7

truncheon baton of office 154.29, 228.6; shaft 327.28

tuilzie brawl, fight 200.1

tumbril cart 254.3

turnkey jailer 316.17

tutor for 225.33 and 225.35 see note to 225.33–37

twinge tweak, prick 175.42

tyring dressing 115.32

umquhile late 230.18, 239.42, 387.20

un-apt not readily disposed 87.1

unbeseeming unfitting; improper 224.42

unbonnet take off one's hat 107.29, 238.41

ungrateful disagreeable 168.13
unrespective heedless, disrespectful 110.7
untoward unseemly, improper 315.27
unwonted unusual 90.28, 133.31, 183.30
uphauld maintain 201.6
usquebaugh *Gaelic* water of life i.e. whisky 297.16
utter offer for sale 60.14
valiancie, valiancy brave or valiant person 238.34 etc.; bravery 349.9
valour person of courage 262.16, 263.34
varlet rascal 75.12, 157.39, 275.8
vennel alley, lane between houses 36.33, 202.35
vestiary room (in a monastery etc.) for storing clothes or dressing in 115.34
videlicet namely 183.37
viol musical instrument with 5, 6, or 7 strings played with a bow 99.22 etc.
violing playing the viol 118.35
visionary imaginary 215.39
visitant visitor 5.3, 270.41
vizard mask 214.39
vulgar common people 8.7 etc.
wad would 201.25
wade *of the sun or moon* move through cloud or mist 258.2
wake parish festival, involving games, entertainments etc. 118.3
walawa, wala wa alas 5.12, 242.4
warder[1] baton used to give the signal to start or stop hostilities at a tournament 228.41, 229.3
warder[2] guard 273.13 etc.
wark work 201.18
warlock wizard 127.40
warstle wrestle, fight 201.15

wassail revelling 177.7, 177.30, 183.29
wastel see note to 75.43
wax grow 146.26 etc.
weal good, well-being 62.27, 70.16, 247.37
wean young child 239.25
weapon-shawing for 35.26 see note
wee small 284.8
ween think, believe 132.29
weird fate 127.42
welked rough, marked with ridges on the flesh 35.2, 238.37
well-coupled referring to the joining of the back to the hind-quarters of a horse 74.3
wem mark of injury 374.26
wether-skin skin of a castrated male sheep, parchment 273.3 (see note)
wert were 35.12 etc.
wha who 201.3, 201.17
whase whose 200.18
whinger short stabbing sword 22.43 etc.
whisht hush, (keep) quiet 355.41
wight fellow 175.25, 207.43, 353.43
wilt will 15.13 etc.
witching bewitching 102.29
without outside 110.26 etc.
wold open country 102.26, 108.4
wont *adjective* accustomed 18.37 etc.
wont *noun* custom 18.28, 78.1, 186.19
wonted usual, customary 51.6, 161.42, 234.25
wot know 22.27 etc.
wrangle dispute angrily 173.16
wrangling disputatious, argumentative 300.40
writhen contorted 8.29, 368.5
wynd narrow street turning off from a main thoroughfare 37.27 etc.
yester yesterday 211.39